A Right To Love

Mark Frew

A Right To Love

A copy of this publication can be found in the National Library of Australia.

ISBN: 978-0-9954440-1-0 (paperback)
ISBN: 978-0-9954440-2-7 (hardback)
ISBN: 978-0-9954440-0-3 (ebook)

Other books by the same author:

Michael and the Multicoloured Gospel
Farewell My Pashtun

For those who have
Ears to hear
Minds to think and
Hearts to love

hearts to love us humans, all of us, all who are descended from the one mother, which therefore makes us all of one tribe and one family, and hearts to love us more than what is written in a book.

To a world which seeks the happiness and well-being for everyone and everything in it.

Contents

Foreword

Quotations from the Koran and chapter and verse numberings were mainly taken from the translation by Maulvi Sher Ali although on occasion some verses were taken from the translation of the Koran by Abdullah Yusuf Ali.

Quotations from the Bible were mainly from the King James Version, otherwise known as the Authorised Version, although on occasion some verses were taken from the New International Version.

Chapter 1

If our lifespan could extend beyond the borders of eternity, would life be worth living for a second if it weren't for love?

Love. A word that conjures up the most euphoric of feelings. A thousand thousand songs have been written in praise of love. Millions upon millions of poems have proclaimed love's qualities. Rivers and rivers of ink enough to fill the four oceans time and time again have been splashed over reams and reams of papyrus, parchment and paper to extol the many virtues of love.

Love has been defined again and again in enough ways to fill a dictionary that would tower over the world: love is patient, love is a many splendid thing, love is a stranger in an open car, love is but a second hand emotion, love is of God and love is God.

Love. Should we feel it or get it, should we do it or live it? Can it be defined? Can it be confined? Can it be contained?

Love has been exemplified, exteriorised and personalised. In ancient times, love ruled within the heavens among the other gods and goddesses, carrying in turn the names of Ishtar, Aphrodite and Venus. Even the dear little godlet, Cupid, also had part possession of a version of love. In classical Greek times, Socrates philosophised about love and then deified it, and later Christianity humanised it, crucified it, monotheisised it and finally monopolised it.

Beyond description, beyond definition, beyond understanding, love defies all our attempts to possess it, to own it, to control it. Religions have tried to set its boundaries and governments have made policies to restrict the extent to which love may move, and yet, love has time and time again crossed beyond each border within which these limits are set. Love is blind to the barriers we set up around it, passing mystically and effortlessly through these futile restraints. Where we blame love for the disasters that occur, it is not love but the bounds we put around love which are to blame.

But while love runs amok, freely and wildly, those stricken by love suffer from love's untamable character. A free-running power like the surging waters of a great river, love flows wild and free, rushing, dipping and gushing with interminable force in a direction in which love alone is privy to. To the unwary, love's unwieldy power is overwhelming, frightening and breathtaking. For others who are like white-water rafters, love is a wild and enthralling ride, an adrenalin rush of ups and downs as love carries them blindly and effortlessly in her powerful path.

But I was beyond love. As far as I was concerned, I had closed the door to love. Rejected by the God of love in the religion in which I had grown up, cast away by my parents who could only love me under certain conditions, dumped by partners whose love for me was only as enduring as my usefulness to them, love had absolutely no place in my existence. I felt as if, after having been whisked along mercilessly in the clutches of its fury, I had successfully reached the banks of this tumultuous river and finally been able to pull myself out onto the banks of this river, catch my breath, re-evaluate my situation and begin life anew – without love.

It was a Monday morning, the first day of my working week. I was already out of bed, had showered, was dressed for work, had breakfasted and was savouring a cup of Gevalia filter coffee, the best coffee in the world as far as I was concerned and, along with ABBA and IKEA, a fine product of Swedish workmanship. I was reading the *Sydney Star Observer*, one of Sydney's gay newspapers, a copy of which I had picked up from one of the venues I had frequented during the weekend. Apart from the photos of gay men and women all ablaze in glitzy colourful array or the overt poses of bare-chested men, there were interesting articles I enjoyed reading which showed me the extent to which the acceptance of homosexuality had infiltrated Australian society, well, at least inner Sydney society. And then there were articles that were amusingly pathetic which I just read for a laugh.

They were the articles on gay marriage that I thought were the most amusing. I could not decide to which category of interest these articles really lay. Really, I didn't get it. My gay relationships had never lasted so I could not at all envisage going so far as to marry someone. But further, what was all the fuss about marriage anyway? Marriage was an institution of the straight world, perpetuated from time immemorial, the shackles of which were unfettered in the late 1960s and early 1970s when the western world finally broke free from this absurd idea that people need to stand before an invisible being that some call "god" and make impossible promises of sensual fidelity to their newly appointed spouse, and then sign a paper, which in the eyes of the government or at least of the community to which the newly wedded couple belonged, gave the couple permission to engage in sensual pleasure – at least without having to hide the fact that they had already been doing it, either with each other or with someone else. Marriage was a golden prison cell that the world was beginning to escape from. And here, between the pages of a newspaper which gave voice to those who were once the sexual outlaws, I read how gay men and gay women were fighting to get into this same cage that straight men and women had managed to get out of.

"Give me a break!" I said and chuckled under my breath. "You want a gay marriage? And then what? A gay divorce? Gay alimony? And are you going to call your spouse a husband or a wife?"

I couldn't see the point in getting married. As far as I understood it, marriage was all about being faithful to one person, declaring to the world that you would only have sexual relations with your spouse. Even the straight world could not honour that irrespective of how much they promised before their Supreme Beings that they would love only the one who at the altar stood before them. Years later he would end up humping like an excited rabbit the new blond secretary or she would be gasping in ecstasy to the loving advances of the boss. As far as I could see, they might like to say that love and marriage go together like a horse and carriage, but infidelity evidently and annoyingly buzzed around the marriage like flies around the horse's rear passage. How can people love their partner so much that they would want to have a legal document which binds them to one person and which declares that this is the one and only person they will ever make love to?

This was where the gay world had it all straightened out - ironically! We have a natural urge for having sex with a variety of partners and not one in much the same way that we have a natural tendency towards eating a variety of different types of food and not the same meal day in day out. Marriage, monogamy and fidelity are totally unnatural, human fabrications and, in evolutionary terms, only a recent innovation. The urge to spread one's wild oats has remained an integral part of mammalian behaviour despite this ethereal belief in faithfulness. Further, this was in particular what it meant to be gay, to be out there having lots of sex with lots of different people. This was why the heterosexual world hated homosexuals so much because heterosexuals were constantly frustrated by their sexual droughts and looked on with envy at the accessibility to sex that gay people had.

But having said that, this didn't mean that I believed in sex with wild abandon either. I placed certain limits on sex. For me, sex had to be safe, private, clean and with no negative after effects, both physiologically and emotionally.

With this thought in mind, I looked up at the kitchen clock. It was almost seven thirty. It was about time to leave. So I put the paper down, grabbed my bag and set off for work.

I was an on-line facilitator or trainer for a company called Tevah Am. My primary role was to assist clients to increase their literacy and numeracy skills, and sometimes their knowledge in basic science, in order for these clients to be able to move on and do further training or to get themselves into the workforce. On-line training or facilitating was the new world of learning in the digital age, being a step forward in a brave new world, where now everyone had access to education anywhere and at anytime – at least theoretically.

Tevah Am was a private college which specialised in the training of those born locally who had not been successful through the school system or for migrants who needed to raise their language and numeracy skills in the English language.

The old chalk-and-talk form of teaching had almost completely disappeared and had been replaced by the new on-line-anytime form of training and learning. However, while learning and training were no longer bound by location and time constraints, our salary was still wrapped up in the old system of an hourly rate payment. The only way that our working hours could be policed was for us to be physically present at a particular organisation. Really, in this new digital age, it was possible for me to train someone anywhere in the world because my communication was merely via the computer and through cyberspace. However, our employers were unable to truly see whether they were getting their full money's worth for our employment unless they could actually see us on the premises which meant that our actual working conditions were a throw back to the old on-site system.

Having grown up in the old on-site system of education, the new on-line-anytime system of learning and training was rather strange. There appeared to be no definite structure and it was as if the learners were learning individually in order to remain in their own private little worlds. There was no collective learning and therefore no collective experience of learning that could be shared and joked about as people grew older. Learners increased their knowledge through individual learning programs so although there may be a large number of learners in the one room, each learner was learning their own thing as if they lived in isolation.

Education had now become atomised. At least this was the case with tertiary education. There was no more classroom camaraderie. There was no more common learning. There was no more shared experience. Learning had become individual, own-paced, personal, insular.

Tevah Am followed a new pattern of delivery. It was an open-space version of learning. There were very large rooms, which we called on-line access rooms, and in each room were a series of computers. Instructors like me sat in the room or wandered around helping each student with his or her own personal learning schedule. There could be forty people in the one room at the one time but although they sat in close proximity physically, mentally they were at different ends of the universe.

In short, I hated it. Of the many potential problems that I knew would arise from this new way of learning, it was the atomisation of society and the atomisation of knowledge itself that I thought was the most damaging. In the old school system, everyone learnt the same thing and so there was shared knowledge which created unity among those who shared the same experience of gaining this knowledge.

Even our workplace had become somewhat atomised. The time schedules of each trainer were staggered in such a way that we all started and finished work at different times. This meant that the individual learning centre could stay open for long hours and be manned for the entire time. There were no scheduled morning tea and lunch breaks. Each on-line trainer had a break for morning tea or lunch only when there was a lull so this meant that the chances of two colleagues actually stopping for a break at the same time were small. Having a chat around a morning coffee or a deep discussion over the lunch break were fanciful oddities of a bygone era. We were here to work and to play a supporting role for second-rounders, those who had missed out in their first go in educational life either in Australia or somewhere overseas. But there was no design to make this a social event, either between instructors and learners, or between instructors themselves.

But despite the constraints put on the ability to socialise, the reality was that socialising or at least exchanges in conversation were possible. Although each on-line access room could house around forty learners at a sitting, there were peak times and off-peak times throughout the day. During the off-peak times, there could be as few as two learners on the computers and these two learners may continue their learning without any outside help. It was during these times that us trainers would slowly and naturally get together and make conversation.

Of all the other fellow-trainers I worked with, Nikita was the one I liked the most. Although she carried a typical Russian name, she had earned the name not because of Russian heritage but because of a favourite character out of a novel that Nikita's mother had particularly liked and hence Nikita's mother had decided to personalise this favourite character through one of her daughters.

I really liked Nikita a lot. This was probably because Nikita, like me, was gay. But then, even though our sexuality was on a par, I knew that it really wasn't the similar sexual orientation that united us. In fact, I had learnt the hard way that sexuality had very little to do with human affinity. After all, there were many gay men out there in the world, and there were many among them with whom I would never want to find myself stranded together on a deserted island. By contrast, there were heterosexual men and women in general who I felt very close to and it had nothing to do with any physical attraction.

Nikita had short hair, bleach-blond and spiked in very alternative fashion. This contrasted noticeably with my long below-shoulder-length hair as if Nikita and I had deliberately set out to exchange the short-hair-for-men-and-long-hair-for-women style of hairdo in order to be contrary to years of tradition when in reality we had both simply decided on our hairstyles independently because we simply chose to wear our hair in this way.

I got on well with Nikita. I think this was due to Nikita's cynical approach to society. We both had been scarred by the small-minded intolerance in all religions and in almost all societies simply as a result of our sexuality. Nikita, however, had a double whammy – not only was she a lesbian, she was also a woman. As a woman, at least according to western religions and even classical mythology, she had to bear the brunt of the fault of a primeval woman who was the blame for bringing in all the evils into the world and as a result be condemned along with all her sisters of the human race to bare the blame for causing all of the world's ills. Nikita had nothing but fiery contempt for such absurd myths and she was hostile towards those who maintained that these myths were historical events. I could well empathise with her. When I reflected back both on the Adam and Eve story and the myth of Pandora's Box, I could see that it was hard for a woman to look on the societies which founded themselves on these peculiar stories and not get angry at these societies' ill-directed blame at all women when they simply should be blaming only Eve and Pandora – had these women really existed in the first place. Further, there is a lot of suspicion surrounding these stories as they came from a man's hand. Would a woman writing a myth be as harsh towards her own sex? When looked at in this light, I wondered how women could ever ascribe to any of these religions at all.

And yet there were women who embraced these religions with open arms. Not the least Hebbeera, another colleague who worked with us. Her dedication to Christianity, at least her version of the religion, was unequalled in sincerity. Hebbeera was odd and mysterious in many ways. She was religious and in particular Christian but the denomination of the Christianity she ascribed to was not clear and she was not very forthcoming about it either. For all we knew, she was a Sunday Christian and she believed in much of the external trimmings of Christianity such as the need to go to church on Sunday, the ferocious need to celebrate Christmas and Easter with full religious zeal, and the strict observance of sex only within the marital state. Even then, her approach to sex was that the entire idea was quite grotesque, and men and women only engaged in such a disgusting activity when the couple desired to sire offspring. I often thought that she would have made a great Essene, a religious adherent to an ancient yet odd Jewish sect, a religion which flourished in the Dead Sea area around the time of the formation of Christianity, which held among other beliefs the idea that sex was purely for procreation. And the Essenes followed this precept to its logical conclusion in a way that most Christians today would find uncomfortable. Husbands and wives in the Essene cult only ever had a sexual encounter when bearing offspring was the motive but then they separated and lived away from each other for the rest of the time without any physical contact whatsoever. The way Hebbeera talked about it, she had this same approach to intimacy.

Her cultural background was just as mysterious. Although on the whole she spoke English with the Aussie twang, there was something in the way she pronounced certain vowels that revealed a foreign touch to an otherwise fully Aussie-grown English. Her name itself, Hebbeera, was unusual. I had never heard anyone carry this name before, neither by an Anglo-Celt nor by anybody from any of the countries from which many of my acquaintances and learners came from. The name sounded like a blend of two names although I was never enlightened as to the actual source of the name. My suspicions were that she was of Middle Eastern extract of some kind, either fully or partially, and belonged to a denomination of Christianity which had an orthodox slant, and yet, much of what she said about Christianity was creepily similar to the Protestant Bible-believing varieties that I was familiar with in my growing up. My reasoning for this analysis of her was that she spoke Arabic well as well as Farsi. But she also spoke Urdu. I remember when in fascination I asked her why she could speak these languages that she gave me a deadly look of what seemed like anger as if I had asked her a personal probing question about the intimate details of her sex life. So, I knew never to ask again. It also made me even more curious to know her origins. After all, Arabic, Farsi and Urdu were three languages spoken in predominantly Muslim countries and yet Hebbeera was vehemently Christian. I had to make second guesses about her history and grabbed small snippets each time I overheard in fragmented form the conversations she had with the on-line learners, particularly when she spoke in Farsi which I to a certain degree understood.

Her religiosity was somewhat annoying. She often made comments that were stingingly condemning of those who did not believe in her religion, comments which angered Nikita and me. She even made comments from time to time about Nikita's and my hairdo, and how that God expected our hairstyles to be opposite to what we had. Because of her judgemental attitude, Nikita and I never let on about our sexuality. Because Hebbeera knew that I was single, she often asked me when I planned to get married and made helpful suggestions regarding the right woman to catch for a wife. Because of her fanaticism and because I had to work together with her at least a couple of hours of every day, to avoid an unnecessary confrontation, I simply did not let on why I would never marry, at least, not in a way that Hebbeera thought I should. Yet, we lived in the twenty-first century in Sydney, Australia, where I could live my sexuality openly, and being open to Hebbeera would have helped to bring her boldly up to date to the point at which our civilisation had brought us. But I didn't feel it was worth an argument. The terrible thing for her was that, because of this, Nikita and I did not feel comfortable engaging in conversation with her because we had to be careful of what we said, so Nikita and I always tried to avoid engaging in conversation with her. However, Hebbeera didn't seem to be aware of this. Rather, when it was a slow-moving morning and the learners were well occupied, Nikita and I got together to have our own private conversation until Hebbeera intruded on our conversation and then domineered it.

There were a number of other colleagues who worked with us but because they came at the time that I usually knocked off for the morning, I did not have much of a social interaction with them as much as I had with Nikita or Hebbeera. Hebbeera, Nikita and I were the odd threesome, the not-very-holy trinity of the morning session of Tevah Am. Students, or using the twenty-first century lingo, learners dropped in at any time throughout the day, starting at about 8 am and continuing right up till about 10.30 at night. Much of the content of their studies was carried out using Moodles which had all the learning content, e-documents to read, recorded lectures which the students could watch again and again, and on-line tutorials. We, the trainers at the drop-in centre, had the job of facilitating the learners, that is, when everything else on the Moodle failed, the learners had someone on site who they could ask for guidance. This was where we came into the picture. Nikita was strong on maths and English. So was Hebbeera, but she had the added benefit of speaking the popular languages of some of our students, namely Arabic and Farsi. I was employed because of my science background which also meant that I had a good level of maths, but I was also like Hebbeera in that I could speak some of the languages of the learners.

My hours were also rather irregular. I worked a split shift. I had a morning shift which began at 8.00 and continued till 12.00. I then took on the night shift three nights a week from 6.00 till 10.30. The other two days I worked the afternoon shift from 1.00 to 5.00. I was the only trainer at this training centre who worked two shifts during the day. The other trainers only accepted four hour teaching blocks in the middle of the day. These working hours attracted those with school children because it enabled the trainers to drop children off at school, come to work and then pick children up later in the day. The evening blocks attracted people who had other jobs during the day and wanted a second job to enhance their income. More women than men worked during the day shift because, even though we live in a society which believes in the equality of both sexes, in married relationships there was still the throwback to the ancient custom of the man being the primary breadwinner and therefore a woman worked to supplement the family income, not to contribute to it equally. This also explained why many who worked the day shift at Tevah Am were rather religious because religious women were willing to continue this tradition of playing the subordinate role to their husbands in obedience to the injunctions in their religious books.

Of course, Nikita and I were different. Nikita held another job which she did in the afternoon. She did not want, like me, to work entirely for Tevah Am and so she had a job in a different area. She also had a long-term partner who had a steady and well-paying job. Because it was so hard to find willing employees to work the night shift, I was happy to take on the additional work even if it meant splitting my workday in two. It was an odd workday but it worked for me.

There were some beneficial side-effects of this job. Although our role was simply to aid the learners through their learning programs, friendships did develop. Sometimes in the course of an explanation, a subsequent conversation would ensue and this would somehow lead to a friendship beyond the bounds of Tevah Am. However, more often than not these relationships tended only to be ephemeral.

There was one young guy called Daniel. A Dinka from the south of Sudan, Daniel fell into the hands of marauders from the north where he was then reduced to slavery. After years of ill-treatment and privation, he managed to escape and flee to Egypt, call on the help of the UNHCR and finally be granted permanency in this great island continent. He was a pleasant guy and I visited him a few times at his place. I even showed him how to cook some basic meals as he was totally inept at this skill and had been relying on junk food as his staple diet. His aim was to get a job to support himself so that he could later marry and start a family. After completing his learning program at Tevah Am, we maintained a friendship during which time I assisted him to get through an apprenticeship as a car mechanic. But it was a friendship that didn't last. Daniel eventually drifted quietly out of my friendship circle and I discovered later that he had finally married and moved to Perth.

Then there was Elliot, an Aboriginal guy from Victoria. I really loved Elliot and we had a short relationship. Elliot had a tragic childhood, born into a household of many children with a father who abused him physically and emotionally. When his father died, Elliot moved to Sydney and lived with an uncle. This uncle helped him to get back on his feet and introduced him to Tevah Am which is where Elliot and I met. It wasn't long before the feelings between us were made clear. We often went out together and Elliot stayed over at my place some nights. However, he told me that the trauma of his upbringing created a yearning for him to trace back his history and find meaning in his aboriginality. He told me that he wasn't deserting me completely but as soon as he could make the connection with his distant past, this would make things easier for him to develop the future connections he had with me and help move into a new future together. He moved back down to stay with his community in Victoria but then I learnt that he had tragically died in a car accident. That was a tragedy that took me a long time to get over.

Another learner who became an ephemeral friend was Musa. Musa was an Iraqi who escaped his country of birth during the Saddam Hussein era. He had also been for a time an inmate of the infamous Abu Ghraib jail. Although willing to show me the permanent reminders on his chest, back and legs of the torture he experienced while in prison, he left it to my imagination as to how these horrid scars came about. His daring yet successful escape out of the prison and the country was further evidence of what humans can achieve under extreme circumstances. I visited Musa on a regular basis as Musa was happy to help me to learn Arabic. Musa took great pleasure in my name as it was the name of one of the archangels shared by Jews, Christians and Muslims. Often when I knocked on the door and Musa asked who it was, when I called out that it was Michael, Musa would say in Arabic, "Michael from heaven!" and then laugh. He would then ask in Arabic as I entered the flat, "Who are you?" and then answer in Arabic his own question, "I'm Michael from heaven" and laugh. I never understood the joke but then I guessed that it was also Musa's mind which had suffered from the effects of the Abu Ghraib prison which caused him to act so strangely, albeit harmlessly. I guess that this was also the reason why one day he just simply disappeared without a trace and with no explanation. Simply one day when I arrived at his unit, he didn't answer when I knocked on the door and no longer answered his mobile phone when I rang or sent an sms. Whatever became of him has ever since remained a mystery.

Then there was Faraj from Iran. Faraj fled Iran in his early thirties. He had been the member of an opposing political party of the state. His party operated clandestinely, and he and all the members thought that the government didn't know what they were doing. But the government was well aware of every step that was taking place. When one of the party members mysteriously disappeared, the other party members knew that there was no alternative except to flee the country. I always found this a horrible prospect. In Australia, the current major political parties are Labor and Liberal. Putting this into an Australian context, this is equivalent to saying that if the current ruling party is Liberal, but you are a member of the Labor party, if you continue to meet with other Labor party members in order to try to get voted in, the Liberal party members would imprison and even execute you and all your other Labor party members if they caught you having clandestine meetings.

What happened to the members of opposing parties who were caught was not pleasant. They often first had a jail sentence. Faraj told me that one of the most "popular" ways to dispose of such "renegades" was to wrap them up in large hessian bags, fly them to a great height hitched to the bottom of a helicopter, and then jettison them onto a rocky outcrop hundreds of metres below. What mind comes up with these ideas to dispose of people?

Being a member of an opposing political party which worked against the state subsequently put Faraj's life in danger and therefore led him to his eventual flight halfway across the world to Australia.

Faraj had become quite a good friend. He was an avid body builder and had a body that would have been the envy even of Achilles. Faraj was someone I socialised with often and we spent time either exploring the suburbs or simply at one another's places. Faraj was an odd friend in the sense that he was a heterosexual to the extreme and yet accepted my homosexuality without flinching. In fact, he was someone with whom I could really discuss just about anything. Faraj maintained that he was a Muslim but he lived a life markedly different from the pervading view of Muslims in the general public. He was nothing like the type we heard about in the media, those who killed people simply because they did not follow their versions of Islam. Faraj was amazingly open to alternate views and alternate beliefs while at the same time maintaining a strong dedication to his own religion.

Outside the working arena was a very good friend of mine, Khatyn. Khatyn had been a colleague of mine when we worked at a college called the Australian English Language College, or AELC, but when this college closed down, Khatyn and I found new jobs in different workplaces. But we had established a strong friendship that was now quite fixed and firm. We were quite close and I had dubbed her The Woman I Would Marry If I Wasn't Gay, a title I thought she would find offensive but in fact made her laugh. Khatyn knew that the pay at Tevah Am was average and the only reason I had sought a job there was because there wasn't much else out there in the work market which needed my skills. The work at Tevah Am was suitable for me because it used both my linguistic and my scientifico-mathematical skills, skills that I had acquired because my first degree at university had been in chemistry and I had worked as a research chemist for many years before going back to university to pursue a course which was more in line with my interest in linguistics. However, although this was a rather unique blend, it was not reflected in the way I was paid. To at least make my pay substantial, this was another reason why I worked the three night shifts, especially because the hourly rate for working at night was enticingly much higher.

No doubt to help me get ahead economically, Khatyn always brought to my attention overseas postings of exceptionally good pay in countries eager for native English speakers to teach English. I remember that she first told me about the opportunities to teach in Japan. Then there was Hong Kong. And then there was mainland China. And then once she told me of excellent opportunities in Dubai.

"And the pay's fantastic!" she exclaimed. "I've heard of people going to Dubai for a year and when they return, they have earned so much money that they can buy their own house!"

I would always reply with an expression on my face that Khatyn called The Look.

"Khatyn, how would I survive in this country for a year? Dubai is an Arab country, no doubt very Muslim, and therefore very severe against homosexuals. How would I survive there? How would I get away with nobody knowing that I'm gay? Truly, is it really worth it?"

"It would only be for a year," Khatyn assured me.

A year. I couldn't last that long trying to pretend I was something I was not. I had done that for the first twenty-odd years of my life. Since then, I had been living very openly so it would have been next to impossible to go back and live in the closet again. I was too content with my life in Australia anyway to go and live somewhere else where I would have to pretend I was something I wasn't just to make other people happy.

Then one day, Khatyn showed me an advertisement in her local newspaper. It was all about an organisation called the Msingi wa Mungu Project. The organisation asked for volunteers to go to Tanzania to participate in programs there. People could participate in a variety of programs: engineering, building, information technology, science and maths. And there was one program which required the teaching of English. The article was lengthy and talked about how people could go there for as short as a two week period or for longer stretches such as six months. The organisation claimed to be non-denominational and had both Christian and Muslim backing.

"Wow! That would be curious!" I said with a laugh. "At the moment, the Christians and Muslims around the world are bitter enemies and here is an organisation being run in harmony by these two supposedly opposing factions."

"Well, why don't you give them a ring and find out? It would be interesting. You could have a little working holiday and maybe pick up another language. I mean, what language do they speak in Tanzania?"

"Swahili," I replied.

"There you go. And haven't you noticed that a lot of your African learners speak Swahili?"

This was true. The two most popular languages spoken by our sub-Saharan African learners were Dinka and Swahili. However, I noticed that Dinka was only spoken by some, but not all, Sudanese who had sub-Saharan African physical features, an example being Daniel. By contrast, I discovered that sub-Saharan Africans who spoke Swahili came from a wide range of countries, such as Ethiopia, Somalia and even from the Congo. When I had asked these students why they could speak Swahili, they explained that they had learnt the language while living in refugee camps in Kenya or Tanzania. Because of this, I had bought a couple of books and CDs in order to learn Swahili so that I could communicate with these students, even though it was only at a rudimentary level of the language. It was also my first introduction to a sub-Saharan African language.

But to go and live in Africa, even for only a couple of weeks? You've got to be kidding, I thought. I enjoyed the modern luxuries the twenty-first century had to offer me in my wealthy country, my comfortable soft bed and pillow, my unit with all the electronic devices that came with it, my car, tarred and sealed roads to drive on, supermarkets filled with a vast array of food, nightclubs and bars, even fresh water at the turn of a tap. Why would I want to exchange all this for a straw hut on a dirty, dusty floor, a tree for a toilet, a bucket for a shower, a donkey for transport, water from a well I had to first walk kilometres to get to and then boil the water before I could drink it? Why would I want to go to such a place just to pick up a language? I had managed to learn communicable Swahili in the comfort of my own country and what I could speak was usable.

And, I mean, these people had left their countries to come to mine so they had more of an incentive to learn English than I had to learn Swahili.

I thanked Khatyn for showing me the article but declined the offer. It would take a mercy mission of extreme proportions to dislodge me out of my comfort zone and coax me to spend time in a country that still operated in an epoch a couple of centuries behind my own. The pay wasn't bad enough at Tevah Am to entice me to rough it for better pay, even for a short period.

How little did I realise at the time that this article was to change the very course of my destiny.

Chapter 2

"Michael?" Peter called me one morning in the tone of an old school principal as I passed his office.

Peter was our new direct line manager although his title did not bear much weight. Rather, he was simply a trainer-in-charge, which translated as someone who had managerial responsibilities but was only paid pathetically little more than a trainer. Peter's job was quite demanding of his time so much so that Peter looked constantly gaunt and tired as he put long hours into the job simply to get a couple of extra dollars in his weekly pay packet. Although the position itself was not glamorous, it came with the promise of a step up into a higher managerial position, although as the months rolled by this promise looked more and more illusive than real.

This made Peter rather dry and cynical but he managed a self-composure so as not to take out his frustrations on those lower down on the echelons of the company.

Of the many tasks assigned to Peter, one was to interview referrals to Tevah Am and assess their abilities in English, maths and science, and then find out what their future goals were. From this he designed a personal program for the learner, analogous to a personal trainer designing an exercise program for a newcomer to a gym. Tevah Am with a logic of its own called each program an *Occurrence*. This Occurrence was then divided into individual units: reading units, writing units, numeracy units and science units. Each unit had an hourly rating assigned to it. There were some units assigned with ten hours, some with fourteen, some with twenty, some with twenty-seven, some with fifty and so on, and Peter's job was to produce an Occurrence of 200 hours made up of enough units that when totalled together made the proscribed 200 hours. However, the units couldn't simply be selected at random. There were rules as to which units could be used together and which couldn't but it was quite a complicated affair. For example, if a learner did, say, Unit A, that learner could not do Units F, G, I or P at the same time. If a learner did Unit B, that learner couldn't do Units D, H, Q, Y or Z at the same time either. Trying to assign enough units to make up 200 hours for each learner was like an IQ test in itself or a series of general ability questions in an entrance exam into a selective school. Who decided on this system remained a mystery but I surmised that whoever designed it either did it while he or she was drunk or it was intended as a gag but was then passed through as a brilliant idea by some bureaucrat who knew nothing about education. However, in order for Tevah Am to receive appropriate funding, Tevah Am had to comply with this form of training.

During the assessment period, if the new learners were migrants who came from a country in which English was not the first language, Peter would find out the migrants' first language and if they spoke a language that Hebbeera, I or any of the other staff members were proficient in. Peter would then inform the learners that there were on-site trainers who spoke their language and the times at which those trainers were available. Peter would then make us aware of the new learner who was coming to the centre so it didn't come as a surprise when a new face fronted up at the door. Because Peter was the new trainer-in-charge and had replaced the previous one who had moved on to newer employment, Peter still had to double check what skills each of us trainers possessed that matched the needs of our potential learners.

The way Peter had called me into his office sounded more like a reprimand than a call for my attention. I skulked into his room with what must have been a guilty look on my face.

Peter laughed. "Have you done something wrong?"

I looked at Peter. "Well, I don't think so, but the way you called me, it sounded as if I had."

Peter laughed again. "You speak Swahili, don't you?"

"A little," I replied.

"And you speak French?" Peter asked.

I admitted that I did speak French reasonably well. I had learnt French because a previous partner of mine was a Francophone. However, French certainly wasn't a favourite language of mine. This former francophonic partner was always disgusted whenever I admitted that I preferred speaking German. The relationship with this French speaking partner had been fleeting. My ability to speak French continued long after the relationship had ended. Nonetheless, even though French was not on the top of my list of languages I had to learn before I died, it still held some fascination for me. As my proficiency in this language increased, I became impressed to discover to what extent French vocabulary had infiltrated the English language. But what really fascinated me about French was finding out who actually spoke the language. French was a useful language to know because it came in handy when dealing with Vietnamese, at least of an older generation, with some Lebanese, Syrians and Egyptians, and from time to time we had students from francophonic sub-Saharan countries such as Senegal and the Congo.

"*Oui,*" I replied.

"*Bon, alors,*" Peter replied, showing the extent of his high school French. "We have a young boy coming on the program and I have told him to come in the morning when you are on site. Apparently he has only recently arrived in Australia so his level of English is not very high. He speaks Kirundi, Swahili and French."

I had never heard of Kirundi but guessed it was simply another sub-Saharan African language.

"Okay, that's fine," I replied. "What's his name?"

Peter looked at the interview form that the learner had filled in during the preliminary interview with Peter. "Polycarp. Polycarp Bilayakosa."

I laughed. "Are you serious?"

Peter looked at me puzzled. "What's so amusing?"

"Don't you know who Polycarp was?"

"Who he was? What do you mean, who he was?" Peter asked bewildered. "I guess he has always been Polycarp! He's a bit young to have been anything else."

"You know! St Polycarp, the disciple of St John, the fourth gospel writer."

Peter just gave me a smarmy look.

"Well, I don't think it's the same Polycarp."

Polycarp. The name itself comes from the Greek words *poly* meaning "many" and *karpos* meaning "fruit". But the only Polycarp I knew was one of the early Church Fathers. Polycarp's claim to fame was that he was a disciple of St John, one of the twelve disciples of Jesus. Like St John who wrote one of the Gospels and later three general letters or *epistles*, all of which constitute books of the Christian Bible, Polycarp also wrote an epistle, ancient copies of which still exist today. Polycarp's letter was written with the same love and devotion as his master's writings, written to the congregation of Christians in a city called Philippi, a city to which St Paul had written a letter many years earlier.

Polycarp probably left his mark because of the acclaimed miracles that occurred at his martyrdom. Polycarp was one of the presbyters of the ancient city of Smyrna, one of the seven cities to whom John the Revelator wrote his famous Revelation, a city which exists today in modern Turkey under the name of Izmir.

Polycarp was captured by the Romans and brought to trial. He was told to give up his Christianity and declare that Caesar was Lord. But Polycarp refused. As a result, Polycarp was condemned to be burnt at the stake. When the fire was lit, to the amazement of all the onlookers, the fire formed a large circle around Polycarp like a halo but the fire did not burn him. This was evidence of Polycarp's holiness. In frustration, and quite indifferent to the miracle, one of the executioners decided to pierce Polycarp in his left side and, lo and behold, another miracle occurred: a dove appeared from Polycarp's pierced side in a similar manner as a pigeon from a magician's hat. Needless to say, apart from this aviarial wonder, blood also flowed out in abundance from the wound and eventually, despite all these divine wonders, Polycarp was burnt to death anyway. The magic show was spectacular but not miraculous enough to prevent Polycarp's inevitable end at the hands of the Romans.

So holy and venerable was Polycarp that his martyrdom was written down by Ignatius, one of Polycarp's disciples. However, Polycarp was not holy enough to have his writings considered as part of the New Testament. Polycarp's writings were most probably outvoted because Polycarp was not a direct disciple of Jesus but rather a disciple of a disciple of Jesus, or in other words, a grand-disciple of Jesus. As a result, although Polycarp's letters are studied by students of theology, to the general Christian population of today, Polycarp and his writings remain largely unknown.

"When will he be coming?" I asked.

"Today, I guess."

"With a Roman legion?" I asked jestingly.

"If you want to arrange it," Peter replied dryly while handing me Polycarp's interview form. I took the sheet of paper and walked back to the on-line access room.

There was only one on-line learner all consumed in his studies, earphones on, eyes intently fixed on the screen and hand on mouse. There was therefore nothing for me to do at this point in time except simply stand and wait in case this on-line learner looked up and made signs that he wanted my attention.

I took out my smartphone from my pocket to see what the time was. My smartphone threw at me the noise of falling rain and windscreen wipers which was supposed to reflect the weather we were experiencing outside. However, one look through the window and it was obvious that it was a sunny morning. I noticed this happened often with my smartphone. There were times when the weather according to my smartphone was contrary to what the weather was really like outside. There had been times when I had relied on my smartphone for the current climatic conditions and subsequently ended up with washing on the line while it rained heavily outside or me deciding not to go to the pool when in fact it remained sunny for the entire day. I later learnt that it was better to rely on what I observed around me than what was written on my smartphone.

I slipped my smartphone back into my pocket. I could have simply sat or stood idly without moving which would have been as boring as being a shop assistant in a slow shopping moment. However, my father had taught me how to use my time efficiently. Moments of simply standing around doing nothing could actually be used effectively if you knew how. We were, however, forbidden to wear earphones connected to iPods and smartphones while we worked because our ears had to be open for an inevitable call for attention. However, because I was an avid language learner, I used these vacant moments to learn new vocabulary. At home, I always had a book lying somewhere in my unit, on the coffee table, on my work desk, on a lounge and so on. It was always a book in one of the languages I wanted to keep my proficiency in. Each time I read a word I didn't understand, I looked it up in the relevant bilingual dictionary and then wrote both the foreign word and its translation on a scrap piece of paper. This piece of paper would soon have a list of new words I wanted to commit to memory and I would then carry the list in my back pocket. During these lull moments, I would take the paper out and commit the words to memory. Being environmentally conscious, the scraps of paper I used were usually photocopies only used on one side destined to be thrown away and I gave these sheets of paper a second use before they ultimately were thrown into the recycling bin. I could memorise vocabulary and keep an eye on the learners at the same time so this helped me through the boring moments of my day.

It was early morning and quite quiet in the on-line access room except for the soft clickings of the mouse from time to time by this on-line learner. If no other on-line learners came in before Nikita did, at least when Nikita arrived the two of us could chat to pass the time.

With that thought, I became all involved with my vocabularly learning when I heard a noise at the door. I simply thought it was Nikita so when I looked up, I was expecting to see Nikita's smile and hear her greet me. However, what was at the door was a total stranger. It was a young sub-Saharan African boy and I knew immediately who he was – Polycarp. He entered the on-line access room slowly as if he were unsure whether to take another step. Although very dark skinned, his face seemed to sparkle and shine like polished ebony. He was medium height and fairly well-built which could be seen through the neatly ironed shirt he was wearing, with a sober coloured tie and dull navy blue trousers, as if he were dressed for an office job or at least for an interview.

He had the most beautiful features. His hair had been shaved to a manageable and neat length so that it covered his skull in perfect symmetry. The whites of his eyes contrasted greatly with the darkness of his skin but appeared as white as milk and without a blemish. His nose opened out to two large nostrils but it appeared purposely and correctly designed to appear that way. His lips were ample, sufficient but not excessive, and he had a strong, square, finely-shaped jaw.

His entire face shone with youthful innocence. I guessed that he was sixteen. He looked as if he were an angel who had inadvertently broken a wing and fallen from heaven and into my personal space. The Christians had got it all wrong: not all angels were beings that were bright, as white as snow and shiny - some were dark, as black as pitch, and youthful.

Polycarp just stood there all forlorn, not daring to take another step until I said something. Immediately a swell of feelings of pity overwhelmed me. I wanted to rush over to him, hold him and protect him from the evils of the world, to not allow his heavenly innocence be tainted by earthly affairs. I didn't want him to become entangled with the lusts and desires of the world so that, when his wing was repaired, on his flight back to heaven, God would not mistake him for one of His enemies. He may not have been the old, venerable Polycarp I had read about in history books but this modern day Polycarp lived up to his namesake's saintliness all the same.

"Please, come in and take a seat," I said to him. Polycarp looked at me with wide eyes which contrasted so distinctly from his dark skin. I realised I had spoken too quickly for him to understand and so I repeated the statement in Swahili.

"*Unasema kwa Kiswahili?*" Polycarp then asked with obvious delight. I understood that he had just asked me if I spoke Swahili. However, as he took his place, he went off on a tirade in Swahili and I didn't understand a word he said.

"*J'ai entendu que tu parles le français aussi,*" I then said to him, which is French for "I heard that you speak French as well". Polycarp was even more astounded and began rattling off in French although this time I understood every word, even though he spoke French with an accent typical of French speakers from sub-Saharan Africa. I told Polycarp to choose a computer and that I would help him to log in. I asked him for his documentation as he was issued with a unique identification number and various passwords he needed to get onto the computer, one to get onto internet and one to gain access to his particular Occurrence.

I spent about half an hour with him. I communicated with him in French because it was the only language between us that both of us could speak comfortably. I also was familiar with French vocabulary associated with computer technology and internet access. During this preliminary introduction to Tevah Am, I had the impression that Polycarp had actually never used a computer before in his life and he confirmed this when I asked him about his past use of the computer. Polycarp negotiated very slowly around the screen which meant that I had to be patient as I helped him to get onto the Moodle that contained his units. The computer, usually annoyingly so but this particular day fortunately, was so slow that it matched the speed at which Polycarp himself operated. This also allowed me in between times to engage in small talk and hence get a brief overview of who he was and why he was here.

In this short period of time, I discovered that Polycarp was a refugee from Burundi but had spent much of his time in a refugee camp in Tanzania. His first language was, in fact, Kirundi, the national language of Burundi. It was then that I discovered in which country Kirundi was spoken. However, he was only a young boy of about thirteen when he arrived in the refugee camp and it was there that he had picked up the national language of Tanzania, Swahili. He had learnt French because French was the language of instruction in Burundi and he had done all his schooling in French at least up until the time he had fled his country of birth. I could tell that he spoke a rather basic level of French typical of a twelve year old and I found sometimes that I had to simplify my French so that it was compatible with his level. While in one of the refugee camps, he had worked in a rudimentary way as a nurse and from that moment he realised that this was his vocation and hence career of choice. His first step in this direction was to learn English and this is what landed him in an Occurrence at Tevah Am.

I then discovered that Polycarp was twenty and that he had a nephew who he looked after. I asked him where his nephew's father was. Polycarp went really silent. I realised then that not all refugees were willing to divulge everything about their past. After this long pause, I noticed tears form in Polycarp's eyes. Eventually he said to me that a lot of things happened in Africa, terrible things that he preferred to forget. I realised then that there were limits to the questions I could ask him about his past.

Different refugees obviously have different reactions to their painful past experiences. Musa and Faraj were quite open when it came to relating to me their experiences in their countries of origin, and why and how they came to Australia. I also remembered when I worked as an English teacher at AELC that I constantly had classes full of refugees. The first refugee to divulge to me his entire story was an Afghani called Faisal. He was quite willing to tell me everything and to answer all my questions. In fact, Faisal and I developed quite a deep friendship which lasted for many years. My relationship with Faisal made me realise that perhaps refugees actually didn't mind relating their past experiences after all and that was why whenever I met refugees, I simply asked about how they came to Australia. However, Polycarp was obviously an exception. And his reaction to my question was a signal to me not to further probe into his past.

Getting Polycarp set up and on the way to his own independent learning took some time. I didn't even notice when Nikita had arrived along with a few other learners. When Polycarp was finally ready to continue on his own, I looked up. Nikita on the other side of the room nodded and smiled at me from a distance a non-verbal greeting to which I responded accordingly. This was also a signal for me to wander over to her for a social chat as all the other learners were now well and truly occupied. The morning progressed with the occasional assistance given to Polycarp who every so often lifted up his head and raised his hand for help. It was understood that Polycarp fell under my particular responsibility and so I responded to his silent pleas for help in either French or Swahili.

Soon Hebbeera arrived which signalled to me that I was now halfway through my shift and only had two more hours before I could clock off for the morning. Odd that she was, Hebbeera at least was a good colleague in that she cooperated well with the handling of learners, and so when I wandered over to her and explained that we had a new addition to the fold, I knew that she would know how to take up where I had left off when I had finished up for the morning.

When it got to about 11.00, I thought it wise to let Polycarp know that I would soon be leaving so that if he needed any help, he simply needed to speak to any of the other trainers who remained in the on-line access room. However, Polycarp's response to what I told him was quite alarming.

He just sat there motionless as if I had actually told him off. I looked at him and then noticed in his eyes tears begin to well up. Immediately I felt a lump form in my throat and then drop to my stomach.

"Is everything okay?" I asked him.

Polycarp didn't say anything immediately. He just looked at me. Then, slowly he raised his hand and took mine in his.

"Can I stay with you? I don't want to go home. There's nothing there."

I felt as if my blood had suddenly turned to ice.

"Is everything okay with you at home, Polycarp?" I asked him. "Is your nephew okay?"

At first, Polycarp just stared at me and it appeared as if he were straining to prevent himself from crying. Eventually he was able to speak.

"My nephew is at school and he won't be home until later. I don't want to go home to an empty house. I don't know anyone here."

I looked up at the ceiling and took a deep breath. My heart had been touched. Why couldn't I just be a trainer and turn off my feelings towards my learners? The cold, calculating side of me just thought, well, he is not your problem. The government brought him here. Your job is simply to direct him in his training and when that's finished, your responsibilities are over.

However, the more emotional side of me told me that this young boy was now a part of my community and so I had as much of a responsibility as anyone to do something.

"Polycarp, I will be finishing here in about an hour. If you want, I can drive you home and spend the afternoon with you until your nephew gets home. Would you like that?"

Polycarp nodded his head.

"If you have finished here, you can go to the canteen and grab yourself a cup of coffee or go to the shops. In an hour's time, just come back and meet me here. Okay?"

Polycarp nodded again but this time it was accompanied with a smile. He then slowly logged off the computer, gathered all his things into his bag and then left the room.

At about ten minutes before it was time for me to leave, Polycarp was already at the door of the on-line access room waiting. I pointed at the imaginary watch on my left wrist and then flashed the ten fingers of both my hands at him. He then disappeared. When I finally left, I met him just outside the building.

"Okay. Come on! Let's go," I said to him and off we went.

Polycarp told me his address but he didn't know how to get to his place by car as he was totally reliant on public transport and he really had no idea of the layout of the Sydney suburbs. I simply used my street directory to find the street he lived in and knew that once we had reached his street, he could direct me to his place.

Polycarp didn't say much as we drove home. There was a gentle silence in the car as he stared out the window. I didn't feel comfortable in the silence. But then I didn't know what to ask. Any question I wanted to ask led back to his past: So, how's your family? So, is the weather here different from your home country? So, how's life here compared to what it was like in your home country? Despite the discomfort of the silence, I felt I had no choice but to simply grin and bear it. And Polycarp didn't seem to mind. I thought he may comment on things that he saw out the window but he just sat motionless and observed the Sydney suburbs move idly by through the passenger side window.

We finally arrived in the street of his residence and then Polycarp guided me to his block of flats. He had a car space and told me I could park there. Polycarp then led me inside his flat.

Once inside, I looked around. My first reaction was to burst out laughing. Scattered around in the loungeroom was an assortment of furniture which did not match or go together at all, neither in colour nor in style. There were a number of different lounges and armchairs, some leather, some upholstered in fabric but all totally unmatching in colour co-ordination. There was an assortment of wall units. In particular, there was what looked like a beautiful ornate hutch in period furniture style decked out on top of two what looked like classroom desks. Underneath the dining table were six chairs but only one of the chairs actually matched the table. All the others were obviously from different diningroom sets. It reminded me of the native bower bird which collects and gathers anything according to a logic of its own to create its bower. What I saw was what would happen if a child was given his or her own house and allowed to furnish it without any adult input.

"Wow! You have a lot of furniture," was the only way I could actually address what I saw. "Where did you get it all?"

As if I didn't know.

"Off the street. Australia is great! People throw away such nice furniture so I pick it up and bring it home."

I could understand where Polycarp was coming from. Furniture was so easy to come by in Australia because a lot of furniture was often cast onto the street. You can judge the wealth of a nation by the type and amount of rubbish that a nation creates. A number of times a year, there is a council cleanup where people are invited to put any unwanted furniture on the street and then the council takes it away. As this day approaches, the mounds of unwanted furniture form a wall along the kerb almost as impressive as the Great Wall of China. At the same time, you see people stop and rummage through what has been placed there. As for what happens to the furniture when the council picks it up, this is something I have always wanted to know.

Apart from the great quantity of clutter, there wasn't much to make me laugh about the flat. When I entered the kitchen, it was small with tiles missing and had the stench of rotting wood. I opened one of the kitchen cupboard doors and looked inside only to be overcome by both sight and smell before closing it again.

"Have you spoken to your real estate agent about this?" I asked him.

"Yes. They know there is a problem. I've told them a few times. But they don't do anything."

The kitchen stove looked old and I could tell by the temperature range in Fahrenheit that this was an antiquated model. The fridge, however, looked brand new.

"That was given to me by the government," Polycarp explained.

I opened the fridge door and inside I saw yet more clutter. There were vegetables and fruit, tins and cans of so many varieties, bottles and containers of many things, as if there was almost no more room to put anything else. And this was for two people.

There was some food on a plate. I wasn't sure exactly what the food preparation was supposed to be.

"Who made this?" I asked Polycarp.

"I did. Would you like some?"

The food preparation looked like it was supposed to be a salad but the colours and my inability to determine the different food items used to make this illustrious cuisine didn't give me the courage to be able to even try a taste. I turned it down.

"That's okay. I'm not hungry. What about you? Are you going to eat?"

"Not now. Maybe later when my nephew gets home."

"Can I just have a look around in your flat?" I asked, although I had every intention of doing so anyway.

"Yeah. Sure."

I looked inside the bathroom. Once again, it was about as bad as the kitchen. Some of the bathroom floor and wall tiles were missing, there was no shower curtain for the shower recess and there were pit marks over the bathtub. The wooden bathroom cabinet was rotten and what should have been two sliding mirror doors on the vanity unit was simply shattered glass.

"How long have you lived here, Polycarp?"

"Only one month."

One month. This could not be a result of Polycarp's mistreatment of the place, surely.

Polycarp came across as such a placid young man that I couldn't even imagine him hurting a cockroach. But why was he given such paltry conditions to live in? I asked him how much rent he was paying and, when he told me, the blood rushed to my head in anger. He was paying almost the same amount of rent I was paying and yet the quality of his flat was not almost the same as mine. Even if we took into consideration the location, it was true that I lived in an area where flats were relatively cheap but even so, the quality of Polycarp's flat did not reflect the rent he was paying. I had the suspicion that the real estate agent was playing on Polycarp's total ignorance of value, what he could and should be paying. Also, because Polycarp spoke to his real estate agent and did not write a letter to explain the problems with his flat, this was most likely the reason why nothing ever got done. And knowing how basic Polycarp's English was, no doubt whenever Polycarp spoke to the real estate agent, the real estate agent could argue that they didn't know what he was saying anyway whenever Polycarp came to make requests and complaints.

This, or so it appeared to be at least, was what was going on. After all, real estate agents aren't famed for their brazenly immaculate honesty. This was also a clever strategy, to take in refugees from non-English speaking backgrounds and then do nothing to improve their living conditions. After all, one of the stipulations for having repairs done in a flat is to send a list of repairs in writing. Refugees from non-English speaking backgrounds on the whole can barely speak English so how on earth would they know the first thing about writing a complaint letter? They also probably don't understand everything written in the lease agreement especially as the language is termed in complicated legal language. The real estate agent no doubt gave him the lease agreement and just showed him the bottom line where to sign without explaining that any repairs that need doing, he simply needed to send a written request.

"Polycarp, have you told the real estate agent about all this?"

"Yes," Polycarp answered definitively. "But they do nothing. They just say, 'yes, yes' but nothing happens."

I rubbed my chin and thought.

"Polycarp, we need to write a letter to the real estate agent. That's how things get done here."

We moved from there to the two bedrooms. The bedrooms, however, looked okay. There were scratches and colour pencil marks over the walls but at least there was something about this flat that was tolerable. In each bedroom, the beds looked new. These, so Polycarp explained to me later, were provided for him when he moved into the place. But the cupboards looked old so I guess they were taken off the street.

We then made our way back to the loungeroom. Polycarp had a balcony, a very small one, almost like mere scaffolding than an actual balcony but there was room enough to put two chairs. Polycarp asked me if I wanted anything to drink and so I asked him for a cup of tea. I was going to sit and wait for him to make it but decided that to ensure I got a cup of tea that tasted like a true cup of tea, it was better that I made it myself. Polycarp came with me to the kitchen and pulled out an assortment of teabags from which I chose one of my liking. I offered Polycarp a cup as well and he obliged.

We went back out on the balcony. The view was nothing to get excited over, just more old, run down flats in the neighbourhood. But it was still a balcony and there was still a view. I really didn't know what to talk about with Polycarp. Africa seemed to be well out of the question. And I couldn't think of anything else to talk about. I was hoping that Polycarp would ask me some questions but he didn't seem to have the social skills or understanding that to get a conversation going, you actually have to ask questions.

I asked him what time his nephew was coming home. We had at least some time then to do something. In order to actually have a topic of conversation, I asked Polycarp to provide me with a pen and some sheets of paper so that I could write a letter to the real estate agent about those things that required fixing.

While writing the letter, I explained to Polycarp the importance of the written word in Australia. For everything we do, we need written evidence. It is not enough to just say something, you have to have a piece of paper to show evidence that you have actually tried to do something. I said this to be instructive but also to get him to open up about his adventures in Africa. But he didn't say anything. I was hoping he would say something like, "Well, in Africa, it's different. We do it like this." But he just listened and nodded his head. I also thought that because this was probably the first time he had had social contact with a local of his new country of residence, he would be interested in knowing something about me and therefore ask me questions. But he didn't. He didn't seem to be at all curious about me and my background, where I lived, whether or not I was married (although I was glad he didn't ask me that anyway), if I liked my job or anything of that nature. So, our conversation was simply about what we needed to write in the letter.

This, at least, made the time pass. Some time later, while we had been working on what to write, I heard a noise at the front door and in came a little young African boy. He was small and looked as if he were eight years old. As soon as he came in, he called out, "Eh weh", the Kirundi form of "hey, you." Polycarp then got up and went inside to greet him and I followed. I was expecting a typical parent-child greeting where the child jumps up and wraps loving arms around an awaiting parent. But instead, he just said hello to Polycarp bluntly and without any signs of emotion. Suddenly he looked at me and went completely silent. The whites of his eyes widened like two dishes on a black background, as if he were terrorised to see a white person.

"This is my nephew, Jeremiah," Polycarp said in order to introduce Jeremiah to me. I stuck out my hand to shake Jeremiah's but Jeremiah just stared at me.

"Who's this?" Jeremiah asked in Swahili, not realising I understood him.

"He's my teacher. And you can speak to him in Swahili. He understands."

Jeremiah stared at me for a moment and then said in Swahili, "So, you can speak Swahili?"

"*Ndiyo*," I replied, using a Swahili word with a similar meaning to "yes".

Jeremiah then looked at Polycarp and said, "I'm hungry." He may have been shy or shocked but obviously his shyness and initial shock went away very quickly. He disappeared into his bedroom to drop off his bag and then headed for the kitchen. Polycarp left Jeremiah to his own devices. I heard noises of clanging crockery, the fridge door opening and then banging closed again. Soon Jeremiah came out into the loungeroom with a bowl full of ice-cream.

I looked at the big bowl of ice-cream and wondered how so much ice-cream could fit inside such a little boy. I turned to Polycarp.

"Polycarp, is Jeremiah going to have tea?"

"I don't know. Right now, no. He's having ice-cream. He loves his ice-cream!"

I could only guess that if Polycarp allowed Jeremiah to eat ice-cream or anything Jeremiah so desired at any time that he wanted, Jeremiah was probably not being well fed. This made me evaluate the situation. Our country was humane enough to welcome refugees fleeing from the atrocities in other countries to find peace and tranquillity here. But once the refugees arrived in Australia, they were pretty much left to their own devices. No thought was put into whether or not these refugees knew anything about Australian society, whether or not refugees knew where to shop, what was a balanced diet, what was good hygiene, in short, how to survive in a modern nation like our own.

What made the situation even more difficult for Polycarp was that on paper Polycarp was twenty years old but emotionally he was still a child. He had come from a refugee camp in Tanzania and therefore no doubt knew nothing about how to live in Australia, how to raise a child, what foods to eat, nutrition, discipline and so on. We welcomed him into the country, gave him a flat and some furniture, and then left him to fend for himself and for a small child without checking whether or not he knew how to function correctly in this new life. There seemed to be no support for him. I could also imagine that in the refugee camp, food was scarce as is the general picture of sub-Saharan Africa, and therefore once in Australia, Polycarp and Jeremiah just felt that there was food in abundance to have and enjoy without any consideration of health issues that can result from this abundance. I was beginning to question what life skills Polycarp actually had.

"Polycarp, children shouldn't eat so much ice-cream. And Jeremiah should wait till dinner and then have ice-cream after he has eaten a healthy meal. He should eat fruit or some other snack at this time of the day." I said this in Swahili purposely and not in French as much for Polycarp as for Jeremiah.

Jeremiah looked up at me from behind his mountain of pink, brown and white snow in horror as if I had threatened to send him back to the country he had come from.

Then I thought of the overall picture of how these two were living. I began going through a mental checklist of things that we take so much for granted in the way we live in Australia. Did Polycarp know how to cook, to clean, to wash clothes, to use cleaning chemicals, the danger of overuse of cleaning chemicals? I realised that these kids really needed some guidance.

As a result, I volunteered to visit these kids regularly. I decided that I would come over on the two evenings during the week I wasn't working and make sure everything was okay, that Polycarp knew what to cook and how to prepare nutritious meals for both him and Jeremiah, that he knew how to deal with the everyday issues of living in a modern world, how to pay rent, which phone and electricity company to choose, where to shop and so on.

The first evening I came over to Polycarp's place, Jeremiah was a lot more respondent towards me than the first time I had met him, at least acknowledging that I had come. He showed no particular excitement that there was a visitor in the house who had come to rescue him and his uncle from the general indifference of the general Australian society.

That evening I decided to show Polycarp how to make a base red sauce. I find that a red sauce is an easy thing to start with and it can be used to prepare a variety of different foods with pasta, casseroles and so on. With a red sauce, you can add fish, chicken, beef, vegetables, and make a variety of quick meals. I thought that this was a good place to start when showing someone how to cook.

That night, we ate spaghetti with tuna. This was the first time that the boys had eaten spaghetti. I showed them the technique of holding the fork with its head on the spoon and then twirling the spaghetti around so that there was enough to get it into the mouth. Poor Polycarp had great difficulty co-ordinating this but Jeremiah, true to the nature of children, quickly learned how to get this all together.

After dinner, Polycarp brought out a large A4 envelope he had received that afternoon in the mail. He wanted me to read what was inside and explain it to him. I pulled the contents out of the envelope. There were reams of official documents. These were obviously official United Nations documents about the two boys. I was familiar with what UN documents looked like from my involvement with Faisal because I had to help Faisal understand what was written in official United Nations documents that were related to him.

"What are these, do you know?" I asked Polycarp.

"I think they're all my papers. When I was interviewed at the refugee camp in Tanzania, the UN officials told me that they would give me a copy of all the papers that I had to fill out to get a visa. These must be them. But what am I supposed to do with them? Can you read through these and tell me?"

"Yeah, okay," I replied.

I leafed carefully through the documentation but much of it was just photocopies of documents with Polycarp's and Jeremiah's photos on them, health reports and so on. As I came to each of them, I explained to Polycarp what they were. At this point I was conversing in Swahili and that was when I realised how rudimentary my Swahili was because I didn't know official words such as "health report", "photocopy" and so on.

For those things I didn't know the Swahili word, I said the word in French. However, Polycarp didn't know many of these French expressions either so on these occasions I had to beat around the bush to explain what the expressions meant. My lack of vocabulary when trying to explain all this officialdom that I was reading reminded me of the game *Taboo*.

Eventually I arrived at a series of documents which had a copious amount of writing, lots of reporting about something. I showed Polycarp and asked him if he knew what they were. Polycarp replied that he didn't and asked me to read them to find out what they were all about.

I looked at the dates at the top. There were series of UN reports stapled together. I sifted through them and then sorted them out into chronological order. No doubt, I thought, this would at least help me to work out how things went.

"Okay," I began in Swahili. I took the first document. I quoted the date at the top and then translated what the different aspects of the document were. The document was the result of an interview with Polycarp about his past in Africa. There was a preamble about who was present at this interview, the translator, the language used to translate, the date, the time and the location. Past this introduction, there was a summary of the interview. This summary, typed up as a computer generated document, summed up the details of the interview.

As I began to read the summary, my ability to read aloud evaporated. The summary spelled out how Polycarp no longer had anywhere back in Rwanda nor Burundi to return to and thus he came under the protection of the United Nations. The details were sketchy but enough to provide the general outline of what had possibly happened to Polycarp's family.

What shocked me at first was that Polycarp and his brother, the father of Jeremiah, were not the only children of Polycarp's parents. Rather, Polycarp was the youngest child of eight children, with two brothers and five sisters. The whereabouts of all his family members were unknown but most probably they were all deceased. As for the father of Jeremiah, not only was it certain that he had been killed, Polycarp was a witness to this horrid event. Jeremiah was only a baby at the time. Jeremiah's mother survived but later remarried, returned to Burundi, and then it was speculated that she also was killed along with her new husband. Polycarp was left alone with his nephew. Using the estimated dates of different events recorded in the report, this meant that Polycarp was about thirteen or fourteen years old when he became suddenly the carer of a child. Polycarp, a child himself, suddenly found himself with the responsibilities of raising a child.

I looked up at Polycarp but I was unable to say anything. I looked at this sweet, innocent-looking kid and realised that behind this innocent façade hid a history of horror stories. This kid was definitely hiding a lot of nightmarish memories.

"What is it?" Polycarp asked me quizzically.

I didn't know what to say at first. Then I just stammered, "L-l-let me just read on a bit first and then I'll explain."

I pulled out the next document. This document looked similar to the first and appeared to be the result of yet another interview. This one, however, was more detailed. Polycarp had been asked more questions to substantiate everything that was summarised in the earlier document. There were pages and pages of information which I needed to read through. Each page painted the picture of what this young man from Africa was hiding inside that young head of his.

The document explained the full name of Polycarp's father, mother, two brothers and five sisters, their respective spouses for those who had them, and all of Polycarp's nephews and nieces. The story was that Polycarp was originally born in Kigali, the capital city of Rwanda. But although he was born there, he and all his family members were considered refugees because Polycarp's parents and older siblings had escaped a war in Burundi and found refuge in Rwanda. But the Rwandan government only considered their refuge as a temporary measure and it was made clear through the identity cards everyone had to carry that for the whole time they lived in Rwanda, Polycarp's family were and always would be refugees.

Then there was another war. I guessed that this was the infamous war between the Tutsis and the Hutus. As a result of this war, the entire family had to run away. However, during the scuffle, the members of the family got separated. However, what caused the separation was not made clear.

Only Polycarp, his brother and his sister-in-law managed to escape to Tanzania to a city called Kigoma on the banks of Lake Tanganyika. They were gathered into a refugee camp alongside all other refugees from the same war. While in the camp, one night some hoodlums with guns managed to get inside the camp and went around on a killing spree. One of the victims of this killing spree was Polycarp's brother. Polycarp managed to hide during the shooting but although he was out of sight, he was not out of earshot and he heard the sounds of shooting followed by the torturous sounds of people dying.

At that time, Jeremiah was only a baby. Because of this attack by hoodlums, the Tanzanian government decided to move the refugees to another refugee camp. Polycarp's sister-in-law refused to go. She was too frightened to move. She also no longer wanted the responsibility of Jeremiah as Jeremiah was a reminder of her late husband. As a result, Jeremiah came under Polycarp's responsibility. Polycarp, a child himself, became responsible for a child.

Eventually, the UN became involved with Polycarp's case. The report indicated that there was nothing in Polycarp's answers that gave any suggestion that Polycarp was lying. The report further explained that Jeremiah was happy to be with his uncle and that his uncle treated him well. This meant that they should remain together.

Eventually, so the report continued, Jeremiah's mother went back to Burundi and remarried. There were reasons to believe that she and her new husband were murdered.

Polycarp and Jeremiah had no family members left except themselves. It was then up to the UN to decide where to send them. The possibilities were the UK, Sweden, the Netherlands, Canada, the USA, New Zealand or Australia. The UN chose Australia. And here these two were, in this little flat in the suburbs of Sydney.

I sat up and looked at Polycarp. I could feel tears in my eyes.

Polycarp looked at me disturbingly. "Is everything alright?" he asked.

"Have you read this report?" I asked.

"No, I can't understand it. What is it about?"

"Now I know what happened to you in Africa."

With that, I gave him a big hug. Polycarp responded but it was a hug that was not reciprocated, as Polycarp did not quite understand why I had become so emotional. It took me a moment to pull myself together again before continuing the conversation.

"Tell me. It says in these reports that the members of your family cannot be located. Is it possible that they could still be alive? Any of them?"

Polycarp bowed his head. "No. I'm sure they're all dead." There was a slight pause. Polycarp then looked away.

"I don't want to think about Africa anymore. I just want to forget everything and start again."

The tone in Polycarp's voice said it all. There were a lot of questions I wanted to ask him about what had happened in his past and about the war from his perspective. But it was very clear that there were a lot of memories that were much too painful for Polycarp to bear.

According to Polycarp, everything was lost, everything, all his possessions but also his entire family. Family is what gives us some sort of identity, and tells us who we are and where we belong. Polycarp no longer had anyone except his nephew. However, according to the UN report, the only definitive information about Polycarp's family was that all the other members of his family simply went missing. There was nothing to say that they were definitively dead. The possibility still remained that members of his family may well be still alive.

But how was Polycarp going to find this out? From his response, it sounded as if he didn't want to even try. All hope was lost. He had resigned to the fact that he was starting from zero, a new life in a new country with total strangers. I could also tell that he did not even want to try and find out if it were possible that any of his family members were still alive. After all, what would happen if he tried to do so and after all this trying, he discovered that, yes, it is true, all his family were dead? I could understand what was going on in his mind. He wanted a complete break from the past. It was no use turning back. It was time for a new beginning, a new tomorrow, a new start to life. The past was too painful a memory and it was time to make new, fresh, positive and happy memories.

But then a thought crossed my mind: what if I tried to find out for him without Polycarp knowing what I was doing? I could do the research. If any of his family still existed, this would be wonderful news for Polycarp and would give him at least a remnant of a family to which he belonged. Alternatively, if it could be confirmed that all members of his family were in fact dead, then this chapter of Polycarp's life could be conclusively closed. And all this could be done without Polycarp's knowledge so that he would not need to relive the memories of his past.

A few days later, I did an internet search to find out the contact details of the United Nations High Commission for Refugees, or the UNHCR. There was a website which presented a variety of programs run by the UNHCR around the world. The UNHCR, so I discovered, did work that was quite extensive. It helped to improve educational facilities in underprivileged countries, to help communities improve their drinking water, their sanitary systems and their general infrastructure. However, I was simply interested in getting details of Polycarp's family. Eventually I found down at the bottom of the web page as I scrolled down a tab entitled Contact Us and the corresponding contact details. I immediately composed an email and sent it. Within a few days, I received a reply from the UNHCR in Canberra. The UNHCR contact replied that the UNHCR office in Australia only concerned itself with Australia, New Zealand,

Papua New Guinea, the Solomon Islands and the South Pacific. For further information about Polycarp, I would need to contact the UNHCR office in Arusha, Tanzania, as this office concerns itself with countries in the sub-Saharan African zone.

Tanzania. As soon as the name of this country left the pages of this email and entered my consciousness, it matched up with the organisation Khatyn had told me about in the same country, the Msingi wa Mungu Project. The UNHCR and the Msingi wa Mungu Project both had similar ideals, at least where education was concerned. Was it possible that those who worked at the Msingi wa Mungu Project also had intercommunication with the UNHCR in Tanzania?

But what if I physically had to go to Tanzania to get this information? Would I be prepared to do this? For a helpless and innocent young boy like Polycarp I would be prepared to do much more. Roughing it in a foreign country for a short period of time would be nothing compared to finding out conclusively whether or not a nice kid like Polycarp still had other family members.

The next time I saw Khatyn, I asked her for the contact details of the Msingi wa Mungu Project. Once I had these details, I rang the office and spoke with the receptionist. The receptionist suggested I come in for an appointment. She emailed me a form that I needed to complete and then asked me to come in for an interview.

A date was made and soon I was on my way.

Chapter 3

The Msingi wa Mungu Project sounded rather ambitious in its claims to be run by people who all believed in God, irrespective of their religious backgrounds. Before making a phone call, I did an internet search on them and discovered that they had as their basis that all religions were basically and fundamentally the same. The basis of all religions was respect, tolerance and helping people. The runners of the project were even able to demonstrate this by quoting from sections from the well-known holy books to substantiate this claim.

The Msingi wa Mungu Project was not the only time I had heard of an organisation or group of people who had come up with the idea that all religions were fundamentally one and the same. The Hindus for centuries had always been welcoming of other religions and the reason why Hinduism appears on the surface to be an incomprehensible conglomerate of divine beings is because of this all-inclusiveness. An example is how elements of the Christ, under the guise of the god Krishna, on close scrutiny are recognisable to modern day Christians. Whereas in Europe where the worship of the Christ completely took over the worship of the Roman gods and goddesses, Christ in the form of Krishna simply blended in with all the other gods and goddesses of the Hindu pantheon when Christianity was brought to India. Even heroic figures from the past were accepted into the Hindu godhead, such as the god Iskander, who is in fact simply the great historical figure of the Greeks, Alexander the Great.

Later, when Europe began to wake up from its intellectual slumber when the Enlightenment began to take on its full effect, the German philosopher, Immanuel Kant, arose out of the religious turmoil of the time and made the surmisation that although all religions seemed different, they all really had the same objective. Putting aside all the external trimmings of religion such as hierarchical order and superstitious rites, the core of religions such as tolerance and moral behaviour showed that those of all religious persuasions had a common ground which united them altogether.

Then later, in 1844, an Iranian called Siyyid Ali Muhammad Shirazi believed that God had inspired him to lead a movement that united all religions, or at least the main well-known religions of the time. This eventually led to the development of the Baha'i faith or Baha'ism, a religion which recognises all the holy books as equally divine, at least all those acknowledged as holy books at the time of his ascent.

Again, later in the same century, another visionary, a Punjabi by the name of Mirza Ghulam Ahmad, who claimed not only to be a prophet but further the returning Jesus Christ himself, began an alternative form of Islam, the Ahmadiyya Muslim Community, a movement which developed almost in parallel with the formation of the Baha'i faith. Contrary to our conventional understanding of Muslims, Ahmad claimed that not only was Muhammad a prophet of God, Ahmad also acknowledged the major prophets of the Judaeo-Christian Bible. He even went further and welcomed other great figures of antiquity who formerly had no particular religious affiliation, such as Socrates, the Buddha and Confucius, into the Al-Ahmadiyyah Islamic fold.

So the Msingi wa Mungu Project was nothing new. It was just another organisation which struggled with each religion's claim that those who belonged to the religion alone held the truth and those who did not follow the truth were just loathsome, dirty, evil people. This unfortunately did not match up with reality because, despite what anyone of any religious persuasion wanted to believe, there were after all nice Jews, nice Christians, nice Muslims, nice Buddhists, nice Hindus, nice Zoroastrians and simply nice people in all walks of life, even though those outside the religion did not hold the same beliefs as those within.

However, although cynical about the idea that all religions could somehow be united, I had to be honest and commend such organisations. Usually religious people broke into warring factions so it was nice to know that there were religious people out there who attempted to do the reverse, that is, try and bring them all together.

The day that I went to the Msingi wa Mungu Project office, I was somewhat nervous of what would transpire. The office was situated in North Parramatta in a little but modern office above a shop front on one of the main roads which leads out of Parramatta. The office was quite small and cluttered with papers and other objects stored around the place as if this were a small warehouse for outgoing goods.

I was introduced to Angela Wennings. She was the Msingi wa Mungu Project representative in Sydney at the time. Angela greeted me politely and we went into her office. She asked me some preliminary questions and once I had said I was an ESOL teacher, that is, a teacher of English to those who spoke other languages, there was a sound of "Ah! An English teacher!" which gave me the impression that this was a positive sign that I had been accepted into the project. Angela then took the form

I   had completed which included questions about my background and my experience with sub-Saharan Africans. Angela then asked me what I knew of Africa itself. How much knowledge, I asked myself, did I need in order to win an opportunity to go there and find out about Polycarp's family? What I did know of Africa was what I had seen in documentaries in various times during my life. Of course, there were also the images of constant war and civil unrest as came out from time to time on the news broadcast, and the images of famine and starvation as advertisements for charity organisations and child sponsoring always indicated. There were also the stories of pillaging and torture as related to me by my students. Is this the type of answer Angela was waiting for?

"Pfer! Well…I…um…well…from…er…what…," I stuttered as a beginning.

"So, only what you've seen on television?" Angela helpfully suggested.

"Well, er, no," I first lied and then admitted, yes, that was the only knowledge of Africa that I had. Having said that, I was ready to get up and thank her politely for the interview as I obviously didn't know enough about Africa to form a part of this team.

However, Angela smiled.

"And what do you know about Tanzania?"

Tanzania. I knew very little about Tanzania. I knew that it was one of the three countries that made up, along with Kenya and Uganda, East Africa. I at least knew that Tanzania was often confused with our island state, Tasmania. I also knew that the official language was Swahili, a language that we often associated with gobbledygook.

I shrugged my shoulders as my answer.

"That's fine. Just to let you know, it's not all that bad," she reassured me. "It is true that many of the African nations that we see portrayed on television have problems. Tanzania, however, is a little different. It's a very peaceful country, albeit poor, so you shouldn't have any problems with safety."

Hope returned that I would still be able to go.

"Now, one thing you should be prepared for is that where you are going, the conditions are not like here. You will be residing on the school premises themselves in a dormitory where the students usually sleep. The rooms are very small and you will have to share with someone else. There is a communal bathroom for everyone in your block and the bathroom is basic to say the least."

"That's okay," I replied, relaxed to hear that the conditions I had just heard about were nothing as bad as what I had originally thought. To me, it sounded like I was going on a camping trip.

There was a cost, however, for going. It was an unusually small sum of about ten dollars a day to pay for food and lodging. This money was to help the project. So much, then, for going overseas to earn a bit of money! But for the mercy mission I was about to undergo, it didn't worry me to pay.

Angela then explained how I was to organise my trip. I needed to arrange to get my passport if I didn't have one. I also had a choice of travelling together with a group of other people going to the Msingi wa Mungu Project from Australia or I could simply organise my own trip as long as I arrived at Kilimanjaro Airport at a particular date and time. I opted for the latter.

Angela then explained that I would need to obtain a visa to enter Tanzania. I could get the visa on arrival in the country but to make things easier for me, I could organise my visa early by sending my passport to the Tanzanian Embassy in Melbourne. I thought that the latter was the better option. I wanted everything to be done before I left the country. I was going to arrive in Tanzania completely on my own so I wanted to make sure that all possible issues were dealt with before I left Australia and not have to deal with them on the Dark Continent.

Even though I had decided to organise my own travelling arrangements, Angela urged me to attend a meeting where I would meet other members of a group going from Sydney. That I had to meet this group obviously meant that I was definitely going.

"So, do you have any questions?" Angela asked me as a finale.

I paused for a moment. I knew it wasn't really the business of the Msingi wa Mungu Project to deal with lost relatives but being an organisation with a humanitarian interest, the least I could do was ask. After all, this was the real reason for my involvement.

"Angela," I said, "I am very happy to help out with your organisation because your project follows the principle of helping others which is a principle that I follow. The real reason why I decided to get involved was because of a refugee boy where I work."

With that, I explained the entire story, what I wanted to do, where I needed to go and what I wanted to find out. Angela sat there and listened. I thought this was going to create a complication in my application and therefore cause me to be rejected. Once I had finished, Angela smiled.

"Wow, Michael, you really are a good man! That's fine. We can organise something. I'll let you know at the group session how we can help you. I'm sure we can organise this. We will probably organise someone to accompany you to Arusha."

Angela asked me if I had any more questions. She did not write anything down or appear to make any notes about my request. So I was sure that once I had left her office, my special request would soon be forgotten and the real reason for going to Tanzania would be squashed and I would end up participating in an activity I didn't really mean to get involved with.

"Oh, one very important thing!" Angela then added as an afterthought. "You need to get vaccinations before you go. Have you had vaccination shots for travel before?"

I shook my head slowly.

"That's okay," Angela then continued. "It's not too hard to get them done."

Angela then opened a draw, pulled out a business card and then passed it to me.

"Here's the contact details of a doctor in the Parramatta area who specialises in vaccinations for travellers. You just need to make an appointment and then bring your vaccination card with you to the group meeting so we can verify that all has been done."

Angela then smiled at me. "So, do you have any more questions?"

"No, no," I replied. "That's all. I guess I will see you at the group meeting."

Both Angela and I stood up. Angela then shook my hand.

"Pleasure to meet you, Michael. I look forward to seeing you at the group meeting."

I walked outside and onto the street. I looked down again at the business card and saw that the suggested doctor had his office near the centre of Parramatta, about a twenty minute walk from the Msingi wa Mungu Project office. I thought I may as well walk to the doctor's office and organise an appointment while I was in the area.

I reached the building as indicated on the card and walked inside. I was greeted by the receptionist who asked me if she could help me. I told her about my plans to go to Tanzania and my subsequent need for vaccinations. I was expecting her to organise an appointment in the next couple of days or so. However, she looked down at her appointment diary and then said, "Sure. There's been a cancellation today so we can schedule you in to see the doctor in about ten minutes."

Ten minutes? I thought. This was rather sudden and unexpected. I hadn't had the time to appreciate that the doctor was about to prod and prick me. I remained speechless for a moment and so the receptionist, who sat there in expectation, prodded me for an answer.

"So, is that okay?"

"Yes, that's fine."

"Just take a seat, then. The doctor will be ready with you in a minute."

In the reception area were seats strategically placed around the walls and in the centre of the room was a large, square coffee table with an assortment of out-of-date magazines. I reached down, picked up one of the magazines and then began leafing through it. But I found that articles about famous actors and their tragic love lives and how they first get married and then divorce not long after as if marriage were a trivial affair, or new and improved ways to diet and finally lose those unwanted kilos simply did not interest me. I placed the magazine back on the coffee table. I sat back and looked across from me to see a white stand decorated with an assortment of brochures with information about travelling. They spoke about a variety of travel issues but it was those about diseases that caught my attention. There was one brochure with the ominous title, *Before You Travel, Consider This!* I got up, walked across the room and took one of these brochures from the stand. I opened the brochure and the central pages spread out into a large A3 sized beautifully decorated and coloured map of the world. Each colour represented a disease which required vaccination, and where more than one of these diseases was prevalent in an area, instead of one single colour, the area was striped with each colour for each disease. I looked first at Australia which appeared to be completely disease-free. And then I looked at Africa. In various parts of the Dark Continent there were all the colours of the rainbow, indicating that this continent had a risk of all these horrid diseases. I didn't like this brochure at all so I put it back.

I noticed other brochures, some of which only talked about one particular disease: Cholera, Scarlet Fever, Hepatitis A, Dysentery and so on. I don't know why this thought suddenly came to mind but I thought to myself, if the Creation Story as recorded in the Bible were true, then when were diseases created? When the writer of Genesis wrote that on the fifth and sixth days God created all the birds, fish and land animals, did this include bacteria and protozoa, seeing these are by biological definition living creatures?

And what about viruses? According to conventional understanding, viruses are not living creatures at all but simply a genetic code, something akin to a computer program. When on their own, viruses are no more living than a rock or a grain of sand. But once inside a cell, viruses can change the program of the cell and create multiple copies of themselves. On which day, then, were viruses created? On the second day when the dry land was created or on the days when the animals were created?

And what about the story of Noah? Did Noah take into the Ark two of every bacterium and protozoon?

Not only so, in the Bible, we don't really hear much about diseases until we get to the story of Moses and his exposition of the Law. And then the only disease we really hear much about is leprosy. Nothing, however, is mentioned about how this disease is spread and there is, strangely enough, no cure. Rather, Jesus, in his form of Jehovah, commands Moses to condemn those unfortunate to catch this horrid disease to leper colonies to suffer the indignity of the disease itself and the stigma of being separated from loved ones and from the general community until their ignominious death. But then, a thousand or so years later, this same Jesus then comes out of heaven and goes around healing a smattering of lucky lepers at random with a simple but miraculous touch before disappearing back into the sky leaving all subsequent lepers condemned to a life of misery - until the mid-1900s, however, when a cure for leprosy was finally developed, not via the voice from a burning bush but through simple medical research.

I then wondered how Jews and Christians treated lepers today. If Jews and Christians believed that Jehovah gave Moses the Law and the Law is eternal, then Jews and Christians were forced to continue to segregate lepers into leper colonies for the rest of their natural miserable lives. After all, this modern cure is not mentioned in the Bible and so therefore it is not of God. And if it is not of God, then the only alternative is that it comes from the enemy of God. Therefore, irrespective of how enticing it is to take this cure and gain the enjoyment the cure brings, we should not be tempted by the enemy of God to take it because anything that doesn't come from God can only do us harm, despite how deceptively good it appears and how successful it has been for those who don't believe in the Bible. But how one approached the Torah depended on whether or not one had leprosy. For those who weren't suffering from this debilitating disease, it was so easy to stand there grim-faced, arms folded tightly and tapping a foot like the Wicked Witch of the West, declaring that seeing the Bible says that lepers had to remain in leper colonies and suffer the misery and indignity of this disease, this was after all what Jehovah had commanded in His Book. After all, who are we to question Jehovah? However, for lepers, irrespective of how much they believed in the Law of Moses, being offered an extra-toranic cure that actually completely cleared up the leprosy was a much more enticing alternative which would make obeying the Bible implicitly a little harder to do.

Another thought that went through my mind was that Christians in my church used to say that God gave the medical doctors the knowledge they have today. One has to ask, then, why Jehovah didn't give the knowledge of the cure for leprosy when He gave Moses the Law but rather waited over three thousand years during which time lepers through the millennia had to suffer horrendously.

And further, why did Jehovah create the disease in the first place when there seems to be absolutely no advantage whatsoever for its existence? And Jehovah in his incarnation as Jesus seems to confirm this when he rids people of this horrible disease. While Christians marvel at how miraculous Jesus was to be able with a touch to remove the leprosy from those suffering from the disease, there aren't any Christians as far as I know who stand back from the overall picture and say to themselves, "Now, wait a minute. Jehovah created this disease and made people miserable as a result. Wouldn't it have been nicer if Jehovah in fact had not given people leprosy in the first place rather than give them the disease and make them suffer, and then come along later and remove the disease?"

I then saw a brochure on AIDS. Although I was now quite familiar with this terrible disease, I decided to take this brochure out and have a read of it. However, as I pulled the brochure from the stand, the receptionist called my attention and I saw at the reception desk a man standing there wearing a white coat which was a giveaway that he was a doctor.

"Michael?" the doctor called as an echo of the receptionist.

There was nobody else in the room so there could only be one person the doctor was addressing. That I was in the process of taking a brochure on AIDS suddenly filled me with absolute embarrassment as if I had been caught out. Although it had long been known that AIDS doesn't discriminate because of one's sexuality, AIDS still carried the stigma of being a gay disease. Hence my interest in the brochure about AIDS was like a silent assertion of the type of physical activities I got up to. I could feel a tingle in my face which meant that I was blushing. In my embarrassment, I pushed the brochure back in its place but unfortunately in my haste to get the brochure back in on the stand, somehow all the remaining brochures on AIDS fell chaotically onto the floor. Right in front of the brochure stand was a carpet with AIDS, AIDS, AIDS in parquetry fashion all around my feet. I crouched down to collect all the brochures when I felt a presence behind me.

"That's okay," the receptionist said in a gentle tone. "Give them to me. I'll put them back. You just go with the doctor."

The receptionist smiled as she took the mess of brochures from my hand and with that I followed the doctor into his little room.

This doctor specialised in vaccinations for travellers but his surgery was very much the same as the surgery of my GP. The doctor was a rather large fellow, almost as wide as he was tall. I asked myself the question how a doctor, who was supposed to administer health, was not a walking example of health. But knowing that he would soon be wielding sharp pointy objects and plunging them deep into my body, I decided to leave this comment in the recesses of my mind.

The doctor asked me which country I was planning to go to and when I was planning to go there. When I told him I was going to Tanzania, he then asked me if I had been immunised against polio, tetanus and whooping cough apart from the time I was immunised against them as a child. When I replied in the negative, the doctor explained that I would need a booster shot for these childhood vaccinations but also be vaccinated against a plethora of other dangerous diseases including Yellow Fever and Cholera. The doctor also suggested that I get immunised against Hepatitis A and Hepatitis B. Although it sounded like an attempt at upselling, a side of me acknowledged that it was better to be protected against these diseases than to fall victim to any of them in a faraway country.

However, there was no vaccination for malaria and so I had to take preventative medication, which was a series of tablets which I had to begin taking two weeks before I left but also continue taking four weeks after I got back to Australia. And even then this medication was not one hundred percent effective. Ouch! This malaria business was quite an unnerving affair.

"Okay," the doctor continued. "I guess you don't need me to tell you, unless you've been living under a rock, that AIDS is a big problem in Africa. Here is a booklet. This booklet will give you a breakdown of the possibilities of catching AIDS by country. Let me show you."

The doctor opened the booklet at random to one country. Next to the name of the country was a percentage. If I understood the doctor correctly, this percentage meant that this was the chance of catching AIDS if I had unprotected sex with one of the locals.

The doctor then flicked the pages to Tanzania. Next to the name Tanzania was 33%. This meant, or so I understood it, that in Tanzania, there was a 33% chance of catching AIDS if someone had unprotected sex with a local Tanzanian. A 33% chance of catching AIDS in Tanzania? I wasn't sure how to understand this statistic. Did this mean that 33% of the inhabitants of Tanzania were victims of AIDS?

I then cast my mind back to when I first started making myself familiar with AIDS and another statistic I had learnt in my research. When I asked how AIDS spread, the nurse at the sexual health clinic where I had my regular checkups showed me stunning medical information. Statistically, a man who is the receiver in a sexual encounter with a man who has AIDS has something like 50 times the probably of catching AIDS during unprotected sex than anyone else in any sexual encounter. This means that, if a man is the actor in unprotected sex with a man who has AIDS or with a woman who has AIDS, that man has only one fiftieth the chance of catching AIDS compared with a man who is the receiver in sex with an HIV positive actor. This meant that if AIDS was so prevalent in sub-Saharan Africa and the disease was spreading so determinedly, these statistics were inadvertently revealing something about some of the Africans' true sexual activities.

"You have got to be kidding!" I told the doctor. "I thought AIDS was predominantly a homosexual disease. You know what this means, then." This was meant partly as a joke but inside there was an element of seriousness in the statement.

The doctor didn't say anything. He just raised his eyebrows in a way which indicated that he didn't want to commit to a comment either way to the implication. With that, he inserted the needle for my last injection, then signed and stamped my immunisation booklet.

Once finished, the doctor went back behind his desk, opened the top drawer, pulled out a package and handed it to me.

"Here. Take this with you as a precaution. Irrespective of whether or not you are in the giving or receiving end, just make sure you use them."

I looked down at the package. Although nicely wrapped up in transparent plastic, I could tell that the contents were a couple of condoms and lubricant. For a second time, I could feel my face tingle so I knew I was blushing. My comment made it obvious which team I bat for. The doctor's subsequent reaction made it obvious that he did not judge me for it and that he was interested in my protection, which really was for everyone's protection.

I looked up at the doctor. "I'm not going there to have sex," I said by way of protest. "I'm just going to help out with some volunteer work and also find out information for this student of mine."

"Just make sure they go with you in your luggage," the doctor said gruffly. "You just never know."

I made the statement that the package would never be opened. However, I acknowledged that I would obey the doctor's orders nonetheless.

Before leaving, the doctor wrote out a certificate to carry with me through immigration. It was a certificate indicating that I would be carrying malaria medication into the country. I needed that, so he explained, because otherwise I could be picked up as drug dealing and the Tanzanian officials could turn a simple trip to the country into a nightmarishly complicated legal affair. The doctor also asked me if I was taking any other medication. He suggested that I take medication in case of headaches and diarrhoea and to include the names of each type of medication on the certificate.

At the end of my consultation and the various jabbings, the doctor wished me an enjoyable trip. I duly paid the receptionist and took one last look at the brochure stand to see that all the brochures were tidily back in place before leaving to go home.

If the Msingi wa Mungu Project was an attempt to find unity in the world, the United Nations Organisation was even more so. The United Nations Organisation symbolises just how populous our planet has become and how much we need an organisation which helps all nations to come together. It has been the dream of many empire builders to be the rulers of the entire globe and today there is an organisation that in a way does just that. The United Nations Organisation symbolises that humans have reached a point in their development where they can no longer live in isolated pockets working independently.

This is because no one nation can act alone without affecting other nations. All new developments end up in the environment, and the environment does not respect the clearly marked borders we draw on our maps. Rivers flow relentlessly past border posts, the air blows dauntlessly across boundary lines. And now the advent of internet has shown just how international we are. We have access to any piece of information from anywhere on the globe, in any language and at any time.

The UNHCR, which acts as a branch of the UN, also gives an idea of how far reaching the events in one country affect other countries, not only neighbouring countries which share borders but also countries half   a world away. Many of the learners who came to Tevah Am clearly illustrated this. Social unrest is no longer a local phenomenon but affects everyone on the globe.

The UNHCR also is the link between the countries from which refugees flee and the countries to which refugees find refuge. The UNHCR helps to re-establish contact between displaced persons overseas and their families back in their home countries. And it was this vehicle that I was about to use to find out whether or not any of the members of Polycarp's family were still alive.

It was only a couple of days after having my vaccination shots that I was back at Polycarp's place. The tradition had become that when I arrived, I spent some time first with Jeremiah helping him with his homework. I then cooked tea. Then I spent the rest of the evening with Polycarp right up until bedtime. It was when I was cooking that Polycarp's situation really affected me. Polycarp would come to the kitchen with his exercise book and pens, and work on some of his units, at least the writing and maths units. I wondered how he felt. It must have been in a way a relief for him to be able to relinquish for a moment the duties of parenthood and simply be a child for a number of hours. I can only guess that he was happy to have someone else take on the duties of a parent for him, even if those parental duties were simply cooking the evening meal a couple of nights a week and helping with homework.

When I had finished cooking, I called the boys together and the three of us sat down and ate as a family. Jeremiah recounted the events of his day at school in the typical eight-year-old fashion. Polycarp, however, did not say much. His only conversational topic was how delicious the food was, which was a grand compliment for me. But apart from that, Polycarp barely said a word. There was an eagerness on my part to know what was going on inside that head of his and it was frustrating not being able to ask outright.

I had become for a moment a surrogate parent, in a way both father and mother. But I didn't want this relationship to build. I assured myself that this was a temporary arrangement until I could find out whether or not other members of Polycarp's family were alive so that all could be reunited once again. Alternatively, if it could be confirmed without a doubt that Polycarp and Jeremiah were the only survivors of their extended family, my temporary role would be to ensure that they had established themselves in Australia firmly enough in a job and within a social group in which they finally felt they belonged. I was beyond emotional involvement - call it love or what you will – and that if I developed any for anyone it would certainly come back and hurt me.

I could feel the spray from the splashings of that mighty river sprinkling on my skin. I just needed to back away on the bank and not get too close to the water.

Chapter 4

Soon after my interview with Angela at the Msingi wa Mungu Project, I told Nikita of my proposed journey to Tanzania.

"So, you're going to follow Khatyn's advice after all?" Nikita asked.

Nikita had been aware of Khatyn's constant suggestions of going overseas to teach English and hence come back to Australia with enough money to buy my own place and a few additional luxury items. She was also aware of my refusals to do so and the reasoning behind such refusals. She was therefore surprised to learn that I was going and I actually had to pay for the privilege.

"Yeah, but it's only for two weeks. Well, that is, I will be taking two weeks leave from here. I will only be over at the Msingi wa Mungu Project for nine days."

"Only nine days? That's not enough time to do anything!" Nikita replied bemused.

"Well, unfortunately, the trip over there takes at least two days. There's no direct flight from Sydney to Kilimanjaro Airport."

Nikita's facial expression communicated to me that this was an uncomfortable proposition.

"I tried all the permutations possible," I continued. "To fly to Tanzania, you can only go up to Asia and then down again or fly directly west to South Africa and then up to Kilimanjaro. It doesn't matter which way I go, all trips take at least thirty hours."

"Thirty hours of travelling? You must be keen!"

I paused for a moment. "No, Nikita. It's not out of keenness. It's because of Polycarp."

"Whoa!" Nikita innuendoed. "You must really love this Polycarp!"

"No, Nikita," I rebuked. "It's not what you think. I mean, anyway, Polycarp is young enough to be my son and guys his age don't interest me."

Nikita's facial expression changed from a cheeky look to a more serious expression.

"Michael, you're seriously going to go out of your comfort zone for this young guy for no ulterior motive?"

"Nikita!" I sputted. "I thought you knew me better than that! And in any case, does every action have to be motivated by a sexual impulse?"

Nikita's furrow dropped. "Are you doing it then for…for…"

"Love?" I interjected. "Of course not! I'm not motivated by love. It's more of a communal thing. I mean, I believe in humanity and it's all of our business to help anyone in need."

"Settle down, there, old boy!" Nikita then said. "There's no need to get emotional about it!"

Fortunately Nikita knew me well. When I reflected on the conversation that had just transpired, I realised that I definitely had worked myself up. Fortunately Nikita knew not to take my emotional outbursts personally.

I went silent for a moment and really didn't know what to say. However, Nikita then laughed. "You know, Michael, 'love' really wasn't the word I was going to use! But yeah, that's a good motive!" She then paused and changed tone. "Geez, Michael. You're going to be granted sainthood one day! And I thought you weren't religious!"

"Only if you're the one who grants it," I replied in an attempt to change my tone from the earlier seriousness to a more jovial one. "You know, it's a bit of a shame I'm not religious anymore. I'm going to do a good deed and I know that there is no reward in the end for doing it."

"No reward for doing what?" Hebbeera interjected, appearing from out of nowhere and entering the tail end of this conversation. As soon as Hebbeera appeared, both Nikita's and my shackles went up.

"Going to Tanzania to help someone," Nikita answered abruptly for me.

"Tasmania?" Hebbeera asked with a face expressing complete incredulity. "But I thought you hated the cold weather."

"No," I replied, trying hard to suppress a rude comment. "Tanzania. And you stress the i, that is, tan-zan-EE-a."

Hebbeera looked at me with a strange expression. "But where is Tanzania? Is it really a country?"

"No, of course not," I replied rather derisively. "It's a completely made-up country. When I went to the travel agent to book my ticket and organise my accommodation, my travel agent was very happy to accept my hard-earned cash in order to organise a trip for me to a land of fantasy. I'm flying Air Pegasus and staying in the Inn of the Three Bears."

Hebbeera looked at me blankly and I had the impression that she really believed what I was saying.

"Of course, it's a real country!" I finally blurted out. "It's one of the three countries known as East Africa."

I was quite surprised that Hebbeera had never heard of the place. I could remember at school learning about Kenya, Uganda and Tanzania being three countries of East Africa that formed part of the British

Commonwealth. Although I was more familiar with Uganda because my early childhood coincided with the infamous rule of Idi Amin, and Kenya because of the ads we often saw of filter coffee from Africa, I didn't really know terribly much about Tanzania, but at least I knew where it was.

"What are you going to do there?" Hebbeera continued.

"I don't know. Go on safari, shoot a few lions, get caught up in one of their perennial wars, catch an exotic disease."

"He's volunteering to work at the Msingi wa Mungu Project," Nikita replied for me.

"The what?" Hebbeera asked with a tortured expression on her face.

"There was an ad in the newspaper about it not long ago," Nikita replied. "The Msingi wa Mungu Project is asking for volunteers to help out in East Africa at various colleges to teach English or do other volunteer work."

Nikita paused and then continued. "It's a religious organisation that helps people in need. This organisation takes volunteers from wealthy countries like Australia to give up themselves and help the underprivileged on the African continent."

I could tell by Nikita's tone of voice and by the way she stressed certain words in her sentence that she was in fact having a go at Hebbeera, someone who claimed to be a committed Christian and believed everyone should follow the Bible implicitly, hence implying that what I was going to do in Tanzania should be what Hebbeera should be doing as her Christian duty. But Hebbeera's blank expression revealed that she didn't pick up the insult but rather she looked on in expectation for Nikita to continue, which she did.

"Michael has decided to volunteer for a couple of weeks."

"Nine days," I corrected her.

"Oh, but in Africa!" Hebbeera stated both with her lips and her entire body in a way that exaggerated her disgust, as if the word "Africa" was synonymous with the word "vomit".

"I would never go there," Hebbeera continued after a momentary pause. "What a dangerous place! You have to get vaccinated against so many diseases and yet there are some diseases you can't get vaccinated against. I hope you know not to swim there. And be careful not to get bitten by insects because you could easily catch malaria or some other unusual parasitic disease! You be careful there."

She paused for a moment and then added as an afterthought, "And where are you going to stay? Will you have access to running water? Is it clean?"

When Hebbeera had posed that question, suddenly the focus of my thoughts went from her to my upcoming trip to Africa. Hebbeera had a point: Where *was* I going to stay? Suddenly this realisation filled me with anxiety. The people at the Msingi wa Mungu Project had told me that there would be simple accommodation, that everything would be provided for, sleeping quarters, food and all other essential facilities. They also told me that these facilities would only be of a basic nature. What did all this really mean? I remembered that as a child I had been on scout camps and all provisions were very simple indeed. We had communal sleeping quarters, communal eating halls where basic food was provided for us and common bathroom facilities, which meant that whether we liked it or not, we had to strip down and shower together with fellow scouters whether or not we liked the idea of being naked in the presence of other people. Was this what the accommodation was going to be like over there?

For days after, these frightening, unknown aspects played on in my psyche and made me ask myself what I was getting myself into. How was I going to survive in these primitive conditions? What made it all the more difficult was that the images of Africa that we were always fed with were of an immense stretch of land which could swallow you up whole. The land was vast without the slightest hint of there being any civilisation. Travel brochures and all advertisements associated with any part of Africa always exhibited a picture of open country, tribespeople or safari animals and not once in such travel brochures did they ever show photos of towns, cities or any other evidence of civilisation.

Yet every time I saw Polycarp, my heart just went out to him. I really wanted to find out whether or not he was completely alone in the world without family or whether there was after all a spark of hope that one family member of his may just be still alive. I was willing to put myself out for another person in need. It was a principle I held to and followed. It was not due to a belief in a being greater than all of us who demanded of us to do good to others nor the idea that there would be an eternal reward after the grave for all our good works done in this life. Rather, I had long recognised that we all lived on this one planet and whether we liked it or not, we all had to share it. And it simply made sense to me that if I could help someone, if I had the time and the means to help, then I should do it. The Msingi wa Mungu Project entered my consciousness at the time that Polycarp had wandered into my enclosure. It was perfect timing. Someone who needed help and the means by which help could be provided were both there before me so it made sense to me to act appropriately. I was only going to be in Tanzania for a short period anyway and the worst that could happen, as long as all my vaccinations worked and no-one found out what really went on in my head – or other parts of my body – was that it could once and for all be confirmed that all members of Polycarp's family were definitively deceased and we could finally make closure.

Before I left, I told Polycarp that I was going away for a two week vacation. I didn't tell him the destination in order not to cause him to fret, fret about my safety but also because it would have stirred up unpleasant memories from his past. Polycarp was obviously a little distressed that I wasn't going to be around for a couple of weeks to help him with his on-line training at Tevah Am nor during the two days that I visited him to play the part-time parent role. I assured him that the other trainers at Tevah Am would be of assistance and in any case the two weeks would go by very quickly and it wouldn't be long before I was back again. Fortunately, Polycarp didn't ask any questions regarding the reason for my sudden need for a holiday nor where I was going. In fact, Polycarp showed no interest whatsoever about my short term absence except that I wouldn't be around during that time.

It definitely was a long trip. My first destination was Hong Kong. I had never actually been to Hong Kong in my travels and hence decided to take the opportunity of having a night's stay and find out what was so spectacular about this place. I soon discovered the attraction. Hong Kong was alive twenty-four hours a day. It was modern, glistening and bustling. I walked around the streets close to my hotel for a couple of hours, soaking up the magic of the place. It also seemed to be one huge shopping complex with street vendors and shopkeepers competing with signs and billboards for our custom. On just about every street, someone was encouraging me into their shop to buy a watch, a T-shirt and even a woman for the evening. Not long after, I sought a restaurant for an evening repast and soon I was back in my hotel room and fast asleep as Hong Kong continued well into the night.

My flight out of Hong Kong was not scheduled till the following evening so I had almost a full day there the following day. I decided to go on a morning tour and gain an appreciation of the place. The tour was in fact more of a shopping tour than an educational one as we were taken to various workshops where we saw craftspeople manufacturing local wares such as traditional clothes or jewellery. The tour through the factory was concluded with the strong encouragement to actually purchase something although many of us on the tour were, unfortunately for the tour organisers, not very interested in doing so.

What was most fascinating about the tour for me was when we passed a very tall building which had a purpose-built large hole in the centre of it. The tour guide pointed this building out on passing and explained that the hole was intentionally included in the construction to allow for the dragon of the water to pass up into the mountain and not get obstructed. According to the locals, so the tour guide explained, water symbolises money and if the building obstructed the flow out of the sea and onto the mountain of this water dragon, then money would not flow into this building and hence the business would not survive. I just listened in complete stupefaction. How could this great city, pulsating with modernity, hold onto such achaic superstitions to the point that they affected how a building was constructed? And in any case, how did they make the connection between water and money? And did anyone seriously ever see this dragon move up out of the water, up into the mountain and then return to the sea, moving through the hole in this building? It was an absurd idea. But in a way it gave this building and hence the area an extra dimension than simply being a bland agglomeration of buildings. And no doubt this building got business because this absurdity made people want to go and see the building.

That evening I continued my flight. My next stop was Bangkok but only as a stopover to pick up passengers. Then it was a night flight over the Indian Ocean to Nairobi where I had to get out and catch a different flight from there to Tanzania.

The contrast between Hong Kong Airport and Nairobi Airport was striking. Hong Kong Airport itself was huge and very much like one large shopping metropolis. Nairobi Airport was small, dank and lifeless, at least at the time I arrived there which was very early in the morning just before sunrise. It only took about ten minutes to walk from one end of the airport to the other along what appeared to be a long hallway. There were the occasional duty free shops with traditional African stuff for sale. I spent much of the day there before my flight was due to depart from Nairobi but I was not interested in buying any of the goods on offer once the shops had opened. I spent much of the time in Nairobi Airport walking up and down, counting the minutes before my flight was due to depart or just looking at the type of people who would be travelling through Nairobi. It was terribly boring but I accepted this as part of international travel.

Just when it was getting close to the departure time, an announcement was made that my flight was delayed an hour. This was frustrating but I was familiar with flight travel and I knew these things happened. This simply meant that I would arrive an hour or so later than planned but I was sure that those at my destination would soon be aware of this.

Finally it was time to leave. There weren't many people on my flight. The plane was only about half full. I had a window seat on the left side of the plane far down the back so that my view wasn't obstructed by the wing. By this time, the sun was well and truly up in the sky and provided a spectacular view of the African landscape below us. This was the first time in my life that I had seen the African continent with my own eyes.

It seemed as if I had only begun to enjoy the view below me when I heard the captain announce, "Ladies and gentlemen, this is your captain speaking. We will soon be making our descent into Kilimanjaro Airport."

And there below, on the ground, the great African landscape stretched out in all directions beyond the horizon, a vast stretch of grey-green carpet interspersed with brown dust and sand, a parched earth waiting thirstily to be quenched.

I could see the runway, a small strip of dark grey like a small patch of metal on an immense carpet. But I could see no signs of life. There were sparsely scattered dwellings interspersed within this dustbowl but there appeared to be no roads or townships. What on earth was I going to do in this vast desert? Where were the offices I needed to visit? Where was the Msingi wa Mungu Project? The travel brochures were right: where was civilisation?

Once the plane had landed, I noticed a vehicle with a stepladder straddled to its back like a campervan come towards the plane.

"Goodness," I said to myself. "Does that mean we have to walk from the plane to the airport?"

Sure enough, that was what we had to do. Once I walked out of the plane and onto the tarmac, the heat and dryness of the place hit me as if I had walked into a drying room. The heat and the parchness of the place immediately wrapped themselves around me and tried desperately to suck out every bit of moisture from my tongue and eyeballs. I carried my shoulder bag with me, following the trail of the other arrivals to this lonely outpost in the middle of the Dark Continent.

The airport arrivals lounge was small and stoic. Its decoration of concertina panelling, glass shutters and dark wooden ribbed interior hinted that this building was erected during the 1950s or 1960s and the style had not been updated since then. The smell and appearance betrayed an attempt to give the airport an upkeep but there was no suggestion that there was any thought about modernising the airport and bringing its decor into the twenty-first century.

The queue slowly built up as we approached immigration. Some people had stopped and were busily writing at makeshift desks. I guessed these people had opted to apply for a visa on arrival because there were signs everywhere indicating that for those who hadn't yet obtained a visa, this was the moment to do so. I felt a sense of relief that I had already obtained mine before leaving Australia as to apply for a visa at this part of the trip would have been a painfully slow process. I was eager to get out of the airport into whatever accommodation being offered me, to get freshened up and maybe have a sleep.

There were two women ahead of me on the queue. They were speaking English and I guessed from their accent that they were from North America. They were quite agitated and nervous, and soon the reason for their agitation was made clear. They were commenting on our late arrival and had therefore assumed that the arranged transfer from the airport would have already gone. It soon became evident why they had come here: they also were here to participate in the Msingi wa Mungu Project. I couldn't understand their anxiety. Did they really believe that the organisers of the Msingi wa Mungu Project would stick to a particular time for those arriving from overseas and if these people were late, the organisers would simply leave the airport and leave us stranded, left to our own devices?

The queue progressed very slowly. It appeared as if each person's case was being assessed minutely. This already gave the impression that this was a sinister sign that things were not going to go well as we passed through.

When the women ahead of me finally made it to the window, they gave their passports to the immigration officer. The immigration officer took their passports and began slowly to inspect them. The women continued to express their agitation. Because the immigration officer took his time to give the final stamp for the two women to get into the country, the women began to get excited. The immigration officer abruptly stopped what he was doing, sat back and looked at the women.

"What seems to be the problem?" he asked deliberately slowly.

The immigration officer looked quite threatening and quite frightening. If he had addressed me in this manner, I would have been speechless and possibly pooed my pants! However, these women were obviously a lot more courageous and brazen than I could ever be.

"We arrived late and we don't want to miss our bus. We were supposed to be here about an hour ago."

The immigration officer just looked at them with a gruff, arrogant expression as if to say he couldn't give a toss what happened to these women once he had finished his line of duty. The women continued to shuffle around in an agitated manner while the immigration officer just sat calmly and looked straight at them. Eventually, the women calmed down. Once they had stopped moving, the immigration officer continued.

"Now that you're settled, we can continue," he said, and slowly and deliberately began looking at all their documentation before finally giving them the stamp in the passports they most desperately were seeking. Once their objective was achieved, the women scurried off.

I had already learnt from this charade how I wasn't supposed to act. I walked up to the immigration officer, terrified inside, but calmly presented my passport and documentation to the immigration officer. The immigration officer slowly checked everything, checked that the photo in my passport matched my real facial features, stamped the appropriate pages and then presented me once again with my passport. Obviously I had played the game correctly because the immigration officer did not hinder my progress into the country. I smiled at him and said "thank you" in Swahili but he just looked at me gruffly and passed a glance at the person who was after me in the queue.

With such an introduction to the country, I already felt unwelcome and realised why Tanzania did not feature as a well-renowned and popular destination for vacationers.

Unlike the women ahead of me, I didn't rush to get away from the immigration counter. After all, we still had to collect our check-in luggage. The luggage carousel was just around the corner from immigration and was in a small hall, a room which looked only big enough to fit about a hundred people comfortably. The two agitated women were standing there staring at the motionless carousel as if all their hopes and dreams of entering the country were as lifeless as this baggage belt.

From the luggage collection room there was a clear view out onto the tarmac and the awaiting plane from which we had disembarked. Luggage was being unloaded and, from our vantage point, the luggage appeared to fall from the back of the plane as ungracefully as business from a bird. The luggage was then loaded onto the carrier trailers and then eventually driven to the outside of the carousel. Suddenly the carousel came to life. Fortunately for these women, their luggage was among the first to appear and soon they were loaded and then disappeared out of the airport.

Not long after, my only check-in bag finally arrived. Along with my hand luggage, I walked briskly through the Nothing to Declare doorway and suddenly found myself walking through a set of glass doors which finally led me straight out into Tanzania.

Once outside in the open air, the heat and dryness once again hit me. It wasn't too unpleasant as I was familiar with such weather conditions back home, particularly as I had been to the interior of Australia on a number of occasions on holidays. And especially as I was someone who enjoyed hot weather, I didn't find this heat too uncomfortable, hot and dry as it was. The dryness was slightly uncomfortable but the heat was pleasant.

In the outside area which looked something like a bus terminal were parked a few small minibuses and a few coaches. I wandered over to where they were all parked to see if I could find the shuttle bus I was supposed to take to get to the Msingi wa Mungu Project.

"Are you right there, sir?" a voice from behind me called.

I turned around to see an officially dressed, well-presented black Tanzanian man looking at me and smiling.

"I'm here with the Msingi wa Mungu Project," I replied cautiously.

"Yes, come this way," the gentleman said and led me in the direction of one of the coaches. The hatches to the underpart of the coach were open obviously in order for our luggage to be stored during the trip and in this fashion the coach looked like an enormous beetle with its wings opened up to reveal its guts below. One of the people near the bus, who I assumed to be someone from the Msingi wa Mungu Project, took the larger of my two bags and placed it in the storage section. He then invited me to board the bus with my smaller bag.

Once inside the bus, I saw the two women who were in front of me in the queue when we were going through immigration sitting in one of the seats. They obviously had managed to get on their bus after all. However, now they were in an agitated state because the shuttle bus wasn't moving. Obviously the coach was waiting for everyone else who was supposed to attend the Msingi wa Mungu Project to arrive and no doubt other passengers on our flight who had yet to pass through immigration would soon be accompanying us. I couldn't therefore make out what it was that was making these women so impatient.

Slowly, more and more people got on the shuttle bus. Soon there was a lull and it looked as if there was no-one else to get on. I saw one of the officials walk back to the airport terminal and disappear into the building, only to return about ten minutes later and give the signal to the driver to get underway.

The drive out of the airport was a long road. It seemed to go on for kilometres and kilometres. I had a full view out of the side window and during our trip I saw people along the road, walking or riding bicycles. It struck me as quite odd. Were there that many flights in and out of Kilimanjaro Airport? Why was there so much traffic, even with people coming and going on foot or on bicycles along this road which ultimately only led to the airport? Not only so, from where had they come? From the sky there appeared to be no townships at all as far as the eye could see, at least looking out of the side of the plane that I was on.

This length of road met up at a T-intersection with a main road which stretched out in both directions into the mere nothingness which made this vast continent. There was clear signage indicating that in one direction the road led to Arusha, and the other, which was the direction in which we were to go, led to Moshi. Apart from this sign and a few buildings, there were absolutely no other signs of civilisation.

Once we were on this stretch of road, the scenery was just as bare and bleak as it had been from the trip from the airport to the main road and confirmed the dismal and empty view of the land as seen from the air. And as it was from the air, the land just seemed to go on and on forever and ever out to the horizon and beyond. My two female travelling companions in front of me first of all looked out into the vast nothingness agape in horror. Finally one of them said to the other, "My goodness! This land is so empty. It's dry and dusty. How on earth do people survive in this place?"

I wanted to burst out laughing. From the sound of their accent, I guessed they were from the United States. Surely there were places in the United States where the land is dry and vast just as we were seeing it here. After all, for me, this outstretch of vast nothingness was similar to what I had seen on trips to the interior of Australia. On one trip with my parents and my sister, Karen, we travelled from Sydney to Perth along the Nullarbor Plain by car and caravan, and another time we travelled to Alice Springs and Uluru, and these outback scenes were similar to what I was seeing here. Hadn't these two seen such landscapes in their own country? After all, American Westerns, which are a popular form of cinema, are always set in the far west which is hot, dry and dusty, very much the same as the view from our windows here.

Eventually, the emptiness was beginning to take its toll on me. We had travelled for quite some time and still there was no sign of a township. Where on earth was this Msingi wa Mungu Project actually located?

Finally a township broke the monotony of the emptiness of the land. This small township suddenly appeared out of nowhere and was announced by the bus running over a section of ribbed road which no doubt was deliberately made to slow vehicles down as they passed through this small township. The loud roar as we careened over the ribbed section of road announced that we had arrived and on both sides of the road were groups of buildings which looked like makeshift houses and most probably served as sidestreet shops. People were swarming around like ants. But there were only buildings along the side of the road and not beyond. Surely this was not our destination, I thought, because there did not seem to be any place for a large school to house a project like the Msingi wa Mungu Project. My suspicions were soon confirmed when once again with a loud roar we passed over more ribbing on the road which indicated that we had reached the other end of this township and were once again travelling through open land. Because we had passed a township, I thought this meant that Moshi must soon be up ahead.

But this was a false dawn. Once we had left this township, the land returned to its former emptiness, empty of towns, empty of buildings and empty of people. A silent, lonely land once again stretched out to the horizon. This was increasing my anxiety. Where on earth was this Moshi? But also, why did they place the airport so far away from the township of Moshi?

Once again the roaring sound of ribbing on the road indicated that we had entered another township but this township was no bigger than the first one and was similarly built, with buildings simply lining either side of the road with very little or no habitation beyond these. Then once again, we heard the roaring sound as we travelled over the ribbed road and once again we were back into the emptiness of the continent.

Finally, signs of a larger town began to emerge. Houses began to appear, first sporadically, then as parts of a neighbourhood with one house fenced off against the next. And then the number of people began to increase, first they were on their own, then in small groups, then finally in large crowds. But there was nothing in particular of note to observe. We hadn't entered much into these first signs of civilisation when suddenly the bus slowed down and then made a sharp left turn. We then continued along what seemed like a major road which was lined with very large houses with vast gardens and other buildings which seemed to indicate that they were hotels or restaurants of some kind simply because of the advertising that screamed out at us. All these buildings looked rather opulent and upmarket. Even a view of the cars parked in the driveways revealed that those who lived in these houses certainly had money, and certainly more money than I had ever earned. What was this, then, that I was doing here helping the poor? What poor people? And in this neighbourhood?

Eventually the bus made yet another sharp left turn and came to an abrupt halt. From my vantage point, I saw a boom gate and a couple of black Tanzanians dressed in white uniform who I guessed were guards. The guards came round the bus before signalling the driver to pass through the boom gates. I also saw a large placard indicating that this was the compound of the Msingi wa Mungu Project. We had finally arrived. But with such a number of security guards stationed at the entrance to the project, I surmised that this wealth along this section of road was not universally shared throughout other parts of the country.

There was a sense of relief when we finally arrived at our destination. The compound into which we entered had the appearance of a school or a scout camping ground. As we passed through the gate, one of the organisers finally made an announcement and this was the first and only announcement on the entire trip. He explained that once we got off the coach and had claimed our luggage, we were to make our way into the central office area where we needed to sign our names in the registry. We then had to move to another building where we would be assigned our rooms.

I got off the bus, collected my other suitcase from the guts of this enormous insect we had been travelling in and followed the crowd to the main building. This building was like a large school entrance with an imposing reception desk where we were to sign in the registry. We then continued through the building, out into the compound and into another building which looked like from the outside a small house and the room in which we assembled together looked like the diningroom. Everyone looked tired and exhausted after such long trips. As well as the obvious newcomers who were all surrounded by luggage, there was about an equal number of much fresher-looking people, the majority of them being obviously of European background. There were a few dark-skinned sub-Saharan Africans who I assumed to be locals but because of the scarcity of black Africans in the room, I asked myself the question whether or not I had actually arrived on the Dark Continent.

Once we had all entered this large room, an elderly looking gentleman took centre stage and introduced himself as the director of the project. His name was Gordon McMahon and he was an emeritus Anglican minister.

"Good afternoon, everyone," Gordon began. "Welcome to the Msingi wa Mungu Project. I know you have all travelled from very far to be with us here today and I know you are all tired from such long journeys. So, before I begin debriefing you about the program, I'm sure you would all like to take the time first to find your rooms, settle in and freshen up."

There was a communal sigh of appreciation throughout the crowd. Gordon then gave us a time at which we needed to return to this diningroom-looking room where we would have tea and then be given instructions about how the program would pan out during the week.

Gordon then explained that we had all been assigned rooms in the dormitories. He warned us that some of the dormitories were still under construction so some of us would have accommodation which would be extremely stoic. This really was a reinforcement of what we had been told in Australia before we had left to come here so it was no longer new news. We would be accompanied by one of the long term residents to our sleeping quarters. Once Gordon called out our names, we simply needed to follow the person assigned to take us to our rooms.

Gordon then began calling out people's names. When the person in the crowd heard his or her name, Gordon told these people who among the group of long-term residents on the other side of the room would accompany them to their quarters. It appeared that many of the people came in pairs or groups. This suddenly made me realise just how alone I was. I was in a foreign country and even though there were white compatriots among the group, I didn't know anyone at all. A momentary feeling of fear and anxiety rushed over me.

Gordon continued calling out names. Groups of people got up and one of the long term residents in the room came over and soon that group disappeared.

Soon it was my turn.

"Michael Farril?" Gordon called out.

"Yes, that's me," I signalled to make myself obvious.

"Okay, Michael. Ibrahim, would you like to show Michael where he will be sleeping?"

I looked across the room. Once Gordon had called Ibrahim's name, from the sole person who got up, I knew which one was Ibrahim.

This image that walked towards me, this was not a man. It was a walking artistic masterpiece. It was a Greek sculpture lovingly created by one of the masters, either from the Greek classics, such as Praxiteles of Athens or Polyclitus of Argos, or one from the Renaissance artists, such as Michaelangelo or Donatello. Whoever created this masterpiece was a master craftsman in ebony, who knew how to perfectly curve every muscle and sinew of the human body in perfect symmetry and proportion. I could almost see the craftsman at his work, gently chiselling around the eyes in such a way that it appeared as if water had once dropped from a height down onto the nose and then flowed away both left and right over each eye to leave a beautiful and perfect teardrop shape. I could see how carefully and delicately the artist had sanded away at the chin so that the lower jaw stood out strong and firm with great pride which was clearly evident even though it was covered in a generous layer of black sheep's wool. This ebonite masterpiece looked at me with a bright smile through his beard which had been carefully moulded and trimmed around his face. He had flecks of grey hair among what was a crop of abundant curly black wool over his skull. I could see how the artist had polished carefully the entire surface until that deep, dark ebony shone with a brilliance that reflected the light. I could also make out the contours of what appeared to be a somewhat thin and yet athletic build, the resulting sculpture of a David or a Discobolus. Here in little Moshi was a living statue, an example of classical artistry come to life.

As he approached me, I said under my breath, "Wow! You are beautiful!"

"I'm sorry?" Ibrahim asked as he extended his arm to greet me, obviously having heard my comment, or at least acknowledging that I had spoken as he approached me.

This guy must have bionic ears! I thought to myself and was suddenly embarrassed by my spontaneous outburst.

"I said, I'm Michael," I lied, and then extended my arm out to meet his so that we could greet each other with a sturdy handshake.

"Hi. I'm Ibrahim," he said. He then paused and looked up at the crown of my head. "You have long hair," he then commented and smiled.

So what? I thought. Is there a problem with that?

This made me feel very uncomfortable. Was he scolding me? His comment sounded like my mother's criticism, that a man should not have long hair because St Paul wrote in I Corinthians 11:14 that "if a man have long hair, it is a shame unto him". Paul may have thought so but I certainly did not feel ashamed for growing my hair out long. In fact, I had decided to do so simply to see what it would look like and the longer it grew, the more I grew to like it. No-one at the Msingi wa Mungu Project in Sydney had commented on my long hair in the group meeting so why did Ibrahim have to say something about it?

"Here, let me take your luggage," Ibrahim continued and reached for the larger of my two suitcases.

My sudden flash of irritation was suddenly replaced by embarrassment as Ibrahim took my luggage. It was the twenty-first century and trade in slaves from Africa was well and truly over. I made sure that I took at least one of the bags to show that although he was Tanzanian, as humans we were still equal.

Ibrahim. I knew that the name Ibrahim was the Arabic version of the English Abraham. This meant that if his name was Ibrahim, he had to be Muslim. Despite my acquaintance with Faisal and Faraj who were both Muslim but also rather tolerant of non-Muslims, I began to build a picture of what type of person this Ibrahim was. After all, this Msingi wa Mungu Project was a rather religious organisation. Faisal and Faraj by contrast claimed to be Muslim but really didn't follow their religions religiously as neither regularly went to the mosque nor did much of what staunch Muslims were known to do. The Msingi wa Mungu Project, by contrast, was a religious affiliation of some description. Therefore, Ibrahim, being Muslim, and hence being quite a strict religious Muslim, had to have a very closed-minded outlook on life, especially concerning the free life I led. I had to admit that he had some sort of tolerance towards non-Muslims because he was here with non-Muslims at this Msingi wa Mungu Project. However, I decided that this was probably a façade as very religious Muslims in general are quite intolerant of other ways of viewing the world. Ibrahim no doubt had a wife but she was kept at home wrapped up in layers of cloth, while he professed an arrogant outward show of morality but most probably frequented places where women of ill-repute sold what was valuable to most heterosexual men. This impression of him completely swallowed up the positive one I initially had of him.

He was also immaculately dressed. He wore a crispy white shirt, spotless tan trousers and impeccably shiny, polished shoes which signalled to me that he thought of himself high on the socioeconomic scale and those below him were unfortunate but really none of his concern. Nonetheless, he certainly had a gentlemanly way about him.

With a clear and firm hand gesture, Ibrahim opened his arm to indicate the direction that we were to go. I hesitated to move and then said to him, "Maybe it's better that you go first. You know where we're going."

Ibrahim gave me a humble nod of acknowledgement and then smiled to show that he agreed with what I had said. He then moved in the direction we were to go and offered me to follow him.

We walked out of this small building. There were a couple of steps down from what seemed like the patio at the back of this building and onto the bare dirt. Once my feet hit the soil, an odd but pleasant feeling passed through me as I realised that this was the first time that I had put my foot down on the African soil. There was a sense of connectedness, of belonging, that somehow this land was welcoming me back as if at some time in my past I had left it. There was a strange but beautiful sense of attachment, as if the soil were saying to me, "Welcome back, my child. Your ancestors left this land many epochs ago and you have returned to the land that first bore you." It was as if the theory of the evolution of humanity was right, that all humans in the far ancient past were once born in this Dark Continent and from there peopled the rest of the globe. In some strange and esoteric way, I was coming back to the mother of our being.

Ibrahim led the way along a dirt path to another building in the far distance. There were other buildings scattered around but all far from each other as if each building needed to be aware of the existence of the others but be at a safe distance away in order not to interfere with each other's business. Between each building were stretches of fields with a splattering of trees here and there as if we were on somebody's farmland. There were areas of land where vegetables were growing in neat rows and Tanzanian gardeners were hard at work watering them or digging the dirt to plant more. What surprised me the most was that the landscape looked quite familiar. As a child, whenever we watched movies or TV series set in the sub-Saharan African landscape, such as *Tarzan* or *Daktari*, the land was a wild, untamed forest with tall trees and thick, impenetrable forests, with wild lions and leopards lurking in the shadows. The landscape I was seeing around me here was familiar, as if I were on a farm on the far side of the Blue Mountains, in Bathurst or Dubbo. If it weren't for Ibrahim, a typical, black African man, and the other sub-Saharan Africans I had seen on my journey from the airport up to here and those I saw working in the gardens, I could have sworn that I was still in my home country.

The walk to our dormitory was along a dusty pathway where puffs of fine dust formed small dust clouds with every step. I was amazed how the dust so easily got into the air and yet Ibrahim's clothes remained impeccably clean. As we walked along, Ibrahim pointed out certain landmarks on the compound to help me get my bearings as to where I was and how to get around.

We eventually arrived at a building which from the outside once again looked quite familiar. It was a brick construction and similar to buildings I was acquainted with at home. It was obvious that this building had only been recently built and it still showed evidence that it had not as yet been completed.

Ibrahim led me down a corridor and then finally we entered what appeared to be a rather small room but hitched out with two very large double beds. On first impression, each bed appeared so big that I thought it could hold four people. Hovering above the bed was a mosquito net, tied up in a bun, waiting for someone to untie the knot so that its lace network could hang lazily around the one who occupied the bed.

"My goodness!" I exclaimed. "These beds are huge!"

Ibrahim laughed. "Yes, this is a temporary arrangement. The second teachers dormitory hasn't been completed yet and these beds will eventually go there. This building hasn't been finished yet but once it has, some of the students will occupy these rooms and smaller beds will be put in here. I hope you don't mind it being so cluttered in here with two large beds."

"No, that's fine," I replied, thinking how comfortable it would be in such a large double bed on my own.

In one corner of the room was what looked like something of a cupboard, or really it looked like a bookshelf with four shelves. Two of the shelves were already cluttered with personal items so these must have been the other occupant's belongings.

"I suppose I can put my things on one of these shelves," I commented.

I walked over to the bookshelf. I saw an assortment of toiletries on display on one shelf and on the other were a number of books. There was one book lying on its own. It had a dark green cover and on the cover was writing in beautiful calligraphy and in Arabic script. I recognised it immediately. It was the Koran. An instant shudder went up my spine. I knew instantly that I would have to be completely on my guard about anything I said and did as the person I would be sharing the room with represented totally everything that I was not. And more, he would no doubt kill me for being so.

"I can see my roommate has already set himself up," I said, turned around and smiled at Ibrahim.

"Yes. That's me. I'm your roommate," Ibrahim replied.

Something inside me like a large heavy object dropped through to my feet when I contemplated that I would have to share a room with this complete stranger from a country I knew was not very tolerant of my kind of people. But even further, I knew deep down I was scared of Ibrahim because he was so many things I was not. He was black, he was a heterosexual family man and, possibly what scared me the most, he was a strict, religious Muslim. For nine days I would be sharing a small confined space with this total stranger, totally strange in so many ways.

"And tomorrow I will be accompanying you to Arusha to the UN office," Ibrahim further added.

"Oh, great," I replied but inside my muscles further tightened. However, what else could I do? Ibrahim would only be a part of my life for what would be less than a sand grain of time in comparison to my entire existence, so all I needed to do was play the charade and be polite and be whatever else Ibrahim would like me to be for nine days. After all, I was here on a mission, to find out if Polycarp had any surviving relatives, and once there was an answer either in the positive or the negative, my reason for coming to this Dark Continent would be complete and I could return home to my normal life.

Ibrahim sat on his bed.

"Do you want to have a bath before we go to dinner?" he asked.

"A bath?" I asked.

"Yes, you know, wash your body."

Have a bath! I then remembered what I had learnt in my Swahili book about the expression used to mean to have a shower. This was obviously a throwback to the colonial days when washing was originally by bath.

"That would be a great idea," I replied.

It had been an exceptionally long journey and I could feel that I needed a complete overhaul, a good shower and a shave. The last decent shower and shave that I had had was in Hong Kong and that was almost twenty-four hours before.

Ibrahim led me to the other end of this short building into a large open space and then we entered what appeared to be another corridor. Along one side were all the toilet cubicles and on the other all the shower recesses. It was very Spartan and it was difficult to say whether this was because the building had not yet been completed or these were what the facilities were supposed to be like for the students who would later reside here.

The toilets were simply holes in the ground, or what we in Australia call Asian toilets. I looked at these with a shudder. Would I have to put up with using this type of toilet for nine days?

The shower recesses were just as sparse if not moreso. They were simply rooms with a small hole in the centre of the floor. There was no shower rose. Ibrahim must have read my mind because when I turned around to look at him, he said to me, "I'll just get you the water."

Get me the water? What did that mean? Ibrahim disappeared while I examined the bathroom in more detail. There appeared to be no wash basins where I could shave and brush my teeth. I guessed that I was going to have to shave while I had a shower and, without a mirror, I would have to shave like a blind man and simply feel around to ensure that I had done a good job.

A few minutes later, Ibrahim came staggering in with a bucket of water in one hand and what looked like an empty margarine container in the other. Ibrahim put the bucket gently down inside the shower recess without spilling a drop.

"Do you know how to wash like this?" he asked. Once again, he must have read my mind!

Ibrahim then explained to me the process. I simply needed to take a cup full or two of water and pour this over my body. I then simply needed to lather my body all over and then pour the rest of the water over me, rinsing out the soap. I shuddered at the thought. However, I was so in need of a shower and there was no alternative, so I had to go through with the process. This was what washing my body would be for the next number of days.

Ibrahim then left me, saying he would be waiting for me in the room, and soon he was gone. I touched the water. I was expecting it to be ice cold but it was quite tepid. And because it was such a hot day, my first Tanzanian shower wasn't too bad after all. In fact, by the time I had emptied the contents of the bucket over the last remnants of lather on my body, I discovered that although not as luxurious as a shower at home, it really wasn't that bad after all. I then guessed that the reason for such a shower for the students was so that the students wouldn't spend hours under the spray wasting water. When the students came to live here and they needed to have a shower, the amount of water they were given to wash with could easily be controlled.

Or was it simply to save money on plumbing?

I then further realised that not only was this a sensible step when dealing with children, this was a great environmental innovation. At home, it was now a requirement that all water taps and shower roses had a maximum flow rate of nine litres per minute to limit the use of water. Here, each student would be given a ten litre bucket of water and it didn't matter if they took a minute to shower or an hour, they only had ten litres to wash with and hence the amount of water was completely controlled.

Although an ingenious water saving and environmentally sensible innovation, I could barely imagine this type of system hitting it off in Australia.

When I had finished, I realised I had not thought ahead and had not brought a clean change of clothes to get into. This meant that I had to get changed back in the dormitory. I wrapped my towel around my naked body and returned back to the dormitory carrying the clothes that I had travelled in.

When I arrived back at my room, Ibrahim was lying on the bed reading. As I entered the room, he looked up at me and smiled.

"I forgot to take with me a clean set of clothes," I said as a confession, feeling embarrassed that I had walked into the dormitory with only a towel wrapped around my waist but leaving me bare-chested. I wasn't sure what the protocol or the culture was in Tanzania. Was it okay for a man to walk around almost naked in front of another man?

I turned around to my bed and opened my suitcase. I took out a clean T-shirt and a pair of boxer shorts. This was a strategic choice. We would later have to come back here to go to bed and so the T-shirt and boxer shorts could be my pyjamas which meant I did not have to remove anything and reveal parts of my anatomy which may cause offence. But while putting on my boxer shorts under my towel, a shudder went up my spine as if I could feel Ibrahim staring at me. Once my boxer shorts were on and I could remove my towel with decency, I turned around. Ibrahim was indeed staring at me. I could not decipher from his facial expression whether he was staring in disapproval because I had broken an unwritten social custom or that he simply was watching what I was doing because this was the only movement going on in the room. This made me feel even more aware of what lack of clothes I had on and so I was just as eager to put on my jeans and a T-shirt to cover much of my body.

I looked outside and the sunlight was obviously dimming. It would soon be night time. This was when the mosquitoes would be out in full force. I had brought along a generous amount of tropical strength mosquito repellent and began spraying this over the exposed parts of my body and face. Once done, I could feel the tiredness begin to creep over me.

"Okay," I said as an indication that I had completed what needed to be done. "I'm ready."

Ibrahim put his book down and then sat up.

"Do you want to put the mosquito net down now? Then we don't have to worry about trying to do it when we get back in the dark."

Ibrahim pulled the mosquito net out of its bun and just as it is in the movies when women with long hair pull the bobby pin out and their hair falls down loosely and freely, so the mosquito net cascaded down like a lace river over the four sides of the bedframe, draping over the bed like a protective shield. We then left the dormitory and made our way to the community hall.

The community hall was simply the first place we had all grouped together when we had arrived. There were four tables to seat about ten to fifteen people per table. When we arrived, all the tables looked full. We stood in the dining hall hesitantly surveying the scene. Ibrahim then finally pointed in the direction of one of the tables and said, "There's a place over there. I'll sit over here."

This meant that Ibrahim and I had to squeeze in at different tables.

For me it was a relief to get away from Ibrahim for a moment.

As the others at the table made room for me to squeeze in, each threw me a welcoming smile and a cheery welcome. I responded politely and cautiously.

As nice as these people appeared to be, I did not feel comfortable among them. After all, it is really difficult being among religious people when you are gay. I was all too familiar with what Christians thought because the only significant story where men who want to have sex with men make a show in the Bible is when we read about the inhabitants of Sodom and Gomorrah. This therefore means that when Christians discover that a man they know is gay, the Christians view this man not as a normal, average guy on the street but rather as some raging monster with a rapacious sexual appetite who, like the inhabitants of Sodom, begins salivating at the sight of any fresh male flesh he can get his hands on, banging on doors and yelling at close range that he wants to "know" him, and chafing at the bit in order to fulfil his insatiable desire irrespective of whether or not the target of his lust consents to it.

Fortunately for lesbians, an equivalent story about female homosexuals finds no biblical cognate.

And to really rub salt into the insult, St Paul later writes in the first chapter of his letter to the Romans that homosexuals, both male and female, are evil, insolent, arrogant, boastful, deceitful, malicious, gossipers, slanderers, greedy, depraved, murderers and really just outright heartless people. This certainly doesn't help if you are in the church trying to deal with your sexuality as it was for me back in my teens. So, not only are homosexuals attracted to their own sex, according to the Bible, homosexuals have the social skills of an uneducated but ruthless dictator.

With such a thought, this should mean that if the Bible is so accurate in its accounts of people, the most violent and heartless misfits of society should also be gay. And yet, oddly enough, I have never once heard a Christian make the statement that terrible tyrants of history such as Genghis Khan, Catherine the Great or Josef Stalin clearly illustrated through their actions the evidence of their sexuality. And the dictator of all dictators, Adolf Hitler, somehow managed to escape the accusation that his actions were clear signs of which side of the sexuality fence he sat on. But then this would make it all the more confusing because Romans 1:32 then says that homosexuals "not only do the same but have pleasure in them that do them" because Hitler certainly was not pleased with the doings of homosexuals in 1940s Germany since the plight of homosexuals under the Nazi regime was no better than it was for the Jews.

So, in this group of only religious people, I knew I had to be careful of what I said and the way I acted. If any of these people discovered I was gay, they would generally assume that they had a frightfully evil monster in their midst. And if Ibrahim, who was now my roommate, found out, the consequences would surely be lethal.

Although my Christian upbringing was something well in the distant past, I was still familiar with what were the right things to say and the correct ways to act in such an environment. However, because I was obviously a lot further advanced in years and therefore at an age that I should have a wife and grown up children, I knew that by confessing that I had neither would be a glaring irregularity. So, I knew I could not let any of our conversations steer towards this topic of conversation.

I was unsure what to say and so was happy to suddenly be interrupted by some sort of clanging noise which obviously was to get our attention. Once everyone was silent, a local Tanzanian called us to attention.

"Good evening, everyone. I would like to say that dinner is now ready. Before we start, I'd like to open with a word of prayer."

Everyone dutifully bowed their heads and clasped their hands. The man out the front then strung out a rather verbose rendition of gratitude for the food that we were about to eat. I followed along with the charade.

Grace. I remembered as a child that we had to say grace before we ate a meal. Since leaving the faith, whenever I sit down to a meal, I just start eating without a second thought. So, these days I notice what a strange and rather superstitious practice saying grace actually is. Religious people go to the extent of talking out loud saying a whole lot of thanks but there is no evidence that anyone is actually listening, apart from those who are together in the same place. How do those who say grace know whether anyone else apart from themselves has actually heard their prayer? And does the food taste any better by saying grace?

I was also extremely curious as to what was going to be said for grace. Because the Msingi wa Mungu Project was all about being open to all religions, I was curious to hear who exactly the grace was going to be said to. The grace that was said, sure enough, was open to interpretation. The prayer was only made out to "God" and "the Lord" or the combination, "the Lord God". There was no mention of names, of Jesus, Mary, Allah, Brahma, Shiva, Zeus, Athena, Marduk, Ishtar or any of the plethora of other gods and goddesses known to have been prayed to at various times in history.

It took some time to get through the grace but we finally arrived at the Amen.

"So, let's go and get something to eat," said one of the people at my table.

There was an orderly scramble towards where the food was being served and an eventual organised and civilised queue formed. As the queue eventually made its civilised composure, I could not believe that in the shuffle to create an organised line I managed to get Ibrahim directly in front of me.

"Hey, Bwana Michael," Ibrahim then said to me to acknowledge that he realised that I was directly behind him. There was a momentary silence as if Ibrahim wanted to say something and really didn't know what to so he simply added, "So nice to see you again."

Well, I couldn't say it was particularly nice to see you, I thought to myself but simply replied to his comment with a nod and a smile.

The food was served as if we were in an open cafeteria. I noticed that it was clearly indicated whether or not the food contained meat, whether the meat was halal or otherwise, or animal products of any other description. This Msingi wa Mungu Project had certainly expected and successfully catered for people of a wide range of dietary laws. Obviously, then, the Msingi wa Mungu Project catered for all religious codes, not just simply Christian and Muslim. A further furtive glance at the crowd of people and I could see a few men and women dressed in what appeared to be typical Indian attire so these people perhaps were the vegetarians or even the vegans the project wanted to cater for.

When Ibrahim reached the food table, contrary to what I expected, Ibrahim avoided the meat. He even avoided the halal meat. He only chose food that was vegetarian. This was totally unexpected. He did not look like a vegetarian. He did not look like a vegetarian especially as he was a somewhat fitted-out looking guy and I always expected vegetarians to be rather thin and emaciated because they can't get the protein necessary to build their bodies out. But then I thought that this wasn't true anyway because Khatyn was a vegetarian and she looked as healthy as any meat eating person among my acquaintances. I guessed, however, that Ibrahim probably was not aware that the halal meat was there and to be sure he simply avoided anything that had meat in it.

During dinner, all of us at the Msingi wa Mungu Project made our acquaintances. It was amazing how it was organised. We were all here for a variety of different functions. Some of us had come to teach, or at least teach the teachers at the school, others were engineers or tradespeople who were going to help out with construction work. Most were here on a six month contractual basis but there were a few like me who were here only for a short two week period. I wasn't sure how all this was going to work. There didn't seem to be any particular continuity. I knew I was here for only nine days, for example, and I would impart my knowledge and skills in teaching in that brief period. But the person who followed me would probably have different ideas. This would inevitably create a lot of confusion for the local teachers as far as I could see. However, in the end it was an economical way to build this school up using volunteers.

Once we had eaten, Gordon called us all to attention and handed out a sheet of paper which showed what the program was for the next two weeks. Gordon first began talking about the program for the teachers. The first two weeks were a series of workshops where the teachers from overseas would have the opportunity to talk to the teachers at the Msingi wa Mungu Project and talk about teaching strategies, how to adapt local resources to local teaching, how to implement modern pedagogic principles and so on. There was also a series of debates for the students to participate in and for those teaching the English component to assist in developing the skill of debating.

Gordon reiterated what we were going to do the following day. He then turned to me and said, "Now, Michael, you're not attending the workshop tomorrow because Ibrahim is taking you to the UN office in Arusha. So the other teachers can debrief you tomorrow evening about what they did during the day."

I was stunned! This Gordon may have come across as an elderly man but he obviously had not lost any of his mental capacity. On one meeting he not only had remembered my name, he knew why I was really here and what I really wanted to accomplish. And he had organised everything for me.

"Now before you all go," Gordon concluded, "you will notice that there are lights on on all the buildings in the compound. They will stay on all night. There is all-night security and we have watchmen around the compound. So anyone who goes sleepwalking at night, you will be okay."

Everyone laughed at that comment. That signalled that this was the end of the debriefing and so we were dismissed. A rumble of noise suddenly formed as the groups of people began to get up from the tables and make their way back to their dormitories. I was waiting for people closest to the door to move so that I could leave when I suddenly felt two heavy hands plant themselves quite firmly on my shoulders. I turned around. It was Ibrahim.

"Okay, Bwana Michael," he said. "So, let's go back to our dormitory."

We walked out of the eating room and then out under the African night sky. It was now dark outside. A light cool breeze blew across my face which filled me with a positive sense of purpose as to why I was here, a small reward for my effort for coming here.

As we walked away from the common eating hall, the surroundings became darker and darker with no electric lighting to guide the way. In the obscurity, I happened to look up into the night sky. For the first time in a long time, I could see the night sky besparkled with millions upon millions of glittering diamonds. In the suburbs of Sydney where I lived, I had never seen so many stars. The heavens at night here stretched over the Tanzanian interior looked as if they were a glass roof completely black but where millions upon millions of sparks had dropped on the upper surface. It was also the first time for a long time since I could remember seeing the Milky Way and why it was so named.

I had to stop and comment on this nocturnal spectacle. Ibrahim stopped with me and looked up into the heavens. Ibrahim agreed with me about the wonder of this heavenly scene but it was obvious that he had seen this many times before. I just wanted to soak up this beautiful vision, I was just so captivated by it.

Suddenly Ibrahim broke the silence. "Haven't you noticed that the stars all look the same and yet they are fundamentally completely different? Yet, altogether in the sky, they form a harmonious mix, something beautiful, each star to look at individually and yet together also just as beautiful?"

I looked at Ibrahim. In the darkness, I could barely make out his features.

"Wow! That is so profound," I commented. I had a fairly general idea of what he was on about. Although the stars on face value all looked the same, at the same time, which was the entire paradox of it all, they were all entirely different. For a start, the five planets visible from Earth with the naked eye, namely, Mercury, Venus, Mars, Jupiter and Saturn, were not stars at all and the source of their light was merely a reflection of the large fiery ball at the centre of our solar system and not due to a light inherent in these celestial bodies. What was even further revealing about these planets was that although they were similar in the way they reflected the sun's light, each planet was curiously different in its own makeup.

But there were also other sparkling nightsky bodies which had no inherent light of their own. Called asteroids, coming from the Greek words *asteros* meaning "star" and *oidos* meaning "similar to", asteroids on close scrutiny were merely lumps of large rocks, each their own size and shape, and only appeared as stars from the earth because they reflected the sun's rays.

But even the stars themselves were all different. Although from Earth they simply looked like pinpricks of light through a dark canopy, each star was at its own stage of evolution, from a brown dwarf to a red giant.

It was a beautiful insight of what the starry night sky represented. That was how I understood what Ibrahim wanted to say. With that, I made a move to continue our journey to the dormitories. Ibrahim responded to my movement but added a further comment.

"The stars in the night sky are a wonderful reflection of humanity. Like the stars, all of us humans are completely the same, yet at the same time, we are completely different from each other. But if only we all appreciated each other's differences and didn't try to dominate each other or feel superior to each other, like the stars, humans would reside in heaven."

I was already captivated by the wonderful night sky. But as soon as Ibrahim had said these words, I was overwhelmed by a tingling sensation that started from deep within my chest and spread out to my fingers and up through the back of my neck.

I just turned around to look at Ibrahim while he continued to stare up into the sky. I just wanted to reach out and hug him, what he said was just so beautiful. But like a wave at the beach which suddenly appears from nowhere and completely wipes out the sandcastle you have painstakingly tried to build, a wave of fear, which I took to be a return back to reality, overcame me and my initial image of Ibrahim, the heterosexual, highly religious intolerant Muslim man, returned to me. This might be a beautiful saying but I was sure that Ibrahim meant that each star had to be a Muslim star to be worthy to shine in a Muslim-only night sky. Those outside this realm of belief were simply worthy of nothing more than to be completely annihilated.

With that, I made a move to go in the direction of the dormitories and Ibrahim followed my lead. As we approached, the light shining from the corner of the dormitory lit up our path so we could see where we were putting our feet down.

Once we were back inside our dormitory, my bed appeared to be beckoning me. I could feel that I was very tired and could not wait to lie down in a bed for the first time after such a long trip from home. Ibrahim disappeared to the amenities for the last time to offload before going to bed.

The light on the building outside provided some sort of light inside the dormitory so we could make out to some extent the interior of the room. As planned, all I needed to do was to remove my shoes and socks and then my jeans, and dressed in T-shirt and boxer shorts slide under the mosquito net and then into bed. We had both a sheet and a blanket to slip under but because it was quite warm, the sheet was ample covering.

Once under the sheet and my head on the pillow, I was ready to leave the real world for the evening and venture into the land of dreams. I had only just settled when Ibrahim walked into the room. In the semidarkness, I could still make out his features.

Ibrahim stripped down and like me he had a pair of boxer shorts on under his trousers. But he then removed his shirt to reveal his bare chest. There was enough light streaming in from outside to allow me to make out the contours of what I thought was a well-formed African body. I could also make out in the semi-darkness a generous layer of chest hair from his neck to his navel all in tight curls like the looped surface of Velcro.

Whoa! I thought. What an eye-rinse! A sculptor in ebony could not have been prouder of such a wonderful piece of sculptured work! I wondered if he was naturally this shape or he had to work at it to keep in this fit state.

His carpet of chest hair was also something amazing. I had always thought that Negroids were completely hairless. I thought chest hair was only a feature of Caucasian or Middle Eastern men.

Ibrahim then lifted up the mosquito net and climbed onto his bed. But before lying down, he sat on the bed with his legs crossed with his hands lying relaxed, palms up and his eyes closed in what looked like the lotus position. He closed his mouth and I heard the air rush first in and then out of his nostrils once and then there was silence.

"Not a Muslim way to pray," I thought to myself. "Very strange!"

Even so, I just shrugged off the absurdity of prayer, rolled over and soon was sound asleep.

Chapter 5

It was the urgent morning need that pulled me out of bed the following morning. Already it was dusk and the confident sun was already pouring a new batch of sunrays onto the African continent and I guessed – and hoped – that this dispersed the malaria-bearing mosquitoes so that I was not attacked once fully exposed to the environment.

It took a moment for me to successfully pull the mosquito net up enough for me to slide under it. My initial reaction was to pull the mosquito net to one side like large curtains over a bay window but after two tugs in this fashion, I became fully enough awake to know that this was not the correct procedure. Finally I managed to pull the mosquito net high enough to allow me to slip onto the floor and finally make the fifty metre dash to the toilets.

The concrete floor allowed me to make my way to the door in silence in order not to wake Ibrahim. I tried to open the door without making a sound but the door betrayed me with a slight click, soft but audible, and soon I was out the door and moving swiftly along the corridor. There were yet three more doors I had to pass, two which were closed, the last one open ajar but enough for me to see inside the occupants fast asleep also in large beds. The thought quickly dashed through my mind that I could not recall hearing anyone else in the dormitories the night before so they must have come later after I had fallen asleep.

When I returned, it became obvious that my attempts to be discreet had been futile as Ibrahim was already awake.

"Good morning, Bwana Michael," Ibrahim slurred through his attempt to wake up.

I slid back under the mosquito net and then under the sheet.

I had learnt that the Swahili word *bwana* meant "mister" and was used as a sign of respect. A bit odd, however, for two men who were, so I guessed, of similar age.

"Good morning, Bwana Ibrahim," I replied in an attempt to use the same respectful Swahili word.

"Did you sleep well?" Ibrahim asked me.

"Yeah, very well, thank you."

Ibrahim then sucked in noisily a good volume of air into his lungs and rolled onto his back. He then looked at his watch.

"What time is it?" I asked.

"Just after seven o'clock," Ibrahim replied.

"What time do we have to leave?"

"Oh, we have plenty of time," was Ibrahim's answer.

That's not an answer to my question, I thought enervated. I wanted to make a sarcastic quip against this answer but then just thought to myself that it wasn't worth it. I am only with this stranger for eight more days, I reminded myself. I took a few deep breaths to calm myself down and then said, "So, do we leave at about 9 o'clock?"

"Eight thirty," Ibrahim replied.

It was now just after seven o'clock and we didn't have to leave until about eight thirty. What was I supposed to do in the presence of Ibrahim for another hour and a half? I lay on my back and looked up at the ceiling through the mosquito netting with the hope that I may just drift back off into sleep. However, I felt wide awake. I wondered how long I could go without having to have any conversation with this stranger who now occupied my personal space.

I heard Ibrahim breathe deeply again as if his body needed a further kick start and hence needed an extra helping of oxygen to get himself going. I heard the bed move which indicated that Ibrahim was turning over.

"You must have slept well!" Ibrahim commented.

I rolled over and looked at him.

"Why do you say that?" I asked.

"As soon as I got into bed, I asked you a question and you didn't reply. You must have gone to sleep as soon as your head hit the pillow!"

"Yeah, I'll be honest. It was a long trip."

"So, where are you from?" Ibrahim asked as he got up on one shoulder and leant on his hand.

"I'm from Australia," I replied.

"Oh, from Australia," Ibrahim commented as if this information confirmed him of something. "From the direction of the rising sun."

"Yes, from the east," I replied in a way to be a little sarcastic to what sounded like a roundabout way of saying from which direction I had come, as if Ibrahim didn't know the English word for "east" so he used the movement of the sun as the means of orientation.

"Oh, which part of Australia?"

"From Sydney."

"Wow," Ibrahim said. "That certainly is a long way from there to here. How long did it take you to get here?"

"About thirty hours."

"Whoa! I can understand why you were so tired, then," Ibrahim replied. "How long are you staying here?"

"Oh, not long, really. I'm going back next week," I replied.

"Oh, only for a short time. Are you here on your own?" Ibrahim asked. "Did you come with your wife or did she stay home in Australia?"

No, I wanted to reply, I'm not married nor will I ever be married. I will never have children of my own and increase the population and continue to increase the problems that humanity is now causing with the increase in population. I am a screaming queen and have sex freely and openly, totally unlike the situation in this closed-up country of yours.

But I couldn't say that, even though I really felt like saying so. I was here for such a short period so it wasn't worth the outburst. However, I decided in a way to answer his question honestly.

"No," I replied. "I'm not married. I have no wife." And then as an afterthought I added, "Nor do I have a girlfriend."

"Oh, okay," Ibrahim replied. I interpreted his body language as an indication that my answer was an uncomfortable one for him. I was expecting him to question me more on the topic but he stopped there.

There was a slight silence and then I decided to quiz him. "How about you? Are you married?"

Ibrahim rolled over noisily onto his back and looked up at the ceiling as if the answer were written strategically on the painted surface of the ceiling. He then looked back at me with a smile.

"Well, I was. But my wife died some years ago."

Whoa! That knocked the wind out of my sails. How was I to answer that? I just looked at him for a moment and then replied, "I...I'm really sorry."

Ibrahim nestled his head back onto his pillow. "That's okay," he said and seemed to shrug this piece of information off as if it were now past history, no longer to be considered.

That piece of information was a road block in the conversation. I wanted to ask what she died of but just felt that this was extremely inappropriate. But I didn't want the atmosphere to stagnate back into silence. After a moment's pause, I threw in another question.

"And do you have children?" I asked.

"Yes, six children. Five sons and a daughter."

"Oh, wow! And are they here at the Msingi wa Mungu Project?"

Ibrahim laughed.

"Oh, no. One of my sons lives with his wife and children in Zanzibar. I have another son in Dodoma. Two of my sons live in Dar-Es-Salaam.

Another son and his family, and my daughter and her husband live in Tanga."

I now had a general overview of Ibrahim's family. From this description, I could further fine tune my estimation of his age and that we both belonged to the same age bracket.

Once again, a lull hung in the air. I didn't know what else to ask him for a moment until my mind was brought back to the Msingi wa Mungu Project.

"So, how long have you worked here at the Msingi wa Mungu Project?" I asked him.

Ibrahim rolled onto his back.

"Ever since it started. I was one of the people who helped to get it started."

"And you live here on the premises?"

"No, no," Ibrahim said. "I only work here from time to time. I'm staying here at the moment because of a particular project I'm involved in and it's actually easier for me to stay on site for the next couple of days. In reality, I live about twenty kilometres from the centre of Moshi but on the other side. And I work at the International School. I help out here from time to time."

"Oh, so you work at a school? You're a teacher, then?"

Ibrahim rolled back onto his side to face me.

"Yes, I teach English and history."

"History!" I said as this created some interest. "What history do you teach?"

"Mainly Ancient History, you know, Egypt, Greece and Rome, and some modern history."

"Do you teach any African history?"

"No, that doesn't form part of the curriculum. But I have read about African history."

"Which history do you like in particular?"

"I like all history," Ibrahim commented. He then paused for a moment before continuing. "You know, every time I learn about the history of any civilisation, to me it shows just how wonderful all humans are. Many people when they study history they think that the history of Europe is only for the *Mzungus,* Asian history is only for the Asians, African history is only for the Africans and so on."

"*Mzungus*? Who are they?" I asked bewildered.

"White people, European people, people like you."

This cut me short. I wondered if this word *Mzungu* was in fact an insulting slur at Europeans. It made me feel uncomfortable as if Ibrahim were casting an aspersion at me. I was later to discover, however, that the word *Mzungu* was in fact benign in meaning and in a way a compliment.

"And you've studied the history of Asia? And of Australia?"

"Asia, yes. I've read a lot about the history of India and also about China. Australia, however, no. I haven't read anything about your country yet. Eventually I'll find out."

This was all interesting but then it was the end of this line of conversation. I needed to find a new topic.

"And what are you doing here?"

"I am involved with the recruitment of teachers."

I was going to make a comment to help the conversation flow. But while I was framing a question in my mind, Ibrahim looked at his watch.

"I guess we should start getting ready. I'll go and get some water so we can have a bath."

Ibrahim climbed out of bed, stood up completely erect and then stretched. I was absolutely captivated by the sight. Unfortunately, my body responded accordingly and I had to wait until Ibrahim had left the room before I could get out of bed because I didn't want Ibrahim to realise the effect his physical appearance had on my hormonal stimuli.

When I finally got to the amenities, I stood and waited with my towel held in front of me to hide the morning broom handle. When I saw Ibrahim come into the amenities block carrying a bucket of water for me, it made me feel rather awkward. Ibrahim was waiting on me, a white guy, or *Mzungu* as he called it, in the same way the Europeans in the past forced black Africans to wait on their white masters. But I couldn't see any way out of this situation. Ibrahim knew where to get the water from and he did not show me. But then I had another thought: what if Ibrahim were white-skinned or a *Mzungu* like me? Would I think of this gesture as being master-slave or would I simply accept that this was a kind action by one person for another?

We went into separate cubicles. The water was once again tepid and in this heat, even at this early hour of the morning, it wasn't too uncomfortable to pour this luke-warm water over my body. Although slightly uncomfortable at first, once dry, the coolness of the water made me feel quite refreshed.

Ibrahim was first to finish and I heard him leave the amenities. Once he was gone, I allowed a couple of minutes before I left as well and made my way back to our room. Once I had arrived, Ibrahim was already partly dressed, wearing a freshly ironed white business shirt and a pair of navy blue business trousers. I couldn't get over how handsome he looked. But also, I realised how embarrassed I would be if I decided to wear T-shirt and jeans. Fortunately, most of the clothes I had brought along with me were, after all, business clothes because I knew I would be working with other teachers at this project and I had been advised that business-type clothes were the type of clothes teachers wore in this part of the world. So, I decided to dress in par with Ibrahim.

Breakfast was at the same place where we had eaten dinner the night before. However, unlike the night before, Ibrahim and I were the only ones there apart from the woman in the kitchen who organised the food who I found out was Mrs Clarsson. Mrs Clarsson welcomed us in and told us to sit down at one of the tables. She offered us for breakfast an omelette with some bread. Both Ibrahim and I were happy to have a stiff cup of coffee as well to accompany breakfast. Once we had finished, Mrs Clarsson brought out a large bowel of fruit. There were a number of large avocados in the bowel.

"Wow! Is it alright if I have one of these?" I asked.

"Of course," Mrs Clarsson replied. "I'd rather you ate them than throw them out. We have so many on the tree that sometimes we have more avocados than people to eat them and so we have to throw them away."

Too many avocados? Throw them away? There are too many on the tree? I thought about avocados in Australia and just how expensive they were there, and here I was being told that there were so many that people here were happy I ate them because otherwise this delectable fruit would be thrown away. Wow! I felt as if I were in paradise! And these avocados were huge. They weren't the scrawled up, tiny shrivelled up, rough dark skinned things we saw in the shops in Sydney. These were large, emu-egg sized, smooth green skinned things with a more than adequate amount of flesh within. Mrs Clarsson told me to eat as many as I wanted and I did. However, once I had eaten my third one, I could not eat any more.

I walked away from breakfast bloated, strangely enough in this continent that was supposed to be so poor that people were starving to death. Obviously they weren't getting enough avocados wherever these starving people were.

Ibrahim and I were then taken to the bus terminal which was in the centre of Moshi town by one of the drivers. Moshi was my first introduction to an all-out African town. The name itself comes from the Swahili *moshi* meaning "smoke". It gets its name from its appearance from a distance, particularly in the morning or afternoon when mist hangs over the township and looks very much like a layer of smoke. What amused me about the word "moshi" is that when repeated, that is, "moshi moshi", this is the expression used by the Japanese when they first pick up a ringing phone. To a Swahili speaker, it must sound amusing to hear a Japanese answer their phone saying "smoke smoke!" which may also sound alarming as if the Japanese were close to saying "Fire! Fire!" In fact, I was later to discover when I became very familiar with the Swahili language how similar in sound Swahili and Japanese were to each other.

Moshi was a quaint little town. The buildings were in general made of concrete but obviously from a bygone era as the concrete was chipped and cracked like well-used crockery. By contrast, those walking around these chipped and chapped buildings were women and men dressed in African attire which looked clean and pure as a soul cleansed of sin. Many of the women wore the familiar *kanga* material wrapped around their bodies, and a smaller portion around their heads, in the typical style I was familiar with of African women I had seen in Sydney including some I had seen in the on-line access rooms at Tevah Am. The men wore familiar looking shirts and trousers which were typical of western style but the colour co-ordination was extremely different. Unlike the drab white shirt and choice of navy blue or black trousers typical of the official male garb of the city office worker, the men wore shirts and trousers in a combination of colours that could only be compared in nature with flowers and butterflies. Really, it was extremely pleasing to the eye, and the dark skin below the clothes only brought out the colours even more definitely.

Our transfer dropped us off at what looked like a central bus station as there were small and medium-sized minibuses dotted around with teams of people moving around them like ants around their booty.

As soon as our transfer had dropped us off, Ibrahim and I began walking in the direction of where the buses were. As we took our first steps, suddenly a crowd of men came running at us armed with manila folders and what looked like raffle ticket books, already yelling out as they charged at us. My first reaction was to scream and run in the opposite direction yelling, "Help!" but because Ibrahim kept walking on nonchalantly like a superhero ready to combat the enemy as if it were part of a day's work, I resisted my first emotional reflex. Suddenly all around us was a barrage of what looked like angry men flashing folders and ticket books at us, pens at the ready to accuse us of any false statement that we made, pretty much as if Ibrahim and I were politicians suddenly surrounded by the paparazzi. Instinctively, I just pushed closer to Ibrahim.

Ibrahim raised his left hand in the air as if to signal them all to silence which they all automatically did.

However, the silence was only momentarily observed when suddenly a flurry of voices and shaking of paper resumed again. Throughout all this anarchy, Ibrahim appeared to be weighing up in his mind his next move. Eventually, he directed his attention to one of those in the crowd and asked in Swahili the cost and other details of the trip to Arusha. With that, the rest of the crowd slowly dispersed and there was only one man left from whom Ibrahim bought and arranged the tickets.

We were led to the coach that was to take us to Arusha. I was rather impressed by it. It looked like a modern coach, the type I would catch between major cities in Australia. Ibrahim politely and gentlemanly let me have the window seat and he sat next to me against the aisle.

Once we were all on the bus, the bus pulled out of Moshi town. As we moved out of the town, I watched the people around the sides of the highway walking around, cycling, peddling, pushing oxcarts and running. It was as if we were being farewelled by a crowd of well-wishers for a safe trip to one of the big cities of Tanzania.

The further we went, the number of people along the side of the road became less and less. The country became more and more deserted but also extremely beautiful. For some reason, this second view of the landscape seemed so much nicer than the day before after arriving from such a long trip from Asia. I noticed that the landscape was much greener than my first impressions, not possessing the deep, rich verdure of a northern European landscape, but certainly much greener and lusher than the typical bone dry brown and dusty Australian outback.

I had been so engrossed for some time in watching the scenery that I realised I had completely neglected Ibrahim seated beside me. He may have been this scary religious Muslim but he still was a human being and I felt a bit rude simply giving him my back. I turned to look at him and noticed that he was reading the *Mwananchi*, one of the local newspapers.

"Beautiful countryside," I said to him with a feeling of overwhelming satisfaction.

Ibrahim simply smiled at me.

"You've no doubt seen this several times before," I commented.

Ibrahim laughed. "Yes, you could say that. But I agree. It's beautiful countryside."

I stared back out the window. I felt that maybe I should try and be a bit more social with Ibrahim and actually make small talk with him than totally ignore him. But I really didn't know what topic to introduce.

I always find it difficult talking with people from other cultures because you never know what topic is taboo so it's hard to find out where exactly to start. As the only thing we had in common thus far was the Msingi wa Mungu Project, I thought I may as well start there.

"I think it's an impressive attempt for people of different religions to try and work together like they do at the Msingi wa Mungu Project," I said. "At this time, Christians and Muslims in most parts of the world are really at loggerheads, and here in the heart of Africa, you're showing that Christians and Muslims can really get along if they tried."

Ibrahim laughed as if this were an indication of his joy of the success of this project.

"Yes, I like it very much. It is like the first step back on track towards the principles of *Ujamaa*."

"I'm sorry?" I asked. "The principles of what?"

"Of *Ujamaa*. This is what the founding father of our nation, Mwalimu Julius Nyerere, was leading us towards."

"Mwalimu Julius Nyerere?" I asked mystified. "Who was he?"

"Ah, Mwalimu Julius Nyerere," Ibrahim said with a sigh and leant back in his chair as if the name itself were the invisible armchair into which he was finding comfort.

"Mwalimu Julius Nyerere was the father of our nation. It was he who led Tanzania into independence in 1961."

"And you were a witness to that?" I asked.

Ibrahim laughed. "Of course not! I was born around that time, though. And I saw him when he came to Moshi when I was a child."

I turned to look out the window. Then I turned back towards Ibrahim.

"And what are the principles of *Ujamaa*?" I asked inquisitively.

Ibrahim was still looking forward down the front of the bus but his face seemed to shine as if he had entered a sort of reverie. He then sat forward and looked at me.

"That all of us are equal, you, a *Mzungu* and a Christian, me, a black man and a Muslim, men, women, irrespective of our religions, we are all part of the human race and we can all contribute to society. It doesn't matter our differences, as long as our differences do not impinge on someone else's freedom."

It was the second time that a tingling sensation went up my spine and into my fingers and toes. What were these wonderful words that Ibrahim was expressing? Further, who was this Julius Nyerere who first proclaimed these beautiful words upon which Ibrahim based his statement?

"And if you don't believe in any god? Can you still be a part of this *Ujamaa*?" I asked rather cautiously but also out of curiosity.

Ibrahim looked at me with a strange expression on his face.

"How can anyone not believe in God?" he asked.

This put my shackles up. I had an answer to that question. But this certainly wasn't the place to argue the point.

"Well, I know people who don't," I replied, any anger in the tone of my voice thankfully masked by the sound of the travelling bus.

Ibrahim shrugged his shoulders and screwed up his face in a way which indicated that he had never thought of this before.

"I suppose, yes, there is no need to believe in God or have a religion under the principles of *Ujamaa*. To be part of *Ujamaa*, you need to be a human being. As long as your beliefs do not cause you to adversely affect other members of a society, even those who have no belief in God are welcome in this society, as long as they contribute to that society."

I was quite stunned by the comment. How could Ibrahim, a Muslim, embrace such a universal, cosmic belief in the unity of all humankind and yet say that he was a Muslim? Further, how could Ibrahim unabashedly and without difficulty accept a non-religious human being, someone who said that he or she did not believe in the existence of any gods, including the very God of his religion, into this *Ujamaa*? I was fully aware of Muslims' reactions to those who said they did not believe in God. Anyone who made this declaration in front of Muslims had to be suicidal because Muslims were known to kill people for this simple declaration, even if that person had good reasons for making this claim, and even though this confession did not affect Muslims in any way. If an atheist were throwing rocks at Muslims, or raping their women, or molesting their children, or killing members of their religion, or stealing things from their homes, I could understand Muslims getting together and killing that person. But by simply stating that someone does not believe in the existence of God surely could not warrant the outrageous enraged outburst of a group of people to the extent that they had to kill this person.

But Ibrahim, on the contrary, was not moved, or so it would appear, by the possibility of people who believed there was no god living in his *Ujamaa*. Non-religious people were welcome in the society that he and his former idol believed in. But how could that be? I was sure that it said in the Koran – although I had not read it at this stage but I would find out later that this was so – that Muslims could only associate with Muslims. Non-Muslims had to be eradicated from the face of the earth as quickly as possible.

I wasn't quite sure what to say right away. There was a mixture of confusion inside of me about Ibrahim and what he said he believed. I was also moved by this Julius Nyerere and this *Ujamaa*. This *Ujamaa*, if I understood Ibrahim correctly, was my belief.

I also wondered where "my kind of people" fit in within this utopic society. Gays and lesbians are hardly known to have been welcome into any society in the past. There have been rare occasions when they have. And modern western societies at least accept gays and lesbians although gays and lesbians still have to hide their identity under certain circumstances. This was definitely the case for Nikita and me. As trainers, neither Nikita nor I could ever admit openly to the learners our sexual orientation. I had also heard in the American army that there was a policy of "don't ask don't tell" where gay men and women were accepted into the armed forces but could not openly reveal their true sexual identity while their heterosexual counterparts could openly talk about theirs.

"What was Julius Nyerere?" I asked. "Was he a prophet?"

Ibrahim laughed.

"No," Ibrahim said. "He was the president of our nation in the 1960s."

He then changed his expression from comical to rather serious.

"However, he was a visionary. So, I guess in that way he was like a prophet."

Ibrahim then descended into deep reflection. A painful thought passed through his mind.

"You know?" Ibrahim said, turning to face me, "Mwalimu Julius Nyerere was like our Moses leading us to the Promised Land. He was building our nation upon the principles of *Ujamaa* and this was turning our country into a land flowing with milk and honey. But then he died. He died while we were on our journey. He died and left us wandering around lost in the wilderness."

Ibrahim said this with a hint of pain in his eyes. This Julius Nyerere really meant something to him. But what was amazing was that Ibrahim spoke about Julius Nyerere as if he had known him personally. But from what he himself had said, Julius Nyerere died when Ibrahim was only a child. Julius Nyerere, however, had to have been a significant figure if he still held significance in Ibrahim's life.

Ibrahim then looked outside as if something had caught his attention. I felt that it was important then to change the topic and stop the trauma that I had just caused.

"Is the UN office far from the bus station in Arusha?" I asked.

"It's probably too far to walk," Ibrahim replied. There was a slight pause and then Ibrahim added. "By the way, why do you want to go to the UN office?"

"Because…," I began and then stopped. I thought about it for a moment and then realised I had to go right back to the beginning. So I began. I explained what I did for a job, how I had met Polycarp, that I had read Polycarp's UN reports about his past in Rwanda and then in the refugee camps in Tanzania, about the ad about the Msingi wa Mungu Project and how this all finally connected up and ended with me sitting on this bus next to Ibrahim on the way to the UN office in Arusha.

Once I had explained all this, Ibrahim's eyes lit up and he smiled. "Wow, Bwana Michael," he exclaimed. "You must be an angel!"

I wanted to laugh at that comment. If he had known everything about me, would he have made the same comment?

With that, it became apparent that we had finally reached our destination. The coach suddenly made a sound as if it were slowing down. I looked out the window. Sure enough, we appeared to have arrived in a town of some description. I turned to Ibrahim.

"So, where are we?" I asked.

Ibrahim craned his neck to look out the window.

"We're here in Arusha," he replied. "We're arriving at where we get off."

Soon the bus came to a standstill. As we stepped out of the bus and onto the concrete platform where the buses were parked against, Ibrahim looked warily around as if he were a spy on the lookout. As we walked along, Ibrahim asked me if I preferred to take a taxi or was I okay to take the daladala.

"The daladala? What's that?" I asked perplexed. I had never heard of such a form of transport.

"Daladalas are small buses that travel all around the city. As we entered the city, did you see the small buses that we passed along the road?"

"Yeah," I said.

"Well, those are daladalas," Ibrahim said. "They're not the most comfortable form of transport but they are certainly much cheaper than a taxi."

I was working on a strict budget. The only reason why we were taking public transport was to get from point A to point B. Surely we weren't going to be travelling for hours as we had just done, so a couple of minutes of discomfort far outweighed spending an excessive amount of money just to feel comfortable for a few moments.

I just shrugged my shoulders in complacency. "I'll follow you," I replied.

We arrived at a siding and once again were bombarded with a crowd of people demanding our attention. I felt as if I were a world-renowned singer or actor crowded in by journalists and paparazzi trying to get a piece of my attention. For the first time I understood what it felt like to be famous.

Ibrahim grabbed my hand. No doubt the idea was to keep me together with him. But it was an unusual gesture, something I was not familiar with, a man holding another man by the hand. The only time this happened in the Australian culture was when the two men loved each other intimately. It took me well by surprise. Even though I was the type of guy to enjoy holding hands with another guy, the instinctive fear of showing affection towards the man one loves in a sea of hostile, intolerant homophobes that I was sure made up Tanzanian society caused me to tighten up. Once the reality of the paparazzi still yelling at me for their services became once again lucid in my consciousness, my next reaction was to hold tighter to Ibrahim's hand so that I wouldn't become lost within this mass of people.

Ibrahim dragged me through the raging mob until we were at a clearing at what looked like a bus stop beside what looked like a major road. Already there were daladalas waiting alongside and people trying to get into different ones. The daladalas had names along the sides of them, I guess indicating their ultimate destinations.

Ibrahim looked at me. "Are you prepared to ride in one of these?" he asked with somewhat of a concerned tone.

Each daladala looked as if it had been stuffed with as many people as possible in an attempt to enter the Guiness Book of Records as being the minibus that could hold the most people before it just exploded from the pressure of the internal contents. I had never seen such a thing in my life. At first, a sense of fear overwhelmed me. Would I seriously be able to breathe and survive in such packed conditions? But this was soon followed by an exciting sense of adventure – I had to try this out to see if it were true!

"That's fine," I replied. "I don't mind."

Ibrahim looked at the different daladalas until he found the one that he wanted to get on. A man at the door of the daladala shook a stack of coins at him, creating a loud clinking sound and I guess to get our attention to pay for the trip. Ibrahim allowed me to enter the daladala first before getting in after me.

When inside, I saw there were people sitting in every conceivable seat, some even doubling up. Then there were people standing in every conceivable place. I could not see anywhere where I could actually place my foot on the ground. However, I could feel Ibrahim behind me pushing so that he could get on and so I had no other choice but to slip my foot down somewhere although I couldn't see where, hoping that I was not standing on someone's foot. Once Ibrahim was inside with me, the daladala made its attempt to move.

Once I had settled, I looked around me. I was expecting the people on the bus to stare at me because I was the only *Mzungu* on the bus. However, everyone just sat there dispassionately, totally indifferent to my presence.

In the position I was in, I couldn't see much out of the window. My view was simply a small crack between bodies pressed hard against the window and a partial view of the road below. What we were passing all this time was beyond my knowledge. I couldn't even move around to get a better view because of the crowds within the daladala. I just hoped Ibrahim knew where we were heading.

We were first off to a flying start but then this gentle flow changed to spurts of stops and starts, as if the daladala journey were conveying a message in Morse Code. All I could do was hang on to the roof to prevent myself from falling. The other passengers seemed well adjusted to this form of irregular spurts of movement.

The trip was certainly adventurous. Every now and again, I heard someone call out *shuka* which Ibrahim later explained was the Swahili word for "get off" or "get down", and in this context was a short way of saying that someone wants to get off. Soon after, the daladala would come to a halt and certain passengers would then squeeze through the crowd and onto the street, to be replaced by more passengers wanting to get on. From where I was standing, if you could call it standing, I could see the daladala conductor clicking his stack of coins and mumbling something which I could only guess was to advertise to those around the final destination of the daladala. Even though the daladala was packed full, the bus conductor felt that he could still almost literally squeeze in a few more passengers. It certainly was a different ride to any I had experienced before.

We eventually arrived at our destination although I could not work out exactly how Ibrahim knew where we were. I could hear the sounds of people outside so I knew wherever we had arrived, it was about as crowded outside as it was inside the daladala.

Although an adventure, it was great to get out of the confined space of the internals of the daladala. As I stepped out, I felt as if the air around me were expanding in response to the increased space around it.

We walked onto the kerb and away from the general crowds around the other daladalas which had also arrived at the same place. But although we had escaped these crowds, there were still other crowds to contend with on the side of the road.

I took a look around me. The area certainly had a town sort of feel with buildings around us, cars and daladalas, and people everywhere, but it all seemed simply to be Moshi magnified. The buildings themselves were not high-rise skyscrapers as is often the case in large metropolitan areas but they were tall enough nonetheless. The buildings, however, looked as if they were starting to fall apart and could do with some major renovations and repairs. Before us stood a single-storey building with the style and colours of the 1960s.

"Okay," Ibrahim said, looking around as if he were planning his attack. "The UN building is in the next block, not far from here."

Ibrahim then began walking in a particular direction. I just went along with him. We had to walk along the road from time to time and share the bitumen with cars, daladalas and other pedestrians.

As we walked along, I saw signs in Swahili. My linguistic curiosity came out. I read them out loud and asked Ibrahim what they meant. Ibrahim translated them for me and I tried to then commit these to memory. Ibrahim then asked me if I could speak Swahili. I explained that I was in the learning stage of the language and that if he wanted to, he could speak to me in Swahili but he would probably have to repeat things or translate them until I got a feel for the language. So our conversations ended up being switches back and forth between Swahili and English.

We finally arrived at a building that didn't look like anything in particular. We then went in. It had some resemblance of a small shopping complex but unlike shopping centres I was familiar with in Sydney, the central area was bare. There was access to the shops and offices inside along the left and right hand sides of the building.

We finally came to an office with an indication that we had reached our destination. I pushed the glass doors open and entered, Ibrahim following behind me. We were welcomed at the reception desk by a rather young, well-dressed and very beautiful Tanzanian woman.

"Yes, can I help you?" she asked but she didn't smile as she said it.

"*Jambo! Habari yako?*" I said using one of the standard Swahili greetings for "hello, how are you?"

"*Safi tu!*" the woman replied with one of the standard replies to this Swahili question and this seemed to melt her attitude as this brought a smile to her face.

"I am here to enquire about some refugees from Burundi," I began. "I have a friend in Australia who was originally from Rwanda but escaped to a refugee camp in Tanzania. He got separated from his family and wants to know if any of his family members are still alive."

"Is that your friend there?" she asked, indicating with her face Ibrahim who was standing behind me.

"Oh, no. This gentleman here has simply accompanied me from Moshi. The person in question is in Sydney, Australia. I am here on his behalf."

"Okay, then," the receptionist replied. "Just one moment and someone will be with you shortly."

I turned to look at Ibrahim and then moved away from the reception desk. I looked around the room. Suddenly a Tanzanian man dressed in a suit and tie came to the counter.

"Can I help you?" he asked.

"Yes," I replied and then repeated what I had initially said to the woman who had first spoken with me.

"I see," the man behind the counter said. "And what is your relationship to this man?"

"I am a friend of his," I replied.

"And where is he?"

"In Sydney, Australia," I replied.

"Then why didn't you enquire at the UNHCR office in Canberra?"

"I did but they told me that I could only get the details from the UNHCR office here in Arusha."

"A long way to travel to get this information," the man said but did not smile so I guess he did not mean it as a joke. "And which organisation do you represent?"

Which organisation did I represent? What difference did that make? I wanted to ask him if I did not represent an organisation but was only here on behalf of Polycarp, did this mean that Polycarp was therefore doomed to continue to live in ignorance, never knowing whether or not any of his family members were still alive?

"I...well...I...," I stuttered but then Ibrahim interrupted.

"We're with the Msingi wa Mungu Project," Ibrahim said with all authority.

I turned to look at Ibrahim. Ibrahim looked at me and then turned again to the man behind the counter.

"Ah, the Msingi wa Mungu Project," the man behind the counter said, his features relaxing as if to indicate that he was aware of the project and this then gave the green light to continue with the inquiry.

"And do you have your identity card from the Msingi wa Mungu Project?" he asked.

An identity card? I thought to myself. What on earth for? Ibrahim, however, pulled out his wallet and from his wallet he pulled out what looked like a business card and handed it to the man. The man behind the counter then scrutinised it. A smile of satisfaction beamed over the man's face.

"Ah, you're the co-manager of the project," he said.

I turned once again to look at Ibrahim. The co-manager? I thought he was simply a lowly teacher like me. But he was actually the co-manager of the project? Who, then, did he manage the project with?

The man behind the counter wrote Ibrahim's details down and then handed back Ibrahim's card. He then began completing the form. He finally took some further details from Ibrahim and me, including all the names of Polycarp's family that I had brought along with me written on a sheet of paper. Once he had completed the form, he passed the form over to Ibrahim to sign. Ibrahim took the pen the man presented to him and signed the document with his left hand.

"You're left-handed," I said quietly to Ibrahim. Ibrahim looked up at me and smiled embarrassedly.

"Yes, yes!" Ibrahim replied hurriedly and continued writing. The look on his face gave the impression that this was an embarrassing confession.

"That wasn't a rebuke," I then said. "I simply just noticed you were left-handed, that's all."

It had only struck me that Ibrahim was left-handed simply because it made me realise just how universal left-handedness was among the human species.

Ibrahim finally completed the form and handed it back across the counter.

"Thank you, Bwana Ibrahim," the man behind the counter concluded, taking back the form. "Now, I simply need to run the names through the database but at the moment our computer system is down. But once it's up and running again, it should only take a matter of minutes to get any details. The system should be running again soon although we don't know when for sure. Do you have a number I can ring you on?"

Ibrahim gave the man behind the counter his mobile phone number. The man behind the counter then said that he would ring as soon as the system was up and we could return to get the details. With that, Ibrahim and I left the office.

Once out on the street, Ibrahim looked right and left and then turned to me and asked, "Well, what would you like to do now?"

"I would like to change some Australian dollars into Tanzanian shillings if I could," I replied.

"Okay, let's do that. Let's go."

We wandered around the streets of Arusha. It was obviously a major tourist destination because there were lots of *Mzungus*. Also, a lot of them were dressed up in traditional tourist clothes. It was as if they had read a manual which gave details of the tourist uniform and they had followed the details to a tee.

It was a bustling atmosphere of people everywhere, the noise of cars, daladalas, motorbikes, of people yelling or calling out. But even so, the pace was quite slow and unhurried. What most impressed me were the outdoor tailors. Here were people who sat outside in the dust, the car exhaust and the crumbling concrete, making clothes on old sewing machines that used a push pedal to get them going. It was like stepping back into the very distant past, about one hundred years ago. But again, it was the unhurried pace at which they did their work that appealed to me as if there were no business objectives to complete by a very short deadline.

There was something about this, a return to the days when we weren't rushing around from morning to night to fulfil work objectives, to answer emails, to check the details out on someone's Facebook page or Twitter. It had a real carnival feel about it. If people weren't dawdling around, they were sitting in front of shop entrances just staring out into space as if they were in a statue contest to see how long they could sit as motionless as possible for the longest time.

We finally made it to a *Bureau de Change*. I could never work out why the English expression for such a place had to be in French. When I looked at the name of this office in the other languages, the other languages had their own name for it. Why did English have to use French?

We walked inside. The internals looked old and run down. Anything that was made of wood appeared to be painted in the old mission brown of decades gone by, that dark brown of colonial times. What was not brown looked as though it had once been white but over the decades because of absolute neglect had been tarnished to a drab grey colour by the accumulation of pollution, like the soul of a sinner blemished with sin.

We had to make our way over to the counter. Over the counter was a partition made of glass which supposedly was to allow both the service person behind the counter and the customer to see each other but prevent any physical contact between them. But because of the dimness of the room and the fact that the people providing the service were themselves dark skinned made visibility as difficult as out in the outback on a moonless night. The lack of material, except for what looked like a black curtain draped partly over the glass partition, a totally unsuitable colour for this already dark interior, caused the noise out on the street to enter the office and ricochet throughout the room making it seem much noisier in the office than it was out in the middle of the street.

Because of the brightness of the outside Arusha day, it took me a moment to become accustomed to the dark interior, to be able to get my bearings and even know in which direction I was to walk. But like a bat, I was first guided by sound when I heard over on the left of me somebody say something which sounded like, "Yes, sir, can I help you?"

Ibrahim and I then walked in that general direction. Ibrahim seemed quite at ease in this sudden change of light intensity to the extent that I guessed that Tanzanian eyes could readily switch from light to darkness much more readily than a foreigner.

When we reached the partition, I could hear the voice speaking but could barely make out the figure behind the counter. I could see the eyes and teeth reflecting the incoming light from outside but for the rest of the facial features, I could barely make out anything else about the person, whether they were a man or a woman, old or young. With the constant noise buzzing around like the internals of an echo chamber and the lack of suitable light, I felt as if I had suddenly become partially deaf and blind.

"I would like to change some money, if that's possible, please," I said in extremely polite language.

I heard the voice, which sounded more like the voice of a woman than a man, say something but I did not understand it at all. I went to press my ear onto the glass when Ibrahim said, "Yes, we are together."

Goodness! I thought. These Tanzanians have good ears as well!

There was a slight pause and I waited for the next step. The woman, whose features were slowly becoming more and more into focus as my eyes adjusted to the darkness, appeared to be adjusting the swivel stool she was seated on so that she could get into a more comfortable position.

"And how much would you like to change?" the woman asked and this time I could hear her much clearer.

I thought about it for a moment. I was here for about two weeks. I wondered how much I would spend in that time at home under the same conditions. I had to pay for my accommodation and maybe I would buy some souvenirs.

"Two hundred Australian dollars," I replied.

The woman behind the counter looked at me rather unimpressed as if I had just told her that her attire was adequate but she could have dressed better if she had tried. She took some time before she reacted to my comment as if we were talking to each other via satellite from two completely different time zones.

"Can I have your passport," she asked.

My passport? I thought to myself. I wasn't changing traveller's cheques. Why did she want to see my passport? But I needed the money so there was no point arguing. I struggled to take out my passport from under my clothes which meant now my shirt was hanging out over my trousers as if I were in the middle of getting dressed. I passed my passport over to her. The woman then looked at the photo page and then began slowly to flick through the pages almost as if she were reading a novel. What on earth did she want to know?

Finally she stopped and looked up at me. "And your money?" she asked.

I handed her four golden Australian 50 dollar notes under the glass partition. The woman took the money with a scowl, picked up the notes and then thumbed through them to check that I had provided the amount of money I said I would give her. She did this so meticulously. I thought to myself, there are only four notes. It's not like I'm changing a couple of thousand dollars in five dollar bills where you need to count all the money.

The woman then slid my passport back under the partition.

"Just wait a moment," she said and moved away from the counter.

The black curtain, which was more suitable for a photographer's dark room than an office window, slid over the glass partition so that I could no longer see where she had gone.

A sudden feeling of horror overwhelmed me. Where did she go? She had taken my money and then simply disappeared! I turned around to look at Ibrahim who was not behind me but actually sitting on the only chair in the room. He looked at me and smiled but did not move. This led me to understand that he knew that what I was experiencing about changing money was the standard procedure and I should just wait a moment like she had told me to. This relaxed me somewhat and so I just turned back to look at the partition and leant on my elbows.

The clamour from outside came in waves as cars drove by at irregular intervals, and various groups of people made their way past. Time just seemed to be going by but this woman had still not appeared.

Finally she reappeared at the window holding what looked like two decks of exceptionally long playing cards. Around each deck was a white paper strip. The woman then took one deck, broke the paper strip and started counting as she placed each card on the bench in front of her as if we were about to play a hand of poker. But as she started counting, I realised that these were not cards but Tanzanian shilling notes. I didn't know what she was saying at first until I heard her say "eight" and then I mentally followed her counting. When she had finished with the first deck, she proceeded with the second. This took quite a few moments to get through because it was as if she were counting every single card from a deck of fifty-two cards. Once she had finished these two batches of money, she opened a drawer in front of her and then took out a few more notes and a couple of coins. She then shoved the pile of money under the counter.

I took the two piles of money the woman had given me. I was stunned to see how much money I had in each hand. It was like I was holding two bricks. Where was I supposed to put all this money? I knew it wasn't going to fit in my wallet. I hadn't quite resolved this issue when the woman behind the counter then said, "And here's your receipt."

This was one of those moments I wished I had a third hand. I had two piles of money, one in each hand, and then I was supposed to pick up the receipt. While trying to resolve this issue, I suddenly heard a voice behind me and the woman behind the counter turned to look over my shoulder. A voice over my shoulder said something in Swahili and the woman started to respond. I realised this was a new customer.

Just hang on! I thought. Can't you just wait till I've finished?

I then saw a shadow in the semi-darkness approach me from the left hand side. Was this it? Was I about to be robbed? The shadow on my left picked up my receipt and the loose change, and then said, "Here, come over here."

It was Ibrahim. He must have seen my dilemma and immediately rescued me in this situation. We went over to the side of the office while I had two piles of notes to hang onto.

"Don't go showing people outside you have all this money," Ibrahim warned. "Arusha is not the safest place in Tanzania, especially with tourists around."

I thought about it for a moment. There was no way I could put all this money in my wallet. I then remembered a friend of mine telling me on one of his overseas trips that he carried surplus money in a strategic place where thieves most unlikely wanted to fossick around in. So, in the semi-darkness, I placed the money as best I could in this secret place. I had in the order of two hundred and fifty thousand Tanzanian shillings so as an extremely rough estimate I considered one thousand shillings to be equivalent for calculation purposes to one Australian dollar. I guessed how much I needed to give Ibrahim later for the bus trip to and from Arusha plus a bit of extra money should we stop off to get something to eat. Pretty much all the money that was given to me at the *Bureau de Change* was in two thousand shilling notes except for a few ten thousand shilling notes so I still had a considerable layer of money to jam inside my wallet. The rest of the money was tucked away skilfully yet uncomfortably.

Once everything was set, Ibrahim took us outside.

"Just keep an eye on your wallet," Ibrahim warned. "There are pickpockets everywhere."

To avoid being a target of such theft, I put my wallet in the pocket of my trousers and then just walked around with my hand in that pocket. The only time I took my hand out was whenever I desperately needed the use of both hands.

"Okay," Ibrahim said. "We have to wait till the UN office calls me. What would you like to do now?"

I shrugged my shoulders. What was there to do in downtown Arusha?

"Are you hungry?" Ibrahim asked.

"Not particularly. I wouldn't mind something for morning tea, though. It's a bit early for lunch."

"Let's go and have a cup of tea and some maandazis," Ibrahim replied.

"Maandazis? What are they?"

Ibrahim smiled at me. "Let's find out!"

He then grabbed my right hand and started leading me through the crowd. It felt really weird that he grabbed my hand like this so openly and overtly while walking in public. But I had been warned that this is what Tanzanian men do in public and they think nothing of it. But it had the strangest effect on me. Because the holding of hands in my cultural context meant that the two people in question were in an intimate relationship, it made me feel that Ibrahim and I were partners and he was unabashedly showing his love for me in front of all Tanzanian society. Poor Ibrahim! I knew if he knew what thoughts were going through my head at that moment of time, the typical Muslim that he was, I would be dead meat! But Ibrahim couldn't read my thoughts and there was no way I was going to tell him what was on my mind anyway. So I just went along with it. It was a wonderful moment, a small secret fantasy that would soon vanish like the early mist on a warm winter's morning.

But also I realised I was starting to warm to Ibrahim. After all, he was not a bad guy. Up to this point he had been quite caring towards me and yet he was one of the managers of the Msingi wa Mungu Project. He therefore wasn't some orderly assigned by an authority to bring me to the UN office, he was partly involved in the decision making of the entire project. But also what he had to say about this *Ujamaa* originally purported by this unknown Julius Nyerere fell in line with my own understanding of how the world should be. I was fully aware that I was actually beginning to like this guy very much.

But it was all a fantasy for the moment, I thought. In any case, he was a Muslim and a widower. And I would simply be someone in his personal time-space dimension for a number of days before I disappeared again out of his life almost imperceptibly and immemorably.

So, in the middle of all this noise, the crowds and the dust, I soaked up as best as I could and for as long as it would last this wonderful, beautiful moment.

Chapter 6

Ibrahim eventually led me to a place which could loosely be described as a restaurant. But as with much of the township, the internals of this restaurant looked old and worn out, as if after its first erection, there had been little if nothing done to update the décor and bring it into the twenty-first century. The building was made of concrete and the walls were obviously painted over with a yellowish-beigish sort of colour, what looked like what once had been a white wall but had since been stained by cigarette smoke equally over the entire surface.

There were about twenty tables spread out around the restaurant. Each table and each of the chairs looked like the cheap type of furniture used in meeting halls which are readily folded up and put away for storage in readiness for the next function. Over the tables was spread a cheap looking plastic tablecloth, some of them with tears in them as if they really needed to be replaced. There were various bottles on the table of various sauces, I guess tomato sauce or barbecue sauce, as well as salt and pepper, and sugar.

The place was half full. Ibrahim led me to one of the tables and we sat down. We had barely sat down when one of the waiters, dressed in a dull coloured uniform but at the same time very formally attired, approached our table. Ibrahim and the waiter exchanged words of which none I understood. In the middle of this exchange, Ibrahim then stopped, looked at me and asked, "So, would you like maandazis and tea?"

Being the adventurous type and because I like to try new things at least once, I simply smiled and nodded in agreement. Ibrahim then conveyed this back to the waiter and the waiter then left.

I took a brief glance around the room. I noticed at one table three middle-aged men well dressed in suits sitting together, obviously business men or government officials of some description. They had a rather dismissive behaviour towards the waiters and those around them as if these people were somehow below them and weren't really quite people at all. At another table was a family of four, mother, father, and two small children. I saw at another table two middle-aged women.

I turned back to look at Ibrahim.

"So, you're the manager of the Msingi wa Mungu Project," I stated.

Ibrahim displayed an embarrassed smile as if admitting to this was something he found hard to do.

"Well, I am one of the managers," Ibrahim replied.

"One of them?"

"Yes, there are seven of us."

"Seven managers?"

"Yes, seven managers. We all have separate responsibilities. I manage the teaching staff, that is, I organise the teachers, what they need to teach, how many classes we might need, how many classrooms we need to organise for the future, things like that. There are managers for different aspects of the project, such as the engineering manager who oversees the construction of the buildings, the catering manager who is responsible for organising all the meals, and so on."

"But why then are you sleeping in the students' dormitories with me?"

Ibrahim laughed.

"Why? Don't you want me to sleep there?"

"It's not that. Being a manager, I thought you would at least have a special section of the project in which to sleep, a special section for the managers."

Ibrahim laughed again.

"I'm a manager, not a king!"

I laughed at that comment. It was quite obvious that Ibrahim had a sense of humour.

"Yeah, but what I mean is that you, well, you know, slept in the same sleeping quarters as the plebs."

"The plebs?" Ibrahim asked.

"You know, the plebeians, the workers, the common people."

Ibrahim laughed again.

"What do you mean? Because I am a manager, I don't do any work?"

That question stopped the flow of the conversation for a moment. I wasn't sure how to reply to that. What Ibrahim was asking was correct. Just because he was a manager, this did not mean that his work was any more or any less than anyone else's at the project.

Just then, the waiter arrived with our food and drink on an ordinary plastic tray which reminded me of the types of trays which were the in thing in the 1970s. He first placed our plates in front of us which contained two maandazis, and then placed our cups, which looked more like mugs, and saucers on the table, and then left.

I looked at the maandazis. They looked like brown cushions, about the size of a bread roll. I then looked up at Ibrahim. Ibrahim took a bite of one of his maandazis. I noticed that inside, the maandazi looked a light yellow colour, something like the colour of beach sand. It looked like bread. So, I picked up one of mine, sniffed it at first and then took a bite. It was quite tough to chew through. As I chewed, the flavour became apparent. It tasted very much like a doughnut but less sugary. In fact, I was later to discover that the translation for maandazi is "doughnut". Although similar to a doughnut, maandazis are still a different thing and so I preferred to call them even in English maandazis.

The maandazi was rather dry and so with the first mouthful I needed to wet the internals of my mouth. So, I grabbed my tea and took a sip. It was still quite hot so I could only take a sip. My tea was very milky. I noticed that the maandazis and this milky tea went very well together, as if I could not enjoy the one without the other. However, the maandazis being quite oily and the tea being so milky, I thought I could not really have too many of these in this hot climate, otherwise I would have a weight problem in no time.

After a few more sips of tea and bites of maandazi, Ibrahim brought back the conversation as if the service of the tea and maandazis had simply been an intermission of the conversation.

"Mwalimu Julius Nyerere taught us that just because someone is educated and has a job managing or running a system doesn't mean that that person is somehow above and beyond the people he is managing. We are all part of the society. I am part of this society. My role in this society is no more important than the farmer who tills the ground and provides our food or the cleaner who keeps the school yard clean. These people no doubt are like me, that they get hungry and thirsty, and have various physical desires as I have, avoid sickness and pain as much as I do, and look for companionship and support as much as I do."

Once again, a tingling sensation went up my spine. Ibrahim's thoughts were my thoughts, his beliefs were my beliefs. Ibrahim based his beliefs on this former Tanzanian president, Julius Nyerere. This entire idea was similar to what St Paul the apostle wrote how that all Christians were members of the church like different organs working together in the body, which really was an idea he got from Socrates who, through Plato, said that in an ideal society, everyone was part of the body with their own functions to play but overall everyone had an equal share in the benefits of this society. Was this then how this African nation, Tanzania, functioned, based on these principles?

I was beginning more and more to be filled with admiration for this guy sitting across from me. His vision for humanity, at least within the borders of this East African nation, was very much the same as mine.

And then I thought about my sexuality. Could gay men and women live comfortably within this type of society that Ibrahim believed in? They did in mine.

I was beginning to see that I quite liked this man, Ibrahim, and his views on life. I could see that a good friendship would no doubt develop between the two of us. It would be too much of a shock for him to find out everything about me here and now. However, if we continued our friendship, in the safety of my home in Australia where I would be 12,000 kilometres away from him, I could raise this issue. It wouldn't matter, then, how Ibrahim reacted to this.

"What you have to say about Julius Nyerere and *Ujamaa* is very interesting," I commented. "To be honest with you, Ibrahim, I believe in much of what you are saying about the principles of this *Ujamaa*. And if your president started this *Ujamaa* here, I can understand why people say that Tanzania is quite a safe country compared to all the other sub-Saharan African nations. You must be happy to be living here in Tanzania."

Ibrahim leant back and laughed.

"Yes, on the whole, Tanzania is a peaceful country. We don't have the same problems as our neighbouring countries. One of the reasons why Tanzania doesn't have the problems that other African countries experience is because Mwalimu Julius Nyerere abolished the idea of tribalism."

I took a sip of my tea. "What do you mean by that?" I asked.

"If you take a look at our northern neighbour, Kenya, for example. Although Kenya is one country, there are many different African tribes living within the country. But even so, the Kikuyu tribe is in the majority and therefore pretty much rules the country. This causes social unrest between the different tribes. I mean, a clearer picture is your friend, Polycarp. The terrible fighting in Rwanda was a result of the fighting between two main tribes, the Tutsis and the Hutus. Mwalimu Julius Nyerere recognised that tribal conflict was damaging to society and so he succeeded in uniting Tanzania by getting rid of the concept of tribes."

"Wow! How did he achieve that?" I asked.

"When we went to school, we had to move around. If we went to one school for our primary education we had to go to another school to complete our secondary education. We had to do this so that while we were at school we learnt together with other people from different tribes. Nyerere was also strict on getting everyone in the country to speak Swahili and not continue to speak their own tribal languages. Nyerere also encouraged people to intermarry between tribes. So now we have a generation of children born from a parent of one tribe and another parent from another. This means that no one tribe is now dominant in the country and this keeps the country stable. Mwalimu Julius Nyerere also encouraged Tanzanians to move around and live in different parts of the country and not remain in their own tribal pockets."

When Ibrahim said this, the picture of multicultural Australia came to mind. I couldn't help but see that multiculturalism was really just multi-tribalism with a different name. Like the different African tribes, the different cultural groups which came to Australia had their own languages and customs. Each cultural group settled in isolated pockets within the country, particularly within certain suburbs of the major cities. Just in Sydney, in many suburbs it was equivalent to entering a mini-China, a mini-Turkey, a mini-Iraq, a mini-Vietnam, a mini-Sierra Leone or a mini-Brazil. Many of the people living in these suburbs remained within their own cultural groups, socialised within their own cultural groups and even identified themselves only within their own cultural groups. I was even familiar with the new terminology these people were using to identify themselves. Whereas in my growing up there were only Australians – with the unfortunate exception that Aboriginal Australians had been sadly considered outside this group – today we talk about Anglo-Australians, Asio-Australians and even Aboriginal Australians. What Julius Nyerere was doing in Tanzania was the reverse. Instead of Tanzanians identifying themselves with a specific cultural group, that is, a specific tribe, Nyerere courageously brought Tanzania into peace and unity by eradicating this form of specific identity so that Tanzanians identified themselves simply as Tanzanians. And the reason he did this was to avoid the problems associated with tribal factions and social unrest evident in the other sub-Saharan African nations.

This Julius Nyerere was a visionary. His views were not specific to sub-Saharan Africans. I could see how his views were universal.

There was a moment of silence after Ibrahim's comment. Ibrahim and I continued eating our maandazis and drinking our milky tea. All this new information required digestion as I placed it in my memory network for me to process later.

Ibrahim then smiled in the middle of one of his chews and then asked me through clenched teeth to prevent bits of maandazi crumbling out onto the table if I thought what I was eating was okay.

"Yeah, it's not bad," I replied.

"Would you like some more?" Ibrahim then asked and he made a movement with his head which showed that it looked as if he were   going to beckon the waiter to come over and serve us with more. I energetically replied in the negative, saying that these two were enough and that I could wait till lunch for something more to eat.

"Are you sure?" Ibrahim insisted.

"Yes, that's fine. I've had enough for the moment. But thank you anyway," I said emphatically to show that I definitively did not want to eat or drink any more and that I wasn't just saying that to be polite.

Once we had finished our small morning repast, Ibrahim then looked at me and smiled.

"What would you like to do now?" he then asked me.

We were in a new town in a new part of the world. What better thing to do than to go around and explore the place. I made that suggestion and Ibrahim acknowledged non-verbally with a move to leave.

We got up and Ibrahim walked back to the counter. I walked behind him. When we arrived at the counter, I saw Ibrahim pull out his wallet so I knew he was about to pay.

"That's okay. Let me. It's my shout," I volunteered.

"It's your what?"

I realised I had used a typical Australian word which no doubt had not caught on here on the African continent.

"It's my turn to pay," I translated.

I pulled out my wallet but Ibrahim tried vehemently to prevent me. "That's okay," he said. "You're my guest."

"I know," I replied. "But I'd like to do something to show my gratitude for your help."

There was a bit of toing and froing between Ibrahim and me as to who was going to pay when the man behind the counter stood erect, folded his arms and in an unimpressed manner said, "Is anyone going to pay for this?"

Ibrahim finally relented. I did a mental calculation in my head. In Australia, a cup of tea would cost about $2.50 and some sort of small cake about $3. Because the exchange rate was approximately 1,000 Tanzanian shillings to the Australian dollar, I estimated that it would cost a little under ten thousand shillings. I took out a ten thousand shilling note and handed it to the man behind the counter. The man behind the counter kind of snarled at me and humphed in a disapproving manner, walked away and came back with lots of notes and coins. Obviously the cost of our refreshments was much lower than I had anticipated!

We stepped back out onto the noisy street with people walking everywhere, the smell of dust and car exhaust filling our noses, the sounds of people, bicycle bells and squawking animals welcoming us back onto the street.

We had hardly taken a few steps when Ibrahim stopped and pulled out his mobile phone. He went off in a flurry of Swahili for a moment, then paused for some moments, then answered with a *ndiyo*, that is, "yes", and a *sawa*, that is, "okay", and then placed his phone back in his pocket.

"We have to go back to the UN office," Ibrahim replied. "They have news for you."

Ibrahim was about to lurch ahead when he stopped and turned to me. "Where's your wallet?"

"In my pocket," I replied mystified.

"Just hang on to it. There are pickpockets everywhere in Arusha."

I dipped my left hand into my pocket to check that my wallet was still there. When I couldn't feel it, I panicked. But then I realised I had instinctively put my wallet in the right back pocket of my trousers and hence I returned the wallet to this front left secret location, and then kept my hand in my pocket while walking around. Ibrahim occupied my right hand by grabbing and holding it, once again in what was no doubt an innocent gesture on his part but which I secretly enjoyed.

Ibrahim manoeuvred us around through the Arusha streets until we finally made it back to the UN office. A flurry of butterflies opened up inside my stomach as we entered the office. The same receptionist greeted us once again but this time with acknowledged familiarity.

"Yes, just one moment," she said. "I'll get him for you."

Finally, the officer to whom we had originally spoken came out of the back office to the front desk.

"Mr Farril," he said. "Unfortunately we have bad news for you. The people you are looking for, they are confirmed deceased. All of them. I'm sorry."

There was a moment of silence while I tried to digest the information. Poor Polycarp. It was now confirmed that his entire family had been completely annihilated out of existence. How was one supposed to interpret this, to understand what this meant? What did it mean when one day you have your mother, your father, your brothers and sisters, their spouses and all their children, and then the next day they are all gone, each and every one of them, and you have no-one in your family because none of them any longer exists? One of the ways in which we define ourselves, in which we understand who we are and our identity within the greater framework of the universe, is our relationship to family members. However, Polycarp, like the last skittle left standing when all the others had been knocked down, was now all alone in the world. That was the overwhelming sensation that took over me as if it were my family and not someone else's.

Eventually I was brought back to the real world. I thanked the man behind the counter. I asked if there was anything I needed to do but the man behind the counter replied in the negative. So that was it. My objective had been achieved. There wasn't anything more I needed to do here.

We left the building and were once again back out on the street. Although the every day sights and sounds blared at me, they seemed more to be coming from a distant place. Ibrahim seemed to understand exactly what was going through my mind. He just took one look at me and then said, "Let's go back to Moshi."

With that, he led me by the hand and took me back to the bus station where we caught the next available bus back to Moshi. We had to wait quite some time before the next bus to Moshi was ready to depart.

On the trip back, I just stared out the window and out onto the vast stretch of African land. The emptiness of the land was like an exteriorisation of what I was feeling within. But why did I feel this way? It wasn't my family which had disappeared.

It was a long trip but we finally arrived back at Moshi. Once we had descended from the bus, Ibrahim walked us away from the crowd and over to where there was a collection of buildings as if it were some sort of shopping centre or office buildings. Ibrahim suddenly came to a stop. He looked around as if he were trying to get his bearings.

"How are you now?" he asked so kindly.

"I'm okay, I suppose," I replied.

"Are you sure?" Ibrahim asked. It seemed so kind of him to ask like this that it took the bite off the terrible news of the day.

"Yeah…yeah, I'm okay," I replied and this brought me out of my despondency. I looked up at Ibrahim and smiled in a way to show that there was nothing more we could do and I needed to get out of this morose mood.

Ibrahim looked at his watch.

"It's just after lunch time. Are you hungry?" he asked.

I looked up at him and then my glance casually moved back to the bus station where I had seen a clock mounted on what looked like a clocktower. I could see that it was already afternoon.

"Yeah, I guess," I replied.

Ibrahim laughed. "Well, you're either hungry or you're not! It's not something you need to guess."

His comment made me laugh. In a way I liked it because it was the type of sarcastic comment I would have made if someone had given me this type of answer.

"Okay, yes, I'm hungry," I replied.

"What would you like to eat?"

What would I like to eat? I thought. I mean, was Ibrahim able to miraculously provide me with any food I so desired here in this poky little town in the middle of Tanzania? Was there some sort of eatery like they have in Sydney where all foods from around the world are on offer in one small area?

"I dunno," I replied. "What's something typically Tanzanian I can eat?"

"Have you ever eaten ugali?"

"What's that?" I asked.

Ibrahim smiled.

"That's what we'll have now," he said. "Let's go."

Ibrahim took us to what I guess was a restaurant but looked very similar in quality, or lack of it, to the place we had had the cup of tea and maandazis in Arusha. The place was almost completely full as it was after all around lunch time and no doubt these people at this restaurant were workers from the surrounding office buildings I had passed. I guessed this because the men were meticulously dressed in shirts and ties and the women were similarly dressed in office fashion. Ibrahim led me over to one of the few remaining tables and we sat down.

"You can go over there to wash your hands," Ibrahim said and indicated where the tap was with a movement of his head. I looked over and saw a sink in the corner which seemed so out of place in a restaurant and was more typical in a public toilet. There was a man already standing there washing his hands and he concluded with a good rinse of his face before standing up again erect and looking at himself in the mirror. I was firmly settled and didn't want to leave the table but as the saying goes, "When in Rome do as the Romans do". So I struggled between the tables and walked over to the wash basin. I gave my hands a good wash. Once I was back at the table, Ibrahim got up and did the same.

I didn't understand why it was so imperative to wash my hands before eating. However, I really appreciated this sense of cleanliness by the Tanzanians.

Ibrahim sat back down again.

"So, what would you like to eat with your ugali?" he asked.

I smiled shyly and shrugged my shoulders.

"Surprise me!" I replied.

"Okay. Is there anything you don't eat?"

"No," I replied. "I eat pretty much anything. I mean, I don't mind trying something first. I'll tell you if I don't like it."

Ibrahim then craned his neck around to get the attention of one of the waiters. There was a waitress not far from our table.

"Aunty? Aunty?" he yelled.

Aunty? Is that what they call waitresses? I thought. It sounded so odd but so nice.

The "aunty" came to our table. Ibrahim then rattled off in quick Swahili the orders for our meals. The "aunty" nodded and then said something back. Ibrahim then turned to me.

"Would you like anything to drink? A beer?"

"Okay," I replied.

"What beer would you like?"

"I don't know. What beer do they have?"

Ibrahim started saying names and when he mentioned Kilimanjaro Beer, that sounded like the right beer to drink in this part of the world and I chose this one.

Once the "aunty" had gone, Ibrahim sat back in his chair. He then leant forward on his elbows.

"So, are you okay now?" he asked.

"I'm sorry?" I asked back in bewilderment.

"I was worried about you and the news about Polycarp's family."

"Oh, yes, I'm okay," I said and looked down at the table.

"You really love this Polycarp very much, don't you?" Ibrahim asked.

I was quite struck and taken aback by the comment. I looked up at Ibrahim. There seemed to be a touch of undertone or innuendo in the question. Or was I just reacting supersensitively to this comment?

"I guess, yes, you could say I love Polycarp," I replied cautiously.

"You must seriously do," Ibrahim replied. "I could tell by the reaction when you heard the news about his family members. But also, you have come all this way from your country to Tanzania to find out this information for Polycarp. You didn't have to it but you did. How many people would do that?"

"Well...I...," I stuttered as a commencement to the sentence but as my mind flicked through all the people I knew, I could not imagine any of them actually doing what I had done.

"You really follow your religion truly," Ibrahim then said.

But I don't have a religion, I thought. But I knew I couldn't say this here in Tanzania, in front of this big, African Muslim man. Not only was I concerned for Polycarp's life, I was also concerned for my own. But I had to play along with his comment.

"Well, yes," I said with a cautious start. I looked down at the table and then back at Ibrahim. "You know, Ibrahim, to me, what I'm doing, this is religion. This idea that religion is regularly reading a holy book or going to a church or a mosque or a temple or a synagogue, saying prayers and trying to convert people, this is not my idea of what religion is all about. To me, religion is looking at people around us, finding people who are disadvantaged and saying, 'What can I do to help that person?' This to me is what we should be doing. All of us."

Ibrahim just looked at me with wonderment in his eyes.

"Wow, Bwana Michael! You must be an angel from Allah! You are really special!"

I didn't know whether to laugh or get angry. What kept going through my mind after he said that was, yes, but I'm gay, I'm gay, I'm gay! I know what you as a Muslim would think if you knew that. What I'm doing for Polycarp and for anyone else, all these are looked on as wonderful things to do which make me look like a saint. But for some strange reason, all my great works would be negated simply because I am gay. Suddenly I would become some sort of evil being, equivalent to Adolf Hitler or Idi Amin simply because I like to lie naked next to another naked man. My sexuality shouldn't have anything to do with it but you would make a huge thing out of it.

The thought lingered in my head so much that I was so close to just standing up in front of everyone in this restaurant and yelling at Ibrahim. This man across the table from me, there neat and tidy in his good clothes, with a good position in life, I wanted to yell at him and say how much of an easy life he had because he's not gay. Because he likes to lie naked next to a naked woman, everyone is happy with him and he can aspire to any height he wanted. But I am limited. I don't have the same freedom.

I don't know why this thought came to me when Ibrahim had been so kind in his comment, even though I felt it was rather misguided.

Fortunately the waitress arrived with lunch so it broke the frustration and the annoyance of the moment. The food came out on what looked like food trays from an army barracks mess hall with various separations where different types of food were on different parts of the tray. In one segment there was a large white mountain which looked like a helpful serving of mashed potato. In another segment was clearly a large cooked fish. And in the other segment was what looked like some stew with a tomato sauce base with cooked vegetables through it. I looked over at Ibrahim's tray and his was the same minus the fish. In place of fish, he had what looked like baked beans.

I instinctively went to grab a knife and fork but then realised there weren't any.

"How do we eat this?" I asked.

"With your hands," Ibrahim replied. "I'll show you."

Fortunately I had been with people from other cultures who eat their food without eating utensils. The first time this happened was when I first went to Faisal's place. I guessed it was a common practice in the Middle East. The difference was that instead of using bread as the edible eating utensil, here in Tanzania, and I was to learn later that this is the same throughout much of sub-Saharan Africa, they use this large snow white mountain that in Tanzania they call ugali.

The ugali looked like mashed potato and so I was expecting it to feel soft when I dug into it. However, it was hard, somewhat of the consistency of dough. It was also very hot and I almost burnt my fingers during my first plunge into what looked like something that was supposedly cold.

There was definitely a technique to it. Ibrahim took a small portion of the ugali, about the size of a pebble, manipulated it in his right hand and then took a portion of his baked beans or vegetables before plopping the lot into his mouth. His dexterity made it look so easy. However, although I successfully got a mixture of the ugali, fish and the vegetables into my mouth, my manner of eating was not as elegant.

I tried the ugali on its own to see what it tasted like. It was almost tasteless. I discovered later that this was a staple diet of sub-Saharan Africa and ugali is the base food like rice in South East Asia and bread in Europe, and like rice and bread, ugali on its own is just a tasteless base.

The fish at first looked very unappertising. It looked as if it had been washed up on the shore and lain there for days, died and dried, and then someone had scooped it up and brought it to this restaurant to be placed on my eating tray. However, although somewhat dry and hard, it was very delicious. I couldn't believe the contrast between how it looked and how it tasted. Ibrahim told me that it actually came from Lake Victoria and the fish from this lake is well known for its excellent taste. The vegetable "stew" was simply okay but it added to the nicety of the rest of the food.

While we were eating, the waitress came once again to our tables, this time carrying a tray with two very large bottles of beer and two glasses.

"Kilimanjaro?" she asked as she arrived at our table.

Ibrahim signalled to place the bottle in front of me. The waitress then placed another bottle in front of Ibrahim. She then placed small serviettes which appeared no bigger than a sheet of toilet paper on the table and then our glasses. She then held the tray under her arm as she removed a bottle opener from her pocket, uncapped each bottle of beer and then poured some into our glasses.

I watched how she put the beer in the glasses. In Australia, we tilt the glass so that as the beer flows in, it doesn't form a big head of froth on it. However, this waitress poured the beers directly into our erect glasses energetically with the expected result of the glass being more froth than beer. The waitress then walked away.

I looked at Ibrahim's beer. Ibrahim noticed that I was looking at his beer.

"I prefer Safari Beer," he said. But that wasn't why I was looking at his beer. Ibrahim was a Muslim so why was he drinking beer? I thought Muslims didn't drink alcohol.

I had seen this before in Australia. Just about all the Afghani refugees I had met in Australia said they were Muslims but they all drank alcohol. I had met a few Iranian refugees who said they also were Muslim but they also drank alcohol. And here was Ibrahim, a self-confessed Muslim drinking alcohol. What was it, then, when we hear that Muslims don't drink alcohol?

Ibrahim picked up his glass in a way that invited me to pick up mine. "Cheers," he said, and took a mouthful. I imitated him silently.

"So, how do you like the food?" he asked.

"The fish is really delicious!" I stated. At least this was something positive at this table.

I then looked at his tray.

"What are you eating?" I asked.

"Oh, these are beans. And these are vegetable greens," Ibrahim replied.

"Do you like fish?" I asked.

"When I used to eat it, yes, I did like it. But now I'm vegetarian."

Vegetarian? Since when were Muslims vegetarians? I knew that Muslims didn't eat pork but a Muslim who doesn't eat any meat at all?

A Muslim who is vegetarian, who drinks alcohol, who prays more like a Buddhist adept than following the conventional Islamic mode of prayer, who participates in a major way working with people of other religions? Ibrahim, I thought in bewilderment, who the hell are you?

I wanted to stand up and yell at Ibrahim that he was a hypocritical piece of work. Your kind, I wanted to say to him, spend your time suicide bombing and rampage killing those who don't believe what you say and yet you yourselves don't even have a consistent view of what you all believe. But like a pressure cooker, I had to keep a lid on my emotions, inside the pressure building up enough to cook everything inside to a pulp, on the outside looking calm and shiny as if all was sunshine within.

I had only been here a day. I had already got what I came for. But I had committed myself to this project for another eight days – eight more days to continue this charade that I was deeply religious and to put up with the hypocrisy I was so used to seeing in religious people. What difference would my opinion make anyway?

I took a few deep breaths, took a good swallow of beer and threw a two-faced smile at Ibrahim.

"Cheers!" I chirped and clinked Ibrahim's glass.

Chapter 7

When we had finished eating, pretty much my entire right hand was covered with leftovers of ugali, fish and vegetables. By contrast, Ibrahim's hand was for the most part quite clean with only a few of his fingers being noticeably soiled by food. I wiped my hands with the toilet-paper-sized serviette but in so doing the serviette broke up into fragments which stuck around my fingers so that my hands looked worse than before. Ibrahim invited me to go over again to the wash basin and clean my hands. I felt like a complete klutz with pieces of serviette around my fingers as if I had cut myself shaving my hand. However, it was a relief to wash away the stupidity.

We soon made our way out of the restaurant, back onto the street and then headed for the Msingi wa Mungu Project. It is amazing how filling a mountain of corn flour and a schooner of beer can make you feel. I felt rather bloated and, had the contents of my stomach been hydrogen, I would have certainly floated away at that moment. Ibrahim suggested that we walk back to the Msingi wa Mungu Project as it was a pleasant walk. I didn't mind the walk as it was an opportunity to see a bit more of the township of Moshi. I also knew that the exertion of energy would activate my stomach into digestion and help to clear the excess luggage in my stomach.

As we walked along, I looked around at the place. Moshi certainly was very different to Sydney. However, it reminded me of country towns I was familiar with. I had been to Broken Hill, the furthest town west from Sydney within the state of New South Wales and I saw a similarity in Moshi with its cracked roads and the guttering with no clear definition, dusty pathways and old buildings which really could have done with a face lift. This was the best comparison I had of Moshi with anything I was familiar with in Australia.

One thing that was certainly different was the people. Everywhere I looked, everyone was dark skinned. I became more and more aware of how different I was. Nonetheless, nobody looked at me strangely or made me feel that I didn't belong. Rather, their reactions or lack of reactions indicated that they couldn't care less that I was there, that I was simply one of the many other incognitos walking around the Moshi township.

While deep in this contemplation, Ibrahim broke the silence. "So, Bwana Michael, what's Sydney like?"

I was absolutely amazed by his question. Had Ibrahim been reading my mind? But I wasn't sure how to answer the question at first. Sydney was such a large place and there were different parts to it. The question was similar to me asking what Africa, or America, or Europe was like. It all depended on which part you were in.

"It's a big city," I said by way of reply, with some hesitation before going on with my description. "You have the main city centre of Sydney. No doubt you have seen photos of the Harbour Bridge and the Opera House."

"Yes, I've seen these in photos."

There you go, I thought. So, Sydney is not too unknown here in Tanzania.

"Well, that's the city itself. That is only the actual city itself with all the buildings. But Sydney is not only that."

I paused and looked around me and then continued. I described the city of Sydney with its skyscrapers, the City Circle Railway System, Martin Place, Centrepoint Tower, Hyde Park and Darling Harbour. I explained how these were features of the city itself and were really centres of attraction and tourism. I talked about the ferries and how they travelled out to different parts of the city that were connected by waterways.

I then went on to talk about the suburban areas and how the metropolitan area radiated out far and wide from the city centre and how different suburbs and even different areas of the metropolitan area differed, whether you lived in the north, the east, the south or the west.

I described the suburbs in general and then went on to explain that the different suburbs these days no longer simply are different because of their proximity to the city centre or the wealth of that area but now they are agglomerations of people from different nations of the world. Some suburbs, so I explained, are predominantly Chinese, others Vietnamese, others Turkish, Iraqi, Korean, Indian, Afghani and so on. At one time I said African and then realised that this was too generalised and so I delineated this to those from Sierra Leone, Sudan and Rwanda.

"So, there are Africans in Sydney?" Ibrahim asked and he stopped walking to ask this as if to emphasise the question.

"Oh, yes. We've had a large influx of Africans over the past number of years."

Ibrahim looked into the distance as if this answer needed complex contemplation.

"So, if I lived there, I wouldn't be the only African in Sydney?" Ibrahim then asked.

Although a serious question, there was something amusing in the way he asked the question which made me laugh.

"Of course not," I replied definitively. "Polycarp and Jeremiah are not the only Africans in Sydney these days. For example, when I catch the train into the city, I would say that about one out of every five people I see on the station is African of some description. It's not like here. You know, we've walked this far and we've only seen Africans and I'm probably the only *Mzungu* here. Sydney, by contrast, is more like the Msingi wa Mungu Project where there is a mixture of people."

As soon as the words were out of my mouth, I was able to put my mind into gear and understand the real import of Ibrahim's question. Was Ibrahim contemplating on moving to Sydney?

Ibrahim had a neutral expression on his face after I had said this and it was impossible to know what was really going through his mind. But suddenly, without warning, he took a step forward which was a silent indication that we were to continue walking.

Ibrahim's lack of reaction to my last statement completely washed away the conversation and so there was a moment of silence as we continued on. We continued our walk to the Msingi wa Mungu Project and eventually arrived at the project entrance. I had a much better view of the layout of the entrance than I had when I arrived the day before by bus. The entrance consisted of a grand avenue, lined with trees which led for about one hundred metres before entering a clearing which opened onto what looked like a central courtyard with a flagpole centrepiece and the Tanzanian flag flapping majestically atop the pole.

We entered the main office and greeted the receptionist who reminded us that we needed to sign the registry to indicate that we were back on the Msingi wa Mungu Project's premises.

From there, Ibrahim led us back to our dormitory. It was still early afternoon and there was a hive of activity all around of people working on the construction of new buildings or gardeners working in garden plots. There appeared to be no educational activity going on but I simply guessed that this was occurring in one of the many classrooms scattered around the compound.

Once we were back in our dormitory, my bed looked so inviting as if it were welcoming me to nestle into its soft body and hold me in comfort. The beer had also had the effect of making me feel exceptionally sleepy. I knew an afternoon nap would help to wash away the effects of the alcohol. Ibrahim disappeared for a moment and I could only guess he had simply gone to relieve himself. With that I just kicked off my shoes and lay on my bed. I began to feel rather relaxed and could start to see the dream world superimposed on the world of reality when Ibrahim returned and pulled me completely back into our current space-time dimension. Ibrahim turned and saw me lying there and smiled.

"You feel like a sleep?" he asked.

"Is that alright?" I asked.

Ibrahim laughed.

"I guess it's alright! You can have a sleep. Don't sleep for too long or you won't be able to sleep tonight."

"Yeah," I replied emptily.

"There's a debate on this afternoon before dinner down at the Nyika," Ibrahim continued, "that starts in about an hour."

"What's the Nyika?" I asked inquisitively.

"Remember when we walked in at the entrance to the project?" Ibrahim asked.

"Yeah."

"On the left side as we entered, there's an area where a few trees are growing in what looks like a wilderness. That's the Nyika. That's where we usually hold debates."

"Why do they call it the Nyika?" I asked inquisitively.

"Because *nyika* in Swahili means 'wilderness' or 'grassland'. This is an area of the project that hasn't been touched. No buildings have been made there and so the area has continued to grow wild like a *nyika* so we call that area the Nyika."

I had a vague recollection of seeing something like that near the entrance but didn't really take it into account.

"Anyway, have a sleep. I'll come back in an hour and wake you so we can go together."

"Thanks," I replied.

Ibrahim fiddled around with something in the room but I didn't take any notice of what it was. Not long after he had left the room, I felt as if my entire body could lay back and relax.

I stared up at the roof through the bunched up mosquito net above me. Suddenly the events of the day replayed through the recording device in my head. Polycarp's family was gone.

While swimming in my cogitations, suddenly I felt a hand on my chest and a gentle whisper calling my name. Was this Polycarp? Was he appearing in my dream? As my mind staggered out of the daze, I realised it was Ibrahim. What was he doing waking me up? He said he would come back and wake me up in an hour.

"Bwana Michael. Did you sleep well?" Ibrahim asked.

I looked sleepily into his face which was still a blur and then around the room.

"What time is it?" I asked.

When Ibrahim told me the time, I realised I had been asleep for about forty-five minutes. Once over the shock of being suddenly awakened, I realised that I had been in a deep sleep and I felt quite refreshed from this short cat nap. I rubbed my eyes to remove any remnants of sleep I had left in them and then tried to sit on the edge of the bed.

Ibrahim then went over to the bookshelf and started looking business-like at a series of papers.

"What do we do now?" I asked.

Ibrahim turned to look at me.

"There's the debate at the Nyika. We can go and watch that. Alternatively, you are free to do whatever you like until they serve dinner."

"What's the debate?" I asked.

"Oh, the students practise their English by engaging in a debate."

"So, what's the topic?" I asked.

Ibrahim looked down at the piece of paper he was holding so then I realised that he had the program in his hand.

"Um, 'Is the theory of evolution compatible with religious belief?' Er, no, that was yesterday. 'Will the introduction of the internet help Tanzania to prosper?'"

There was an internal sigh of relief that the evolution/religion question was not the topic of the debate. Knowing that this religious group would eventually play in favour of religious belief winning trumps against everything else would have made me feel extremely uncomfortable. And what if Ibrahim asked me afterwards what I thought of the debate? A topic about technology and Tanzania's prosperity sounded like a much more neutral topic. In a way it would be quite entertaining. It would be impressive to watch students try to argue a point and use a language which was not their first to be able to support their argument.

I said that this would be an interesting prospect and so I agreed to go to the Nyika to watch the debate. Ibrahim then told me that he had an errand or two to do beforehand but that he would try to be there later.

When I arrived at the Nyika, there was only a handful of people there. Gordon was among the few people there and as soon as he saw me he smiled and greeted me.

"So, you're already back from Arusha?" he asked. "How was it?"

The pang of the recollection of what had transpired earlier in the day hit me like a punch in the gut.

"Gordon, it wasn't good," I replied. I wasn't sure what to say next but Gordon immediately understood.

"I'm very sorry, Michael," he replied by way of comfort.

"It's okay," I replied. "I mean, no, it's not okay."

Gordon put his arm around my shoulder.

"I'm very sorry, Michael. Unfortunately a lot of terrible things happened a little further west from here."

I looked up at Gordon to at least show that as sad as the news was, I wasn't destroyed by it. I knew that this news was a possibility so I had been psychologically prepared for this possible outcome. Gordon removed his arm from my shoulder and then added a comment.

"We're not always supposed to know why God allows these things to happen."

This comment was said as a comforting remark from Gordon's world view but it caused a well of anger to build up inside. How can you sincerely believe in this God of yours who allows these things to happen? I thought. How can you believe that God is Almighty and that God is love and is compassionate, and then He allows such horrendous situations to occur?

Fortunately Gordon diverted my thoughts away from this immediately.

"And Ibrahim looked after you alright?" Gordon asked.

"Yeah, yeah," I replied but really wasn't sure what he meant by the question.

"Ibrahim's a good man, you know," Gordon continued. "You have to be careful sometimes with the locals. However, Ibrahim is very trustworthy. That's why I didn't mind allowing him to share the dormitory with you when he asked me. The other managers are sleeping in a different dormitory but there wasn't enough room for all of them as their building isn't complete. Ibrahim volunteered to share with one of the people coming from overseas and he also volunteered to take you to Arusha so it was decided that he may as well share the room with you. I knew you wouldn't have any trouble with him. He is a very fine gentleman. I have known him now for just over two years and really he has been an asset to this project."

This sudden confession by Gordon about Ibrahim increased the positive appeal of this man.

"And he was very happy to look after you," Gordon continued with a perplexed look on his face as if the prospect of Ibrahim wanting to look after me was some sort of riddle. "As soon as I told him that a man called Michael was coming and needed someone to escort him to Arusha and back, Ibrahim was more than happy to help. Your name seemed to fascinate him for some reason as if it meant something to him."

"Well," I replied, "I can't see what's so fascinating in the name Michael. It's a pretty ordinary name really." I paused and then continued. "And Ibrahim helps manage the place?"

"Oh, yes," Gordon replied. "I'm retired now and I felt led by the Lord to establish a school over here and help the poor. We advertised for local Tanzanians in Moshi to help manage the project and Ibrahim was one of the first to volunteer. The idea is to raise the education level of the people here, in particular those who cannot afford to go to school, as well as take in orphans so they have somewhere to live and get an education at the same time. Once we get one project up and running, we can start another and then another so that the education level of the people here can be raised and hopefully this will in turn raise the country itself out of its overall poverty."

"And what does the government feel about this?" I asked.

Gordon laughed. "We had to obviously get the agreement of the government to allow the project to go ahead. We had to get special visas but apart from that the government was very happy for us to get involved. Once we had completed all the governmental formalities, we started advertising. And now here we are!"

I looked around.

"There aren't many students here," I commented.

"Not at the moment. There are about a hundred students here now. Each student has to be sponsored. We run the project despite the number of students. We advertise around the world for people to sponsor children to attend school here. The more sponsors we get on board, the more students we can accommodate at the project."

A hundred students? Where were they all hiding? I hadn't seen any during my first twenty-four hour stay here.

The sounds of people arriving at the Nyika cut the conversation short. Gordon looked around and then began directing people to different places in the Nyika. This was the first time I saw the students and was amazed at how many there actually were.

Gordon then came back to me.

"Hey, Michael, how would you like to adjudicate the debate this afternoon?" he then asked me.

"Adjudicate?"

"Yes, that is, adjudicate their English. Make corrections. Show them what they could do to improve their English. I always ask one of the English teachers to do that and seeing you're the first English teacher here, I thought I'd ask you."

I agreed to the task. It didn't sound too difficult.

The number of people slowly began to increase at the Nyika. At one point, a few students came out bearing furniture, a number of school desks and school chairs, and set them up like an outdoor courtroom. The few trees in the Nyika served as a backdrop in front of which were placed two rows of tables and chairs, one row on the left and one row on the right, each row for each side of the debate. A third row of desks and chairs was placed to the side for the three judges, two who would decide who performed the best and which team won, and one for me, the adjudicator, to provide feedback as to their ability to express their ideas in English. The rest of the people from the project were invited to sit on the grass.

There was something about doing the debate outdoors that appealed to me. A feeling of freedom of conducting a debate out in the open was like the feeling of taking off a straight jacket or simply removing tight clothing. This entire atmosphere put me in a good mood and it was refreshing to have something positive for the day to lift my spirits.

Soon everyone was settled and Gordon, who now took on the role of the MC, stood centre stage and introduced the topic of the debate. He gave a neutral introduction of the internet, about how powerful a tool it was and how widespread it had become. He made anecdotal comments about the type of information that was available, including sites that provided on-the-moment news, immediate answers to questions such as what the capital of Burkina Faso was and things as simple as how to cook a pavlova. Of course, the internet also provided access to education, which was what the Msingi wa Mungu Project was all about. It was a nice introduction, not too long, and with a bit of humour thrown in. Once this introduction was over, Gordon then threw the stage open for the first speaker for the affirmative to take the floor.

The first to stand up and speak was a small, forlorn looking young Tanzanian girl. In my mind, I gave her the nickname Thumbelina. She approached centre stage in front of the two rows of desks. My initial reaction was to make sure that I wasn't too hard on her. I knew what it was like to learn a foreign language and the difficulty of making sure one spoke accurately, which was not always accomplishable. I knew that it was beneficial for someone to correct grammatical mistakes so that learners of the new language spoke the language as well as possible so that their language ability sounded good to a native speaker's ear. I made a mental note to make corrections and suggestions in a gentle way so as not to overwhelm her and destroy her confidence.

However, this analysis of this small person was totally changed as soon as she opened her mouth.

"Ladies and gentlemen," she started with a bold voice and then welcomed all those there, teachers, guests from overseas and then her fellow students. It was a bold introduction without one grammatical mistake and, although with a typical Tanzanian accent, very clear pronunciation. Whoever had trained her to speak in this way had done a wonderful job.

Thumbelina then went off on her speech. She used in her speech some of the elements from Gordon's introduction and showed how this was beneficial to Tanzanian society and further helped to advance the Tanzanian economy. The speech was bold, convincing and in very good English. She made only one or two minor grammatical mistakes and I noted them down so that I had at least something to make a comment about. I was completely amazed. I gave her a thumbs-up as a silent congratulations of a speech well-done, however, Thumbelina did not see this and simply returned to her place behind the desk.

Thumbelina's speech was applauded and then the first speaker of the opposition was invited to stand up and speak. The first speaker of the opposition was a rather large boy, like a monument to the word "ample". He was pleasantly plump. He was the African answer to Humpty Dumpty. Everything on him looked plentiful, his wide round eyes, his wide flat nose, and his ample lips. For a child brought up in poverty, I questioned how poor he really was and guessed he ate one too many meals of ugali than he was allotted.

He was big in body and even bigger in speech. He produced a fiery speech against the advances of the internet, focusing on the access that internet has to not-so-pleasant information such as home-made bombs and violence. The internet, so he argued, also gave access to the ideas portrayed in decadent European countries. He gave the example of the Netherlands where the idea of making marijuana legal would fill the minds of Tanzanians and distort them into thinking that marijuana could be considered okay and on par with alcohol, the legal intoxicant in most countries including the African nations. Humpty was then welcomed to sit down with an overall applause from the crowd.

The next speaker for the affirmative was a young boy much more in keeping with the general stereotype of a poor nation, a tall but emaciated young man who could do with the surplus bowl of ugali that Humpty had eaten. He had rather different features to the stereotypical Africans I was familiar with. His eyes were almond shape, almost South East Asian looking, and he had high cheekbones and a fine nose. Although I didn't have the anthropological skills to determine the source of these features, I knew that this young man obviously came from a different tribe than others in the area. However, although timid looking, obviously he was deliberately handpicked to give his viewpoint of a strongly argued case for technology. Somewhere in his speech he finally revealed the source of his features as he was the descendant of the Masai Tribespeople.

The speeches continued, one for the advancement of internet, the other against. It was obvious that those chosen for the debate were deliberately selected because of their brazen boldness and their willingness to strongly argue a side in front of a large audience in a language that was not their first.

All arguments had been put forward and now it was the last speaker of the opposition to speak. This was a young man, very handsome and very athletic looking. He appeared to be the darkest of them all here and at the same time the most handsome. He wore his school uniform correctly, shirt completely tucked in, his belt well in line with the button line of his shirt and his shoes meticulously cleaned. I was immediately taken in by his handsomeness. I was fully conscious of the effect he had over me. I had the impression that everyone was going to stand up and applaud him simply because of his sheer beauty. I looked around at the judges and then at the audience but no-one seemed to react any differently to him than they had to the other speakers. I suddenly became aware that this was my own personal appreciation of him and so I pushed the thought aside and prepared myself for his speech.

This ebony Adonis gave a speech that was no more or no less confident than the previous speakers. In a similar manner to those on his team for the opposition, he spoke about how Tanzanians using internet have easy access to the decadence of the West. We had heard this in the previous two takes of the opposition and this ebony Adonis appeared to simply reiterate this. However, then his speech took on a much deeper course. The decadence of the west was not simply the freedoms we enjoyed. The internet gave access to pornographic sites that   would otherwise have not been accessible without this new computer invention. This seemed to be what his entire argument hinged on. Free access to pornography and the explicitedness of what people supposedly can do in sex would suddenly make those who have internet access want to try all this out. People would be encouraged to imitate the acts they saw on these sites.

Then he dropped the bombshell. Not only is there access to heterosexual pornographic websites, there is access to gay websites as well. I was initially impressed by his use of the word "gay" and not "homosexual" which meant that whoever had coached him had taught him this word. Homosexual pornographic sites would then encourage more boys and girls to become gay.

What? I thought. I had to fight the urge to actually stand up and scream at him at how ludicrous this statement was. Since when had homosexual pornography ever been the source of anyone wanting to have sex with someone of their own gender? I had absolutely no access to homosexual pornography when I was a child and indeed I didn't even know homoerotic pornography actually existed and yet I still turned out to be gay. Also, I remembered once showing Faraj some homoerotic pornography, and the way he reacted to it did not support what this ebony Adonis had said because Faraj never showed any sudden interest in having sex with other men – much to my disappointment.

But then the ebony Adonis said something that at the time didn't quite mean anything but later seemed like a peculiar thing to say. Those who look at these gay pornographic websites – and it was obvious that this had a male bias to the comment – would then become intrigued and want to go to some seedy place in Moshi, the name of which I didn't catch, and then try what it was like to have sex with another man. It intrigued me later when I had settled down because I asked myself the question: how did he know about this place? Or whoever had coached him?

The way he talked about the homosexual issue made it clear that homosexuals and homosexuality was looked on as completely disgusting and perverse and therefore a very wrong thing to do, the view that had persisted in the western world for thousands of years right up until my father's generation.

That was the only comment that this ebony Adonis made about the effects of the internet on promoting homosexuality. He moved onto his next argument as to why the internet was actually a negative force in Tanzania, something that had nothing to do with sexuality. But my emotions had put my brain into shut down.

This gave me an opportunity to see how things in the world really were. My life in Australia at this current time in all eternity was like a paradisiacal bubble. Of all the times and places in eternity for a homosexual to be born, this was an ideal one. I realised how fortunate I was to be living in Australia and the freedom to live my life the way nature had programmed me to be. I had always appreciated this as if the world had woken up and crawled out of its cocoon to welcome a new dawn. For the first time I understood first hand that had I been living here in Tanzania as a Tanzanian and discovered that my sexual attraction was pre-programmed towards my own sex, I would have been doomed. It was bad enough growing up in Australia in a Christian family where this rude awaking had long-ranging consequences but at least it only caused a disruption with the relationship with my parents, not complete isolation and damnation within the society in which I lived.

I felt the twinge of fear and pain of each and every male and female homosexual in that crowd of students who was aware of his and her sexuality as if they had channelled all their feelings to flow into my own soul. I felt the societal oppression weighing heavily on me as if columns that supported the vault of the sky had suddenly collapsed and the firmament had fallen and was now resting on my shoulders. I felt as if every male and female homosexual in that group of school students had turned to look at me, begging me to do something, all saying at once, "Please, Sir. Help us. Please help us." But what could I do? Could I there and then stand up before everyone and confess that I was gay and that such a comment by the ebony Adonis was unwarranted, even discriminatory?

This last speaker for the negative finally finished his speech and it was time for the judges to announce their verdict. However, I didn't listen. I don't know which they finally decided was the winning team. My eyes sailed over to the speaker of the opposition, the ebony Adonis, and I just stared at him. He just sat at his table like a typical school child who had performed an assignment for school. But I wanted to walk over there, grab him by the front of his shirt, shake him hard and tell him a thing or two I was so enraged. My mind was so otherwise occupied that I didn't even hear when they called me up to give my commentary of each student's use of English. One of the judges next to me had to nudge me to get my attention. I dutifully got up and took centre stage. It took some moments for me to gain my composure. I took a few deep breaths and ruffled through my notes to stall time and to help me focus solely on the task I had been invited to undertake. Pushing my annoyance and frustration to backstage, I put on my friendly façade and gave my analysis. I first praised the students for their wonderful ability to speak English at such a good level and commented that I understood how difficult it was to stand up in a crowd and deliver a convincing speech in a language which was not one's first. I then commented on each student's speech using a praise sandwich, first commending them for their speech, then mentioning one or two mistakes in English that they had made and offering a suggestion, and then finally praising them for their effort overall. When it came to giving feedback to the ebony Adonis, I had to swallow large doses of my anger before giving him the equivalent feedback I had given the other students.

It was late when we finally made it back to our dormitory. After the debate, we had dinner and then Gordon gave a talk to update us with what the program was for the upcoming week, followed by a Devotion, that is, some sort of discussion about the importance of God in our lives. Only a small part of my mind was involved in all this while my main concentration was on what had happened at that debate. It made me feel angry and sick. I wanted to get out of here, get out of Tanzania and back into the solace of my safe haven of Australia. I then felt angry at Polycarp. Why did he have to crawl into my heart and affect me so much that he caused me to end up actually making a trip to this horrible place?

When we reached the dormitory, Ibrahim suggested that we have a bath before getting ready for bed. As usual, he fetched the water while I waited in the shower amenities. There were other men already there showering, and a number of them were chatting to each other across from one cubicle to another. There was absolutely no sociability inside of me and I looked forward to getting into my bed and hiding from the world.

When we finally got to bed, Ibrahim dressed down once again. Once in only his shorts with his dark-skinned and carpeted chest exposed, I simply and overtly stared at his wonderful physique. There was a certain cynicism inside as I looked at his body. This was the only saving grace about Ibrahim. He came across to me as an extremely good-looking man. But he was a member of this entire anti-gay, anti-technology, anti-openness and anti-freedom society that this religious organisation represented to me.

Ibrahim crawled under the mosquito net and onto his bed. In the semidarkness, he once again took on the strange pose that I thought was odd for a Muslim to pray in. In a short time this was over and then Ibrahim rolled over onto his side and went to sleep.

But I couldn't sleep. I wasn't sure if it was the afternoon nap or the debate or the news about Polycarp or a combination of all of them. Maybe it was jetlag. But I just lay in the semidarkness and stared up through the lace into the darkness.

After a few moments, I groped around on the floor to find my aerosol can of Aerogard and then began liberally spraying it all over my body. With that, I slipped out from under the mosquito net onto the concrete floor and walked over to the window. The external lights were shining onto the dusty compound. I could also see the lights from other buildings across the entire project complex through the leaves of the trees scattered about the place. I leaned on the sill and just stared out into the dark African night.

I hadn't been there long when Ibrahim stirred.

"Hey, Bwana Michael. Are you okay?" I heard him say softly.

"Yeah, I'm okay. I just can't sleep."

I heard Ibrahim then move in the bed so I guessed he was rolling over.

"Still thinking of the news about Polycarp?"

Ibrahim was partly right. There was something in his empathy that put my anger against this man on hold. At least the Polycarp situation was a safe conversational topic.

"You really love this Polycarp, I can tell," Ibrahim continued.

A chill went up my spine as he said this. There was something innocent about the way Ibrahim commented on this, a comment without rebuke but with what I assumed to be underlying innuendo. And it was the second time he had said it. I wasn't sure how to respond to this at first. Suddenly the vindictiveness as a result of the comment made by the ebony Adonis stirred up inside me.

"Yes, I love him very much," I replied. I paused for a moment before I made the next comment. I chose to word it in a way that was ambiguous. "If things were different, I would marry him."

I chose to make the comment that way because the expression "if things were different" could mean anything. Ibrahim sounded as if he had taken a deep breath to prepare for the next question he had to ask.

"What do you mean? Can't men marry men in Australia?"

Fortunately it was dark. I could feel a flush in my face and was sure that my face had gone a few shades of red. The feeling of being in imminent danger suddenly overwhelmed me.

"No, they can't," I finally replied. "But would it worry you if they could?"

There was total silence. I knew what his answer was going to be. The ebony Adonis had spoken on behalf of all Tanzania and no doubt on behalf of the whole of sub-Saharan Africa. Men who loved men and women who loved women, these people needed to be severely dealt with, beaten up, put in prison or stoned to death. Their very existence needed to be expunged from even the thought of existence. A sense of despondency then overwhelmed me as if I simply didn't care what Ibrahim did to me. He could get out of bed and beat me to death, I simply didn't care.

I heard Ibrahim move again so I guessed he had rolled over once more.

"I guess it wouldn't, as long as both men seriously loved each other enough to be married," I heard from the silence. This was not what I was expecting to hear at all. I did not believe that he had said that.

I turned towards his bed and could just make out the rough detail of Ibrahim's body. He was lying with his head in his hand and his elbow digging into his pillow.

"Are you serious?" I asked him.

"But isn't Australia like Europe and the United States?" Ibrahim asked as his answer to my initial question.

"In what way?" I asked.

"In the way that men can marry men and women can marry women?"

I looked out the window. The innocence of the question, asked in a way that was devoid of judgement, rather, it was full of curiosity and even care for alternative views. It was a question that sought clarification, information, an increase in knowledge. My earlier concerns and misgivings about talking so openly about this subject were put on hold.

"No, they can't," I replied, staring out into the semidarkness of the Tanzanian landscape.

There was further silence. I heard Ibrahim noisily take in a draught of air through his nostrils.

"Is that why you won't marry Polycarp?"

Once again, a cold chill ran up through my spine. How was I to answer this question? In the end, I simply decided to answer the question as honestly and as innocently as the question which was posed.

"No, that's not the reason why I won't marry Polycarp," I replied. "I won't marry Polycarp because I'm not in love with him. And in any case, he is far too young for my liking. If I were to marry a guy, he would have to be around my age and be of a similar mentality to me."

As soon as the last word had escaped my lips, I realised exactly what I had said. Ibrahim had lured me into a false sense of safety that allowed my heart to speak. But once the words were out, my whole body went tense. This was a confession as clear as any confession I could have given about my sexuality. And I had admitted it to Ibrahim.

This answer was followed by deathly silence. I just stared once again out into the darkness of the Tanzanian landscape. I didn't dare turn around. All was silent both in the dormitory and outside. Finally, Ibrahim made a noise which meant he had moved again in the bed.

"But don't you think that marrying a man, that you are a man, is somehow," and there was a pause before he continued, "not ordinary?"

There was something sinister in the question. Once again, a fresh wave of fear flooded over me like a wave on the surf. What had I gotten myself into? Maybe I should not have gone down this path. However, unfortunately, the words were out, my statements were now ideas in Ibrahim's mind and I could not retrieve them.

I decided to find a way to salvage the situation.

"Tell me seriously, Ibrahim," I began and turned around to look at him in the semidarkness. "Just say, not that this means that this is the way things are, but let's just say that I, as a man, wanted to marry a man. My relationship with this man, how would it affect you?"

There was utter silence. However, the mere silence, the semidarkness, the questions Ibrahim had posed and what my responses to these questions implied now filled me with an intense fear and I could feel my heart beating in my chest and in my neck.

"If you loved a man," Ibrahim then continued but there was a slight pause at the end of this clause. I was struck by the fact that he was not attacking a relationship between two men as either filthy, a distortion of nature or even a repugnant sin against God. He was still discussing relationships between men as a hypothetical. The wave of fear that had earlier overwhelmed me suddenly abated once again as if the wave had suddenly been sucked back out to sea and I could feel solid ground beneath my feet, a sure footing that I was safe. Eventually, Ibrahim retraced his steps and then continued.

"I mean, if a man loves another man," Ibrahim started and then stopped. There was a slight pause and then he continued speaking. "If you loved a man and you thought he loved you but you weren't sure…"

There was once again a long pause.

I turned to look at Ibrahim. His silhouette in the darkness was difficult to make out. I then turned once again to look out into the night.

"…and you, er, wanted to know, er, for sure – *kwa hakika* – what this other man felt for you. I mean," he stammered and once again paused.

This had suddenly turned from fearful to quite amusing. What is it about straight guys that they ask such odd questions? I just continued to look out the window and wait for him to finish the question. It sounded like a difficult question for Ibrahim to get out. For a moment there was once again silence until Ibrahim was able to speak out again.

"I mean," Ibrahim once again continued. "In your culture, if you wanted to marry this man, how does a man in your culture tell the other man he wants to…er…marry him?"

I just wanted to laugh! I don't know why but it sounded just so funny! What a strange question from a heterosexual. What difference would it make to Ibrahim?

"Well, in my culture," I began and tried to think of something that would sound somewhat exotic. After all, back home, the places where I met guys, you just had to look at a guy you liked and with a wink, or a simple twitch with the eyebrows or some other subtle feature of body language, you conveyed your message and the other guy responded accordingly with a form of body language which meant either yes or no. Alternatively, if anyone said anything, they would generally use the well worn out line, "Would you like to come back to my place for coffee?" So many times I had been invited to partake in this caffeinated beverage but had never sipped a drop of coffee on arrival.

Ibrahim had used the word "marry". However, although he spoke English extremely well, I was aware that because of cultural differences, he said things that meant something in my cultural context but something different in his. As it was, when we had a shower, Ibrahim said that we had a bath when having a bath meant something different to me. As for the use of the word "marry", to me it was just a euphemism Ibrahim was using to mean to have an intimate moment.

But I had to say something to Ibrahim. What difference would it make anyway? Was he going to discuss this with other people here in Tanzania about the cultural aspect of how men meet men in the western world and introduce this novel feature into Tanzanian society? My mind went into imagination mode. What was something really elaborate that I could say that would come across as quite interesting?

"Well, when the lover wants to make his intentions known to his beloved," I began. I chose the words "lover" and "beloved" because these were the words used in the English translation of Plato's dialogues about two male lovers and these terms made it easier than saying "one man" and "the other man" which would have made the explanation quite confusing. "Well, the lover walks up to his beloved, takes his beloved's right hand and kisses his middle finger. The lover then kneels down, takes his beloved's hand and touches his forehead with the back of his beloved's hand, that is, the place on his hand the lover kissed, and then brings his hand back down to his side and then stands up again. While still holding the hand of his beloved, the lover says to his beloved, 'My dearest so-and-so. I think I love you and I would like to marry you so that you and I can be one'."

I suddenly saw something dash along the ground and disappear up in the tree closest to the dormitory. I then heard Ibrahim's deep inhalation.

"And how does the beloved show that he has accepted him?"

I thought hard for a moment. What could I say next?

"Well," I said, still fixing my attention on what was occurring outside, "the beloved then takes the lover's two hands and pulls them towards his waist. The lover then accepts this as a sign that he can embrace his beloved. They embrace and then kiss." And then I added as an afterthought, "And anything else that they wish to do together."

There was a momentary pause. Whatever had attracted my attention outside had gone and all was once again still.

"And," Ibrahim then asked so quietly and hesitantly that this time I could barely hear his voice, "do you think such relationships are acceptable?"

I felt a flush through my shoulders and up into my face. But also there was a sense of fear again. The question Ibrahim asked was not like the earlier questions of curiosity. What would happen next?

Then a sudden feeling of anger and rebellion overwhelmed me. Damn him! I thought. Face the truth. This is a reality. So after a slight pause, I turned to face him and even though I could not quite work out his facial features in the semidarkness and whether or not he was looking at me, I just spoke.

"Yes," I replied, "I do think such relationships are acceptable. After all, don't we all have a right to love whom we wish to love? No-one has the right to keep two people who love each other apart. Anyone who tries to separate those who love each other goes against all the teachings of love taught in all religions."

That last bit I threw in without any qualification for the statement. I could at least say that the Judaeo-Christian belief argued for love in general, and Plato's *Symposium* spoke about such expressions of love between two people, two men, two women and between a man and a woman in much more detail. I really had no idea what the Koran had to say about love and relationships, or any of the other religious books, such as the Bhagavad-Gita or the Vedic Scriptures.

There was a deathly silence in the room, almost as thick as the darkness. This caused a tightness about my back and shoulders, that horrible feeling of stress when you feel some awful event is about to happen. Ibrahim was Muslim and so such a comment meant that he had to kill me, and at any moment he was going to get out of bed and fight for his religion.

But finally, Ibrahim once again noisily inhaled and then I heard him move so I guessed he was just rolling over in the bed. Then there was another further silence until Ibrahim spoke again.

"Bwana Michael," he said softly, "you should get back under the mosquito net. The last thing I want is that you catch malaria."

And that was the last comment Ibrahim had to make on that topic. And once again, like a number of his previous comments, it sent a tingle through my body. I had made it quite clear what I thought about the so-called decadence the ebony Adonis had spoken harshly against earlier in the day and yet Ibrahim still continued to care for me.

With that, I obeyed immediately. I snuck up under the lace wall around my bed and got under the sheet. I rolled over and faced the wall, away from Ibrahim. I wondered what he was thinking or if he was going to make a further comment. But not long after the silence of the night had captured the domain of the room, Ibrahim began to snore so I knew he was now fast asleep.

Chapter 8

I awoke early the following morning. As the cobwebs of the night and the dream world slowly dissipated from my mind bringing me back to the conscious world of the here and now, the conversation that Ibrahim and I had had before we had gone to sleep the previous evening came to mind and caused a slight shudder to pass through my body. It was an awkward situation and I knew I had to now be on my guard because of the personal details about myself I had conveyed. How had Ibrahim interpreted what I had said? If he had rightfully understood what I was getting at, how was Ibrahim going to react towards me? And what was more complicated was that I was not in my home country in the world of anti-discrimination and equal employment opportunities where I could fall back on the clemency of national law to protect me. As far as homosexuality went, I had returned to the homophobic and homo-ill-informed times of the pre-1970s. I regretted everything that I had divulged about myself the night previous. However, I simply needed to find a strategy to give the idea that I really was a heterosexual guy. I knew how to play that game anyway. I had to do so to survive all through the years of my growing up. To survive, homosexuals have to learn to listen, watch and imitate straight people and then just repeat what they have learnt at the opportune moment so that nobody suspects a thing.

When Ibrahim wakes up, I thought, I will work out a way to steer him away from the idea that I might have lewd and distorted desires however supportive I may be of people who have such desires.

I glanced at my mobile phone to see what the time was. It was still quite early. The lights from outside were still on which meant it was still dark. However, when I sat up and looked out into the night, I could see that morning was just beginning to make its appearance.

I lay back in bed and stared up at the ceiling through the semidarkness. There were still quite a few days before I could return to my normal life in Australia. I had accomplished my mission, which had taken a much shorter time than I had expected, and now I was ready to return home to my free life. But the deal was to be at the Msingi wa Mungu Project for just over another week.

I began to go into deep, critical reflection. I wasn't terribly happy here. It was too reminiscent of the religious life of my childhood and early adulthood. These were unpleasant memories. Hence, I didn't want to get to know anybody here at the Msingi wa Mungu Project socially. It was too dangerous. One can only go so long pretending someone is something they really are not before people discover what's really going on in that person's head. All these people I had associated with the night before at the dinner table were all treacly sweet but I knew just how judgemental religious people were. They were nice to you as long as you followed the party line. But when they discovered that you were not one of them, they went to great lengths to convince you that their dogma was the all-embracing, unwavering, irrefutable truth. If you raised questions that showed that certain tenets of their belief sounded strangely odd, they threw at you a condescending smile as if you were stupid and that you did not quite reach their height of inspiration. Then they went to great lengths to show that their belief system, despite the irregularities, had an explanation, an explanation that at least made sense to them.

This led my thoughts wandering. I reflected on my childhood days in the church. I remembered grappling with ideas that just made no sense to me. One example was the belief in the trinity. Christians argue vehemently that they are monotheistic and ridicule religions such as Hinduism which believe in more than one god. "Of course, there is only one God!" they scoff at these evil polytheists – and I still don't understand what is so evil about being polytheistic – "the Bible is quite clear in saying that there is only one God!" And then they tell you in the next breath, "This one God is manifest in God the Father, God the Son and God the Holy Ghost. Isn't that clear enough that there is only one God?" Catholic Christians add to this list a myriad of saints who have very godlike powers, no different to the lesser gods in the ancient Greek and Roman religions or even the modern religion of Hinduism.

Those on the outside of the religion clearly see the contradiction. I even saw it when I was in the religion. But those on the inside have developed clever arguments to convince or at least delude themselves that there is no contradiction at all. The explanations are legion but each explanation only makes it clear that they are trying to say that they believe in three gods but at the same time they want to wear the badge that they are monotheistic.

I've had Christians quite arrogantly tell me that I have a problem and that I'm actually stupid not being able to understand the concept of the trinity. I was even in trouble with my parents as a young adult when I tried to make sense of it all. But when push comes to shove, and trinitarians are forced to realise that in fact the idea of a trinity is really an impossibility which forces them to either confess that they seriously are polytheistic and therefore really believe in three different gods, instead of finally admitting it and saying, "Yes, that's right. It's impossible to believe in the trinity and be monotheistic", they rather tell you that the trinity is, after all, a mystery, and that God will reveal this when we reach the next life. But we have to believe in this impossibility in this life or we will be condemned in the next. We have to believe something illogical in this life in order to have a beautiful life in the life after the grave.

Ironically, these same Christians criticise other religions which have odd beliefs. When the Hindus explain that one of their gods, Ganesh, has the head of an elephant because his real head was cut off and therefore he had it replaced with the head of an elephant, the Christians mock the Hindus to scorn at their overt belief in such stupidity and illogicality. How can a god wear the head of one of the animals the gods created? But these Christians don't see that the Hindus have as much right to say to the Christians, "Well, this is a mystery and you have to believe it in this life in order to have a blissful life in the next one and that God will reveal the logic in it all after we die."

What always annoys me about religious people is that they clearly see the inconsistency of the belief in another's religion but they cannot see the same in their own. It's just as Jesus said in the Sermon on the Mount in Matthew 7:3 – 5 that people can see the speck of dust in someone else's eye but can't see the beam of wood in their own. I have never really been able to understand why the gospel writer talked about specks of dust and beams of wood in people's eyes but it always makes me blink thinking of my eye with a speck of dust in it. Imagine how it would feel if there were a four by two in one of them. But the principle is a good one and I wonder if Jesus meant to include the criticism of other religions within this teaching.

Another difficulty I had as a Christian was how Christians can read a passage from the Bible which is quite clear and plain but if Christians were to understand the verse as it is written, this would cause a problem with the entire belief system. However, what amazed me was how the Christians could say without batting an eyelid, "Yeah, but it doesn't mean that."

For example, I remember a friend of mine at school, Troy Krisston, confronting me with the verse from Psalm 93:1 which says, "the world also is stablished, that it cannot be moved" and being told that this is evidence that the Bible is wrong because the earth does in fact move. In fact, the Church, both Catholic and Protestant, used this very verse against Galileo to prove to Galileo that his theory that the earth revolves around the sun and not the sun around the earth was wrong. Because the Bible is always true, so the argument ran, then Galileo had to be wrong. But today, Catholics and Protestants alike believe that the earth orbits the sun. What is not very well known is that the Catholic Church did not apologise for its condemnation of Galileo until 1993, four hundred years later, and this was a moment when the Church was forced to finally admit that it had in fact made a mistake, although the Church did this ever so quietly. As for Protestants, apart from Martin Luther's railings against Galileo, later Protestants gently put to one side their past criticism of the heliocentric system and accepted the current view of our universe, totally ignoring, overlooking or going to great pains to never mention this verse in the Psalms when doing so.

When faced with this verse today, I have had Christians without a hint of hesitation say to me, "Yeah, but this is not what this verse means." In other words, when we read Psalm 93:1 that "the world…cannot be moved", this doesn't mean that the psalmist meant that the world cannot be moved. Oddly enough, the same cannot be said when the Bible speaks against homosexuality. When the Bible says that homosexuality is a sin, strangely enough, Christians don't say, "yeah, but this doesn't mean that homosexuality is a sin."

But who could I tell that to here? But then, what did it matter? I just had to survive for the next number of days and then I was out of here.

With that, the outside lights suddenly flicked off and it was obvious that morning had definitely broken. I rolled over onto my side and looked across the room. When I looked at Ibrahim's bed, I noticed that it was empty. I simply guessed that Ibrahim had gone to the toilet so I lay back and looked up at the ceiling.

"I wonder what I can do now," I then asked myself. What was the schedule for the day? The paperwork with the weekly schedule was wedged within the pages of my diary which was over on the bookshelf that held Ibrahim's and my belongings.

I quietly snuck out under the mosquito net, stuck my feet on the ground and then walked across the concrete flooring with a snip-snap sound till I got to the cupboard.

Once at the shelving, I pulled out my diary and then flipped the pages to where the Msingi wa Mungu Project program was inserted. I pulled out the A4 paper and opened it up, putting it at an angle to gain the full extent of light coming in from the window. This particular day the job for us visiting English teachers was to demonstrate to the local English teachers at the Msingi wa Mungu Project how to prepare and deliver a lesson. The theme of the lesson was the interaction between buyer and seller. Our job was to demonstrate the steps required to teach such an interaction. I had done this now for years that I could do it in my sleep. However, for those who have never taught their language before, it is quite a complex affair.

Even though I knew exactly how to go about this, I needed to make some helpful notes that I could pass on to the Msingi wa Mungu Project teachers. I groped along the shelf where my belongings were for a pen. None of my pens were there so I probably had them in my bag. In any case, surely Ibrahim had a pen on his shelving that I could borrow for a couple of minutes.

I started fossicking around on his shelving. But what intrigued me was that Ibrahim had a number of books in his possession. I picked up the one I had seen the other day and briefly leafed through it. Just as I had surmised, it was the Koran. However, this Koran was bilingual, with the Arabic on the right hand side and an English translation on the left.

I put the Koran back down. It really didn't interest me to read it. I pulled out another book with a similar backing but instead of being a dark green it was black. I opened it up at the middle and leafed through this book. It was in Swahili. By the arrangement of the text into columns with verse numbers and with the names of the books at the top, I could immediately tell that this was the Bible. I turned to the title page of the book and there on the page was *Biblia*.

"So, they call the Bible *Biblia* in Swahili," I thought to myself. I knew *Biblia* was actually the Spanish word for Bible. So, why did Swahili speakers use a Spanish word for the name of the Bible? As far as I was aware, the Spanish did not come to this part of the world.

And Ibrahim had a Bible? Since when did Muslims read the Bible? I had never heard of Muslims interested in reading this literature. Rather, I had heard of stories of Muslims in their curiosity reading the Bible and then being threatened with death for doing so. Alternatively, there were the other extremes of Muslims finding copies of the Bible and simply burning them. After all, Muslims didn't seem to hesitate to set churches alight, so why not the Christians' Holy Book? So, why did Ibrahim have one? Did he read it? Did he intend to read it?

Suddenly I heard the door open.

"Hey, good morning, Bwana Michael," Ibrahim panted as he walked through the door. I was startled. I suddenly felt guilty, caught in the act of intruding into Ibrahim's affairs, and so with swift action, I pushed the Bible back onto the shelf. But in my exuberance, by pushing the Bible against the other books on the shelf, the other books fell onto the floor with a loud clack-clack-clack.

I froze in horror as if I had just dropped the long sought-after Holy Grail. There was a momentary silence.

Ibrahim was breathing heavily which only exacerbated the fear of the moment. Then Ibrahim spoke through his panting, "So, I see you have taken an interest in my collection of books."

This broke me out of my petrified stupor and I immediately began picking up the books and putting them back on the shelf.

"I...I'm really sorry, Ibrahim," I stuttered. "I didn't mean to pry into your personal affairs."

Ibrahim laughed. He walked over to his bed and sat down. He was wearing a T-shirt, sport shorts and a pair of jogging shoes.

"That's okay," he replied. "You are most welcome to read any of my books. They are not secrets. Help yourself. Take one."

"I...I really didn't have any particular interest in any of them," I said in order to say something. Ibrahim seemed to suspect that I didn't believe it when he welcomed me to his little library.

"Please, Bwana Michael, it would be an honour for me to see you read my books. You would give me great pleasure."

I hesitated. Now I was stuck in a bind. I couldn't just return to bed and leave his books because then it would seem as if I were snubbing his offer. At the same time, I only knew the content of two books that he had on the shelf and neither of them particularly interested me. However, because my job was to play the Christian, I came up with an idea that fit within the context. I picked up the Bible.

"I just wanted to see what it was like reading the Bible in Swahili," I replied.

I then once again picked up the Bible and walked over to my bed, slid back under the mosquito net and then lay in a way which enabled me to appear as if I were reading. Ibrahim grabbed a hand towel from the end of his bed and began wiping sweat from his face. There was once again a momentary pause and then Ibrahim spoke.

"Would you like me to get you a Bible in Swahili?" he asked once again through his panting although his breathing was coming back to normal.

"No, no," I replied shyly. "That's fine. I have enough Bibles at home. In any case, when I read the Bible, I read it in the original languages, in Hebrew and Greek."

Ibrahim breathed with that noisy ventilation sound that he often made.

"Wow, Bwana Michael. So you can read Hebrew and Greek? Could you teach me?"

"Teach you?" I said through a smile. "Ibrahim, I'm only here for another week. I can't teach you Hebrew and Greek in a couple of days. It took me ages to learn these two languages."

"Yeah, that makes sense," Ibrahim puffed. "It's a shame though because I would really like someone who can read the Bible in these languages to teach me so that I can read the Bible in the original languages as well. I can read Hebrew a bit because it is similar to Arabic but I am not that good with Greek."

I put my head in the cup of my hand and leaned my elbow on the pillow.

"Why do you want to read the Bible in the original languages?"

Ibrahim threw the hand towel back onto his bed and then sat back with his hands behind him.

"I think it's important," Ibrahim replied, "to read the Holy Books in the original languages. I mean, it's great that people have gone to the effort and translated them into English and Swahili and the other languages of the world, but I feel to really get a greater understanding of Allah, we need to go back to the original languages. I was required to do this when I was studying the Koran and I am glad that I learnt Arabic to be able to read the Koran in Arabic. But I have not as yet had the same opportunity with the Holy Bible."

It took a moment to digest what Ibrahim had just said before I was able to ask the next question.

"You mean to say that you believe that the Bible, the Holy Book of the Christians and the Jews, is as much a holy book as the Koran?" I asked hesitantly.

Ibrahim laughed. "Well, if I didn't, I wouldn't be a true Muslim, now would I?"

Ibrahim now had my full attention. I sat up on the bed and crossed my legs.

"Why wouldn't you be a true Muslim if you didn't consider the Bible as a Holy Book as much as the Koran?"

"Because the Koran says the Bible is a Holy Book as much as the Koran is."

A tingle went up through my spine up to my neck. "It does?" I asked almost in a whisper.

Ibrahim lay back on his elbows on the bed. "Yes, in many places."

I was speechless. Here was a Muslim actually defending the Bible as a holy book. I had never heard of such a thing in my life. From what we saw on the news and from things that Faisal had told me, the Bible was like an enemy of Islam which needed to be rooted out and destroyed. And now Ibrahim was telling me that the Koran itself said that the Bible was as equally holy as the Koran.

"But where?" I asked.

"Well," Ibrahim began and sat up. "Do you mind if I quote from the Koran?"

"Hang on," I interrupted. "Can I use your Koran to read the passages?"

"Of course, you can," Ibrahim replied and laughed.

I slipped onto the floor and made my way to Ibrahim's collection of books. I took the Koran and brought it back to the bed, got once again under the mosquito net and then onto the mattress. This was the first time in my life that I had ever opened up a Koran and actually read its contents.

"Okay," Ibrahim began. "The first surah to make reference to the Bible is Al-Imran, the third surah, where it says in verse 4," and then Ibrahim quoted the verse in Arabic. In fact, each time he quoted a verse from the Koran, he said it first in Arabic and then translated it into English. And when he spoke in Arabic, the sound was melodious.

"Hang on, hang on," I replied nervously. "What's a surah?"

"It's like a chapter. The Koran is made up of different chapters called surahs."

I opened up at the front of the Koran. The contents page had the name "List of Surahs" and then the page number for each surah. I looked down the list and saw the word "Al-Imran" and turned to the page number where this surah started.

"I'm just looking for it." I noisily flicked through the pages till I had arrived at the correct page and then looked for the verse in question.

"Okay, got it," I then said.

"Okay," Ibrahim then said. "This verse says, 'Allah has sent down to you the Book containing the truth and fulfilling that which precedes it and He sent down the Torah and the Gospel'. In this verse, it is quite clear that Allah is telling us that He sent down the Torah and the Gospel in the same way he sent down the Book, that is, the Koran."

I wasn't sure if the Torah here in this passage only referred to the first five books of the Old Testament or the Old Testament as a whole. I knew that in Hebrew that *torah* simply meant "law" and for Jews and Christians this "law" simply referred to the first five books of the Old Testament, namely, Genesis, Exodus, Leviticus, Numbers and Deuteronomy. But somehow it also sounded as if the word "torah" in this context was a shorthand way of saying "Old Testament".

In the same way, I didn't know if what was meant by the Gospel referred to only one gospel in the New Testament, the four gospels as one unit or the entire New Testament as a whole. It seemed strange that the verse mentioned the word "gospel" in the singular when the New Testament actually contains four and we usually refer to the gospels in the plural.

As for "the Book containing the truth", it didn't come across to me as apparent that it was, in fact, the Koran being referred to. From my little understanding of how the Koran came to be, the Koran was made up of recitations that Muhammad received from the angel Gabriel but was not actually put into book form until decades after Muhammad's death. But I didn't want to interrupt Ibrahim's flow of argumentation.

"Later in the same surah," Ibrahim continued, "when the angels spoke to Mary before she gave birth to Jesus…"

Angels? I asked myself. I thought only one angel spoke to Mary, the angel Gabriel. But again, I wanted Ibrahim to keep the flow of his monologue.

"The Koran," Ibrahim continued, "says in verse 49 that the angels said to Mary, 'And Allah will teach him' - that is, Issa, - 'the Book and Wisdom and the Torah and the Injil'.

From the context, I realised that the name *Issa* was the Arabic name for "Jesus". I had to keep this in mind because whenever Ibrahim spoke of Jesus, he always used the Arabic name, Issa.

I also realised that the Arabic *Injil* was the English "gospel". I could see where this word came from. The English word "gospel" comes from the Greek "euangellios". Change the g to j and you get "euanjellios" and then shrink this down and you get "injil". So I had to keep a mental note of this: Issa is Jesus and Injil is Gospel.

"The Koran," Ibrahim went on, "later says in verse 85 of the same surah that Muslims are commanded to say, 'We believe in Allah and in that which has been revealed to us, and in that which was revealed to Abraham and Ishmael and Isaac and Jacob and the Tribes, and that which was given to Moses and Jesus and other Prophets from their Lord. We make no distinction between any of them'. In this case, what was given to Moses was the Torah and to Issa the Injil. Because this verse also says 'other Prophets', this means that there are other books by other prophets that have all been revealed by Allah to us."

Other prophets? I thought to myself. This certainly could mean the other prophets of the Old Testament both major and minor so this extended the acceptance of the Old Testament to include all the prophetic books from Isaiah to Malachi. But it could also mean other prophets from other religions, such as Zoroaster and Socrates. This then explained how Mirza Ghulam Ahmad gained some wiggle room from the Koran to develop his version of Islam to incorporate other prophets from other religions into his own.

"Then, in the following surah, Al-Nisa, in verse 137," Ibrahim continued, "the Koran commands, 'Oh you who believe! Believe in Allah and His Messenger, and in the Book which He has revealed to His Messenger, and the Book which He revealed before it. And whoever disbelieves in Allah and His angels, in His Books, and His Messengers, and the Last Day, has surely strayed far away'. The Koran commands Muslims to believe in His Books."

Ibrahim took a pause and then sat up as if to emphasise his statement.

"Notice how the Koran commands those who say they believe in Allah must believe in His Books. His Books, plural. Not one book, the Koran, but His Books, all of them. To believe in Allah's Books, we have to read them."

Ibrahim was now beginning to get worked up. There was a passion in his voice as if in frustration he was trying to get his message out to the world, not simply trying to answer my original question.

"In the next surah, Al-Ma'idah, verse 44, the Koran talks of, 'The Torah, wherein is Allah's judgement' and again in the verse that follows, Allah states emphatically, 'Surely, We sent down the Torah wherein was guidance and light'. And then, further in verse 47 the Koran says of Issa that he is one 'fulfilling that which was revealed before him in the Torah; and We gave him the Injil which contained guidance and light, fulfilling that which was revealed before it in the Torah, and a guidance and an admonition for the God-fearing'. In this surah, the Koran clearly tells us that the Torah and the Injil are a guidance and a light for all those who believe. Those who believe in the Koran must therefore believe in the Torah and the Injil as a guidance and a light. To believe that they are a guidance and a light means Muslims must use them as a guidance and a light. And to use them as a guidance and a light, Muslims must read and learn from them."

There was something magic in the passion in Ibrahim's words. What was also rather unusual was that Ibrahim, a Muslim, sounded at this moment so much like a Protestant preacher in the pulpit.

"And again," Ibrahim continued, "further in verse 111, Allah spoke to Issa and told him that, 'I taught you the Book and Wisdom and the Torah and the Injil'."

I took a pause in thought when Ibrahim stated this verse. Here, there is a mention of "the Book" as a separate entity to "the Torah and the Injil" and Allah taught each of these to Issa, that is, Jesus. Historically, this Book could not be the Koran because the Koran as far as I understood it was not revealed until about 600 years after Jesus and was revealed to Muhammad, not to Jesus. So, what was this Book? And was this Book the same as the Book mentioned earlier in Ibrahim's exegesis?

"And again," Ibrahim continued in his passion, "in the next surah, Al-Anam, verse 90, Allah tells us that it was to the Jews that Allah gave His revelations where it is written, 'It is these to whom we gave the Book and dominion and prophethood. But if these people are ungrateful for them, it matters not, for We have now entrusted them to a people who are not ungrateful for them'. If the Jews no longer follow the Torah, so the Koran says here, it no longer matters to Allah because Allah has now entrusted the Torah – Allah is talking about the Torah here – to people who are grateful for receiving the Torah, even if these people are not Jewish. And further in verse 92 it is written that Allah 'revealed the Book which Moses brought, a light and guidance for the people', and further in verse 155, 'again, We gave Moses the Book – completing the favour upon him who did good, and an explanation of all necessary things, and a guidance and a mercy – that they might believe in the meeting with their Lord'."

Once again there was this mention of the Book. But in this case, the Book in this context had to be the Torah because this Book which was given to Moses was the Torah. Ibrahim also understood this Book to be the Torah when he explained the meaning of the verse to me.

I was becoming more and more amazed at all these verses Ibrahim was reciting to me. Ibrahim didn't quote only one verse from the Koran, he was quoting verse after verse after verse. And these verses weren't ambiguous and vague, they were quite clear.

"Again," Ibrahim went on, "in the next surah, Al-Araf, verse 158, it says, 'Those who follow the Messenger, the Prophet, the Immaculate one, whom they find mentioned in the Torah and the Injil'. That the Koran tells us that we find mention of the Prophet in the Torah and the Injil means we should read the Torah and the Injil to see this.

Again, in the next surah, Al-Taubah, verse 111, it says, 'A promise that He has made incumbent on Himself in the Torah, and the Injil, and the Koran'. See how Allah equates the three books, the Torah, the Injil and the Koran equally."

This was distinctly clear. As Ibrahim mentioned, the three holy books, the Torah, the Gospels and the Koran, all three, were grouped together on equal terms. There was no mention or even hint that the one superseded the other.

The more I listened to Ibrahim, the more I questioned the entire history of the Islamic world. How is it that through all these years the Koran has clearly told believers in the Koran that the Bible is just as much the Word of God as the Koran is and yet we don't hear of Muslims upholding the Judaeo-Christian holy books with the same vehemence as the Koran?

"Again," Ibrahim continued, "in the next surah, Yunus, verse 38, it says that 'The Koran …fulfils that which is before it'. Then in Bani Isra'il 17:56 Allah says that 'to David We gave the *Zabour'* that is, the Psalms."

Okay, now I could include the Psalms among the other Old Testament books that the Koran admitted were part of the Word of God.

"Later," Ibrahim went on, "in the surah Al-Mu'minun, verse 50, Allah says that, 'We gave Moses the Book' and again in the surah Al-Furqan, verse 36, Allah says, 'We gave Moses the Book', and again in the surah Al-Qasas, verse 44, 'And We gave the Book to Moses' and again in the surah Al-Sajdah, 24, 'And We did give Moses the Book'. Allah said this four times in four different surahs. And which Book did Allah give to Moses? It was not the Koran. It was the Torah."

We? I thought to myself. If Muslims are strict monotheists, why does Allah use the first person plural in the Koran of all places to refer to Himself? Who apart from Himself is included in this "we"?

Ibrahim then paused, took a deep breath and then breathed out as if he had just completed a marathon.

"Those, therefore," Ibrahim concluded, "who believe that the Koran is a revelation from God are required to acknowledge that the Torah and the Injil are equal to the Koran. This therefore means that those who believe in the Koran are required to honour the Bible in the same way as they honour the Koran, in both reading it and observing it."

Wow! I couldn't believe what I had read in the Koran and also Ibrahim's analysis of these verses, which stood well to reason. But if these verses were so clear in stating this case, what was this about Muslims destroying churches and synagogues, and burning Bibles?

At least it was the first time that I understood how it was possible for Muslims to be united with Christians in an organisation like the Msingi wa Mungu Project. In fact, it meant that those who believe in the Koran are in fact discrediting their own holy book and working contrary to their own religion if they didn't make some connection with these other "people of the Book" or at least acknowledge and read the Book or Books that formed part of the Judaeo-Christian religion.

But this raised the question. If this is what the Koran says, weren't Muslims also bound by the commands to turn the other cheek, to do unto others as you would have them do unto you and to "love one another as I have loved you"? Blowing up synagogues and churches, and in some cases the mosques of rival denominations of the one religion, or simply killing people who just did not believe in any religion whatsoever simply did not seem like a confirmation of the teachings of the Gospel that the Koran claimed it was an extension of.

What Ibrahim had told me and the verses he had quoted which I had read personally, at least in translation from the original Arabic, was an Islam I was quite unfamiliar with. Or more to the point, it was an Islam quite unheard of. This only made me more curious about what the Koran had to say. I now really wanted to read it and know what it said within the pages.

But if Islam acknowledged the Judeao-Christian Scriptures as part of its corpus of holy literature, I was sure that this was going to cause many more problems than met the eye. After all, I remember growing up in the church and being told that the New Testament was an extension of the Old. Even in the Gospels themselves, Jesus often says that if you want to understand Jesus, you have to search Moses and the Prophets, that is, the Old Testament. And yet, some of Jesus' teachings were quite at odds with the Law of Moses.

Another teaching that would create problems would be the very nature of Jesus himself. According to the Gospels, Jesus is the only begotten son of God, and to attain eternal life, one has to believe this. Even Jesus himself in John 14:6 made it clear that "no man cometh to the Father but by me". But from what I understood of Islam, the only way to heaven was to believe that Muhammad is God's prophet. Those who believe in the Koran and therefore believe that the Koran is a revelation and an extension of the Torah and the Gospel, how do they account for this?

And who cares anyway? was my next thought. That is a holy quagmire religious people, and in this case, believers in the Koran are going to have to sort out for themselves. It didn't affect me. It certainly put the Koran under a different light than my previous understandings of it, but that was about as far as my interest in all things religious went.

This religious conversation no longer was of any interest to me. I decided to completely get away from this topic and so I changed the subject abruptly.

"So, where have you been?" I asked.

"I went for a run," Ibrahim replied and then sat back again on the bed.

"Do you always go for a run in the morning?"

"Not every morning. Whenever I can."

Ibrahim then breathed one last deep breath and then said, "And now I need to go for a bath."

Ibrahim was soon gone and I was alone in the room. I decided to get out of bed and get ready for the day. I wanted to check what the day's program was and start getting prepared for it. The program simply said that those helping out with the teaching of English were to visit a classroom, give a lesson about how to buy things at a shop and then take the students to the markets where the students would be required to carry out the interaction in English. And that was it. Nothing was said about the type of students we were getting but I simply assumed that these students no doubt already had a basic enough level of English to carry out an over-the-counter exchange. I also assumed that the other teachers who were participating had similar training and experience as I had of teaching English of this complexity.

I thought about how people buy things in Tanzania. When I started learning Swahili from books and CDs, the exchange between shop assistant and customer was a parodied argument. For example, when the shop assistant names a price, the customer might say something like, "Are you kidding? That's expensive! Hey Mister/Missus, reduce the price for me. I'm not a *Mzungu*!" The shop assistant argues back that this is not expensive and asks the customer to name a price. The customer then names a ridiculously low price and the shop assistant says something like, "Hey, customer. This is not the benevolent society! I'm running a business! I have a wife/husband and children to feed." And this goes on until both buyer and seller reach an equitable price. At first, it appears as a real out-and-out argument but people who shop like this every day consider this the normal way to shop. What appears to be an argument is not a real argument at all but just a routine way to haggle. This meant that the students had to learn how to parody this argument but using appropriate English in the process. I guessed that the other English teachers participating in the project appreciated the complexity of teaching this.

I wondered how much the students already knew. After all, there were so many things to teach just to go shopping. For example, the students had to know the names in English of all the typical items one can buy at a market. Just take one group, fruit. How many types of fruit are there: apples, bananas, pears, grapes, oranges, peaches, mangos, pawpaws and so on. And vegetables: potatoes, tomatoes, eggplant, carrots, celery, broccoli, et cetera. Then there are clothes: shirt, trousers, skirt, blouse, bra, underpants, socks, shoes and so on.

But not only did the students need to know the names of each of these items, they also needed to know how to make the noun plural. Usually to make a noun plural, we just add s, for example, one apple, many apples. However, we add es to words that end in ch, s, sh and x, which means that not only do we add a sound to the end of the word, we add an extra syllable. For example, one peach, many peaches, where *peach* has one syllable but *peaches* has two. And in some cases, the item in question is already a plural word, such as trousers, pants, shorts and scissors, that to talk about singular or plural we have to begin with *pair of*, for example, a pair of scissors, many pairs of scissors.

Then there's how to address the shop assistant. From my Swahili book, I learnt that you can say things to the shop assistant like, "Hey, Mister, these bananas, how much?" which would be considered quite rude and abrupt in English and therefore a much more congenial way to ask is "Could you tell me how much the bananas are?" Also, polite markers, such as "please" and "thank you" are essential for a successful transaction within an Anglo-Celtic context, something which is considered quite bizarre in many other cultural contexts, including Swahili speakers where words like "good" and "fine" carry the same task. I had also learnt that in Swahili when a shop assistant tries to up-sell a product and the customer doesn't want the extra item, the customer simply says "I don't like that!" which is quite a respectable and polite way to refuse the up-sell in East Africa but which comes across as extremely rude and brusque in English, where the Anglo-Celtic alternative would be something like, "Ah, no, thanks!"

I therefore assumed that what we were going to do in the classroom this particular day was a summary of all the work that the local teachers had been doing over the past several weeks to build the students up to the task.

Ibrahim accompanied me to breakfast. Breakfast was once again for me a few large avocados and a cup of coffee. I relished these avocado moments because I knew when I got back home to Sydney, I would have to pay through the nose to enjoy this luxury item that was so abundant in this land of supposedly perpetual famine.

The English teachers were to meet at reception and Gordon would then take us to the classroom where we would be teaching. Our little group consisted of six people. There were the two women from the USA, Kathy and Cindy, the two women who were agitated at the airport when I first arrived, and three young women in their late teens, two from the UK and one from Canada, with the rather bizarrely similar names of Joanna, Rohanna and Susanna, who I nicknamed, but not out loud, the Anna sisters. And then there was me.

"Wow! Six teachers!" I thought, and hoped that we would be teaching a large class where we could divide the students into large enough groups for each teacher.

While we waited for Gordon, I asked the women if they knew what we were supposed to be teaching. The women spoke with relaxed confidence. This gave me the impression that they had done this before in their home countries. They also gave the impression that teachers who had been at the Msingi wa Mungu Project before us had done the groundwork so that what we were going to do was merely a summary lesson to consolidate all that the students had learnt the previous weeks and then do an eventual dress rehearsal for the real thing later in the day when we went to the market. However, I had not as yet been filled in with the essentials of what was going to happen in the classroom. What part would I play? Kathy asked me if I had taught before and I answered in the affirmative. She then said that I simply needed to play along with the teaching. I interpreted this to mean that I would play the part of a teacher's aid, handing out handouts, writing on the board, helping the slow students find the right page in their textbooks and so on. That was fine. I had done that before as well. It also helped me to overcome my nerves because without the essential preparation, I certainly did not want to walk into a classroom completely ill-prepared.

Eventually Gordon came and led us through the compound and finally to the building. I was expecting to hear the noise of rowdy students spilling out over the window sills when we arrived but there was an eerie silence as if the teacher had beaten the students into submission.

Gordon knocked on the door and soon the door opened. The man at the door was a typical Tanzanian, very well dressed and quite an ample man with hanging cheeks and matching pot belly, almost as a boast to his opulence and status. But he welcomed us with a sincere and friendly smile. From the conversation between Gordon and this teacher, Padri Mchungakondoo, I discovered that this teacher was not only a teacher but also the pastor of the local church. Padri Mchungakondoo welcomed us into the room and soon left as if this were a change of shift.

We walked into the room. The first thing that struck me about the room was the décor. I felt as if we had stepped back into the time when my parents were at school. There was a huge chalkboard hanging at the front of the room. Chalkboards were a thing of the past even when I was at school when whiteboards and marker pens were all the rage. I wasn't sure if I knew how to write with chalk if I were called to do so. It was also evident that this chalkboard had been well used and had hung there for a long time or had hung somewhere else before being brought here, as it showed peaks and valleys in the left and right edges as if rain had trickled down its surface and now left rivulet tracks in its place.

Our audience was a group of about thirty men of what seemed like all ages, mainly middle-aged men but with three young boys who looked about twelve interspersed among them. These boys and men were seated at old styled desks with sloped desk tops which could be opened and inside all the necessary school items, namely, exercise books, textbooks and pens, could be conveniently stored. Not only did these desks reflect a past style of classroom, these desks looked as if they actually dated from this ancient past with areas of the wood chipped or ribbed with wear.

The students were wearing a variety of attire, some of them in casual wear, in T-shirt and jeans, and some in formal attire, wearing a tie, smart shirt and dressy trousers. This unusual audience looked up at us but it was difficult to ascertain what exactly they were thinking as a small group of *Mzungus* suddenly invaded their presence.

Gordon came to centre stage. He then introduced us, speaking in Swahili with a heavy English accent. Even though I couldn't speak Swahili flawlessly, I immediately recognised how different Gordon's Swahili was to a native speaker's. Gordon explained who we were, that we were here to teach these students English and to prepare them for an afternoon at the market where the students would be able to practise their English. I thought it was odd that Padri Mchungakondoo had left the classroom because I was of the impression that the whole idea was for us *Mzungus* to show the local Tanzanian teachers how we taught English as a second language in our respective *Mzungu* countries.

Once Gordon had left the room, we were left to do the teaching. Because Kathy and Cindy came across as the leaders of our teaching party, I waited on the sideline to be called up when necessary.

Cindy took centre stage and then introduced herself. "Good morning, students," she began.

"Good morning, teacher," the students all replied in unison, in a fashion reminiscent of old time schooling where the students were ultra-obedient.

"Today you are all going to the market to practise your English, aren't you?" Cindy continued. She spoke in her North American accent and with a rapidity that I myself found difficult to follow even though I speak English as my first language.

"Now, when you go to the market, you will want to buy something, right?" she asked and when she said "right?" her voice went up in the tone of a question but her head nodded with affirmation to which the students studiously imitated.

"So, when you see something you want to buy, say, for example, you want to buy a loaf of bread and a container of milk, what do you ask? You say, 'I would like a loaf of bread and a container of milk', right?" she continued, once again nodding her head on "right" as if to emphasise the certainty of the comment. All the students nodded with her.

"So, let's practise this," she continued. Cindy then grabbed a stick of chalk that was lying idly on the teacher's desk and then wrote along the chalkboard in a good teacher's neat handwriting, "I would like to buy a loaf of bread and a container of milk." She then turned back to the students.

"Okay, repeat after me: I would like to buy a loaf of bread and a container of milk," she said.

The students first stared at her and it was obvious that they had no idea what she was telling them to do. Cindy seemed to be a bit embarrassed and so Kathy came to the rescue. She walked to centre stage, raised both her arms to signal the students to imitate the sentence and said, "I would like to buy a loaf of bread and a container of milk". This had the desired effect as a few students began saying the sentence and by mid-sentence the entire class had joined in in unison.

Kathy and Cindy got the students to say the sentence again, and then got them to repeat the sentence again. The three Annas smiled in approbation and also joined in with the rest of the room as if they were chorus girls supporting two lead singers.

I just looked on in total incredulity. Were the students learning to communicate with the shop assistants at the market or to chant a mantra in devotion to two common commodities in the developed world? I then asked myself while the chanting went on, do these students actually know what a loaf of bread and a container of milk are? Is this a Tanzanian staple diet? From what I understood of Polycarp, bread in the form of white slice and milk coming in waxed-lined containers were quite foreign concepts. The time with Polycarp and my brief outing with Ibrahim indicated to me that there were other foods that formed the staple diet of Tanzania, such as ugali, maandazis, beans and fish.

But the five women chanted with beaming smiles, smiles which were reciprocated by the students and which appeared to indicate that everyone understood what was happening and all were enjoying the proceedings.

Kathy then turned to the chalkboard and wrote, "Here's five thousand shillings. And you can keep the change." She then turned around to the class and, using a double arm upward movement to indicate that she wanted the students to repeat what she had written on the board, she began the second part of the chant which the students dutifully and, from the expressions on their faces, happily imitated: Here's five thousand shillings. And you can keep the change.

After this charade, Kathy looked at Cindy and raised her eyebrows which communicated, "What else could we teach them?"

There was a momentary pause when Rohanna stepped forward.

"This is too small. Do you have one in size eight?" she suggested cheerfully.

The look on Kathy's face showed an expression of enlightenment as if Rohanna had revealed the answer to the meaning of life. Kathy then wrote this sentence on the board and then gesticulated for the audience to follow: This is too small. Do you have one in size eight?

While the audience gleefully repeated the sentences over and over again, I looked at the board and read out each sentence in my head: "I would like a loaf of bread and a container of milk. Here's five thousand shillings. And you can keep the change. This is too small. Do you have one in size eight?" Looked on in isolation, these sentences had as much meaning as a coded message in a cryptic crossword puzzle. So what did the students understand by all this? Their smiles certainly indicated that they were gaining a lot of pleasure out of the exercise but I questioned whether they were drawing any meaning out of it.

Kathy and Cindy, like the main singers in a band, with the three Anna sisters in the chorus group, once again went through all these sentences with the class. I felt that if they kept going, they would eventually put the words to music and have a number one single out on the Tanzanian pop charts. But these students were soon going to go to the markets and would have to actually communicate in English to buy something. If the students simply imitated these sentences like parrots, they were not going to achieve anything. I waited patiently for   a moment to interject and the moment arrived when there was a slight pause after repeating all these sentences for the fourth time. Kathy and Cindy looked at each other and the Anna sisters looked on in expectation. There was a slight pause as if the women were conferring about the next brilliant sentence one could say in a department store when I just stepped forward onto centre stage, turned to the room of students and asked in Swahili, "Do you understand?"

There was a sudden silence in the room, so thick you could have suffocated in it. I felt like Paul the Apostle in Jerusalem in the incident at the end of Acts 21 and the beginning of Acts 22 when Paul started speaking Hebrew, an action which stunned the Jewish authorities because they thought Paul could only speak Greek.

Suddenly, one of the students in the audience cut through the silence with the statement in Swahili, "Hey! The *Mzungu* speaks Swahili!" and this was followed with cheers of exuberance as if I had just done a back flip. I turned to look at the women and they too had faces expressing delight.

"Do you speak Swahili?" Kathy asked.

"Yeah, a bit," I said slowly and measuredly.

"Oh, that's great! Why didn't you tell us? Can you lead us in the teaching?"

Cindy and the Anna sisters looked at me with pleasing smiles as if Kathy had asked me to lead the teaching only if it pleased the court, which it evidently did. I turned back to the class and looked at the students. I had been teaching for years and knew exactly what to do.

There was a moment of silence and then I turned to address the class.

"Okay," I began and then spoke in my basic, broken Swahili. "Now, before I start, please remember that I don't speak Swahili very well. When you speak, please speak slowly because if you speak too fast, I won't understand. When I speak in English, I will speak slowly so you can understand. Okay?"

The cheers that arose in the room were as if I were the champion of a competition I had won for the students. The students were so excited that this *Mzungu* could speak Swahili but contrary to what I had told them, they spoke with a rapidity that did not enable me to understand a word they were saying.

Eventually I was able to get the class back on track to what we were teaching. I began by asking about the sentences the students had been reciting. As I had feared, the students did not understand the sentences at all. None of them knew what a loaf of bread was, and what they understood by the word "container" in "a container of milk" was the Swahili word *debe*. A *debe* is a four-litre metal container, the type of metal container used in Australia to carry petrol or the type of container olive oil comes in at the supermarket. Although someone could carry milk in a metal four-litre container, so the students mused, they couldn't understand why anyone would want to do so because no-one keeps such a large quantity of milk because it goes off too quickly. Rather, it was common for Tanzanians who lived in villages where they had no refrigeration to buy milk in powdered form in small tins.

The students then asked what *would* meant in *would like*. They were familiar with *like* and with *want* but did not know what *would like* meant. As I did not have the depth of Swahili to explain it, I simply told them that they needed to look at the two words, *would like*, as one unit, that it is a politer version of *want*. I further explained that the *would* in the phrase *would like* was a carryover of something from an ancient form of English but that it required a lengthy explanation which was not useful for them anyway.

The students then asked about the following sentences: Here's five thousand shillings. And you can keep the change. When I made it to the end of my translation, there was a sudden uproar which frightened Kathy, Cindy and the Anna sisters. I didn't understand anything within the cacophony except that I heard the word "Wazungu", which is the Swahili plural form of *Mzungu*, mentioned a few times. I signalled to the class to calm down and once I had gotten the class back to its original tranquillity, I asked what the issue was. One of the students explained that five thousand shillings might not be much money for *Mzungus* but for Tanzanians that was a lot of money. Five thousand shillings was for many a week's salary. Although the student who made this remark was rather hostile when this comment was made, I couldn't help bursting out laughing.

With this explanation, this meant that five thousand shillings may have been equivalent to about five Australian dollars when we compared shilling for dollar but the actual buying power of the shilling in the Tanzanian context was much higher. When buying some milk and bread, which in Australia would cost something in the vicinity of three to four dollars, the sentence, "Here's five thousand shillings. And you can keep the change" might be equivalent in the Australian context to saying, "Here's five dollars. And you can keep the change", hence the shop owner gets a small but nice tip. However, within the context of Tanzania, it was equivalent to going into the local corner shop in Australia to buy milk and bread, and then saying, "Here's five hundred dollars. And you can keep the change."

I then turned to Kathy, Cindy and the Anna sisters and asked if it was okay to rub out the sentences that were originally chalked onto the board. The women replied with all encouragement. I tried to dust off the words and in their place was a foggy white smear, obviously a result of an ineffectual duster and the dubious surface of an aging blackboard.

I then wrote a typical dialogue between shop assistant and customer, using as my background typical markets from many places in the world of my experience as well as those in Sydney such as Flemington Markets, where items are clearly displayed and it was only a matter of pointing to something and asking in polite English how much it was. I threw in a few exchanges where the customer disagreed with the price and haggled the shop assistant to a more acceptable price. I totally avoided the "and you can keep the change" bit seeing in the real world, the customer haggled the price down so it would be totally illogical to pay the final haggled price and then give the shop assistant extra money, let alone additional money which would bring the total sum to the original price quoted by the shop assistant. My dialogues were limited to calling any item "this" because I was familiar that at markets the item on display was clear for all to see so it was unnecessary to actually name the item. This also helped to avoid having to go through an inventory of names of objects when there wasn't time in this simple class to learn them.

When we had finished going through the explanation of the different parts of the dialogue, I divided the class into pairs where one student played the part of the shop assistant and the other the customer. I asked my five co-teachers to sit in on one of the pairs, listen to the dialogues and help the students if they got stuck or said something incorrectly. Each of the pairs struggled through the dialogues. Some were better at it than others, some having to pause and think what the next word was in the sentence whereas for others the words simply flowed uninhibited from the tongue.

We were part way through this when there was a knock at the door. Padri Mchungakondoo had arrived. It was now time to go to the markets. Padri Mchungakondoo would lead the way.

We teachers were to assemble at the entrance office and wait for the students as Padri Mchungakondoo said he needed to explain something to the students before we left. As we walked over to the entrance, my co-teachers began to comment about this morning's class.

"Michael," Kathy began, "that was very well done! Even I learnt something from that lesson! Is that how you always teach?"

I was surprised and rather put back by the compliment. My original thoughts had been that these people were embarrassed or even insulted by the way I had completely taken over the class and even overrode what they were originally teaching. However, rather than being indignant, they were thankful. This made me feel a little bit ashamed of myself about how critical I was of them.

"Ah, well, yeah," I replied. "I mean, this is what I learnt about teaching English when I did my postgraduate in the Teaching of English to Speakers of Other Languages, that is, TESOL."

"Oh, so you learnt this at university?" Cindy asked.

"Maybe *we* could learn something from you!" Kathy continued.

"But didn't you ladies go to university to learn to teach English?" I asked rather puzzled.

"No, we are volunteers at our church," Kathy replied. "When new migrants come into our city, they are welcome to drop in at the church during the week. We have set times, usually in the evening so that these migrants can come after work."

I asked the women, then, what they knew of teaching English, what they knew of English grammar, what they understood of texts both written and spoken, if they appreciated the difference between colloquial and formal language, if they knew what word stress and sentence stress were, consonant clusters, the change in meaning when using short and long sounds which change the entire meaning of a word such as "much" and "March", if they knew the science behind learning and what things enhance and what things impede memory. I even asked them if they spoke a second language. Neither of them nor the Anna sisters were familiar with any of this. They had believed that all it took to be able to teach English was simply the ability to speak it.

Kathy laughed. She agreed that the students sometimes asked tough questions that she was unable to answer. She remembered one student once asking her about the *would* in *would like* just as one of our students had asked and she was puzzled why this student bothered to ask. *Would like* is just *would like*, she thought. Didn't the student just get it? Another student had asked what the *been* meant in a sentence like *What have you been doing lately?* She also remembered a student asking the difference between *The train arrived* and *The train has arrived* when in both cases the verb is in the past tense and yet the two sentences do not have the same meaning.

"So, what did you tell the student?" I asked.

"I told the student that we say 'the train has arrived' when we are at the station and 'the train arrived' when we are not."

"And did the student understand that?"

"Well, yeah," Kathy replied, "but then he asked, 'So, when I say 'he has been to San Francisco', that means he is in San Francisco and when I say, 'he went to San Francisco', he is no longer in San Francisco?'"

"And what did you say to that?" I asked.

Kathy laughed again. "I said, 'no, it's the other way around. If he has been to San Francisco, he is no longer there, but if he went to San Francisco, he's still there'."

I wasn't sure whether to laugh or cry. I wondered if the student ever discovered the pattern or found another teacher who had a good grounding in grammar to finally give the proper explanation.

I then asked the three Anna sisters if they could explain these features of English and they confessed that they couldn't. But then they further admitted that they had come to the Msingi wa Mungu Project as volunteers just after leaving school as something they felt that God had guided them to do during their gap year.

In any case, all of us, Kathy, Cindy, the Anna sisters and I had paid to come here so it wasn't as if the Msingi wa Mungu Project was paying for teachers without any experience. But then, bringing inexperienced teachers to the field seemed like a means of bringing in a failure.

But these women wanted to know more. I was touched by their frankness and openness to their lack of knowledge and their receptiveness to new ideas. They were honest about what they didn't know and were willing not only to admit it but also to find out more. I therefore felt all the more ashamed of my condescending thoughts towards these women as they didn't consider themselves as expert teachers even though they had been offered the role through the organisation.

Eventually Padri Mchungakondoo arrived with his flock of students at the entrance and soon we were on our way to the markets.

The markets were near the centre of Moshi town so it was about an hour's walk from the Msingi wa Mungu Project. Gordon had suggested that we walk because it was good exercise and it was a way to get a feel of Moshi. Kathy, Cindy and the Annas were all in agreeance with this and so was I, even though I had already been to the town centre before with Ibrahim.

As we set off on our walk, our large group broke up into smaller groups. Three of the students came straight over to me, Jehoshaphat, Enoch and Apollo. I wanted to laugh when I heard the names of Jehoshaphat and Enoch. These were the names of two people in the Bible, but they were such old names no-one called their children these days, at least, not those born in Australia. It was like Polycarp and Jeremiah. But then, when I thought about it a little further, why is it that we consider these names now old-fashioned simply because they come from the Bible? After all, there were other personalities in the Bible, the names of whom people in the twenty-first century carry and no-one thinks these names are odd for modern people, names such as Daniel, Simon, Sarah, Ruth and Rachel. Even I carried the name Michael after one of the supposed archangels. There were even men today who bore the name of the oldest man to have ever lived according to the Bible, namely, Adam. So why couldn't a Christian, after all, name his or her child after other personalities in the Bible, such as Isaiah or Salome?

Apollo's name, however, stuck out as unusual and I thought it rather odd but also it made it sound as if he were the child of someone who was educated in western history and who was familiar with Greek mythology. However, so it turned out, Apollo was not named after the god Apollo of antiquity but after Apollo 11 when this spacecraft made its famous landing on the lunar surface in July of 1969. This meant that Apollo not only bore a name of a significant historical event but it also bore testimony to what year he was born, at least for those who knew the year in which the namesake of the spacecraft that landed on the moon occurred.

Because I had already taken a walk between the centre of Moshi and the Msingi wa Mungu Project, I was at least familiar with this small township and what appeared to be the residential area of the place. As a result, it was nothing for me to become completely absorbed in the conversation that developed between me and these three men, although it was really Jehoshaphat who did much of the talking. From his intent interest in me, I had the impression that this was the first time he had ever had direct contact with a *Mzungu* and the fact that we communicated in Swahili bore evidence of this supposition. The difficulty was that he spoke rather quickly and I had to get him to slow down to a comfortable pace until I was able to partake in this foreign exchange on an equal footing. However, because there was no way out other than to speak only in Swahili, it was amazing how quickly I was able to get up to speed with the language. I could feel whenever I spoke that my Swahili was quite sloppy and no doubt broke many of the grammatical rules that would otherwise justify this fine sounding language but Jehoshaphat was extremely enthused in obtaining information about the outside world through me that it was obvious that my lack in the language was simply overlooked as a minor trifle. Enoch and Apollo through their body language showed that they were as much intrigued and absorbed in the conversation even though they were simply a silent audience to the conversation that ensued.

The questions Jehoshaphat threw at me really brought out to me the vast difference between our lives. These men, so I soon discovered, were being trained in the Anglican Church to become priests and one of the unfortunate prerequisites for them was the mastery of English. They were brought to the Msingi wa Mungu Project, an organisation that claimed no particular affiliation to any church or any particular religion, simply because the Msingi wa Mungu Project had already gained fame as a prestigious learning institution which was funded from outside – that is, from outside the country, particularly from English-speaking countries such as the UK, Canada, the US, Australia and New Zealand. Other *Mzungu* teachers had come to the Msingi wa Mungu Project but this was the first time that a *Mzungu* had come to teach who also spoke a sufficient level of Swahili to engage in a fairly in-depth conversation.

But their questions about life in the land of the *Mzungus* revealed an overly ambitious, even esoteric and almost fictitious one. Their expectations of the country of my origin made it sound as if I had descended from heaven like a demigod or a supernatural being of some description and condescended to dwell among the mortals. Mzunguland was like the paradise of fiction, as described in the holy books, where much is gained where little effort is put in. To some extent I could agree with what they were saying. Clean water flowed freely right into our homes, food of varieties from all over the world were readily available at a reasonable cost in close proximity to our homes, it wasn't difficult to earn the money to buy a car, even if one settled with a second-hand car like I had which ran quite well with only occasional problems. And, of course, we had access to all the new electronic gadgets that became available, iPods, laptop computers, smartphones and iPads. Electronic gadgetry was inexpensive and readily available.

I did counter this comment, though. I questioned whether or not these people had adequate food. Jehoshaphat was quite an ample looking man so his access to food was obvious. I commented on the access they had to fresh food and vegetables, mangos, pawpaws, avocados and bananas which seemed to drip from trees in their plots. There was something more natural, more untainted, much tastier in the fruit and vegetables that they grew compared with the fruit and vegetables that arrived processed in cans, bottles and jars on our supermarket shelves or even those claimed to be fresh from cool rooms and specially treated because of the long haul to the marketplace from where they had been grown.

We finally made it to the market. But I was totally unprepared to see the vast amount of fresh fruit and vegetables on sale. What intrigued me the most was the special care taken to organise the fruit into geometrical arrangements especially at the stalls where they sold spherical shaped fruit and vegetables such as oranges and tomatoes. This seemed to be the only care taken in the entire market. Apart from that, it appeared that the building had ceased to have any maintenance or repair work done from the day Tanzania had obtained independence from the British. There were wooden structures throughout the building which appeared to conduct two purposes, one to separate the different stalls from each other and the other to keep the roof far up above to protect those below it.

We soon passed through to what I thought was the other end of the market but then I realised that this was simply the entrance to a part of the market which had no roof and hence was exposed to the elements. In this open air courtyard was a sea of bananas. There were bunches and bunches and bunches of green bananas. I was absolutely impressed at seeing so many. Within this courtyard there were various people scattered around amongst the bananas but I couldn't work out who were the vendors and who were the customers. I wondered if Queensland could compete against such stiff competition.

I turned to Jehoshaphat and asked him in English, "So, would you like a banana?"

Jehoshaphat turned to me with a deadpan expression on his face which illustrated that he really didn't understand what I had said. It would have required too much of an explanation to get the joke across so I just shook my head as an indication that what I said had been nothing and that Jehoshaphat need not worry about it.

We continued on into the next building. It was semidark inside. In this section of the market there seemed to be lots of grains, cereals and other forms of dry food. I saw such a variety of beans that I had never seen before. In Australia, there is a variety of beans and lentils that we can get from the market and I often go to the local Arabic or Indian shops to stock up. But here in this market, there was such a variety of beans in a wide range of sizes, shapes and colours like I had never seen before. I was particularly impressed by some beans that were of a light green colour but had a black dot in the middle, resembling a black-eyed bean but of a different colour. I was so impressed by what I saw that I wanted to buy some and take them home but I guessed I wouldn't have been able to bring them into the country because of our quarantine laws.

We wandered around but the students weren't buying anything and therefore were not practising their English. They seemed to be quite disinterested in either trying to improve their linguistic skills or making any purchases. Padri Mchungakondoo did nothing to encourage them either. This appeared more of a sightseeing trip or an excursion. And then the thought came to me: do these men have any money at their disposal to actually buy anything?

Eventually it was time for us to walk back to the Msingi wa Mungu Project. Jehoshaphat, Enoch and Apollo once again clambered around me to continue our conversation. I asked them about where they lived and what their future goals were. Because they were training to become Anglican ministers, I asked them what they thought of the Msingi wa Mungu Project and its affiliations with other non-Anglican belief systems. Jehoshaphat's answer was not very clear or at least I did not really understand what he was trying to tell me.

However, in that same conversation, and so I guess within the context of my original question, Jehoshaphat asked me about gay marriage. I wasn't fully sure that I had understood him correctly when he asked me and so got him to repeat his question much slower. He used the word *mshoga* which I had never heard before but everything else in the context of the sentence sounded as if this was what he was talking about. I rephrased the question by asking him if he meant a marriage between two men and two women and he replied in the affirmative. This meant that the word *mshoga* meant "gay" and I later learnt that it was specifically used to refer to male gays. I remembered a long time ago hearing that the Swahili words for "gay" were actually *msenge* and *basha*. This word, *mshoga*, I could only guess was a new word.

Jehoshaphat's mention of *mshogas* and my understanding of the word caused a flush in my face.

My first reaction was to take the hostile stance and show that Christianity was all lies and fundamentally flawed which is why on the argument of gay marriage Christianity should not interfere. But then the voices of all those young gay boys and young gay girls within that crowd at the Nyika during the debate came back to mind as if I could hear them calling me, "Please, sir, please. Speak out on our behalf." It was the sound of those who needed help. When people needed help, someone had to speak up for them. I needed to be courageous but also fair in my approach.

I wasn't sure at first how to approach the argument. But then the idea came to mind. Put it forward as a supposition. Propose it by saying, "Well, what if I were gay, and I wanted to marry another man, how does that bother the rest of the people in society?" Beginning with this platform was then the answer.

The only problem was that the way to form a conditional sentence in Swahili is not the same as it is in English. In English, all conditional sentences use the word "if" but it is the tense of the verbs around the "if" which determines whether the proposition one is making is real or imaginary. For example, if I said, "If this object conducts electricity, it is a metal" this is real but if I said, "If I had wings, I would fly" this is purely imaginary. It was only later when I had developed my Swahili that I discovered that Swahili has different words for "if", one for sentences which are real, the other if they are imaginary. Little did I realise at the time that I was using the "if" that expresses real situations.

I continued with the argument. What I had to say sounded ordinary and clichéd from where I had come but I guessed it was new for these people who came from a remote and isolated area of Africa. I first explained that whether we liked it or not, there were men in the world who liked women to have sex with, and some men who liked men, and there were some women who liked to have sex with men and some women who liked to have sex with other women. Why should only those men and women who like making relationships of the opposite sex only have the opportunity to create unions where the couple share their lives together and have all things common between them protected by law so that if one of the two dies the other receives the goods and benefits of the deceased partner. If I were gay, so I thought I had put it correctly in Swahili - but only found out later that I had said something like, "because I am gay" - and I had married a man, and he and I were here at the Msingi wa Mungu Project, how would we as a couple affect all the other people at the Msingi wa Mungu Project, and indeed, throughout Tanzania?

There was some silence at first. What surprised me was the lack of reaction. There was no attempt to refer to the Bible's commands against homosexuality or the condemnation of male homosexuals as it is supposedly clearly stated in the Bible. But then, Jehoshaphat made a reply.

"But I couldn't imagine walking around in Moshi town or in my village holding another man's hand as if we were a married couple."

It took a moment for me to digest what Jehoshaphat had just said. Then it occurred to me. Is this what the resistance to the legalisation of gay marriage is?

"But, Jehoshaphat," I replied after this moment of reflection, "nobody is saying that if gay marriage is legalised, this means that everyone has to marry someone of the same sex. What we are saying is that we recognise that some men don't like women and don't want to make a relationship with a woman but rather would like to make a relationship with a man. In the same way, there are some women who don't like men and would rather make a relationship with another woman. Because you can't imagine yourself walking around Moshi town holding a man's hand as if he were your husband but you feel more comfortable doing this with a woman, that's fine. No-one is condemning you for that. But just say my feelings are the opposite, that I don't feel comfortable walking around with a woman as my partner but rather feel comfortable with a man. What the gay marriage law allows is that everyone is allowed to marry whom they love and not whom society tells them they ought to love. Prohibiting gay marriage takes us back to the old time when our marriage partners were chosen for us by the society within which we live and not on the basis of the love between the two people being thus joined."

Jehoshaphat, Enoch, Apollo and I continued our walk in utter silence. I was absolutely surprised. For those on their way to enter the priesthood in the Anglican Church, I was expecting them to appeal to the myth of Adam and Eve and the not-so-impressive worn-out saying of Christians in Australia that "God made Adam and Eve, and not Adam and Steve" as their final and conclusive support that two men or two women should never be allowed to marry. Rather, there was total silence on the matter.

Suddenly we heard a noise behind us of motorbikes which broke the silence. Jehoshaphat grabbed my hand and pulled me to the side of the road to help me avoid getting run over by this sudden intrusion. This also had the effect of breaking the freeze in the conversation which then took on a completely different course.

We finally made it back to the Msingi wa Mungu Project compound again. Once we had reached the entrance, the *Mzungus* and the Tanzanians separated ways. But before we did, the three students who had shared the walk with me from the Msingi wa Mungu Project to the markets and back asked for my contact details. I was quite surprised that they wanted to maintain contact with me especially after my outright appreciation of gay marriage. In any case, I never heard from them again anyway.

There was nothing scheduled for the rest of the day. Rather, on our program, it was written that the afternoon was simply free time. Kathy, Cindy and the Annas wandered off to their respective   dormitories, conveniently away from the men's, which meant that I was now alone to wander back to where I had been sleeping for the past number of days.

When I reached the dormitory, it was quite quiet. In a way I was happy to be back in my solitude, away from the religiosity of the place and the constant reminders of the oppression I had lived under in the earlier years of my life. I could breathe a bit of freedom in my solitude even if it was only for a short time.

Once inside the dormitory, I flopped onto my bed with my back on the mattress and stared up at the ceiling. But it was such a sunny day outside. I didn't want to lie indoors, and I certainly didn't want to sleep now and then be unable to sleep during the night. It certainly would have been nice to simply sit outside under the great sunshine, lying in a park somewhere in total solitude with a good book to read.

I turned over onto my side and looked at the bookcase. Ibrahim had a series of books there. Were there any that would be particularly interesting to read? Then I thought of Ibrahim's argument about the Koran and how that the Koran claimed to be equivalent or on the same footing as the Torah and the Gospels and therefore all three, the Torah, the Gospels and the Koran should be considered by those who believe in the Koran as equal revelations from God. And yet, I had never heard before this time of Muslims openly making this claim.

Rather, what I knew of Islam and Muslims was this. Islam began with Muhammad. One day, so Muslims claim, the angel Gabriel, the same angel who had six hundred years previously told Mary the mother of Jesus that she would give birth to a baby boy even though she was a virgin, appeared to Muhammad in a cave somewhere in the middle of the desert on the outskirts of Mecca. Gabriel told Muhammad to recite everything Gabriel told him, all of which were messages directly from God, and Muhammad was then to get others to memorise these with him. Of the many things Gabriel told Muhammad to recite, those that we were familiar with were that God wanted men to grow their beards, God wanted women to cover themselves up completely when they were in public, God wanted everyone to stop drinking alcohol, God wanted everyone to stop eating meat from pigs, God wanted everyone to pray towards the city of Mecca five times a day and the way they were to do this was to kowtow in the direction of Mecca on small decorated mats, God wanted people to worship Him in buildings called mosques, God wanted people to worship

Him particularly on Friday, God wanted people to stop eating during the daylight hours during the month of Ramadan and God wanted those who believed in Him to go out on jihad and kill everyone who didn't follow the religion of Islam. So on the surface, Islam certainly did not look like a religion which was an extension of Christianity or Judaism. Islam was certainly quite different from Christianity and the teachings of "love thy neighbour as thyself" and "turn the other cheek" so central to the Christian faith.

And then there was Ibrahim. Ibrahim claimed to believe in the Koran as well as in the Torah and the Gospels. This was evident because he had all three in his possession. But also he proved quite conclusively that the Koran told him to do so. But Ibrahim was also vegetarian, something that was totally unheard of within the Islamic world. Ibrahim also drank alcohol, although I was quite familiar with those who say they believe in the Koran but then drink alcohol in the freedom they experience in Australia. Also, when Ibrahim prayed, his mode of prayer resembled more the Buddhist meditation than the traditional kowtowing we were all familiar with. The curiosity then led me to find out what exactly was written in the Koran.

I slid off the bed and wandered over to the bookshelf. I grabbed the Koran and opened it up. I had to leaf through several pages at the front which were an introduction explaining why there was a need for a new holy book and the justification of Muhammad as the prophet of God for this new age. I wasn't interested in reading this. I simply wanted to read what the Koran itself had to say. I finally reached the first chapter or "surah" as Ibrahim had called it.

The name of the first surah was *Al-Fatihah*. From my basic Arabic, I knew that the verb *fataha* meant "to open" so I surmised that *Al-Fatihah* possibly meant something like "the opening" which made sense for a first chapter of a book. It was a very short surah made up of seven small verses. But the surah didn't really say much of consequence and really didn't add to what the Bible already said about God. This surah sounded something like a psalm or even a hymn, or rather a plea. The surah ended with a petition to ask God to guide those who read this surah to follow the right path, that path being the one on which God granted His favours and not the one which attracted His wrath and led people astray. I looked up. It was quite an innocuous surah with a yearning to it. However, contrary to my understanding of the formation of the Koran, this surah seemed more of a prayer, a yearning from within rather than a proclamation from the heavens to the inhabitants on the earth. I tried to imagine the angel Gabriel telling Muhammad that this was a command from God when really it was a plea from a person's heart.

Then I thought of the Bible, especially the Psalms. The Psalms were also in a way a plea to God. How then could these be God's words? Did God tell all humanity through David how to plea to Him?

I took a glance at the Arabic script. I had only learnt a bit of Arabic from Musa, a former learner from Tevah Am. Even so, I was at least familiar with Arabic script because I had learnt Farsi with Faisal, and Farsi also uses Arabic script.

I therefore tried to sound out the letters. I started right at the beginning: bismi allahi. I recognised the second word, allahi, as being the God of the Koran, Allah. When I sounded it out again, I made the words run together and came up with "bismillahi". As soon as I had said it, I immediately heard in my head the epic song *Bohemian Rhapsody* by the 1970s pop group *Queen* and the lines that run, "Bismillah, no, we will not let him go, Let him go, bismillah".

"Oh, so *that's* what they're saying!" I said out loud to myself as I looked up in the air with satisfaction and finally realised what that part of the song actually meant. "Bismillah" so I discovered by looking at the translation meant "in the name of God". I worked this out using both the English translation on the left hand side and my knowledge of Hebrew which is a sister language of Arabic because in Hebrew the word for "in" is *be* and the word for "name" is *shem*, and therefore the Arabic *bismi* would be similar to the Hebrew *beshme*, meaning "in the name of".

I continued reading through the Arabic script and was amazed that I was able to recognise some other words, those which were similar to Hebrew. There was the word "rabi" translated as *Lord*. This word was similar to the Hebrew word "rabbi" which any reader of the English Bible would also be familiar with because the same word is used in the Gospels.

Another word I recognised in the Arabic version was "maliki", translated as *Master* which was similar to the Hebrew word "melek" meaning "king", a word that came into the English language in the name *Malcom*.

There was also the word *yom* which means "day" and hence I discovered that it was a word common to both Arabic and Hebrew. I was particularly familiar with the Hebrew word *yom* meaning "day" as it is used in the Hebrew Bible when talking about the six days of creation. This same word, *yom*, has also been used by some modern Christian sects to lead to an understanding that the six days of creation are not really six twenty-four hour days but simply six periods. This was done by explaining that the word *yom* was similar to the Greek word *aeon* which means "an age" or "a long period of time" and therefore used to help prove that when God created the world in six days, the world was in fact created in six aeons, that is, six very long unidentified periods which could then help to marry the theory of evolution into the original story of creation.

But they were the only words I recognised in the Arabic version of this surah. A familiarity of the Hebrew language and Arabic script therefore meant that if I were to put my mind to it, I could probably eventually learn to read the Koran in the original language.

I looked out the window at the beautiful sunshine and thought that I really should be spending my time outdoors and not inside this room. I helped myself to Ibrahim's Koran and simply went outside onto the front porch of our dormitory and sat with my legs dangling over the edge. There appeared to be nobody about and it was after all free time so there was no reason for me to go anywhere or do anything at this stage. The next event on our timetable for the day was to have tea and that was hours away.

I turned the pages to the next surah, *Al-Baqarah*. There was no indication of what this word meant so I assumed it was meaningless, although it sounded similar to the Hebrew word *baqar* meaning "cow" or "ox". The thought put a smile on my face that there was a surah called *The Cow* but that sounded sacrilegiously cheeky and I guessed that the word meant something more esoteric and holy. It only made me laugh later when I eventually began to dabble in Arabic to discover that *Al-Baqarah* actually does mean in Arabic "the cow".

Al-Baqarah began once again with the same opening verse as *Al-Fatihah*, namely, "In the name of God, the gracious and merciful", and then the second verse was simply three Arabic letters: alif, lam, mem. It was like saying that the second verse said A, L, M. There was no indication of what A, L, M actually meant. What, then, I thought, was helpful in this verse for the daily lives of those who believe that the Koran is the venerable Word of God?

In the next number of verses, all the way down to verse twenty-five, there was a lot of effort to convince the readers that what they were reading was the venerable truth, talking about those who say they believe but actually don't and what will happen to them. It puzzled me why so many verses were dedicated to saying "this is the truth, this is the truth, this is the truth, this is the truth, and if you don't believe it you will be tortured in hell".

When I reached verse twenty-six, I felt that I was now about to read something with substance. Here the verse says that those who believe and do good works have prepared for themselves a beautiful garden through which rivers flow. I sat up and looked across at the Msingi wa Mungu Project compound and thought about it. What, according to the Koran, is a good work? I remembered Faisal telling me about good works and people who had good hearts. That I had helped him to gain his permanent residence in Australia was viewed by him as a good work. But was suicide bombing a group of innocent people, including small children, or exploding a bomb inside a mosque of Muslims who belong to a different version of the Islamic faith even though these people are on the surface fellow-Muslims, were these later explained in the Koran as an example of a good work?

I continued reading and when I reached verse thirty-one, I realised that this was the first mention of something that I was familiar with as a Christian, the creation of humans. Verses thirty-one to thirty-four talked of a story of how God spoke to the angels and said He would create a representative on earth and then how God taught Adam the names of all the objects on the earth.

When I reached verse thirty-five, I noticed that the narrative had completely changed its focus. Whereas the first thirty-four verses talked of God in the third person, that is, "He", so that the narrative was originally being presented by someone speaking on behalf of God, assuming Gabriel, suddenly the narrative changed abruptly where the narrator was now "We". It was obvious from the context that the "We" that was narrating this part of the story was God. But it struck me as strange that God was using the first person plural, "We", and not the first person singular, "I". I thought the Koran presented a fiercely monotheistic religion, a religion where there was only one God. Who were these other people amongst the "We" whom God was talking with? However, it had such a similar ring to the first chapters of the Hebrew Bible where God also speaks in the first person plural saying things like, "Let us make man in our image, after our likeness" and later "Behold, the man is become as one of us".

I recognised in this part of the recount that the Koran taught that it was Satan, who the Koran also gives the name Iblis, who deceived the first humans. However, what was written in the Koran was not a reflection of what was actually written in the Hebrew Bible. In Genesis, there is nothing that even suggests that the snake which tempted Eve was Satan dressed up in animal clothes. The Genesis story when read honestly indicates that the snake which tempted Eve was the actual reptile that slithers along the ground today and the idea of a Satan or even of ethereal beings that fit the description of angels is completely absent from the original story in the

Torah. The Koranic version was obviously a reflection of the later interpretation forced onto the Creation Story, that the snake in the original Garden of Eden story was Satan.

I continued reading and when I reached verse forty-one, I noticed how the narrator changed from the first person plural, "We", to the first person singular, "I", and that it was still God talking. But then it reverted back to "We" in verse fifty. The continual oscillation from "We" to "I" to "We" reminded me of the days when I was an avid Christian and this was used to explain the trinity. God was both one entity and three entities at the same time. The Koran appeared to subtly imply the same thing or at least that God was both one and more than one at the same time. This struck me as very odd for a religion that was ferociously monotheistic.

When I reached verse fifty-four, I read for the first time what Ibrahim had told me about how the Koran insists that it was simply an extension or an addition to the Christian Bible, and not a replacement. After all, verse fifty-four said to remember,

> *when We gave Moses the Book and the Discrimination, that you*
> *might be rightly guided*

The only book that God gave to Moses that everyone is familiar with is the Old Testament, or at least the Pentateuch. If God gave Moses this book which was to guide His people, God who never changes, and therefore His guidebook which never changes, should be read by those who believe in Him. God then gets angry in verse eighty-six at those who only believe in part of the Pentateuch but don't believe in other parts. Then in verse eighty-eight, God is heard saying,

> *And verily, We gave Moses the Book and caused after him*
> *Messengers to follow in his footsteps; and to Jesus, son of*
> *Mary, we gave manifest Signs*

It struck me so powerfully how that the Book of Moses, the Torah, was again and again being hailed back to with regular insistence. With such strong and regular referrals to the Torah, did this mean that there were Torahs held in veneration in every mosque around the world?

The surah then continued to unfold in verse one hundred and thirty-seven where God seems to cry out with great earnestness

> *Say, 'We believe in Allah and*
> *what has been revealed to us, and*
> *what was revealed to Abraham and Ishmael,*
> *and Isaac, and Jacob*

I sat up and looked out across the compound and thought. This was similar to one of the verses Ibrahim had quoted me but now I had time to actually meditate on what it said. Those who believe in the Koran believe in all these prophets and make no distinction between them. But that's not what Muslims ever seem to say. Rather, the way Islam is perceived, those who believe in the Koran believe that only Muhammad is the prophet to believe in, as if Muhammad had eclipsed all the other prophets before him and that he has no equal. However, the Koran clearly states that those who believe in the Koran must believe in all the prophets and make no distinction between them. I read the verse again and again to make sure that I had read it clearly and there was no other way of understanding it.

I looked up again across the compound at the Msingi wa Mungu Project. This was the first place in the universe where I had seen Muslims, or at least one Muslim, actually acting according to the writings of their own holy book. Ibrahim had in his possession the Holy Bible and those who attended the Msingi wa Mungu Project were people who claimed to be in unity with both the Christians and Muslims, and even other religions.

I was twinged with a bit of anger. The images we saw on TV of those in Muslim countries fighting each other or of Muslims going on the rampage against Christians, the stories that came out about Muslim Egyptians attacking Christian Egyptians, Muslim Sudanese against Christian Sudanese, Muslim Nigerians against Christian Nigerians, these Muslims were acting against their own Holy Scriptures. And no-one was saying anything or pointing this out.

I then looked back down at the Koran and continued reading. In verse 143, the English version used the word *qiblah* and I recognised the same word in the Arabic script. However, there was no explanation as to what the word meant. However, the following verses talked about the Holy Mosque and that those who followed the Koran should turn towards this Holy Mosque. I guessed that what was being talked about was the direction in which Muslims were supposed to face when they prayed, that is, when they prayed, they should pray to Mecca. So I guessed in the context of the passage and of my general understanding of Islam, the *qiblah* described the direction of prayer towards Mecca.

I was intrigued how in verse 145 Allah, now speaking in the first person plural, that is, using "We", mentions people turning towards the heavens when they prayed, but now God was telling them that when they prayed, they were to pray to the Holy Mosque. But the problem was the matching up of the pronouns with the nouns they were apparently referring to. At the beginning of the verse, we read how "We see you turning your face" and from the context of the earlier verses, it is assumed that this "We" is referring to Allah. However, it says at the end of the verse that "Allah is not unmindful of what they do". If Allah is mentioned here in the third person, then He cannot be the "We" of the earlier portion of the verse. At least in English it doesn't work this way.

I found this verse rather bizarre. God dwelt in the heavens, at least this is what the Jews and Christians believe and indeed those of most if not all other religious persuasions. I guessed that those who believed the Koran also believed that God dwelt in the heavens. Why, then, did God want believers in the Koran to pray to the Holy Mosque? To me, it was like saying to my learners one day, "You know, I notice when you come and ask me a question, you look me in the face. Well, in the future, when you want to ask me a question, don't look me in the face but rather stand facing in the direction of where my house is located."

The next thing to go through my head was the word "mosque". For some reason, it suddenly occurred to me that if Islam was an extension of Judaism and Christianity, why did Muslims suddenly come up with a new word to describe the building in which they worshipped? The original building according to all three Abrahamic faiths where the devotees were to worship was called the Temple. This Temple was situated in Jerusalem but the Temple was completely destroyed in 70 AD and only the Wailing Wall remains as a remnant of this holy building. The present day building in which Jews gather to worship is called a synagogue and I knew that this word came from the Greek *syn* meaning "together" and the Greek *agein* meaning "to bring", that is, a synagogue is a building which "brings together" the Jews. The synagogue was not instituted by Yahweh in the Law of Moses but developed around the time of the Diaspora when many Jews were taken well away from their homeland to dwell in countries far flung from the original centre of worship. Jews who lived far from the land of Israel still needed to keep in contact and so in the townships where they had settled down, they established buildings where those of common faith and heritage could come together and still practise their religion, even though in a fragmented way to how the Law of Moses originally required it.

The word *synagogue* does not make its appearance in the Old Testament. Rather the first mention of the word in the Judaeo-Christian holy books is in the New Testament. According to the Acts of the Apostles, the Christians continued the practice of gathering together in a building in the same way as the Jews, first actually coming together in the synagogues themselves, and then, when Gentiles were welcomed to the faith and the Christian religion slowly but surely moved away from its Jewish source, a new name was given to the building of worship. In English, this word is *church* coming in a roundabout way from the Greek *kuriakos*, a contraction of the Greek *kurios*, "Lord", and *oikos*, "house", hence, "house of the Lord".

So, what about *mosque*? Why did Muslims call their holy building a mosque? I did eventually find out. It actually comes from the Arabic *sajada* meaning "to prostrate". In Arabic, the word "mosque" is actually *masjid* the *ma* prefix turning the verb *sajada* into a noun, hence a *masjid* is a "prostrating" and by extension "a place of prostrating". The word then came to English through the French rendition of the word, namely, *mosquée*.

I read in verse 174 that it says that believers in the Koran were not to eat blood, the flesh of pigs or anything on which the name of God had not been invoked. Except for the forbiddance of pig meat, I saw a similarity with the Christian injunction, where Christians are told in Acts 15:29 that they are forbidden to eat blood.

Verse 175 intrigued me where it said

> *Those who conceal that which Allah has sent down of the Book…Allah will not speak to them on the Day of Resurrection, nor purify them. And for them is a grievous punishment*

All that I had read thus far and what Ibrahim had told me about how the Koran is a revelation equal to the Torah and the Gospel, all these were what Allah had sent down in the Book. However, the Bible was really 66 books and the Koran was really 114 surahs although I wasn't sure if this could be interpreted as 114 books or simply 114 chapters of one book. Even so, whenever the Koran mentioned "the Book", sometimes it meant the Torah, sometimes the Gospels, and sometimes it implied the Koran. Which book was this verse referring to? However, from this constant use of the singular "book" to refer to all the holy books, I had the impression that the Koran collectively called all holy literature all one book. This did make some sense to me because I was familiar with how the Christians call all 66 books of the Bible one book.

With this understanding, I wondered how believers in the Koran understood this verse. Many of those who believed that the Koran was the Word of God had actually been concealing what Allah had sent down in the Book, especially what was sent down to Moses and Jesus, for a very long time. Weren't Muslims therefore afraid of the grievous punishment that awaited them in the next life for doing so?

I then discovered the origin of the fast of Ramadan. This was found in verses 184 to 188. But it was verse 188 which intrigued me where it said

> *Eat and drink until the white thread*
> *becomes distinct to you from the*
> *black thread of the dawn.*
> *Then complete the fast till nightfall…*
> *thus does Allah make His commandments clear*
> *to men that they may become secure against evil.*

It was very clear to me that the fast at Ramadan required no eating and drinking during the daylight hours. The explanation of the timing when the fasting should begin was very clear, when "the white thread becomes distinct to you from the black thread". There was nothing which said something to the effect of, "however, if you live in the far northern or far southern latitudes, it is understood that in summer, the daylight hours are extremely long and in some places in the extreme north and extreme south, there is no night at all for many months, so in these cases, simply look at your watch and fast for 12 hours and then eat for 12 hours." Rather, as soon as you could distinguish between a white and black thread, you had to stop eating. I discovered later that I was not the first to actually ponder on this thought and no doubt many a poor inhabitant of countries which enforce the Koran have difficulty dealing with this verse when they think about countries much closer to the two poles. In fact, in one Iranian movie, *Marmulak*, a young novice asks innocently an imam what a Muslim is supposed to do during the month of Ramadan if he finds himself at the North Pole. The only answer that the imam gives is that the young novice is not about to take a trip to the North Pole so why is he bothering with the question.

I continued reading. There were times when certain things that were mentioned earlier in the surah were once again repeated, such as you must pray regularly and do good works. I didn't really understand why it needed to be repeated.

There was then a long section about what a man does if he wants to divorce his wife. I thought this was quite curious because Jesus also talks about divorce. But the conclusion Jesus makes was quite different to what was written here in *Al-Baqarah*, a surah which was supposed to be a summary and an extension of the Torah and the Gospel. Jesus said that once a man and his wife marry, they were married for life and divorce was almost impossible. However, in *Al-Baqarah*, marriage and divorce seemed as sterile as a business contract for the purchase of a good or service.

In verse 247, the surah tells us to remember what the chiefs of the Children of Israel said to their prophets, that they wanted a king to rule over them. I was familiar with this story in the book of I Samuel. However, what followed was a story about someone called Talut and then another called Jalut and that David killed Jalut. There was nothing in the account in *Al-Baqarah* that I was familiar with. I wondered at first if Talut was the Arabic version of King Saul, but then there was this Jalut whom David killed and I wondered if this was the Arabic version of Goliath. Even if it were, I could not quite match up the story. The story in *Al-Baqarah* was quite vague and I wondered how anybody listening to this surah at the time could seriously understand what the story was about.

Then I read verse 254. This verse said

> *These Messengers have We exalted,*
> *some of them above others: among*
> *them there are those to whom Allah spoke;*
> *and some of them He exalted*
> *by degrees of rank.*

The difficulty was trying to work out who was talking. At first, I assumed as earlier in the surah that the "We" was God but then the verse mentions Allah in the third person using the pronoun "He". What struck me about this verse was its total contradiction of verse 137 which said

> *Say, 'We believe in Allah*
> *and what has been revealed to us, and*
> *what was revealed to Abraham and Ishmael,*
> *and Isaac, and Jacob and his children,*
> *and what was given to Moses and Jesus, and what*
> *was given to all other Prophets from their Lord.*
> *We make no difference between them'*

I looked up across the Msingi wa Mungu Project compound and thought about these verses. One verse says that all the prophets are equal and those who believe in the Koran are not to make a distinction between them. But then later in the same surah, the Koran says that there is a sort of hierarchy of messengers or prophets, where some are exalted above others. Those who believe the Koran is a revelation from God, what are they supposed to believe about the prophets? Are they to make a distinction or not?

I continued to the end of *Al-Baqarah*. There was something about giving alms, how lending with interest was evil and what you're supposed to do when you lend money. The surah then ended with a few comments that had been repeated earlier, such as Allah makes no distinction between the prophets.

I looked up again and shook my head to help my eyes readjust to the afternoon. Reading this surah was quite heavy going but I could not say that it was invigorating. It was certainly enlightening because it was my first window into the actual belief of this religion.

The difficulty of the surah was the way it shifted from one subject to another with no particular connection. And the use of pronouns were not clear as God was referred to as "He", "We" and "I" throughout, but also the "We" sometimes in context referred not to God but to an unknown group who spoke about God.

I turned to the next surah, *Al-Imran*. Once again, the surah began with *bismillah* which once again caused *Bohemiam Rhapsody* to flow through my head. When I got to verse 4, I read where it said

> *He has sent down to thee the Book*
> *containing the truth and fulfilling*
> *that which precedes it;*
> *and He sent down the Torah and the Gospel*
> *before this, as a guidance to the people*

It struck me so powerfully. It was quite clear. The Koran was sent down in the same way as the Torah and the Gospel. I could not understand how anyone could take this in any other way than that the Torah, the Gospel and the Koran are all equal. Those who believe the Koran by default believe the Torah and the Gospel. Those who criticise the Torah and the Gospel criticise the Koran which supports and speaks highly of the Torah and the Gospel as equal to the Koran.

This made me feel so angry. Why is it that those who believe the Koran do not read and keep the Torah and Gospel as part of their Holy Writ? If I were to believe the Koran were a holy book, not only would I need to read and believe the Koran, I would be forced into believing that I must read the Torah and the Gospel as well. And yet, I have never heard of anyone who says that the Koran is the holy book of God making this claim when the Koran was so clear in saying so. Except from Ibrahim. There was nothing in what I had read, and I would discover that there is nothing at all in the entire Koran which suggests that the Koran supersedes the Bible nor is in anyway better than the Bible. According to the Koran, the

Judaeo-Christian Bible and the Koran are all three equal books. Those who honour the Koran, honour the Judaeo-Christian scriptures. Those who despise and criticise the Judaeo-Christian scriptures, despise and criticise the Koran which compares itself with these scriptures.

Just at that moment, I looked up and could see Ibrahim coming in my direction. The sight of him caused to bubble up inside me the anger I had against the book that I was holding and the people who were upholding it. I wanted to get up quickly and return the book to Ibrahim's shelf before Ibrahim had a chance to know that I had invaded his privacy by helping myself to one of his books but Ibrahim was much too close now for me to pretend that I hadn't seen him. If I got up now, it would appear that I didn't want to talk to Ibrahim and that would come across as very rude.

When Ibrahim finally made it to the landing, he stopped and greeted me. He then looked down at the book that I was holding and trying to conceal. This seemed to make it more obvious that I had something in my hand to hide from him.

"You're doing some reading I see," Ibrahim commented with a broad smile.

I felt as if I had been caught out in the act of doing something wrong. I lifted the book out from beneath my knees.

"Yeah, sorry, Ibrahim," I confessed. "I know I should've asked but I just wanted to have a look."

Ibrahim looked at me with a free expression on his face.

"I told you before that you're most welcome to any of my books, Bwana Michael," Ibrahim replied.

"It's just," I continued, "that I have never read the Koran before and I just wanted to read it in more detail. What you told me earlier today just increased my curiosity and seeing I had nothing else to do, I decided to read it."

I was holding the Koran in both hands, my left hand nursing the spine of the book with the rest of the book closed around the index finger of my right hand which I was using to mark the page I had just been reading. With that, Ibrahim took both his hands and placed them around mine. There was a tenderness in which he held my hands and a sparkle in his eyes.

"You can keep this book," he replied. "It's a gift from me. You can have it."

I was speechless for a moment as the tenderness of the touch of his hands, the penetrating glance of his eyes and his broad smile penetrated to the depths of my heart. Time came to a standstill as I looked Ibrahim in the eyes and saw what appeared to be an abundance of kindness and love. There was a long moment of stillness as we looked each other squarely in the eyes. For some reason, I had the sudden impulse to reach out and kiss him on the lips. But eventually the raw reality of the information I had been reading in the book between our hands and the reality of what those who believe this book to be the venerable Word of God do in the name of this book once again overwhelmed me and I then moved my hands back towards Ibrahim.

"That's nice of you, Ibrahim," I replied. "But that's okay. I can't take something that's yours."

Ibrahim pushed back the book wrapped in four hands, two black and two white, towards my body gently and purposefully.

"I would like you to have it. It would give me pleasure to give it to you."

There was a momentary pause. What did he mean by this? There was something loving and gentle in what he said. But what did he want to do? Make me believe that this book is the divine message from God?

The silence was broken by a number of labourers passing by, a hoe slung over one shoulder, in dusty shirts with evidence of holes from overwear and gumboots caked with soil. The labourers threw a greeting at us as they passed by and Ibrahim replied in return with a few salutary remarks. Once they had passed us, Ibrahim looked up in the sky.

"Dinner is going to be ready soon. Do you want to go and have a bath now?"

Ibrahim then got up and we made our way to the amenities to wash off another day's efforts.

The rest of my time at the Msingi wa Mungu is a bit of a blur. Obviously nothing controversial or that evoked my emotions actually occurred. I began to get on well with Cindy, Kathy and the Anna sisters the rest of the time I was there. The more I got to know them, the more ashamed I felt of myself for being so critical of them that first day in the classroom. They were receptive to new teaching methods as much as the local teachers were but they also came up with great ideas themselves that I knew I could use in my teaching.

But because I was scared of them finding out my true identity, at the end of the day I made sure I left them before our work conversations could turn into social ones. We all knew which countries we all came from but I didn't know anything else about them and I didn't want to ask because I didn't want them to ask anything about me.

It was a bit more difficult with Ibrahim. Ibrahim and I shared the same room so at the end of the evening, in the privacy of our dormitory, there was always an hour or so after coming back from dinner and Devotion before we went to sleep. Ibrahim usually went to sleep not long after we got back to the dormitory only because on some mornings early in the morning he went for a run. This made for one conversational piece because Ibrahim asked me at one stage if I did anything sporty. I said that I actually was a swimmer and back home I went to the swimming pool almost every day all year round. However, I was aware that there would be no swimming pools at the Msingi wa Mungu Project so I just thought I would take a rest from physical exercise for this short time. What was quite amazing about Ibrahim's jogging and my swimming was that our ideas about fitness and the body were similar. My doctor had told me that once I was over forty it was important that I maintained a healthy regime which included some regular sporting activity. I had already been a swimmer from my teenage years so for me it was a matter of simply continuing the exercise. I explained to Ibrahim that our bodies were like machines and if we didn't keep them in good order, they failed us. Ibrahim didn't quite like the idea that I compared the human body to a lifeless machine but he did agree with the concept. However, as he always did, he threw a religious slant on the topic. He told me that he thought it was strange that religious people spent a lot of money to keep churches, mosques, synagogues, temples and all other religious buildings looking fresh and new but they did not do the same to their own bodies. Our bodies, so he explained, were the true temples of God. God created our bodies whereas people created the buildings of worship. So it was of more honour to God for us to keep in good condition the body that God had created for us and not the buildings we created for Him. Ibrahim viewed it almost as a sin when God's people could not be of assistance to the poor and needy all because their own bodies failed them simply out of neglect of the maintenance of their own bodies. This then explained his somewhat athletic physique. I thought everything he had to say about exercise and God was quite quaint and really it was quite insightful but I had never heard this coming from a Muslim before. Or any religious person for that matter. Faraj was a Muslim and he did weight-lifting but I didn't think he did weight-lifting because of his religion. Was I going to read something to this effect in the Koran?

Another evening Ibrahim asked me about living in Sydney again. This was a regular theme that Ibrahim pursued but I could not work out why. In any case, I gave him a broad outline of the place and tried to explain to him my daily routine, what the weather was like, typical distractions and nice places to visit. Ibrahim then asked me what it was like to teach secondary school students as he had once applied to participate in an exchange program with a teacher from one of the International Schools in Sydney although he believed after the long silence his application had not been successful. I replied that I wasn't totally familiar with the students at International Schools in Sydney but I did know that secondary school students in Australia in general were not nice creatures to teach. I had done a short stint of teaching in a high school and vowed and declared that I would never do it again. This must have completely dissuaded Ibrahim from pursuing this and he told me that obviously God knew what He was doing.

I wanted to tell Ibrahim at one stage that I was not religious at all. However, I just couldn't. What I eventually did was find a sort of middle ground. I admitted that I was not a Christian but rather a Socratist. That Ibrahim was aware of Socrates indicated that Ibrahim had quite a solid education. It made sense though because Ibrahim had said that he was a teacher of history and so he had to be familiar with ancient Greece especially when teaching in an International School which had a European basis. There was a bit of a debate about whether Socrates was simply a philosopher or it could be argued that he was a prophet. I argued for the latter and explained what I had read in the dialogues of Plato about Socrates having momentary trances and then later confessing that he had been inspired by God. What intrigued me about Ibrahim was that he listened. He didn't bombastically object and state that I was wrong but rather admitted that he wasn't aware of where it was written in the dialogues although he didn't really believe that Socrates was a prophet, at least not in the conventional religious sense. However, he also admitted, which was a real plus for him, that he could not further comment on what I had told him until he had reread Plato's dialogues. I was quite impressed when he mentioned that he had actually read Plato's dialogues in the first place. I didn't know many people who had actually done so.

The more I got to know Ibrahim, the more I realised there were quite nice elements about him. Although much of what he did and believed involved God, if I took God out of the equation, Ibrahim's views of life, the world, the people in it and our responsibility towards those people were very much the same as mine.

But the religiosity did annoy me somewhat. It made me feel uncomfortable only because of the dreadful experience I went through growing up in a religious home and the terrible consequences I had to face when my parents first found out that the religion no longer made any sense to me and later found out I was gay. This was often repeated during the course of my life when I met other religious people and their reactions only reinforced my initial feelings towards religious people in general. And one only had to listen to the news to be further aware of the destruction of the planet and the abuse of human rights at the hands of the religious. Ibrahim was nice and the people at the Msingi wa Mungu Project were nice but it was a niceness with strings attached.

In any case, the only reason I had come to the Msingi wa Mungu Project was to complete a mission and not participate in the project at all. The reason why I had come here made me suddenly realise how much I missed Polycarp. Each day slowly passed and brought me closer to the time I could return and see him. It was true that I had no good news for him. But now that Polycarp had no-one left in the world and this reality had been confirmed, I made a quiet promise that I would look after Polycarp, get him on his feet and help him settle within Australian society. Then when the time came that he was well established, my mission would be complete and I would be ready for the next person to help and look after. I noticed of all the people I had tried to help in the past, Polycarp had needed the most help. This was because he had come to Australia at such a young age and almost completely alone.

I saw this as my life's mission, the reason why I was here on the planet. In some ways, my objectives were similar to those endorsed by the Msingi wa Mungu Project. But my objectives came with no strings attached. Those I helped did not have to ascribe to my religion or lack of religion to get further help. All that concerned me was to get them back on their feet.

It was now the second-last night at the project. As we made our way out of our dormitory to dinner, the sun had just set and we had entered a sort of twilight. There was a certain relief and eager anticipation on my part that in twenty-four hours from this time, it would be my last night at this place and the following morning I could return to my home of freedom and civility, escaping the oppression of the religion and my inability to live openly who I was. Another way of putting it although not so elegantly was that I couldn't wait to return to Australia to give open expression to my hormonal urges.

Ibrahim managed to find a space for both him and me to sit together at one of the tables. At our table sat Kathy and Cindy as well as a number of familiar faces, the names of whom I have now forgotten. I must have been in a good mood because I was chattier than ever. We had finished our second last dinner that I would share with these people forever. Then it was time for Devotion and then we could go to bed

As it had been for each previous night, Gordon led us in prayer, the prayer being made out to a nameless God, a universal prayer that Jews, Christians, Muslims and those of any religious persuasion could ascribe to. Gordon then chose to read from the Gospel of Matthew, chapter twenty-five, verses thirty-one to forty-six. I was familiar with this story, the so-called story of The Sheep and the Goats. Jesus tells his disciples what will happen on Judgement Day, that he will separate the righteous from the unrighteous in the same way as a shepherd separates the sheep from the goats. The sheep, that is, the righteous, will go to his right and the goats, the unrighteous, to his left.

Because I was familiar with the story, I allowed my mind to wander off for a moment as Gordon went on to explain the details of the parable. While he digressed into a long explanation, I pondered on the view of sheep and goats according to the Gospels. I wondered what those in the animal kingdom would have thought if they were able to read the Bible. Sheep always were portrayed as innocent, righteous and never doing anything wrong. Sheep first get their rise to popularity with King David who exonerated sheep in the well-known twenty-third Psalm where he portrayed Yahweh as his shepherd and himself as a sheep. King David, having first been a shepherd, seems to have risen sheep to stardom because of his own association with these beasts, and forever after sheep have always been viewed in a favourable light. Later, Isaiah prophesied how Yahweh's servant would be led like a lamb – a baby sheep – to the slaughter, a prophecy which the New Testament itself acknowledges as a reference to the coming Jesus Christ. Jesus himself, according to John the Baptist, is the Lamb of God, and even in the Revelation, the book prophesying the end times, the sheep, in its infantile form, is hailed in honour when the Beast makes war against the Lamb. Because of this continual reference to sheep, this meant that wherever Christianity was preached in the world, sheep had to be introduced into that country for otherwise much of the message of the Bible would have been incomprehensible. I thought about Australia before the arrival of the British. If missionaries had gone to Australia to convert the Aboriginals before the British had established themselves there, how would these missionaries have explained all these references to sheep when there were no such animals that resembled sheep on this vast continent?

The goats, by contrast, would no doubt be very cheesed off to read that they were considered the unrighteous only because they had been born goats. They were born with a physical attribute that they had no control over but were condemned regardless as a result. I could well empathise with the goats' discontent. What was so innocent about sheep anyway? Why were they the stars of the animal kingdom? From my experience of farm animals, sheep were actually the dumbest.

"Now, listen carefully to what Jesus is saying in this story," Gordon continued and somehow this signal brought me out of my thoughts. "This is not a parable. It is not a metaphor. For those teachers of English," and when he said this, Gordon looked across the room at us English teachers, at me, and Kathy and Cindy and the Annas in a way that indicated that we ought to be well aware of this particular technique. "This is a simile. Jesus simply says that he will separate everyone from all nations into two groups, the righteous and unrighteous, *like* a shepherd separates the sheep from the goats."

Gordon paused here as if he wanted all of us to reflect back on our high school English where we had to analyse poems and find the poetic techniques used in them.

"But what made the two groups different?" Gordon then continued. "Did Jesus say to the righteous, 'Come, inherit the kingdom prepared for you, because you went to the synagogue every Sabbath or to church every Sunday or went to the mosque every Friday and never missed a day, or you observed every Ramadan faithfully and never ate or drank during the daylight hours, you read the Torah, the Gospels and the Koran regularly, or you studied the Torah and the Talmud regularly or went to Bible Study every Friday night and never missed it or to Koranic school and memorised the Koran completely, or you never drank alcohol, never ate pork, or you wore something on your head when you prayed or prophesied or covered your face when you were in the company of a man'?"

Gordon paused for a moment to let it sink in. He was making a poignant point and it was obvious that he wanted everyone to understand it.

"No," Gordon then continued, getting us out of the suspense. "The only thing that separated the sheep from the goats was what the sheep and goats did and didn't do to others, 'Inasmuch as ye have done it unto one of the least of these my brethren, ye have done it unto me'. Jesus said that for all of us, for you and me, to make it into paradise, our lives should be dedicated to feeding those who are hungry, giving those who are thirsty something to drink, giving clothes to those who have nothing to wear, looking after the sick and visiting those who have been imprisoned."

There was once again a pause. Gordon was obviously using these pauses to really make us think.

"Notice how Jesus says in this parable that our entrance into paradise is based on the good things we do for others. There is nothing in what Jesus said about how many people we converted or forced to convert to the religion, how well we knew what was written in the Holy Books, how many times we prayed, how many times we fasted, how many times we did things that really are only external trimmings of the religion and really are secondary to how we live our lives for others, how we help others, what we do for others."

There was something absolutely beautiful and deep in what Gordon said. It was the first time in the entire time I had been here that I was interested in what he had to say during the Devotion.

Gordon went on. He referenced this parable with what Jesus said in the Sermon on the Mount in Matthew chapter seven where there would be those on Judgement Day who would question God by saying, "Lord, Lord, have we not prophesied in thy name? and in thy name have cast out devils? And in thy name done many wonderful works?" God, however, will tell them quite literally to "go to hell" because they did not keep God's commandments. And God's commandments, those He wants us to keep and ensure that we enter paradise, are the way we look after other people and get people out of their distress.

I wondered about other verses in the Bible which talked about the Day of Judgement. I later looked up what it said in Revelation 20:12 how John the Revelator saw all those who had died, "small and great stand before God" and how everyone was judged "according to their works". In reference to Matthew twenty-five and the story of the Sheep and the Goats, those works were how those people treated other people in their distress.

While Gordon kept talking, I pondered on everything I had learnt as a child about Christianity. However, I could never remember once in all the years I had been to church and all the times I had gone to Bible Study anyone saying anything like this. My whole Christian life was one of striving to read the entire Bible and then trying to follow every commandment, and usually the unusual and least practical ones, to the nth degree. The way the Bible and Christianity were fed to me during my growing up was of a religion where if you falter in one little thing, that was it, your entire salvation would be destroyed. As a result, Ruth, a school friend of mine, was originally going to hell because she believed in the Catholic Church, prayed to Mary, did the rosary, took the Eucharist and confessed her sins to the priest. A Jewish friend of mine from university, Joseph, was going to hell because he did not accept that Jesus was the Messiah. Rosemary, a friend from my local church, was going to hell because she believed Joseph Smith was a prophet, read the Book of Mormon, abstained from alcohol and caffeinated drinks and was baptized for those who had died. But in these stories of the Judgement Day, that's not what counted. What counted was how you treated the poor, the sick, the imprisoned and anyone who was down and out or treated unfairly.

I was particularly intrigued by the part where Jesus had said that he had been in prison and the righteous had visited him. What was Jesus in prison for? As we learn from the story, it is not Jesus *per se* but the "least of these my brethren". What were these people in prison for? Why did people go to prison? Jesus did not say that these people were innocent of the crimes they were accused of and forced into prison wrongly accused. So, these "least of these my brethren" must have been among other things thieves, rapists and murderers. Jesus did not endorse the crimes that they were in prison for, simply that the righteous went and visited them.

Gordon then made an end of his portion of speaking and then looked towards Ibrahim for him to speak. Ibrahim then wriggled out of the seat he was in next to me and made his way next to Gordon. Ibrahim thanked Gordon and reiterated in summary form everything that Gordon had to say. Ibrahim then picked up a Koran lying on a table close to him, obviously not the one that he had given me earlier. He then began.

"In the same way as it says so in the Injil, so it also says in the Koran. As it says in the second surah, in *Al-Baqarah* verse one hundred and seventy-eight.

It is not righteousness that you turn your faces to the East or the West, but truly righteous is he who believes in Allah and the Last Day and the angels and the Book and the Prophets, and spends his money for love of Him, on the kindred and the orphans and the needy and the wayfarer and those who ask for charity, and for ransoming the captives; and who observes Prayer and pays the Zakat; and those who fulfil their promise when they have made one, and the patient in poverty and affliction and the steadfast in time of war; it is these who have proved truthful.

Yes, we are called to believe in Allah and the Last Judgement, to believe in all Revealed Books and in all the Prophets. But believing is only something that occurs in our minds and is something between us and Allah. But as Allah said through Issa and Muhammad, it is what we do for other people which is the most important. Allah did not tell us through Muhammad that we should show our love to Allah by only spending money on the kindred, that is, fellow-believers of the Koran, but also on orphans, the needy, the wayfarer, those who ask for charity and for freeing those who were captives and made slaves. Allah through Muhammad did not say that we must only do good to orphans, the poor, the needy, the traveller and for the freeing of prisoners only if they are Muslim, or only Shi'ite Muslim or Sunni Muslim or Ahmadiyya Muslim or Wahabbi Muslim. Allah doesn't even say to do it only to those who are believers. The call to do good is a necessity to all people irrespective of their beliefs."

Ibrahim paused just like Gordon had as if both had rehearsed this speech especially with these pregnant pauses to make us think. But the message touched me right to the heart. But I could not remember reading this verse in the second surah. There was so much in *Al-Baqarah* that dazzled and confused me about what the Koran was trying to say that I could not remember this verse being there. But there it was. But it also made Ibrahim look even more beautiful, much more angelic than I had ever noticed him before.

"And notice," Ibrahim continued, "that Allah, through Muhammad, calls us to believe the Book. Although Allah mentioned 'the Book' singular, he meant all revealed Scripture. And all revealed Scripture contains the same message. Even Plato records Socrates' words, words Socrates received from Allah, about Judgement Day."

When Ibrahim mentioned Socrates, I felt once again a tingle right through my body. Ibrahim was looking directly at me and I knew he was deliberately making reference to Socrates as he had heard me say before that I was a Socratist. He then had my full attention. Ibrahim looked directly at me as if a message from God had gone through him to me to tell me something and to ensure that I was listening to His message. Once he was satisfied that my eyes were on him and therefore I was completely listening, he continued his speech with an overall glance at all present to show that he once again was addressing the entire audience.

"In Plato's Republic, Part X, Socrates tells the story of a man called Er who dies and witnesses Judgement Day. Like the prophet Issa says in the Injil, Socrates explained that all those who die will face the judges, and the righteous and the unrighteous will be separated, the righteous on the right and the unrighteous on the left. And how does Socrates describe those who are righteous and those who are unrighteous? The unrighteous are those who did bad things to other people, those who killed others, maimed others or enslaved others. The righteous, however, were those who had shown kindness to all people, to their parents and to Allah."

Once again, a tingle of excitement ran up my spine, into my fingers and throughout my entire body. What were these wonderful words that Ibrahim was advocating and supporting from what he called the Revealed Books, not just the Koran, but from the Bible and now the Dialogues of Plato? And Ibrahim was emphatic, as it was in the Koran, that those who believe in the Koran do not only believe in one revealed book but in many, in particular the Torah and the Gospels.

I reflected on Ibrahim's reference to Plato's *Republic*. I had read this dialogue before but could not remember this particular part of the story of Er but decided to read it later when I had an opportunity. When I did read it again later, I was amazed at the uncanny similarity between the story of Er and the parable from Matthew 25.

Ibrahim finally finished his preaching and all those in the room gave out an emphatic Amen which signalled Gordon to close this Devotion in prayer and allow us to return to our dormitories to sleep. Once said, everyone slowly got up, made their way out the door and into the African night.

Once out of the house and on the earth beneath us, Ibrahim and I made our way back to our dormitory. Ibrahim's speech moved me and I was filled with an overwhelming feeling of love and acceptance because of it. It made me view Ibrahim in quite a different light, dragging out quite forcefully feelings for Ibrahim that had been lying buried and veiled because of the assumptions of the religion that he was said to hold. Once we were about halfway to our dormitory and fully enwrapped in the darkness, I took the opportunity of the privacy to express my thoughts about the wonderful words he had to say.

"Ibrahim," I began. I meant for us to continue walking as I spoke but for some reason, Ibrahim decided to stop in answer to the call of his name.

"I…I didn't mean for you to stop," I said. "But I just wanted to say, I really enjoyed what you had to say tonight."

I paused. Then I continued.

"I know you mentioned Socrates, and you mentioned him because of me. That was the first time I have ever heard any religious organisation appreciate the words of Socrates. But your words were, what can I say? They were beautiful. I just wanted to say thank you."

In the semi-darkness, I perceived a smile from Ibrahim. His eyes and teeth were the only features which lit up in the otherwise darkness of the area. Ibrahim took my hand and gave me a small tug. This was the signal for us to continue on to the dormitory.

"Yes," he said, almost imperceptibly, "I mentioned Socrates specifically for you."

Once again, that characteristic shiver went up my spine, that feeling of excitement.

It wasn't long before we had reached the spotlight of our dormitory where everything was well-lit. We climbed up the small set of stairs that led to the landing and then into the building which led to our dormitory.

Once inside the dormitory, we both began to get ready for bed. As had been customary for me, I stripped down to a T-shirt and boxer shorts before slipping under the mosquito net and then under the single sheet under which my body received protection from what was not really a very cold night. Ibrahim stripped down to simply a pair of shorts, once again exposing the rest of his manhood for my eyes to soak up and he was soon in bed himself. The light from the outside poured in and kept the dormitory in a semilucid state.

Ibrahim did his lotus-sitting prayer and soon was settled under the sheet. I heard him breathe noisily and then there was silence. I guessed he was now asleep.

But I couldn't sleep. My mind was racing with so many thoughts. I knew I wasn't going to sleep, at least not straight away, so I sprayed myself with a second dose of insect repellent, slipped out onto the floor and stood looking out the window. I began pondering on the beautiful words that Ibrahim had spoken that evening. Although I no longer embraced the Christian faith nor any faith whatsoever, this evening's Devotion encapsulated my entire world view, what I believed what life was all about. This was a world view I lived by.

But while floating on this wonderful cloud of wonderment, I was suddenly taken back to the debate in the Nyika. One of the arguments about modern technology was that it would cause more men and women to become gay. And this to them was some sort of sin or crime. But nowhere in the verses from these Revealed Books that Gordon and Ibrahim quoted was the subject of sexuality raised. The only goodness was the way people treated others. The unrighteous were accused of either simply neglecting to help those in need or outrightly hurting and killing them.

Despite the beauty of the message from Gordon and Ibrahim's Devotion, there was also a feeling of despair. Although I didn't believe in God or the Last Judgement or in angels or that these Revealed Books were dictations from God, the message Gordon and Ibrahim were advocating was my way of living. I also believed that our lives here were all about helping the down-and-out when we had the means to help out. I wanted to be part of this, part of the Msingi wa Mungu Project, part of this world where people wanted to help other people. But these religions had shut those like me out. We were not welcome to share in the wonderful world of doing good to others. But how did my feelings for men hinder me from helping others? In fact, if there was anyone I was willing to share my life intimately with, this other person would have to share my ideals. Imagine if the Msingi wa Mungu Project or any religious organisation accepted people like me. Imagine how much more the project would grow. We would be people without the responsibility of children and therefore we could put all our energies into helping children without parents, or anyone who needed any form of help. Just look at the example of Polycarp. If I had been married with children, it would have been difficult, even impossible for me to be doing what I was doing for him as I would have had to relinquish my duties as a husband and a father to be able to put the amount of time I had put in to help Polycarp and Jeremiah. Because my sexuality had freed me from familial responsibilities, it had freed me up so that I could help others. But religions shut people like me out so that people like me have to help others independently and on our own. I thought of how much I would have liked to have been part of an organisation like the Msingi wa Mungu Project because as a combined force we could achieve so much more.

I stood there in the semi-darkness lost in my thoughts when Ibrahim broke the silence.

"Bwana Michael, are you alright?" he asked. It was obvious from the way he spoke that he had not actually been asleep at all.

Ibrahim's voice gave me a start.

"Yeah, yeah," I finally replied. "I'm alright. I just can't sleep. I just wanted to look out the window for a bit until I started feeling tired."

There was a moment of silence. I heard Ibrahim move so I guessed he was rolling over on the bed.

"So, Bwana Michael," he continued. "Tomorrow night will be your last night here."

"Yeah, it will," I replied. There was a slight pause.

"I will miss you, Bwana Michael," Ibrahim continued.

I felt a flush in my face. It was very touching what he said. But I did not feel the same in return. Should I say something of similar value? But I didn't feel it. So why should I say it?

There was a long silence. No sound was coming from Ibrahim's direction so I wasn't sure if this meant that he had gone to sleep or not. My thoughts then returned to concentrate on looking out the window.

Soon, I heard Ibrahim once again noisily inhale and the sound of him moving in the bed. Ibrahim then took a breath.

"May I," Ibrahim began and then stopped. There was silence again. "May I," Ibrahim started again, paused and then continued. "May I join you?"

Yeah, you can join me, I thought to myself but didn't say this out loud. It's not like I own this part of the room and therefore it's private property. I'm not really doing anything except standing here anyway, looking out the window and letting my mind wander.

I then turned to Ibrahim and simply shrugged my shoulders as an indication that he had my permission.

I turned to look out the window and then heard a gentle thud. I turned around to see Ibrahim sitting up in his bed, feet on the floor and the mosquito net pulled up.

I could only make out his silhouette but could not read the expression on his face. Ibrahim then stood up slowly and began walking over to the window where I was standing. It appeared that he had now become interested in finding out what it was that had me transfixed on the outside world. He walked over to the window and stood next to me and looked outside. There was a long pause while we both looked silently outside even though there was actually nothing in particular to look at.

Ibrahim then made a move which made me turn to face him. I looked into his face. He had a concerned look on his face. What was concerning him?

Ibrahim then reached out his left hand and slowly and gently took my right hand in his left and brought my hand up to his lips with a soft and gentle movement. And then he gently kissed my middle finger. He then slowly knelt down, pulled my hand up so that it touched his forehead and then brought it down to my side again and then slowly stood up. He was holding onto my hand when he began to speak.

"My dearest Michael," he started. "I think I love you and I…"

He then paused. I was taken so much by surprise. I wasn't really sure what was happening. Then Ibrahim continued.

"And I…er…I," he began and then coughed to clear his throat before continuing with, "and I would like to marry you so that you and I can be one." This last part of what he had to say trailed off into a quietness that was almost inaudible.

I was completely stunned. I couldn't move. The curtain from the angle at which Ibrahim was standing cast a dark shadow over his face and I could barely make out the contours of his face. But what I could make out was a desperate yearning, a humble plea for me to respond to what he had just said. I was so taken aback. I just did not know what to say at first. I couldn't move.

Ibrahim must have realised that what he originally had said was so quiet that I probably didn't hear it because the second time he said it a little louder.

"I would like to marry you so that you and I can be one," he repeated.

Suddenly flashbacks of all the nice moments I had had with Ibrahim from the time I had arrived here, when I first saw him on my arrival at the Msingi wa Mungu Project, the first night when he removed his shirt, the comment he made about the stars, holding his hand while strolling around in Arusha, all these memories flooded into my head and filled me with euphoria. I instinctively grabbed his hands and brought them to my waist.

Ibrahim immediately responded and next we were in an embrace.

And then things went on from there. But before going too far into the event, Ibrahim took precautions to lock the door and to close the curtains enough to obscure as much of the view from outside as possible.

What followed on from there, all those who have ever been in love, both gay and straight, know just how much of a wonderful night it was.

Chapter 9

A pleasant night for me is often followed by an awkward morning. When I woke up, Ibrahim had me fully in his grip as if he simply didn't want to ever let me go. The morning light was already straining through the curtains draped across the window. I felt the morning urge upon me and needed to unload my bladder. I struggled through Ibrahim's grip which was actually quite loose as Ibrahim was still deep in sleep. I quietly dropped onto the floor, grabbed something to cover my naked body and then made the dash to the amenities to offload.

When I returned, I quietly closed the door behind me and gently replaced the lock in position. But instead of returning back to bed with Ibrahim, I made my way onto the big double bed that had been initially reserved for me. Once under the safety of the sheet, I looked across at Ibrahim in the other bed. Our adventures of the night before came to mind and filled me with pleasurable feelings. But now it was the morning after. The magic of the night was replaced by the full realisation of what had happened the night before and it just made me feel so uncomfortable. I had made love with a black man, a Muslim man, an extremely religious man, a man who had once been married, a man who came across as very masculine and with not one ounce of the stereotype that we see of men of my calibre. There had been nothing in his behaviour prior to this time which gave me the slightest inkling that he may actually fancy another man. But the passion of the previous night certainly proved otherwise. Something about the entire affair made me feel extremely uncomfortable.

Suddenly Ibrahim stirred. He made moves to show that he had just come out of sleep. He then made gesticulations to show that he was now aware that he was alone in the bed and he groped around in the blindness of sleep to capture that which was originally within his grip but which had since got away. It was obvious that this caused slight confusion as he opened his eyes and began looking around him like someone who had misplaced something. He then sat up, looked over in my direction, and once he had caught my attention, he smiled.

"Bwana Michael," he half whispered. "You're so far away! What are you doing all the way over there?"

I just smiled. I didn't have a satisfactory answer. This then made me even more embarrassed. What could I say? We had been so intimate the night before. What would be the explanation for me suddenly being so far from him?

Ibrahim then threw back the sheet that had been the only covering over his naked body. He then looked around on the bed until he found a pair of shorts which he then slipped on before slipping himself onto the floor. He sat and looked across at me, smiled and rubbed his eyes. He then got up, unlocked the door and disappeared. There was no guessing where he had gone.

Soon he was back. He quietly and gently locked the door behind him in very much the same way as I had done. But instead of going back to his bed, he took one look at me, smiled, and then crawled under the mosquito net and into the bed with me. He climbed right on top of me and kissed me before lying back on his side. I rolled over to look at him in the face.

Obviously my sudden desire to be away from him did not bother Ibrahim or deserve a comment from him. I still felt uncomfortable but could not really work out why. Nonetheless, now that Ibrahim was back in bed with me, I was ready for open dialogue. That what had happened the previous night actually took place was totally unexpected and I wanted to find out how Ibrahim knew to take the steps he did.

"So, tell me," I started. "How did you know that I would respond?"

Ibrahim smiled and shook his head in indication that he had not understood my question.

"I mean," I rephrased the question, "how did you know that I would be interested in you in this way?"

Ibrahim laughed and leaned his head back before turning to face me.

"I knew from the first moment I saw you. I noticed the way you looked at me when you greeted me. I also noticed the way you looked at other men and didn't show much interest in women." Ibrahim paused there and then continued. "Also, you said you didn't have a wife or a girlfriend so I could only therefore guess the reason was that you weren't interested in women." He paused again and then added. "Also, the way you held my hand whenever we were out on the streets. There was a certain intensity in it that men usually don't have, at least Tanzanian men, when they hold hands." There was a further pause and then Ibrahim added, "Also when you spoke about Polycarp, there was an intensity in how you spoke about him that seemed more than just feelings of friendship. At first I was jealous of Polycarp. But then you said that you were only interested in men of your age. I knew then that there was hope for me. I still had to double check by asking you what you really thought about a man marrying another man which is why I asked if you thought such a thing was ordinary. When you gave me your answer, I was elated. All I needed from then on was the right moment to be with you like we are now."

I reflected back on that conversation. If I had only known! However, in a way, it was actually good that nothing had happened earlier. During the week, through the conversations between Ibrahim and me, I was able to gain a true appreciation of Ibrahim's personality without this appreciation being clouded by intimacy. Had we had an intense moment right at the beginning of my stay, I would simply have gained a false positive image of the person simply because intimacy blinds us to the true personality of a person.

"Why did you wait till last night to take the first step?" I then asked.

"I had to make sure," Ibrahim replied, "that I fully understood what type of person you were. I needed to know how you viewed things, what was in your heart." Ibrahim paused there for a moment and then continued. "I was also very nervous. There were a few times earlier in the week I wanted to approach you but I was afraid. Even last night I was afraid. But last night I especially knew that there wasn't much time left and I had to act quickly. While I was in bed, I couldn't sleep, trying to think of a way to let you know my feelings and to find out if you had these feelings for me. I prayed to Allah to provide an opportunity to let me make my feelings known to you. Suddenly you got up and went to the window. I then understood that Allah had answered my prayer."

Poor Ibrahim! I thought. And I thought I had experienced a difficult week hiding my feelings!

However, there were still questions I needed answers to.

"Then," I continued, "what about your wife and your children?"

"What about them?" Ibrahim asked.

"Why did you marry and have children if you don't like women?"

Ibrahim touched my cheek with the side of his hand.

"Because that was the thing to do. In Tanzania, when a man reaches his maturity, it's time for him to marry. So, when I had finished school and my university studies, my parents made it clear to me that it was time to marry and so they helped me find a wife."

I had heard this many times before from gay men and women from different countries, especially countries where homosexuality was a crime. The idea that a man gagged at the thought of having to be intimate with a woman or that a woman enjoyed the affections of another woman and not a man, these were simply not part of the thought process within these oppressive societies. So, these unfortunate gay men and gay women are forced to go through the motions of outwardly demonstrating that they thoroughly enjoyed the intimacy of someone of the opposite sex even though it makes their stomach turn and makes them want to vomit when they have to actually perform the act. But what else can they do? The alternative is simply not to be married. But a single life in many of these societies can be a very difficult one, especially when people depended on children in their old age for support.

"Did you love your wife," I asked almost as a whisper.

Ibrahim rolled onto his back and looked up at the ceiling.

"Yes, I did love her. She was my wife."

"I mean," I once again rephrased the question, "did you like, um, well, did you like loving your wife?"

Ibrahim turned around again to look at me. He smiled and there was a softness in his eyes.

"I tried to."

Although the answer was meant in a kind way towards his late-wife, it told me a lot of what he had gone through to please everyone else in his community. The thought made me shudder when I contemplated how I probably would have had to do the same if the society in which I lived had been like Ibrahim's. What was an unnerving thought was that not only was it an unwritten societal rule for Ibrahim to exercise his sexual energies contrary to what his body dictated, according to the legal system of the country, exercising his natural sexual energies was against the law. So, if Ibrahim at any time allowed his body to exercise its sexual expression in the way his body naturally wanted to do so, it was crucial that he made sure that it was done in a way so that no-one ever found out.

And it was clear that Ibrahim was aware of this at this particular time. After all, Ibrahim had taken precautions. The door was securely locked even though there was no reason for anyone to actually enter the room. The window was completely covered with the curtains so that it was almost impossible to see inside the room from outside.

"You've obviously done this before," I commented after this observation.

"Done what?" Ibrahim asked inquisitively.

I laughed.

"Done what? What we did last night!"

"Well, yes, because I was married."

It took me a moment to get what he said before I realised what he meant.

"No, no," I said. "I mean, done it with another man."

"No, I haven't," Ibrahim half-whispered and he hugged me, bringing me closer into his sphere of influence. "You are my first man."

He then kissed me on the forehead.

"And you will be my only one," he whispered, more as a plea than as a statement.

This last statement was open to many interpretations. I first interpreted it to mean that after me, he would probably get married again or simply no longer have sex because there was no alternative in his society. But slowly, the force of the way he had said it and the kiss on the forehead, something about what he had just said and done, this made me shudder. Did he really expect that we would somehow become an item, a couple? But as I thought about it more, it was a pipe dream, an illusion. I was here for just another twenty-four hours and then I was going back home, back to my Sydney life, far away from this African nation. What Ibrahim and I had experienced the night before would simply have been a wonderful moment that we had shared together and that's where it would end. The very idea, the very possibility that we could create something out of what we had done the night before was completely ludicrous if not preposterous. No, Ibrahim did not really mean that. It was his emotions of the moment creating an illusion that this could last for a long time. So, I simply ignored it. Once I was out of Tanzania, all this would be a pleasant memory I would leave behind.

Eventually we had to get out of bed and get ready for the day, especially as we had to wash away the evidence of what had transpired the night previous. When we went to the bathroom, Ibrahim once again fetched the water but this time there was a pleasure in the fact that he had gone to fetch water for me. It wasn't back in the colonial times when African slaves served their European masters. This was the act of a lover doing something for his beloved.

But we could not carry out the event to its fullest. I wanted to share the shower with Ibrahim, to wash his body and allow him to wash mine, a romantic act that both gays and straights engage in as part of the courting ritual. But we couldn't. Back out in the exposure of the general Tanzanian society, we had to act as if there was nothing more between us than a casual friendship and a general business relationship.

The day crawled by while I was separated from Ibrahim. This was my last day helping out with the teachers of English while Ibrahim was involved with his responsibilities. I spent the day looking at my mobile phone every ten minutes to see if it was time my Msingi wa Mungu Project work had ended.

When the afternoon came, I almost ran back to the dormitory to see if Ibrahim had already returned from his duties. But I had to wait. That longing to see him again filled me with great expectations. Now I couldn't wait to see him. And it was the last day. Every minute counted.

He did finally come and his greeting showed that he was just as happy to see me as I was to see him. Wow! I hadn't had this feeling for a long time! I had forgotten what it was like to have someone to love and someone to be loved by. It was fleeting and it would not last, I was totally aware of that. But I cherished the moment while it was there.

"Would you…um…like to go out tonight? To eat? Somewhere else?" Ibrahim asked.

"Go out? Don't we have to have dinner here at the project?" I asked. "Don't you have to take part in the Devotion?"

"Yes, usually I do," Ibrahim replied. "But I told Bwana Gordon that because it is your last night here, I thought it a nice gesture to take you out somewhere else and have one last African experience away from the project."

You mean so that we could go out on a date, I thought to myself. You obviously couldn't say that to Gordon.

"I'd love to," I replied.

Yet another experience I hadn't had for a long time, getting prepared for a date. We were in the same room to do so nonetheless but there was a wonderful feeling as I went through my luggage to find what I thought were the nicest clothes to wear. Most of the clothes I had brought were business shirts and trousers accompanied with good black business style shoes anyway. There were only a couple of shirts and trousers left that I hadn't worn thus far. Those that I had already worn had been placed in plastic bags for me to wash when I returned back to Australia.

It wasn't long before we were both dressed and ready to go. Ibrahim just looked like the most beautiful man in the universe the way he was dressed. I thought he looked just as wonderful with clothes on as he did without them.

Once out of the project compound, Ibrahim led us down the road in the direction the English teachers had gone to the markets with the students just over a week earlier. In fact, where Ibrahim took me was not far from the markets. It wasn't a flash five star restaurant. Rather, it was similar to the restaurant we had gone to in Arusha. It was a simple plastic-tables-and-chairs affair on a solid concrete floor so smooth it felt as if you could ice-skate over the surface. Above the tables were large beach umbrellas advertising popular beers. Even before we had arrived at a table, the welcoming aroma of well-cooked barbecued meat wafted through the air and welcomed us to the restaurant. To one side there was what appeared to be some sort of pavilion which served as a bar, as evidence of the display of different bottles of alcoholic beverages and I guessed within the doors of this small building the chef was busy cooking. The restaurant was half full so it was easy to find a table.

Once seated, Ibrahim invited me to wash my hands and indicated with a movement of the head in which direction the basin was. Again, the place to wash our hands was outside against a wall, a bathroom basin like the ones we have inside our homes in Australia, equipped with a small mirror for those washing their hands to inspect their facial appearance on completion of the hand-washing. Once I had returned and sat down, Ibrahim got up and echoed what I had done. Soon one of the waiters arrived and asked us what we wanted to drink. Ibrahim ordered our beers, Kilimanjaro Beer for me, Safari Beer for himself. When the beers arrived, I heard Ibrahim in Swahili order fish for me and beans for himself. The waiter then opened the beers for us and filled our glasses again with a quickness that caused a large frothy head to sit on the rest of the amber liquid. The waiter then left. Ibrahim raised his glass and signalled to me to do the same. He then clinked my glass.

"Cheers!" he said. I replied and we both took a mouthful before returning the glasses back to their spots on the table.

"Bwana Michael, I'm going to miss you," Ibrahim began. "But not for long."

The first part of what Ibrahim said was touching. But the second part troubling. Ibrahim was going to miss me. I felt the same about him. But not for long? How could he say that? Okay, this was a wonderful moment. But it was impossible for this to go on. It was a magic moment, two days in an entire existence, a magical two days. No doubt this was Ibrahim's coping mechanism.

"I will miss you, too, Bwana Ibrahim," I replied but I made no comment about the second part of his original statement. There was a moment of silence and then Ibrahim spoke again.

"Do you believe in dreams?" Ibrahim continued.

I took a swig of beer. I screwed up my face as a precursor to my answer.

"Yeah, of course I believe in dreams. I dream every time I close my eyes and go to sleep."

Ibrahim laughed a bit.

"I mean, do you believe dreams are messages in disguise?"

I felt the earnestness in the question and understood that Ibrahim believed this in all seriousness. I was a lot more skeptical about it.

"Well, not really," I replied. "But why do you ask?"

"I had a dream some time ago. Well, I know when it was. It was three months ago."

I didn't understand at first why it was so important that the dream was three months ago.

"Yes," I replied cautiously. "Go on." My mind had already begun looking at the calender inside my head and then I realised that it was about three months before my trip to Tanzania that I had made contact with the Msingi wa Mungu Project office in North Parramatta. This was not of any significance at first but when Ibrahim explained to me the dream and what it meant, there was something eerily coincidental about the timing.

"I dreamt I was standing on the seashore and before me was the vast ocean. I heard the waves crashing on the shore. I was facing east. It was night time. Suddenly I saw something rising from the east. It was very small and very bright. At first I thought it was a star but as it approached the shore, it became bigger and bigger, when I realised it was an angel, a human form with wings, a man with wings to be exact. But as it approached, I realised that it wasn't moving in the conventional way. The angel was in a way flying but he was riding a fish, a large fish, red in colour, intensely red, like the colour of blood.

The angel came to me on the beach and greeted me. The angel was in the form of a man but with bright long-flowing hair. On his head there was a crown, and in the crown was a blue star, with a blueness which was much more brilliant than anything that can be blue on earth, like the blueness of the perfect sapphire.

The angel greeted me. It was Michael the archangel. He told me that I bore the name of Ibrahim because I would follow in the steps of the first Ibrahim. But whereas the first Ibrahim acted alone, I, the new Ibrahim, would be reunited with my twin, that, in fact, Michael the archangel was in some way this other twin, and we together would work with the other twins to complete the work we were set to do. To do this, I would have to return with Michael across the sea, towards the rising of the sun, to a new land not mentioned in any of the holy books.

And then, from the place in the east where we were finally to return, there came a great light which shone and illuminated the whole earth. But as I stepped onto the water to go back with Michael to the land of the rising sun, before us was a tall mountain, so high that its peak disappeared into the sky like Mount Kilimanjaro. Michael led the way, climbing the mountain. I knew I had to follow him and that the only way to reach the other side was over this very tall mountain."

Ibrahim paused. I looked at him. It certainly was a strange dream. But I had strange dreams as well so it didn't sound any different to the dreams I had from time to time. Then Ibrahim continued.

"Don't you see what the dream means?"

I smiled and shook my head. Was there supposed to be a meaning to it?

"The archangel's name was Michael," Ibrahim continued, "and your name is Michael. The angel came from the direction of the rising sun and you come from Australia, which is in the same direction. Michael the archangel and you both are men and both have long hair."

Suddenly the comments that Ibrahim made to me the first day I met him that I had long hair and that I came from the land of the rising sun suddenly made sense. Those comments he made on our first meeting were actually in reference to this dream. I stared at Ibrahim in disbelief. He had seemed such a level-headed guy and the night before had been a wonderful event. But what he was telling me now was so twilight zone.

"So, are you implying that I am an angel?"

I looked over each shoulder to illustrate that wings were missing from my body. I then felt my head to show that there was no crown on it.

Ibrahim laughed.

"Bwana Michael, dreams are symbolic. Haven't you noticed that the dreams as recorded in the Bible and the Koran, and those in our religious traditions are all symbolic?"

I had to concede that. When I thought of dreams in the Bible, the first dreams that came to mind were the dreams of Joseph. Each of those dreams on their own were rather bizarre but when interpreted had some sort of prophetic power.

"Then what's the symbol of the dream where this Michael, the archangel, has wings?"

"Bwana Michael, you are Michael. And the archangel is Michael. Like the archangel, Michael can fly, you can also fly as you came to Tanzania by plane."

"But you said that this Michael came riding on a red fish. I didn't come riding on a fish, and I guess that means that Michael came by ship. I came by plane. And I took quite a circuitous route to get here."

"Yes," Ibrahim replied. "But this is all symbolism. Don't you realise that the red fish represents Christianity?"

I looked up above me and then back at Ibrahim.

"And this represents my Christianity?" I asked.

"It represents this clearly," Ibrahim replied.

"But you know that I'm really not Christian," I objected.

"But you grew up as a Christian, didn't you?" Ibrahim asked.

I was stunned. I had actually never told Ibrahim that I was brought up in a Christian home. However, I did say that I read the Bible in the original languages and who would take the effort to read these books in this way if they weren't first of all religious themselves.

"And the blue star?" I then asked. "Is that supposed to represent Judaism?"

I said this really as a joke. I made this match because the red fish that Michael was riding was interpreted as a religion and hence I made the association that therefore the blue star must represent a religion and I was familiar with the blue Star of David as a symbol of Judaism. I was, however, stunned by Ibrahim's reply to this.

"In the same way as the blue star on the Israeli flag."

I laughed.

"But I am not Jewish, nor do I have Jewish heritage," I replied and took another mouthful of beer.

"Are you sure?"

"With a name like Farril," I replied, "there's definitely no Jewish connection. In fact, no-one knows for sure where the surname Farril comes from except that it comes from the British Isles, but no-one knows if it is Anglo-Saxon or Celtic. But it's definitely not Jewish."

Ibrahim smiled. He made the comment that the fact that Farril is of unknown origin provides a leeway to the possibility that Farril might actually originate from a distant Jewish name. I simply dismissed the thought. I was sure that if there had been a Jewish connection in my ancestry somewhere, somehow it would have trickled down through the generations.

But this began to disappoint my appreciation of Ibrahim. He seemed like a regular sort of guy despite his religion, but now he was entertaining these fantasies.

"So, you're some sort of prophet, then?" I asked and took another mouthful of beer. I looked around the restaurant and thought how uncharacteristic and how ordinary this basic restaurant setting was for a modern day prophet.

"No," Ibrahim replied with a gentle laugh. "I'm not a prophet. Allah spoke to me in a dream. Allah speaks to all of us in dreams. I'm not unique in this way. We simply need to respond to what Allah is telling us."

"I thought God only spoke to us through the holy books," I replied.

Ibrahim sat back in his chair and placed his hands in front of him with the tips of the fingers on his right hand touching his left. It was the posture of a confident, almost arrogant, authoritarian about to dispense with his decrees of truth. But what came out of Ibrahim's mouth was in fact a question.

"Why do you say that, Bwana Michael?" Ibrahim asked with an honest expression of inquisitiveness on his face.

But I didn't say that, I thought. You, the religious people, you all say that.

"Well, I don't say that," I replied.

Ibrahim paused and looked earnestly at me. However, the way he looked at me, as innocent as he was, it was as if his eyes bore a hole right into the centre of my soul.

"Then why did you say that you thought Allah only spoke to us through the holy books?" he asked.

I felt my shackles going up. This conversation appeared to be riding down the avenue where we were about to have a very uncomfortable argument simply over religious beliefs.

"Because that's what religious people always say," I replied. "However, I do not hold to this belief."

Ibrahim then put his hands clasped and upside down as a cat's cradle in his lap. He looked as though he were about to say something but I decided to throw the ball back into his court before he spoke.

"So, you, as a Muslim, what do you believe about how God speaks to us? Despite the fact that you believe the Koran is a holy book which is the medium through which God speaks to us, how can you, as a Muslim, believe that God speaks to us in other ways apart from through the holy books?"

Ibrahim laughed gently again. There was something gentle and noble about his reactions to my pointed questions. Religious people have a tendency to become quite bold and forthright as soon as they are presented with a challenge as if any question on a religious matter that compromises the religion they believe in is a personal insult. But when Ibrahim spoke, there was a complete assuredness in what he had to say, as if his entire belief did not crumble at the first sign of a problem with his belief.

"It's not *despite* the fact that I'm a Muslim that I believe it but *because* I am. As the Koran says, in Yunus 10:48, 'And for every people there is a

Messenger. So when their Messenger comes, it is judged between them with equity'."

I looked at Ibrahim. On face value, there was nothing in that verse which supported Ibrahim's belief. There was definitely a quantum leap between the meaning of this verse and the answer to my original question and I made that point. However, Ibrahim came back with an answer.

"When it says 'people', the Arabic word is *ummah*. Now *ummah* really means 'community' so it can refer to a group of people holding a common belief, such as the *Ummatialislamiyah*."

I shook my head and closed my eyes. "The Ummati…the what is it?"

"The *Ummatialislamiyah*, the Muslim community. All the Muslims together as a group."

"Go on," I then said and took another mouthful of beer.

"*Ummah* can refer to a nation, like Tanzania, or it can refer to a tribe, like one of the many tribes across Africa. So each tribe has received a messenger at one time."

"So, there has been a prophet to every tribe in Africa, to every tribe of the Aboriginal Australians, to every tribe in every place on the globe where they have had tribes, to every nation and so on? And does that mean that for every new country that forms, God must send a prophet to fulfil this verse?" I stated militantly.

Ibrahim made a movement with his head which indicated that he was rather taken aback by my brazen attack. But in the same gentle way as he always had, he replied.

"Not a prophet," Ibrahim corrected me, "but a messenger. Now the Arabic word used here is *rassool*. Examples of *rassools* in the Koran are the prophets among whom is Muhammad. But other *rassools* are angels. The angel Gabriel, for example, was a *rassool*. Angels are supernatural beings which exist in the spiritual world. This means that some *rassools* appear to different nations and different peoples not in the guise of a human being but in the form of a spiritual *rassool*. When a *rassool* in the form of an angel appears to humans, normally he appears during a dream, as was the case with the angel Gabriel when he appeared to Mary and Joseph as recorded in the Injil. A messenger has appeared to many tribes around the world through the portents and dreams through the medium of the *waganga*, then to the people. If you examine the peoples in all places of the world, many will have received a *rassool* in this way."

"I'm sorry," I threw in. "What's a *waganga*?"

Ibrahim took a sip of his beer and I followed his lead. I felt as if both of us needed to lubricate our mouths because we had to take a sip of beer before we spoke.

"The *waganga* are the special men and women in our tribal cultures who both cure diseases and communicate with the spiritual world."

"The medicine men or witchdoctors," I interjected.

"These are two ways to translate the word," Ibrahim replied.

Immediately I thought of the Aboriginal Australian concept of the Dreaming. All Aboriginal Australians, as far as I was aware, had a belief like this, where some time in the Dreamtime, somewhere in the past, a messenger in the form of a supernatural being brought laws to these people.

Once again, a shiver passed through my body because of the all-inclusiveness of Ibrahim's belief which oddly was built on Ibrahim's Islam. Or more correctly, on what was written or at least implied in the Koran.

"But if this is true," I continued, "then we would expect that all beliefs and all religions to be fundamentally the same. But they're not. There are vast differences between the different religions and the beliefs around the world."

At this point, the waiter arrived with our food. Once again, the food was brought out on metal trays, the trays appearing as if they were surplus from a preceding war and the Tanzanians simply made use of this surplus. Once the waiter had gone, I looked at Ibrahim's tray of vegetarian food which had not a scrap of meat on it. How was it that he was a vegetarian and yet he claimed to be a Muslim? Not once had I ever heard of a Muslim making the claim that animals should not be killed and eaten. The only animal that Muslims were not allowed to kill and eat was the pig.

Ibrahim dipped his right hand into his food which was the signal to begin eating. With that, I took a small piece of ugali, began rolling it into a ball and then collected a small piece of fish. I could tell that this was fish from Lake Victoria because it tasted so much like the fish I had the first time Ibrahim took me out to eat.

Ibrahim swallowed the first portion of food, picked up his beer and washed down what remained in his mouth and then continued.

"Are religious beliefs and traditional rites really different? Or are there underlying similarities between them?"

"Goodness!" I retorted. "They certainly are all very different."

"For example?" Ibrahim invited.

I took another handful of ugali and mixed it with some more fish. I knew there was a conflict of desires here, a desire to eat this delicious food and a desire to continue in this conversation. But I managed to do both.

"Well, for a start, they all believe some mythical being in the past brought to them from a lofty domain in the heavens a set of laws for their community to live by. I mean, for example, the Arrentje tribe of Central Australia believe that some mythical being in some form or other came to their tribe with a set of laws for them to abide by. This supernatural being came out of the sky and settled in the centre of Australia and gave these people everlasting laws.

The Torres Strait Islanders believe that their god, Marlo, came to their islands from the west after descending out of the sky, and while Marlo moved through the water, he took on various forms, first the form of a whale, then the form of a canoe and finally the form of an octopus before finally settling in the Torres Strait Islands and giving laws to the people who live there.

The people of the Polynesian Islands have similar beliefs where they believe their supernatural beings in the past appeared to them in strange forms out of the sky and established laws for their communities to live by.

By contrast, the Christians believe that God, in the form of a lightning and thunder on top of Mt Sinai, first appeared to His people, the Israelites, and gave them His laws through Moses, and then later God appeared on earth in the form of a man called Jesus to update the laws that God had originally given to Moses."

Ibrahim nibbled on one of his fingers to remove food trapped in one of the joints and then continued.

"What you are telling me, is that a difference between all these tribes or a similarity?"

"Well," I replied as if it were very clear, "they are all very different. The way that these different tribes explain the attributes of their gods, their gods are all different and in different forms."

"But," Ibrahim answered, "when you look at the way you explained it, the way these messengers came to the different tribes may be different but overall they explain the same message, that a messenger came from some place, and from the supernatural way these beings travelled, the place they came from must have also been supernatural in a way. Each messenger appeared to each of these people bringing them laws. To me, this is a fulfilment and a confirmation of what the Koran says in Yunus 10:48 'And for every people there is a Messenger.' The Koran does not explicitly state that each messenger was in the form of a human, the way we usually associate messengers, such as the prophets. Even as the Koran shows, the archangel Gabriel was also a messenger, but this messenger was not a human being but an angel."

Ibrahim made an interesting point. Ibrahim's explanation of the sphere of interpretation of the word *rassool* instantly brought to mind the strong similarity with the word "angel", but not the English word but in the form the English word comes from, that is, from the Greek word *angelos*. The Greek *angelos* simply means "messenger". The traditional translation of *angelos* into the English "angel" is often accompanied by the interpretation that the *angelos* was an avio-humanoid creature. However, when we examine the use of the word *angelos* in the New Testament, it is uncannily similar to the way Ibrahim understood the Arabic equivalent, *rassool*.

In Luke 1:26, for example, the Gospel writer writes that "the angel (*angelos*) Gabriel was sent from God". We have been conditioned, from our Sunday School teachers, our church leaders, from the great artworks of the Renaissance and by all the traditional images at Christmas that Gabriel the *angelos* was some sort of ethereal being from another world, human in form but birdlike in propulsion. But then we read in Mark 1:2 that God says, "Behold, I send my messenger (*angelos*)" and it becomes clear only two verses later that this *angelos* is John the Baptist who, as far as all the classical artwork and church teaching goes and as it is clearly portrayed in the Bible, was a human being like everyone of us. The Bible makes no distinction between the *angelos* Gabriel and the *angelos* John the Baptist in the use of the word in Greek. Rather, they were simply beings sent from God. The New Testament *angelos* could take on different forms, either in the form of a being from a different realm outside the physical universe we live in or in the form of another human being.

In fact, the word *angelos* simply comes from the Greek word *angelo* meaning "to bring news" and is encapsulated in the English word *evangelist*, the *ev* being the Greek for "good", and so an evangelist originally meant "someone who brings good news".

I further saw a similarity in the broader understanding of the Greek word *angelos* and the use of the Hebrew word *malak* as used in the Old Testament, again sometimes translated as "angel" and sometimes as "messenger". In Genesis 22, in the story where Abraham was told by Jehovah to sacrifice his son, just as Abraham was about to give his son the death blow, it says in verse eleven that an angel called out to him not to do so. The word "angel" in the Hebrew is *malak*. It has always been understood that this *malak* was some sort of ethereal creature in human form but with extra aerodynamic limbs. However, in II Samuel chapter eleven, in the story where King David sees Bathsheba washing herself outside on her roof, it says in verse four that King David sent messengers to bring Bathsheba to him so that he could be intimate with her. These messengers in context were simply normal human beings, part of the people who made up King David's court. However, the English translation of "messengers" in this verse is also from the Hebrew word *malak*. In fact, the last book of the Old Testament is called Malachi and simply means "my messenger".

The Arabic word for "angel" is also *malak* as it is in Hebrew and is used in the Koran, often translated as "angel" in the English translations. And like the Hebrew word, it can be a messenger of many different forms.

This made me ponder on another Greek word used in the New Testament which was similar in meaning. This was the word *apostle*. Anyone who has read the Old Testament and New Testament in their entirety will notice that in the Old Testament, those who were sent by God to deliver a message on God's behalf were called prophets. But when we read the New Testament beginning with the Gospels, we are introduced to a new name to describe messengers, namely, "apostles". When I was a child growing up in the church, I had the impression that apostles were special people who were distinct and unique in their identity and function. However, on close scrutiny, the apostles were no different to any of the prophets in the Old Testament.

That the word *apostle* was similar in use to the word *angel* was brought out in my readings of the New Testament, especially when I read the New Testament in Greek. Most Christians say that there were only twelve apostles. But on closer scrutiny, the reality is that there were nineteen mentioned by name. The traditional twelve are named in Matthew 10:2 – 4, Judas Iscariot being replaced by Matthias in Acts 1:26.

However, Paul was also an apostle and this is clear because he calls himself an apostle in many of his letters.

Then in Acts 14:14 we read about "the apostles, Barnabas and Paul". Barnabas, as we read in the early part of the Acts of the Apostles, was a later convert to the Christian faith after the death and resurrection of Christ and was not one of the original twelve, and who was for a time Paul's travelling companion.

We also read in Galatians 1:19 that Jesus' brother, James, was also an apostle. Jesus' brother James was definitely not one of the original twelve apostles because the fathers of the two Jameses mentioned in Matthew 10:2 – 4 are Zebedee and Alphaeus and not Joseph, and in any case, Jesus' brothers according to John 7:3 - 5 did not believe Jesus was sent from God while Jesus was alive.

Two other travelling companions, Silvanus, also known as Silas, and Timotheus, otherwise known as Timothy, are implied as being apostles in I Thessalonians 2:6 because the pronoun "we" in this verse refers back to the very first verse of the entire epistle where the author of this letter is "Paul, and Silvanus, and Timotheus".

And the greatest apostle of them all is Jesus Christ himself, as Hebrews 3:1 makes very clear where it says, "Wherefore, holy brethren… consider the Apostle…Christ Jesus."

The word *apostle* today has an elevated meaning and sounds as if it refers to special holy people. But the word *apostle* simply comes from the Greek *apostolos* meaning *someone who is sent*, coming from the verb *apostello* meaning *to send out*. When we look at the actual function of the apostles in the New Testament, they were simply sent out as messengers to preach the gospel to the whole world. In the Acts of the Apostles, we read how Paul was sent to the west of the Roman Empire and Philip was a messenger to the Ethiopians. Beyond the accepted canonical books of the Bible, there are also traditions that the other apostles went further afield, such as Thomas Didymus, who was a messenger sent to India.

In this light, the interpretation of the verse in the Koran from Yunus 10:48 "And for every people there is a Messenger" and accepting that the Koran acknowledges the Old and New Testament as the Word of God equal to the Koran, and the understanding that *rassool, malak, angelos* and *apostolos* all can be interpreted as "messenger", it means that Jews, Christians and Muslims could appreciate that messages sent by God to all humanity came more often through human agents and not-so-human agents than via books. That is, messages from God are not confined to the medium of a book but can today as they have in the past come to us via other media such as through dreams.

I really didn't know what to answer at first. What Ibrahim had told me was true, that all these tribes and peoples of the world all talk of some sort of messenger, different in form but similar in determination, sent from some supernatural place to bring laws for these societies to live by.

"You know, you've got a point there," I replied.

Ibrahim made no remarks or comments to indicate that he was right. Quite the contrary. He did not portray the usual arrogance I was familiar with when religious people try to push their point and prove that they are right. Rather, the way Ibrahim presented his point and allowed me to accept it was no different to a scientific experiment. It was like Ibrahim knew the answer but was helping me to find the answer for myself. Whether I believed his view of the cosmos didn't seem to worry him. Ibrahim was assured of his belief and did not seem affected if I had only just come to this realisation.

"Well, then, if it's not the way the messenger was sent or the message was given, then it is the way that different peoples of the world understand their divinities. Some believe there is only one god, one divinity, but others believe there are many. Simply on this score, the messages are different."

Ibrahim grabbed for some more ugali and beans, and plopped these elegantly into his mouth, took a number of chews, and then swallowed the mixture with a beer chaser.

"But again," Ibrahim replied, "is that a similarity or a difference?"

I snorted.

"I think it is quite clear that there is a difference between one and many!" I replied rather arrogantly.

However, Ibrahim sat and listened before offering his own explanation.

"I can see why you say this," Ibrahim continued. "But there is also a way to see that this is really not a difference. Let's start with Christianity, for example. As a Christian, you say," Ibrahim began but then stopped and smiled. "Okay, you said you weren't a Christian. Christians say that there is only one God and then that there are three, God the Father, God the Son and God the Holy Ghost. So Christians already have an appreciation of the oneness even in plurality, or of a plurality in oneness. But go back to the beginning of the Torah and read the first verse: 'In the beginning, God'. The word 'God' in this verse is not a singular word, *eloha*, but the plural word, *elohim*, that is, *gods*."

When Ibrahim said this, I felt a mysterious tingle flow through my veins once again. I was amazed at his knowledge of the Bible, even this particular point from the original language. I was also familiar with the fact that just about all the references in the Old Testament to God use the Hebrew word *elohim* which is the plural of *eloha*, "god".

"But also in the Koran, we see this feature also quite clearly. In almost every surah of the Koran, Allah uses the plural, that is, 'We', to refer to Himself."

I remembered what I had read in the second surah, *Al-Baqarah*, how the Koran switched from the first person singular to the first person plural to the third person singular, almost like a schizophrenic. But it was amazing to hear that this reference to God as "We" and "Us" was prolific throughout the Koran. This was extremely bizarre, especially in light of the hostility Muslims have towards those who believe in more than one god. I would have thought that the Koran would have been extremely unequivocal about the oneness of their deity, ensuring that the only pronoun ever referring to God was always singular.

I was familiar with the Jewish argument that the use of the plural word "gods" and the use of the first person plural really was a sign of respect. If this is the same in the Koran, it means that whoever wrote *Al-Baqarah* oscillated between respect and disrespect towards the deity without any distinct pattern or reason because the writer moves back and forth from "we" to "I" to "we" in reference to God.

"Also notice," Ibrahim continued, "that other religions on the surface appear to believe in many gods but in reality these gods are only one god. The Zoroastrians believe in seven gods, the highest of them all being Ahura Mazda. But in reality, the seven gods, the holy heptad, are not separate beings but really seven ways of looking at the one god.

The Hindus also make the claim that they believe in many gods, Ganesh, Shiva, Vishnu and so on, but as Swami Dayananda shows in the *Satyartha Prakash*, these different deities are not separate and distinct but a reflection of the plurality of the gods in the oneness of God.

If you were to continue to look into all the beliefs in all the tribes and peoples around the world both past and present, you would discover that this same principle exists throughout."

I sat and thought about this for a moment. I took a mouthful of beer and then set my glass down.

"So, what are you trying to say?"

"That the idea that there is one God and many gods really is saying one and the same thing. I mean, even Muslims themselves admit with pride that there are many names for God. As it says in Bani-Isra'il 17:111, 'by whichever name you call God, His are the most beautiful names'. Why does Allah need many names if Allah is completely one? What this shows is that, yes, there is only one God, but in His oneness, there is plurality in His singularity."

"So, are you saying that, like, when the Greeks said that they believed in many gods, they really believed in one God? When the Greeks said that Poseidon was the god of the sea, Pluto was the god of the underworld, Aphrodite was the goddess of love, Ares was the god of war and so on, the Greeks really meant that there was only one God with lots of names?"

"When you think of it," Ibrahim replied, "why not? The Greeks believed that each of these gods had supernatural powers but what would be the difference in their godness? When you look deeper into what the

Greeks were saying, they were saying the same things that the Koran is saying, that God has many names, the God of the sea, the God of the underworld, the God of love, and so on. This one God is many faceted and is all of these. In the same way, Muslims say that God is truth, God is compassion, God is all-forgiving, God is mercy. In a way, Muslims are saying that there is a god of truth, a god of compassion, a god of forgiveness, a god of mercy, but it is also true that these different aspects are the one god. So it is when we look at the traditions and beliefs of tribes who have received their laws from messengers of the past. When they say that they believe in many gods, they really mean that these are merely different aspects of the one God."

Ibrahim took another mouthful of beer.

"In fact," he continued again full of religious fervour, "the Koran shows us this relationship between plurality and singularity in other ways. At one time the Koran tells us to believe in the Messenger, singular, and later the Messengers, plural. The Koran also tells us to believe in the Book, singular, and the Books, plural. The Koran tells us that the Gospel, singular, was revealed by Allah, when we know that there are five Gospels, plural. The Koran also tells us that there is a Satan, singular, and also that there are Satans, plural. Allah's understanding is much higher than ours and He knows that on a spiritual level, plurality and singularity co-exist quite comfortably and those who read the Koran carefully recognise this. What causes the unrest in the world over religion is simply this misunderstanding."

"Five gospels?" I queried. "I thought there were only four."

Ibrahim gave me a strange look and then said, "I thought there were five: Matthew, Mark, Luke, John and The Acts of the Apostles."

That was a point, I thought. Traditionally, it was Luke who wrote the third gospel and also the Acts of the Apostles, so it stood to reason that if his gospel was inspired by God so was his treatise to Theophilus.

I was beginning to see that Ibrahim had an incredibly admirable view of the world and different religions. Yet, he supported his beliefs on verses from the Koran. As a result, his entire world view was just so different to our understanding of Muslims. Some Muslims were absolute fanatics demanding everyone to only do things and worship in one way and that was the Muslim way. Those who did not do this were to be obliterated.

I still felt that what Ibrahim was saying was not right even though Ibrahim had provided me with answers to show that I was wrong. There was a side of me that wanted Ibrahim to finally confess that my initial statement was in fact correct.

"Okay, then," I then said further taking up the challenge. "If it is the same god who appears to all these people, why are all their rites and rituals so different? We can immediately tell if someone is a Jew, a Christian or a Muslim, simply by their mode of prayer, days they commemorate as sacred, the day of the week they consider holy and so on. But also in various places around the world, different tribes have adopted their own practices to the deity and they are all different. If it is the one God who brought all these practices, why are they all different?"

"Bwana Michael," Ibrahim replied. "Allah says quite clearly in Al-Hajj 22:68 that 'to every people have We appointed ways of worship which they observe; so let them not dispute with you in the matter'. Allah appointed different ways of worship but for Allah it is still the worship of Allah. They all might seem on the surface to be different but ultimately they are all in worship of Allah."

The Koran said that? I thought to myself. So then why are there Islamic bullies around the world pushing people to worship God in only one way, and in particular, their way?

But also, how was it that Ibrahim could read the Koran and other people who call themselves Muslims could read the same Koran and yet Ibrahim and these people were as different as apples and buttermilk? One wanted to narrow the world view to only one perspective while the other appeared to be open to all views as if they were all one and yet both used the one book to support these opposing views.

All this talk made Ibrahim come across as both quite an amazing person with a beautiful and yet different perspective of the Islamic religion I had been so familiar with. But at the same time, it made him come across as a little odd. But that didn't matter. This was my last night in Tanzania, on African soil, and I would soon return to the sensibility of my Australian life, back to my unit, to my comfortable bed, my modern shower and bath facilities, my car and my modern life. Ibrahim would be an odd but pleasant memory, one of those men who I had had a great time with however fleeting the event and how bizarre the topics of conversation had been.

And I just didn't buy into this otherworldly thing. There was no evidence as far as I could see that a world beyond the one we experienced really existed. And I was definitely no angel in any interpretation of the word, neither winged-creature nor messenger from a personage in a lofty dimension.

"Then, what about your dream? Is this yet another message from God?" I asked.

"It has to be," Ibrahim replied. "It has begun to be fulfilled."

"So," I then said, "God speaks to you in dreams?"

"God speaks to all of us in dreams," Ibrahim replied. "As it is written in Joel 2:28, 'And it shall come to pass afterward, that I will pour out my spirit upon all flesh…your old men shall dream dreams, and your young men shall see visions'. Allah sent messengers in the past and now He sends His message to all of us through our dreams and it's up to all of us to listen to what He has to say."

No, He doesn't, I thought. Dreams aren't messages from God. If they were, the messages God sent to me in dreams were incomprehensible gibberish. However, if Ibrahim believed this, so I continued to think, then let it be. As odd as this dream he had related to me earlier was, at least it was harmless.

When we had finished eating, Ibrahim paid the bill and then signalled me to go over to the basin in the corner of the room to wash my hands.

We walked out of this little restaurant and out into the night. There was very little light so it was difficult to see. However, far above us I once again took a glimpse of the beautiful starry night and the millions upon millions of tiny diamonds glistening far above us. This brought back pleasant memories of the first night of my arrival and the wonderful statement Ibrahim had made back then. He might be a bit off the beam this Ibrahim but his intentions were certainly commendable.

Ibrahim pulled me out of my thoughts.

"Would you like to go and have another drink?" he asked.

"Yeah, sure," I replied. "Why not?"

Ibrahim instinctively grabbed my hand and off we went walking into the Tanzanian night. We started walking back in the direction of the Msingi wa Mungu Project but soon turned into a side street which had a row of houses on one side and open land on the other. It was semi lit with some semblage of street lights. Ibrahim led me to what appeared to be some sort of shop. Really, it was like a large box with a hole and chicken wire. It reminded me of little corner shops and unassuming little edifices in small country towns of Australia.

Ibrahim yelled out something to get the shopowner's attention and soon a little what looked like a young Tanzanian with the patchy attempt at a beard appeared at the window. There was an exchange of friendly dialogue and soon the little man disappeared, only to reappear with two plastic chairs which he carried over to the empty land across from his shop. The little waiter gesticulated to me with extreme respect for me to sit on one of the chairs and then he offered Ibrahim to sit in the other.

The young man disappeared only to reappear not long after with a plastic stool which he placed in between Ibrahim and me to serve as a table. The man then went back over to his shop, entered it and for the first time I saw a light go on. He returned with two bottles of beer, the respective beers being placed in front of Ibrahim and me.

When the waiter had gone back to his little shop, Ibrahim raised his glass as a signal for me to raise mine and with that we clinked glasses.

That we had come to have a drink was like seed crystals in a crystalisation experiment. Not long after sitting down, other groups of people began to arrive out of nowhere or so it seemed and impromptu tables and chairs were set up in other areas on the vacant lot.

The atmosphere was beautiful. I was taken by the simplicity of the atmosphere. In Australia, at least in the city and in the suburb where I lived, we couldn't just sit outside on plain plastic chairs in a cheap little street bar like this and have a simple drink in the open air, be served cheaply in such a make-shift way. We could do something like this if a group of friends organised a night in someone's backyard but I felt that it would not have the same bar feel.

The simplicity and spontaneity of the moment was just wonderful. An outdoor bar, on the street, the warm night, the open sky, and of course, in the company of Ibrahim, despite his odd beliefs, this was a moment I wanted to capture and, like Oliver in the story *Oliver Twist*, place it all in a box so that I could once again later see it at my leisure.

Our conversation at the make-shift bar was more banal and mundane than at the restaurant. The subject matter oscillated between the events of my time at the Msingi wa Mungu Project and what my life would be like when I returned back to Sydney.

We had a couple of beers. I was worried that I would end up sozzled and would stagger back into the Msingi wa Mungu Project like a real drunkard and make a real spectacle of myself which would not have made a great impression of me for my last night there. But once we were up and on our way, I noticed that I still clearly had my faculties.

We finally made it back to the dormitory. Our room was made secure against all intruders, both of the human and insect kind, before we climbed in together into Ibrahim's bed and engaged in one of nature's most fundamental urges.

Once the job was complete, we lay still in the bed. I pondered on my adventure here in the Dark Continent. The search for Polycarp's family, a noble quest, was duly rewarded in the end. I would soon leave Africa with a pleasant memory.

Chapter 10

The sounds of the morning and the feeling of Ibrahim's grip around my body woke me. Ibrahim's deep breathing indicated to me that he was already awake. There was an earnestness in the way he gripped me, as if he thought that if he let go of me even for a second, I would simply float away from him. The sounds of the morning had also taken on a new turn as I could hear the sound of rain. This was the first time since I had been here that I had heard it rain. It sounded so out of place.

"Morning, Bwana Michael," Ibrahim whispered in my ear, obviously realising that I had left the world of dreams and was slowly entering the real world.

"Is that rain?" I mumbled sleepily.

Ibrahim breathed in with that whistling sound through his nostrils I had become familiar with.

"Yes, it's raining," he replied. And then there was a long pause. "Even nature is sad to see you go," Ibrahim added. He punctuated this last statement with another squeeze on my body. "But it won't be long till we are together again, forever."

This last statement was a little disturbing. Ibrahim was continuing to maintain that this would go on forever when to me it was totally impossible. We should leave it as a wonderful adventure, a pleasant memory of a wonderful moment together and move on with our lives. But then, what did it matter if I just played along with it? In a number of hours I would be on my way out of the country and Ibrahim could believe what he wanted to believe about us.

It was the morning of lasts: my last shower using only a bucket of water, my last shave without a mirror, my last breakfast of avocados, my last walk on African soil.

Among the things I packed in my bag was the Koran Ibrahim had given me. This book had once terrified me because of its association with intolerance but now it meant something to me, at least this particular copy, because it was a gift from Ibrahim. His hands had held mine while I held this book. This made the calligraphy on the cover look more ornate and more beautiful than it originally had.

The Msingi wa Mungu Project had organised a driver to take me to the airport. I first had to go through last minute formalities of signing out. Gordon came to the front office and presented me with a certificate of recognition and an official thank you for my participation in the project. Gordon once again expressed his condolences for the bad news about Polycarp's family, then wished me all the best for my trip back to Sydney and told me that I was welcome to return and participate once again should I wish to do so. I replied with a solid handshake.

Ibrahim accompanied me to the airport. I sat in the front passenger seat next to the driver and Ibrahim sat in the back. In a way this was quite disappointing because I really wanted to have some sort of physical contact with Ibrahim for the last time while I was in his proximity.

The long drive out to the airport was done in silence. I don't know what was going through Ibrahim's mind but I didn't really know what else to say to him. He had developed into such an odd character for me. He said he was Muslim and definitely testified to this by his constant references to the Koran. However, he was quite universal and all-embracing in his ideas of the universe, both the one we can see and the one Ibrahim claimed to exist but can't see. He was very tolerant and open to other ideas which was very different to the general view of Muslims in the world. And he was a good-looking man, at least for me, and a wonderful bed companion.

But it was only an adventure. I had come to Tanzania to accomplish a mission and in the process had had a magical moment. Once I was finally on my flight, my entire adventure would disappear into my past as a beautiful memory.

When we arrived at the airport, the driver parked to allow me to get out and collect my luggage from the boot. Ibrahim came to help. The driver mumbled something unintelligible to Ibrahim in Swahili and his body language indicated that he was in rather a bit of a hurry. Ibrahim debated with him somewhat but the driver didn't relent.

Ibrahim then escorted me to the entrance of the airport.

"The driver said he has to return now back to the Msingi wa Mungu Project. Unfortunately he can't just wait around –"

"Yeah, I understand," I interrupted, finally realising what the issue was.

I took one look at Ibrahim. And then we just hugged each other. We hugged each other tightly. I could feel the passion in the strength by which Ibrahim held onto me. Tears began welling up in my eyes much to my frustration. I did not want it to be known how deeply I was going to miss him. This was one of the longest, most loving embraces I could ever remember having with anyone.

But it was in eternal terms an embrace of short duration. The driver yelled out something and that was the signal for the embrace to end.

Ibrahim turned and walked back over to the transport vehicle. I watched as he got inside. The driver was soon inside on the driver's side, reversing out and making his way out of the airport. I saw an arm from the passenger side of the car stick up out in the air and wave. I watched on until the car was obscured from view by the other cars and the trees scattered around in the car park. He was gone so quickly. I was absolutely amazed at how quickly he suddenly was no longer in my life.

I turned around and entered the airport. Once all the airport formalities were complete, it was simply a matter of waiting in the airport for my plane.

Kilimanjaro Airport is certainly not a big airport. The waiting area is about the size of a school hall and consists of uncomfortable plastic chairs held together on long rods of metal so that when someone a couple of seats down sits down and moves around, the entire row of chairs including those further down the rod move along with it. Very annoying when young kids who can never settle at the best of times decide to rock and roll in their chairs and can't keep still to the annoyance of the other patrons.

However, the view out of Kilimanjaro Airport is fantastic. There is a complete cinemascopic view of the airport and hence planes can be seen far in the distance come gliding down softly onto the tarmac, all completely noiselessly as the airport is hermetically sealed, and finally taxi to within close proximity of the airport building. I saw a few small propeller planes fly in before the large jet engine that would take me on the first leg of my journey out of Africa finally touched down. Once my plane had parked close to the building, the passengers for my flight were called up and invited to board the plane. As it was when we arrived, we were required once again to walk out of the building and all the way up to the plane, and mount the ladder before entering inside the guts of this huge metal bird.

I fortunately had secured a window seat and doubly fortunate to be able to look back down at the airport building. The memory of my arrival here which seemed like only a day ago went through my mind. I wondered what it would be like if I could meet the arriving me and recount how my life would change because I had come here.

Ibrahim, of course, was on my mind. All I could think of was Ibrahim, Ibrahim, Ibrahim. But while I thought of him, I realised that I had strong feelings for him. This wasn't the result of a sudden infatuation after a couple of nights together in the physical. There was more to Ibrahim. I had enjoyed him physically. But I also enjoyed his values, his outlook on life, his care of all humanity, his desire to raise the happiness level of the world through education. These values were my values.

But he was a religious man, and in particular, someone who ascribed to a religion that I feared. This was particularly awkward because religion had been completely wrung out of me and I had come to the conclusion that there really is no place for religion in my life. How could I develop a relationship with someone who held strongly to religious beliefs when my feelings towards religion were quite the opposite?

Soon the plane was ready for take-off. The flight attendants went through the safety procedure before the plane began to taxi out onto the runway. Then the engines revved up and this mighty metal machine picked up speed and rapidly rode down the runway before tipping its nose towards the heavens, and the African earth beneath slowly but surely slipped away.

This sudden disconnection from the African continent did something to me. I don't know what it was but suddenly I felt so empty and so alone. I watched as we ascended further into the sky, and the airport below became once again a patch of metal on a grey-green carpet.

"Good-bye, Ibrahim," was all I could think.

It was certainly a long trip home. There were two stops on the way and in each airport in which I stopped I had to wait hours for the next connecting flight. The sterility of the internals of these airports helped to sterilise my feelings for the African continent and in particular those for Ibrahim. Surely by the time I got home, Ibrahim would have become a passing memory, a wonderful moment of my African experience, a memory to pull out whenever I felt down and blue. And that would be it. That wild river would never succeed in pulling me back into its tumult. I was beyond it, out of its grip. In any case, even the idea that Ibrahim and I could actually become partners was just totally preposterous. It just couldn't happen. Ibrahim may believe his dreams but his dreams could never really take place. He just told me his dreams to try to make me think that we could ever be together.

And on my trip back to Sydney, I thought once again of Polycarp. The reason for my trip to the Dark Continent was because of him. I began to feel for him. His parents, his brothers and sisters, his nephews and nieces, all the members of his entire extended family now ceased to exist. And this had been completely confirmed. This sat heavy in my heart. I realised just how difficult this concept was to grasp. How awful! How are we supposed to comprehend this?

The day after I arrived back in Sydney I was back at work at Tevah Am. The jetlag knocked me around a bit but apart from that my work life returned to its ordinary blandness. On my first morning back at work, when Nikita finally arrived to begin her shift, because there were only a handful of learners pre-occupied with their Occurences and didn't need any help, she was eager to know of what had transpired on my trip, in particular, what I had found out about Polycarp's family. I relayed to her the tragic news and Nikita offered her condolences, although the condolences really should have been directed at Polycarp as I was merely the messenger. I then began giving her a rundown of my time, first of the long trips to get there and then what had occurred at the Msingi wa Mungu Project itself.

While in conversation, Hebbeera eventually arrived to begin her shift. She saw Nikita and me in full conversation and as there was still only a handful of learners fully involved with their Occurences, she came over and burst into Nikita's and my conversation.

"So, how was it?" she asked.

"It was okay," I replied. I had not mentioned to Hebbeera the real reason for my trip so she had simply assumed that my whole intention was to participate solely in the Msingi wa Mungu Project. So, I only talked about the highlights and what I thought were the interesting aspects of the project. I deliberately emphasised the role the Msingi wa Mungu Project played in actually doing as was understood what religious people were supposed to do, that is, put themselves out and help other people, but Hebbeera obviously missed the subtle attack against her lack of response to the requirements of her religion.

"I hear African women are very beautiful," Hebbeera then said. She then smiled in a cheeky way and added, "You didn't meet someone special while you were over there?"

"Yes, I did," I replied.

Nikita looked on with surprise, Hebbeera with wide-eyed delight.

"I hope it was a good Christian girl," Hebbeera said. "A good Christian girl would make a wonderful wife."

Nikita covered her mouth with her right hand and her eyes betrayed that she was stifling a burst of laughter. Hebbeera was facing me from a different direction so she did not notice Nikita's reaction.

"No," I then replied rather brazenly, "in fact, the special person I met was a Muslim man."

Nikita's movement made it look as if she were trying to stop herself from laughing out loud completely. Hebbeera's eyes changed from delight to deathly horror.

"A Muslim man?" Hebbeera gasped. "No, you don't want to go out with a Muslim man."

"Why not?" I replied emotionlessly. "If I met a nice guy and he happens to be Muslim, then why what?"

Hebbeera looked as if she were going into cardiac arrest. I wasn't sure at first which was more repugnant to her, the fact that I said I had met a man or that I had said he was a Muslim. Hebbeera then caught her self-composure.

"No, no, no," she then said. "You don't want to go out with a Muslim." She said this with a grave tone in her voice.

"Why not?" I asked.

Nikita turned to look at me over Hebbeera's shoulder. Nikita's eyebrows were raised as a question mark and she had a cheeky smile as if to question where this conversation was leading.

"Those who follow Muhammad," Hebbeera continued, "are following the Beast of the Revelation."

"What?" both Nikita and I exclaimed in unison.

"Muhammad is the Beast, the mystery 666."

I took a quick glance around at the learners, hoping that none of them had heard what Hebbeera had to say. If there were any Muslims among them, Hebbeera's outburst was no doubt going to cause an uproar. Fortunately, the five learners had their earphones on and were intent on looking at their screens.

"How do you come up with that?" I asked puzzled.

"Oh, but he is," Hebbeera continued bombastically. "When you see what is happening in the world among Muslims and read the Revelation, it is clear that the Beast is Muhammad. The number six is the number of a man and Muhammad's name adds up to 666."

I raised my eyebrows. Seeing the Revelation was written by someone who was steeped in Jewish thought, it had always been assumed in the church I went to as a child that the calculation of the name of the Beast was based on the name of the Beast as it was in Hebrew. I was aware that in Hebrew, the letters of the alphabet had both a sound value and a numerical value. Only the consonants were written in Hebrew which meant that Muhammad's name in Hebrew was M-H-M-M-D. I knew that in Hebrew the numerical values of each of these letters was that M = 40, H = 8 and D = 4. From this, I did a quick mental calculation.

"No, it doesn't," I objected. "Muhammad's name only adds up to one hundred and thirty two. That makes him five hundred and thirty-four short of being the Beast."

Hebbeera glared at me.

"The Koran, however," she then said, "shows that it was written by a man because it carries the number six. Anything that has the number six in it is clearly from a man. The mystery 666 is three sixes together so it is the number of a man three times, an unholy and human imitation of the holy trinity. It would only be of God if it carried the number seven."

"How does the Koran carry the number six?" I asked puzzled.

"There are one hundred and fourteen surahs in the Koran. If you add up the digits in the number one hundred and fourteen, that is, one plus one plus four, you get six."

Nikita laughed. "And the Bible has sixty-six books. So it is the number of a man two times. Further, if you take the Bible and the Koran and put them together, you get 666. So these holy books together must be the mark of the Beast."

Nikita's comment jarred my senses. Usually I would have found such a comment amusing but this time it was like an affront to Ibrahim and his belief that the Torah, the Gospels and the Koran were all holy books. Hebbeera looked on in horror and her facial expression said it all. She just turned around and walked off in a huff.

Nikita then turned to me.

"Are you serious when you say that you met a Muslim man?" she asked in all seriousness.

I didn't know what to say. The truth was that I had. But the truth was also that it was merely fleeting. I had had a good time with one but now it was over.

Nikita laughed. "I'm surprised you're still alive!"

Nikita asked me where I had met him and where we did it. Nikita went into further laughter knowing that all this had occurred on the Msingi wa Mungu Project's own grounds. She was in particular happy that I had done it with a religious guy because this brought out quite pronouncedly the hypocrisy of religious people and how that it doesn't matter what religious people say, biology will always triumph over ideology.

Usually I would agree with Nikita but what she was saying in a way made me feel uncomfortable and moreso that I was betraying Ibrahim. To a degree, Nikita was correct in that Ibrahim was caught within the confines of religion even though his religiosity was much more universal than the average fundamentalist Christian or Muslim. However, quite oddly, Nikita's insults were therefore not only insults against the closed-minded religious, in a way they were insults against Ibrahim and in this case her attacks hurt me as a result.

Nikita was also correct about the conflict between religious ideology and biology. Christianity I knew for sure, and I was later to find out that this was the same in Islam, was totally intolerant of homosexuality. However, Ibrahim, as beautiful as his attempt to find a universal ground amongst all religions and also to find an opening for Socratists like me, was in direct opposition to the religious views of the intimate relationship that could develop between two men as it had happened between the two of us on two occasions.

This created a problem in the way I viewed Ibrahim and it made me more determined to simply view him as a holiday adventure that would soon become a pleasant memory of a distant past. I was back in Australia, in my safe haven, in my permissible world where there were no absurd constraints on my freedom.

A few days later I stayed over at Polycarp's. My first day back with Polycarp, however, was very emotionally draining. The day I arrived at his place after this trip, as soon as I saw him, I just gave him the squeeziest hug I could ever give someone. I now fully knew the total loss that he was experiencing. But I couldn't tell him, at least not now. But on seeing him, it made me realise just how much we should not take life for granted, that the people we associate with, who we help, who become part of our lives, these people every day mean something because tomorrow they may no longer be around.

Poor Polycarp was quite taken aback by my overtly and superfluous expression of emotions. At first his grip on me in return was feeble but then it was reciprocated. When we had separated, he didn't ask me the reason for this sudden outburst of emotions but seemed to understand.

"Yes, I missed you, too, *baba*," he finally said to me.

I was completely taken aback by the word "baba". This is the Swahili word for "dad". Polycarp wanted me to be his father? If we considered the age difference between us, I was old enough to be his father. So if it meant something to Polycarp to call me father then I was content to take on the role and consider him as my son. After all, I had no family, no wife and no children, so I wasn't encumbered with other familial duties which hindered me from taking on the relationship building between the two of us. And all the more so because it meant that Polycarp at least had a new family member.

But as happy as I was to take up the duty as his father, I felt that Polycarp would consider me in this role only as long as he needed someone in his new country to depend on and provide him with a link to this new community that he was being initiated into. This, too, would pass. Nonetheless, deep down, I didn't mind. People come and people go, that was just the way life went.

In a way, I felt that helping people was my calling. When Faisal first came to Australia, I helped him to integrate into Australian society and when he finally had settled down and his entire family was reunited with him in Auburn, and he had settled himself into a job, the contact between us mysteriously ended. It was understandable, though. Faisal had now a wife and eight children to contend with, six children who were born in Afghanistan, and then two subsequent children when his family was finally reunited in Australia. It also made sense because he had not seen his wife and children for such a long time and no doubt he had so much catching up to do. This no doubt absorbed all of his time as he had to find a suitable house, try and help his children get into school, get himself a job and many other things. On the few occasions that I did ring to speak to him, we spoke for a short time with the promise of getting together for longer at a later date, a date which never eventuated.

At about this time, Faraj entered into my sphere of friendship. He was originally a learner at Tevah Am but then we became friends outside of my workplace. Faraj was a very intelligent man and this came out through how quickly he picked up the English language and from there did several courses to get working skills such as the ability to drive a forklift, to operate a cherry picker, do first aid and so on. This made him very employable very quickly. Faraj was also adaptable. He moved where there was work irrespective of how far it took him, within the Sydney metropolitan area, down to Victoria, to South Australia and even to Western Australia.

Faraj loved women as much as I loved men, and our zest for sex was quite comparable. Faraj guessed I was gay in the early days when we began to socialise. He was talking about women one day and he noticed that I did not respond with the same relish which made him ask me at point blank, "Are you gay?" The question hit me right out of the blue. But the frankness of the question was akin to him asking me, "Are you vegan?" I met the frankness with a direct answer in the affirmative. Faraj didn't even bat an eyelid as if he had already surmised the answer and was only waiting for a confirmation. From then on, he was happy to compare notes about sex and sexuality from my world-view and sex and sexuality from his.

Faraj wasn't a married man and this was quite odd in the society from which he had come. But it was obvious from his relish for women that it would be hard for him to settle down with only one. His honesty appealed to me. He never led on to women that he was looking for a relationship but was happy to have sex for the sake of sex. And he knew where to find the type of women who were happy to oblige. I could imagine he was quite a success with women because he had a great built-out body as he was a fanatic body builder. Faraj obviously was aware of how to get the right muscle tone to master the correct streamlined, aerodynamic body that the classical sculptors would have loved to have used as a model. Faraj was rather a disappointment in my life because we got on oddly well and if the physical attraction had been requited, a serious relationship could have well been in the making. But this, unfortunately, was not to be.

Faraj showed his diligence and aptitude to developing his English in quite an odd yet ingenious way. Whereas the average Australian gets flustered at the arrival of door-to-door salespeople in what is often the most inconvenient of times, Faraj welcomed these people into his home and served them tea and nibblies while these salespeople displayed their wares. The salespeople at first were no doubt encouraged by the invitation thinking that they were going to get something out of the sale, only to be later frustrated to find out that the person gaining anything from the encounter was Faraj. Faraj had only invited them in so he could use the opportunity to practise his English.

Not long after I had returned from my trip to Tanzania, Faraj told me that he had had a visit from the Jehovah's Witnesses and the Mormons. When the ambassadors of each of these religions had been invited in, they no doubt believed that they were in luck in bringing a new convert into their folds. In fact, Faraj didn't turn them away empty handed on the first encounter but allowed these missionaries to return time and time again. Faraj asked them difficult questions and these missionaries weren't able to answer the questions themselves on the spot and therefore had to go away and find someone in their religious establishments that could. These religious ambassadors also brought lots of literature for Faraj to read, all in English, although out of the deal Faraj managed to score himself a Bible in Farsi, obviously these missionaries thinking that this would enable the conversion to go much smoother than if Faraj still had to battle through the Christian holy book in English.

"And have you read any of the Bible?" I asked inquisitively.

"Bits of it. I read a few things at the beginning and there were things in there I knew about because I am a Muslim," Faraj replied brazenly.

"So, you had no difficulty reading the Bible?" I continued.

"No, not really. Why?" Faraj asked with a question mark in his voice as if I thought he may have found the Bible a very complicated book to read. Once I realised that this was the import of his question, I reframed the question.

"What I mean is, as a Muslim, what did you think when you read the Bible? I mean, I thought Muslims don't believe in the Christian Bible."

"No," Faraj came back with, "of course Muslims believe the Christian Bible. We believe in all the prophets and if so we must believe in the books written by these prophets."

What? I thought. Are you serious? Could you then tell all the Muslims in the world who attack Jews and Christians and their holy books what you have just told me? That's not the general picture we are getting of Muslims and their beliefs.

"It's funny but Ibrahim said much the same thing," I replied.

"Ibrahim?" Faraj asked.

"Oh, he's this guy I met at the Msingi wa Mungu Project in Tanzania." I then went on to explain to Faraj exactly what the Msingi wa Mungu Project was, what I had done there, and a brief summary of the dialogues I had had with Ibrahim.

"But what I would have liked to have asked Ibrahim was how he, as a Muslim, gets around contradictory teachings between, say, the Gospels and the Koran."

"What's that word? Contra…?" Faraj interjected.

"Contradictory. 'Contradictory' means when you have two statements and both statements say the opposite. So if you have a contradictory teaching, it means one teaching, say in the Injil," and I slipped straight into the Arabic word because I had heard Ibrahim use it so often. At that point I interrupted myself and explained to Faraj why I had used that word and not the English word "Gospel". I then continued. "And another teaching, in the Koran, and both are opposite. That is a contradictory teaching. So, if Muslims believe that the Injil is from God and the Koran is from God, then when there are two teachings that are opposite, you have a contradictory teaching."

"For example?" Faraj asked in anticipation.

There were so many, I thought, but I decided to choose one that wasn't very controversial.

"Let's take divorce. What does the Koran teach about divorce? Can a man divorce his wife?"

"Yes," Faraj stated quite emphatically as if this were obvious.

I chose this topic because I knew of the stark contrast between divorce in Islam and divorce in Christianity. In Islam, all a Muslim man had to do was say to his wife *talak, talak, talak*, meaning "I divorce you, I divorce you, I divorce you", and the divorce took place there and then. Both ex-husband and ex-wife were then free to marry someone else. By contrast, Jesus said in the Sermon on the Mount in Matthew 5:32 and to the Pharisees in Mark 10:11, 12 that a husband and wife should never divorce, except if one of them has an affair outside the marriage, and if they should happen to divorce, they were no longer allowed to marry anyone else.

Faraj's Farsi Bible was handy so I looked through it to find one of the passages and then passed Faraj's Farsi Bible over to him for him to read. I watched Faraj read this with intent and I was curious to know what his answer was going to be. He had a deep furrow while he contemplated the text. I was expecting him to be speechless when he had finished reading it, or at least say that the Gospels were no longer reliable which is why we have the Koran. But rather he had an answer to provide.

"Look, you know, you're a teacher, aren't you?" he began. "You set strict rules when you teach, what you expect from people who don't do their homework and what is a pass or a fail in a test, don't you?"

"Yeah," I replied hesitantly.

"Now you set these expectations really high because you want your students to do well, don't you?"

"Yeah," I replied just as hesitantly.

"Sometimes, just sometimes, you have students who don't perform as well to these rules so sometimes, when by these rules these students should just fail, you take other things into consideration, like they have family responsibilities or work responsibilities which prevent them from doing all the homework and passing all the tests, although on the whole they work hard as students."

"Yeah," I replied once again in the same expectant tone.

"Well, it's the same here. No doubt God wants people when they marry to stay married for life. But sometimes, even with the best intentions, a married couple find that they no longer can live with each other and so God makes concessions for them and allows them to divorce."

I don't know what appealed to me the most, the amazing level of Faraj's English to express this really complicated idea or the way he beautifully maintained the unity of the New Testament with the Koran. He did not, as I would have expected and have heard from other Muslims, completely disregard the Injil at all with a side remark that the Injil has been tampered with and we can no longer trust it. In his answer, he maintained the integrity of both holy books.

This then made me think. What did I really know about Islam? Was the Islam that we saw in the world of bombing and killings of the infidel really what Islam was about or was there another side to Islam that I was missing?

"You know, Faraj," I started. "Can we go back a bit to the beginning? Like, I don't know much about Islam except what I've heard, such as, you have to pray five times to Mecca every day, Friday is the Muslim holy day, you have to fast during the daylight hours during Ramadan, women have to wear veils and the Koran is the holy book. When I met Faisal, I never asked him much about Islam because I felt too uncomfortable asking in the case that if I said I didn't agree with something he said about Islam, Faisal would do something bad to me. But when I was with Ibrahim at the Msingi wa Mungu Project, Ibrahim told me a side of Islam which is different to what we see on the news. Can I ask you some questions about Islam? I mean, it's not that I want to convert to the religion, it's simply that I would like to understand more about it, what the religion really teaches."

Faraj looked at me with a serious but calm expression.

"Sure," he replied. "You can ask me anything about Islam. You can even tell me that you don't believe in the religion and that the Koran is just rubbish. That might be your opinion. But I believe it, it's my religion. You can ask any question you like. I don't mind."

Wow! Faraj doesn't mind people asking about his religion and doesn't mind someone even saying that they thought the Koran was rubbish. Faraj would not maim or kill or do anything to a person who criticised his religion but would shrug it off. If only this could be the universal reaction of all believers in the Koran.

"Oh, okay. Well, let's start at the beginning. First of all, Muhammad was visited by the angel Gabriel and it was Gabriel who gave Muhammad the Koran."

Faraj acknowledged that this part of the story was so.

"Now, can I just stop there? This is another reason why I really question a lot about the Judaeo-Christo-Islamic belief. All these religions say that angels have wings and they fly from the throne of God down to earth. The throne of God is somewhere high up in the sky, further away than the sun. Now, when NASA began the space program in the 1960s, wings were found to be totally unnecessary for space flight because there is no air in space. In order for wings to function, on both birds and on planes, and hence on angels, the wings need to be in a medium of air. In the vacuum of space, wings are totally useless. So although the wings on angels are functional within the earth's atmosphere, what propels angels once they enter the vacuum of deep space?"

Faraj laughed. He then thought about it.

"I don't know exactly but maybe it's like the space shuttle. The space shuttle has wings but it only has wings to enable it to fly back from outer space. Once the shuttle leaves the earth's atmosphere, it doesn't use its wings. Maybe it's the same with angels. I don't have a definite answer for you at the moment."

I liked the answer. I didn't agree with it but I thought Faraj's off-the-cuff answer with no preparation was not a bad one. I could have pursued this and then asked that if angels were not made of the same matter as humans and the entire universe we experience, what was the necessity of wings at all? After all, as angels were supposed to be made out of some ethereal substance not affected by matter, angels therefore wouldn't have had the need for wings for propulsion anyway because gravity and wind resistance which occur in the world of matter would have absolutely no effect on them. But this was getting right off the track of my actual enquiry.

"That's okay," I replied. "Now, how did Muhammad get the Koran? Did it come down all at once in book form?"

"Oh, no," Faraj replied. "Muhammad was illiterate so the angel had to recite the Koran to Muhammad and then Muhammad had to memorise it. Friends of the prophet wrote down what Muhammad said to them. But the Koran was not put together as a book until the time of the Caliph Uthman or certainly under the Caliph Abd al-Malik."

If that is the case, I further thought to myself, all the references in the Koran regarding "the Book" can't really refer to the Koran because the Koran did not take on book form until much later after Muhammad received the message from Gabriel. But this seemed like too much of a complicated topic to go into and so I left it.

"Once Muhammad got the Koran," I continued, "how did all this business between Sunnis and Shi'ites begin?"

"That happened before Muhammad died," Faraj replied. "Before Muhammad died, he knew he had to name a successor. One day, it was a really hot day. Muhammad was in the middle of the city when he received a revelation from God. Muhammad demanded a great…um…like a high stage or something like that."

Faraj stopped to find the word.

"Like a platform?" I volunteered.

"Yeah, a platform," Faraj replied but I guessed he only agreed because he had never heard the word "platform" used in this way and it fit. I wasn't sure if this was really the word he was looking for but it didn't take away from the story so I just let him continue.

"Anyway, once the platform had been constructed, Muhammad climbed up and sat at the top with his first cousin, Ali. Muhammad raised Ali's hand high up in the sky in front of everyone, so high that Muhammad's sleeve fell down so that you could see his armpit. He then cried out to everyone…um…I don't know how to translate this exactly."

Faraj thought about it for a moment, first said it in Arabic and then gave his translation,

"'To whomever I am his Lord so this Ali is his Lord'."

"In other words," I suggested, "Muhammad said something to the effect of, 'to those who consider me as their Lord, then they should consider Ali as their Lord'."

"Yes, that sounds right."

But Faraj repeated his translation so I had to guess that this was a word-for-word and therefore more direct translation from the Arabic. But it didn't matter. I got the point.

"So, when Muhammad died," I commented, "Ali became the next leader of the religion."

"He was supposed to," Faraj replied. "But when Muhammad died, there was a big argument over who should take over from Muhammad as the Caliph. Although Muhammad received a revelation that Ali should succeed him, there was a great argument between the different parties. So, Muhammad's son-in-law, Abubaker, became the Caliph after Muhammad's death. Ali didn't put up any resistance because he risked getting killed by Abubaker's supporters if he tried to demand his claim as Muhammad's successor. After Abubaker died, Omar, Muhammad's father-in-law, became the second Caliph and then after him the next Caliph was Osman. Then when Osman died, finally the people begged Ali to take the rightful place of becoming the Caliph as Muhammad had first said. At this stage, Ali really didn't want to take the position but felt pushed into becoming the fourth Caliph."

"Hang on," I interjected. "Let me get this straight. Muhammad received a revelation from God telling him to tell everyone that when he died, Ali was to be his successor. But when Muhammad died, even though everyone believed Muhammad was a prophet, the people chose someone else to be Muhammad's successor instead of the person Muhammad the prophet had named. So this means that these Muslims at the time of Muhammad didn't show by their actions that they believed Muhammad at all. Rather, they showed a total disrespect and disregard for this prophet of God."

"And this is the problem," Faraj continued. "This has caused the fighting between the Sunnis and the Shi'ites ever since. The Sunnis believe that Abubaker truly was the successor of Muhammad but the Shi'ites don't. The Shi'ites believe that Abubaker took leadership when he shouldn't have but because Islam was only a small tree that needed guarding, they allowed Abubaker to take the power. It wasn't until Ali finally became Caliph that Islam became strong."

I liked the imagery of Islam as a small tree that needed guarding. I thought this was very poetic. But at the same time, it raised another question. If God is Almighty, it doesn't matter how small His tree is because no-one could harm it anyway. So why did Ali and his supporters believe that they needed to give away the rightful place of the Caliphate to Abubaker in order to protect this new religion? If God had intended Ali to be the successor after Muhammad, who on earth could be strong enough to resist God's will? If what Faraj was relating to me were true, Abubaker was able to override God's will. But further, if Abubaker became the ultimate leader of the Muslims after Muhammad's death thus disregarding this revelation from God through Muhammad, it showed that Abubaker and all his supporters had great contempt for God and His messenger. But it added to the confusion that if Abubaker took the place of Muhammad, how could Abubaker make the people follow any of the other injunctions that Muhammad had given to the people if Abubaker couldn't even obey Muhammad's injunction to make Ali Muhammad's successor? I didn't want to say anything or ask Faraj anything about that but Faraj must have read my thoughts because he added to what he had just been talking about.

"Because Abubaker became the next Caliph after Muhammad against the revelation from God through Muhammad, this created a spiritual problem for Muslims. The Muslims who say that Abubaker was the rightful successor of Muhammad are the Sunnis. The Sunnis say that, in fact, Muhammad did not say that Ali was his successor. What Sunnis say is that when Muhammad said, 'To whomever I am his Lord so this Ali is his Lord', that the word 'Lord' in Arabic is *mo'lai* and that in Classical Arabic you will find that *mo'lai* really means 'friend'. So Sunnis say that when Muhammad took the time to organise the construction of the platform, you imagine, it probably took hours, then Muhammad climbed up onto that platform in the middle of the hot day and raised Ali's arm so high that you could see his armpit, he simply wanted to tell everyone that whoever is Muhammad's friend is also Ali's friend."

I laughed. I laughed at the sheer cynicism and the criticism Faraj was expressing towards the Sunnis because of the interpretation of this statement. Faraj appreciated the humour in what he had said and how I reacted to it, and smiled in reply.

"I mean," Faraj continued, "if you ask a Sunni just like that, without any reference to that sentence, what *mo'lai* means, they will tell you it means 'lord'. You try it. The next time you meet a Sunni at your work, before you ask anything about his religion, just ask him as if you are asking out of curiosity what does the Arabic word *mo'lai* mean and he will tell you that it means 'lord'. But if you then ask why then they don't believe Ali was the rightful Caliph after Muhammad when Muhammad had said, 'To whomever I am his Lord so this Ali is his Lord', then he will say, 'Oh, yeah, but you have to remember in Classical Arabic that the word *mo'lai* really means 'friend' and that's what it means here' and so they will go on."

What struck me about the split between the Sunnis and the Shi'ites was how much it seemed like an echo of the split between Catholics and Protestants, although the split between the latter followed the split between the two Muslim groups. Both Catholics and Protestants read what Jesus said to the apostle Peter in Matthew 16:18 that

Thou art Peter, and upon this rock I will build my church

but they come up with different interpretations. The Catholics claim that this verse means that Peter was the rock upon which Christ built his Church. Their justification for this is lost in the English translation. But in the original language of the New Testament, Koine Greek, the name, Peter, and the word, "rock", are *Petros* and *petra* respectively, and this supposedly was intended as a play on words to show that Peter and, what the Catholics then assume, all Peter's successors represented through the subsequent popes are the rock upon which Christ's Church was to be built. By contrast, when Protestants read this same verse, they admit the play on words but say that Jesus is referring, not to Peter, but to himself, and that the play on words means that in the same way as Peter's name means "rock", so the Church is built on a rock but that this rock is the confession that Peter made a few verses earlier that Jesus was the Messiah. And then the Protestants extend this to mean that because Christ is the rock, this therefore means that the Bible is that rock. After all, so the

Protestants argue, if Christ had intended to build his Church on Peter, he would have said, "Thou art Peter, and upon thee I will build my church". The Catholics then make the counterclaim that Protestants only began to see this alternate interpretation fifteen hundred years after Christ had made this statement, when Martin Luther, John Calvin, Henry VIII and all the subsequent breakaway factions from the Catholic Church began their own private churches, and so to keep the integrity of this verse they had to reinterpret it.

A lot of arguing over a statement of twelve words. But, as a result, there have been hundreds of years of slaughter within Europe and outside Europe in countries where Europeans have spread the two factious versions of Christianity, all because of an interpretation of a verse about who or what is the rightful successor of the Church after Christ's death. In the same way, there has been ruthless slaughter between Sunnis and Shi'ites throughout the history of Islam over the interpretation of a saying of Muhammad and about who should be or should have been Muhammad's rightful successor.

"But we Shi'ites believe," Faraj continued, "that Ali was the rightful Caliph and he only became Caliph after Abubaker, Omar and Osman had been Caliphs before him."

"So, there are Caliphs today who are the successors of these Caliphs," I asked.

"No. After Ali, Ali's first son, Hassan, became Caliph. When Hassan died, his brother, Hossein, became the next Caliph. When Hossein died, then his son became Caliph and the Caliphate passed down from father to son down to Mehdi. Mehdi was the twelfth Caliph. But Mehdi didn't die. He's still alive living somewhere in Arabia. When he got old, he retired and now lives in a tent but he wanders around in Arabia. He only interacts with Muslims when there's a big dispute."

I looked on with incredulity.

"Wow! He should participate in the United Nations."

"No," Faraj replied in all seriousness. "The Mehdi no longer speaks to humans directly. There are two…er…*na'ib*…er…someone who speaks for someone else."

"A representative?" I asked.

"Yeah, a representative. There is a *na'ib khaas*, that is, a special representative. He is the only one who can speak with Mehdi. Then there's the *na'ib aam*, or public representative. Mehdi speaks to the *na'ib khaas* and the *na'ib khaas* then speaks to the *na'ib aam* who then speaks to all the Muslims and tells them how to settle their disputes."

"And he's still alive today? After how many years?"

"It's about," and Faraj looked up at the roof and then said in the intonation of a question, "eight hundred years?"

Did Faraj seriously believe this? Didn't Faraj see that this could easily be made up because no-one could ever see Mehdi and therefore prove that he was alive or dead? The lines of communication were complex to ensure that the evidence that a man eight hundred years of age and still living today remained unprovable.

"This Mehdi," Faraj continued, interrupting my thoughts, "is the one we believe who will come back riding a white horse, like it says in the Revelation in the Bible."

"You mean, the verse which says in Revelation 19:11, 'And I saw heaven opened, and behold a white horse; and he that sat upon him was called Faithful and True'?"

"Yeah, yeah, that one," Faraj replied in confirmation. "We believe that it won't be the prophet Issa who will ride the white horse. It will be Mehdi."

"Well, if Muslims believe that it will be Mehdi riding the white horse and not Issa," I questioned, "and the Revelation says that it will be Issa and not Mehdi, how do Muslims match this up if they believe the New Testament and the Koran are both revelations from God?"

"I don't think it says in the Revelation the name of the person riding the white horse," Faraj replied.

I didn't have an English Bible with me and I really didn't care who was on that white horse anyway so I let this point go.

"But, why," I continued, "is Mehdi still alive after all this time? Why is it that God allowed Mehdi to stay alive all this time for all these hundreds of years to be the vehicle through which God speaks to the Muslim world in times of disturbance and distress, and yet allowed the greatest prophet, Muhammad, to die?"

Faraj gave a deep sigh. "It's not ours to question God. God has a reason for what He does and if He prefers to do it this way, who are we to question Him?"

And how do you answer that? The eternal religious answer to an impossible question.

However, this began to fascinate me more about the Muslim religion, strangely enough. Ibrahim had given me a Koran so now I wanted to know more about what it said within. But I wanted to start with what Faraj had been talking about.

"So, Faraj, where in the Koran does it talk about the *mo'lai* and the succession of Caliphs?"

"It's not in the Koran," Faraj replied. "It's all in the…er…*hadith*." Faraj looked up at the ceiling as if his roof were a bilingual dictionary.

"Oh, yes, the Hadiths," I replied. "Yes, I've heard about these. And that's what we call them in English."

"Then the Hadith," Faraj replied. "There is a collection of books called the *hadith nabavy,* that is, the Hadith of the Prophets."

When he said this, I realised that the Arabic word for "prophet" must be "nabi" and it struck me how similar it was to the Hebrew word "nevi", a word I was familiar with in particular in what the Jews call the Old Testament, namely, Torah, Nevihim, Uchtuvim, where *nevihim* means "prophets". Hebrew and Arabic are both Semitic languages and I was seeing more and more relationships between the words in these two languages.

"But hang on," I then asked. "I thought only the Koran was the Word of God."

"No, not entirely," Faraj replied emphatically. "But that's what the Sunnis say. The Sunnis only believe what is in the Koran. Sunnis don't believe in the Hadiths or in the Tafsir Al-Mizan. They believe only in the Koran."

"The what, the who? The Taf what, what's his name?" I asked trying to make sense of all this sudden new information.

"The Tafsir Al-Mizan. It's not a person. The Tafsir Al-Mizan is an explanation of the Koran written by Allamah Sayyid Mohammed Husayn Tabataba'i."

I burst out laughing. The name sounded so funny that I thought Faraj was actually joking. But Faraj just looked at me in all seriousness, not understanding why I had laughed. I suddenly felt embarrassed. I coughed and tried to compose myself, removing any signs of jocularity from my face.

"I'm sorry, Faraj. The name sounded funny. Continue."

"Well," Faraj continued, obviously not offended by my outburst of laughter, "he wrote a collection of writings to explain the meaning of the Koran. He was a great man, a great philosopher, who wrote great explanations of each verse of the Koran so that we could all understand what the Koran was saying."

I had to think about this for a moment.

"But don't Muslims simply believe that God sent down the Koran so that everyone knows what's the right thing to do?"

"Yes, that's right. But there are verses in the Koran that are not clear and so the Tafsir Al-Mizan explains in detail what they're supposed to mean."

"So, this means that Muslims believe in the Koran *and* the Hadiths *and* the Tafsir Al-Mizan."

"Yes, that is, Shi'ites do. You can't have the Koran without the Hadiths and the Tafsir Al-Mizan. But the Sunnis say that we should only believe the Koran. Sunnis don't believe in the Hadiths or the Tafsir Al-Mizan."

"But the Sunnis do have a point," I threw in. "From what I understand, the Koran, and the Koran alone, was revealed to Muhammad by the angel Gabriel. The Hadiths and the Tafsir Al-Mizan were written by other people and are therefore the opinion of these people. They are therefore not revelations from God and therefore cannot be used to decide what Muslims are supposed to believe or not believe."

"But you cannot understand the Koran on its own," Faraj objected. "There are verses in the Koran that are not easy to understand or are written in only a few words. The Tafsir Al-Mizan explains these words and verses in greater detail so that people can understand what the message God is trying to give us."

Faraj's explanation of the need for other works such as the Hadiths and the Tafsir Al-Mizan to help us understand such a complicated book as the Koran was quite a strange concept for me. God, so we were led to believe, wanted to convey His message to everyone in the world. This would mean, at least how I understood it, that the message would have been framed in the simplest of language so that even the simplest of minds could understand it for otherwise it would be a message out of reach to the average person on the street. Not to mention, the Koran, as I would read later, makes the claim in Al-Nahl 16:104 that it is "plain and clear" to understand, written, so it says in Al-Zukhruf 43:4 in "clear, eloquent language that you may understand it".

Faraj's argument also meant that the Koran cannot be a guide book of salvation to everyone but only for those who have access to the Hadiths and the Tafsir Al-Mizan. Further, the Koran along with this encyclopaedic library of literature is only for literate and well-read people, and more specifically, well-read people literate in the Arabic language, and even more specifically, people who at some time in their busy lives actually had the time to read all this literature. Were there that many people on the globe and in all history who throughout their lifetimes had actually not only made it through reading all this literature but also been able to remember everything that is written within in order to apply it all to their daily lives? And did we really need so much information to know how to make the world a great place for everyone to live in? Wasn't Jesus' saying to "do unto others as you would have them do unto you" – although better said, "do unto others as they would like to be treated" – clear enough in its simplicity?

Further, it created another issue as there was no agreement amongst Muslims themselves about what is a revelation from God and what is not. It made it even further complicated for us non-Muslims because we spend so much time trying not to offend the Muslims but when it came down to it, after fourteen hundred years, Muslims themselves hadn't quite made it clear either amongst themselves let alone those outside the faith what things exactly offended them and what didn't.

But again, what struck me was the similarity between the Shi'ite-Sunni controversy and that between the Catholics and the Protestants. Protestants claim that Christians need the Bible and the Bible only as a guide through life in very much the same way as Faraj's description of the Sunnis and their relationship to the Koran. Anything beyond this is superfluous and definitely not to be considered. By contrast, the Catholics, although they also believe in the Bible, say that Christians must in addition believe in other traditions handed down by the apostles that are not written in the Bible, and in the proclamations made by successive popes *ex cathedra*. This was similar to Faraj's explanation that the Shi'ites believe in the Koran, the Hadiths, the Tafsir Al-Mizan and the communications from the living Mehdi who passes on extra messages through the *na'ib khaas* to the *na'ib aam* then to all other Muslims, and I guessed in context this meant only Shi'ite Muslims because I could only guess that Sunni Muslims don't believe in the Mehdi.

"And is it ever possible that the Sunnis and Shi'ites will ever be once again united so that there is one Islam?"

"It's not just the Sunnis and the Shi'ites who need to unite if there is to be one version of Islam. There are other versions."

"Other versions?" I asked in stupefaction. "I didn't know there were more than the Sunnis and the Shi'ites."

"Oh, yes," Faraj replied. "There is Wahabism, Ibadi Islam, the Koranists, Yazdanism, the Nation of Islam, Sufism, the Salafi, Al-Ahmadiyyah Muslims…er… that's those I can remember."

Different versions of Islam? And as many as this? The general picture that we got from the media was of a unified group of religious people called Muslims and they all belonged to the one religion. But Faraj had just rattled off ten different factions, and if the Sunni-Shi'ite dispute was anything to go by, these different factions were not united in the slightest. Once again, it was like a mirror on Christianity. There are times when we hear in the media about the Christians as if all Christians belonged to one united front. But there are many versions of Christianity beyond the simple Catholic-Protestant divide.

What struck me of interest was how this showed that when a new religion formed, when the leader of that religion died, instead of there being unity among all the believers in that leader to carry on the religion, factions developed quite soon after the leader's death. I was familiar with this from my knowledge of the history of the Christian Church. Now I was hearing the same thing about Islam.

What intrigued me was that this same phenomenon was evident in all religions, even the not-so-well-known ones and those a bit off centre from the mainstream. For example, I remember in my Bible-believing days, I had originally thought that the Mormons were one united group of people, supporters of their leader, Joseph Smith. However, I discovered that when Joseph Smith died, immediately his religion split into factions and it is only one of several opposing factions who have missionaries who annoy us at our door.

Even the Jews weren't unified. According to the Gospels, at the time of Jesus, there were three major parties, the Pharisees, the Sadducees and the Herodians, and from Josephus there was a fourth group in this divide called the Essenes. The Jews today are still divided between the liberals, the orthodox and the ultra-orthodox even though they all claim to descend from one patriach, Abraham, and have one law-giver, Moses.

But that was enough of Islam and comparative religions for the day. It certainly opened up my eyes to the reality of Faraj's religion.

"I appreciate, Faraj," I concluded, "that you don't get hostile and want to kill me because I don't believe in your religion."

"Each to his own religion," Faraj replied. "I'll tell you something. I had this dream once."

Oh, no, not another dreamer, I groaned inside. Is this yet another Muslim thing?

"I dreamt," Faraj continued, "that I was standing next to a suitcase and Jesus was standing in front of me."

It struck me that this time Faraj called him Jesus and not Issa.

"Jesus then said to me, referring to the suitcase, 'Lift it'. I tried but I couldn't lift it. Then Jesus said to me, 'Go on, lift it'. I said to him, 'But I can't lift it'. Jesus then smiled at me and said, 'It is well that you said you can't lift it. Each to his own religion. We can only lift what we can'.

And when I woke up, I realised that God had sent me a message and I understood what he was trying to tell me."

This was getting a little too much twilight-zonish. But I didn't want to make it obvious that Faraj's recount of his dream was to me a little odd. So, I used it as a conversation piece.

"Yes, Ibrahim had dreams and he said one involved me," I added.

"Ibrahim? You mean, this Ibrahim you met in Africa?"

"Yeah, that one."

"You mention him a lot," Faraj commented. And then a broad smile appeared right over Faraj's face. "You love this Ibrahim, don't you? You've mentioned him so many times in this conversation! There's something going on between you and him!"

I could feel the flush in my face so I must have gone beetroot red. And it was quite apparent as Faraj pointed out to me quite frankly.

"Did you have fun with him?" Faraj added.

A second wave of flushness surged through my body towards my face and Faraj laughed almost uncontrollably.

What intrigued me about Faraj was his total acceptance of my homosexuality even though he was a Muslim because I was aware that homosexuality was a crime worthy only of death in Muslim countries, especially in Iran where Faraj was from.

But I was also aware of Faraj's background and the quasi-totalitarian regime he had escaped from and the difficulty to survive under such a regime. Faraj had made it clear to me from several of our conversations that a life where people are forced to live a particular way was an unpleasant one. As a result, this is what made him so tolerant of people who followed other religions and commendably enough even towards people like me who did not ascribe to any particular religion at all. On top of that, he had no problem accepting the fact that I fooled around naked with guys. To Faraj, this was okay as it was private fun that I was having and I wasn't hurting anyone in the process. This in particular no doubt was a result of his own lifestyle where he had fun with women naked, none of whom were his wife. Faraj seemed to appreciate my sexual freedom because he could relate to it from his own life experience.

"So, are you going to go back there and meet with Ibrahim again?" Faraj continued.

"No," I replied slowly. "I can't go back. I mean, it's quite expensive to travel there and it would take me a while to save up."

I stopped there for a moment. And then I continued.

"You know, Faraj, Ibrahim was a really nice guy. I admit I had fun with him and it was good. But Ibrahim was something different."

With that, I went on to explain all the wonderful qualities I saw in Ibrahim, our conversations, Ibrahim's religious views and his overall views of humanity. As I described him, and it was the first time I had spoken to anyone about him in such detail, I realised just how deep-seated my admiration for him was. Faraj looked on silently as I went off in my verbal reverie. When I had finished, the expression on Faraj's face said it all.

"Wow, Michael! He sounds like the right guy for you! Don't let this guy get away from you!"

I sat back in my chair in exasperation.

"But how can a relationship develop between us? Seriously. Ibrahim is in Tanzania and I am here in Australia. And really, I don't know the guy that well."

"It sounds like you know him well enough!" Faraj suggested.

"Well, that would then mean that one of us has to move from his country to live with the other one. I think it's a foregone conclusion that Ibrahim would have to move here because there would be no way in the world that we could live together there. And then that means I have to sponsor him. How do I do that? And I'm only a simple trainer, and only a casual trainer on sporadic work. To do something like that, you need lots of money and I certainly don't have lots of money."

Faraj's face relaxed into a smile.

"Hey, Michael, when it's love, love will find a way. And if it's God's will, He'll make a way, even if you have to walk on water or ride on the back of a fish to get to him, it will happen."

When Faraj mentioned the riding of a fish, it sent a tingle through my whole being. Ibrahim had said that in his dream, this ethereal being, supposedly me, came riding on the back of a red fish to bring Ibrahim, my supposed twin, back to this faraway land to the land of the rising sun, at least the land of the rising sun in respect to Tanzania.

Faraj then looked at his watch and jumped up off the lounge.

"Ooop! I have to go to work now."

Faraj then began busying himself preparing for work while I stood waiting for him. I then accompanied him to the station which was not far from his unit before returning back to my car and then driving home.

The conversation I had with Faraj really brought out further my curiosity regarding Muslims and Islam. But it was Faraj's final comments in relationship to Ibrahim that really stood out. Faraj had commended me to Ibrahim to the extent of encouragement. The fact that I had spoken about Ibrahim openly to someone also brought out my feelings towards Ibrahim to the fore. Yes, he would be the type of man I could live with. I didn't simply think of him as a wonderful African jungle adventure. I had deep feelings for Ibrahim and I could actually imagine sharing a life with him. It was like a missing piece of a puzzle which had finally been put into place.

But that would have been easy had we met here in Australia, if Ibrahim had been a learner at Tevah Am, for example, or a member of Polycarp's community in Sydney. But Ibrahim was a Tanzanian man with a life in Tanzania, in a country which was so hard to get to from Sydney. There was a great mountain to surmount for there to be any chance for Ibrahim and me to ultimately live together. But it was just impossible. I knew I shouldn't even venture into this thought because it was delusional and I would in the end end up extremely frustrated and hurt.

But also, the very idea of getting into a relationship with someone troubled me. I had been in relationships before but they had been ephemeral and ended unpleasantly. The alternate free life I led where I could have a different sex partner was much more appealing. But Ibrahim had upset the oxcart. He made me think once again of the possibility of getting involved with the one person. I had to speak to someone about it.

The following morning at Tevah Am, when there was a lull in our workplace and Hebbeera had not yet arrived, I struck up a conversation with Nikita.

"How long have you and Pace been together," I asked.

"Oh, about three years," Nikita replied.

"Are you happy in your relationship?"

Nikita gave me a funny look. "Why, you suddenly have an interest in going out with me?" she asked and smiled.

"No, don't be silly," I replied meeting her joke. I then returned to being serious. "Are you happy being in a relationship?"

Nikita looked at me for a moment and then spoke. "Michael, what are you getting at? Is this about Ibrahim?"

I took a deep breath and then sighed. "Yes, okay, it's about Ibrahim."

I was silent for a moment and then continued. "I mean, it's totally impossible that we could ever be together as a couple. But even if we could, I don't know what's better, to stay single and enjoy my single life where I can pick up different guys at different times or to actually have the one person in my life."

Nikita smiled. "You really are serious about this Ibrahim, aren't you? This was no holiday fling."

I shrugged my shoulders and raised my eyebrows as a silent answer which was a noncommittal yes.

"I dunno," I continued. "I can't see how being with the one person all the time is better than the free life I live now with no commitments. I mean, don't you get sick of Pace sometimes and wish you were no longer together so that you could have a bit of fun with someone else as a bit of variety?"

Nikita laughed. "Of course, I sometimes feel that. That's only natural. But, Michael, it's not a question of whether being single or being in a committed relationship is better. Neither life is perfect. Nothing in life is perfect. So, you have to make choices. Which do you prefer, to remain single and have random affairs or live with the one person for the rest of your life?"

"And do you like having only Pace?"

"Yes, very much," Nikita stated emphatically. "She is a great partner."

"But don't you ever get tired of her? What happens if you want to have sex and she doesn't feel like it and vice versa? What happens if Pace just lets her body go and makes herself unattractive? What happens if you see another woman and you want to make out with her one night?"

Niktia laughed again. "Michael, like I said, neither life is perfect. You have to make choices. The single life is not always that enticing anyway. Being on your own can be quite lonely. It might be true that you can have sex with whomever you want but you have to find someone first to do it with her. It's not like as soon as you feel like having sex, a woman you like having sex with is waiting for you there and then. You have to go out and find her. And then you might become frustrated because you can't get anyone. So, the single life is not always as attractive as it sounds. But I understand also that being in a relationship isn't always attractive either. I try to make sure that I keep physically attractive for Pace because my body now belongs to her and I should keep my body the way it was when she first saw it. I'm sure, however, that Pace would continue to love me nonetheless. But in a relationship, I can't think of myself anymore, I have to think of Pace. I have to say to myself whenever I do anything, would I appreciate this if Pace did this to me? If I let my body go, or if I leave the home a mess, or if I want to go out, or even if I look at another woman, I have to ask myself, how would I feel if

Pace did this to me? Being in a relationship is quite challenging because it's not simply about having sex with your partner. It's about living with your partner on a day to day basis where sex is actually a small part of the package. And then there are other issues that can cause problems like how to spend your time and your money. It just so happens with Pace and me, these issues are not a big problem. I mean, we have our moments but on the whole Pace is a wonderful woman and I'm glad I have found her and all the positives of being with her far outweigh the negatives."

I stood there and thought about it for a moment.

"If you do meet someone you love," Nikita continued, "that person is much, much better than all the one-night stands you could ever have. Sex is so much nicer with the person you love than with a total stranger. And then there is so much more. There is the cuddling up together either in bed or even sitting and watching a movie with a glass of wine and a box of chocolates."

I shrugged my shoulders because I really didn't know what to say to this.

"Also," Nikita continued, "I understand that finding that special person is not easy. But if you do, you want to hold onto her, in your case, him, because it's not easy to find that someone special to share your life with."

"But Ibrahim lives in another country," I replied.

"It doesn't matter. When you have found that special person, you want to reach out and hold her and not let her go."

I reflected a moment.

"To be honest," I admitted, "I don't know if it's just an infatuation, a holiday affair or something deeper."

"You certainly talk about him a lot," Nikita replied with a laugh.

"Yeah, okay, so I do," I said. "But if I were to get into a relationship with him, or with anyone, before making a commitment, I would like to get to know the person well. I'm sure you knew Pace well before you moved in together with her."

"Yes," Nikita replied. "That's true. We knew each other for about two years."

"But how can I get to know Ibrahim better?"

"You're still in communication with him, aren't you?" Nikita questioned me.

I sighed. "No, I'm not. I don't have his contact details."

"You've got to be kidding!" Nikita remarked.

"Well," I replied, "Ibrahim seems really religious or at least has some really strong religious ideas."

"That's not a good sign, then," Nikita said abruptly.

"Well, yeah. Said like that. The thing is," I continued, "that his odd religious ideas fit in snugly with my world view."

I then paused for a moment of reflection before I added.

"It's really strange," I continued. "We shared the same room for just over a week and yet at no time did I feel uncomfortable with him as a roommate. I only felt uncomfortable with him because of his religion but then when we did the deed, Ibrahim embraced what we did into his religious views."

Nikita threw me a strange look. "I thought you said he was a Muslim," she stated.

"Well, he said he was and he even quoted from the Koran. And from the Bible, surprisingly enough!"

"Sounds a bit too creepy to me," Nikita stated emphatically.

I thought a moment.

"But what if Pace," I continued, "told you that she still embraced a religion, say, Christianity, and felt that she could be both a Christian and be your partner and somehow she didn't find this incompatible. Would you have moved in with her?"

"Probably not," Nikita answered without hesitation.

I wasn't satisfied with the answer and so I decided to attack it from a different angle.

"Okay, then, what would you do if Pace came home one day and said that she had this dream that God had spoken to her but what God had said to her really had no effect on your lives together but simply on her outlook on life? Like, Pace said God told her stuff but none of it was that your relationship was wrong and you had to go to church or anything like that, just that she felt God told her to be nice to everyone?"

Nikita laughed. "I'd divorce her."

"Seriously," I said.

"If Pace came home and told me that," she began and looked up at the roof as if she had to be careful what she said because there was a CCTV recording everything. "I suppose if she said that God spoke to her and her ideas were a bit strange and yet she still thought that being with me was fine, I mean, knowing Pace, I would find this hard to believe she would even say such a stupid thing, but if her belief in a god was not the male chauvinistic destructive Jehovah but some other benevolent more feminine or at least balanced feminino-masculino God, I suppose

I would think it a bit odd but I would still love her. I mean, it would depend on what this belief really was all about and what it was leading her to do."

Nikita paused. She then added, "You know, Michael, the first thing you must do is be honest. Tell Ibrahim honestly what you feel about religion and why. If Ibrahim truly loves you, your different views about religion will not be a hindrance. I can tell you, if he said something to you like, 'I don't care that you don't follow the same religion as me, I love you anyway and my love for you I can work into my faith', this means he sincerely loves you. That's true love in my book."

Nikita then looked in the direction of the door and then the expression on her face changed.

"Speaking of God, here she comes now," Nikita finally said.

I looked in the direction Nikita was looking and saw that Hebbeera had arrived. This signalled the end of this conversation.

I wasn't quite satisfied with what I got out of the conversation with Nikita. What I did realise was that I knew very little about Ibrahim except what I could glean from the week together and also the comment Gordon had made about him which also was a positive comment.

That night, I sat on the balcony of my flat, glass of wine in hand, and stared out at suburbia around and below me. I had lived alone for a long time and I enjoyed my solitary life. But because of Ibrahim, suddenly I felt as if I needed someone to share my life with. That is, not just someone, I wanted Ibrahim. But I realised that not only were there so many insurmountable obstacles that lay in the way of such an idea coming into being, I didn't even have any contact details. When I had left the Msingi wa Mungu Project, I wanted to make the separation total so I didn't ask for Ibrahim's contact details and, oddly enough, Ibrahim didn't ask for mine. So maybe he really didn't have feelings for me as strong as he expressed them while I was there. Maybe as it was for me, for Ibrahim I was just an exotic adventure, a stranger from a faraway land. Eventually we would forget about each other as we moved on with our lives.

But surely, I thought as an afterthought, it still wouldn't hurt if we were at least penfriends. We could write to each other and continue to exchange ideas. That would be something. But for that to happen, I needed his contact details. I could get them if I went back to the Msingi wa Mungu Project office in Sydney where all of this had begun.

I therefore resolved to speak to someone at the Msingi wa Mungu Project office in Sydney at my next available moment.

Chapter 11

To accomplish my mission, I knew it would be better to physically pay a visit to the Msingi wa Mungu Project office in North Parramatta than to ring or try to make contact by email. After all, I had no particular reason why I wanted to specifically communicate with Ibrahim so I had to come up with a strategy to explain this odd request.

Before reaching the office, I had invented a reason why I needed to get Ibrahim's specific contact details. My scheme, so I thought, was cleverly devised and soon I would be able to re-establish contact.

Once inside the office, I asked to speak to Angela but discovered that she was now over in Moshi. The receptionist at the desk was not the same one I had met on my first visit and so I had to give some background of who I was and why I was at the office making enquiries.

"Well, I was at the Msingi wa Mungu Project at Moshi some time ago," and I stated the dates of my arrival and departure, "but when I returned home, I noticed my personal diary was missing. I like to keep a personal diary and write down my thoughts, and especially as this was a great adventure from my home country, I certainly wanted to write down my thoughts about it. I have searched everywhere at home, however, and I can't find it. I'm sure I left it in Moshi. I shared a room with a Tanzanian guy called Ibrahim. Do you know Ibrahim?"

The receptionist shook her head and confessed that she hadn't actually been to Tanzania before.

"Oh, okay. I'm sure Gordon knows who he is. If I could just have Ibrahim's contact details, then I can send a message to him so that I can get my diary back."

"Oh, you don't have to worry about all that," the receptionist replied. "If you describe what the diary looks like, I'll organise Gordon to retrieve it for you and bring it back with him when he returns."

A fluster of frustration caused my hands to clench but fortunately I held these behind my back out of the receptionist's sight.

"Ah, well, I'd rather speak to Ibrahim directly. Ibrahim probably would know exactly what the diary looked like because he saw me writing in it a couple of times."

"Well, that will make it easier," the receptionist said cheerfully as if she felt she were actually helping me out. "I'll just ask Gordon to speak with Ibrahim and if Ibrahim knows what it looks like, he will have no trouble locating it."

I scratched my ear and screwed up my face in exasperation trying to think of another tactic to get the prize I had come for.

"Well, the problem is, you know, it's a personal diary and I don't want people to inadvertently read the contents. I mean, I don't mind Ibrahim reading it because I noted down some of the things he told me. But I don't want other people there reading it because, I don't know, maybe they will take offence."

"Ah, sir, but that's not a problem. We will get Ibrahim to wrap it up so no-one with prying eyes will be able to look inside and read it."

No doubt the receptionist was trying hard to be helpful but she was destroying all my attempts to get what I had come for. I stood there flustered, trying to think of something to say when finally, in exasperation, I blurted out, "I spent nine days sharing the same room with Ibrahim. We became friends the whole time and I really want to get back in contact with him. However, I lost his contact details. We had some really interesting conversations and I really wanted to continue our discussions even if we do it from a distance. But I don't have his contact details and I need them!" The poor receptionist looked at me rather timidly and finally said, "Oh, okay. Why didn't you say that in the first place? Here, you can write to the Msingi wa Mungu Project in Moshi."

The receptionist then clacked on the keyboard of her computer with amazing speed. I then saw her press Print, the printer made clicking and whirring sounds, and out came a printed document with the Msingi wa Mungu Project contact details in Moshi.

"You can send an email to this email address," the receptionist then added, "and I'm sure someone could pass it on to him. If it's personal, you might have to write a letter by hand and just post it to this post office address."

Once that sheet of paper was in my hand, the feeling of relief was like finally making it to the toilet after fighting a desperate urge. I thanked the receptionist profusely for the address. I don't think she fully appreciated why the address was of such importance to me but at least I got what I came for.

That night, once again on the balcony of my unit, a glass of red wine on the balcony table next to a fresh new writing pad, I sat with pen at the ready. This was the first time in a long time since I had ever written a letter to anyone. Writing letters, so I thought, was a means of correspondence from a bygone era. We had now entered the world of Internet and

Facebook, where written communication was done through tappings on a keyboard or hand movements over a screen. But I was about to write a letter by hand onto a sheet of paper using an ink pen. Fortunately I still often took notes or wrote minutes at meetings by hand so I still had maintained this skill.

But it wasn't the fact that I was about to write a letter by hand that was delaying me. It was the fact that I simply didn't know what to write. In a way, I felt extremely guilty for having left Ibrahim with absolutely no possibility of him being able to get in contact with me and I had not taken the effort until now to actually get back in contact with him. An apology was a definite requirement. Even my reservations about the possibility of us ever having a serious man-to-man relationship no longer constituted an excuse. I could have been honest and simply told Ibrahim that it was not meant to be but that we could still be friends, even if it simply meant we were correspondents from different continents because part of what brought us together was the sharing of our ideas and this easily could continue despite the distance between us.

I stared at the paper, then out at suburbia, then at my glass of wine and then at the paper again. I simply didn't know what to write. Feelings of guilt were blocking the flow of thought. I sat back in my chair, took a sip of wine and looked once again beyond the railing of my balcony. Maybe this was a silly idea. Re-establishing contact with Ibrahim would create the false idea that Ibrahim had in his dream that we would eventually be together. Even though I knew it would never happen and Ibrahim was simply deluding himself, by creating communication channels between us, wouldn't I be guilty of leading him on into thinking that his delusion would one day come to pass?

While I sat back and enjoyed another sip of wine, allowing the coolness of the evening to gently breeze over me, Faraj's words came back to me in replay: Hey, Michael, when it's love, love will find a way. And if it's God's will, He'll make a way, even if you have to walk on water or ride on the back of a fish to get to him, it will happen. Don't let this guy get away from you.

This was like the command to remove the blockage, open the flood gates and let the ideas flow. I put my wine down, picked up my pen and began to write.

I stopped here and thought: What if someone else read this letter before Ibrahim did? What if this letter arrived at the Msingi wa Mungu Project, even though it was personally addressed to Ibrahim, the receptionist or some other person who collected the mail decided that it was his or her job to open and read incoming mail before passing it on to the specific addressee? But I didn't want to cross out what I had just written. So I just left these words stand and then continued in a less emotionally packed tone. I talked about our conversations, about the goals of the Msingi wa Mungu Project, our trip to Arusha to the UNHCR office, and I alluded in the most cryptic of language, in a way I hoped Ibrahim would understand but nobody else could, of the last moments together. I then wrote a bit about my return to normal Sydney life and how I had seen Polycarp since I had returned although I had not let Polycarp know anything about my going to Tanzania in the first place. I concluded the letter in a less emotionally charged way than I had previously planned, signing off as if I had been writing simply to a dear friend or even a cherished brother, and not an intimate lover.

When I had finished, I realised that I had actually written five handwritten pages of this large notepad. I reread the letter and tried to imagine a neutral third party who had inadvertently managed to get their hands on the letter and what they would have understood of the contents. I satisfied myself that any other reader apart from Ibrahim would simply understand the letter as a correspondence between two very close male friends, nothing more.

I then folded the letter up, placed it in an envelope and wrote Ibrahim's name and the postal address of the Msingi wa Mungu Project in Moshi. I wrote my return address on the back of the envelope and then turned the envelope once again to the front. In the old days of letter writing, if you wanted only the addressee to see the contents of a letter, you had to write Private and Confidential in clear letters at the top, and so I did.

At least that was an upside of the old handwritten letters. The only way handwritten letters got read by anybody else was if someone else actually physically opened the letter and had a look. Then the receiver would know that the letter had been tampered with. These days, electronic letters are freely available once they are put into cyberspace and anyone computer-savvy enough to intercept and read them can do so with the sender and receiver being none the wiser. In fact, e-letters can readily be duplicated or even multiple copies made, and the copies can go viral revealing anything personal the sender and the receiver hoped to conceal from all but themselves.

The following day I had to go to the post office to buy a stamp so I could send it. Wow! That was something else I couldn't remember doing for such a long time. It was like taking a stroll down memory lane, a bit of childhood nostalgia of a simpler life.

I plopped the letter in the post box outside the post office and heard it clunk before I set off. I really didn't know how long it would take before I would finally get a reply from Ibrahim but as soon as the letter was in the post box, I tried to simply forget all about him.

It was time to put all my energies back into Polycarp and Jeremiah. With no family and it was beginning to become apparent that even with no community support here in Australia, Polycarp was sure to flounder if he didn't get some support.

My routine with Polycarp and Jeremiah had now become three nights a week where I came over to their place, two during the week and one on the weekend. On these evenings, I cooked tea, helped first Jeremiah with his homework and then helped Polycarp until there was no more energy left in my mind and so I had to go to sleep. On these three evenings, I slept at Polycarp's place and went to work from his place the following morning.

Because of Polycarp, I suddenly found myself in a situation where I now had to put full effort into learning Swahili. This was our mode of communication and I needed it more than ever. I needed it to help Polycarp who was himself going through a crash course in learning but for him it was learning English as well as other basic schooling. Because of the war and the atrocities Polycarp went through in East Africa, Polycarp had interrupted schooling so there was a lot he had missed out on. Further, all his initial schooling was conducted in French.

When the war started and the massacre between tribes forced the mass exodus of Rwandans from their home country, Polycarp spent his early teens simply running and trying to survive. Trying to find metaphors in an obscure and not-very-interesting poem or trying to calculate the equation of a parabola was certainly of no importance at this stage in his life. When he finally found refuge in a refugee camp at the north western extremity of Tanzania, although not the same conditions as they were in his childhood days, in the refugee camp Polycarp was able to continue some semblance of schooling that he had been denied prior to this time. In the refugee camp, schools were set up and children could continue to get an education. The teachers continued the tradition of conducting the schooling in the language of learning, that is, in French as it had been so in Rwanda.

When I looked at a map to find where Rwanda was, I was quite amazed to see how close it was to the east coast of Africa. From my knowledge of history, I was aware of the English-French rivalry in Africa and how France won domination of the west of Africa and Britain of the east. I had always thought you could run an imaginary line through the middle of this continent and this would roughly show the divide between French and British Africa. However, if such a line existed, France had penetrated much further east over this line reaching east as far as Burundi and Rwanda. However, I was later to find out that Burundi and Rwanda were not originally French colonies but rather Belgian, and that Burundi and Rwanda were originally not separate countries but part of the Congo.

Polycarp was later to explain to me that Burundi and Rwanda were originally one country but were then split into two, one called Rwanda and the other called Urundi Rwanda. *Urundi* is simply the Rwandan word for "other" so *Urundi Rwanda* simply means "the other Rwanda". Eventually, the name Urundi Rwanda was reduced to Urundi. But Urundi simply meant "other". It sounded odd that a country was simply called "other". So, someone came up with the idea of putting a b at the beginning of the name and hence the name of the country Burundi came to be. It was like, say there was a country that we called *Other Australia*, then we dropped the *Australia* and because it didn't make sense to call a country *Other*, we added a consonant like d and made a country called *Dother*. I thought that was such a cute way for a country to get a name!

But as much as Polycarp and I could speak French and this could be a common language between us, I preferred speaking Swahili. In a way, it was a way of getting away from the dominance of a European *lingua franca*.

But now there was a further impetus to learn Swahili. Swahili was the national language of Tanzania, and this was therefore Ibrahim's mother tongue.

Because of the interruption in Polycarp's education, Polycarp needed to at least get his School Certificate. After working through two Occurrences at Tevah Am, he then attended a special school which specialised in teaching the School Certificate particularly for migrants who were over the school-leaving age.

Spending time with Polycarp made me realise just how important parents' input into their children's education was. Parents who involved themselves in their children's education ensured their children greater educational success.

However, Polycarp had not had this support until now. And everything was doubly hard for him. Polycarp, however, made me feel very proud. He definitely was a fighter. He had so many obstacles in his way: he had to learn a new language, he had to improve his education level, but he also had to look after a nine-year-old child, ensure Jeremiah was settled in school, did his homework, was correctly clothed and fed. Meanwhile, he had to ensure the rent was paid, negotiate with the real estate agent to get repairs done, do the shopping, prepare meals, keep his unit, his nephew and himself hygienically clean, pay electricity, water and phone bills, and somehow study and do homework himself, get some sleep, keep himself healthy, overcome the atrocities of his past and somehow through all this keep his sanity, all without anyone to support him, except now from me. Polycarp didn't realise it but he was a real inspiration to me.

The role I took on was to be, just as Polycarp had called me, a type of father. The difficulty for me was that I had no idea what it was like to be a father. So this was a learning experience on its own. But I fortunately only had to be the father of a grown up child, so at least this was no doubt a lot easier than what fathers have to go through as a child goes through all the stages of life before reaching adulthood. The real function that I played was to cook tea for Jeremiah and Polycarp so that at least three nights a week Polycarp was relieved of this duty so he could concentrate on his studies. After we had eaten, I then put Jeremiah to bed, sometimes even sat and read a story to him, and then spent the rest of the evening explaining to Polycarp what he had learned that day at college, explaining it to him in Swahili and then helping him with the homework he had been given to complete for the next day.

It was as a result of the cooking that yet another dimension came out about Polycarp and Jeremiah. There had been a time when I had made the discovery of kangaroo meat on sale at the local supermarket and I thought I'd give it a try. It took a while before I mastered the best cooking technique for this strange meat which resembled beef in colour and texture but just did not perform the same way when subject to the same cooking regimes. When I barbecued or grilled it, it became as tough as leather as if I were eating the straps off a saddle. I tried stir-frying it in my electric wok but the meat disintegrated into the consistency of a morcel of meat that somebody had already had a good chew on. Eventually I discovered that baking the meat or any form of slow cooking of the meat such as in a casserole or a stew rendered the best results. I also made the amazing discovery that if you marinated the meat in a mixture of soy sauce and sesame oil and then baked the combination, the result was an amazingly delightful cuisine which could not be replicated using beef or any other red meat equivalent.

Now that Polycarp and Jeremiah were in Australia, I thought it would be a great idea for them to be initiated into the wonders of eating the local fair. So one evening I decided to ask them if they wanted to try it.

We were all seated at the table having tea. The boys made me feel honoured that everything I cooked for them was delicious. But then, it probably proves the saying that "the best meal is the one you didn't have to cook yourself".

"So, what would you like for the next time I come over? Would you like to try kangaroo meat?"

"Kangaroo meat? Do you mean the national Australian animal?" Polycarp asked in surprise verging on horror.

"It tastes nice. I mean, it's meat like any other meat. I know how to cook it to get the best taste."

"But Jeremiah and I can't eat kangaroo," Polycarp replied. "We are *sabato*."

Polycarp said this in Swahili. What he actually said was *Sisi ni sabato*. I knew that *sisi ni* meant "we are" but I had never heard the word "sabato" before. In the context, I assumed that it meant that they were allergic to certain foods. Unfortunately, I didn't know the Swahili word for "allergic". But the way Polycarp had said that he and Jeremiah were *sabato* sounded the same in the context as if he had said that they were both lacto-intolerant or ciliacs.

"*Sabato*? Is this a sort of sickness?" I asked to clarify the meaning.

Polycarp looked at me in horror and disgust.

"No, we are Christians but we are *sabato* Christians."

Christians who are *sabato*? Polycarp's reaction was embarrassing and I realised I had said something wrong. So, I tried to work out the meaning of *sabato* within this new context. What was something in Christianity that sounded like *sabato*? The stress pattern of the word *sabato* was the same as the word "tomato" but apart from rhyming with *sabato*, I had never heard of a religious group dedicated to the eating of this red vegetable. The word continued to stir in my mind while I tried to find an association with the word and a possible meaning. Suddenly I made the connection. *Sabato* was similar to the Hebrew word *shabbat* which is in English *sabbath*. This meant that Polycarp and Jeremiah were "Sabbath" Christians and then I realised.

"Oh, you're Seventh Day Adventists!" I said in English.

It had taken me quite a lot of mental energy to actually work out the meaning of the word as if I had been participating in a quiz show or doing a cryptic crossword on national television. Once I had finally got the answer, I was expecting Polycarp to praise me with something like, "Yes! Well done! You've got it!" But he simply and unemotionally acknowledged that this was the English translation from the Swahili *sabato*.

I didn't know much about the Seventh Day Adventists except that they went to church on Saturday, the Jewish Sabbath, and not on Sunday. Apart from that, I had assumed that they had a diet like the average Christian, and Christians had no dietary restrictions as far as the New Testament was concerned, except that they weren't allowed to eat blood.

"So, why can't Seventh Day Adventists eat kangaroo?" I asked.

"We are not supposed to eat any meat," Polycarp replied.

I felt a flush in my face. For all this time I had been preparing meat dishes. So why hadn't Polycarp mentioned this before?

"If there isn't enough food and we have to eat meat, then we're allowed to. But we can only eat meat according to what is written in Leviticus," Polycarp explained.

I couldn't believe my ears. It was one surprise to discover a group of Christians who said they were vegetarian, another to hear that they restricted their meat consumption in line with the Mosaic Law. Didn't Seventh Day Adventists read the Bible where it was written in the Acts of the Apostles in chapter ten about Peter's vision of the cloth that came down from heaven with all the animals of God's creation and how God told Peter to kill and eat all of them? Didn't they read how when Peter, a Jew, told God that he would not eat unclean animals, God told him that He had now cleansed all animals, even the animals which had previously been unclean, so that all could be eaten?

Didn't Seventh Day Adventists also read how Paul later confirmed this in his letter to Timothy in I Timothy 4:4, 5 where he wrote

What was becoming more and more evident was that I was being hemmed in on all sides by religious people and vegetarians.

I was mentally too tired to have a religious debate over this and really I didn't see the necessity of it. I wasn't religious and Polycarp's dietary restrictions were easy for me to get around. In the end, I decided to simply cook vegetarian meals for them on the nights that I came over. I could simply eat meat the other nights of the week if I really was desperate for a meat meal.

"But why didn't you tell me that before? When I'm with you, I don't mind cooking vegetarian," I replied. "All the while I've been cooking meat meals you have never said anything."

"That's okay," Polycarp replied. "You were being so kind to come and cook for us that I didn't want to say anything."

Yeah, but how do you think I would feel now if I had cooked something with pork or bacon in it? I thought to myself.

But Polycarp was a Christian, and a Bible Christian of some description. My familiarity with Seventh Day Adventists was that on the whole they were very much the same as Protestant Bible Christians but with a few minor variations, one being that they went to church on Saturday and not Sunday, and now I had discovered that they were also vegetarian. Although I didn't agree that Christians had to observe the Jewish Sabbath, nor did I care any longer on which day Christians went to church anyway, I could see how Christians could stake an argument in favour of Saturday as the church-going day because the Christian God, who is the Jewish God, had originally blessed Saturday as the Sabbath.

But that a Bible Christian organisation could make the claim that Christians should be vegetarian? I had read the entire Bible, even in the original languages, and I couldn't remember ever reading such an injunction. However, although it may not be a Christian teaching to be vegetarian, at least from the point of view of the lives of animals and even from an environmental point of view, being a vegetarian was certainly not a bad thing.

This then made me reflect back on Ibrahim. He was vegetarian. But he said he was a Muslim. I had never heard of Muslims wanting to be vegetarian either. Apart from abstaining from pig meat, Muslims as far as I was aware were free to eat all meat as long as it was halal.

All this stuff about different religions, who could eat what, what people believed, what was a revelation, what we are allowed to do, what is offensive, this was all becoming very complicated indeed. In Australia, in order not to offend anyone, we have to constantly keep abreast of all the new developments in thought in all the religions and cultures that come to our shores. I often asked myself the question, though. Do these newcomers to Australia ever go through the same quandary, trying to keep abreast of what each religion and culture believes and then making sure they don't offend anyone else in the process?

But Polycarp did not mention any more about religion after that. Strangely, and fortunately, he never asked about my religion, if I had any, and if I did, whether I should consider transferring my allegiance to his. I could only guess that for him he was thankful that someone came around regularly to his house to ensure that he and Jeremiah were fine, that Jeremiah's homework was being done and later in the evening Polycarp's assignments were being explained and completed, and that someone came around three nights a week who prepared three evening meals with enough leftovers for the following day. If such a person was helping them out, did it really matter on which day that person went to church, or was it important that that person went to church at all or even followed any particular religion or believed this or that prophet? Would the affiliation or lack of affiliation to a prescribed religion or holy book change how helpful the help was? And would the sexuality of that person really matter?

Added to the help, the letters I had originally written to Polycarp's real estate agent on the first day I had come to Polycarp's place finally bore fruit. As time went by, repairs to the unit were made which made the unit a lot more livable. I was particularly glad to see the vanity unit in the bathroom replaced because it worried me that Jeremiah could have cut himself with the shards of glass. The shower recess was finally provided with a new shower curtain. But the best surprise was to find that the entire kitchen was completely refurbished. This, however, also came with an increase in rent. Fortunately Polycarp's rent assistance also went up to match the increase.

There were a lot of pleasant and memorable events that came out of this relationship between me and these two boys. That the boys had come from a completely different culture had some amusing outcomes. Meeting people who come from other countries has shown me an odd reality on how we place certain values on objects which only mean something when a group of people share that same value but which for those outside the group is simply an object. Linked to this, at least in the case of Jeremiah and Polycarp, there was not only a difference in culture, there was also a difference in physiology that fascinated me, and that was their hair. Sub-Saharan Africans have tightly curled black hair which resembles sheep's wool. This has both its advantages and disadvantages that I was completely oblivious to until my intimate relationship with Polycarp and Jeremiah.

One Sunday I decided to spend the day with the boys and so treated them to a day at the local swimming pool. It was a nice time where we splashed around and jumped in the water. I also showed them a few tricks like diving in with my hands at my side and not stretched out in front, and doing a back flip into the pool. Jeremiah insisted on learning how to dive and during his first attempts he learnt what a belly flop was and how painful it could be.

But when we came to the end of the day, while my hair was straggled and dishevelled in every which way which meant that I needed to wash and brush it so that it looked respectable, Polycarp's and Jeremiah's hair stayed completely in place. They didn't have to do anything to their hair at all. If we had to go out to a dinner straight after the swimming pool, while I would have had to spend some time ensuring that the crop of my head looked respectable, the boys could have simply put on the appropriate attire and gone without any worry at all about their hair.

The downside was that droplets of water apparently get trapped in the curls and somehow these droplets accumulate and later at a most inconvenient moment suddenly flow out from the tangle. This can be particularly annoying after having a shower at night before getting into bed. I remember one evening when I had stayed over, and Polycarp and I had spent hours on one of his assignments. It was getting close to eleven o'clock at night when Polycarp said that he wanted to have a shower before going to bed. While he showered, I myself got ready for bed. When Polycarp came from the bathroom, I went to wish him goodnight. There on his head was a nice floral showercap. It was an absolute shock that left me speechless for some moments.

What do you do in a situation like that? How was I supposed to react? Was this the revelation of a fettish? Was Polycarp soon to slip into a lace-embroidered cotton nightie and carefully crocheted slippers? Was he then going to put facial cream on every conceivable area of skin except his eyes where two slices of cucumber would be placed to conceal his vision? If this was his fettish, it was his business as it didn't affect me. However, I wondered that if this became public knowledge, it would be difficult for him to deal with in a cruel, racist world especially as he was already dark-skinned.

Once I could gain composure, I decided to ask him bluntly. "Polycarp, why are you wearing a showercap?"

I used the Swahili word *kofia* which really means "hat" as I didn't know the Swahili word for "shower cap" or even if there was a Swahili word for it.

"Oh, this?" he said, touching the cap. "It's just that after I have a shower and then go to bed, during the night, water drips out of my hair so I put this on to stop it going on my pillow. Otherwise my pillow gets wet and it wakes me up."

I really didn't know what to say to that. A general discussion went on in my mind. You can't wear that. Showercaps are only for women, especially floral showercaps. A very sweeping sexist comment but whether I liked it or not, it was the value we placed in Australia on floral showercaps and showercaps in general. But Polycarp's answer also showed that he was not aware of this value. As a result, this unusual object had a practical application which suitably solved what was for him an annoying problem.

"Oh, okay," I replied in a way to show at least what he had said made sense. My only concern was that if during the night some intruders broke into the unit and saw Polycarp with this thing on his head, I wondered how they would react.

There was another night during winter when I arrived at Polycarp's house after work. Jeremiah opened the door and I gave him my usual hug and then made my way into the kitchen to see if Polycarp was there doing his homework. This particular night, when I reached the kitchen, there was Polycarp at the kitchen table, studiously writing – and wearing a Santa Claus hat. It was so amusing to see a black kid with the typical red coned hat, the top flopped to one side with a large white pompom on the end dangling in all gaiety.

At first I was speechless. It took me some moments before I could say something.

"Polycarp, why are you wearing that hat?"

Polycarp looked up from his homework and in all innocence answered my question.

"It felt a bit cold so I decided to put this hat on."

My mouth opened to frame the words of an objection to say that after all this is a Christmas hat and should only be worn at Christmas. But then, what if this was the only hat that Polycarp had? Again, I realised that we in Australia say that you can only wear a red conical hat with a white pompom on the end around the end of the year during the Christmas period. Polycarp, however, was totally unaware of this and thus for him, such a hat was a convenient form of attire to keep his head warm from the cold.

In fact, it was in relationship to Christmas that I was left speechless about a particular cultural aspect of ours.

There are aspects of Christmas that I really love. Although I no longer believe in the Christian religion, I still enjoy certain aspects of Christmas, especially those in Australia. In Sydney, during the weeks before Christmas there are nights in local parks where we have Carols by Candlelight. Families and friends gather together on picnic blankets in the park and when it's dark, everyone lights candles and in the cool of the night, while holding the candles in the darkness, the entire crowd of people sing together Christmas carols. I love singing the Christmas carols. My favourite is *Hark the Herald Angel Sing* and I know all three verses by heart. The words are beautiful even though I know it's all a fantasy, but it's a lovely fantasy nonetheless.

Other aspects of Christmas are really for children but because I did not have any children of my own until Polycarp and Jeremiah entered my life, the fantasy of Santa Claus no longer had any particular appeal. However, some weeks before Christmas I guess what had happened was that during class at Jeremiah's school one day, the teacher had talked about Christmas and in particular about Santa Claus. I surmised this from Polycarp's reaction.

While the tradition was to put up a Christmas tree, decorate it and place presents below it, it was obvious that Polycarp and Jeremiah were totally unaware of this tradition. One evening while eating dinner together, Polycarp suddenly blurted out with, "Is it true that at Christmas there is a man who comes into everyone's homes?"

Well, it isn't really true, is what I thought but I wasn't sure what to answer at first. I mean, how do you answer this with Jeremiah at the table and this idea of Santa is supposed to be a story we want our children to believe.

"Well, what we say," once I had found a tactical answer to the question, "is that a man called Santa Claus comes down the chimney, and if you don't have a chimney, he just comes in through the door and puts presents under the Christmas tree…" and at this stage I stopped. While I paused to try to find a way to give some background to the story, Polycarp used this pause to offer his thoughts.

"Well, all I can say is that if someone tries to get into my house, I'll attack him and make sure he leaves and knows never to come back!"

Polycarp said this in all seriousness. In a way it was quite interesting to hear him say this because it showed that he was very protective and also very brave.

I wanted to laugh but at the same time knew I couldn't because Polycarp would not have understood the joke. I then realised that it was necessary to explain the background of the tradition. But as I thought about it, I thought just how absurd the explanation really was to someone unfamiliar with the tradition. We teach our children that there is this magical man who one night of the year mystically flies from the North Pole to every home in the world riding in a magic sleigh that somehow flies through the air with reindeer which mystically run on invisible roads. In Australia, we put a slight slint to this story and say that when Santa reaches the southern continent, because reindeer don't like the heat, Santa unshackles the reindeer somewhere before the great south land and hitches six large white kangaroos called Six White Boomers, and they carry on the task of what the reindeer were doing in the rest of the world. When he arrives at each person's home, he places presents under a decorated tree, drinks a glass of milk or beer or whatever the parents decide is appropriate refreshment for Santa, gets back on his sleigh and continues until he has delivered presents to everyone.

However, I wanted to continue and say that this is not a true story. But we tell our children this story every year. But then, why do we tell our children a lie every year? How was I to explain this? I knew very little of Polycarp's background so I didn't know if in Burundi or Rwanda parents had a tradition of telling their children stories like this to add spice to their children's lives. Even so, I realised that the possibility of Polycarp having shared in such a cultural experience was highly unlikely because of Polycarp's rather unpleasant time during his youth.

There was also an irony in Polycarp's reaction to this story. We in developed countries laugh at the simpleton beliefs of those who live in developing countries. And yet, when we consider the Santa Claus story which is promoted energetically at the end of the year through many TV programs, on junkmail flyers and in every shopping centre, were we any different from them? This relationship with Polycarp had really opened my mind a lot wider than I ever thought possible and made me see things that I had never seen before, despite all my past experience with people from other countries.

Yet, despite our cultural differences, a very close relationship had developed between us. It was Polycarp who started calling me "father", sometimes calling me the Swahili "baba" sometimes calling me "papa", and through this he had inadvertently entered the innermost part of my being. There was something significant and beautiful about it.

So, if Polycarp called me father, then this meant that he was my son. I had a son. So I stopped calling Polycarp by his first name and started calling him *mwanangu* which is Swahili for "my son".

I now had a son. Wow! It was a concept that was so foreign to me! All through my growing up, everything in my culture, the books we read at school, the movies we saw on TV, the songs we heard on the radio, everything geared us to believe that when we reached a certain age in our growing up, we would eventually get married, settle down and then create families of our own. However, my very being was obviously strong enough to get through this cultural indoctrination unchanged because not once in my growing up did I feel that I wanted to do any of this. I simply had no desire to replicate my genes and keep them alive in the next generation. Something in my physiological makeup simply went contrary to this flow and managed to unaffectively remain so.

This no doubt must have broken my parents' hearts. That they had a son who was gay meant that the continuity of their genetic material was broken. No doubt my parents had been caught up in this indoctrination believing that now that they had passed on their genes to the next generation, they would see their genes once more replicated a step further down the line and, if they lived long enough, they would see their genes replicated even further. This no doubt was one of the many reasons why my parents cast me out of home when they found out my sexual orientation because all their hopes of seeing the continuation of their genes through me were completely shattered.

Strangely, I didn't feel that I was missing out on anything by not having children and so I would have continued my life as an isolated individual with no real affinity to anyone. However, Polycarp had now entered my life and it was he who had begun describing our relationship as father-and-son. It gave me great pleasure to provide him with the prospect of belonging to a new family now that his previous family no longer existed.

Strangely, this importance of family, of belonging to a wider community in which everyone was now somewhat related suddenly began to pick up pace. Not only was a new branch forming in my family tree with Polycarp grafted into it, parts of my family tree I was completely ignorant of were beginning to come to light. But this was happening despite the cracks and fissures long established in my family connections.

My relationship with my mother during my adult life had not been close. The relationship was cleanly severed the day my parents discovered my sexuality. Sent away from the home I was brought up in, I thought that I would never see my parents again. This statement was fulfilled in half. For about thirteen years, there was no contact between my parents and me. Then one day, I heard that my father had died.

I have no way of explaining the feeling of loss this brought to me. Anyone who has lost a father understands this subsequent feeling of loss. But my feelings were of a double loss. In a sense, my father had died the day I was banished from the family home, but then my father died a second time when his death was total. At least while my father was alive, although hurtful the separation between us had been, there was a glimmer of hope, no matter how slight this hope was, that one day my father would see it in his heart that despite my sexuality I was still a human being and moreso that I was still his own flesh and blood. However, once my father had died, this light of hope was extinguished forever.

My father's death somehow brought a jolt to my mother's consciousness, bringing the reality of our mortality to the fore. Somehow my father's death caused her to suddenly reconsider her complete break in communication from her son. My father's death must have made my mother realise that although she had been treating me as though I had died, I was actually still out there in the community alive and well, and that there would in reality come a time when I too would be forever dead just like my father. Death was no longer a supposition, it was a cold reality. But the relationship between my mother and me was no longer the same as it had been when I was a child. Like the atom which is kept stable by the balance between attractive and repulsive forces, so my relationship with my mother was one of the balancing act between the biological connection I had with her as my mother on the one hand and the feelings of anger and hurt on the other as a result of having been no longer considered worthy enough to be her child simply because of what I liked to do in private. The most difficult part for me was to move forward and realise that despite how painful the past had been, there was no longer anything I could do to change it.

My father's death must have affected my mother deeply because her whole attitude to family had changed. Jesus' injunction in Luke 14:26 that to be his disciple Christians must hate all members of their family may be an easy commandment to follow in the fiery strength of middle age when people can support themselves. But in the cool twilight of advanced years, family members actually provided the support needed as the natural strength fades away, irrespective of whether these family members hold the same beliefs in Christ or not.

My father's death somehow also made my mother look for her place in the extended family because she began searching through our family tree to provide her with an identity. As a result she began researching her genealogy and the genealogy of my father. Because Anglo-Australian culture, based on British culture, is male-biased, it didn't take long for my mother to trace back the Farril ancestry to its first arrivals in Australia. Thomas Farril, sent out from Scotland as a convict, came to Australia in the late 1700s when transportation had just started and, on his emancipation, he decided to stay. He married Susan Crelley, also sent to Australia as a convict, and in obedience to God's commandment both to Adam and Eve and then later to all the survivors of the Flood, Thomas and Susan were fruitful and multiplied. This was evident by the popularity of the surname Farril. As to the surname Farril, there were no records in Australia which explained the origins of this surname but my mother was somehow able to confirm what had already once been suggested that in reality no-one really knew where the name actually came from or whether it was an Anglo-Saxon name or a Celtic one.

Trying to find my mother's ancestry was a little harder because traditionally women had to lose their surname on the day of their wedding and take on the surname of their husbands. For each step back through the female line, there was an extra step where my mother had to find out what the maiden name of each married female ancestor was.

The universe must have been listening to my mother's desperate plea to find the people who she was related to on this big family tree because one day she received a letter in the mail from someone who claimed to be a distant relative. Not only was this distant relative making enquiries about living descendants of a common ancestor, this living relative had already done much of the research on my mother's side of the family tree right back to our first ancestor's arrival on the Great South Land. This extensive research had been compiled into a comprehensive book and this distant relative was inviting all the descendants to a great gathering in order to launch the book and also to provide an opportunity for all those of the family to meet each other.

It was during a visit at my mother's place that I received all the news.

"We've all been invited to a reunion of the…" my mother began and then paused in order to work out the pronunciation of the word, "the *rize* family or *reez* family."

I asked her to pass me the letter. I read down the page till I saw the surname that reflected the pronunciation my mother had attempted.

"Oh, the Riese family!" I stated.

I looked up from the letter and scanned the room while my mind took the word *Riese* and scanned my internal dictionaries.

"Riese. That means 'giant' in German. But surely our ancestors weren't German," I said but it was really more of a question.

"Well, you can find out more when we go to the reunion. One of our distant relatives who is organising the reunion has written a book which has all the information. You can buy the book when we get there."

"What's this relative's name?" I asked.

"It's there in the letter. The person who sent the letter."

I looked down to find who had signed off at the bottom. At the bottom of the letter was scribbled a very old-fashioned stylish signature and below that was typed the name Johann Riese.

Johann. What name could be more German than that? "Johann" was the German equivalent of the English name "John". But if his first name was German, and Riese was a German name, then we had German ancestry. I had Teutonic blood flowing through my veins and for all these years I had never suspected it.

This made me go back to the letter and read the contents slowly and in detail. The letter began with a welcome to all members of the Riese family and the opportunity for all descendants of Gottlieb and Martha Riese, the first of our ancestors to leave Germany and come to Australia.

I sat up and looked at my mother. She noticed a bewildered expression on my face and asked the reason for it.

"This Johann who is asking for the reunion is not one of our ancestors who came to Australia, surely?" I asked in surprise.

"No, no," my mother replied. "I think when you read the letter, he says he is one of the descendants."

As I read on, I discovered that Johann Riese was simply someone on our family tree, a second or third cousin or however one describes the side connection of a relative a couple of places removed. Like all of us invited to the reunion, so the letter explained, we were all descendants of a great patriarch and matriarch who were the father and mother of four sons: Gottlieb, Gottlob, Gottfried and Gotthilf.

"Mein Gott!" I commented to my mother but because my mother did not understand German, she didn't know what I had said and therefore missed the joke. All the better because she would have considered it blasphemy that I used God's name in vain.

At first, I wasn't sure if this was some sort of joke. But there was nothing to indicate that what was written in the letter was meant to be taken lightly. This indicated that old patriarch and matriarch Riese were extremely religious to the extent that they had to have the word "God" in each of their sons. They had no daughters.

From the four Gott sons, we were descended directly through the second son, Gottlob. "Lob" is the German word for "praise" so Gottlob means something like "Praise of God" or "God's praise".

This made me reflect back into my own personal history. There were elements of my person which began to make sense. As early as I could remember, way back in my childhood, the German language had fascinated me and I was determined to learn it. In 2nd grade, at the age of eight, I had a German teacher and I remember asking her to teach me German words and expressions. I remember at about this time discovering a book in our primary school library which taught German. When I reached high school, German was an elective subject in Year 9 and not only did I vehemently choose this subject, I excelled in the subject so well that I was top of the class. Even when I had left school, I tried to maintain my German. I read novels, I joined the Goethe Institute and I watched the German news on SBS. Now with the latest technology, I download German programs onto my iPod and listen to them when I travel in the car to and from work. This fascination, this attraction to things German now began to make sense. As a linguist, I was fascinated by many languages but there was always an underlying tug at this great Teutonic language.

What fascinated me even more was that I was drawn to my mother's side of the family. Because of the male-bias of family trees, it was assumed that the surname and therefore the ancestry of the male surname held dominance in our being. With a British name like Farril, coupled with a history of Australia dominated by the arrival of the British over two hundred years ago, the overriding pull should have naturally, or at least presumably, been towards the British Isles. There had been no hint in my family, even in my mother's family while her parents were alive, that there was anything German in our ancestry. Yet my fascination for Germans and all things Teutonic had been there.

I had been aware of the Germans coming to Australia and establishing the Barossa Valley in South Australia. This was a silent piece of Australian history which not many Australians were aware of. Yet I had sought it out, or as it seemed to me, it had sought me out, and had formed a part of my knowledge base of the development of this Great South Land.

"So, with a name like Riese, we had an ancestor who was a giant, I suppose," I commented partly as a joke but partly with some seriousness. I knew names had meaning and there had to have been a reason for our ancestors having this surname.

"You will have to come to the reunion, son, and find all this out," my mother replied. "I don't know. I just got the letter."

"Where's the reunion?" I asked and then scanned down again through the letter. There was a section in the letter which indicated the date and time of the reunion, and the location.

"Walla Walla?" I asked and then looked up at my mother. "Is that a typo for Wagga Wagga?"

"I don't know. There's a map in the letter."

I looked through the other papers to find the map. The map looked like a nice stylised map from a tourist bureau. The centre of the map was Albury, a large township right on the border between New South Wales and Victoria. Sure enough, it was not a spelling mistake. The location of the reunion was at Walla Walla.

"Is Karen coming?"

"Yeah, I think she is," my mother replied. "Apparently Peter is working so he won't be able to come with us, though."

This was going to be fascinating. We were going to learn more about our hidden history at this reunion.

I cast my mind back to my school days. All our history lessons had been very Anglo-centric. Apart from a brief interlude into the Roman Empire, all I remember of my history lessons were the Kings and Queens of England from William the Conqueror in 1066 with emphasis on King Henry VIII and Queen Elizabeth I. Then greater time was spent on Anglo-Australian history, how that because of the search for spices in the eastern hemisphere, the Europeans sailed all over the world and eventually discovered that there was another continent as opposite as one could get from Europe. We learnt about Vasco da Gama, the first known European and the first Portuguese to enter the Indian Ocean. The Portuguese were followed by the Dutch who were responsible for making known to the Europeans the existence of this great southern land and giving it the first European name, New Holland. History of Australia then took on its dominant British flavour with the arrival of Captain Cook in 1770 who was the first known European to see the east coast of Australia and who painted such a pleasurable picture of the place that not long after, hordes of British came and took the land. All through our history classes, it was presented as if only people from the British Isles came to Australia and that was what the population of Australia was made up of until around the 1970s when mass migration from other nations began. That there were other people who had come to Australia from other countries during this period was not mentioned and hence gave the assumption that only white Britons came to this great southern land. Not only so, those who had migrated to this great southern continent thousands of years before the British knew of its existence were barely mentioned but when the Australian Aboriginals were presented in our history classes, they were presented as some sort of nuisance, a hindrance to the progress of this new British colony, as if they suddenly appeared out of nowhere as an obstacle in the path of British expansionism.

According to this history, as far as I was aware, like all my white compatriots, I was a purely British descendant. The Germans did not even feature in Australian history. The first known mention of the Germans in my history classes was Otto von Bismarck and then later Adolf Hitler. The Germans, for all we cared, were just a bunch of krauts who were ruthless barbarians who because of Hitler's Nazism interrupted the wonderful journey of progress into the twentieth century. That Germans had anything to do with the early history of Australia did not become apparent until I took a trip to the Barossa Valley once and discovered the rich Teutonic history in this part of our country and how this dated back to the very early years of British settlement. Even then, this was merely a small curiosity that made very little change in my view of Australia as an extension of Britain.

But from this letter, I discovered that on my mother's side, not only was there a German phase in the history of Australia, this German heritage ran through my veins and I was very much a part of it.

I gained some sort of pleasure from this knowledge. The idea of being a person of one cultural heritage made me feel rather one-sided, as if I were one-dimensional. Having ancestors from a variety of different sources gave me the feeling that there was more to me, as if I were multifaceted. It was true that the rich history of the British Isles held something I could relate to because to a degree I claimed descent from Britain.

However, I could now lay claim to being a descendant of another great nation, the German nation, and share with its rich history.

But there was more to this dimension that was yet to be discovered.

Chapter 12

Having been born before the computer revolution, I was a witness to what life was like before and after computers, in particular, how computers had shrunk the world we live in. In my primary school days, to have a penpal from another country was an exoticism. I had many penpals in my early years. I would write a letter describing what life was like in my home town, go to the post-office and send the letter, and then wait for weeks before I would discover with delightful pleasure a letter from another country with the description of things from the perspective of another culture. The envelopes themselves were exotic. Different countries had their own types of airmail envelopes, usually a coloured envelope, not the standard white but usually light blue or yellow, with alternate blue and red diagonal stripes around the border. What was also exotic was the stamp which betrayed the country from which the letter had originated.

Opening the envelope and looking at the contents that lay within was like opening up a pouch holding a small portion of the country from where the letter had come. On occasion, my penpals and I included in our letters small trinkets that would otherwise be considered as rubbish to the average citizen of that country, such as chocolate wrappers, bottle labels or even a junk mail flyer. We also exchanged cut outs from newspapers of TV programs or weather maps. This made each letter a unique personal peak at what life was like in another country, a window into another world.

Part of the fun of having a penpal was the waiting for the letter. Once I had plopped my letter in the letterbox at the post office, it was often at least a month's wait before I heard the latest news from my penpal who would not only answer my questions of curiosity about his or her home country but tell me about the trivialities and interesting features of this foreign land.

With the advent of the internet, this wonderful feature of international communication has been replaced. We now have the possibility of having friends from all over the world and know everything about them and the country they live in all in an instant. In fact, the internet has shrunk the world so much that we don't even need to have friends in other countries to find out the latest in any particular country. There are English newspapers in almost all countries of the world and simply by finding the website that holds these newspapers, we can find out instantly what is happening far away. Because of my interest in languages, I have the further dimension of being able to read newspapers in the local languages. I have discovered many websites which have electronic versions of the local newspapers in the different countries of the world and I can read what's going on anywhere in the world, even as far away as Luleå in Sweden if I really wanted to.

While the internet brings the advantage of instant international knowledge, it takes away that wonderful moment of anticipation. There was something sweet about seeing my letters go in the post box and the anticipation every day from then on waiting for a letter to arrive in the letter box at home weeks later and read the news about this foreign land. Another advantage of this was that letters long anticipated were read and read thoroughly and many times so that for years after I was still familiar with certain details about my penpals' lives. By contrast, today with the internet, we have so much internet overload that the memory of our e-friends really is quite fleeting to the point that we almost forget from one week to the next details about those we communicate with. If I were to ask the next generation today what one of their Facebook friends told them last month, I'm sure by now they would have forgotten and they would have had to forget it in order to keep up with the torrent of new information streaming through the net.

The advent of the internet also has sped life up. People seem to be constantly having to put up images and comments daily to keep up with the information they constantly receive from their e-friends. And because they have so many e-friends, they don't seem to have time to digest the information. It's like we are all running through a tunnel and on the walls around us is information of our friends but we don't have time to stop and process any of it as if we have to hurry on to the next lot of images pasted to the wall.

Writing a letter, therefore, to Ibrahim was like a momentary lapse into a bygone era where life was slower and we had time to savour moments of anticipation, wondering what to expect when we received the next letter, savouring each word and letter and enjoying them again and again as we held the letter in our hands.

I arrived home one evening to find in my letterbox a letter in the old airmail envelope I had thought no longer existed. I instantly knew who it was from and a quick glance at the stamp on the top right hand corner confirmed that the sender had come from Tanzania. It was such a wonderful surprise. I was so excited I nearly dropped the keys as I rushed to unlock my unit door.

I entered my flat and unceremoniously tossed my bag and whatever else was in my hands on the floor, shook my shoes off and immediately went to the closest lounge chair to sink into it and readily tear open the letter to read its contents. Warm feelings of positive emotions rushed through me like a wave in the sea once I began with the introduction: *My dearest brother Michael.*

Unlike my letter to him, Ibrahim's letter was unrestrained about his feelings. There was little doubt how he felt towards me. The feelings this wrought in me! It had been such a long time since I had felt that someone loved me this much, as much as Ibrahim was telling me in his letter.

I also enjoyed the fact that his letter was not simply an expression of his love. It was also a newsy letter, filling me in with the latest at the Msingi wa Mungu Project but also his work at the International School.

Later that evening, I sat out on the balcony with a glass of red wine and Ibrahim's letter. I read the letter again and again. Each reading of the letter made me a little tipsier in the same way as the red wine was doing. I looked up into the night sky and saw the three-quarter moon. I read the letter and then stood up and held the letter to my chest as I looked out onto suburbia. I then read the letter again, held the letter to my chest in ecstasy as if I were holding Ibrahim himself. Ibrahim loved me. Or at least he had deep feelings for me. Really, I knew Ibrahim loved me but I just didn't want to use that four letter word.

I then sat down on one of the balcony chairs and sighed. The ecstasy slowly gave way to a feeling of frustration. It may be true that we had feelings towards each other. But whereas it would have been nice to be able to actually sit together in the same time-space dimension and have a conversation, this was totally inconceivable. Ibrahim lived a third of a world away from me.

Ibrahim included in his letter an email address. This therefore brought our penpalship back into the twenty-first century. In a way this was a little disappointing because I was happy to return to an earlier epoch where life was simpler and correspondence had greater currency because it took so long to write and receive a letter which made the correspondence all the worth waiting for. It was much more different than our current forms of electronic communication where correspondence was happening so quickly and what's more people were communicating such trivial information such as what they were having at this point in time for lunch or where they were at that moment on their walk through the suburbs.

But there were also the advantages. Because I now had Ibrahim's email address, I knew that as soon as I pressed Send on my computer, my email was already in Ibrahim's e-mail box 12,000 kilometres away, and I didn't have to wait weeks for him to receive my letter and even more weeks to receive a reply.

My first email to Ibrahim was rather cautious. I provided some subtle enough indication of how I felt about him, enough for Ibrahim to understand, although the passion was diluted enough to be reinterpreted quite differently to the intended meaning should other prying eyes see my message. I sent off my email and was surprised and happy to receive a reply within twenty-four hours. By contrast, Ibrahim's email was jammed packed full of passion. The passion in his email was much stronger and certainly unequivocal so I realised that he was in a situation where he could correspond freely via this electronic medium.

As I read through the first couple of lines, I could visualise that river of passion rumbling along in strong torrents. The clearness and freshness of the water was alluring and inviting, overriding all my objections for ever getting back in. Each jet of water that sprouted through the air was like a wave which beckoned me to enter and partake of the cool and refreshing waters. If the waters looked fresh and clean, imagine how they would feel wrapped around my body, tingling with sensation every part of my being.

Reading Ibrahim's email was like standing on the edge of this river bank. His words were beautiful, enticing me into believing that he really loved me and that it was possible that there could ever be something between us more than this holiday romance.

But as beautiful as his words were, I balked at replying. What could I say? I didn't want to lead him on.

But less than twenty-four hours later, I received another email from him. When I looked at the timing of his email, although my computer indicated that I had received the email in the afternoon, when I took the time difference between Sydney and Moshi into consideration, I realised he had sent it early in the morning. But this email message was a message of quite a different turn.

My dearest Michael,

I had a dream last night. In the dream, I was on a flat plain and in the distance was a mountain range with defined peaks. All the peaks were like ordinary mountain peaks. But the tallest peak, the father of all these mountains, reached much further into the clouds, just like Mount Kilimanjaro. As it is with dreams, as soon as I became curious of this one object, I was immediately brought into close proximity of it. In fact, I was standing at the top of this peak. It was not the peak of the mountain, however, which disappeared into the sky. Rather, atop this mountain were two trees. Each tree grew close together and was very tall. I leant against the trunk of one of these trees and there I saw you resting against the other. You were smiling at me and then you indicated with a move of your eyes to follow the trees up into the heights. As my eyes followed the trunks, I noticed that at a point further up into the sky, the two trunks merged into one and from that point were full of fresh green branches. This was different to the two trunks below which were dry and branchless with the bark peeling off with what looked like chip marks as if a feller had tried to cut the tree down but abandoned the task, and sap oozed from these chip marks, as if the trunks were dead and lifeless. At the very top of the tree, which I could see very distinctly despite how far into the sky the tree entered, was an abundance of small white flowers. I could see the flowers detaching from the top of the tree and entering the sky, becoming the very stars that fill the night sky while some of the flowers gently fell to the ground, so small and so gentle, and formed the shoreline of the coast.

"Ibrahim and his dreams!" I muttered to myself. There was a tingle of excitement when I read about the dream. I immediately understood what he was trying to get at. I guessed that each of the two tree trunks represented each of us, which was obvious from the fact that Ibrahim had been leaning against one trunk and I against the other, and the merging of the two was his hopeless fantasy that we would one day be together as one. That he saw the two trees on a mountain peak seemed odd but not too out of the way for a dream. The flowers becoming the stars and dropping down onto the shoreline sounded as if he were saying that once we were together, everything would be beautiful for us both above us and below us.

It was very beautiful. But it was also very impossible. We were both a third of a world away and the possibility that we would ever be together in a partnership was just totally inconceivable. The facts before me were that Ibrahim and I lived worlds apart and neither of us had the means nor the resources to live in the same three dimensional space-time for the rest of our natural lives. We could remain correspondents but that was it. We had to be true to ourselves. There was no way we could ever be together for ever like the fairy tales say for the reason that it would require a lot of red tape to get through to sponsor him to live in Australia.

Further, not only were we world's apart in physical space, our minds lived in different universes. Ibrahim was religious, a firm believer in an intelligence greater than ourselves guiding our way, and a dreamer who believed his dreams were messages from another dimension, including this dream that implied that we could ever be together. I, on the other hand, was totally unreligious, someone who did not believe anything beyond what I knew for sure through my senses and through my logic, that there was no evidence of a Grand Plan, that everything happened by pure luck and chance. I was a realist. Ibrahim believed in the possibility of gods and angels, things that as far as I knew had no evidence of existence. There would definitely come a time when these two universes would clash and we would not only strongly disagree with each other but it would cause the relationship itself to crash. This had to be made clear. Yes, physically it was beautiful between us. But the physical doesn't last long and is not what holds a relationship together. Our mental differences would eventually cause definite problems.

I then thought of what Nikita had told me. If Ibrahim truly loved me, it wouldn't matter that his mind was filled with religious things and mine was not. What was important was for me to be honest with him right from the beginning. If Ibrahim had no problem that he held to strong religious views whereas I didn't and yet Ibrahim still expressed his love for me, then he loved me indeed.

And I had not been completely honest with Ibrahim about what I thought of otherworldly things so it was time that he knew. That would help to put the brakes on his feelings for me.

I stared at the computer screen for some time reflecting on what it was that I was going to write. A sledgehammer approach would certainly not do.

Eventually, I was able to turn my thoughts into words on my computer screen.

Dear Ibrahim,

Thank you for your nice email. It was well received.

I stared at these words but wasn't sure if this was simply too pithy to write in this manner. But then I thought I may as well continue. I could come back and change the beginning when I had finished what it was I had wanted to write. I continued with the body of the email.

I spent a wonderful time with you at the Msingi wa Mungu Project. I mean that in all ways. Yes, I enjoyed the passionate times. But I also enjoyed our conversations about religion, about the spiritual world and about our place in the universe.

I can see you are very religious. You are completely in touch with the religious side of the world and in a way I can see that you live a life which really

And so I went on. I wrote positively about Ibrahim's outlook on life and how his religion, his personal version of Islam was all-encompassing and how he showed this by his involvement in the Msingi wa Mungu Project. I closed off the email with expressions of affection and then signed off.

I sat back and sighed. This would probably be the email message that would finally quench the passion that Ibrahim had for me. There was nothing more unforgivable for a religious person than the frank rejection of a supreme deity and its world of demons and spirits. I stared back at the screen and the words in my message. But the other side was that no serious relationship could develop between us and one of us had to be honest about it. I was prepared to approach the topic rationally even if Ibrahim could not. At least what I had written was better than telling Ibrahim blankly and honestly that we could never continue this relationship. Long distance relationships just never work and we had to face this reality despite what our passions may have dictated to the contrary. Once I had fully convinced myself that this was the right thing to write, I read once more through my email and then clicked Send. I was quite sure that I would not receive an email again from Ibrahim and what had been between us would finally be over.

And poor Ibrahim and his dreams. They were a nice delusion on his part. They were lovely but they were in the end unreal and the unreality had become obvious because his dreams would after all not be fulfilled.

I finished one more glass of red wine and then headed for bed.

As I had predicted, there were no emails from Ibrahim the following day nor the day after. The more the days continued without a response, the greater the relief it felt on me. I could turn my feelings off from Ibrahim and get on with life.

A few days later, after finishing the morning shift and getting ready to go for a swim, I noticed on my smartphone that I had received an email message. I clicked on the button to open my email inbox to check whether or not the email was an important one or could wait till later. I immediately recognised the sender. It was from Ibrahim. I paused for a moment and then thought to myself that I could wait till after my swim to read it. It would no doubt be an email of condolences, expressing Ibrahim's disappointment in my lack of belief and how our wonderful moment together should now finally come to a close as a result.

Once my swim was over, I totally forgot about the email. It wasn't till late in the evening when I got home from work that I remembered Ibrahim had sent me the message. I grabbed myself a glass of red wine, turned on my laptop, opened the email message and began reading.

The message started out with the usual greeting and then an entire introductory paragraph to ask how I, Polycarp and Jeremiah, and my entire family were. My expectation for the second paragraph was an expression of regret and disappointment for my lack of belief and infidelity to the spiritual world. However, the message was quite different to the one I had expected. Instead of an admonition, Ibrahim's message jumped into a parable with no indication that he had changed the direction of his correspondence.

There was once a Caliph of a great dominion. This Caliph was powerful but he was also noble and wise. He established laws throughout his dominion that were fair and equitable that he himself abode by. Because of the righteous and just rulership of this Caliph, this Caliph was honoured and respected by his subjects.

This Caliph had divided his dominions into wilayas.

I was intrigued that Ibrahim had used the word "Caliph" for his description of a ruler and not the traditional European word "king". However, the word *wilaya* I didn't understand at first but guessed from the context that it meant something like *district* or *state* and when I looked this up in my Swahili-English dictionary later in the evening, I found out that this was correct. The email continued.

Every seven years, the Caliph called together the heads of these wilayas to bring tribute and to make an account of the activities of each wilaya.

Because the Caliph's dominion was so extensive, it took many days to reach the border regions. There was one wilaya at the far reaches of this dominion. When it was the turn of the head of this wilaya to give an account of the activities of his wilaya, this head of the wilaya addressed the Caliph by saying, "Mfalme Mtukufu."

I knew *mfalme* meant "king" in Swahili so I guessed in the context that *mtukufu* meant something like "honourable" so that *Mfalme Mtukufu* meant something like "Your Royal Highness" and with a later check of the dictionary this turned out to be correct.

"Mfalme Mtukufu. There are subjects among my wilaya who do not believe that you, O Mfalme Mtukufu, exist. They say there is no ruling Caliph over many wilayas. Because they have no means of travelling beyond the borders of the wilaya of which I am the head, they say that there is no other wilaya beyond the one in which they live."

The Caliph was astonished. How could subjects of his dominions be ignorant of his existence when this great Caliph had established equitable and just laws to make the lives of his subjects peaceful? But the Caliph needed more information.

"Are these subjects troublemakers? Do they refuse to pay the zakat?"

I remembered first seeing this odd word *zakat* when I read the surah, *Al-Baqarah*, on the patio of the dormitory at the Msingi wa Mungu Project. I later asked Faraj what the word meant and discovered that it was equivalent to the English word *tithe* and hence paying the *zakat* was akin to paying tithes.

"No, O Mfalme Mtukufu," the head of the wilaya continued. "Quite the contrary. They are noble citizens. They respect your laws and they pay the zakat. They believe these laws are equitable and true even though they do not acknowledge that they come from our great Caliph. They also pay the zakat willingly because they understand that the poor and the needy are the responsibility of all the

*citizens in the wilaya, knowing that if their own fortunes fail, they also may need
to rely on the zakat themselves."*

The Caliph leant forward.

*"Why did you tell me that these subjects do not believe I exist?" the Caliph
then asked the head of this wilaya. "They obey my laws and they show respect to
their fellow citizens."*

*"But, O Mfalme Mtukufu, isn't this a sign of disrespect when your subjects
deny with their mouths that The Great Caliph exists?"*

*The Caliph leant back in his throne and then said to the head of the wilaya,
"Leave them in peace. It is not those who say with their mouths, 'I don't believe
the Caliph exists' who are kafiri. The kafiri are those who say with their mouths 'I
believe' but say with their hearts and actions 'I don't believe' because they trample
under foot my holy laws and lie to, steal from and murder those my children who
were created in my image."*

Once again, a magic tingle passed through every part of my body.
In this short story, which resembled so much a parable of Jesus, was a
teaching from a religion that was similar to Christianity but with elements
of Islam woven in. The use of the word "Caliph" for "ruler" was typically
Arabic as was the Swahili word *kafiri* which I knew came from the Arabic
kafir and meant "unbeliever" or "infidel", the very word used by the Koran
to describe those who do not believe in Islam.

The last words of this parable revealed the true identity of the Caliph
where it said "those my children who were created in my image". This
was obviously an echo from the Creation Story where it says in Genesis
1:27

> *So God created man in his own image,*
> *in the image of God created he him;*
> *male and female created he them.*

But what really made the poignant point was that according to this
parable, God considers infidels those who lie to, steal from and murder
those "my children who were created in my image". All humans, "male
and female", Jew, Christian, Muslim, Hindu, Buddhist, Taoist, even
atheists, according to the Creation Story are all created in God's image
and could all be considered in a way God's children. So, the implication of
this parable was that anyone who lied to, stole from or murdered another
human, any human, was considered by God an infidel, a *kafir*, irrespective
of whether the liar, thief or murderer said that he or she was religious
or not, or whether the victims of the lie, theft or murder who were also
created in God's image ascribed to any particular religion. Immediately

I thought of the violence committed by what the media calls terrorists and suicide bombers. In light of what Ibrahim had written in his email, these unfortunate terrorists and suicide bombers, while they consider themselves as believers doing God's favour by murdering infidels, they were showing by their murders that they themselves were *kafirs*.

This part of Ibrahim's message spoke to my heart. It penetrated deep within a part of my inner being so deep within me. His parable had God in it but with the God element removed from the story, this parable was my parable. Anyone who lied to, stole from or killed innocent people, irrespective of the motive behind the lying, stealing and murdering, were simply evil people. Falling back on the premise that they believed it was God's duty to commit these crimes did not rub off on me. In my world view there was no god and hence this revealed the true barbarism and the beastly, animalistic nature of such people.

I noticed even more than before how in some ways Ibrahim's and my thinking were similar. We may have had different starting points but our paths converged and we were walking the same path.

I looked back down at the screen and continued with the message.

But in a way, Bwana Michael, it shocks me to hear that you don't believe in any religion at all.

As soon as I read this sentence, my suspicions were finally satisfied. Yes, Ibrahim is religious and religious people just can't bear those who admit that they have absolutely no religious persuasion.

I read on to see what he had to say about this.

This is something I would expect to hear from someone with superficial knowledge of the world. But not from you. In the days that we were together, I had the opportunity to discover what type of person you are, that you are someone who reflects, who contemplates, who reasons. Moreover, you said that you are a follower of Socrates, that great Greek philosopher who you even claimed to be a prophet.

However, now I understand a dream that I once had.

I stopped when I read about the dream. "Oh, Ibrahim," I spoke out loudly as if by speaking into the computer screen Ibrahim could hear me, "You and your dreams! Do you have to have a dream for every occasion?"

And then I read on.

I dreamt that the angel with the blue star in his crown was walking along in a deserted place. There were no roads, no signs, no directions. The angel walked on and, as it is in dreams, I realised the angel was blind, or at least was not using his eyes to know where to go. I noticed also that the angel's wings were broken which is why he had to walk.

Then, like it is in a movie, I was pulled back to see the entire scene, the angel in the centre and a deserted landscape with barely any signs of life. In the distance was a mountain range. The angel had to climb the highest mountain. Despite the angel's blindness, it knew how to reach the highest peak. That's when I realised that it was using its heart to guide him. When the angel reached the top of the summit, he looked up into heaven, even though he was blind so I don't know why he looked up. But the angel looked up in expectation. Soon, it began to rain. It started out with single drops but then continued until it was raining heavily over the summit. When the rain hit the angel, parts of it soaked into the wings to heal them while the rest dripped onto the ground. The rain, however, was not like normal water but shone like silver as if drops of silver fell from the sky.

Eventually it was raining very heavily and soaked the angel and the mountain top throughout. The angel then unfolded his wings and they were whole. The angel then ascended into the sky with healing in his wings and flew across the desert plain, causing the silver rain to drop on the sandy plain below it and wherever the drops of rain fell, a small form of vegetation grew.

Was he once again making an inference about me? I had never been so idealised or idolised before! It was touching that he felt that I was something so special that I was equivalent to an angel, but there was a lot in the story that didn't seem apparent, at least not to me. I understood the blindness of the angel and that he was inferring that my lack of belief in a spiritual world was my blindness but that I had managed to find my way using my heart because I followed an ethical guide that all religions are supposed to follow, a core belief in love and respect for all humanity.

I read his email further.

I am curious, however, to hear why it is you don't believe. Further, how is it that you don't believe and yet you pursue these noble elements of truth, love and justice? That someone left the safety of a wealthy country and condescended to live with those in a poor country to find out whether someone's relatives were still alive can only mean that this person believes and worships God. How, then, can someone like you do such a thing, to put yourself out for this Polycarp and yet say you hold no religious views?

I need to end here, my dearest Michael. My dearest, dearest Michael, how I miss you, how I miss your touch…

and so the email ended very intimately. The memory of our intimacy, coupled with the effects of the wine had a direct effect on my physique and made me miss Ibrahim all the more.

I looked up into the night sky. Taking into account how late in the night it was and the time difference between us, Ibrahim would be able to look up at the evening sky, which would only be dusk where he was, and see the same stars that I could see. At least this provided in the physical world some sort of connection between us. But now, how I missed him. I wished I were that angel he spoke so often about, with wings fully healed and ready to fly, and that I could fly up in the air, over the western horizon and into his loving arms once again.

In a way, Ibrahim had provided a way for himself, a very religious person, to become emotionally involved, intimately involved, with someone with very non-religious views. But I didn't know to what extent this was a façade to get me to believe or say I believe in some way that I myself were religious and then make me into a religious person.

Ibrahim had asked the question and I was going to answer it as honestly as I could. I was determined to nip in the bud what was growing between us before it bloomed into a complicated mess that would be difficult to untangle from later.

My dearest Ibrahim,

Each time I think of you, I cannot help but remember the wonderful moments we spent during my last days at the Msingi wa Mungu Project.

I met his intimacy with expressions of intimacy as descriptive as his had been to me. I then moved on to the matter he had asked me about.

But it is this same intimacy that we shared, you and me, two men, that is condemned by all religions as being an act that God disapproves of greatly. In the Judaeo-Christian belief, in the Zoroastrian religion, and in all religions I'm familiar with, even in recently formed religions such as Baha'ism, views of the love between two men and two women are presented as something decidedly evil.

This to me is the first piece of evidence that all religions are wrong. All religions view the love and intimacy between two men and two women as evil, as sinful, and therefore unfortunately for all these religions, it shows that these religions cannot be revelations from an all-knowing, all-loving God.

All religions, at least the well-known religions, condemn the intimacy between two men and two women, but do not then explain how a man is attracted to another man or a woman to a woman. None of these religions explains why the idea of two people of the same sex being intimate with each other is wrong except to say that it is disgusting. This therefore means that what is a disgusting thing to do is a sinful thing to do.

But if intimacy between two people of the same sex is repulsive to everybody, then surely nobody would ever want to indulge in it. As a result, there would be no need to make laws forbidding it. It would make absolutely no sense for God to include in His laws that two men or two women who have sex together are committing a grave sin if it were universally appreciated that such intimacy was disgusting.

But does it follow that whatever is disgusting is therefore sinful? And further, disgusting to whom? I think the idea of a man having sex with a woman or two women having sex together is disgusting. I think the idea of obese people having sex together is disgusting. Does this therefore make it sinful? If two very ugly people have sex together, while this to me may be disgusting, does it follow that this is therefore sinful?

Which then leads onto another point: what makes something sinful? The impression I got while I was growing up in the church was that certain actions are sinful because of the damage they cause to another person. For example, it is clear that stealing is a sin. I might enjoy taking something that belongs to someone else simply for my own greed but by doing so I do something that is hurtful to someone else. It is clear that murder is a sin. Again, I might kill someone for some personal gain but by doing so I do something that is hurtful to someone else. It is clear that gossiping is a sin. I might get a kick out of saying something nasty about someone behind that person's back but this is hurtful to that person. It is clear that rape is a sin because the rapist gains pleasure but the victim is severely hurt.

The converse is also true, that is, an inaction which causes harm to someone else is also sinful. For example, an old lady tries to get on a bus and she cannot get up on the first step and I do nothing to help her up. My inaction is harmful to that person and therefore it is sinful. Someone is sick and needs someone else to visit and help with household chores and I have the time to do so but I don't help out. This is harmful to that person. What I understand as being sinful is any action that I do that I may enjoy doing but at the same time harms someone else, or any action I do not do simply because of my laziness or lack of concern for other people. At least, this is what I understood from my growing up as a Christian. When Adam and Eve committed the first sin, so I was told in the church, they became sinful beings which meant they now had the capability of doing bad things, hurtful things that affected other people. To stop His creatures hurting each other, God had to keep bringing in laws to show which actions were beneficial for everyone and which were hurtful.

But being intimate with someone who equally wants to be intimate with me? Who does this hurt? Who receives harm from it? So, how can it be classed as a sin? And yet Jews, Christians and Muslims, as well as Hindus, Zoroastrians and many of the other religions that I know, acknowledge that this is a sin. I am yet to find an established religion that actually confesses that intimacy between two people, irrespective of their gender, is good as long as both consent to it. But none of them do. Quite the contrary. While God looks on disapprovingly and yet benignly at the continual raping, stealing and murdering He sees being committed by His creatures, the only time in history, according to the Bible, when God stepped into action and actually forced His creatures to stop sinning was when He destroyed the cities of Sodom and Gomorrah.

But while these religions condemn men who love men and women who love women, they do not ask a fundamental question: what is the source of homosexuality? Or even more fundamentally: what is the source of sexuality? Sexuality, the force within us that drives us to be intimate with another person according to all these religions can only come from the Creator. According to the Bible, there is only one Creator, Jehovah. Jehovah, through Isaiah, tells us, "I form the light, and create darkness: I make peace, and create evil: I the LORD do all these things" (Isaiah 45:7). This implies that only God can create. The implication becomes a clearer confirmation in the Gospel of John, where it says of the Creator, "All things were made by him; and without him was not any thing made that was made" (John 1:3). Therefore, sexuality, all sexuality, was created by God. So this force that is within me that drives me to love you, my dearest Ibrahim, like the forces of electromagnetism and gravity, in this context was created by God. If God, then, created my sexuality, created this force that brings me to be with you as we were on the Msingi wa Mungu Project, why, then, do all religions view it as a sin? If God finds homosexuality such a disgusting thing, He is the Almighty and with a word He can simply say, "Let there be no more homosexuality" and it would no longer be so. The electromagnetism that draws two people of the same sex together would instantly cease along with God's supposed disgust for it.

So, every religion's insistence that homosexuality is a sin shows that all these religions are not revelations from an intelligence higher than ourselves.

There is only one person I am aware of who claimed to have revelations from God and also confessed that sexuality, all sexuality, was of God and that was Socrates. However, unlike the Jewish god, or the Christian god, or the Muslim god, or any of the gods from any of the other religions that I know of, Socrates' god was drowned out. There are no temples to God and His prophet, Socrates. As much as I admire Socrates as a great philosopher, and more than a philosopher, Socrates' god is not the all-powerful, almighty being that the other religions confess the gods to be. Rather, Socrates' god disappeared behind the scenes of world history, only remaining noticeable to those who preserved and studied Socrates' words through Plato. As noble a character Socrates' god may be, Socrates' god has not championed the world stage to allow sexuality, all sexuality, equal acceptance.

But a more fundamental one is that, if there is a god, why does he or she hide him or herself? We only know of his or her existence through intermediaries, people we call prophets. These intermediaries claim that God or the gods spoke to them or at least communicated to them in some way. Why do the gods only speak to certain individuals and not to all of us? According to the Bible, we are all descendants of Adam and Eve, and therefore all equally sinful. These prophets cannot be sinless if they are the descendants of Adam and Eve. So if prophets are just as much sinners as all humans are, why did the gods speak to these people only and not to all of us equally? Even if these prophets were more righteous than all other humans, there is nothing in the writings of each religion that confesses that any of these prophets were in fact sinless. Even though the Bible claims that Noah, Abraham and Moses, for example, were all men who communed directly with God and therefore earned the right to be called prophets, each of them still proved their humanity, their ability to succumb to fleshly weaknesses. Noah became drunk and lay naked on his bed. Abraham lied to Pharaoh and had an affair with his wife's handmaiden. Moses killed a man and disobeyed one of God's commands. These men were just as human and just as sinful as the rest of us. If God could speak directly to them, then if He exists, He can speak directly to all of us. But religious people do not confess this. Religious people say that God spoke to these men who in turn spoke to us on God's behalf.

And how can we be sure that these people who claim to be prophets really received information from the gods? How can I be sure that what Moses said, or what Elijah said, or what Isaiah said, or what any of the prophets said were messages passed on to us from an almighty being and not simply something that came from their own imagination? In fact, I can show you that what the prophets said in the Bible cannot have come from a power greater and higher than ourselves.

So as you can see, my dearest Ibrahim, as painful as it may come to you, the gods of the peoples of the books cannot exist. You asked me the question and I have answered your question truthfully. I admit that I was not completely truthful to you while I was there on the Msingi wa Mungu Project but that was because I was afraid of what would happen if you or anyone found out that I was a complete disbeliever. But now that I am in my home country where I am free to speak out what is in my heart without being criminalised for it, I am telling you this now.

I ended my email with a closing expressing my feelings but there was much more of a reservedness in it than my previous email as I prepared for a gradual distancing and then complete break from Ibrahim. Ibrahim with his devotion and complete conviction of the existence of the God of the Bible and the Koran certainly would not like to develop a relationship with someone who held diametrically opposing ideas, denying the existence of gods and totally unconvinced that these books were divine inspirations. I was sure that Ibrahim, like all religious people, would not like someone like me criticising these books and finding fault with them. The belief in and veneration of these books is much stronger than any human relationship. And this would no doubt be the last I would hear from Ibrahim.

Ibrahim. Beautiful Ibrahim, with his strong beliefs and his fantastical dreams. However, despite his wayout views, he had been a really nice guy. I did appreciate that. But it was a wonderful moment which would soon remain a memory, a pleasant memory that would become more and more distant as time moved on.

Chapter 13

As expected, I did not hear from Ibrahim for days. As the days passed, the more I didn't hear from Ibrahim, the more I realised that I never would. I could concentrate once again my energies on my life back in Sydney.

I put all my energies into helping Polycarp and Jeremiah as I could see an end goal in sight. Also, because Polycarp and Jeremiah absorbed a lot of my time and my mental space, this helped me to forget Ibrahim.

The weekend of the great Riese family reunion finally arrived. We all met up at mum's place, me, my sister Karen, and Karen's foster daughter, Tabitha, who was originally only a temporary addition to our family but through an odd series of events had become the permanent responsibility of Karen and Peter so now Peter and Karen were in effect real parents for life.

There was something peculiarly odd about this. Neither Karen nor I would ever have our own children and this must have been of great frustration to our parents. But by a strange twist of fate, despite the physical inability to sire children, Karen and I in the end granted our mother her wish to finally have grandchildren.

Tabitha was to join us but Polycarp and Jeremiah could not spare the time, or at least Polycarp couldn't, so I left them behind.

My mother had peculiar traits about her. As the family shrank, her possessions grew. From a humble small house during my growing up, mum and dad had finally moved into a huge house with four bedrooms and a huge yard that could hold a soccer match and yet only two people resided here, and then when my father died, only one. In the same way, my mother had decided to have in her possession a huge car, all for one person. I didn't quite get it. Wouldn't it have made more sense to have these huge things when the family was huge and then scale down as the population of those residing with her reduced? But for some reason, my mother was of the idea that big is beautiful and she wanted to excel in beauty. As a result, there was no need to travel down from Sydney to Walla Walla in more than one car as the one car that my mother owned had enough room for all of us to ride in.

Although the reunion was to be held in Walla Walla, we had decided to book in at a motel in Albury, the largest town in that area.

From my mother's place, Albury was about a six hour drive down the Hume Highway which these days is a major road with two to three lanes which snakes its way through the country area of southern New South Wales.

Because we set off early in the morning, we managed to reach Albury in the early afternoon. This gave us the opportunity to settle in our motel and then take a leisurely drive out to Walla Walla.

The road meandered through farmland. When we finally reached the sign which welcomed us to Walla Walla, I was first struck by the smallness of the place. There were few houses. The main road, which at first looked like the only road in the entire township, was dominated by small businesses, the names of which revealed the German heritage of this township. It didn't take long before the one and only church which dominated the entire area came into view. It was a grandiose building, impressionable, domineering and possessing a beauty of its own, well-maintained as it looked like it had been newly built. Its grandiose appearance gave the impression that this was a mighty bulwark to protect all those who inhabited the township.

We stopped the car, got out and strolled cautiously over to the church as if we were afraid of defiling holy territory. The church was deserted. Across from the church was a small area, like a small park with a tree as a centrepiece. Under the tree was a rock and affixed to the rock was a metal plaque. We wandered over to have a look. The monument was dedicated to a Johann Gottlieb Klemke and his wife, Anna Rosine, who were the leaders of a group of Lutheran families who way back in 1869 had travelled across from Ebenezer in South Australia to reside in Walla Walla. The names Johann and Gottlieb were definitely German.

"Does this mean that our ancestors, the Rieses, also travelled from Ebenezer to come here?" I asked.

"I can only guess so," my mother replied.

There was another building on the church grounds a little further away. I decided to walk over to it to investigate. When I turned to see the front of it, I was amazed at what I saw. This little building was a large display case, large enough to house the entire bullock dray set up inside and a few extra what looked like museum pieces. But what particularly caught the eye was a massive mural hanging on the back wall of a map of the south eastern area of mainland Australia, in wonderfully coloured design with native Australian animals in various poses. But what was clear to see was the stylised trip those in the bullock drays followed from Ebenezer to Walla Walla, following the Murray River the entire way.

"At least now I know where Ebenezer is," I mused.

I was impressed by the spectacle. I walked a little to get a better view of the bullock dray. Displayed on old wooden planks were the surnames of other families who had made the trek along the Murray River from South Australia to southern New South Wales. There were a variety of surnames, all typically German. But there was no Riese. The Riese family it appeared was giant in surname but not giant in importance among those who had made the trek.

But what impressed me the most about the bullock dray and the other historical artefacts was that for the first time in my existence it brought history to life. In school, when we studied history, the history of Europe, of America, and even of the early colonisation of Australia, it was a history of other people. What we learnt about, the people we studied, they were all sterilely distant, important because of the impact they made on our modern lives but still too far removed to be of any personal interest. But this bullock dray, these ancient artefacts, these weren't remnants from a past era, they were remnants from *my* past era, from *my* ancestors, from those people who were directly responsible for making me me. Unlike the artefacts on display in other museums which contained an interesting but yet cold and distant connection, these historical artefacts here on the church precincts in little Walla Walla had once belonged to my forefathers and foremothers and so there was a personal connection to them.

When we returned the next day, the place did not hold the same serene tranquillity of a country town as it had the day previous. It had suddenly increased in population as crowds of people, all descendants in one way or another from old ancestor Riese, descended on the place. These were people who I had only met for the first time in my life and yet we were all related, all descended from the one mother and father.

When we arrived at the church, we were greeted at the entrance with a number of tables and chairs and those seated behind them who welcomed us as if we were attending a voting booth on Election Day. We were asked which of the sons of old patriarch and matriarch Riese we were the descendants of. We were then issued with a coloured adhesive circle, each colour representing a different son. Our circle was blue. We could distinguish the other descendants from the red, green and yellow circles the other family members were wearing.

We were encouraged to sit in the church with the other members who wore the same coloured circle and, true to our German heritage, this orderliness was well respected.

As I looked around at the mass of people in this church, all descendants of old patriach and matriarch Riese, and more particularly, how we were assigned a specific colour to designate which of the four sons we came from, I couldn't help but notice how much this reminded me of the stories in the Old Testament of the descendants of the twelve sons of Jacob. Whereas these stories held a cold remoteness and lack of relevance when I read these stories in the past, for the first time these stories came alive. Like the descendants of Jacob's twelve sons who established themselves in defined areas within the land of Israel, so we had been assigned defined areas within this church to sit. We had been asked to which son we belonged. We could have just as well been asked to which tribe we belonged.

This was the first time in my life that I actually felt what it was like to belong to a tribe. The idea of belonging to a tribe, so I had thought throughout my life, was an ancient idea. Modern humans no longer thought of belonging to tribes and only traditional and backward-looking people who could not progress with the times continued to hold tenaciously to this ancient idea. However, some modern people still appreciated the idea of tribe. Faisal was aware of the tribe to which he belonged, the Pashtun tribe, and through my learners, especially those from sub-Saharan Africa, I was aware that other people from other nations continued to perpetuate this ancient idea that they belonged to certain tribes, like Daniel to the Dinka tribe of Sudan.

Now, here I was, sitting with other members of my tribe. After all, what is it that made a tribe? This then further brought it home to me what exactly it means to belong to a tribe. A tribe was, in the end, a group of people who traced their ancestry to a common ancestor, some significant person in the past. This significant person distinguished himself or herself by separating from a particular group to form his or her own nuclear family which then grew abundantly with each successive generation until the family was so big it was no longer small enough for each member to specifically know how everyone was connected but at least enough to know from which ancestor they had descended from.

For the first time in my life, also, I realised the impact that this idea of belonging to a particular tribe had on me. Suddenly there was an immense sense of belonging, not simply to one small nuclear family but to an entire crowd of people. These people were not simply unknown members of a community. What linked us all together was that we were in fact related, and we were related because we all had descended from one man and one woman.

The person who organised this immense reunion was himself a Riese, Johann Riese, who had done research on Gottlieb and Martha Riese who had made the great journey from Germany to Australia back in the early 1800s. Gottlieb and Martha had settled in Ebenezer, just as the monument had indicated, but then uprooted themselves and travelled with their four sons and their four sons' wives to Walla Walla some years later. But the Rieses were not among the first families to emigrate from Ebenezer to Walla Walla and this is why they weren't monumentalised like the other German families. They came with later waves of Germans which was why we didn't see the Riese name on the bullock dray.

Johann Riese told the story as to why the Rieses had immigrated to Australia. In Silesia, at that time a part of the old German Empire but today now in Poland, a group of Lutherans were in conflict with Kaiser Wilhelm III, the then ruling monarch, who demanded that all his subjects follow only one religion, the state religion. Many Lutherans living in Silesia as well as other parts of the country believed that Kaiser Wilhelm's version of Lutheranism violated the Holy Scriptures and these Lutherans believed that they should have the right to worship God according to their own conscience. However, Kaiser Wilhelm III's answer to this was that if they wanted to remain under his rule, then following their conscience was not an option.

At that time, the British had newly taken control of a new southern land, vast in space. Somehow, a representative of these frustrated Lutherans came to an agreement with the British authorities which allowed these Lutherans a refuge in this new southern land. What these Lutherans could offer was an extra boost to the white population in what was originally a land inhabited by dark skinned people, and help the British to Christianise these "barbarous" people, even though the Lutheran religion wasn't quite in tune with the teachings of the Church of England. Somehow this was not a problem for the British authorities.

These Lutherans made there way to Australia, in particular, to South Australia, and these Lutherans were responsible for establishing the Barossa Valley, the well-known wine district north east of Adelaide which still preserves echoes of its German past.

Although many of the Lutherans remained in the Barossa Valley, the Barossa Valley had its own share of hardship. In particular, the weather conditions weren't the most favourable and the farming communities of the Barossa Valley faced problems of drought and flood. Word came to the Barossa Valley Lutheran community that land grants had been made available in Walla Walla. Hence, any of the Lutherans who had any interest in making a change in scenery were invited to buy land in the Walla Walla area and start anew. The area was supposedly better   because of its much more favourable weather conditions and soon groups of Lutherans were to leave the state of South Australia and form a part of New South Wales.

And through my mother, I was a descendant of these Germans. I was so gobsmacked by the entire story. The only history I knew of Australia was of the British coming to Australia to establish a new white, European settlement on the other side of the globe. Apart from the Portuguese who were possibly the first Europeans to have actually seen the land, the Dutch who were well-known to have not only seen it but also to have named and mapped it, and the Aboriginal tribes who had inhabited the continent for millennia before that, my history of Australia had been a story of settlement and establishment by the United Kingdom.

It must have been a shame at the time to have been German in Australia for this story not to have survived into the twenty-first century. I was later to find out that my grandparents spoke German but obviously did not pass this on to their children. I had learnt the language at school totally oblivious to the fact that my ancestors had spoken it as if I were awakening a dormant but significant historical aspect of myself.

The afternoon was spent going through ceremonies and having photos taken. In fact, there were five group photos, each of the four tribes of Gottlieb: Gottlieb, Gottlob, Gottfried and Gotthilf, and then a final photo of the entire group of the descendants of the Rieses.

The coloured dots that we wore on our clothes helped us to instantly fall readily into our tribes. Those with the same coloured dots mingled together and we spent time trying to work out in what way we were related. It was the first time that I had met so many of my distant relatives and further that I was aware that any of them existed.

To complete the entire ceremony, we were all invited to attend a final ceremony at the gravesite of our great patriarch and matriach. The cemetery itself was further up the road from the Lutheran church and in what first looked like more farmland but turned out to be the entrance to the cemetery. Old, ornate stone structures, built with care of the time although now stained and weathered over the past hundred plus years stood as silent sentinels as we entered the graveyard. We were finally led to a gravesite that was somewhat isolated from the others. The tombstone was an impressive tall block of rock, resembling a stele with two side posts higher than the midsection, purposely constructed to make the tombstone look like an opened scroll. The inscription was in traditional Gothic print and it was in German. Johann asked if anyone among the extended family spoke German so that they could translate the inscription. It became obvious that no-one in the crowd could. I put my hand up but Johann probably didn't see me because he then decided to read out aloud the inscription himself in German and then translate the inscription into English.

We were all descendants of this old German patriarch and matriarch who no doubt spoke as their first language German. Yet, among all the descendants, all four tribes of people who descended from them, it appeared that there were only two of us who could actually speak the language of old patriarch and matriarch Gottlieb and Martha Riese. This made me reflect on the newcomers to Australia today, those who have come from countries where the first language is not English. No doubt in a couple of generations, the descendants of these newcomers will be faced with viewing the languages of their forebears as a completely foreign language.

When this part of the ceremony had finished, the crowds began to disperse. By so doing, this made the way clear to the gravesite for those of us who had not had an opportunity to view the tombstone in detail. I managed to get right up close and even to touch the headstone. But what intrigued me was the ornate pattern above the inscription. This tombstone had been delicately worked with an intricate floral design at the top. The design was like a network of briers or some overgrowth of some description, something like the pattern of the golden wattle which wraps around the Australian Coat of Arms. In the centre of this briar work was what appeared to be a cross from which all the branches of these briars emanated. But above the cross was what looked like a star. It was quite small so not quite obvious to the casual eye. But I was drawn to get a closer look at it. And I was quite surprised at what I saw. The star resembled the Jewish Star of David. But was this purely a coincidential resemblance or had this been deliberately woven into the pattern? If the latter were true, then it showed that our patriarch and matriarch had been pro-Jewish, very much like my immediate family had been. Our ancestors had therefore acknowledged their indebtedness to the Jews for the Christian faith.

Was this deliberate? Was this a way for the Lutheran community of the time to show to the Australians of this epoch and at a later time that not all Germans were supporters of the Nazi outlook that Jews were *Untermensch*, that is, subhuman?

As the afternoon progressed, people dispersed slowly but surely. The novelty for me was beginning to wear off and I went looking for my mother so that we could start making our way back to the motel. When I found my mother, I saw that she was speaking to a rather elderly gentleman who despite the appearance of old age, he still had his full faculties. When I approached the two in conversation, my mother turned to me and then turned to this gentleman again and said, "And this is my son, Michael."

The old man extended his frail hand to greet me.

"And this is your great uncle," my mother said to me, "my mother's brother."

"It is a pleasure to meet you," I welcomed.

"It is a pleasure to meet you, too, young man," my great uncle replied.

"We've been invited for dinner at uncle's place," my mother continued. "I'm sure this would not be an inconvenience."

"No, of course not," I replied. "It would be great."

My mother's uncle, my great uncle, carried a truly Anglo-Saxon name, William, in fact, so British that it was a popular name used in the British Royal Family. I could only guess that his parents had chosen this name to depart from their Teutonic heritage and try to adapt to the more Anglo-centric and Anglophilic milieu of the time. I was later to learn that it was an astute move on the part of many of those in his generation who had Germanic heritage in order to blend in better with the people of the time who viewed the British Empire and the descendants of it as acceptable and even preferable. Unlike the Aboriginals of the day who could not hide their physical features which betrayed a non-Anglo-Celtic heritage, the descendants of these Germans who were now well and truly established Australians, having white European features enabled them to hide their German heritage, so successfully in fact that successive generations were totally oblivious to the fact that their ancestry was not traced back to the British Isles. It was only now, in the twenty-first century, where a great number of people living in Australia had ancestors from many countries of the world besides the UK, that it was safe and even fashionable to reveal the true identity of the ancestors of those of us with long family histories in Australia.

In a way, it explained a lot, at least to me. There now was a reason for my pro-Teutonic stance, my desire to learn German when I was at school and a desire to maintain this skill as an adult. It also explained my view that Nazism was not the focal point of the Germanic people but rather a shameful but fortunately short-lived period of the illustrious Germanic history. There was a much greater connection with Germany and all things German, their philosophers, their artists and their way of life. Whereas in the past my interest in all things German seemed to simply be a way to appreciate the world through a second culture and not only through the eyes of the Anglo-Celtic world, now there was a definite connection to this other culture.

Uncle William lived in a relatively large house in the centre of Albury. Somewhere in our conversation he mentioned that he was ninety-six years of age. I was quite stunned. Although he had all the appearance of someone who was well into his twilight years, he still had strength and fortitude enough to be able to continue to live on his own. His wife, my great aunt, had died a few years before simply in her sleep. It was a tragedy to learn that she had only died a few years earlier as I was robbed of ever meeting her.

Accompanying Uncle William were his three daughters, Pamela, Veronica and Rebecca. His two sons had moved to Melbourne and were unable to come to Albury for this giant Riese reunion. These three women were my mother's cousins, cousins whom my mother had not seen for years and whose existence I had not even known about.

But when my mother began speaking to them, it was obvious that they had shared some pleasant moments in their childhood. The relationship between my mother and her cousins was fractured when my mother's parents along with my mother's siblings left the Albury area to move to Sydney. In those days, internet and smartphones didn't exist and so as soon as a physical distance separated two groups of people, the separation was almost total. Apparently there was communication by letter from time to time and the occasional phone call. But then my parents' religiosity created a further fissure between them so that the mere existence of my mother's cousins was forgotten. And I had never once in my life ever thought to ask if my mother had any cousins.

Now that my mother was fast approaching her own twilight years and she was not the fiery, energetic woman of my childhood, the fire inside that burnt wildly for her religion no doubt had cooled down somewhat so that differences of belief were no longer a reason to keep her separated from other family members.

What was tragic was that this separation was not due to a complete difference in religious belief but simply a difference in the version of that religion. My mother's cousins as well as my mother had been brought up in the Church of England. But unlike my mother who with my father became members of the Baptist Church, my cousins had remained in the Church of England, going through the time when the Church of England had an appellation upgrade to the Anglican Church. My mother had broken all ties with the Anglican Church even in my childhood memory and broken all associations with those associated with this church, including members of her own family. After all, hadn't Jesus said that believers in him should dissociate themselves from other people in order to follow him fully, even if those one dissociated from simply worshipped a slightly different version of the Jesus one worshipped?

Amongst the group of people who had come to Uncle William's that evening were Veronica's daughter, Jasmine, who looked about Karen and my age, and two of Jasmine's grandsons, Rupert and Angus, who were thirteen and ten respectively.

We all sat around the diningroom table and were served tea and a variety of cakes, biscuits and other nibblies. The room became alive with my mother and her three cousins in animated conversation, Jasmine and Karen also were caught up in their own conversation. Tabitha went with Rupert and Angus to another room to play which left me with Uncle William. This actually pleased me because Uncle William to me was the window to the past world of my ancestors as he was a child when those at least five generations before me were alive. But it also seemed to please Uncle William to provide me with all this information.

I must have asked the right question because this set a course for Uncle William to begin the history of our ancestors. Uncle William was able to enlighten me about his life and the life of his ancestors here in the Albury area. His life was a simple one, of life on the farm in the Walla Walla district along with all the other members of the Lutheran community which had been established in the area. Uncle William told me of life at the time, the old, traditional, colonial life out on the farm, where mechanisation had not yet made its appearance. It was fascinating to hear about his reaction to new fandangled apparatuses such as radios and cars which although had been invented years earlier did not reach a country town like Walla Walla until my great uncle's and thus my grandparents' early childhood.

Uncle William recounted to me what transpired during the Second World War, how he, my grandfather, who was a second cousin to Uncle William, and many of those in the Walla Walla district were unable to participate as soldiers because of their German heritage and how they were under watch by the authorities. However, while they didn't cause any trouble, they were allowed to continue working on their farms producing goods that were then used to help the war effort.

Because of the Second World War, all things German became a shame. Even towns with German names had to be changed. Holbrook, for example, a township north of Albury, originally carried the name   of Germanton but its Teutonic heritage had to be erased. Even

Uncle William's name was changed from the original Wilhelm, the name his parents had given him, so that he carried a much more respectable English name. Also, both Uncle William and my grandfather changed their surname from Riese to Reace which then became the surname that my mother and her cousins grew up with.

At one point, I heard the expression "gay marriage" mentioned. My mother and her cousins had somehow entered into this topic of conversation. This wasn't too surprising because it was a constant topic on the radio which was enough to separate the nation into two poles. I tried to maintain my concentration on what Uncle William was telling me with an occasional diversion of attention to this other conversation developing in the room. I didn't want to get into a heated argument so I tried to keep my attention back on Uncle William. At one point I heard one of my mother's cousins say something to the effect of, "Well, I can't agree with it because the Bible speaks against it," and then heard my mother's placid approval.

I realised then and there how much my mother was still very much against the idea of homosexuals. She tolerated me but it was impossible for me to even mention my interest in men, and had I been in a serious relationship with another man, it was obvious that this would have caused an even stickier situation.

Then I thought of my mother's mention of the Bible. How can the Bible be the final answer to anything? How is it that we have made it into the twenty-first century and on so many accounts proved the Bible to be an unreliable reference source? The Bible has, on various accounts, been proven wrong at least over the past four hundred years and yet it still is given licence to invade the public sphere.

Uncle William was still talking but my mind was now occupied with other thoughts. I began to think about the inaccuracies of the Bible. Just on matters of geography the Bible has been incorrect. The Garden of Eden, for example, was located according to the Bible on a river which split into four branches, two of these being the Euphrates and Tigris Rivers which meander through the left and right hand side of modern day Iraq, but then Genesis 2:13 tells us that another of these branches encircles Ethiopia. One look at a map of the Middle East shows that this is a geographical impossibility, at least it is today.

On matters of cosmology the Bible has been a failure. The case of Galileo Galilei should have finally put to rest forever our dependence on the Bible for truth. Galileo was tried by the Church for pushing the idea that the earth orbits the sun. After all, the Bible tells us that Joshua commanded the sun to stand still for about a day in Joshua 10:12 and 13, and for Joshua to command the sun to stop meant that the sun was in motion and not the earth. Also, the prophet Isaiah caused a miracle for King Hezekiah in II Kings 20:9-11 where the shadow was brought back ten degrees which meant that the sun was moved backwards. And if there was any doubt, the Psalmist was quite clear in saying in Psalm 93:1 that "the world also is stablished, that it cannot be moved". Because the Bible is unequivocal in this verse in its declaration that the earth does not move, it should be clear that the Bible can be wrong in other matters and therefore should not be sought as a reference point.

I wanted to speak out and say something. But at the same time I did not want to destroy the convivial atmosphere of the moment. This is the terrible thing about speaking out against what religious people have to say. Religious people are happy to bombastically push their points in the public sphere and yet get extremely worked up if anyone points out an irregularity or impossibility in their religions. And in so doing, the atmosphere becomes explosive. But this creates a dichotomy. To what extent are we simply to sit silently and allow religious people to make their unfounded declarations in public space which can harm the lives of other people while we remain quiet simply to keep the peace?

At this point, Tabitha, Rupert and Angus came bursting into the room. Tabitha went straight over to Karen and forced her way onto Karen's lap rather obtrusively while Karen was in mid-conversation with Jasmine. Rupert and Angus came over to the table near to where I was seated.

"Where are your manners, boys?" Jasmine scolded the two. "Now, have you said hello to Uncle Michael?"

"Hello, Uncle Michael," the two boys said in unison although Rupert said it much louder which made Angus sound more of an echo.

The two boys looked on with a bit of shyness and then Rupert had the courage to speak.

"So, what's our relationship to you?" he asked.

I smiled. There was something special in meeting these boys and knowing that they weren't simply the children of friends but were somehow related to me even if only distantly.

"Well," I began. "Uncle William is my mother's mother's brother. And Uncle William is your great-great grandfather. So that makes us..."

I paused for a moment. We have no word to describe such a relationship. I thought long and hard about it until I finally said, "And so that's how we are related!"

I then thought about it a little more.

"If you think of it this way," I added, "my great grandparents were your great-great-great grandparents."

The boys, particularly Rupert, seemed satisfied with this explanation. But now that we had established how we were related, this exhausted this topic of conversation. I then grabbed at something to continue the conversation.

"So, how old are you, Rupert?" I asked.

"Thirteen," he replied.

"So, you're in Year 7 or – "

"Year 8," Rupert finished my sentence proudly.

"And what about you, Angus?"

"I'm in 5th grade. And I'm ten but I'll be eleven on the 21st June."

"Oh, wow!" I replied trying to make this significant birthday sound important when it was still some months away. But the date was familiar and I decided to use this as a topic of conversation.

"So, your birthday is on the winter solstice?" I asked.

Rupert and Angus looked at each other puzzled and then back at me.

"What's that?" Rupert asked inquisitively.

"The winter solstice. This is the shortest day of the year. In the southern hemisphere, it falls around the 21st June while this is the summer solstice and longest day of the year in the northern hemisphere. And do you know why it is called a solstice?"

Rupert and Angus shook their heads and looked on with interest. I could tell by the sudden silence behind me that the conversation had stopped between everyone else while everyone listened to what I was talking about.

"Well, it comes from the Latin word *sol* meaning 'sun', and the Latin word *sistere* meaning 'to stand still'."

"So, the sun stops moving at the winter solstice?" Rupert then asked puzzled.

"Have you ever noticed the sun stop moving at any time of the year?" I asked.

Rupert looked at me and squinted his eyes as if there were a trick to my question. He then slowly shook his head.

"What it means," I continued, "is this. You see, we are told that the sun rises from the east and sets in the west. What we're not told is that the sun doesn't set at exactly the same point on the horizon every afternoon. At the moment, if you watch the sun set everyday, you will notice that each day the sun sets just a little bit north than the day before. This continues until we reach the winter solstice. On this afternoon, we see the sun set at its northern most point on the horizon. And then it stops. It stops setting further north. The day after the winter solstice, the sun begins each day to set a little further to the south and this continues until around the 22nd of December when it once again stops setting further south and then starts setting each day a little bit north than the day before. This is how people in the past, before they realised that the earth orbits the sun, knew how to calculate a solar year. The number of days it takes to get from one winter solstice to the next winter solstice is approximately 365¼ days."

"Well, there you go," I heard one of my mother's cousins comment. "I didn't know that!"

"Yes," I said and turned around to face all those behind me. I then turned back to the boys. "Even though people were aware of a solar year thousands of years ago, they weren't aware that a solar year was also the time it took the earth to orbit the sun. Rather, they believed the sun orbited the earth. No doubt you have heard of Copernicus and Galileo, at least you have, Rupert."

Rupert confessed that he had never heard of these men. Was this deliberate? Did the education system purposely omit the mention of these famous scientists? Was it by design and not an accident that the great court case of the millennium had been readily forgotten? This brought it out so much clearer to me the adage that "those who do not learn from the past are doomed to repeat it". This is why the Bible is still allowed to take centre stage and meddle in public affairs because we have not as a society learned from the past what happens when we do so and therefore many of us suffer as a result of it.

"You see," I continued. "Copernicus and Galileo were scientists who from scientific observation and measurement showed that a universe where the earth orbits the sun fits the data better than the sun orbiting the earth. The Church did not like this because this idea went against the teaching of the Church. This is because the Church relied a lot on an earlier scientist, a man called Aristotle. Have you heard of Aristotle?"

Rupert and Angus shook their heads.

I could tell I had the entire room listening to my lesson.

"Well, Aristotle was a Greek scientist and he lived more than two thousand years ago. He was so clever that just about everything he said everyone believed and didn't question. And this included the Church. But many of the things Aristotle said we discovered later were in fact not really quite right. However, he wasn't always wrong, though. There was a dispute over whether the earth was flat or whether it was round. Aristotle argued quite amazingly for his time, you imagine, it was more than two thousand years ago when we didn't have telescopes or computers, that the earth had to be round."

"The Bible says the world is round," I heard my mother comment.

I could not contain myself. I took a deep breath and contemplated what I would say next. I had the choice to ignore this comment and keep the peace but then my mother's comment would be taken as a confirmation that what she had said was true. This would then give Rupert and Angus the message that the Bible, even with its inconsistencies and inaccuracies, had a right to be considered in public space or at least it could not be criticised in public, that when religious people say something absurd, we should sit quietly and allow these people to continue in these beliefs even to the detriment of other people.

By speaking up, however, I was risking a heated argument where I would no doubt be on one side and this room of people who held religious beliefs on the other. But then the voices of the boys and girls at the Nyika once again resounded in my ears: "Please, Sir! Please, help us!" And I thought of all those who had suffered throughout antiquity at the hands of believers in the Bible and if I didn't say something, many more would be victims as a result. This gave me the strength to speak. I was even prepared after making the atmosphere uncomfortable to get up and leave even if I had to walk back to Sydney that very night. This was where the security of belonging to a tribe showed its downside. There is security within the tribe to a degree. But if for some reason your physical makeup or your way of thinking, despite the fact that neither of them would cause harm to anyone else, were to go against the general tribal party line, you would be cast out of that tribe and left to fend for yourself. It was a situation of damned if you do and damned if you don't.

I looked at my mother, at my mother's cousins, at Karen, Jasmine and finally at Uncle William, that grand old man who had invited us to his home to enjoy a pleasant evening. I then looked at the two young boys who were yet to grow up in a world where religion was making an unfair comeback and, unless someone stood up and spoke against it, millions of people were going to continue to suffer as they had done in the past.

"No," I began somewhat gingerly, almost apologetically. "The Bible does not really say the world is round. Rather, the Bible says the world is a circle. As it says in Isaiah 40:22, 'It is he', that is, God, 'that sitteth upon the circle of the earth'. This verse does not say the world is round like a ball but rather that the world is a circle, that is, round like a plate."

I felt my confidence building and so to emphasise the point I picked up one of the plates from the table and balanced it on the ends of the fingers and thumb of my left hand.

"And in the original language, in Hebrew, the word used is *khoog* which means 'circle', meaning that the world is round like a flat plate. This is further obvious because when the Jews translated this verse into Greek, they chose to translate the word *khoog* as *gyros*, which is the Greek word for 'circle', from whence we get words like *gyrate* meaning 'to move in a circle' and *gyroscope*, a mechanism with a flat circular metal plate. Had this verse meant that the world was round like a ball, the Jews who translated this verse from the Hebrew would have chosen the Greek word *sphaira* meaning 'ball' which is where we get the English word 'sphere'."

There was a thick silence in the room. But I didn't allow it to stop me.

"Now, let's see just how geometrically accurate the Bible is. Rupert, have you done any geometry at school?"

Rupert nodded his head quite innocently and fortunately quite oblivious to the negative static now building up in the room.

"So, tell me, Rupert, what is a pentagon?"

Angus piped up as if he wanted to prove that he also was smart enough to participate in this philosophical conversation.

"A pentagon is a shape with five sides," Angus answered proudly.

"Good. And why is it called a pentagon?"

"Isn't it a Greek word?" Rupert volunteered. "Doesn't *penta* mean 'five' in Greek and *gon* mean 'side'?"

"Not bad," I answered. "What you say of *penta* is correct, although the *gon* comes from the Greek *gonia* meaning 'corner' and which is used in these shapes to refer to the angles. I mean, when you think about it, the number of angles a shape has also means the number of sides it has. But correctly, *pentagon* means 'five angles'. But what about the shape that has four angles? What's this called?"

There was a moment of silence as the boys sat and thought about it.

"A square," Angus then burst out cheerfully.

"Or a rectangle," Rupert added. He then paused for a moment and then said, "And a rhombus and a trapezium."

"Very good," I replied, giving Rupert his due praise for extensive knowledge of shapes. "Now, tell me, how many angles does a circle have?"

"It has no angles," Angus replied with haste to beat Rupert to the answer.

"It has an infinite number of angles," Rupert said by way of correction.

"Okay, it has no angles or it has an infinite number of angles. But does a circle ever have four angles?"

"No," Angus once again piped up in haste to beat his brother to the fray, "because then it wouldn't be a circle anymore. It would be a square or a rectangle or those other shapes."

"Very well answered," I complimented. "Then if I gave you four small objects," and I took four peanuts from one of the bowls in the middle of the table and handed them to Rupert, and then held the plate in front of him, "and I told you to place them at the four angles of this plate, what would you say?"

At first, Rupert looked at the peanuts, then at the plate and finally Rupert laughed as if he had worked out the trick.

"But that's stupid! No-one can put four objects at the four angles of a plate because a plate doesn't have any angles to put the objects on."

"Very good," I continued. "It is amazing, then, how you two boys, one in Year 5 and one in Year 8, know that a circle has no angles – or an infinite number of angles if you wish – and not four angles, because then it would no longer be a circle but a quadrilateral shape. And yet, John the Revelator tells us in Revelation 7:1 that he saw 'four angels standing on the four corners of the earth', the word 'corner' here being the English translation from the Greek word *gonia*, the same word used in the shapes pentagon, hexagon, heptagon and so on. So if Isaiah 40:22 says that the world is a circle and in Revelation 7:1 it says the earth has four angles, it means that the Bible writers do not understand plain geometry, something that even a thirteen year old and a ten year old child readily understands."

I concluded by really pushing the praise for these two young boys and their brightness in mathematics. The two boys stood now proud and tall.

"So," I continued, "if the Bible writers couldn't get basic geometry right, how can we trust the Bible on any other issues?"

Rupert and Angus gave me an innocent look as if they had learnt something in a school room setting. However, I could feel the ice crispness of the room as a result of showing up a major fault in the Bible.

"Yes," I then heard from one of the cousins and I turned around to see the sheepish look on her face, "but the Bible is not a science textbook."

The Bible is not a science textbook. I had heard this so many times before when Christians were forced to acknowledge that the Bible made obvious mathematical and scientific bloopers. I could never understand this point, however. I totally agreed that the Bible was not a science textbook. Neither was Gibson's *The Decline and Fall of the Roman Empire*, which is a historical treatise. But if Gibson had written in his great work an event in history and in this account he had mentioned something that was impossible scientifically or mathematically, anyone who knew basic mathematics would argue that his account was not true. No-one would say, "Well, *The Decline and Fall of the Roman Empire* is not a science textbook so despite this mathematical impossibility, the account Gibson gave of this event in history is still true." Rather, because of the mathematical error in the account, every sensible person would admit that the account as it has been recorded is simply not believable.

On an even more practical level, a shopping docket is not a science textbook either. But if I went to the shop, saw an item on special for four dollars and decided to buy two of them, if I then handed the person at the cash register $10 and received the shopping docket which said that I had to pay ten dollars, I wouldn't happily shrug my shoulders and say, "Oh well, after all, a shopping docket is not a maths textbook. So, any mathematical error on it can simply be disregarded". Rather, even though the docket is not a maths textbook, I would still know something was mathematically incorrect which means that someone had made a mistake. And I would ask for my two dollars change.

However, this was too complicated to explain at this point. However, I decided to try a different tact. If the Bible is not a science or mathematics textbook, then what type of book is it?

"Okay," I said and turned around to Rupert and Angus again. "Let's try some basic ethics."

I was sure that neither Rupert nor Angus even knew what ethics meant but I just continued straight into the conversation. After all, although I was talking to these two boys, the argument was intentionally to everyone else in the room who believed the Bible was the perfect guide to good living.

"Let's say I was the president of Australia."

"But there is no president of Australia. Only the prime minister," Rupert contradicted me as if to show now that he was quite an intelligent young man.

"Yes, I'm aware that there is no president of Australia at the moment. But let's say that one day in the future, Australia becomes a republic and I become the president. Now, the day I become president, I decide that there will be ten rules everyone must follow."

I wasn't sure whether or not Rupert and Angus knew what the Ten Commandments were and was hoping that they didn't because this would have made the argument all the more pronounced.

"Now, in my second rule, I say no-one is allowed to make statues. No-one can make a sculpture of a person or an animal or any creature you might find in the sea, on land, in the air or even in the world where God lives. No-one is allowed to make any of these, not out of stone, not out of metal, not out of wood, not out of anything. Then I command one of my ministers to make me a box and on top of the box I want two animals that look like humans but have birds' wings. What would you think of me and my rules?"

There is nothing more beautiful in a situation like this than the innocent, uncomplicated understanding of a child.

"That wouldn't be right," Rupert said in all confidence. "You would be breaking your own second rule."

"And what if I said in my sixth rule that no-one was allowed to kill? And then I told some of my cabinet ministers to kill a whole group of people. What would you think of that?"

The answer was obvious and Rupert seemed to be really enjoying how smart he was that he was able to answer all my questions.

"And yet," I continued, "when Moses gave the Ten Commandments in Exodus 20, his second command was to not make statues and his sixth command was not to kill. But then, not long after, he told the Israelites to make a box, which he called an Ark, to have two statues of angels sitting on top of it. And then when he received the Ten Commandments, when he returned to the camp where the Israelites were waiting for him, he ordered his ministers to go and kill quite a number of people in the camp."

"Well, Moses was just wrong, then," Rupert replied in all confidence.

I turned to look at those around the table.

"So, if the Bible says so, does that mean we shouldn't allow gay marriage?"

The atmosphere was suddenly electrified. It was as if there only needed to be one false move and the electricity would be discharged and cause absolute havoc to all present. There was silence so thick it was almost suffocating. I looked at Uncle William, then my mother's three cousins, Karen, Jasmine and finally my mother. My mother's face had become stone cold, with a grim firm stare at something before her on the table. I was familiar with this ice cold glare whenever someone said or did anything against her specific interpretation of the Bible. But what did I have to lose? What was the worst my mother could do to me? Not talk to me ever again? She had done that before for thirteen years. I had learnt to live without my parents acknowledging my existence.

But this moment also showed me one of the problems of religions. Each religion assumes it has the total truth. Any criticism is met with violence, whether it be by words in an ugly argument or actual physical violence which results in others being wounded or even killed.

But the electric atmosphere didn't last as long as I thought it would. Jasmine played the part of the lightning pole to draw the danger away.

"You're just like Uncle Luke," she said quite casually and with the obvious coolness to show that my comments weren't taken with the same affront against the religion as many religious people do. "He's also a free spirit and doesn't believe in all of this."

The three cousins relaxed and agreed making comments about this uncle's New Age outlook on life and how Uncle Luke was quite the radical of the family.

Even Uncle William was not as offended as I thought he may have been by what I had said but he did have something to say of it.

"So, you mean to say that the Bible is all wrong?"

It was quite a strong statement. But the look in Uncle William's eyes and his facial expression was much softer than his niece's and seemed to be enquiring after information, not looking for a debate. In fact, Uncle William's soft elderly voice was more of a request for an explanation, to draw truth out into the open and this is what opened me up to speak.

"It's not a matter of right or wrong," I replied. "I mean, that question is already loaded. I'm not saying that the Bible is right or wrong. The point is, there are things in the Bible which are obviously not real or even possible. Angels standing on the four corners of a circular earth just proves this point. When I think of this, I can't help but see in my mind an Escher drawing of an impossibility, something that does not exist in this world we touch and see. It is for this reason that the Bible should not be used as a final appeal, a final basis on which everyone should be forced to live by. I mean, it is amazing how four hundred years ago, Europe realised that it needed to separate Church and State because of the conflict between what the Bible's view of the universe was, that is, an earth-centred universe around which everything else revolved, and the reality, that is, that the earth orbits the sun, and that our entire solar system is in fact an insignificant speck in the entire cosmos. And yet there are still people today who have not learnt from this and cause untold misery to other people because they continue to insist on using the Bible as a final basis."

Everyone in the room listened with interest and the electrified atmosphere appeared to have been diminished as if we were now undergoing a simple discussion, even though we were still   gingerly moving along a topic of conversation that was still quite sensitive. My mother, however, continued with a grim expression at the table. I could only imagine that below the table her foot was twitching in earnest.

"So, you don't believe God created the world in six days?" Aunt Pamela asked.

"Again, this is a loaded question," I replied. "What you are asking is if I believe the account in Genesis chapters one and two is actual history. There are really two questions in your question. The first one is, putting aside the Bible for a moment, is it possible that a mighty, intelligent being greater than humans created the universe in a time span equivalent to six earth days? This is one question. I acknowledge without further investigation that, theoretically, this is quite possible. However, apart from the biblical account, we have no evidence for it.

The other question is, the account of the creation of the world as recorded in the Bible, is this describing the universe in which we live? To this question I can answer quite affirmatively with a definite No. I mean, if you read the account carefully, the universe described in the Genesis story does not describe the universe in which we live and what we observe."

"But it does describe the universe we know," Aunt Pamela objected.

Tabitha began asking Karen when we were going to go back to the motel and Karen made a comment that we would go soon. Jasmine suggested to Rupert and Angus to take Tabitha with them and find another game to play. The boys duly responded and soon the children left.

"Well, not really," I continued. "Every Jew and Christian really needs to read the Genesis account carefully and then compare this with what we now know. I mean, let's start right at the beginning: 'In the beginning, God created the heaven and the earth.' Okay, that starts out okay. Then we get to the second verse: 'And the earth was without form, and void; and darkness was upon the face of the deep. And the Spirit of God moved upon the face of the waters.' Now, the universe that is described here is one where it is completely dark and there is a lot of water. What is not so clear is what this 'deep' was. In Hebrew this word 'deep' is *tehom*. The Jews who in 280 BC wrote the Septuagint, which is the Greek translation of the Old Testament from the original Hebrew, chose to translate this word into Greek using the word *abussos*, which in English is 'abyss'. So, this verse could be read as 'and darkness was upon the face of the abyss'. So, the picture we have of the universe, as recorded in the Genesis, is of an abyss, a bottomless pit, and I can only assume, as it does not say this clearly, that the abyss was filled with water, and God hovered over the water which filled this abyss. Now an abyss is simply a bottomless pit.

A pit does not exist in empty space but has to be surrounded by some medium, such as soil or rock. I mean, that is what a pit or a hole is by definition, a gap in a medium such as dirt. But we are not enlightened as to what medium this abyss is deep in. Further, God hovered above the water layer but there is nothing to explain what existed, apart from God, above the water. As for the water and the material in which the abyss was situated, there is no suggestion that God created either of them. In this part of the narrative, God had not yet started His creative work and yet, water and a material in which there was a hole were already in existence. Who put them there? And when? And why?

As for the water, we all know that water only exists as a liquid at certain temperatures. Just go outside on a cold winter's morning and you will see frost on the grass which is simply dew which has frozen. But later in the day, that frost will melt and turn to liquid water because of the heat of the sun. At an even more practical level, put water in the freezer and you get ice-cubes. Then when you heat water, like when we boil it to make tea, it turns to gas. Anyone who has done basic science will have learnt that, more specifically, water exists only as a liquid between the temperatures of $0 °C$ and $100 °C$. What, therefore, was the source of the heat which was keeping the water liquid because without a heat source water remains a solid? Again think about winter and how cold it gets and what we have to do to keep warm. So what was heating up the entire universe to keep the water liquid?"

I wanted to take this along a further dimension and explain that it's not only heat that keeps water a liquid but also pressure. Water is a liquid on earth because of the pressure of the air pushing down on us and that's what keeps water a liquid. However, in the vacuum of space, there is no pressure and so water only exists as a gas, even when it's cold. So this meant that there had to be something that not only was supplying the heat to keep the water a liquid but also the pressure. But I knew that this would be too difficult to explain because this was something that I had studied in my chemistry degree and I guessed that those around the table had not studied science at university level.

"When we read on," I continued, "we find that God created heaven by separating the water in the abyss. As it says in verse 6, 'And God said, Let there be a firmament in the midst of the waters' and then in verse 7, 'God made the firmament, and divided the waters which were under the firmament from the waters which were above the firmament'. What exactly is a firmament? We get this from verse 8 where it says, 'And God called the firmament Heaven'. This means that the sky above us is the firmament, the heaven.

So, to get the full picture, first we have a dark abyss filled with water, then God made a bubble in the water and this air bubble then had water above it and water below it.

Then, in verse 9 we read that 'God said, Let the waters under the heaven be gathered together unto one place, and let the dry land appear' and then in verse 10 we read that 'God called the dry land Earth; and the gathering together of the waters called he Seas'. So, now our picture of the universe is that the earth is in an abyss, above it is the sky or the heaven, and above the sky is more water, all within an abyss. This picture also then matches with Isaiah 40:22 that the earth is a circle, a flat round disc within an assumed round hole. The assumption is that if we go far enough north, south, east or west, we should eventually arrive at the walls of the abyss. Further, what also makes this story impossible is that the waters under the firmament were gathered together into one place. But the *tehom* or abyss has no bottom which implies that the pit has infinite depth, which means that there was an infinite amount of water below the firmament to create the earth which in itself is not a physical possibility. Or perhaps, all the water that was below the firmament was enough to make the earth, which then implies that, if we were to dig down deep enough, we would come to the bottom side of the earth and further below we would stare into utter darkness down a tunnel which has no end.

So, do I believe in the Creation Story of the Bible? My answer is, it's not a matter of whether or not I believe it but rather the Creation Story does not describe the world or the universe in which we live, see and feel."

Karen and Jasmine had begun another conversation quietly at the other end of the table about something else. Mum, however, continued her cold stone glare at the table. My three aunts had relaxed their faces a bit and listened on intently.

"Then do you think we should not read the Bible?" Aunt Pamela then asked. "Do you mean to say the Bible is a bad book?"

"No, that's not what I'm saying," I replied. "The Bible has its place in history as a significant piece of literature. I mean, I still read the Bible from time to time because I was brought up with it. I have some connectedness with it because it has a link with my past."

"Well, that's a bit odd," Aunt Veronica then blurted out and she showed that she aligned more with my mother's feelings. "First you say that the Bible is wrong and then say that you read it. If it's wrong, it doesn't make any sense to me to read any of it at all."

"It does if you compare this with other forms of literature. I mean, Shakespeare's writings are revered within the English speaking world, in fact, even throughout the non-English speaking world as well. His plays are studied and enjoyed the world over. But no-one would confess that Shakespeare was divinely inspired. And if someone told me that, I would show them that this is not the case. His plays may have some historical basis but Shakespeare also embellished his plays to suit his audience. For example, Shakespeare's play *Macbeth* is based on a real Scottish king called Macbeth. But the real King Macbeth did not really kill King Duncan, at least, there is no historical evidence to show this. Yet, we still learn that we should not let our ambitions get so out of hand that we try to achieve what we want at the cost of other people's lives. And if I learn to 'neither a lender or borrower be', it is because Shakespeare's play *Hamlet* tells me this, even though there was never a Prince Hamlet of Denmark in history to have said this. However, at the same time, I would not make it legislation that no-one in Australia is allowed to lend or borrow simply because Shakespeare said so.

This is my approach to the Bible. Further, I read the Bible in its original languages, that is, Hebrew and Greek, because I think it is much more enriching than reading a translation. But just because I don't believe the Bible is divinely inspired, this doesn't mean I cannot read it."

Uncle William must have sensed the distress my exposition of the Bible was having on my mother and so he took on a tact to save the atmosphere.

"So, Michael," Uncle William said. "Come with me. I've got something I'd like to show you."

With that, one of my mother's cousins asked everyone who remained at the table if they wanted another cup of tea. This broke up what seemed to be built up tension. My mother's face relaxed but she did not look in my direction as Uncle William and I got up from the table and left the diningroom.

Uncle William led me to another end of the house. He led me into a room which appeared to be one big library. Around the walls were beautifully ornate bookcases filled with books, neatly arranged and arrayed as if we had entered a library of the educated.

Uncle William walked over to one of the shelves and pulled off a book which was covered in black leather and had the appearance of a Bible. The cover showed a bit of wear but in all had been well preserved. Uncle William handed me the book.

"Can you read this?" he asked.

I took the book from his hand and opened it up at the middle. The odour of the oldness of the book was quite prominent. But once I got over this, I noticed, to my surprise, that the book was the Old Testament in Hebrew. I looked up at Uncle William.

"Where did you get this?" I asked.

Uncle William smiled. "Oh, it belonged to my great grandfather. It was one of the few possessions he brought with him when he left Silesia to come to Australia. I've kept it as an heirloom but it does nothing else but sit on the shelf because I don't know anyone who reads Hebrew. I certainly don't. But now that I know you do, it would be a great pleasure to give this to you, to keep it in the family but also know that it will actually be read."

I looked down at the book and then back at Uncle William.

"Why did your great grandfather Riese have the Bible in Hebrew?" I asked puzzled.

"Well, he was a pastor of the Lutheran church in Silesia then in South Australia. Pastors have to learn the Hebrew and the Greek."

I looked back down at the Bible.

"There is also the suspicion," Uncle William continued, "that there was another reason. There is a belief that the Rieses originally were Jewish."

I felt like a shot of lightning flash up my spine.

"How?"

"Well, for a start," Uncle William explained, "why did our ancestors win the surname Riese? 'Riese' in German means 'giant', so there must have been a very large ancestor in our family."

Uncle William then laughed at this comment. It was rather amusing for me as well as I certainly was not a giant, nor was my mother who was much smaller than me.

"There was a time in Germany," Uncle William continued, "or the Holy Roman Empire as it was then, back around the sixteen hundreds, when one of the reigning monarchs of the time insisted that Jews with non-German surnames had to have their surnames germanised. Wealthy Jews were able to buy a good surname, such as the Rosenthals. But poorer Jews, which must have included our ancestors, had to be happy with the surname given to them by the government. When these Jews entered the registry office to receive a German surname, the German official looked at the person and from their characteristic gave them a surname. So, if a person was particularly dark in colour, they received the surname Schwarz, meaning 'black', or if the person was particularly white, Weiss, or small, Klein. Our ancestor, therefore, must have been particularly large, so large that he was given the surname Riese, meaning 'giant'.

At some point in history, some of the Rieses decided to convert to Lutheranism. There would have been a lot of sense in doing so because it helped to overcome the prejudice of being Jewish in the anti-Semitic environment of Europe at the time – and which continues to be so even till now. Not all the Rieses converted to Lutheranism because there are still Rieses today who are still Jewish. I've visited a few Jewish cemeteries around the world and discovered that the surname Riese appears amongst the other Jewish gravestones in Jewish cemeteries the world over. Also, there was a time when there was a Rabbi Riese in the United States who we were distantly related to."

Uncle William then paused before adding, "So, there you go. We have Jewish ancestry. We, Rieses, were most probably originally Jews."

I thought I was going to faint. I thought of the star in the pattern on old Gottlieb and Martha Riese's gravestone. It was even more significant now why that star was there and what it really was trying to communicate. And then I thought of Ibrahim's dream. Michael, with the long flowing hair, with a blue star in his crown representing the Star of David meaning that I was Jewish. Through my mother, then, through the Riese family, I had Jewish ancestry.

"Are you sure?" I gasped.

Uncle William laughed his warm laugh.

"Almost a hundred percent sure. The only piece in the puzzle that I haven't been able to ascertain for certain is whether great ancestor Riese originally was Jewish and had a Jewish surname which was then changed. It makes sense historically and the fact that there are Jewish Rieses around the world also strengthens this suspicion."

Uncle William then pointed with his forehead at the book in my hand.

"It would also explain this. After all, great grandfather Riese kept this book as a prize possession. He possessed nothing of similar value that would be similar to the Greek New Testament, or anything from the New Testament, or anything that was particularly Christian."

The book in my hand suddenly felt warm.

"And do the other members of the family know this?"

"Of course not," Uncle William replied. "It was difficult enough being German here in Australia in a British environment. It was further difficult being Jewish in a Christian environment. I think my second cousin, your grandfather, knew. But he would have kept it a secret. My sister, your grandmother, didn't know. None of my children know, either."

I didn't know what to think. How was I supposed to react to the idea that I, in fact, was of Jewish heritage? What was it supposed to mean?

"Then why did you tell me?"

Uncle William laughed another warm laugh. "I've had this Hebrew Bible for years. I really wanted to give it to someone in the family so that it stayed in the family. However, as nobody in the family that I knew could read the Hebrew, I thought I would give it to a museum. However, one night I had a dream that I had taken this Hebrew Bible from the shelf and was about to offer it to a museum of some kind when an angel appeared to me and told me not to do so but give it to one of the descendants who was especially chosen to fulfil a task. The angel said that I would know who that person was because he would be able to read the Hebrew. And so it has finally happened. And because you can read Hebrew, this had to mean that you didn't mind knowing of your possible Jewish heritage."

You had a dream about an angel? I asked myself in thought. Was I supposed to believe you? And was I chosen to fulfil a task? Me, a complete skeptic when it came to issues about religion? However, I didn't want to disrespect Uncle William by telling him what I really thought of his dream and how it made him seem a little odd. In any case, his dream was benign and actually required him to do a nice thing by keeping this old Hebrew Bible in the family line. The angel in the dream hadn't told him to go out and beat people into submission because of his unique interpretation of a religious ideology. But also, the dream was creepily more than coincidental. After all, this was the first time I had ever met Uncle William and knew of his existence. There was no way in the world that Uncle William would have known that he had a grand nephew or anyone in the family for that matter who could read the Hebrew.

We suddenly heard laughter from the other end of the house so this was a sign that the atmosphere had relaxed. We then returned back to the diningroom which was well in animation. My mother was back to being quite cheerful and the conversation was obviously on a lighter topic. On my appearance, my mother looked at me and smiled. I guessed that she knew that there was no use getting angry at me for what I had said earlier because this would lead nowhere, especially as we later had to share the confines of a motel room and the even confiner room of the car on the long trip back to Sydney.

The evening moved on quite nicely. There were a lot of stories from these women's childhood that came out, stories about my mother and her cousins that I had never heard about before which were extremely entertaining.

Finally it was time to go. Tabitha came back running into the diningroom and forced herself between my sister's knees in an attempt to sit on one of them, an all-forlorn expression on her face which indicated that she had had quite enough and was ready to go back to the motel and into bed.

We slowly made our way outside. It was a clear night full of stars.

The verse in Genesis 15:5 where God spoke to Abraham came to mind:

> *Look now toward heaven, and tell the stars,*
> *if thou be able to number them:*
> *and he said unto him, So shall thy seed be.*

In the past, this was a special story which related to someone else's history. But for the first time in my life, I realised that this was now my history.

But I also thought of Ibrahim and his comment to me when he looked up at the stars and made the statement

> *The stars in the night sky are a wonderful reflection*
> *of humanity. Like the stars,*
> *all of us humans are completely the same,*
> *yet at the same time, we are completely different from each other.*
> *But if only we all appreciated each other's differences*
> *and didn't try to dominate each other*
> *or feel superior to each other, like the stars,*
> *humans would reside in heaven.*

Both these comments blended into one and brought Genesis 17:5 to mind when God said to Abraham

> *Thy name shall be called Abraham; for a*
> *father of many nations have I made thee*

Abraham, so the Bible prophesied, would be the father of many nations, not just the Jewish nation. If I put the Abrahamic promise that Abraham's descendants would be like the stars in the heaven and that many nations – and did this imply all nations? – would come out of Abraham, and Ibrahim's comment about all humanity being like the stars, was there something significant that came out of this? Was it more than coincidence that the patriarch Abraham and this Tanzanian Ibrahim shared the same name? And through which Abraham was the prophecy in Genesis 12:3 to be fulfilled where it is written, "and in thee shall all families of the earth be blessed"?

Eventually, the coldness of the night took over from the warmness of the comments. We went through a last round of hugs and kisses. My aunts, my mother's cousins, were quite warm in their farewell. Even Aunt Veronica, who I thought was going to be as cold as an ice-cube, gave me a warm farewell.

Saying farewell to Uncle William was the greatest farewell of all the family. At first we shook hands but then I had to hug him. And it felt good. Because of his age, I had the impression that I was hugging good old father Abraham, this great patriarch. I thanked him profusely for the Hebrew Bible. My Hebrew was rusty, I knew, but I decided I was going to read the book he had given me just like great-great-great grandfather Riese must have done.

We eventually made it back to the motel and into bed. The atmosphere had resumed its cordiality, my outburst against religion having been swept under the carpet. But I had to mention what Uncle William had told me. I showed Mum and Karen what Uncle William had given me. I then explained to them what Uncle William had told me about our almost certain Jewish past.

My mother was delighted. I knew that she was going to be. The Jews and Judaism had held a special place in our household because of the connection of Christianity with the characters of the Old Testament and the Old Testament itself. Unlike the general Christian view of the Jews being the Christ-killers, our family had always considered the Jews a group of people to whom Christians should show great respect and indebtedness because of the religion they had brought to the Gentiles.

My mother made a further comment that it was fortunate that her mother had not known because my grandmother, so it turns out, was rather anti-Semitic herself. A good reason for never delving into your family tree because you might discover that a certain group of people towards whom you hold certain prejudices may actually turn out to be one of your ancestors.

But that I had fulfilled what was in Ibrahim's dream was troubling. Ibrahim could never have known that I had Jewish heritage as I had never known nor even suspected this myself.

But it simply had to be a coincidence. I just could not believe that it was anything more than this.

Chapter 14

The trip back to Sydney was long as it had been going in the other direction but this time there was a lot to reflect on which made the journey seem so much shorter.

First of all, we were Jews. Well, not entirely. On my mother's side we were Jews. On my father's side and with an Anglo-Celtic name like Farril, I was a Gentile. But I was still half-Jewish. How, then, was I supposed to react to the Jewish religion? I didn't believe in it as much as I didn't believe in the Christian faith. But there was one principal difference between these two religions: Christians became Christians irrespective of their racial background. By contrast, Jews were Jews because they could trace a direct ancestral line back to the father of the faith, Abraham, through Jacob's fourth son, Judah. Separating faith and family ties in the Jewish world was much more difficult than it was in the world of Christianity. When Jews, therefore, made the claim that they simply did not believe in the Law, the Prophets and the Writings as being divinely inspired, to what extent were these people causing themselves to be disowned from this great family?

Suddenly, this realisation of my possible Jewish heritage made me question to what extent I was supposed to appreciate the Jewish holy texts. In the past, it had been so easy to criticise the Old Testament because it had been written by people I had no connection with. But now that there was a possible ancestral link to these people, suddenly these texts became more personal, more directly a part of me. The Old Testament texts, and in some ways even the New Testament as well, were no longer simply the story and history of a particular group of people. It was now the story of *my* people, *my* group and *my* tribe. To what extent was I disrespecting my tribe when I disrespected documents and the myths within these documents that had been treated with reverence and awe for millennia as the very essence of what made my tribe? And therefore me?

But this whole experience made me realise just how complex my identity was. I had possible Jewish connections and hence all the history of the Jews and their persecution and their achievements were now mine. I identified with these even more.

I also had discovered a connection with Germany, the German language and the German culture. My ancestors were German, at least on my mother's side. They had also been refugees, people who had fled their country because of religious persecution. At least this now created a much greater connection with modern refugees, with Faisal, with Faraj and now with Polycarp.

But also, the surname Farril was a British surname so I still had a connection to the British Isles, whether it was Celtic or Anglo-Saxon. All things British, its history, its literature, its contribution to the world was still something I could identify with as being a part of me.

But what about me, Michael Farril the Australian? I was also Australian. It was in Australia that I was born and raised, within the culture of Waltzing Mathilda, Vegemite and meat pies. What therefore was my identity? To what extent was I to look back into the past and keep the connection with my possible Jewishness and my very certain Germanness and Britishness? To what extent was I supposed to discard these and move into the present and push forward into the future with my Australianness?

In my current historical time zone, I had formed a new tribe and I had accepted Polycarp and Jeremiah as an integral part of it. To what extent should Polycarp and Jeremiah continue to hold on to their Burundian and Rwandan heritage with their myths and languages, and to what extent should they make alterations to their person now that they lived in Australia, especially as they now looked to me, an Australian-born with a white European background, as their father and therefore had become a part of my new modern tribe?

These thoughts of ancestors, tribes and family made me think of Polycarp. When I saw him again after my trip to Albury, the first thing I did when I greeted him was to give him one long hug. I held him close to me as if he would simply vanish if I didn't hang onto him tightly enough. By this stage, Polycarp had warmed to my hugs as if we were biologically father and son.

This relationship that was building between Polycarp and me starkly contrasted with my experience down at Walla Walla. I now realised that I belonged to a greater family, a tribe, a great group of people to whom there was a definite relationship. And yet our extended family was so fragmented. Apart from Karen, Peter and my mother, I had known very little of my extended family until now. But as much as it was exciting for many of the four Riese tribes to meet together in Walla Walla, once we had left, there was very little in the way of keeping in contact, except for my mother's cousins and Uncle William. No-one at the reunion seemed to express any particular desire to exchange contact details and continue to stay in touch. The reunion was simply one of, well, here we are, we're all related. That's lovely. Okay, can we now get a move on with our lives? Very few of the Rieses seemed to care that other members of their extended family existed. So, what allegiance should I really hold to these members of my tribe who had only a casual appreciation that other members of the tribe existed?

By contrast, here was Polycarp, who had no family. Everyone in his family had been slaughtered except for him and his nephew. How ironic. When we have a family, we take no care for those who belong to it. But if the members of our entire family no longer exist, suddenly we pine away because of our feelings of loneliness and lack of family members to relate to. It seemed that we humans were never satisfied.

A week after returning from Albury, I received an email back from Ibrahim. I was rather surprised that I received any email from him at all.

My dearest Michael,

I hope and pray that this email reaches you in good health.

So the email started. His introduction continued and was as ornate as a temple interior.

I have met many people, even those who claim to believe in God, but none so insightful as you.

When I read these lines, I felt the full power of the compliment. That had meaning well inside what I could ever dream. This further led me to read on.

I would like to address each point that you have made and answer them for you in a way that I know best.

You have definitely reached the heart of what all religions try to teach, that we must avoid committing sinful acts and only do those things which please Allah. Allah is our example. As Allah says in Al-Qasas 28:78

> *And do good to others as Allah has done good to you.*
> *And don't seek to make mischief in the earth.*
> *Verily Allah loves not those who make mischief.*

This is quite significant. Allah doesn't love those who make mischief. In Arabic, this expression is rendered as mufseedeenah, *meaning someone who ruins or destroys or causes unrest.*

This verse carried greater meaning than Ibrahim inferred. When I read his explanation of the Arabic word *mufseedeenah,* I couldn't help but think of all the unrest going on in many Muslim countries. Weren't therefore these people aware of what was written in their own holy book?

Didn't they realise that because of their actions, their Koran was telling them that their God, Allah, actually doesn't love them?

I read on.

And what good has Allah done to us? As Allah says in Al-Naba 78:14-17

And We have made the sun a bright lamp
And We send down from the dripping clouds water
pouring forth abundantly,
that We may bring forth
thereby grain and vegetation,
and gardens of luxuriant growth

This is similar to what Issa said in the Injil in Matthew 5:45 that

Allah causes the sun to rise on the evil and the good,
and sends rain on the righteous and the unrighteous.

This is the example that Allah has set for us. Those who follow Allah's will follow this example, and Allah acknowledges the righteous by saying in Al-Dahr 76:9, 10

And they feed, for love of Him, the poor, the orphan, and the prisoner,
saying, 'We feed you for Allah's pleasure only. We desire no reward
nor thanks from you'.

It is also clear that Allah seeks equinimity. As Allah tells us in Al-Hadid 57: 26

Verily, We sent Our Messengers with manifest Signs and
sent down with them the Book and the Balance that people
may act with justice.

The Balance, the scales of justice as they are symbolised in history and indeed in many courts of law, symbolises that Allah expects us humans to act fairly and with justice to everyone for as it says in Al-Mumtahanah 60: 9 "Allah loves those who are equitable".

So, if you do not like someone stealing from you, don't steal from others. If you don't like someone lying to you, then don't lie to others. If you don't want someone to kill you then don't kill others. This is the very essence of what it means to be equitable and to have truly received the Balance that Allah has sent down to us through His messengers. Or, said in another way, as Allah said through the prophet Issa in Matthew 7:12

> *In everything,*
> *do to others what you would have them do to you*

In the same way, if you want others to respect you because of your beliefs then respect others who hold a belief which is different from your own. In the same way, if you want others to respect you and treat you with dignity when you love and are intimate with someone you desire to love and be intimate with, then respect others around you, whether it be your son or your daughter, your uncle or your aunt, your cousin or anyone in your community or anyone in your workplace or anyone in your township, when they fall in love and are intimate with a person they love and desire. For if you prevent others from being intimate with each other, you grant others the right to stop you from being intimate with someone you want to be intimate with.

This is the very command of Allah and is an embodiment of His very essence, for Allah is just and compassionate.

I had to take a pause and a deep breath as these words in Ibrahim's email message simply penetrated into the very central aspect of my being, causing everything from within to tingle and bubble up with an inexplicable pleasant feeling that I could not define. The words were beautiful. They talked of a religious belief in some ways similar to what I was raised on but beyond the limits that this religion claimed to make bounds.

I then read on.

As for your question, "who created sexuality?" Yes, you have answered this question yourself. As you quoted from both the prophet Isaiah and John, Allah creates everything. The Koran confirms this where it is written in Al-Nisa 4:79

> *All is from Allah.*
> *What has happened to these people that they*
> *come not near to understanding anything?*

Everything, even our sexuality, is from Allah. And then Allah goes on to ask why people can't understand this. After all, our sexuality cannot come from anywhere else, not even from Satan, for Satan, like all false gods, is created, and as Allah says in Al-Araf 7:192

> *Those who create nothing ... are themselves created.*

And as it says of Allah in Luqman 31:12

Show me what others besides Him have created.

Allah alone is the Creator. And Allah poses the question to us to find who else besides Him has created anything. As the Koran clearly states, there is no-one else who can create like Allah, not even Satan. So because Satan cannot create, Satan did not create sexuality.

Let me now address another aspect of your email. Like you, I had been convinced that the love between two men or two women was sinful. This form of love so I was told is indecent and evil. Because I had been told this, I believed that my feelings for men were a result of some enticement or some force from a devil, an Iblis. I applied myself wholly and continually to my religion. But then one day, Allah made me aware of this verse in Al-Ankabut 29:46

*Surely, prayer restrains one from indecency
and manifest evil.*

I had prayed regularly, and yet my feelings for men remained. Allah was, however, revealing to me what I should have known from the Koran all along. Because prayer restrains one from indecency and manifest evil, and because I had prayed regularly and my feelings for men remained, this meant that either my feelings for men were after all not indecency and manifest evil, or alternatively this verse was not a revelation from Allah.

Further, Allah made me aware of what He says in Al-Ankabut 29:8

*And as to those who believe and do good works,
We shall surely remove from them their evils*

I spent much of my life trying to do good works, being a good Muslim, praying regularly, studying the Koran regularly, observing all the holy days with passion, trying to be a good son, studying hard at school, doing good to others and yet my attraction to men never went away. Allah, therefore, revealed to me that my attraction to men was, therefore, not an evil that He should try to remove from me for otherwise if this were an evil, it would have been removed from me long ago.

Again, Allah reveals through His Holy Book in Al-Anfal 8:12

He sent down water upon you from the
clouds, that thereby He might purify you,
and remove from you the filth of Satan.

From the time that I read this verse, each time it rained, I went outside and
stood under the rain and felt the water pouring over my body. Although I felt
delivered of all my sins, my feelings for men remained. This had to mean that
either my feelings for men were not filth of Satan or otherwise this verse was not
true.

Again, Allah revealed in His Holy Book in Yunus 10:10 that

But as for those who believe,
and do good works – their Lord
will guide them because of their faith.

I received no guidance to leave my attraction for men but rather I received
guidance to fully understand the fullness of Allah.

Again, Allah says in Yunus 10: 27

For those who do good deeds,
there shall be the best reward and
yet more blessing.
And neither darkness nor ignominy
shall cover their faces.

Allah revealed that my feelings for men were not something I should be
ashamed of or something shameful for me to hide my face.

Allah then revealed to me something that has always been open and clear
for everyone who truly has eyes open to see what Allah's plan is. They tell us as
you mentioned in your email that all religions are against homosexuality. But is
this really true? This would therefore mean that in countries where religions have
been oppressed or criminalised, homosexuality should have been welcomed. But
this is not historically true. Look at Europe during Hitler's regime. Didn't Adolf
Hitler send homosexuals to the death camps during the Third Reich? Hitler did
not acknowledge a belief in God. So it was not due to a religious belief that caused
Hitler to act so cruelly against such people.

In the totalitarian regime under Josef Stalin when the State held the ultimate
power under Communism, a system which denied the very existence of God,
homosexuality was not decriminalised but was made a crime against the state.
What could Stalin's justification for this be if Stalin believed that there is no god?

Many African nations have made homosexuality illegal. But is it in reality because of religious beliefs? As in all totalitarian regimes, we can see the extent of the oppression by the way homosexual men and women are treated. It is only in communities in which Allah's compassion and equity are truly manifested where such people are free to walk with dignity.

All repressive regimes, all dictators who have demanded ultimate control of their citizens have been against homosexuality. What you say about religions being against homosexuality I question, but it is clear to me that when homosexuality is made unlawful or illegal, it is done so under the ruling of an evil tyrant who believes he can control nature. This in itself is a blasphemy against Allah.

And what of those who do not believe in Allah? Or should I say more clearly, those who say with their mouths that they don't believe in Allah? What is the duty of a Muslim? Let the true Muslim read the Holy Koran where Allah commands in Luqman 31:24

> *And as for him who disbelieves,*
> *let not his disbelief grieve you.*
> *Unto us is their return and*
> *We shall tell them what they did.*
> *Surely Allah knows full well*
> *what is in their breasts.*

Muslims are not to be grieved by those who say they are non-believers but to simply leave them alone. After all, Muslims themselves may think these people who say they are non-believers are bad. But Allah knows what is in their hearts. Their hearts may believe in Allah and in His compassion, even though their minds and their lips indicate otherwise.

And so this is how I see you, my dearest Michael. I know that deep down in your heart, you show that you love the all-compassionate, the just and true God because your actions show this. Your mind may not understand it and your lips may not say it but your heart through your actions shows it. And I know Allah knows this. Like a blind man whose eyes cannot govern the way but whose other senses and his heart guide him on the right path, your heart is guiding you along the right path even though your mind's eye cannot see it.

Under normal circumstances, the last comment would have irked me. I didn't believe in God, or more correctly, I could at least show that the gods of the religions which had survived into the twenty-first century did not nor ever have existed. Because I did good things for people was not a result of a belief in anything beyond the world I could touch and see. In fact it was the result of the world in which I lived and perceived that made me want to help others. Had any other religious person told me what Ibrahim wrote in his email it would have annoyed me that that person can only link goodness with a belief in God, even to the point of saying that I believed in God even though I didn't realise it. However, for some reason, it didn't worry me coming from Ibrahim.

Ibrahim's dream then came to mind. Was that what he was implying about the angel Michael who walked around blindly but managed to be guided up to the peak of the tallest mountain? If that were the case, I could not work out the rest of the dream, about the rain of silver and why this angel had to climb the highest mountain to get it.

Ibrahim's email was deep. Despite his belief that the holy books he quoted were dictations from beyond our world, his ability to bring this belief in line with mine, at least in his universal approach to the view of people and the respect we should show to all was quite astounding. I could have replied with another email but I really wanted to speak to him directly. I wanted to discuss this issue in more detail but also I simply wanted to hear his voice again. And of course I wanted to tell him what I had discovered from my trip to Walla Walla.

Fortunately, international communication is very affordable these days. Emailing Ibrahim was almost costless and formed part of my monthly contract with my current phone company. But phoning overseas was also of low cost. This made me stop and think about how far we had come in international communication. I remembered as a child in the days of penpals when I wrote letters by hand and sent them through the post. On special occasions, however, like on my penpals' birthdays, I rang my penpals and spoke to them. I remember at that time it cost something like two Australian dollars per minute and that was a lot of money in those days. My parents only allowed me to speak for three minutes because six Australian dollars was a lot of money for a simple three-minute conversation. These days, international calls can form part of a monthly phone plan. However, as I was no longer in contact with any of my penpals except one, there was really no need for me to call anyone in another country. Nonetheless, for a one-off international phone call, there were phonecards available which cost around ten dollars which, depending on the country you wished to call, allowed you to converse for hours. When I went to the local corner shop to purchase a phonecard to call Ibrahim, I discovered that there weren't phonecards specifically for Tanzania so I had to buy one that was generally for the African region.

I dialled the number on the back of the card and entered my PIN only to discover that I only had an hour of conversation on this phonecard.

That was still enough. Once I had dialled Ibrahim's mobile phone number, I clasped the phone to my ear in suspense. I could feel my heart beating inside my eardrum and each beat seemed to take minutes and make the time go ever so slowly. Each ring through the phone was like an eternity. Eventually I heard a "hello?" which sounded somewhat distorted but I could still recognise the voice I longed to hear.

"Hi, Ibrahim?" I began. "This is – "

"Oh, Bwana Michael!" I heard Ibrahim's distinct voice. Even the distortion of the telephone line could not completely render his voice indistinguishable. It was his beautiful voice.

"Hey, *mambo vipi*?" he asked. This was a familiar and colloquial way of asking in Swahili how someone was, similar to the English, "how's things?"

"*Mambo poa*," I replied using the correct response to Ibrahim's question, which roughly translates as "things are cool".

"Oh, Bwana Michael," Ibrahim said again, without allowing me to get a word in, "it is so nice to hear your voice."

I could feel my throat constrict.

"Ibrahim," I replied, "It's so nice to hear yours as well."

"Bwana Michael," Ibrahim continued without a skip in his breath. "I miss you so much. I would really like to hold you close to me again."

That comment just took the breath out of me. I was struggling not to burst into tears. Suddenly the yearning to be with him, to be physically with him was reawakened.

Our modern technology, our information highway may have shrunk the world but this was only half true. The world had shrunk in the sense that two people on opposite ends of the globe could engage in conversation in real time. But it was untrue in the sense that the distance between them was still there and still real. Ibrahim's voice may be heard right where I was sitting but Ibrahim's physical body was still a third of   a world away. Although I could hear Ibrahim's voice, I could not reach out, touch him and feel his body even though this is what I really wanted to do.

Our conversation got off to a rocky start. We wanted to be with each other, not simply speak with each other but eventually the conversation got going as we both realised that our togetherness on the phone now relied on verbal intercourse.

I started asking Ibrahim about the Msingi wa Mungu Project and how things were getting along. I could easily follow what Ibrahim was talking about as I had already been on the Msingi wa Mungu Project premises and knew where everything he was talking about was located.

Ibrahim then returned the conversation into my arena. He asked me about Polycarp. I gave an update about him and his life here as well as that of Jeremiah's.

Ibrahim listened. This was something I really appreciated about him. I could feel that he took an interest in me, in my conversation, in what I said, as if what I had to say held some value.

Eventually it was my turn to throw questions back to Ibrahim.

"Ibrahim," I began. "I have to ask you. How is it that you, a Muslim, can be so tolerant of other religions, even to the point of working for an organisation and not only working for it but being an active manager of the project, a project that unites Muslims and Christians together, while other Muslims in the world violently attack non-Muslims, particularly Christians, and even other Muslims who do not follow their version of Islam?"

I heard a soft laugh through the other side of the phone.

"Well, obviously, one of us is not acting like a Muslim should."

The perfect argument. I had heard that from people of all religious persuasions. Two people could say that they ascribed to the same religion. However, if one person in that religion did not agree with what the other person did in his or her life or what the other person believed, instead of admitting that the other person was still of that religion, the person would say that the other person was not acting as an adherent to the religion. This person was therefore equivalent to an outsider of the religion and may as well be an infidel.

"Bwana Michael," Ibrahim continued, "when you open the Koran to the first surah, what is the first verse which introduces us to the religion presented in the Koran?

In the name of Allah, the Gracious, the Merciful.

We first read that Allah is gracious and Allah is merciful. This is then repeated in the next verse-but-one: The Gracious, the Merciful."

My thoughts digressed when I heard the expression "the next verse-but-one". It sounded so poetic, so old English and yet so beautiful coming from Ibrahim.

Ibrahim continued. "At the end of the surah, those who read the Koran are urged to look to Allah and ask Him to 'guide us in the right path'. Every Muslim, whether Sunni, Shi'ite, Wahabi, Sufi, whatever denomination we claim to belong to, all of us who pray this prayer every day ask Allah to guide us on the right path. If we all pray this prayer, then in our hearts we must all really be trying our best to follow the path that

Allah 'has bestowed His blessing' as the last verse of this prayer states. All Muslims are required to say this prayer every day. If we must pray it every day, it means that we often stray from this path, all of us, and we need guidance to get back onto that right path. Muslims who kill other Muslims because they feel that these other Muslims are *kafiri* because they don't follow the Koran the way they think they should be are interrupting those Muslims' path to Allah. They are also implying that they no longer need to pray the *Al-Fatihah* because they are boastfully assuming that they will no longer sway from the path and hence no longer need to pray that they don't.

In the same way, in the Injil, the prophet Issa told his disciples to pray saying, 'and lead us not into temptation'. There is a similarity in the prayer Issa asked his followers to pray and the prayer of the *Al-Fatihah*. Allah wants to guide us in the path that leads us, not into temptation, but the one that contains His blessing. This means that even the Christians regularly pray to Allah to guide them, so a true Muslim does not kill Christians nor hurt them because that Muslim would then be interfering with that Christian's call to Allah to guide him or her in the way of Allah.

Anyone, whether he or she is Muslim or not, who maims or kills another person or who destroys anything on the earth, this person is interfering with the plan of Allah. These people are being led astray by the Destroyer."

Ibrahim's words were just beautiful. But it was an Islam I had never heard of before. Ibrahim's belief was nothing like that of the Muslim terrorists of this world, or better said, the Muslim bullies of the world, where the idea was to force everyone to do what these bullies wanted them to do.

"Also," Ibrahim interrupted my thoughts. "It says in the Koran in Al-Fatir 35:46 that 'if Allah were to punish people for what they do, He would not leave a living creature on the surface of the earth'. This shows that every one of us should be punished by death because of our sinful nature. But Allah spares all our lives because Allah loves us and wants us to follow the path back to Him. Anyone who feels that they have the right to kill others to punish them for being unrighteous, this person is boastfully claiming that he or she is now perfect. And this is quite blasphemous."

When Ibrahim mentioned this, this brought a tingle through my body. There was a deep humility in what he was saying. But further, it made me reflect on where it was written in Isaiah 64:6 where Isaiah, himself a prophet, confesses on behalf of all humanity that "all our righteousnesses are as filthy rags" and Paul who wrote in Romans 3:10 that "there is none righteous, no not one". The Old Testament, New Testament and the Koran all equally confessed that every person on the planet was so sinful that God should actually punish every single one of us because of our sinfulness. But He doesn't. There was a deep beauty in Ibrahim's way of viewing God especially as this was not simply derived from something that Ibrahim magic extracted out of nowhere but actually from what was written straight from the Koran.

If this then is what the Koran taught, why was there so much internecine fighting between each of the different Muslim nations or between the different variations of the same Islamic faith? If the Koran taught that everyone was so sinful that Allah should actually punish everyone, then why did some Muslims have the daring to assume that they had a right to kill other people who were, as the Koran clearly confessed, equally unrighteous?

Because of the connection between this verse Ibrahim quoted me and the similarity with the other verses from Isaiah and Romans, this then led me to another thought.

"Ibrahim," I said. "I have to ask you something. I remember you telling me that the Torah and the Injil were from God and that the Koran says so. However, I spoke with another Muslim here in Sydney, one of my learners at work. In our conversation, I asked him if he believed in the Christian Bible. He said that the Old Testament and the New Testament had been distorted by the Jews and the Christians and therefore Muslims no longer needed to consider the Holy Bible. He said that originally the Torah and the Injil were perfect but because people later made changes to them, what we have now is not the pure Torah and Injil that the Koran is referring to. The Koran is referring to a pure Torah and Injil that no longer exist."

Ibrahim laughed through the phone. "Did you tell him to show you where it says that in the Koran?"

"Well, no, I didn't," I replied.

"Go back and tell him to read his Koran. Tell him to read what it says in Al-Anam 6:35 where Allah says

There is none that can change the words of Allah

It must have been important because Allah says it again later in the same surah in verse 116

And the word of your Lord has been fulfilled in
truth and justice. None can change His words

and again in Al-Kahf 18:28

> *There is none who can change His words.*

The Koran says that the Torah and the Injil are the words of Allah. If the Koran says that these are the words of Allah, and the Koran says that no-one can change the words of Allah, how then can a Muslim say that the Torah and the Injil have been changed?

In Al-Araf 7:158, Allah says that

> *Those who follow the Messenger, the Prophet,*
> *the Immaculate one, whom they find mentioned in the*
> *Torah and the Gospel which are with them*

Why would Allah tell us to follow the Messenger mentioned in the Torah and the Gospel that is with them, that is, with the Jews and the Christians, if the Torah and the Gospel that the Jews and Christians have with them have been changed? This verse cannot be referring to a Torah and Injil that no longer exist. Historically we know that the Torah and the Injil that we have today is the same Torah and Injil that Jews and Christians had with them at the time this surah was written. There have been no changes since that time. This shows that when the Koran was written, the very same Torah and Injil that Jews and Christians had in their possession at that time has remained the very same Torah and Injil that the Jews and Christians have in their possession even up to this present day which means that this is the Torah and Injil the Koran is referring to.

Even Muhammad himself acknowledged that the Torah and the Injil are perfect. As it says in Al-Bayyinah 98:3, 4

> *A Messenger from Allah, rehearsing scriptures*
> *kept pure and holy*
> *Wherein are books right and straight*

If Muhammad came rehearsing scripture from books right and straight, from which books was he rehearsing scripture if they weren't the Torah and the Injil? As the verses say, these scriptures contained books, *kootoob*, not one book, *kitaab*, so he was rehearsing from more than one book. And these scriptures which included these books had been "kept pure and holy". So, if they had been kept "pure and holy", Muhammad himself acknowledged that they had not been changed.

Again, in Al-Anam 6:92, the Koran shows how Allah is angry at those who do not believe in the Torah by saying

> *The Book which Moses brought…you treat… as scraps of paper*

Which Book of Moses is the Koran referring to that the unbelievers were treating as scraps of paper if it is not the same Book of Moses, the Torah, the same Torah they had in their possession at the time the Koran was written? Allah was angry at the people because they treated the Torah as scraps of paper and didn't take it seriously as the Koran itself says we should. I cannot see it in any other way but that if I don't believe the Torah is the Word of God, I also am treating it as scraps of paper. Then it means that I am also treating the Koran as scraps of paper as well because there is nowhere in the Koran which says that the Torah and the Injil have been changed."

"Well," I started but then Ibrahim interrupted me.

"The Koran also says in Al-Saba 34:32 that

> *And those who disbelieve say,*
> *'We will never believe in this Koran, nor*
> *in what is before it'*

What is it that came before the Koran that we are to believe in if it's not the Torah and the Injil? And if the true Torah and Injil no longer exist, how can we believe in it? Listen to the verse again, 'and those who *disbelieve*,' that is, 'those who are *kafiri*' do not believe in what was before the Koran. And by not believing in what was before the Koran means that they do not believe in the Koran itself.

Tell this friend of yours that he should heed the warning in Al-Nisa 4:151 and 152 where it says

> *Surely, those who disbelieve Allah and his Messengers*
> *and desire to make a distinction*
> *between Allah and His Messengers, and say,*
> *'We believe in some and disbelieve in others,'*
> *and desire to take a way in between,*
> *These indeed are veritable disbelievers.*

I'm sorry but I can't see how this can be any clearer. It doesn't say that we should believe in Allah and his Messenger, singular, but his Messengers, plural. Those who make distinctions and believe in one messenger, such as Muhammad, but disbelieve in others, such as Moses and Issa, are truly unbelievers, *alkafiroona khaqan*, true *kafiris*. Muhammad is one messenger and we have his book. But so were Moses and Issa, and we have their books as well. The Koran clearly commands us that we shouldn't make distinctions and say we believe in one messenger and not another."

Ibrahim paused for a moment and this gave me a moment to reflect on what he had just said. Has Ibrahim ever said this out loud to anyone else apart from me? If so, why was he still alive?

"Then, what about the Hadiths and Shariah Law that we hear so much about," I then asked, "which even this learner of mine said we should follow?"

"Where does it say in the Koran that we should believe in the Hadiths and Shariah Law?" Ibrahim asked.

Well, I don't know, I thought to myself. I hadn't read the Koran. But the way the Muslim community in the media talked about the Hadiths and Shariah Law, it sounded as if the Hadiths and Shariah Law were endorsed by the Koran. If they weren't part of the Koran nor endorsed by the Koran, then why were Muslims so adamant in trying to establish these all over the world? Ibrahim then made a comment which made it sound as if he had just read my mind.

"Why is it that this Muslim friend of yours believes in the Hadiths and Shariah Law which are *not* mentioned in the Koran but doesn't believe in the Torah and the Injil which *are* mentioned in the Koran?"

He's not a friend of mine, I thought. He was simply a learner who felt he had to tell me about Islam whether I wanted to hear about it or not. Ibrahim's point was pertinent, though, and a very good one. But as much as what Ibrahim said was right, Muslims kill people who tell the truth. Which led to my next question.

"Then why are other Muslims, that is, Muslims not like you, committing so many atrocities in the world, killing themselves and others to try to push their versions of Islam on the world?"

Ibrahim laughed his soft laugh through the phone. I couldn't see how it was something to laugh about but was rather a terribly grave comment.

"My dearest Michael," Ibrahim replied, "these Muslims who are committing these atrocities do them not because Allah has instructed them to do so from the Koran but because the Destroyer has convinced them that this is the will of Allah."

"When you say 'the Destroyer', you mean, Satan, no doubt?" I stated partly as a question. It was the second time Ibrahim had mentioned the word "Destroyer". I originally thought it was an alternative epinym for the devil but Ibrahim's consistent use of the word was odd and unfamiliar as I was only familiar with the name Satan, and had become acquainted with the Swahili-slash-Arabic name Iblis, although this word looked like the Greek word *diabolos* meaning "devil" with the d removed and with some adjustments to the vowels.

"When I say, the Destroyer," Ibrahim replied, "I mean, the Destroyer, the one who is trying to destroy everything good that Allah has created. All those who are out to destroy Allah's world, Allah's universe, Allah's creation, Allah's people, all the descendants of Adam and Eve, all things on this earth that Allah has created, all this is a result of the Destroyer. Allah is the Creator and Satan is the Destroyer. The Destroyer tries to convince all of us to destroy. Those who do not heed Allah fall under its power. You can readily see those who have fallen under the power of the Destroyer. What is heartbreaking is that they go on destroying, believing it is Allah's will without realising that not only does the Destroyer want to destroy Allah's creation, the Destroyer wants those under its power so that in the end they will eventually destroy their own souls, and this will happen in the most horrid of ways, much like drowning slowly in fire. My heart goes out to these people. To save Allah's creation, we must all reach out in love to get them out of the grip of the Destroyer."

"This means, then," I replied, "that those who go out and kill others and themselves thinking they are doing God's will are in fact doing the will of the Destroyer?"

"The Destroyer has no will. It simply has a purpose, to destroy everything that Allah has created."

It struck me that Ibrahim used the pronoun "it" and not "he" as was conventionally the case when referring to Satan.

"You mean Satan is a thing, not a personal being?" I asked.

"The Destroyer," Ibrahim replied, "is not a personal being. It is more like a force, a cancer, eating its way through the fabric of the universe. Anything that gets pulled under its influence hastens the destruction that it wants to complete."

Ibrahim sighed through the phone and then added. "The Destroyer has convinced people that the end of the world can only come when there is an apocalypse, a great war among all people which will destroy this world. The Destroyer has been so convincing that there are many who welcome a great destruction of the world even to the extent of trying to instigate it. But Allah is not a destroyer, He is a creator. He created this world and He created it to be a paradise. It is His plan to maintain the world as a paradise, not to destroy it."

When Ibrahim said this, I couldn't help thinking about what I had learnt as a Christian about the Last Days and the Tribulation as mentioned in the Revelation. During my Christian days, I learnt that the end of the world would come with a great cataclysmic, apocalyptic war which would destroy the world completely but God would then create a new one. The way this picture was presented to us, if we saw nuclear war impending, as Christians we were to simply sit idly by and watch the events unfold because this was part of God's plan. What Ibrahim was now telling me was that such people were deceived into thinking this was God's plan when in fact it was the design of the Destroyer to make people believe that the world had to be destroyed.

"One of the Destroyer's greatest triumphs," Ibrahim added, "was the introduction of AIDS. What better way to destroy humanity than to introduce a disease which takes a long time before any symptoms are revealed, giving the disease the ease to spread like it does."

"The Destroyer introduced AIDS?" I asked. "But I thought you said that only Allah could create and that Satan cannot create anything."

"And that is correct," Ibrahim replied. "The virus that causes AIDS is a creation of Allah. But it originally was benign and had a function in other places in the animal kingdom and did not exist in humans. The Destroyer cannot create anything but it can use Allah's creation to help destroy. And look how successful it was. The Destroyer channelled the disease out of other areas of nature into the human population. And the Destroyer knew which population of people to channel the disease into to ensure that people would do nothing at first to stop it. By the time the disease reached the general population, it had become a major epidemic. And the Destroyer knew human thinking so it knew how to ensure that the disease remained the stigmatised disease that it is today so that few people would discuss it and when they did discuss it, they would not be honest and admit how the disease spreads and worse they would be too embarrassed to speak openly about how it can be stopped."

"You mean," I said to ensure I had understood, "that people will be too embarrassed to admit that man-to-man sex is a way and probably has been the most efficient way for the disease to spread and so they won't speak about such things because this would force them to acknowledge such actions exist. And to talk about it means to get it out in the open. And to get it out in the open is to legalise it, otherwise no-one will admit to such acts and hence keep the disease spreading unabated."

"Not only man-to-man sex," Ibrahim added, "but other means by which the disease spreads that in a way are not bad things in themselves."

I wasn't sure which other ways that Ibrahim meant. However, it was his overall take on the Destroyer that fascinated me.

"So, do you mean," I asked now a little perplexed, "that Satan's angels, or should I say, the Destroyer's angels help to achieve the Destroyer's purpose?"

I heard the air rush through Ibrahim's nostrils. It had become a familiar and now homely sound.

"The Destroyer acts alone. The idea that Satan has angels is a diversion. For those who reflect, it is impossible that there is such a thing as Satan's angels in the way popular myth presents this. If Satan were a ruling angel who had other angels under his command, how could Satan rule them? Satan is supposed to be the opposite of Allah. Allah is compassionate and merciful so Satan must be hateful and hard-hearted. Satan would demand all his angels to be hateful and hard-hearted as much as he is because if any of the angels showed any mercy or compassion, they would be exhibiting attributes of the enemy, that is, Allah. How, then, could Satan's angels work together in unity if they hated each other and were hard-hearted towards each other? How could they show any respect and loyalty to their master, Satan, when respect and loyalty are attributes of Allah? Therefore, if none of the angels has any love or respect towards Satan, how would Satan get them to carry out any of his wishes? And how would these angels help the other angels on their team if they only exhibited hatred and hard-heartedness to their fellow-angels? For a leader to ensure that a group works together, that leader needs to instil into those under his command values such as discipline, obedience, respect and loyalty. For his followers to respect their leader, their leader needs to be fair, equitable, noble, and worthy of respect. A leader who is full of hate and has absolutely no love or compassion towards any of those he leads will not hold command over his group for very long. This means that the Destroyer cannot be a group but is simply a lone individual."

Wow! Now that was a thought. What Ibrahim had said was right. No-one could form a cohesive team without a force that binds the members of the team together and what other force was there that keeps a group together except for love or at least some sense of loyalty? Even if you were part of a team and the leader came across as cruel, that leader would still earn respect and devotion if the cruelty was viewed as equitable and just, that is, the cruelty, or better said, the harsh punishment was dished out because of the serious crimes committed by the team members against others in the group. However, if a leader were unusually cruel and there was no rhyme nor reason for the cruelty apart from the fact that the leader was simply hateful, it wouldn't be long before the group either destroyed or deserted the leader. Satan, if such a thing existed, could not hold the leadership over an entire group if Satan hated everyone in that group and treated them cruelly. Worse, Satan couldn't hold a group together by commanding those in the group to be hateful towards each other nor show one gram of compassion or kindness to each other. Such angels would desert Satan and return to the only other known ruler in the universe and because this other ruler is stronger and mightier than Satan, Satan would not be able to stop them from deserting him. But this was the dichotomy for Satan if such a thing existed. If God was Satan's enemy, and the very attributes of God such as compassion, justice and kindness were things that Satan wanted to ensure his angels avoided because they were attributes of the enemy, Satan would have no other choice but to instil attributes of hate, injustice and cruelty among his group.

I was taken aback very much by Ibrahim's insightfulness. He really thought things through. I was amazed at the conclusions he drew. However, although his description of Satan having a team was an impossibility when looking at this thoughtfully, the problem was that both the New Testament and the Koran spoke of Satan and his angels, and therefore a team of demonic beings which worked together. What was even more curious was, when I did finally read the Koran, I remember reading in Al-Kahf 18:51 that Satan has offspring. How did Satan get offspring? Were there male and female Satans? If so, was it love that brought them together to bear progeny? Did the parent Satans feel parental love and care for their baby Satans as they weaned them and brought them into adulthood? If they did, and love and care were attributes of the enemy that the Satans wanted to avoid, how did they successfully produce this satanic tribe?

"You know," Ibrahim continued, "I had a dream."

Not again! I thought. I guessed that Michael the archangel played a prominent role in the dream as he always seemed to in Ibrahim's dreams and sure enough he did.

"I was walking along a path in the sky, the stars shining all around me. At one point in the path, I came to a crossroads. To the right, the path continued downwards and to the left the path continued up. I wasn't sure which path to take. However, the path to the right looked easier and I wanted to choose this one. Before I went to take a step, I heard someone ask me why I wanted to take this path. I looked around and there was Michael the archangel. He asked me why I wanted to take the path on the right. 'Because this path looks easier to walk down and to arrive at my destination.' Michael then told me to look at the end of the path. Suddenly I could see where the path finally ended. There, the earth, like a large ball, looked desolate and empty, very much like the surface of the moon as photos I had seen of the Apollo moon missions. I saw beyond this desolate moon-like place what looked like the souls of the departed roaming aimlessly about with no place to go. Michael then told me to look at the other path that led upwards. Once again, as miraculously as I could see the end of the downward path, I could see where the upward path led to. At the end, although in the distance, I could see clearly a beautiful garden, a huge garden, through which a river ran, the water of which was as clear as crystal, where the banks of the river were lush and green, trees grew and fruit dripped from the trees in abundance and the people, old and young, black and white, men and women, were just so happy. Beyond this I could see the souls of the departed also in an even more beautiful place reclining in utter peace and happiness. Michael then said to me that this was our choice. Not my choice personally but the choice of all humanity. We can easily go down the path that leads to the destruction of our world and finally allow the Destroyer to fulfil its purpose or we can strive forward to recreate the world the paradise Allah had originally set out to create of our world. If the Destroyer gets its way and destroys this earth, the Destroyer will also succeed in destroying the world that is to come in the next life. If the Destroyer is defeated in this life, not only will there be paradise on this earth, this paradise will continue into the next."

I listened to this description somewhat half-heartedly as I did to Ibrahim's other dreams. However, once he had stopped, I felt I needed to make some sort of comment.

"So, all the prophecies in the Bible about the earth finally being destroyed, you are saying that this is not a foregone conclusion but is ultimately up to us?"

"Bwana Michael," Ibrahim replied, "that is exactly what Michael was telling me. The prophecies weren't given to us to show that what would happen in the future is inevitable. The prophecies were presented to us to show what could happen if we don't all wake up. It is easy just to continue our lives without thinking and this will lead to the utter destruction of the universe. But if all humanity took the effort to think, to reflect, and make the world the paradise for every single person as it was originally intended to be, eventually the Destroyer will have lost the battle and will cease to exist."

Did we really need a visitation from Michael the archangel to show us that these were, after all, the two probable eventualities? But if it meant something to Ibrahim to have a dream which showed this, it certainly was a significant dream for those who believed him.

That Ibrahim had mentioned his dream made me think about another one he had told me in the past. I thought of my trip to Walla Walla and what I had discovered about my possible past. Strangely it took some courage to actually mention it. There was a slight pause in the conversation once we had finished talking about Satan, the Destroyer and the impossibility of Satan's angels. But we had to keep talking to get the full advantage of the phonecard. I took a deep breath and then simply said it.

"Ibrahim, I'm partly Jewish."

I stated this with absolutely no indication that I was changing subject.

Ibrahim laughed. "Then the dream is about to be fulfilled," Ibrahim said without missing a beat and the joy in his voice was contagious.

"Well, I'm not totally certain that I'm Jewish," I hastened to add. "It's circumstantial."

I explained everything that Uncle William had told me and explained that although the evidence was strong, it was not entirely conclusive.

"That's strong enough evidence, Bwana Michael," Ibrahim replied. "That's great. So a child of Isaac and a child of Ishmael are finally coming together to heal the breach."

I pulled my phone away from my ear and looked down at it with question marks and then returned the phone to my ear again.

"What?"

"If you are Jewish, or partly Jewish as you say," Ibrahim said, "and I am partly Arab, then you are a descendant of Isaac and I am a child of Ishmael."

"But you don't look Arab," I replied.

"And you don't look Jewish, either," Ibrahim said with a laugh. "However, through my father's ancestral line, I trace my ancestry to an Arab way back in history who married a Swahili woman of the East African coast. I am mainly Bantu but I have Arab blood."

I wondered then if this was the source of Ibrahim's hairiness. However, all Ibrahim's other features were typically sub-Saharan African and he was very dark skinned. But what was with the healing of the breach?

"The children of Ishmael and the children of Isaac have long been enemies," Ibrahim replied. "This is the cause of much of the unrest in the world and in particular in the Middle East. The sons of Ishmael and the sons of Isaac have not made peace with each other as they should as brothers. The more children of Ishmael who form unions with the children of Isaac, the sooner the world will return to the paradise Allah intended the world to be."

I laughed. It sounded so ludicrous that two very insignificant people on the planet, Ibrahim and I, could play a significant role in world affairs. But then it made me think of Israel.

"Then what about the Jews and the Palestinians? Should they be trying to create unions?"

"Of course," Ibrahim replied.

"So, then," I asked, knowing I was throwing in a delicate question, "what do you think about the claims to land that both the Palestinians and Jews are making in the current state of Israel?"

"What do you think?" Ibrahim then asked.

"I really don't care," I replied. "However, I can understand why the Jews make the claim that Israel belongs to them because they say that the Torah is the Word of God and it says that God gave the land to them."

"Bwana Michael, you need to read the Torah a little more carefully," Ibrahim said by way of a rebuke. It instantly put my shackles up and the argument that Jews and Christians made of Isaac being the true child of promise came to mind. Were Ibrahim and I about to enter a heated argument?

"Allah promised in the Torah," Ibrahim explained, "that He would give the land to Abraham and to Abraham's descendants. Abraham according to the Torah had two sons, Ishmael and Isaac. So the land has to be shared by the descendants of both sons."

Wow! What Ibrahim said made sense. God had promised to Abraham that He would give Abraham the land of Israel. In a moment of doubt, Abraham had an affair with his wife's slave, Hagar, and bore a son. God had made the promise before Ishmael was born so because of Abraham's lack of faith, now there were two sons of Abraham who rightfully could claim the land. Neither of them could claim any greater right over the other if we looked at it in this way.

I laughed. "Does this mean you and I should be trying to live in Israel?"

"Is that what you want to do?" Ibrahim asked.

"Not in particular. I'm only part Jewish anyway and I'm sure I wouldn't be recongised as a Jew. In any case, I'm happy living in Australia."

Because I mentioned living in Australia, Ibrahim abruptly changed the course of the conversation and began once again asking about living in Australia as if he had never asked the question before. I didn't quite get it.

Ibrahim had asked me about living in Sydney on a number of occasions. I had already given him a breakdown, at least I thought I had. Why did he ask me this question so often? In any case, it was something to talk about and for me it was nice from time to time to get off the topic of religion and talk about something else. Once I had spoken about life in Sydney, the conversation then moved on to a variety of topics. We talked about Tanzania, about history, about the Msingi wa Mungu Project, about Tevah Am, about family and friends and so on.

Soon a message came through the phone that we had one more minute of talk time before all the money on the card had been used up. This abruptly stopped us in mid-conversation. I was about to make a comment when Ibrahim beat me to it.

"Bwana Michael, when will you come back to Moshi?" Ibrahim pleaded.

It was a plea that came from deep within and I felt it. It took my breath away and I wasn't sure exactly what to say at first. I tried to gather my thoughts together and say something in return but suddenly the connection was completely cut. I pulled my phone away from my ear and looked down at the screen. It was clear that we had been disconnected.

I then looked up at the sky towards the west at a point that I was sure Ibrahim could see from where he was.

"I don't know," I replied into the air. I felt my throat constrict. "But, geez, I hope it will be soon."

Chapter 15

"Teacher," one of the Chinese learners, May, called out to get my attention. May was a learner doing one of the advanced programs. I was impressed with her progress because despite being a mother of two primary school aged children, she still managed her program. She also had a definite goal in mind when her English was good enough and it showed in her conscientiousness.

"Teacher," she called out again even though I had already begun to walk in her direction. Once I had reached her, I stared at her screen to see what the problem was.

"Do you teach children?" May then asked.

At first I didn't quite get the question. Then, when I realised that her question had nothing to do with her Occurrence, I didn't quite get why she was asking me this particular question in the first place. She knew I taught here at Tevah Am and that all my students were adults so where did she get the idea that I actually taught children. The length of pause before replying must have triggered May into thinking that I had not quite understood what she had said and so she repeated the question but added a bit more to it.

"Do you teach children? You would make a great teacher for children."

"No," I replied quite dismissively. The thought of teaching school children of primary school age or worse of secondary school age was simply a terrible thought.

"I'm sure you could," May insisted.

"I don't have the qualifications to teach at primary or secondary school," I replied.

"But I'm sure you'd be able to teach primary school children."

I did not quite get why she was going down this path of conversation.

"My daughter is not very good at writing," May continued, "and I need an English tutor to help her to read and write. And you explain writing well and you know your English grammar."

That last comment finally put everything into perspective. That's what she was getting at. But private tuition? I'd never done anything like this before. How was it to be done?

"No," I replied. "Sorry, but I'm only good at teaching adults."

"Oh, go on!" May insisted once again. "I mean, are you busy on the weekend?"

I was immediately miffed at the idea that May suddenly was venturing into my private life and my private time. Maybe I didn't have anything in particular to do on the weekend but in the end that was my business and my business only.

"Well, sort of," I replied partly indignantly but also in a way to answer her question somewhat truthfully.

"Just one hour, in the morning," May more demanded than said. "Then you would be free for the rest of the day."

"Where?" I asked.

"You could come to my place. I have a room where a group of children could learn together."

"A group of children?" I asked in surprise.

"Yes, a friend of mine has a daughter and she and my daughter could learn together. We can't help them because our English isn't very good. But you are a very good teacher and I can see that you could help them."

"Look, May," I replied. "I really don't have time for that at the moment. Maybe in the future when I have some free time."

"When will you have free time?"

I was beginning to get agitated that May could not take no for an answer.

"Look, May, I'm just a bit busy on the weekend to do such a thing."

"How much do you charge an hour?" May asked as if she had not heard my last comment. However, this last statement provided me with a means of getting May off my back. I told her an hourly rate that I thought was unusually high and said that I would not teach privately unless I was paid this much. I thought this was the most brilliant dismissive comment to make and it appeared to work. May paused for a few moments and I thought that this was the end of the conversation. I turned around and walked away. When I turned around again, I saw May speaking on her mobile phone in agitated conversation. Not long after, she put her phone down and called me back over.

"I spoke with my friend and she said that was fine."

What? I thought. Did I inadvertently quote the current going rate for tutors? Is that how much they really charged these days?

But now I felt trapped. I had agreed to work at what I thought was an unusually high hourly rate. But May and this friend of hers were willing to pay. This, then, made the tutoring somewhat tempting because what May was willing to pay was a little bit higher than what I was earning per hour at Tevah Am. But was the money overall really worth the hassle of losing a Saturday morning? Although I would be teaching for an hour, I still had to drive to her place and drive home so it was more than a simple hour of a day lost. And what about preparation time? Teaching is not a job where you roll up to a place and start as soon as you arrive but involves hours of preparation before the class starts and then more hours afterwards marking students' work. The hourly rate I quoted was beginning to look less alluring the more this thought went through my mind.

"I tell you what," I then said. "Let's do a trial. I'll do it for a couple of weeks and then see what happens."

We agreed to start the following Saturday morning at 8.30 am. In a way, it was rather annoying to have to wake up early on a Saturday morning to go to work when Saturday had been a sacred day for me to actually sleep in. But I still had Sunday to do this so it was not too traumatic. And then, once the teaching was over, I had a little extra pocket money and the rest of the day was mine to occupy the way I wanted to.

But I was rather at a loss about what exactly I was going to teach these students. I was familiar with teaching adults whose English was heavily influenced by their first language but the daughters of May and May's friend no doubt were born in Australia and although they may look Chinese, in every other way they would be typical Aussie kids. Therefore, I asked May to tell her daughter and the daughter of her friend to write a story in a similar way that they would be expected to do at school and I would use this as a starting point and hopefully this would help me with my first lesson.

It may have simply been private tuition and therefore a casual affair but I decided to dress up in a tie all the same. I had heard from many of my students over the years how that a teacher wearing a tie carried more value than one who came in jeans and T-shirt. To me it was all a temporary pantomime anyway and eventually May would no longer need my services. I thought also that maybe the tie would help to establish a formal atmosphere so that the girls themselves didn't treat the lesson as a game.

When I arrived, May welcomed me and led me to a large room at the front of the house which appeared to be some sort of rumpus room with shelves full of play things, stuffed toys and plastic sports equipment. In the centre of the room were two children's tables pushed together and May's daughter, Lea, and another girl, Rachel, sitting facing each other and looking up at me.

I remembered what one of my colleagues during the night classes who worked at a high school during the day had told me about teaching school students, that is, that you don't smile until Easter. I decided to take on this advice and not show any signs of mirth during the first number of lessons.

May introduced me to the girls. They both looked at my face then down at my tie as if my tie were the centrepiece of my person. When it came to introducing myself and saying who I was, at first I was going to introduce myself as Mr Farril but before the words came out of my mouth, the sound of it in my head made me feel twenty years older than I was. I was aware that, unlike in Australia, in many cultures titles were used with the first name and not the surname and this sounded like a much better compromise. So I introduced myself as Mr Michael, a name the girls accepted without flinching. May then left me alone with the two girls.

The two girls were in Year 4 so they were about ten years of age. Fortunately I had given them work to do for me days before I arrived because it provided me with a plan for the first lesson.

I first asked Lea if I could look at her work. Lea in total silence passed me her exercise book which from its almost pristine state indicated that this had been bought new for my lesson. I picked the exercise book up and first looked at the cover. What caught my attention was the writing in Chinese characters on the front. I read them out.

"Yin yu", I said.

Lea and Rachel looked at me but without one iota of surprise that an Anglo-Australian could actually read Chinese characters. But the characters didn't make sense in the context of an exercise book being used to learn English.

"Yin yu?" I repeated and then translated, "Silver rain?"

"That's my Chinese name," Lea said almost with scorn.

"That's a lovely name," I said. I pondered on the idea of the name and thought that it did have a nice sound. Fortunately, her parents had named her Silver Rain and not Golden Rain because I remembered a Monte Python skit where golden rain was used as a double meaning for urine.

"So, you're learning Chinese?" I continued.

"I have to," Lea complained.

"But it's the language of your ancestors. Don't you want to learn it for that reason?"

"No, it's a boring language," Lea replied.

Whoops! Not a great beginning. And I wasn't here to talk about the Chinese language so my ability to speak and read Mandarin was obviously not going to impress the girls one bit.

I flicked open Lea's exercise book to her narrative. I began reading it in my mind but the silence was too uncomfortable and so I decided to read it out loud with the excuse that any corrections I made to it would be of benefit to both girls, the implication being that they would both get double the teaching in the one hour sitting.

As soon as I had finished reading Lea's not-so-exemplary form of written art, my mind went into teacher mode. The entire story was written in one block with no paragraphs, some sentences trailed along with lines of words and then abruptly ended without purpose, pronouns appeared without any apparent noun to refer back to and tenses were mixed between past and present. In one reading I knew exactly what I was going to do for this first lesson.

After reading Lea's story, I took Rachel's book and read hers. Her attempt was not much better. Rachel's story looked like something she had scratched up five minutes before I had arrived in order to please her parents rather than a first step to improving her writing.

It was clear from the girls' overall attitude that they didn't want to be there and they were doing Saturday morning tuition under sufferance. To me, this was a great sign that I wouldn't have to do this for too long as I was sure that eventually the girls would convince their parents that they didn't need a tutor and soon I would have my Saturday mornings back. Because of this, I put all my effort into the project, developing lesson plans and suitable homework to ensure that the students learnt how to write well in the shortest amount of time. Once this objective was achieved, so I thought, my job would be over and the full Saturday would once again be mine.

Over the next couple of weeks, the girls began to warm to this Saturday morning intrusion. It was as if they had taken on the idea that all three of us were here of a Saturday morning to please the girls' parents. There was no way out for them so they had the choice to make the hour painfully slow or make it a worthwhile entertaining and instructive one.

As the weeks rolled by there appeared to be no sign either from May nor the girls that tuition was ever going to stop. The extra money certainly was nice but not enticing enough to overcome the interruption of my tranquil Saturday mornings. So, it was left to me to bring tuition to an end. It was time to tell May that I no longer could teach Lea and Rachel. I had come up with an elaborate excuse that I thought was very convincing and most ingenious.

I arrived at May's house for what I thought was going to be the last Saturday morning I went there. May welcomed me at the door.   We exchanged our normal greetings and small talk. I was planning to weave into this casual conversation my humblest apologies for my inability to continue with tutoring when in the conversation May said to me, "You know, every Saturday morning just before you arrive, Lea sits at the window waiting for you."

For a moment it was as if someone had reached into my mouth and grabbed my tongue. It took a moment for me to say something in reply to this.

"You're kidding!" I finally stated quite stunned.

"Oh, yes," May continued. "Not only that, I use you for punishment."

"Use me for punishment?" I asked.

"Oh, yes," May continued. "When Lea is naughty, I tell her that if she doesn't behave, I'll tell Mr Michael not to come anymore and she calms down immediately."

Right there and then, my beautiful excuse died. How could I terminate my services now? I just smiled at May while inside I was swearing profusely.

With the extra money, I decided to splurge on another phonecall to Tanzania. That helped me to make the Saturday morning intrusion all the more worthwhile. I decided to ring Ibrahim that evening.

This was a conversation that did not start with any reference to anything religious which for me was a bit of a relief. As much as I liked Ibrahim, and his religious views were much more peaceful and all encompassing than the average religious person, the topic of religion still tended to be rather cumbersome and also for me terribly irrelevant. So it was nice to carry on a conversation that was what I thought true conversations should consist of. In my conversation, I mentioned my new Saturday morning job, how I felt trapped in teaching the two girls but then explained how this enabled me to have the extra money to call Ibrahim.

"But you are a good teacher," Ibrahim replied. "You are still talked about here at the Msingi wa Mungu Project."

I was quite touched by the comment.

"It's really funny though, Ibrahim," I then went on. "The girls' names are Lea and Rachel. Just by the addition of a letter, we could get Leah and Rachel and have the two wives of Jacob. Maybe there's something symbolic in that!"

"That would be so," Ibrahim then joked, "if someone there had the name Jacob."

"The reality is," I continued, "is that they are Chinese, well, I say the girls are Australian and their parents are Chinese. The Chinese have this tradition of having a Chinese name and an English name. They like Australians to call them by their English name."

"Is that because their names are difficult to pronounce?" Ibrahim asked.

"Well," I continued, "I thought the same, that the Chinese think that Australians don't know how to pronounce their names properly. However, because I speak Mandarin, I used to show off how well I could actually say their names in Mandarin. However, I eventually discovered that the Chinese prefer us to use their English names because we don't use their Chinese names properly. What I mean is, the Chinese don't use their first names like we in Australia use our first names. There are only special times and special conventions and situations when their first names are to be used. So, in order not to cause discomfort between us and them, they take on English names and this is the name they prefer us to call them."

"Oh, okay," Ibrahim commented.

"The thing about the Chinese," I continued, "is that their names actually have meaning. I mean, all names have a meaning but in Australia a lot of people don't actually know where their names come from or what they originally meant. But Chinese names have meaning. They are pretty much expressions. For example, I have a learner whose Chinese name is Xiao Hong Li which means 'little red hat', another learner whose name is Huang Shui Ping which means 'yellow water bottle'."

I heard Ibrahim laugh on the other end of the phone.

"Yeah," I replied to his laughter. "I don't know what was going through their parents' minds when they gave their children those names. At least some Chinese parents have a better imagination. The name of May's daughter, Lea, is really Yin Yu which translates as 'silver rain' and I think that name is lovely."

As soon as the words had left my lips, the image of the name and the description of the dream that Ibrahim once had of the silver rain came to mind. It sent a shiver down my spine. And Ibrahim's further comment simply amplified the sensation.

"So, the silver rain is starting, the prophecy is beginning to come to pass." There was a pause and then Ibrahim added, "and we will be together again, Bwana Michael."

I didn't believe it. I didn't want to believe it. It was totally impossible. The world did not work like this. It was merely coincidental.

But the rain did begin. I began receiving phonecalls with similar enquiries: I believe you do tuition. Do you do private tuition? Would you teach my two boys? Would you teach my daughters? Would you teach my son and his friend? Soon I was working for much of my Saturday, from early morning until late into the afternoon.

Because I was teaching school age children for the first time, I started off rather blindly. I was more familiar teaching adult learners especially adult learners who learnt English as a second language where the systematic teaching of English grammar was required.

However, these new students of mine spoke English as a first language so I guessed that teaching grammar was unnecessary. But the more I taught, the more I began to see a pattern in the mistakes the students were making in their writing and it all had to do with grammar.

The teaching of grammar, however, had become outmoded even when I was at school. The belief was that we all learnt to speak and communicate in English in the first number of years of our lives without ever understanding the grammatical principles behind the language and hence the belief was that it was a total waste of time to actually teach it as a subject. Children could feel their way into the language and with lots of practice they would learn eventually to write well.

But this was not what I was seeing. I also noticed a flaw in this line of thinking. It may be true that children learn to speak grammatically correctly in the early part of their growing up, although even this is not quite true, but writing was not a natural form of communication and the way we write is not the same as the way we speak. Writing has structure and certain conventions need to be followed if we want to write well. I felt that without a structured approach to grammar teaching, by allowing students to learn grammar simply through experience was akin to showing small children the letters of the alphabet but not telling them the relationship between the written symbols and their sound value but allowing the children to work it out all by themselves.

I noticed that by teaching some grammatical rules, it made it easier for me and for the students to understand the problems in their writing and to know how to correct these mistakes and avoid making them in the first place.

Not long after beginning to teach grammar systematically, my phone began ringing constantly for my services. This made it clear that I had hit a deficiency in the teaching of English. The parents recognised this immediately and the word spread that I could fill in this gap. It was understandable that the parents of the children I was teaching recognised this because the parents themselves spoke English as a second language and hence they recognised the significance of teaching grammar.

Eventually, not only was I getting phonecalls to teach primary school children, soon I was being asked to teach high school students as well. I was rather reluctant to do so because I didn't want to spend an hour trying to discipline adolescents in the same way as teachers have to at secondary school. However, I soon discovered that in a private tuition setting with only a couple of students at a time, students simply didn't muck up anyway because they didn't have a crowd to please and also the parents didn't want to waste their money.

Teaching high school students and in particular students from Year 9 to Year 12 was actually a bit of a strain because these students were required to study certain forms of literature, a novel, a play, a poem and a Shakespearean play, and then write an essay about what they had learnt. I could barely remember my high school English and what was involved in essay writing but after some groping in the dark, it finally dawned on me that there were really two main elements that I needed to focus on: the theme or themes of the text, and the characters. Some students were also required to work out the techniques used in the text and usually this was of importance when studying poems.

It was the study of poems which I hated the most. I was sure that the education board had combed the world of poems and tried to find the most esoteric and most uninteresting poem to force high school children to analyse. The education board did this as some form of sick joke or perhaps out of revenge against adolescents. This took me back to my high school years. I remembered in English studying poems where we had to pull them apart, find the themes and the techniques, and then write an essay about them. Some poets I didn't mind too much such as Coleridge and his *The Rime of the Ancient Mariner* although his *Kubla Khan* to me was simply esoteric nonsense or, probably more correctly, the babblings of someone tripping out on drugs. At the end of my English exams, I was happy that I would never again have to try and work out whether or not *Kubla Khan* was religious or sexual in nature, or whether he was using symbolism or metaphors, because at the end of the day, I simply didn't give a toss.

But now I found myself back in this arena. Whereas the 4th grade students were my springboard into tutoring, the demand was more for high school students who needed essay writing skills and how to interpret the texts they had to study in their classes. As a result, this meant that if I wanted to keep the students and earn the money, I had to also read the texts.

I found myself reading Shakespeare once again. I didn't mind Shakespeare too much at school. One of the positives of my parents insisting on us reading the Bible in the King James Version was that the English was similar to that used in Shakespeare and so Shakespearean English was not too foreign a language to me when I began reading it. However, the students I was now teaching were the children of South East Asian parents, particularly Chinese and Vietnamese, so I knew that these children had absolutely no exposure to the English of the 1600s before studying Shakespeare's plays.

I thought studying Shakespeare's plays was rather a strange thing to do in a subject which looks at studying English. Shakespeare's English to us in the twenty-first century is halfway to becoming a foreign language because of certain changes in English grammar, the changes in meaning of many words between then and now, and unfamiliar vocabulary used in Shakespeare's time that has since fallen out of use. Seeing no-one was expected to emulate Shakespeare's writing style in the twenty-first century, I could not understand why his plays were presented to high school students as an exemplary form of English writing. Even the themes weren't unique. Shakespeare may have initiated in textual form themes such as appearance versus reality, ambition and love, but these themes also appeared in modern literature written in an English that our students were supposed to imitate.

Not only so, Shakespeare's plays are extremely sexist, racist, anti-Semitic, subliminally anti-gay and outright violent. Had Shakespeare lived in the twenty-first century and tried to publish his plays, his works would never have gotten past manuscript form. Just a look at modern renditions of Shakespeare's plays shows that the beliefs and attitudes of Shakespeare's time are anachronistic in today's world. I remember having to read *Othello* with one of my students and compare this with the modern film, *O*, which was simply *Othello* in a modern setting. The women in *O* were much bolder and more forthright than how they were portrayed in *Othello* because in today's world women are supposed to be portrayed equally as men, not as the frail, subservient creatures that Shakespeare presents them as. The death scenes are also horrific and disturbing in *O* in the same way that they would be if we were watching a modern homicide series or detective story whereas in the original Shakespearean text the death scenes hardly raise any emotions. The familiarity with Shakespeare's plays dulls us to the brutality of the murders within them, the murders only becoming horrific in the modern renditions.

What was captivating about Shakespeare's plays, as far as I could see, was the mere familiarity of them over the centuries. His plays were popular when they were originally written because the events in the   play were considered quite normal and acceptable in the time they were performed. Technology in publishing was still only primitive and quite expensive and so not many people in those days had their works published. As the centuries passed, even though the beliefs about gender, race, religion and even the view of violence changed, what carried Shakespeare ahead was not the greatness of his works but the mere familiarity of them.

This then made me reflect on the Bible. The Bible has been brought into the twenty-first century with all its brutality, viciousness, racism and discrimination but our emotions have been dulled to all of these aspects when we read the events recorded within the pages, especially the stories in the Old Testament. Take any of the violent stories from the Old Testament and attempt to make a modern rendition of them and the events in the story would be horrid and disturbing as they should be understood whereas when read in the Bible they come across as quite normal or at least acceptable.

It was the studying of poems that I found the most exasperating. And so did my students. Some of these poems I didn't quite get on the first reading. Some of them were so obscure, the subject matter so vague and the poem itself terribly uninteresting that I wondered how on earth they ever got published. The publishers who eventually sold the poems must have had an excellent sales and marketing team to be able to get these poems sold and well-known.

I had a pair of Year 8 boys, Luke and Alex, who I taught straight after Rachel and Lea. When I first met these boys, the first lesson was to work on a poem and answer a series of questions about it. The poem went like this:

On Pain and Pleasure

Like twin sisters joined at the thigh
As soon as pain comes, pleasure's close by
A mother in labour her baby awaits
The birth of her baby her heart elates
The pain of hunger can make a man cry
The pleasure of eating will soon satisfy
A painful tooth which causes much grief
The dentist extracts which brings us relief
The pain from an argument the two parties it stings
The pleasure that reconciliation then brings
The discomfort experienced from disease which is chronic
Recovery from this illness a most pleasurable tonic
The pain of death that brings mourning and strife
The joy that soon follows when we gain new life.

Pain with her suffering, discomfort and sorrow
Pleasure her twin sister dispels on the morrow.

The sheet of paper on which the poem was printed was obviously a photocopy and a poor quality at that. However, there was nothing on this poor quality photocopy indicating who had written the poem. It certainly wasn't one of the classical poets and this was obvious from the line about the dentist extracting a tooth which appeared to be a modern reference. I had to admit that although it wasn't a poem that should be put to music and champion the list of pop songs, it was in a way interesting and I got something out of it. Because there was no author, I wondered if the teacher was breaking copyright rules and hence plagiarising. Or was the teacher the actual author of the poem?

"Okay," I started off. "What is the first thing you have to find in the poem?"

The boys looked at me in silence. I didn't want to tell the students the answer but rather get them to tell me what they had learnt at school. I was hoping that they would at least take a guess or even finally admit that they didn't know. But these boys were not very interactive at all. The boys just looked at the poem in silence. The line about the dentist suddenly came to mind and I thought about the amount of pain I was now going through trying to extract information from these boys and how much pleasure it would be if the boys actually said something. But they didn't which meant that I had to.

"Okay," I continued. "Well, you have to look for two main things. You need to find the theme and the techniques. Do you know what it means by the theme of a poem?"

The two boys looked at me as if I had asked them to cut off their left ears and present them to me on silken napkins. It felt more like I was actually torturing the students than tutoring them. I had to take a breath to keep my composure.

"Okay," I continued. "So we don't really know what the theme is. That's okay. That's what I'm here for. Now, the theme is simply the message the author is trying to convey. When you read to the end of the poem, when you walk away from it you say to yourself, 'after reading this poem, I have learnt that blah blah blah' and that's the theme. So, after reading this poem, what have you learnt?"

The two boys looked on at me as if I had been speaking to them in Bhojpourri. They then looked down at the poem and it was as if they were trying to absorb meaning by simply staring at the sheet of paper before them. The silence was killing me more than it was killing them and so I decided I may as well give them the answer.

"Okay, the title itself kind of helps you to know what the theme is. Because the title is *On Pain and Pleasure*, then the poem has something to do with pain and pleasure. As we read through the poem, we notice that every reference to pain is followed by a reference to pleasure. The last two lines then make it quite clear what the poet is trying to say: pain and pleasure are so linked together that when we first experience pain, this is then followed by pleasure, as if pain and pleasure are actually inseparable."

The two boys looked up at me with blank expressions and then looked down at the sheet of paper. Suddenly they showed some evidence of life as they opened up their exercise books and wrote down what I had just told them.

"Okay," I continued, "seeing you have your exercise books open, let's look at the other aspect you have to look for in this poem. These are the techniques. Now, do you know any poetic techniques?"

The boys looked back up at me. The blank look on their faces was making it more and more frightening and I began to wonder whether or not these boys were in fact mentally challenged.

"Okay," I then said. "Just under where you wrote the theme of the poem, I want you to write the title *Techniques*."

The boys looked up at me.

"Yeah, yeah," I then continued, "In your exercise books just under where you wrote the theme."

The boys responded accordingly and wrote down the title.

I thought about it for a moment and then I said to them, "Now, I want you to write down the numbers one to four, then skip a line, then write down the numbers five to eight."

The boys dutifully obeyed and then looked up at me. I began with the first four techniques. I told the boys to write them in the order I gave them and that I would explain why I wanted to separate the first four from the second.

I began with rhyme. Rhyme was a technique, albeit a hard one to write about. I explained that rhyme as a technique was easier to mention if the boys were comparing two poems, one with rhyme and one without.

I asked them why people used rhyme in poems or if the teachers had in fact told them. It became obvious from their silence that they had not been told. I explained that in antiquity people didn't have internet access and so if anyone wanted information it wasn't as readily available as it is now. Even written works were hard to come by because there was no such thing as printing presses or photocopiers and hence all documents had to be hand-written. If you wanted a copy of a book, you actually had to write it out completely by hand. But writing was not very popular and so people related stories through songs and poems. By putting the stories to rhyme it was easier to remember them. I compared this with modern day songs and explained that it is easy to remember the lyrics of a song because the rhyming pattern helps to remember which words were used on each line because the words in the line have a definite pattern. Great works such as Homer's *Iliad* were written using rhyme which is why they could be easily passed down from generation to generation faithfully to a degree without being written down.

I thought this explanation was an eye-opener and the boys were going to be absolutely stoked at this elucidation but they simply looked up at me blankly as if I had been describing the wonders of the colour and texture of sawdust.

Let's move right along then, shall we? I thought to myself.

"Okay, the next technique," I continued, "that I want you to write down is alliteration. Do you know what alliteration is?"

I wasn't sure if I should have asked the question because I was afraid of the blank stares that I would get in reply. However, it appeared that the boys had now begun to come to life.

"Isn't alliteration," Luke began, "like 'Sammy the Snail sipped a strawberry sundae'?"

A corny example, I thought, but a pertinent one. I told the boys to write "alliteration" next to number two and then write the example that Luke gave as it was good enough.

"Good," I continued now that these two cold-blooded students had begun to warm up. "The next technique I want you to write down is assonance. Do you know what assonance is?"

Luke and Alex looked up at me but this time there was more of a sparkle of life in their faces and eyes which didn't look as daunting as when we had begun the lesson.

"No, not really," Alex replied and then looked at Luke who shrugged his shoulders to show he didn't know either.

"Okay," I replied. "Assonance is kind of like the opposite of alliteration. While alliteration is the repetition of consonant sounds, assonance is the repetition of vowel sounds. I mean, you will notice that lots of companies and products use assonance such as Deep Heat where there is the repetition of the 'ee/ea' sound. We also use it in common sayings like, 'easy peasy' and 'super duper' where we repeat the vowel sound, the ea in 'easy peasy' and the u in 'super duper'."

"Oh! Right!" the boys replied and wrote this down. The light was on and we were now in full swing.

"Okay, the last technique in this first group," I continued, "is onomatopoeia. Do you know what onomatopoeia is?"

Luke looked up at me again. "Isn't that where the word represents a sound?"

"Can you give me an example?" I asked.

"Um, bang, splash, um…"

"Pop," Alex threw in, "er…knock knock?"

"Good, yes," I replied. "All of these. So, write down the technique and a few examples."

I knew the boys wouldn't know how to spell such a complicated word as onomatopoeia and so I spelt it for them. I told them that there was no need to worry about trying to remember the spelling of the word anyway as there were very few occasions if any when they would actually have to write it down.

"Okay," I continued. "These four techniques are commonly used simply because of their sound quality. You have to remember that people write poems so that they appeal to more than the visual sense of reading.

Poets often want us to also feel the poem and hear the sounds that are being described so that the poem appeals to more than one sense."

Again, I thought this was a wonderful revelation but the boys just nodded their heads almost imperceptibly as if I had told them something as banal as that I was using a black pen today because I couldn't find a blue one.

"Alright, then," I continued. "Now for the other techniques. Do you know any others?"

The boys looked up in expectation of an explanation without volunteering any answers.

"Well," I continued, "the next one I want you to write next to number five is hyperbole."

"Hyperbole?" Alex said as he looked up at me with a mystified expression on his face and then exclaimed, "Oh, hyper-bowl!"

"If you want to say, 'hyper-bowl', I personally don't mind because if we follow English spelling rules, that's the way we should say it. However, I think your teacher probably wants you to use the pronunciation, 'hyperbole'."

Luke and Alex repeated my recommended pronunciation of the word almost imperceptibly as if it were a swear word and then wrote the word down.

"And do you know what hyperbole is?"

Luke and Alex screwed up their lips and shrugged their shoulders.

"Okay, hyperbole is a form of exaggeration. We use it in common expressions, like, 'I'm so hungry I could eat a horse'. I mean, yes, I'm hungry and I could eat a lot but, no I couldn't eat an entire horse in one sitting. Or another one, 'I hate going to the pool after three o'clock because then there are millions of school kids in the water'. Yes, there are probably a lot of school kids at the pool but it is highly improbable that millions of school children could actually fit in the pool, not to mention that this would imply the entire Sydney population crowded in one Olympic-sized swimming pool."

The boys showed a sparkle of comprehension in their eyes and it appeared that this was turning out to be a little more interesting.

"You will notice," I added, "that we use hyperbole all the time in our everyday language to be, I'm sorry to say this but it's true, to be nasty. For example, I used to make fun of my sister because she used to talk a lot and so one time I said to her that she talks so much that she uses each word in the Oxford Dictionary within a minute."

Luke and Alex laughed. They then looked at each other and grinned mischievously in recognition of some of the other nasty uses of hyperbole they no doubt used in the playground.

The boys then wrote down my bland examples of hyperbole in their exercise books.

"Okay," I went on, "do you know any other techniques?"

"Um…simile?" Alex asked almost apologetically.

"Very good!" I replied. "What's a simile?"

"It's where you compare something using 'like' or 'as', such as, 'he is like a fox'."

"Great!" I exclaimed. "Write that down."

"Metaphor?" Luke then asked.

"I beg your pardon?" I said.

"Metaphor? Is metaphor a technique?"

"Very good," I replied. "And what's a metaphor?"

"That's when you say something is something when it's not, such as, 'he's a fox'."

I had heard this definition when I was at school. This definition, however, just didn't sound terribly helpful. I started to think of examples of metaphors that we use in our everyday language. While doing so, the words "abstract" and "figurative" came to mind as if there were a thesaurus in my head. My mind worked on these synonyms together with the examples of metaphors I was familiar with until it all came together.

"Oh, that's what a metaphor is!" I blurted out as if the conversation in my head had been the conversation with these two boys. "Let me explain. What you're saying in a way is true but it's not a helpful definition. What a metaphor really is is when you explain something in a way that is not real or possible in the world we touch and see. Again, like hyperbole, we use metaphors all the time in our everyday language."

The boys looked on with interest. This was the first time that they actually showed any interest in what I had to say.

"Do you know the expression, 'I have that person wrapped around my little finger'?"

The two boys looked up at me and then slowly shook their heads.

"Okay, well, there is an expression, 'I have that person wrapped around my little finger'. Is that person really, literally, wrapped around my little finger?" I then used my hands to act out wrapping a person around the little finger of my left hand. "What this saying really means is that I have this person under my control."

The boys showed no particular inspiration by this explanation but simply wrote this in their exercise books under the title, Metaphor.

"You will find," I continued, "two other words related to 'metaphor' and that's 'figurative' and 'abstract'. I mean, I could just as easily have said that the expression, 'I have that person wrapped around my little finger' is figurative language, metaphoric language or abstract language, and it would all mean much the same thing."

The boys looked on in silence.

"Another example," I continued even though the boys didn't really show any particular interest in further examples, "is the expression, 'I had the audience in the palm of my hand'. Have you heard that expression?"

The boys shook their heads.

"You think about it. A famous speaker gets up in a large auditorium and there is absolute silence as he or she speaks. That speaker can later say that he or she 'had the audience in the palm of my hand'. Does this mean that every single person in the entire auditorium was standing on the palm of his or her hand?" and this time I held my left palm facing up and with my right hand I drew an invisible circle using my right index finger.

The two boys shook their heads unemotionally.

"It is a physical impossibility for the audience to be in the palm of my hand so this expression is a metaphor. As you can see, a metaphor is used to convey an idea using a physical impossibility to explain a physical reality. I mean, the metaphor is a physical impossibility but you can readily understand the physical reality behind it. It's just like a picturesque way of explaining something, a bit arty farty. But also, in a way, it's also like a shorthand way of conveying an idea. But as you can see, we can describe something as a metaphor but we can also explain the same thing in concrete language, that is, I can say 'I have that person wrapped around my little finger' is a metaphor, but I can also explain this in concrete language, that is, this metaphor means that I have that person under my control. When you read poems, at any time you read something that is physically impossible in this world, you know it's a metaphor and all you have to do is then describe what the metaphor means in concrete language."

This was quite a revelation to me and I thought the boys were going to congratulate me on my insight but they just stared at me blankly.

"Okay, then," I continued. "The last technique I want you to write down is personification. Do you know what personification is?"

"Isn't that when you make some object act like a living thing?" Luke asked.

"You're partly correct. The word is 'personification' and it has the word 'person' in it. That is, you give 'person' attributes to something that is not a person, so it can be a thing or it can also be an animal. Do you know any examples?"

"When the moon walks?" Alex suggested.

"That's fine," I replied. "Write that down."

The boys wrote this down.

"Now," I continued, "these are not the only techniques used in poetry. There are many others, some with unusual names. But these are often the most popular eight you will see in poems. If there are any others, usually your teacher will point them out to you. Anyway, I can point them out to you if I see any today."

Armed with all this explanation, I got the boys to go back to the poem and write down examples of any of the techniques they had just learnt and if they appeared in the poem. We hadn't got far when I looked up at the clock on the opposite wall and realised the hour was up. I suggested for homework that the boys go through the poem, write down quotes from the poem, write out the technique and then explain why they say it is this particular technique. In the following lesson, I would look at what they had written.

So, that morning was torturous but at least the boys had learnt something. The only problem with such a torturous lesson is that it saps out the energy. I still had more lessons to conduct and if this was how my day was going to pan out, I would be mentally drained by the time I got home. During one of the drives between classes, I looked up at the beautiful blue sky and the sun shining proudly. It was a great sunny day. I thought to myself that when I finished tutoring, there would still be hours of sunlight left in the day so I would be able to spend the rest of the afternoon at the local swimming pool first doing my laps and then laying on my outstretched towel relaxing from the rigours of the day.

Finally my last lesson for the day had finished. I jumped in my car and full of anticipation stuck the key in the ignition, started the car up and began my trip back home. I hadn't gone far when I noticed that the sky had begun to get heavy and rather grey. Storm clouds started gathering and it looked seriously like we were going to have a storm.

"That'd be right," I mumbled to myself in the car. "It was a bright sunny day today while I was working but the weather has to change just as I am on my way home and have the rest of the afternoon free. So typical of the weather!"

Very soon it was bucketing down. Not only was the change in weather sudden, so was the change in temperature. This was so enervating. I had planned to go to the local swimming pool. How could I do that now? I might be able to do my laps but there was no way I could lay out under the sun. In any case, if there was a storm the pool would close. The frustration! How is it that the entire day while I was tutoring it was beautiful and sunny but the minute I finish and am on my way home the weather changes so abruptly?

The rain beat down heavily on the windscreen and the windscreen wipers flicked rapidly back and forth. Water tumbled down almost as if it were from a waterfall and the traffic slowed down to make my trip home a lot longer than usual. I looked up through the grey blur formed on the windscreen and yelled out, "So, are you happy now?"

A thought then popped into my head as if someone else had placed it there.

"Who's happy?" it asked. "The clouds in particular or the weather in general? Can clouds and weather be happy? Do they ever express happiness or any other emotions? Are they being vindictive, trying on purpose to make your life miserable? Do the clouds or weather have personal qualities like people? Like persons? Personification?"

Personification? Personification?

"Personification!" I then yelled.

I began to think more about this. Who really is happy now? Is anyone out there actually getting any enjoyment out of spoiling my day? If not, then what possessed me to think that?

Then I began to think more about it. Isn't this what we all do? How many times have I been in conversation and someone complains about a situation, and then they say, "That'd be right! Just when I couldn't have any more problems, this comes along" or something like that, as if there were some vindictive agent in nature which deliberately is out there to spoil our day.

As it was, the weather had changed but it hadn't done so particularly to make me miserable. The weather had changed because there were atmospheric changes in the movement of the air at this particular point in time which caused the resulting storm. It was such a natural reflex to blame the weather for making my day miserable thinking that it had done so expressly when it was all purely coincidental. I focused back on the slowly moving traffic ahead of me and thought of all the other drivers and passengers in the vehicles all around me and thought to myself, do all these other people feel the same as me that the weather has vindictively changed to spoil their days? How is it that I felt that the weather even considered me when looking down onto the earth that I was particularly significant so that it was my day it wanted to spoil? What if the weather was actually vindictively spoiling the day of the driver in the car ahead of me and I was unfortunately innocently affected by the weather's vindictiveness? But again, was it the weather itself that was vindictive? Can the weather be vindictive? Does the weather have emotions?

This started a cascade of thoughts. Natural disasters in times of yore were once considered personified agents that came and caused destruction to groups of people. If the natural disaster did that, and the natural disaster was a personified agent, then the natural disaster carried out its destructive power either because of its vindictiveness, that is, it got some sort of kick out of annoying people, or as payback to a group of people for something these people had done wrong to this invisible agent. As time went by, it was discovered that these natural disasters weren't personal at all so there had to be a personified agent much greater than nature itself that was carrying out all these disasters, once again out of vindictiveness or as payback.

In this evolution of thought, eventually the idea came that there were a number of personified agents and then finally that there was only one responsible for these disasters. In the case of Christianity, this personified agent, called God, had the attribute of being loving and always right, so natural disasters were inflicted on people because of their sins.

Once I had left the Christian faith, I thought that it was absurd that religious people continued to believe that invisible agents greater in intelligence and power than ourselves made changes in our lives beyond our control as reward or punishment for things that we did when there was no such agent to do so. But then I realised that it was actually instinctive for us to have this thought. I had lashed out at the weather and complained because of the weather's vindictiveness when the weather simply had changed without any feelings or any concerns regarding my afternoon plans. It was simply coincidental that the time I was on my way to the swimming pool that the weather no longer was suitable for such a plan.

We did this all the time. How many times have we complained that as soon as we wash our cars it rains, as if the weather is nasty, watching on while we meticulously wash our cars, waiting for the last wipe of the chamois in order for the clouds to gather, drop a load and undo all the effort we have put in? How many times had we complained that when we had put our washing out on the line, when it was almost dry a storm cloud came along and drenched all the washing so that we had to wait until the next sunny day before we could remove the laundry from the line? And in each case we looked on the weather as a personified agent with feelings and emotions. But it also showed just how chauvinistic we were because we felt that the weather which encompassed the large area of air above our heads showed particular interest in our own personal, little lives.

This, then, took me back to the use of personification in poetry. This was why we used personification in poems because it made the subject matter more personal, more relevant to us. In the poem *On Pain and Pleasure*, the last two lines personify pain and pleasure, calling them twins and referring to them as "she" whereas in reality pain and pleasure are not personal agents of any kind at all. What even struck me in my cogitations was that it didn't strike me odd or bizarre that the poet had referred to pain and pleasure as twin sisters. Rather, I thought it sounded lovely and picturesque. But it was nonetheless simply poetic and described an unreal situation. I hadn't questioned the poet's use of personification of pain and pleasure because in the poetic context, it was quite acceptable to personify them. However, had I gone to my doctor with a terrible pain and my doctor found the source of the pain and the appropriate remedy, if the doctor had then told me that he knew the correct remedy for my particular pain because pain and pleasure are after all twin sisters and once he had identified the one twin it followed by course that he could find the other to take its place, I would have questioned my doctor's qualifications and probably even more his mental state.

Why the poet decided to write this poem I was unsure of but at least I understood that it was like all poems. There was a mixture of trying to relay a message, in this case, that it is uncanny that when there is pain it is followed by pleasure as if you cannot have one without the other, and to simply be artistic. The examples given throughout the poem brought this out quite clearly and, except for the reference of the woman in labour in the first example and the obvious religious overtone in the last, all the examples had been pretty much experienced by everyone of us at one time or another which helped us further identify with what the poet was trying to say. Further, the way the poem presented this theme made it more interesting, more pleasurable. If someone had come to me and said, "Did you know that whenever we have pain, this is always followed by pleasure once the pain has stopped?" I would think, yeah, that's true but so what? But by putting the topic into a poem, making the poem rhyme so that it had a rhythmic pattern, throwing in a few unusual but   nice sounding expressions such as "a most pleasurable tonic", it made for a piece of written artwork that made us feel good.

But at the bottom of it all, this personification was totally unreal no matter how lovely and close it brought us to the subject matter. That we have a pain and when the pain goes away the relieving feeling we get after it is extremely pleasurable, no matter how well this poem was written and how much it made me feel good, I knew from my observation and from my logic that it was impossible that pain and pleasure were in fact personal agents who can be "joined at the thigh" or even have thighs or any bodily parts we associate with the average human being.

This then made me reflect on the holy books. For example, St John wrote in one of his letters that God is love. Were we to understand this literally or was this simply personification, that love is really a feeling that we have towards other people, that in the real world love has no personal attributes or physical makeup? In actual fact, John got the idea that God is love from Socrates. In Plato's *Symposium*, the discussion about love being a deity of some kind really brings out the personification in great detail and when we read the discussion between all the people at the drinking party, each try to describe love as if love were an actual sentient quasi-human being.

When John said in the opening verse of his gospel that God was the *logos*, that is, the Reason, the aspect of the intellect which searches out truth using logic, did John literally mean that God was this Reason or was this merely personification?

Further, in the poem *On Pain and Pleasure*, the author and anyone who read the poem were not really supposed to understand that the poet was conveying a literal message. However, there was nothing actually in the poem which said this. Rather, from our appreciation of the poetic genre, we understand that poems convey a meaning using these poetic techniques simply as a vehicle for making the message more interesting or more colourful. But the descriptions in the poem are not supposed to be understood as reality, things that exist in the world we touch and see. No-one is supposed to go out and say that we must believe in the literal understanding of the poem. If they did, scientists would no doubt come along and show that, in fact, pain and pleasure are not human-like in any way and there is clearly no evidence for it. Was this the trouble with those who approached the Bible and the Koran as actual literal accounts and then made demands on others to believe these holy books in this way?

The trouble with the biblical use of personification, and also the koranic use as I was to discover later, is that the personification is, in fact, interwoven within claims of historical narrative. John's gospel opens by saying that God was the Reason but then describes how this Reason really became a human being and then the rest of his gospel is narrative giving the impression that he seriously believed that this Reason was a human being. This makes his gospel in a literary genre of its own where possible poetic techniques are interwoven into supposedly narrative text. Or was the entire gospel actually to be understood poetically?

As for the Koran, in the original Arabic, every surah actually rhymes. This already alerts readers that what they are reading is in fact a poem and therefore various poetic techniques are used within. Like the poem *On Pain and Pleasure*, poetic techniques typically found within the poetic genre, such as personification, hyberbole and metaphor, which are not expected to be taken literally, were expected to be a part of the fabric of the text and therefore physical realities were in fact not actually expected.

So much for the sudden change in the weather dampening my day! These thoughts occupied my time for the long, slow trip home through the traffic and made the trip feel so much shorter.

When I got home, all these thoughts about poetic techniques and the holy books for some odd reason made me curious to read the Hebrew Bible that Uncle William had given me. Although Uncle William had given this Bible to me because it was a prized possession of a distant ancestor of mine and I was the only modern descendant who could read the text, all I had done with the book once I had got back from Albury was to place it in a special box just big enough to hold it so that it wouldn't get damaged.

Once through the door, I tossed my work bag in its assigned corner of the room, made myself a cup of coffee then slumped down in one of the arm chairs. I carefully removed the Hebrew Bible from the box and delicately opened it to the first page.

I knew already how the first chapter of Genesis unfolded and I had been very critical of it. But the appearance of the Hebrew letters and the knowledge that this object in my hands was once held and treasured by an ancestor of mine made me approach the text in a less critical way.

I began reading the first verse: "In the beginning, God created the heaven and the earth". This first verse took us out of the impersonal, cold reality of the universe and presented us with a personalised connection to it, that it once had a beginning and there was something in likeness to humans who created it. There was also something special about reading it in the Hebrew and not in English. Was it because the original language was written by someone I knew, that is, Moses - assuming that Moses was, in fact, the author - whereas the English translation was written by some unknown person? Or was it because of my alleged Jewish connections which now gave me a greater connection to this text and the language in which it was written?

As I read, I read the text as if I were reading a poem which was not to be taken literally in the same way I was to read *On Pain and Pleasure*. When reading the Genesis account in this way, it was quite pleasurable, taking me away into another world.

It had been quite a long time since I had read this story in the original language and hence it was like I was reading this for the first time. Because of this, it was the first time that I read it without any influence from the church telling me how I was to understand what I was reading. As I read it in the Hebrew, instead of the translation I was familiar with from my youth given in the King James where it says

> *And the earth was without form, and void;*
> *and darkness was upon the face of the deep.*
> *And the Spirit of God moved upon*
> *the face of the waters*

the way the Hebrew came across in this fresh, unbiased, uninfluenced reading was

> *And the earth was in chaos,*
> *and darkness on the face of the tehom*
> *and the breath of the gods fluttered*
> *on the surface of the waters.*

Not only was this extremely poetic, it was totally not the story that I had understood it in my childhood. The English translation had completely masked the original meaning and intent of the Genesis account. In particular, the English translation was made in a time when it was a criminal offence to confess that there was more than one god and so even though the original used the plural "gods", to avoid serious legal action and a heavy fine or possibly a prison sentence, the translators had to translate the plural "gods" as the singular "God" in the English.

I felt as if I had entered a dream. The picture that formed in my mind as I read was of a cosmic struggle, of utter confusion, and the gods bringing order out of this disorder.

While reflecting on this, my mind went back to my early twenties when I had become interested in reading books about ancient Mesopotamia, an interest that was sparked from my reading of the historical books of the Old Testament and my attempt to understand the background of the events in these books. This also led me to reading about the ancient Mesopotamian myths. Somehow, what I was reading in Genesis sounded very much like what I was familiar with of the Sumerian myth of Creation when the gods blew on a great body of water called Tiamat and by this act Creation began. And when I reflected on the name "Tiamat", I could see a faint but possible connection between this name and the word translated as "deep" in English, namely, *tehom*: tehom, teom, tiam, tiamat. This then made the connection between the *tehom* and the waters in the Genesis account. In the English version, there is a "deep" and there are "waters" but there is no obvious connection between them or whether the waters are in the deep or the waters are in a completely different place. But if the *tehom* was the Tiamat, this connection becomes clear. The Tiamat *was* the body of water. So this made more sense. Darkness was on the surface of the *tehom*, that is, darkness was on a large body of water, and then the gods blew on the surface of this body of water. And once the gods had done this, the first thing created was light.

And then strangely enough, Ibrahim came to mind. Ibrahim had once said that God is both a singularity and a plurality. This was a plausible concept for Christians who believed God was one and three at the same time. But Ibrahim had also shown that even the Koran suggested a multiplicity in the singularity of God, where Muslims say that God has ninety-nine names and where the Koran has God often speaking in the first person plural. Is this what Ibrahim and all those in the Msingi wa Mungu Project were trying to do, to bring order out of the chaos and light out of the darkness? That when the gods blew together in unison onto the waters, that is, the chaos, light was first brought forth and then order? That instead of the gods being divided, meaning that religions were separate and at odds with each other, and each trying to force everyone else to follow their particular one and in so doing creating utter chaos on the earth, if all the gods of all the religions, which in some mystical way were also at the same time only one god, blew together, out of the chaos would come light and finally order? And peace and paradise on earth? Were we, in fact, reading the Bible backwards, and that what we read in the beginning was in reality what we should be reading at the end?

That was a beautiful thought. This was something I wanted to tell Ibrahim. I wondered what he was going to think when he heard what I had discovered.

This then made me read on. While the storm passed on and the heavy rain continued in its wake, I kept reading. I kept reading until it began to get dark. Because I was reading this text away from the church's influence and as if it were a fresh and new text, many of the stories in the Genesis narrative revealed things I had never seen before. Many of these familiar stories were not understood in the way that the Hebrew was revealing them to me and, so I guessed, how the author originally intended. I knew that in a future conversation with Ibrahim, I would share what I had discovered.

Once I had completed reading the book of Genesis, I then thought of the Koran. Since coming back from the Msingi wa Mungu Project, like the Hebrew Bible Uncle William had given me, the Koran that Ibrahim had given me lay unread in the chambers of my bookshelf. I decided to take it out and continue reading from where I had begun in Moshi. And just like Adam and Eve who ate from the fruit of the Tree of the Knowledge of Good and Evil, my eyes were opened and I saw things that I didn't expect to see.

The private tuition continued in full strength. And I had to read more texts than those that held interest for me. The parents of the students I taught knew that I charged by the hour and not by the number of students. Sometimes parents were happy to have me teach only one of their children at a time. It was when I taught another student called Stuart that I began to see more things come to light.

Stuart was a very outspoken Year 11 student. In fact, I quite liked his character. His cynism made our lessons quite enjoyable.

We carried out tuition in what looked like his parents' study. Although I was provided with a chair to sit beside Stuart, I preferred, as I did with my other students, to actually stand up and walk around with occasional glances back at Stuart and whatever he had in front of him to write in.

One day, Stuart had a poem that he had to write an essay about. The poem was as follows.

The Message

She comes dancing and singing
The plaits of her hair
Tied up with ribbons of amorous pink and pacific white
Which flutter meaningfully in the neuma

Her laughter bubbles up from the abyss of time
And channels forth towards tomorrow
Voices from treasured parchment cry,
"Follow her from your past to your future"

Playfully she rushes forth while
The lines of paper rest firmly behind leaving
A trail of memories
Voiceless faces from the past in silent consent
Guide me forward

She emerges from her cocoon
Of tumbling and bumbling confusion
Gracefully she spreads her wings of harmony
Which flicker majestically across the seven seas
Carrying the nectar of peace and the pollen
Of life to all the regions of the earth

From the exalted peak of the great father mountain
Ascends the crooked belt of Orion
To resume its place within the constellation.
While she flits before the dusk of days
From her silhouette I finally understand
The message

By *Helen Sia Smetterling*

I read through the poem. The first thought that passed through my mind was, what is all this garbage? I then asked Stuart what he understood of the poem.

"I don't understand any of it!" he complained. "It's such a stupid poem and it makes no sense and I don't know why I have to study it."

I could agree with him on that score. The difficulty that this posed for me was that I had to be supportive of Stuart's teacher even though I totally agreed with Stuart that this was an absolutely ridiculous, nonsensical poem and it didn't even sound interesting. At least the poem *On Pain and Pleasure* was catchy and what it talked about was understandable. I shared

Stuart's cynicism of the absurdity of having to study this poem and then write an essay about it. But I couldn't say this out loud.

I had to take the defensive stance. If I expressed out loud that I felt the same as Stuart did, this was likely to strengthen Stuart's discontent and channel it towards his class teacher. After all, it was highly unlikely that his teacher herself had actually chosen the poem but rather it was the school and even higher, the board of studies. I wanted to reinforce the Asian ethic that teachers should be respected, an ethic I think should be instilled in all of us.

"Well," I replied. "Unfortunately you have to learn that in life sometimes we have to do things that we don't like doing to obtain the things that we do like. Your teacher was probably told by the head of English that she had to get you guys to study this poem."

I then reread the poem.

"So," I began, "has your teacher gone through the poem with you and explained what it means and what the techniques are?"

"My teacher doesn't explain anything," Stuart remarked.

"That's a little unfair," I replied to this comment. I really didn't know what to say. How much was Stuart's comment a typical outburst from a student who was simply lazy or even belligerent and hence wouldn't give the task at hand a go and then simply blamed the teacher for his failure? Blaming the teacher was for me too easy a task.

"Well, maybe she has," I then said, "but you didn't understand what she meant. But that's okay. We'll go through the poem together and you can tell me what the teacher said."

"She didn't say anything," Stuart complained.

We really didn't have the time to spend the hour arguing over whether or not the teacher had performed her task but I made the comment that probably he didn't understand and that's why he's upset but not to worry because I am now here and can go through the poem with him in detail.

"Okay," I continued. "So, did your teacher say what the theme of the poem was?"

"No!" Stuart said as an outburst. Stuart must have read the disapproving expression on my face because he then said, "Well, I dunno. Maybe."

"Well, the next time you go to class, simply go and ask her."

"But the essay's due Monday."

Why didn't you tell me that before? I thought. And why didn't you show me this poem ages ago when there was more time to go over it? However, there was no use debating this issue either.

"Okay. It can't be too hard to work out. Let's start with the first stanza. What is Smetterling trying to say here?"

"Something stupid!" Stuart complained. His defeatist tone of voice actually sounded funny and made me laugh.

"Come on," I replied through my laughter. "Let's go through it. Now Smetterling throughout the stanza refers to something that she constantly refers to as 'she'. So whoever this person is, it is a she. Because she dances and sings, and has plaits of hair tied up in ribbon, this gives the image that this 'she' is most probably a young girl.

But notice the words used to describe the colour of the ribbons, 'amourous pink' and 'pacific white'. This is important. The colour pink itself cannot be amorous and the colour white cannot be pacific. So why has the poet chosen to describe these two colours in this way? I think it's because 'amorous' simply comes from the French, *amour*, meaning 'love' and so the pink ribbon represents love, and 'pacific' comes from the Latin word *pax*, meaning 'peace' and so the white ribbon represents peace. Putting all this together, there is a young girl who carries love and peace."

"How can a young girl carry love and peace in her hair?" Stuart asked with obvious sarcasm in his voice.

I laughed. It's a poem, for heaven's sake, I thought. It's not to be taken on face value. You have to dig into it to find out what the author was really trying to say.

"I don't think the poet actually meant that this 'she' was literally a young girl in the normal sense. This young 'she' represents something, she personifies something. There you go, you can at least write down personification as a technique."

I got Stuart to write this next to the stanza.

"Now," I continued, "in the last line of this stanza, the poet uses the word 'neuma'. Did your teacher explain what 'neuma' means?"

"No!" Stuart said emphatically but when he looked up at me and saw the disapproving face looking back at him, he turned to look at the poem.

"Maybe!" he then mumbled.

Stuart then opened up the exercise book he was using for school and flicked the pages noisily until he came across a page which from my angle looked like the mad scribbles of a raving lunatic.

"My teacher said that it was a nonsense word and is being used to describe a substance that doesn't really exist," Stuart mumbled.

Ah! So your teacher did explain the poem, I thought. However, I didn't want to have a go at him because this would have channelled his efforts into trying to justify his contempt for the teacher when I wanted the efforts channelled into actually preparing for the essay. It wasn't important for me to show that I had been right all along that his teacher had, in fact, explained the poem.

I thought about it for a moment and then said, "You know, I don't think it is a nonsense word. This word looks like the Greek word *pneuma* but without the p. Did your teacher mention that?"

Stuart looked at his notes and then mumbled in the negative.

"That's okay. You can add this to your notes, then. To me, Smetterling has used the word 'neuma' not as a nonsense word but because it is the Greek word *pneuma* and she left out the p probably because in English we don't pronounce the p. It makes sense to me that Smetterling actually was using the Greek word *pneuma* because in Greek, *pneuma* means 'wind' but it also means 'spirit'. You see, the Greeks believed that a 'spirit' was a wind of some description. Are you familiar with Christianity?"

"No," Stuart mumbled.

"Are you being serious?" I asked.

"Okay, okay, I know a little bit, like there's Christmas and Easter."

"And do you know why we celebrate Christmas and Easter?"

"Something about Jesus Christ and that he was killed."

"And that's all?"

"How am I supposed to know?" Stuart then cried out. "I'm a Buddhist!"

That wasn't my point, I thought. I appreciated that I had been brought up in a Christian environment so this was why I knew all about Christianity. However, it didn't matter whether or not you were raised in a Christian home in Australia to understand something about Christianity because when it came to Christmas and Easter, the shopping centres were all full of scenes and symbolism from the Christian story of Jesus' birth, death and resurrection. Surely Stuart actually noticed these each time he went to the shops at these times of the year. And surely they talked about it at school before these holiday periods commenced.

His behaviour made me laugh, especially his outburst that he was a Buddhist. I had always pictured Buddhists as being serene, peaceful sort of people who wouldn't hurt a fly and had the utmost respect for all people, especially those in authority. Stuart's reaction to having to do this essay and his comments about his teacher showed that he was like any other obstreperous teenage school student.

"I was just asking," I then said. "The reason I say this is because I think you need to know something about Christianity to understand this poem. If you don't, hopefully your teacher explained this to you."

Stuart looked down at the mad scribblings he had made on the poem but said nothing.

"Okay," I said, realising the silence meant that he wasn't sure and knew what I would think if he said the teacher hadn't told him anything at all. "The 'pneuma' could mean 'wind' but could also mean 'spirit'. Now, Christians say that there is something called the Holy Spirit, and this Holy Spirit is represented as a dove. A dove's wings flutter in the wind, so I guess this is why Smetterling used this particular word here. Also, the dove represents peace and the colour of a dove is white, and this explains the 'pacific white'. As for the 'amorous pink', according to Christianity, the Holy Spirit is God and God is love. So putting all this together, I think Smetterling is personifying the Holy Spirit as a young girl."

Stuart just humphed.

"You see," I continued, "you want in your essay to concentrate on the use of specific words used in very unusual ways. Make sure you comment about them. Also, why did Smetterling use the Greek word *pneuma* and not an English word? I think it's because *pneuma* has a much greater sphere of meaning, and Smetterling deliberately meant both meanings, 'wind' and 'spirit', and so kept the Greek word. If she had chosen to use an English word, she would not have been able to capture the full sense of both 'wind' and 'spirit' which I think she was trying to portray."

"But isn't God in Christianity a 'he'?" Stuart then asked.

"Yes," I replied, "in Christianity God is referred to as a 'he'. But He really can't be a 'he' in our sense of the word because in nature, where there is a 'he' there is always a 'she'. So if God is a 'he' there must also be a god that is a 'she'."

"So, the Christian god is really an 'it'?" Stuart then asked dryly.

"Well," I replied. "We could go on a long theological discussion but we really don't have the time here and it's totally irrelevant to the topic. I think Smetterling appreciated that the Holy Spirit in the conventional sense is really neither 'he' nor 'she' and so she was justified in referring to the Holy Spirit as a 'she'. This may have been because she was taking a feminist stance and making the claim that God could just as well be a 'she' as a 'he'. I also see more to it than this. Young girls generally represent innocence, sinlessness and purity, and hence the personification of the Holy Spirit as a little girl emphasises that the Holy Spirit is innocent, totally without sin."

Stuart looked through his notes. "My teacher definitely didn't say that," he groaned.

"Okay," I then said. "Let's move on because this hour will be over before you know it and I want to make sure you have enough to write about in your essay. Now, when we get to the second stanza, we read how this young girl's 'laughter bubbles up from the abyss of time'. Now, do you understand what this means?"

"That the poet was on drugs when she wrote this?" Stuart said sarcastically.

I just burst out laughing. But I had to also keep on track.

"Come on," I said through my laughter. "Okay. What did your teacher tell you?"

Stuart read the scribblings on his page. "Something about the abyss being a bottomless pit. She said that the abyss of time simply meant eternity, how that time has neither beginning nor end."

"And is that all?"

"Yeah," Stuart said cautiously. I wondered if the teacher had said more but Stuart couldn't actually read his own handwriting which is why he was having difficulty.

"Okay," I continued. "I think there's more to it. Obviously Smetterling had a Christian upbringing because of the constant religious overtones. Again, words are important and you have to watch how words are used. It is true that we think of time as being eternal, but why did Smetterling talk about the 'abyss' of time? Do you know what an 'abyss' is?"

"Isn't it some sort of hole?" Stuart asked, the first time in a way that showed that he was actually trying to co-operate with the task at hand.

"And more than just a hole. It's a hole without a bottom. The English word 'abyss' comes directly from the Greek, *abussos,* where *a* means 'without' and *bussos* means 'bottom' and in ancient Greek literature it usually meant the bottom of the sea, hence, *abussos* means 'a bottomless pit'. So this is a metaphor – there, write down 'metaphor' here – where time is portrayed as a hole. Now, we have laughter here bubbling up and channelling forth. So once again we have another metaphor – again, write that down – of laughter being a substance that can bubble up and channel forth. What does that sound like to you what laughter is here?"

Stuart looked up at me further with a look on his face that he was actually trying to understand.

"Water?" he asked.

"I think so, too. The image is of a hole where water bubbles up and flows out onto the ground."

"So, what happens to you if you drink this water?" Stuart asked, returning to his belligerent attitude. But then his face changed to more seriousness. "Does this mean that you then become happy, too?"

"Yes, keep going," I encouraged.

Stuart hesitated and then added. "If you drink from the Holy Spirit that has always been around forever you will always be happy?"

"Very good!" I praised him. "I think that's what it means, too."

"But I'm a Buddhist," Stuart then objected. "I don't believe in the Holy Spirit."

I laughed. "Stuart, you are analysing a poem so that you can write an essay about it. You're not being asked to believe what the poet is saying!"

Stuart nodded in consent and then began writing down notes, adding to the scribbly handwriting that was already on the page.

"Now," I continued, "the last two lines of this stanza, do you know what they are saying?"

Stuart looked down at his notes. "My teacher said that the 'treasured parchment' is the Bible."

"That could be true," I replied. "But it simply says 'treasured parchment'. Any parchment from antiquity that is treasured could be being referred to here. I think that Smetterling means all documents from antiquity, not simply the Bible, and the reason I say this is because in the next stanza, she writes, 'the lines of paper fall behind leaving a trail of memories' and I believe this means that anything written remains a record of history. All documents written in the past are a record of our past and help us to remember what happened in the past. This then coupled with the 'voiceless faces from the past' I think is referring to those who wrote the documents on parchment, that what they tell us they tell us without a voice, that is, written on the page, and the 'face' really refers to the surface of each page of parchment. The word, *surface*, comes from the French *sur* meaning 'on' and the French word *face* which is the same in English, hence her use of 'voiceless faces'. That is, the pages of parchment speak to us but without a voice, and they speak to us on the surface of the parchment."

Stuart was madly writing all this down. I waited patiently for him to finish.

"And the 'silent consent'?" Stuart asked.

"I think," I began and was getting excited that I could actually see what Smetterling was trying to say, "that the poet means that we must consider all of these documents, not simply pick and choose, that in some way all that was written in the past on parchment somehow agree together and we have to somehow find this connection. Or maybe there are certain aspects of all ancient documents which somehow agree with each other and the Holy Spirit or whatever this little girl symbolises uses the positive aspects of each of these documents or is responsible for these positive aspects being written in the first place. Once we do, this will lead us forward."

Stuart once again madly wrote down what I had said.

"Well, then," Stuart then said as he sat up, "I don't get how this Holy Spirit comes out of a cocoon, unless, of course, in Christianity the Holy Spirit is represented as a butterfly or a moth."

I looked at the poem and then read from the beginning up until the beginning of the fourth stanza.

"Okay," I began. "As far as I know, the Holy Spirit is never represented as a butterfly. Yet, whatever this 'she' is has changed form from a young girl to a butterfly. But you are right to infer that now this 'she' is a butterfly because she emerges from a cocoon, she has wings that flicker and she carries nectar and pollen. But again, we have metaphors here – write that down, metaphor – that is, 'her cocoon of tumbling and bumbling confusion', 'her wings of harmony', 'the nectar of truth' and 'the pollen of life'."

Stuart was busy writing this down while I scanned the page trying to find out what the poet was getting at. The 'tumbling and bumbling confusion' floated around in my mind as if the phrase were trying to find a match in the encyclopaedic network in my head. Tumbling and bumbling, tumble and bumble, tum and bum, tuh and buh, tohu and bohu. It was like a revelation. The Creation story translated in English as "the earth was without form and void" was in Hebrew "and the earth was *tohu and bohu*". *Tohu and bohu* really should be translated as "in confusion" and Smetterling must have known this expression and deliberately used it in her "tumbling and bumbling confusion".

"I think I've got it!" I exclaimed and told Stuart to write down what I had thought. "This means, then, that this 'she' came out of the earth which was in confusion. This 'she' had the power to heal the confused world with truth and life. But why it's the 'nectar of truth' and the 'pollen of life' I'm not sure. Obviously it's imagery – you can write that down, imagery – about butterflies which collect nectar and pollen, but I can only guess that the 'nectar of truth' means that truth is sweet like nectar is sweet. And the 'pollen of life', well, pollen is what makes flowers reproduce so it's symbolic of life."

Stuart finished writing and then looked at me. "So what about the last stanza?"

"Let me think about it for a second," I replied. I thought about the first line of the last stanza: From the exalted peak of the great father mountain. Each time I read "great father" I wanted to follow this with "time" but it was "mountain", so I had to keep going back and read the line again. Was there a connection with great father mountain and great father time? I tried to make that work but it was too much like trying to force a square peg into a round hole. The poem itself had religious overtones so was there something more to the great father mountain that I was missing? The only great father who came to mind was Abraham because he was the great father of Judaism and Christianity and even of Islam. But what was the connection with Abraham and mountains? However, the name Abraham suddenly went clinking round in the recesses of my head. Abraham was originally called Abram, and Abram meant "great father", from the Hebrew *ab* meaning "father" and *room* meaning "high" or "exalted". It was like a strike of a lightning bolt. It now all made sense. Abraham, the "exalted father" was the "exalted peak of the great father mountain".

When I got that piece of information, I then read the next line about the "the crooked belt of Orion". The picture of these three stars came to mind, two greater stars and then the lesser star which was not quite in line with the other two which therefore made the belt of Orion slightly crooked. It then came to me as a great revelation.

"I've got it!" I exclaimed with excitement. "First of all, do you know anything about Judaism?"

Stuart looked at me and his facial expression said it all.

"Okay," I said. "Well, do you know how in the Second World War Hitler sent the Jews to concentration camps?"

Stuart slowly nodded his head.

"Are you sure?" I asked.

"Yes, yes, I've studied that in school."

"Okay, well, the Jews are a group of people who belong to a religion called Judaism. The Jews believe that there was a man called Abraham and he is their ancestral father so all the Jews around the world are descended from this one man."

Stuart went into deep reflection and then asked, "Why did Hitler put the Jews in concentration camps anyway?"

"I'd love to give you an answer," I replied, "but we don't have the time. Okay, now what do you know of Islam?"

"Nothing," Stuart replied.

"Nothing? Are you serious?"

Stuart looked at me embarrassedly.

"Oh, okay," I replied. "That's fine, if you don't know anything about Islam, I'll tell you a little about it because it is relevant to the poem."

But the thought went through my mind. How on earth did Stuart go through life here in Australia and not know anything about Islam? Weren't there girls at his school who wore veils? Didn't he notice that many of the products we buy at the supermarket had *halal* written on the packaging? Didn't he hear about the suicide bombings and other unrest in Muslim countries? Really, I actually envied Stuart's total ignorance and the ensuing bliss that came from it.

I explained that the two religions, Judaism and Islam, both claimed Abraham as their ancestral father. Abraham had two sons, Ishmael and Isaac, and the Muslims claimed descent from Ishmael and the Jews from Isaac. Christianity fit into this picture when considering Jesus, a descendant of Isaac who started the Christian religion. This then explained the crooked belt of Orion. And it was significant, I thought, that Smetterling actually emphasised that the belt was crooked. The three stars that made Orion's belt ascended from the great father mountain which meant that these three stars came out of this great mountain, which was Abraham, so that the stars were metaphorically the offspring and therefore the descendants of Abraham, two directly from him, the third indirectly, which was why the belt was crooked. To me it was a great revelation. To Stuart it was still all stupidity. However, Stuart madly wrote down my explanation. While he did so, I read on. That the three stars resumed their place in the entire Orion constellation implied that the other stars in the constellation were other descendants of Abraham if the stars really meant the actual children of Abraham. However, Jesus was not a son of Abraham like Ishmael and Isaac were so it didn't quite make sense to say that these three stars represented Ishmael, Isaac and Jesus. I guessed that what this really meant was that the three Abrahamic religions, Judaism, Christianity and Islam, came out of Abraham and therefore it was the religions themselves that were symbolised by the three stars. This then implied that the other stars in the constellation were other religions. That these three stars resumed their place in the constellation meant they were originally there as part of a set of seven religions but had at some time come out and now were being put back. What was the meaning of this?

The last lines of this stanza talked of when the belt of Orion had resumed its proper place in the constellation in the "dusk of days" and this implied near the end of time and in particular our time, humanity's time. The entire picture of the sunset created a sense of serenity. I wasn't sure but it appeared to mean that when these three religions finally stopped assuming that they were the only religions in the world and acknowledged that they were only part of a greater picture of the heavens, hence each religion being stars in the sky or "heavens", then peace would come to the universe.

While thinking about this last stanza, suddenly Ibrahim's dreams came to mind, the dreams in which there were high mountains. Were these to be interpreted as Abraham? So what of the high mountain with two trunks which grew apart but which came together?

Once again, it was like an epiphany. Ibrahim had alluded to it in an earlier conversation but now it made full sense. The two trunks were Ishmael and Isaac. That they were two trunks which grew out of this high mountain in a way symbolised that Ishmael and Isaac came directly out of Abraham. A bit of a sexist picture of things, really, because the two boys actually came out of women. However, the image actually made sense. That they were separate trunks meant that they were like separate family trees which continued through history as separate entities. That they would later join up meant that there would come a time when the children of Ishmael and the children of Isaac would eventually join together and when this happened, everything would become fruitful. And then the flowers that came off the top of the tree and formed the stars in the sky and the sand on the shore represented the fulfilment of the Scriptures that the children of Abraham would become like the stars of the skies and the sand on the shore and in this case only when the two sons united. It sent a shudder down my spine. And now I understood the connection between Ibrahim and me, that we were a small example of this unification process that was prophesied to come.

Stuart stared at me waiting and this brought me back to the task at hand.

"Okay," I said and then told Stuart what I had surmised about the belt of Orion, its place in the constellation and the justification I gave for my interpretation.

I then read the last two lines. In my mind I imagined a butterfly flying into the sunset and then I could only make out its silhouette. What message would I get from the silhouette of a butterfly? The image appeared before me in my mind's eye and then I got it.

"I think I understand the message!" I exclaimed. I then came over to Stuart's exercise book. "Draw for me the outline of a butterfly."

Stuart turned the page of his exercise book to a fresh new page with a noise of scorn.

"I thought we were doing English, not art," he complained.

"Just do it," I said.

Stuart made an attempt at drawing a butterfly but it looked like the outline of an indeterminate inkblot from a psychiatric test.

I laughed. "Oh, I get your comment, then."

"Well, I can't draw, okay?" Stuart protested.

"Settle down," I said through my laughter. "That's fine. I'll draw it."

I drew a butterfly, its wings spread out in a way that made the outline look to a degree like a Valentine's heart.

"Now do you get it?" I asked as I pulled back from the desk. Stuart looked down at the image.

"Nuh!" he spat out.

I came over to his exercise book and then drew a Valentine's heart next to my stylised drawing of the silhouette of the butterfly.

"Can you see it now?"

"Mmmm. I guess so," Stuart replied defeatedly.

"It's love! The 'she' talked about throughout the entire poem is love." Suddenly the Dolly Parton song *Love's Like a Butterfly* came to mind and I thought, that is just too corny!

"The message, then, is that it is love that guides us, or should guide us forward. Love brings peace and harmony. Love brings joy. And love is eternal. Love has been there from the beginning of time and at the end of time, it will be love which will conquer and finally bring peace to all the world. It is love that will also eventually unite all the religions together so that they will all live together in harmony. When people of different religions, and Smetterling appears to be having a particular dig at the Abrahamic religions, stop thinking that they are the only religions and reach out in love towards others of other religions, and realise their religions are only one of many and that in some way all religions fit in within the entirety of the heavens, this will finally bring in harmony."

"Oh," Stuart said by way of a groan. "But that does not look like the outline of a butterfly. Butterflies look something like this."

Stuart then drew a butterfly, this time with a lot more artistic skill. His image was more of the traditional image of a butterfly where one wing looked like a capital B, the other its mirror image.

"Butterflies look more like that," Stuart protested.

"I thought you said you couldn't draw!" I exclaimed.

Stuart looked up at me with a cheeky grin.

"Okay, yes," I confessed. "That would be more what a butterfly would look like in outline. But then, what is the message you gain from this in silhouette? That's why I drew my butterfly more like a Valentine's heart. This can be a style of butterfly and then it fits my understanding of the poem. Your butterfly, I agree it's more like what butterflies look like but then what is the message you see in its outline?"

Stuart looked back down at his drawing. "I dunno! Perhaps it is symmetry, harmony, balance."

I looked at the butterfly Stuart had drawn and tried to see something in it. I looked back at the poem and read the last stanza. The Orion image was significant and there had to be a connection. When I thought of the Orion constellation and Stuart's butterfly, I could see that Stuart's butterfly superimposed on the Orion constellation almost with a perfect fit, the only deviation being that the belt of Orion was not straight up and down with the body of the butterfly. But it almost was. Then the four outer stars of the Orion constellation, Betelgeuse, Bellatrix, Rigel and Saiph, traced out the outer contours of the butterfly's wings. This could therefore mean that it was the Orion constellation itself that was the silhouette of the butterfly. But what was the significance? What was the message?

Stuart looked up at me and I could feel his eyes penetrating me which brought me back to reality. I made the comment that Stuart was right to say that the message was harmony although I wasn't completely convinced. There was something more in it but I just couldn't get it at this time. However, I felt that we had analysed the poem enough so that Stuart could write his essay.

"Okay, so do you think you'll be right with the essay from now on?" I asked.

Stuart commented that he could. I told him that when he had finished writing his essay to keep a copy for me and that I would read it the following week even though he had to hand it in the following Monday. At least once I had looked at the final copy he submitted to his teacher, I could get an idea of the type of mark I was expecting him to get.

The final draft that I did see the following week wasn't badly written. Stuart had taken on much of the ideas I had explained to him. His grammar and essay structure weren't quite the best though and I knew these would bring his marks down somewhat. But overall I thought it wasn't too badly done. Hence, I was expecting Stuart to at least achieve an average mark for his efforts.

It was some weeks later when Stuart finally received his mark for the essay. The mark he got was in fact much lower than I had anticipated. I read through the marking criteria but I couldn't see how the teacher had arrived at the final low mark. I needed Stuart to enlighten me as to the reason.

"The teacher said that my analysis and interpretation of the poem was wrong."

Which means, my analysis and interpretation was wrong, I thought.

"Well, what was your teacher's interpretation?" I asked him.

"She said what you originally said, that this 'she' is the Holy Spirit but that it wasn't love at all. The message was that when Smetterling followed the Holy Spirit, her life would be a happy one."

"I can see that to a point," I replied. "But what about the image of the butterfly in the last two stanzas of the poem, the cocoon, the nectar and the pollen?"

"My teacher said that this was just imagery. She said that the cocoon was just a metaphor to describe the earth with all the wars and unrest that happen in it. The mention of nectar and pollen was simply that nectar and pollen are found in flowers and because Smetterling had used the image of the butterfly, that was the only connection."

Yes, that was possible, I thought, but my interpretation as far as I could see was also valid.

"And the treasured parchment?"

"She said that that was only referring to the Holy Bible."

"Well, yeah," I replied. "I can see that this is possible. But because it uses the sweeping comment, 'treasured parchment', there is nothing in this expression that limits it to only the Bible. It could refer to the Bible but it could also refer to any historic parchment that was treasured in the past such as Homer's *Iliad* and *Odyssey*."

I went on through the poem looking at what Stuart's teacher had said should be the right interpretation of the poem and compared these with mine. In some cases I agreed and in some cases I didn't. But even though the teacher did not agree with Stuart's interpretation, which was in fact my interpretation, I thought the entire idea of writing an essay was to show how well you could argue a point. Poems by nature were so esoteric, especially this one, that you could not say for sure whether the poem meant definitively one thing or another. After all, analysing poetry was not the same as doing mathematical problems where there were definite wrong and right answers. After all, that was what essay writing was all about, training us to develop our own opinions by providing evidence for the opinions that we held.

How could Stuart's teacher be so definitive about how the poem was to be interpreted? After all, who wrote this poem: Stuart's teacher or Helen Sia Smetterling? If we really wanted to know what the author really intended, it was necessary to go back to the author herself. If we couldn't, then it was up to each of us to try and work out what the author actually wanted to say. If the author had not been clear in her message, maybe it was deliberately written in this way to allow us to view the poem in more dimensions than just one.

But what was happening here was that the teacher was insisting that there was only one interpretation of the poem, the teacher's. Or possibly higher, that is, it was the board of studies' interpretation. But the board of studies didn't write the poem, Helen Smetterling did. So who gave the board of studies the right to define exactly how Smetterling's poem was to be interpreted? Did Smetterling pass on ownership of her poem over to the board of studies?

I learnt a lesson from this that the next time we examined a text, we had to find out what the teacher wanted Stuart to write and only write that, even if we couldn't understand how the teacher came up with her interpretation and even if we came up with a different interpretation we could actually justify from the text. To get marks, we had to simply regurgitate what the teacher wanted us to say.

Fortunately for me, Stuart wanted me to continue tutoring him because he felt that I had helped him, even though in this case I felt that I had actually failed him. But Stuart admitted that what assistance I did give him prevented him from getting an even lower mark.

While driving home that afternoon, I felt rather stunned but also angry. How was it that interpreting poems had to be done one way? Any time we read a poem or listened to a song, although there may be a particular message in these forms of art, sometimes we got something out of them that spoke to us personally and was different to what someone else got out of them. Wasn't that the whole beauty of songs and poems?

For some reason, this made me reflect back on the religions of the books. I saw a striking similarity between Stuart's teacher and certain religious people. Some people who follow a religion of the book tell others that the religious texts must be interpreted one way: their way. There was no room for alternate points of view and it didn't matter how well someone else demonstrated how they had arrived at a different interpretation. These intolerant people who were nothing else but religious bullies demanded that everyone around them read and understand the holy books in one way, their way, on pain of excommunication or even death. These religious bullies took it upon themselves that they had exclusive ownership of the interpretation of the religious texts as if they had written the texts themselves. And to me, even though I was not myself religious, I felt the blasphemy of it. These people were asserting that they themselves were the very authors of the text, that is, they were inadvertently stating that they themselves were God.

But if the Bible and the Koran were in a way forms of poetry, weren't they also open to interpretation, each person seeing something in them that others may not? And wasn't this the actual idea of poetry, that each of us got something out of the poem, something that spoke to us personally? And instead of the different interpretations of the texts being a cause of dissension, wasn't this God's absolutely amazing way of being able with one text to speak to each and every one of us individually, each of us with our differences, meaning that the texts were purposely written to have multiple interpretations?

Oddly, despite what I saw as my dismal failure to help Stuart, as a result the demand for my services as a private tutor increased. Eventually I was teaching the entire Saturday and when that was full, I used the afternoons during the week between the morning and evening shift at Tevah Am to take on more students. I decided with this surplus money to use some of it to sponsor children at the Msingi wa Mungu Project. Knowing that there were children in the world who had miserable lives and now there was a spark of hope that I could personally provide for them, despite how tiring it was for me now to be working two jobs and fitting in time for Polycarp and Jeremiah, knowing that orphans in Tanzania were receiving a new lease in life gave me the energy to go on.

Also, in this way, it didn't take long to earn the money to fly back to Tanzania.

And when I was able to co-ordinate purchasing a ticket and getting leave from work, I rang Ibrahim to tell him that I was on my way.

Chapter 16

My second trip to Tanzania was a totally positive experience in contrast to my first when I had participated in the Msingi wa Mungu Project. The vast, dry land which had looked empty and inhospitable on my previous trip looked open and welcoming this time round. But what was drawing me down to the landscape of Moshi was not simply the pull of gravity on the plane I was flying in but also the knowledge that the one who I had strong feelings for was somewhere down there waiting for me.

Going through immigration control and through the baggage collection occurred seamlessly as if everyone in Tanzania, even the airport authorities, knew the real reason for my return, as if they all shared my joy.

Once my check-in luggage had arrived on the baggage carousel, I collected it and, along with my carry-on luggage now swung over my left shoulder, I made my way to the exit. I looked at the alternative exits, one following the red line for those with something to declare, and the green line, for those who had nothing. I first glanced at the red line and thought cheekily, "Yes, I have something to declare. I have come all this way to be with Ibrahim and I have strong feelings for this beautiful man!"

There were airport officials dressed meticously and ominously in drab coloured uniforms at the exits and the atmosphere was a lot more serious than it was when I had gone through passport control. If one of the officials had asked me to stop and prove that I had nothing to declare, I would have borne it willingly and patiently. But I hoped that I would not be stopped. As I approached the exit, the last official I had to pass gave me a grave look.

"*Jambo! Mambo vipi?*" I greeted him in Swahili beaming with a smile.

"*Mambo poa!*" the official replied, changing his grim expression to a welcoming grin and signalling me with an overt arm gesture to welcome me to the country. "*Karibu kwetu!* Welcome to our country!"

There was something about the overtly welcoming gesture, the great arm movement and the grand welcome that this official gave me which made me hear in the secret corners of my memory the seventies group *Toto* and their song *Africa,* but in particular the lines, with a change of one pronoun

And I wanted to hurry. I wanted to run! I wanted to be in the arms of this great African man whom I had come to like very much.

And there he was. Ibrahim. The feelings welling up inside me like the surging waters of a great fountain bubbled up into my head so quickly that I thought I was going to laugh, cry and faint all at the same time. When I arrived in front of him, there was no hesitation on either part. Ibrahim wrapped his great African arms around me and I responded just as overtly. And so the next line from *Toto's* song continued in my head

It's gonna take a lot to take me away from you.

All those who have ever been in love, gay or straight, do not have to guess the flurry of wonderful feelings rushing through every part of my body at that moment. I wanted to squeeze Ibrahim so tightly. While in this embrace, the next line of *Toto's* song, although with a slight adjustment on my part, ran through my head

That's something that a hundred men or more could never do

And I could feel that this feeling was reciprocated. The strength in Ibrahim's arms clasping tightly around my body, drawing me deeply into his person. I could feel his heartbeating, I could feel each breath he took, I felt as if I could feel the very inside of his soul.

Once the initial intensity of the moment had subsided enough, I became aware that Ibrahim and I, two grown men, were embracing in a public place, a very public place, in a homophobic society where this expression of love if understood rightly would be considered a crime, a land in which love in its full expression was completely *verboten*. I also became once again conscious of the fact that I had dropped both travel bags and they lay unceremoniously around me on the ground, obstacles in the way of other travellers making their way into the Tanzanian landscape.

As I pulled away from Ibrahim and looked up at him, I noticed his eyes were slightly red and full of tears. This vision of him made me want to burst into tears with him. My goodness, my arrival had brought Ibrahim to tears!

I looked around. Our overtly emotional greeting had created an audience, some looking on in bewilderment, others with smiles on their faces, obviously oblivious to the idea that Ibrahim's and my embrace   was much deeper than a strong friendship between two people of completely different races.

I reached down to grab one of my bags and Ibrahim reached down to get the other. I was so struck by the moment that I didn't know what to say at first. It was obvious that Ibrahim was the same. He grabbed my hand and led me outside to the carpark. Unlike my first arrival into this country, Ibrahim had organised a somewhat more comfortable ride back to the township of Moshi, in what looked like a new car. This was the car of a friend of Ibrahim's from the International School and this friend had also provided a driver in the package. Ibrahim offered me the front seat next to the driver. I guessed in Tanzania, this was the seat of honour. Ibrahim sat in the back. This certainly stifled the passion for a moment. Maybe it was a good idea. Had we sat together in the back, maybe our emotions would have carried us away too far and caused the driver to report us to the authorities.

The trip into Moshi was familiar. The lengthy trip down the stretch of road away from the airport arrived at the junction that continued west towards Arusha or east towards Moshi. As no intimacy could be expressed, Ibrahim and I had to engage in friendly conversation. The wonderful thing about good feelings is that it makes one talkative and we chatted constantly for the entire trip into town.

I didn't know where we were going at first. I assumed we would be returning to the Msingi wa Mungu Project. But once we had arrived in Moshi, instead of going the familiar route to the project compound, we continued through to the township and almost smack in the middle. We were let out and then Ibrahim grabbed the larger of my two pieces of luggage and accompanied me inside a common building within the centre of town. It was a hotel. Obviously not an expensive hotel but at least it would be private.

The externals were concrete and the internals were further concrete. The stairs that led up to the next level appeared to be polished dull grey concrete as if there had been an attempt to make them look clean and shiny for the arrival of a VIP.

Ibrahim led me inside through a heavy set wooden door which creaked on opening. Ibrahim then led me inside and placed my large piece of luggage on what looked like a small coffee table in the corner of the main room. He then closed the door, locked it and drew the thick lace curtains across the window. The sounds of the outside traffic were still clear. The curtain across the window, although it partially blocked the view from outside, only half stopped the hot African sun pouring into this room. Ibrahim then just turned to me and once again embraced me. It was readily reciprocated. And so the morning was taken up with passion. The passion was obviously very strong, too strong to consider other thoughts such as my need to have a shower and a shave. I was sure that I was a bit of an offence for not having bathed or shaved since I had left Sydney about thirty hours before. But then St Peter wrote in the fourth chapter of his first epistle that "fervent love covers a multitude of sins", although I guess he really didn't have what Ibrahim and I were about to get up to in mind when he wrote this.

This physical exertion went on for some time and once completed I felt more than ever the need to have that desired shower and shave although at that point I felt too fatigued and jetlagged to do so. Ibrahim encouraged me to freshen up before having a nap during the day to sleep off the long flight from far away. And he was right. It is indescribable the refreshing feeling brought on after a long and tedious set of flights that a shower, a shave and a brush of the teeth can bring as if the riggers of the long trip wash off the body with the waste water.

I got into some fresh clothes and then lay back on the bed. I could feel the effects of jetlag creeping up on me. But I didn't want to sleep for hours and then not be able to sleep during the night so I asked Ibrahim to not allow me to sleep too long. Ibrahim got on the bed as well and let me snuggle up to his body while he grabbed a book and began reading.

When I awoke, Ibrahim was still in the same position but his book was laying down open on the bedside cabinet and he was asleep holding me with my head on his shoulder. It didn't seem to be the most comfortable position for him and it made me realise just how nice he was to do without some comfort in order for me to find some.

The movement I made when I did wake, even though I thought it was ever so slight, seemed to be enough to wake Ibrahim. Ibrahim gave a deep inhalation with the loud sound that usually went through his nose before holding me close to him and kissing me on the forehead.

"Did you sleep well?" he asked me.

I felt rather groggy. But at the same time, I didn't want to go back to sleep. I asked Ibrahim what the time was and when he replied, I realised it was still only the middle of the day. Ibrahim suggested that we go for a walk in the township of Moshi and even have lunch somewhere.

Moshi is not a large town. It is, to some degree, a tourist town only because tourists can stay in Moshi before making the ascent atop the tallest mountain of Africa, Mount Kilimanjaro. But in this sense, Moshi has to compete with the much larger and possibly more tourist-friendly township of Arusha, the same place I had gone to find out Polycarp's details from the UNHCR. But my time in Arusha had been brief, and Arusha remained a town that heralded sad news so that Arusha remained a town in my psyche where bad things were likely to happen. Moshi, by contrast, held much greater appeal to me because already so many wonderful memories were embedded in it. And now I was back here with Ibrahim to create even more wonderful memories.

Apart from that, Moshi really had nothing about it that particularly grabbed my attention. It was the size of an Australian country town, something like Orange or Tamworth. The buildings, the roadways, the public transport, the shops, every part of its little infrastructure was rather ordinary and bland. One redeeming feature of the place was a roundabout with a monument in the centre, an obelisk about the height of a three-storey building with a clock at the top, surrounded by four radiating hedges on a flat section of lawn. This organised and therefore odd feature of the township spruced up the place a little bit and reminded me of war memorials in many suburbs of Sydney with similar features.

And there was also, of course, the majestic Mount Kilimanjaro itself which created a magnificent backdrop to the township. This imposing natural monument towered up from the otherwise flat land and stared proudly up into the heavens.

The only problem with Mount Kilimanjaro was that it wasn't always obvious. It could be hidden for days behind a veil of clouds in such a way that one would not even suspect its presence. It was only on some evenings when the clouds rolled back like the curtains on a stage when one actually got to appreciate the majesty of this beautiful mountain.

Ibrahim asked me what I wanted to do in Moshi. This was a difficult question to answer because what does one do in a small town? It was like asking someone the same question in a minor suburb in Sydney. What I wanted to do was simply be with Ibrahim. Wherever Ibrahim was, I was also happy to be there. I was happy to simply walk up and down and back and forth through the Moshi streets, criss-crossing the grid patterned streets of this town. And so, that's what we did. I had seen a bit of the township before but now I got a better view of what the town was like.

In Moshi, the arrangement of shops seemed very random. We went past what looked like a supermarket but it was quite small. There was nothing of the equivalence of Woolworths, Aldi or Kmart. I wondered if I were to live here how long it would take me to find out where to get the things I needed. At least for fruit and vegetables, I knew where the market was.

We passed another shop which looked more decked out for tourists than it was for the locals. The shop window itself was jammed full of what looked like a vast array of ebony carvings of typically African figurines.

But I was simply happy to walk around and watch the world go by, at least this little part of the world. I was with Ibrahim and that was all that mattered.

When it got towards late afternoon, Ibrahim suggested that we go somewhere to have tea. In fact, I actually slipped back into English and asked Ibrahim, "What are we going to have for tea?"

When I asked the question, Ibrahim looked at me and gave me a funny look. "For tea? What we are going to have for tea is tea. What? Would you like to go and have a cup of tea now?"

"No, no, no," I replied and laughed. "For dinner. The last meal of the day. Or in Swahili, *chakula cha jioni*."

Ibrahim then laughed himself. "You call the evening meal 'tea', do you? Is that an Australian expression?"

I knew it was originally an English term.

"That's interesting," Ibrahim continued, "because in Swahili, we sometimes call breakfast 'tea', that is, *chai*, because that's traditionally what we have for breakfast. Well, we have more than just tea."

I found this fascinating because I remembered when Faisal was teaching me Dari, he said the same thing. In Afghanistan, they call breakfast *chai* as well. "Chai" was an Arabic word and came from the Mandarin "cha", the same word that the English got the word "tea", although I'm not sure how the word "cha" was converted to "tea" - there was obviously a lot of malletting to change the shape of this word from "cha" to "tea". It was understandable why the East Africans and Afghanis called breakfast *chai* and I could only guess that it was by a similar analogy that in Australia and originally in England, they called the last meal of the day *tea*.

Eventually Ibrahim took us to a bar-looking place and we found a table. It was the same type of down-to-earth place we had eaten in before. Ibrahim ordered beers for us and soon the waiter was back with the respective bottles. When the waiter had gone, I looked over at Ibrahim. Ibrahim raised his glass in an invitation to clink glasses before he took a sizable mouthful and then put his glass down.

I was very happy to be with Ibrahim. That we could finally sit together in the same time-space dimension and enjoy each other's company in so many ways could not be explained in words. I had grown very comfortable with Ibrahim and I knew at this stage that I could actually address any subject with him, including topics of a sensitive religious nature, without there being a subsequent fight. Therefore, watching Ibrahim drink his beer drove my curiosity to the point that I just had to ask him.

"Ibrahim, I'm not asking this as an accusation but simply as a question," I began. "How is it that you are a Muslim and yet you drink alcohol?"

Ibrahim looked at his glass of beer and then back at me. "Why do you ask?"

"Well, I mean, you say you believe in Allah and in the Koran, and yet you drink alcohol. I thought alcohol was forbidden to Muslims."

"Maybe it is and I refuse to obey," Ibrahim replied jovially but I wasn't sure how well he took the comment. I didn't ask the question to scold him or reprimand him or anything. It was purely out of curiosity.

"No, alcohol is not forbidden to Muslims," Ibrahim continued. "Alcohol is only forbidden to Muslims if alcohol takes over a person."

I sat back and my eyes widened to what he said.

"But I thought one of the defining attributes of Islam was the abstinence of alcohol. I mean, it is pretty much universally acknowledged that Islam and alcohol do not occupy the same space."

"Who told you that?" Ibrahim asked and he had quite a cheeky grin when he asked it.

"Well, I…er…it's just common knowledge," I replied. I knew what made me say it. It was such a standard thing. Faisal told me that it was wrong for a Muslim to drink alcohol, Faraj told me it was wrong, others of my Muslim students staunchly opposed it. I even remembered learning how that one of the Tsars of Russia wanted a national religion and had the choice between Judaism, Christianity and Islam. The reason why he rejected Islam was because of this religion's teaching of the abstinence of alcohol which was just too much for the vodka-loving Russians to abide by. The Islamic abstinence of alcohol was as much ingrained in our understanding of Islam as the need for Muslims to pray to Mecca and fast during Ramadan.

"Well," Ibrahim replied, "I follow not what people say but what Allah says. And in this case, the Koran allows for it. As it says in the Koran in Al-Nahl 16:68

And of the fruits of the datepalms and the grapes,
whence you obtain
intoxicating drink and wholesome food.
Verily, in that is a Sign for a
people who make use of their reason.

I am a person who makes use of my reason in the way that Allah has required me to use it."

I just stared at Ibrahim in total disbelief. Was Ibrahim having me on? Was there really a verse in the Koran which actually said that alcoholic drinks, "intoxicating drinks", were actually from God? Had I read this verse and simply overlooked it?

"And Allah has given a sign," Ibrahim continued, "in 'intoxicating drink'," and then Ibrahim held up his glass of beer. "This 'intoxicating drink' goes together with 'wholesome food'. For those who make use of their reason, so the Koran tells us, it is clear that intoxicating drink and wholesome food together occur naturally as a sign from Allah. Anyone who forbids intoxicating drink is forbidding something natural, something that Allah associates with wholesome food."

I stared at Ibrahim in total disbelief. I took a mouthful of beer while Ibrahim continued.

"Muslims who forbid any form of alcohol have not quite understood what Allah was saying in the verse in Al-Ma'idah 5:91 where it says

O you who believe! Wine…is an abomination of Satan's handiwork.

I mean, the usual understanding of this verse is that wine is an abomination of Satan. But how can wine be the handiwork of Satan when Satan did not create wine? As it says in Al-Nahl 16:68, 'the fruits of…the grapes, whence you obtain intoxicating drink' is 'a Sign'. These Signs, these *ayaat*, are from Allah, not from Satan.

But the key to understanding the entire situation is from Al-Baqarah 2:220 where it is written

They ask you concerning wine and the game of hazard.
Say, 'In both there is great sin and also advantages for men.'

If wine has an advantage, it cannot be the handiwork of Satan because nothing from Satan is of advantage to us.

Even the first miracle of Issa was to turn water into wine. As the Injil says in John 2:11, this was the first sign or *ayah* of Issa. If Issa was a prophet from Allah, then this *ayah* shows that Allah has blessed alcoholic drinks. And this sign of Issa is quite significant. We know that water is good for our bodies. Issa turned water into wine. But it was not Issa who really performed the Sign but Allah through Issa. So it was the handiwork of Allah. If water is good, and Allah turned it into wine, how much better is wine to water?"

I was speechless. I was amazed at Ibrahim's understanding of the verse from John 2:11 which in the King James Version contains the expression "this beginning of miracles" in reference to Jesus turning water into wine. But the word "miracles" in this verse in the original is actually the Greek word *semeion*, that is, "signs", and, therefore, Ibrahim was justified in saying that Jesus turning water into wine wasn't merely a miracle but was also an *ayah* or "sign". I just sat there. Ibrahim continued.

"Even the prophet David in the *zabour* says in Psalm 104:15 that Allah gave us wine because it makes our hearts glad. Wine, and in general, fermented juice from fruit, is Allah's gift to humans and it carries many advantages. Even further, as we see with Issa, wine is a Sign, an *ayah* of Allah."

I was stunned when I heard this. That Ibrahim was justifying his drinking of alcohol was one thing. That Ibrahim justified this directly from the Koran was mind-blowing.

"And it is in the Koran?" I asked sheepishly, almost apologetically.

"And quite clearly, 'for people who make use of their reason'. It is extremely clear what is being spoken about when we also compare the words used in each of the verses. The verse in Al-Nahl 16:68 which talks of 'intoxicating drinks' uses the Arabic word *sakaran*. Notice also in the context that it is intoxicating drinks from all fruit, not only grapes. It says the datepalm but it can also include malt or from whatever plant alcohol is made from."

When Ibrahim mentioned "malt", he raised his glass of beer in the air to emphasise this point.

"What the verse is saying is that the fermentation process is natural. Humans did not create fermentation and Satan certainly did not create it either as Satan cannot create. It is a creation of Allah, and in this verse it is also an *ayah*. When you then look at the verses which speak negatively about alcohol, the word used is not *sakaran* but *khamr*, which comes from the word *khamara* meaning 'to veil' or 'to cover'. As soon as your senses are veiled from the drinking of alcohol, you have drunk too much and now the Destroyer has taken control. Allah hates anything that 'covers' or 'veils' a person. It is the handiwork of Satan to 'cover' or 'veil', because covering and veiling cover and veil the truth."

I took a mouthful of beer. It tasted even better than ever. But now I was on my guard not to drink too much and lose Ibrahim's approval.

"Then what do you say to Muslims who abstain from alcohol and preach this?" I asked.

"If people choose to abstain from alcohol, that is their choice. And really, if someone abstains from alcohol because they are afraid that they cannot refrain from drinking too much or they are afraid that they will harm other people under the influence of alcohol, then, yes, it is good for them to abstain. As long as that person only eats wholesome food, they are still doing good to their bodies."

"Wow, Ibrahim! You are incredible!" was all I could say. Ibrahim sat back in his chair and laughed.

"Why am I incredible? Don't we all have eyes to read? Don't we all have minds to contemplate? Shouldn't all our hearts be open to what Allah has to say to us?"

Eventually the food arrived. Ibrahim indicated to me to go over to the basin in the corner to wash my hands before eating. When I returned to the table, Ibrahim then got up and did the same.

When he was back, we both got stuck into the food. I watched once again how well Ibrahim was able to eat the food with his hands without getting much of his hands dirty whereas I seemed to get food right up to my wrist.

I took a glance at Ibrahim's food and once again noticed as I had always done that he had no meat. He had ordered fish for me but his tray was devoid of meat.

"Ibrahim," I started.

Ibrahim looked up at me as he put a handful of food in his mouth and used his eyebrows to signal a reply.

"Ibrahim, I don't mean to keep questioning you on what you eat and drink but you do everything so differently to what I expect of Muslims. Again, I'm simply asking out of curiosity. I notice that you don't eat meat. As far as I am aware, the only meat that Muslims can't eat is pig meat. Otherwise, Muslims are allowed to eat any meat as long as it is halal. And yet, you don't eat any meat at all."

Ibrahim smiled and his eyes sparkled through the smile as if what I had just said was an amusing tale. Ibrahim completed swallowing that mouthful of food before replying.

"Killing and eating animals is not the plan of Allah," Ibrahim replied.

I had already put another piece of fish in my mouth and was in the process of chewing it but once Ibrahim made this comment, I simply stopped chewing. Ibrahim noticed me and then he laughed.

"Bwana Michael, remember that Allah allowed the killing and eating of animals after the Flood as punishment. That's why there has been a long tradition of eating meat. But it was not Allah's original plan."

That lump of fish was not well chewed but I forced it down my gullet and took a swig of beer to ensure that it made it down my oesophagus.

"So, God wants us to be vegetarians?"

"When we are all vegetarians, the world will return back to its original state, back to paradise."

I looked at my half eaten fish which had tasted so delicious when I had eaten the first portions but now the thought of continuing to eat it in light of what Ibrahim said made me feel as if I were on the verge of committing a serious crime. Ibrahim must have read my mind because he looked at me and laughed.

"Bwana Michael, in this instance, I am not your judge. You have to be convinced in your heart not to eat animals. I cannot convince you."

They were nice words but they weren't completely reassuring.

"Bwana Michael, I ordered this meal for you," Ibrahim urged.

This last comment broke the spell. The fish once again took on its full appeal and the guilt of eating it was removed.

"Khatyn will love you," I remarked.

"What's Khatyn?" Ibrahim asked puzzled.

I laughed.

"You mean, who's Khatyn," I replied. "Khatyn is a friend of mine in Australia. She is a vegetarian also. Not for religious reasons though but simply because she is aware that animals suffer when we raise them to be eaten. I mean, she has a point and I totally understand it."

We continued eating and then I asked.

"Where do you get this idea that we should be vegetarians?"

Ibrahim picked up his glass of beer. Each time he took a sip of beer, I couldn't get over the information he had given me regarding the Koran and the consumption of alcohol.

"In the Torah, in the beginning, Allah told Adam and Eve in Genesis 1:29 and 30

> *I give you every seed-bearing plant on the face of the whole*
> *earth and every tree that has fruit with seed in it. They will be*
> *yours for food. And to all the beasts of the earth and all the birds of*
> *the air and all the creatures that move on the ground, everything*
> *that has the breath of life in it I give every green plant for food.*

Allah wanted all animals, not only humans, to be vegetarian, to eat only fruit and vegetables. This was the world in which He created Adam and Eve, the paradise in which He wanted them to live in.

The prophet Isaiah prophesies of the time when we will return to this very state of things. In that time, not only will humans once again return to eating food that only comes from plants, even the 'lion shall eat straw like the ox' as it says in Isaiah 11:7. This can only happen when we make an effort to stop hurting and destroying one another, humans against humans and even animals against other animals. When this occurs, as the prophet says in the same chapter

> *The earth shall be full of the knowledge of*
> *Allah as the waters cover the sea.*

This will be the sign that Allah has won back the world He first created so that it is the paradise He intended it to be from the beginning."

I took a morsel of fish together with some ugali and placed the mixture in my mouth, a sense of guilt once again coming over me as I did so. The world that Ibrahim was painting, one of peace not only between humans but between all living things was certainly a beautiful one and one certainly worth striving for. But was it real?

Biologically, carnivores have a digestive system which can only tolerate a flesh diet. As for humans, all over the world from the time of recorded history, humans have always been omnivorous with meat being part of the diet, even if it only formed a small part. Only in certain pockets of the world has there been a tradition of vegetarians and vegans, such as in India.

For this prophecy to be fulfilled, not only would there need to be a switch from a carnivorous diet to a herbivorous one, the actual digestive tract of our current carnivores would have to adapt in order to effectively digest plant material.

Ibrahim further explained that humans and animals should strive towards a vegetarian diet and not destroy life as the Destroyer convinces them to do. Allah had to relent after the Flood and allow the consumption of flesh. Allah had prophesied that the time would come when we would return to the original state but it was up to us to help fulfil the prophecy.

Once all humanity had reached this stage, the animals would naturally follow suit.

A bit of a pipe dream as far as I could see. It was a commendable idea for all humans to strive towards vegetarianism. But what really intrigued me mostly from what Ibrahim said was that we humans were responsible for making prophecies come to pass. I had always understood that prophecies would be fulfilled irrespective of what humans did. But Ibrahim's implication was that prophecies could consciously be made to happen. I didn't quite agree with this idea but then there was nothing in the holy books that I had read which said that prophecies occurred independently of humanity's attempt to fulfil them.

These conversational topics had satisfied my curiousity about Ibrahim's solid and liquid consumption but then it led me to ask Ibrahim about food preparation. Ibrahim confessed that he actually didn't like cooking and he really didn't have to because he now lived with his mother and his mother's friend, seeing all his children had grown up and married and he no longer had a wife. I told him that if we were ever to live together, I would be happy to take on the role of the chef because I absolutely loved cooking and the kitchen would be my domain. I said that if we ever lived together, I could go part vegetarian but I confessed that there would be times during the week when I would continue to eat meat because I knew that without a little bit of meat in my diet I ended up being anaemic. Ibrahim just laughed and said that it didn't matter. On this score, it was up to the individual between his or her own conscience. But he did add that if we felt we should eat meat, the way animals were killed for our consumption therefore had to be humane. In fact, he said that meat eaters should be the ones who actually do the killing and this would show the cruelty of the practice and therefore possibly alter their eating habits accordingly.

After we had eaten, we took a stroll up and down night time Moshi. Moshi is not the amazing place that you would write home about but because Ibrahim was there it was the most beautiful place in the world. So many beautiful memories were being created in it. And further Ibrahim and I could walk up and down the streets holding hands because in Tanzania this was culturally acceptable. Ah! Tanzania! Because of this acceptable custom, Ibrahim and I could walk openly holding hands and express our affection to each other in public, something I could never do walking the streets of Sydney.

We returned to the hotel, got into bed and continued the romance. Once over, we had our last cleansing before finally collapsing once again into bed for the night.

The next morning we were up late. We had breakfast and then checked out of the hotel. As we left the building, Ibrahim holding my larger suitcase and me carrying the smaller one, I asked Ibrahim where we were going.

"There is someone I would like you to meet," Ibrahim replied. Ibrahim led us to a major road where there were daladalas sitting alongside what obviously was a bus stop. The daladalas were almost empty. There were men standing near the daladalas clinking coins and yelling out what I guessed were destinations. Ibrahim led us to the daladala that would take us to the person he wanted me to meet. Because we were the first passengers, we got the front row seats. Because the daladala was a reconstituted minibus, this meant that passengers who sat at the front had to sit right next to the driver. Ibrahim mounted the daladala first and allowed me to sit next to the window. The conditions were cramped and made even cramper because of my luggage but I didn't mind as we had an excellent view of the road and what was around us.

Some time passed before we finally set off. One of the many things I learnt about my stay in Tanzania was to take things slowly and to be patient. There were no timetables to follow, no busy schedules to observe, no deadlines to meet. Everything happened at a slow pace. In a way, this was actually good for me as I was on holidays anyway and it was good for my system to actually slow down and take everything at a relaxing pace.

Eventually the daladala was half full and then it was time to set off. We travelled in an easterly direction and watched the busy township become replaced by villages. When we came to the next stop, more people wanted to get on and the daladala fast approached its maximum capacity. I wondered if there ever came a time when the owners of the daladalas had to concede that it was a physical impossibility to take in any more passengers.

We continued on, stopping at small village centres. Each time we stopped, whenever there were children at the bus stop, they would look at me and call out, "Mzungu! Mzungu!" and I would smile and wave at them. *Mzungus* were a rare but welcome occurrence in this part of the country, so Ibrahim explained.

Finally we arrived at what looked like a rather deserted country area. There was a sparse number of buildings scattered around in what looked like farmland. I heard Ibrahim tell the driver to stop at the next bus stop and soon the daladala stopped and let us off.

Ibrahim then took one of my bags and led me along a dirt track which led through corn fields and up a hill into a country area where we eventually reached an agglomeration of houses as if we had arrived in a small residential area. We arrived at a non-assuming house.

"Hodi!" Ibrahim called out. I had learnt from my Swahili book that in Tanzania, people didn't knock on the door when they arrived at someone's place but called out "hodi" to get the attention of those inside. This made sense because it no doubt was a practice which began in the distant past when Tanzanians lived in much simpler constructions which

had no door to knock on and hence to get the attention of those inside one had to announce their presence. An elderly woman, dressed well in African style, colours ablaze in all directions, and her head covered in what looked like the hijab but in an array of fine colours emerged from the house. The old woman first of all looked at Ibrahim as if she were sizing him up before her face brightened up in pleasant recognition of the person who had come to her door. Ibrahim and this woman exchanged typical Swahili greetings before Ibrahim turned to introduce me. This woman was Ibrahim's mother. She greeted me in English and from the accent and the way she stumbled over words she was not as fluent in English as her son was. I therefore greeted her in Swahili.

"*Shikamoo*," I said with a smile, using the respectful form of greeting towards those one considers as one's senior.

"*Marahaba!*" Ibrahim's mother replied using the appropriate response to my greeting. She looked at Ibrahim with question marks and Ibrahim smiled and replied in Swahili that I could speak the language. Ibrahim's mother then welcomed us into her home.

Ibrahim introduced me first by pronouncing my name in the English way and then he rephrased it by saying it in Arabic. Ibrahim's mother stopped where she was standing and it was as if she had suddenly received a revelation from heaven the way her eyes lit up.

"Michael, the angel from heaven!" she said in Arabic.

I was quite taken by both the comment and how similar it was to what Musa, a former learner of mine, used to say to me quite often about my name. I felt that I was being brainwashed into believing that I was in fact Michael from heaven. But it did come across as a surprise that Ibrahim's mother actually said this in Arabic.

A conversation ensued between Ibrahim and his mother. Ibrahim's mother invited us into a small room which held a small table with four chairs. We sat down and were served tea. There was another elderly woman who came out and helped with the tea service. I was introduced to her but not explained her relationship to Ibrahim's mother and I didn't think it was my place to ask. When the other woman discovered that I could speak some Swahili, she was delighted and began asking lots of questions about me, where I had come from, what I was doing here, was I enjoying my stay in Tanzania and so on.

Ibrahim explained to me that this was where he lived. Ever since his wife had died and his children had moved away, he had moved back with his mother. However, he and his mother didn't live in the same building. The building in which we were having tea was the house in which his mother and her friend lived. There was another building on his plot of land behind the house we were in and this is where Ibrahim lived.

That afternoon, Ibrahim took me into his house and got me to put my suitcases in the bedroom. I asked Ibrahim why we had stayed at the hotel if he lived in Moshi. Ibrahim explained that he wanted to pass one night just the two of us together in much more comfortable conditions because his own house was rather basic. I replied that Ibrahim's house was a mansion simply because it was Ibrahim's.

I then asked if I could have a look around. It wasn't a large house. The walls were besser brick and the roof was corrugated iron. There was a very small toilet room with an Asian toilet inside and the shower room was small and surrounded with concrete walls. The shower rose was actually not a rose but a pipe which ran up the wall and then hooked over at the top and down onto the person who showered beneath it. There was only one tap and this obviously meant that there was only one temperature of water.

The floor of the house looked as if it were the actual rocky surface of the ground. Ibrahim noticed me looking at the floor.

"I'm really sorry for the terrible quality of the floor," Ibrahim said apologetically. "I haven't had the money to finish doing up the house. I wasn't expecting someone special like you to come to my place so soon."

"It's fine," I replied. "It's your home. And because it's your home, to me it is more beautiful than the most ornate palace."

Ibrahim squeezed my arm in acknowledged gratitude.

Ibrahim then took me on a little tour around the plot. Behind the house the hill continued up. Ibrahim took me to the top of the hill where we were welcomed with a magnificent view of the entire countryside. To the west we could see in the distance the central township of Moshi, to the south and east the land just disappeared into the horizon. To the north was the steep slope of mountain which slowly and steadily reached up into the heavens to form the uppermost peak of Mount Kilimanjaro. What a spectacular view! I just wanted to drink the view in and let it fill my entire body.

That evening, people from the neighbourhood came over to visit Ibrahim and his guest. There was no electric lighting so a few hurricane lanterns hung from strategic places in the area and a few candles were lit on the table to provide light. Even though I was introduced to each guest by name, it was as if as soon as their names were mentioned I as quickly forgot them. What I do remember was some had typical European and some typical Arabic names. And there were a few who had unusual names I had simply never heard before.

But there was one man in particular who I remembered not only his name but also our conversation. This man, from what I could gather from the way he looked and the fact that he looked grown up but had not as yet any grey hairs, was in his thirties and he had come with his parents who looked a lot more elderly. I remember that his name was Babeer. The feature which stood out about him was his beard but it was quite scraggily and patchy as my beard would be if I tried to grow one. It did not look nice on him at all. There were bare patches on the sides of his face where the hair did not appear to be able to grow which gave the impression that these areas had been scratched. In fact, the angle at which these patches were slashed on the sides of his face looked as if he were a cat who had been in one or two night fights and been badly wounded in the process. Also, his left eyelid didn't open as much as his right and looked somewhat deformed. He also had a couple of random teeth missing. His overall appearance was of a back street tomcat that had been in regular scuffles. Babeer came to sit with me and seemed to take great interest in me. I at first guessed that he simply was interested in conversing with me because I was a *Mzungu* and this was his first opportunity to actually speak to one in depth as I was able to converse in the local language.

Babeer asked me lots of questions, about where I came from, what I did in Australia as a job, what was life like in Australia and so on. His questions became more and more probing when he started asking if the pay as a teacher was good in Australia, how many times I had come to Tanzania and if I had left any family at home. He then asked if I was married and had children. I started to become uncomfortable when he asked me these questions. Because Polycarp had called me father, I decided to answer that I had a son but that led to Babeer asking if I had a wife to which I honestly answered no. Babeer had to know why. I answered this honestly by saying that the mother of Polycarp was unfortunately no longer alive and knew that Babeer would not get the play on the description. The usual reaction to this I would have thought was to express one's condolences but Babeer simply wanted to know if I was planning on getting married again.

This strangely and creepily enough led him to ask me how I had met Ibrahim. What was he getting at? Babeer's questions about the relationship between Ibrahim and me became very probing and therefore rather uncomfortable. Babeer was overtly asking these questions not out of curiosity but it sounded as if he were trying to catch me out in something. But I could also sense some jealousy in his questions. How was it that Ibrahim managed to meet a *Mzungu* and be able to invite this *Mzungu* to stay at his place? Was Ibrahim some sort of precious stone? What made Ibrahim better than anyone else that provided him the luck and the privilege of meeting up with a *Mzungu*? But further, what exactly was this relationship between Ibrahim and me?

Babeer then asked, although now it seemed like an interrogation, how I had met Ibrahim. To this question I answered truthfully as I was sure there was no need to lie about it. But why then, Babeer quizzed me, had I come back to Tanzania if I wasn't participating a second time in the Msingi wa Mungu Project but was only spending time with Ibrahim? At this stage, I wanted to tell him to mind his own business but I didn't know how to say this in Swahili and I certainly didn't want to do it here on this first evening at Ibrahim's place.

Fortunately at this point in the interrogation, one of the other guests called for Babeer's attention and he moved away from me.

My face must have been portraying what was going on in my mind because Ibrahim took one look at me and then came over to where I was seated.

"Is everything okay?" he asked.

"Yeah, yeah," I replied, even though I was lying. But how could I tell Ibrahim the truth? And in any case, what did it matter? Babeer surely couldn't do anything to harm me.

Eventually, and to my relief, the guests disappeared into the night and Ibrahim, his mother, her friend and I were alone. Ibrahim's mother and companion soon left us to go down to their house. It was almost pitch black with only one of the hurricane lamps providing us with light. I moved to an area of the courtyard away from the light to look up at the stars. Once again I saw millions upon millions of sparkling diamonds in the night sky, a rare scene. I looked around at the heavenly spectacle when suddenly I saw Orion. Smetterling's poem *The Message* came to mind and I looked at the crooked belt and the four principal stars that formed an invisible encasement around the belt.

I turned around towards Ibrahim.

"Look!" I exclaimed and pointed up at the sky. "There's Orion!"

Ibrahim looked up but he did not show the same exuberance I had on seeing this constellation. I then had to explain to Ibrahim the poem.

"I read a poem for one of my students," I began. "In the poem, the crooked belt of Orion was described as coming out of a great mountain. I interpreted this to mean that the belt of Orion in this context referred to the three Abrahamic religions because the great mountain was symbolic of Abraham, or his original name Abram, which in Hebrew means 'high father' or 'exalted father'. Mountains are high up and so representing Abraham as a high mountain is a pertinent symbol. Three stars coming out of a high mountain would therefore be an apt representation of the three religions that came out of Abraham."

"Bwana Michael," Ibrahim burst out. "This reminds me of one of my dreams."

Oh, Ibrahim, I thought, did you really have to spoil the moment? However, it was Ibrahim and he always had a dream to relate. And in any case although his dreams were odd, they were harmless.

"I dreamt," Ibrahim began, "that I was putting on a belt on my trousers but the belt wouldn't fit entirely around my waist. I could tell with the buckle in my left hand that I had the belt but while I tried to reach around my back with my right hand, I could not feel the other end. I took the belt out again and as I held it up, I realised that it had been cut and all that remained was about as long as my forearm.

I could feel my trousers slipping down and I knew if I didn't find the rest of the belt and use this to hold up my trousers, my trousers would fall and expose my nakedness. I then heard a voice behind me and Michael the archangel stood there with the other parts of the belt, one in each hand and held up high. He commanded me to give him the part of the belt I held in my hand. I obeyed even though I could feel my trousers starting to slip down so I held my knees together to prevent this from happening. Michael then told me that the belt won't perform its function until I had all three parts joined together.

Then I felt as if a large cloth was draped around me over my clothes and it was suddenly removed, and I felt so much cooler and more comfortable as a result. As the cloth was removed, I noticed four what looked like small angels, cherubs, three which looked like young women and another one, and it was difficult to know if it was a boy or a girl, holding the cloth, each cherub at one of the four corners. The cherubs brought the cloth to Michael who then placed the now restored belt in the middle of the cloth like a line along the centre. With that, the three pieces of the belt became three male-looking cherubs which like the other cherubs took hold of the cloth, and all seven cherubs with this large cloth, and I then noticed that the cloth was a beautiful intense blue, like the pure blue of a cloudless sky, flew up into the sky. As I watched them ascend into the heavens, I noticed that the cherubs were each holding against their chests a book. As they entered the sky, the pattern they formed looked like the outline of a butterfly and in fact began to look more and more like a real butterfly with its wings fluttering in the wind. As it went further into the sunset, the outline of the butterfly left an imprint on the heavens forming the seven stars of the Orion constellation. When I woke up, I pondered on what the dream might mean. That the belt was in three parts and I needed the three together was significant. The thought of the Christian trinity came to mind but I knew this wasn't correct because it is wrong to commit *sheerk*."

"It's wrong to commit what?" I asked rather bamboozled.

"*Sheerk*, that is, associating other things with God. The Christians say that Issa, the messenger, is in fact God. But Issa was only a man and so it is wrong to associate Issa the man with God."

I was intrigued, not by Ibrahim's disbelief that Jesus is God like the Christians say that he is, but that there was actually a name for such a "wrongdoing". Ibrahim's comment about committing *sheerk* was so strong as if to do such a thing were a serious criminal offence. However, I couldn't really say that committing *sheerk* was a terribly bad thing to do and I could only equate it with someone believing that the moon was made of cheese. I might consider someone who believes the moon is made of cheese rather ill-informed but I'm not sure if I would put such a person in the same category as a criminal or a wrongdoer.

"It was when," Ibrahim then continued, "I read Al-Taubah 9:111 where it says, 'A promise that He has made incumbent on Himself in the Torah, and the Injil, and the Koran' that it came to me. The Torah, the Injil and the Koran are three and I needed the three together as the Koran stated. Then I understood what Michael was saying. By only having part of the belt, eventually I will be brought to shame."

An amazing interpretation, I thought. I thought it was intriguing but that's about all.

"And?" I asked to get Ibrahim to continue the interpretation of the dream. "What about the butterfly?"

"Butterflies in our community represent loyalty, humility, wisdom and love. We have a story, *Kipepeo Amnusuru Binadamu*, that is, The Butterfly Saves Humanity, about how a butterfly through its wisdom saves humanity from dangerous insects and the diseases they bring. It is the *kipepeo*, the butterfly, through its love for humanity, the wisdom it imparts to humanity, and the humility and loyalty it shows towards humanity that brings us truth and life. But it is not the butterfly itself, the insect, but the principles the butterfly represents that bring harmony, that we humans should live these principles towards all humanity and indeed to all of Allah's creation."

When Ibrahim said this, I suddenly saw the connection. The Swahili word for butterfly is *kipepeo* and it comes from the Swahili word *pepa* meaning "to flutter", hence describing the movement of the butterfly. In Genesis 1:2 it says that "the Spirit of God moved upon the face of the waters" but the word translated as "moved" in the King James Version actually comes from the Hebrew word, *merakhefet*, which like *pepa* also means "to flutter". Was this why Smetterling used the image of the butterfly in the last stanzas of her poem? This was creepily coincidental.

"And what about the cloth?"

"The cloth is a veil," Ibrahim replied, "and veils cover something or hide something. Allah hates that which is covered and wants things revealed, in particular, the truth. That the cherubs removed the cloth from my shoulders meant that they were removing my lack of understanding and revealing to me the complete truth."

"The truth about what?" I asked perplexed.

"About the holy books and where they fit within the entire scheme of the universe."

I didn't know how Ibrahim arrived at this but I wasn't interested enough to ask Ibrahim to provide me with an explanation.

"And what about the cherubs?" I asked.

"The seven cherubs are the seven stars of Orion, the three that form the belt and the remaining four the four corners of the constellation."

"Then if the three stars which form the belt of Orion are the Torah, the Injil and the Koran, this implies that the four other stars must be four other holy books," I said.

"That's correct, Bwana Michael," Ibrahim replied. "The Torah, the Injil and the Koran were written from a man's hand. There are three holy books which were written by three women at some time in antiquity and one was written by someone but we cannot tell whether it was a man or a woman. When these seven holy books are put back together, there will finally be unity. The Destroyer has deliberately caused these books to remain hidden in order to cause instability and imbalance, to make one sex dominant over the other. This is what has caused the unrest and destruction in history. The idea is to make total unrest so that humans will ultimately destroy themselves and everything on the planet. These four books need to be uncovered so that all seven books, the three holy books, the Torah, the Injil and the Koran, and these four hidden books, can be put back in their proper place and in their proper context."

Smetterling's poem came to mind and the image in the last stanza oddly matched up with Ibrahim's analysis. The coincidence between

Ibrahim's explanation of the Orion and the poem I studied with Stuart was frightening.

"But what if we never find these other four books?" I asked.

"They will be found," Ibrahim stated confidently. "In the meantime, Allah requires us to use our intellect and our hearts to breach the gap. And other holy books not part of this collection also have remnants of what we will find written in this set of holy books."

"But why must there be seven holy books? Can't all the holy books in the world simply be brought together?" I asked.

"There are seven holy books because the number seven is holy. The other holy books are like the stars in other constellations that populate the heavens," Ibrahim replied. "They are also important. However, the Torah, the Injil and the Koran have played a dominant role in world history in the same way as the Orion constellation dominates the night sky although it shouldn't because it is only one constellation among many. However, these three books, the Torah, the Injil and the Koran belong with the four other books to create a set of seven holy books because the number seven is the number of Allah. These three books cannot be completely understood without the other four. That seven is needed to complete the set is evident. And this is evident because the number seven repeats itself in nature. Already we have seven days in a week. But also there are seven notes in a musical scale."

Ibrahim paused and then added, "And there are seven continents."

Well, that all depends on what point one is trying to make, I thought. If we consider North and South America as two continents, then we could say that there are seven continents: North America, South America, Europe, Africa, Asia, Australia and Antarctica. However, there are those who claim that America is one continent and not two and this brings the number down to an uncomfortable six. Further, the ancient symbol of the Olympic Games, namely, the five interlocking rings, back in antiquity represented that the Games were held every fifth year. However, people wanted to use this ancient symbol as the symbol for the modern Olympic Games. But for some reason it was decided that the Games would be held every four years and not every five and so this symbol had to be reinterpreted and thus forced upon it was the interpretation that there are five continents. Even so, what is considered a continent is totally arbitrary.

"Also," Ibrahim continued, "you with a chemistry background will know that the elements on the periodic table repeat themselves in seven groups."

Not quite, I thought. There are actually eight. I wasn't familiar with the idea that chemists originally thought there were seven groups in a period. However if this were true, it would make sense because the Noble Gases were unknown to exist for a long time because they were non-reactive. It certainly sounded like something Christians would have bombastically claimed as evidence of the existence of God but then they no doubt would have quietly put this idea aside with the discovery of the Noble Gases and the final formation of the Periodic Table.

I shrugged my shoulders.

"And there are also seven heavenly bodies which orbit the earth," Ibrahim said.

"Well, there's actually nine," I contradicted.

"What do you mean?" Ibrahim asked.

"Well, there are seven we can see with the naked eye, the sun, the moon, Mercury, Venus, Mars, Jupiter and Saturn. This is what led people in the past to believe that seven was the holy number. But then when telescopes were invented, we finally could see Uranus, Neptune and Pluto."

"But notice how Pluto has been proven not to be a planet which means that there are only seven planets which orbit the earth. The sun and the moon are not planets and I am sure for this reason it was corrected that Pluto is not a planet which means that in reality there are only seven which orbit the earth."

"Well, they orbit the sun," I contradicted.

"Yes, in reality. But in a spiritual sense they orbit the earth."

I looked at Ibrahim and frowned. Ibrahim was still looking up at the stars and so he didn't see my reaction. I was going to ask him to explain what it meant by planets spiritually orbiting the earth but then I felt that it wasn't worth the argument.

"There are also seven colours of the rainbow," Ibrahim added.

That's debatable too, I thought. I knew that the seven colours we were told at school were red, orange, yellow, green, blue, indigo and violet, but I could never distinguish between violet and indigo. My suspicion was that some religious person in the past didn't like the idea that there were only six colours in the rainbow because six, as Hebbeera even admitted, was considered by some Christians as being an evil number. Because seven is believed among Christians to be a holy number, two names for purple were invented to describe the last colour in the series to give the rainbow seven colours.

"This means that there are seven in the plurality of the single godhead."

I turned to look at Ibrahim.

"What?" I asked in total surprise.

"In the Torah, we read how Allah created man and woman in His image. As it is written in Genesis 1:27, 'Allah created man in his own image, in the image of Allah created he him; male and female created he them'. Women and men are obviously different so how could Allah create a man in His image and a woman in His image if Allah only looked like a man or only looked like a woman? This further shows the multiplicity of Allah. Look at you and me, we are different in skin colour. Look at the differences in humankind today. We are all different in skin colour, hair type, gender and sexuality. But according to the Torah we are all created in the image of Allah. The Torah says that Allah is all of these which if you look in the world means that Allah would have to be more than one person. But there is only one Allah. So there must be a plurality to Allah in His singularity."

It must be noted that when Ibrahim said all this, he said it in Swahili. Swahili has only one word, *yeye*, which is translated as both "he" and "she" in English. So when Ibrahim used the pronoun to refer to God, when he used the pronouns "He" and "His", these pronouns in Swahili actually could equally be translated as "She" and "Her".

"So, there are in fact seven gods?" I asked.

"No, no, no!" Ibrahim replied as if what I had said was a personal insult. "There is only one God, Allah. But in a way, Allah is also seven. I mean, there are aspects of Allah that make Him one and there are aspects of Him which make Him seven."

"But that's impossible," I objected.

"Bwana Michael," Ibrahim stated in a tone as if I needed to learn something. "You have to understand that sometimes we have to accept what is written in the holy books by faith and not question them. Our minds are not like Allah's mind. Eventually when we finally see Allah, it will all make sense."

I didn't know how to argue that point. But then I didn't want to either. I liked this image of God. It was so fresh and new, and such a progressive view of God than the old male chauvinistic gods of the Abrahamic religions. And yet, according to Ibrahim's interpretation of the Torah, his explanation was in fact the original understanding of the deity as described in the holy books.

"Then why aren't we born as both genders?" I asked.

"I don't know. Only Allah can answer that," Ibrahim replied. "But if a human is born as both genders, they are much closer to being in the image of Allah than the rest of us."

An interesting point, I thought. Although I didn't quite agree with his argumentation, I was interested to know how those who believed in the Torah would argue against it.

"But what about sexuality," I questioned Ibrahim. "Why would God have sexuality? God doesn't need to reproduce."

Ibrahim laughed.

"No, no, no, Bwana Michael," Ibrahim laughed. "Sexuality is simply a force. People don't have sex only for procreation. In fact, most of the time when humans have sex it is not to have children. It is simply a force. And it's a uniting force in the same way there is a uniting force that holds the plurality of the singularity of Allah together. Because Allah is both male and female, He has all the uniting forces between all versions of His person, male to female, male to male and female to female. One way that the Destroyer has created unrest in the world is to make certain of these aspects of the deity appear disgusting and others acceptable. This is very clever because it makes it harder to see what the Destroyer is doing. Had the Destroyer convinced us that all of these uniting forces were disgusting, all humanity would have recognised at once that this is not of Allah because all of us have this driving force within. So, the Destroyer has made one aspect of this force appear good and others evil. Whereas all humanity here on earth should be living with the total unity of the deity with all its relationships, the Destroyer has convinced many that only a small aspect of the deity should be allowed to exist. And look at the unrest as a result."

I liked that point, too. I wished I had seen this in the years I was an avid Christian.

"And you therefore understand the relationship between us, that what brings us two together is a reflection of this uniting force between two male aspects of God in heaven?"

"Bwana Michael," Ibrahim replied in a tone which indicated that he was satisfied that I had finally understood what he had been saying, "I can see now that you truly understand."

Suddenly we heard a noise like the sound of a dull thud and then a groan. I simply froze. I felt all my muscles go tense and the hairs on the back of my head stand up as spikes. Ibrahim grabbed the lantern and moved in the direction from which the noise had come. This caused the area where I was standing to become completely dark which only increased my fear.

I couldn't move. Eventually the light Ibrahim was holding came to a stop and then moved abruptly down which indicated that Ibrahim had just placed the lantern on the ground. He then called me over.

At first I couldn't move. I was so afraid but then I wanted to be where there was light and I knew it was safe wherever Ibrahim was. So I scurried in the direction of the light.

When I arrived, Ibrahim was crouching down around a human figure that was clasping his knee. It was Babeer.

Ibrahim asked him in a serious tone what he was doing there. Babeer was too busy groaning and holding his knee to be able to speak. The courage had returned to me so I picked up the lantern and held it high to provide more light over the area. Babeer was not only holding his knee, he was also rubbing his head and there were signs of blood.

Ibrahim had a good look at the head wound and then asked Babeer again what had happened. Babeer now was able to speak, even though it was more of a hiss through his feelings of pain. He simply said that he had fallen over and knocked both his knee and his forehead on some rocks. Ibrahim asked him what he was doing on Ibrahim's plot to fall over in it and Babeer replied that he could see the light of the lantern still on at Ibrahim's plot and because it was still shining, he wondered if everything was alright with Ibrahim and me. It did not sound like a terribly convincing excuse and I wasn't sure if Ibrahim really believed him or not.

Once Babeer started to show signs that he was in fact okay, Ibrahim suggested that he and I help Babeer back to his place on his plot. Ibrahim walked on Babeer's right and I on the left holding the lantern as Babeer hobbled under our support. Babeer's plot of land was a good fifty or so metres away from Ibrahim's so it wasn't too far to carry him.

When we arrived, Ibrahim called out *hodi* and Babeer's parents came out. When they saw Babeer, they were worried to see their son in this state. They helped bring him into their house. Water was brought for him and used to clean his wounds. The water washed away sufficient blood stains to reveal that the wounds were superficial and harmless.

Once it was established that Babeer was okay, Ibrahim and I returned to Ibrahim's home. We went inside, got ready for the night, got under the mosquito net and then into bed. Ibrahim made sure the curtain in the room, which looked like a used blanket, shielded the window completely and that the door to the bedroom was locked. Once the flame in the lantern was extinguished, it was completely dark inside Ibrahim's room. I could not see a thing at all. I had never for a long time experienced complete darkness like this.

I had to grope around until I could feel where Ibrahim was and then snuggle up to him. We were finally settled and all was quiet. But this disturbance by Babeer concerned me.

"Ibrahim," I whispered.

"Yes, Bwana Michael," Ibrahim replied.

"Do you believe what Babeer said?"

Ibrahim remained quiet.

"Ibrahim, I think he was actually listening to our conversation."

Ibrahim did not make a comment either way. For a moment there was silence. Then Ibrahim moved to get into a better position.

"Don't let it concern you, Bwana Michael," Ibrahim finally said. "Let's get to sleep. We have a long trip tomorrow."

Chapter 17

The next day I left the larger of my two suitcases at Ibrahim's place and took the smaller one with a couple of changes of clothes. Ibrahim also brought along a small carry bag. Ibrahim had organised to take me on a trip to see other parts of Tanzania. The first part of the trip was a long bus ride from Moshi along the north east portion of the country right down to the largest city and early capital of Tanzania, Dar-Es-Salaam. The "salaam" in Dar-Es-Salaam definitely had an Arabic sound to it and even English speakers are familiar with the fact that *salaam* is the Arabic word for "peace". Ibrahim enlightened me by telling me that the *dar* is the Arabic for "harbour" and so Dar-Es-Salaam simply means Harbour of Peace or Peaceful Harbour.

It was such a romantic name and I had this image of a beautiful city with a Middle Eastern flavour, buildings erected in an Arabic style with desert flora such as date palms and coconut palms dotted around the city. But when we arrived at the bus depot, and Ibrahim had finally negotiated among the crowds for a taxi to take us to the actual harbour itself to continue our trip to our planned destination which was in fact the island of Zanzibar, the sights, sounds and smells in Dar-Es-Salaam did everything to jar the senses rather than to pacify them. People, cars and daladalas were scattered around the network of roads like an organised mess, most of the cars and daladalas appeared to have been used beyond their use by date, the roads were not clearly edged with defined kerb and guttering but seemed to be frayed at the sides as the bitumen of the road subtly and undefinedly disappeared into the dust. The infringement on the senses by all that was around us made the name of the city sound more derisive than descriptive.

The trip in the taxi was long and torturous as the driver had to negotiate the tangled and knotted network of traffic from the west of the city, where the bus terminal was located where we had alighted from our long trip from Moshi, to the east coast where the ferry would take us on to Zanzibar.

We finally arrived at the east coast. This was the first time that I had seen the Indian Ocean from its western extremity. I imagined that if I looked hard enough, I would be able to see the west coast of Australia although I was quite sure that this was really stretching the imagination.

We made our way down to a set of buildings alongside the sea, a set of buildings which did not look very imposing but were in fact the very buildings we had to enter in order to acquire a ticket to make the great trek from mainland Tanzania to the island of Zanzibar.

I left Ibrahim to purchase the tickets. What struck me, however, and I would discover throughout the rest of my time in Tanzania, was that there were always two prices, one price for Tanzanians and one price for foreigners, the latter always being a much higher price alongside what the locals had to pay. It filled me with a sense of indignation at first. The country obviously was very discriminatory. I tried to imagine Australia doing the same, making foreigners pay more for services than the local people.

Eventually, however, I got used to it and realised in some ways the fairness. The Tanzanian earning power was significantly lower than that of other countries, particularly Western and Arab countries. If Tanzania only had one price for all, the locals would never be able to afford any of these services and therefore these services would operate solely for the tourist market. Odd as it seemed, this system of different prices for nationals and extranationals ensured equity so that everybody both locally and from outside could benefit and enjoy what the country had to offer.

The trip across from Dar-Es-Salaam to Zanzibar takes about two hours. We had a choice to go second class, which was below deck, or for an extra five Australian dollars go first class, which meant riding right on top of the ferry where at the front of the deck was only the open sky above our heads and a spectacular 360° view of land and sea. I was in a foreign land and I was on holidays so I didn't mind paying the extra money. And once we were on our way I was absolutely happy that I did.

The view from the top of the ferry was just spectacular. Once we had left the coastline of Tanzania and were on the open sea, I took turns to watch the receding African coastline on one side and the approaching coastline of Zanzibar on the other. In fact, we could see a lot of the Zanzibar coastline for much of the trip because we had to travel up from the south west of the island to the north west where the ferry finally docked. During the trip, from time to time we saw dhows sailing around, the characteristic small fishing boats with unusually-shaped sails that had been in use in this area for hundreds of years. At one moment, I thought of Vasco da Gama and his first journey into this area of the world, the first known European to venture this far from Europe and open the way for the subsequent entrance into this area by other European nations.

This was a moment which I enjoyed alone. Ibrahim sat under the shade and read the newspaper. I guessed it was a trip he had done before and hence it was almost akin to a regular bus ride from one destination to another.

As we approached the place on Zanzibar Island where we would eventually disembark, unlike the view of the receding Dar-Es-Salaam, the view of the approaching Zanzibar was as esoteric and exotic as the name of the island itself. The first building on the horizon which caught the attention was a small white tower which looked somewhat Middle Eastern in style. The closer we got, the more of the Zanzibar township was revealed to us, the tower blending in with the rest of the buildings that lined the city entrance, the style a reflection of Arabian architecture from the empire it had originally come from.

Getting off the ferry and the procedure we had to go through just to get onto the island was almost as tedious and complicated as it was for me to actually get into the country once I had arrived at Kilimanjaro Airport. I felt as if we had actually crossed an international border and were passing into another country, not arriving in another part of the same one. The immigration officials, as in any country of the world, were quite gruff. But we got through the formalities eventually and were soon on the island.

Zanzibar. The name sounds exotic, folkloric, romantic. So, entering the island was like entering a mysterious wonderland. Because of the Arabic nature of the name, I felt as if we were about to walk into a Middle Eastern story of genies and flying carpets. But it didn't take long for the fantasy to settle and be replaced by the reality of the place. Zanzibar was simply another township in Tanzania, full of everyday Tanzanians, everyday buildings, everyday transportation and all those everyday things that make up our reality.

Ibrahim led us to our hotel. The hotel itself was not far from where we had disembarked. It was a small but beautiful building and was built in the style of antiquity when Zanzibar was a part of the extensive Arabian Empire. We made it to our room which was small and Spartan, consisting of two large beds with mosquito nets draped over the sides and one small bedside cabinet. The adjoining bathroom was a small room with only a toilet to one side and then the rest of the room as if the entire room were the shower recess, a small plughole in the centre and the shower rose suspended above as the centrepiece. It was Spartan but it was really all we needed especially as I had to be frugal with my money. I wasn't sure how secure the building was to intruders but I kept everything of value on my person and what was in my bag could easily be replaced.

The trip had been long and tiring. But the adventure was not fully over. Once we had had the time to freshen up, have a shower and get into a clean change, Ibrahim had yet another person he wanted me to meet. There were a few times that Ibrahim was on his mobile phone and I recognised from his conversation that he was organising someone to actually come to the hotel in which we were staying. Eventually the guest arrived. I took one look at him and recognised immediately a stark similarity between the two men, the new arrival looking like a much younger version of Ibrahim. After a deeply moving greeting between these two men, Ibrahim introduced me to this stranger.

"Bwana Michael, this is my son, Amani," Ibrahim presented to me.

Amani greeted me with an energetic, hearty handshake and a broad smile which further showed the reflection of his father.

"So, this is the *Mzungu* who is causing my father great excitement," he said full of energy.

Amani then passionately asked his father why Ibrahim hadn't organised for the two of us to stay at his place and not waste our money on a hotel. Ibrahim gave the excuse that he didn't want the two of us to trouble him. I assumed that Ibrahim couldn't really divulge how much we also wanted to spend some time alone together and being at Amani's place would not have allowed us the freedom to express how much we wanted to keep each other's company during my short visit to the country.

Amani led us downstairs where a taxi was waiting. We all clambered in and were then taken to an unassuming small house in another area of the township which didn't seem to be far from the hotel. I could only guess that the taxi fare was rather extravagant especially as Amani did not look like he was the wealthiest of people in the area. I also thought it a burden on Amani's finances when it didn't seem too far to walk. Ibrahim was to tell me later that it was actually a safer option than walking because we had to return later in the evening and it wasn't terribly safe to be roaming the streets of Zanzibar on foot especially for a *Mzungu* because of the general belief that *Mzungus* have lots of money and therefore have no qualms about having their wallets forcefully emptied as their wallets are sure to fill up again in no time.

Also, it was a sign of respect for Amani to pick us up by taxi rather than have us walk back to his place. This was difficult for me because as much as I felt honoured by the gesture, I also felt bad that Amani spent a lot of money in a way I considered unnecessary when he could have used that money for someone who really needed it.

Amani lived in an unassuming house in an unassuming neighbourhood. However, once I was out of the taxi, I could hear children in the area yelling out "Mzungu! Mzungu!" so it was obvious that my presence was completely noticeable.

Once inside Amani's home, we were taken into what resembled a loungeroom with a couple of lounges and armchairs. There was also a television in one corner but somewhat dated and a stereo system of a type that was starting to look old fashioned. But it struck me to see such electrical equipment. I realised that I saw none of these in Ibrahim's humble cottage.

A young woman, dressed in colourful array, her head covered but still with her face exposed, entered the room with a large ornate golden tray with beautiful small glasses, similar to the types of small glasses that Faraj often served tea in when I went to his place which were apparently common tea glasses used in the Middle East. There was also a large ornate glass teapot and the rich auburn tea inside. The woman then placed the glasses in front of each of us and poured tea, smiling in silent offer.

As she was on her way to leave the room, two young girls, one who looked about four and one about two, suddenly appeared. Both stopped and stared at me wide-eyed as if I were a genie from a bottle. The woman made a comment to them and they turned and disappeared.

"My children are curious to see the *Mzungu!*" Amani commented.

"So, you have two children?" I asked.

"Yes, two daughters."

"Oh, that's lovely!" I commented. "They can come here and sit with us. I don't mind."

Amani looked at his father with a look of question marks on his face.

"Invite them in if you want to," Ibrahim then said.

Amani then called for the young woman who I had worked out was his wife to bring his two daughters in. Amani's wife returned with the two girls who came only so far into the room but then wouldn't budge. I realised that they were rather shy and possibly scared as they had never seen a *Mzungu* in real life before. I also appreciated how they felt. I could remember the first time I had seen a black person and was simply amazed but also frightened because he looked so strange.

"Come in and sit down," I said to Amani's wife.

I turned to look at Amani who once again looked at his father as if he were asking a question through his silent stare. I knew this was going to cause a problem and it was deliberate that I did this. In Australia, we are always told to respect other people's cultures and therefore accommodate them. However, when do others accommodate the Australian culture? In my culture, women and children sit together with the men because we are all one community. I knew that what I was witnessing was the Zanzibarian culture where women and children socialise separately from the men. So, in this multicultural moment, whose culture should prevail, theirs or mine?

"Yes, bring them in," Ibrahim said.

Amani's wife tried to push the two girls forward. The younger of the two refused and dug herself into her mother's leg. The other one, the elder of the two, stood there with a finger in her mouth and looked on as she came slowly forward. Ibrahim then simply got up, walked over to her, picked her up and then sat back down on the lounge next to me with his granddaughter.

"Say hello to uncle," he said quietly.

I held out my hand and touched her on the cheek. She didn't flinch but didn't respond in any particular way either. I stuck my index finger into her loose hand and she slowly gripped tightly onto it.

"Don't be scared!" Ibrahim whispered to her.

Amani's elder daughter then released her grip and then stroked the back of my hand. It was probably the first time she had ever felt the skin of a *Mzungu*. I also could relate to that feeling. I remember the first time I had ever met a sub-Saharan African and how I had touched his skin. It's strange but once you've touched the skin and felt it for a bit, the mystery finally goes away and the person who looked so strange and bizarre suddenly becomes a normal human being. Once Amani's elder daughter had touched my skin, she then smiled.

"Do you want to come and sit on my lap?" I asked, clapping my hands on my knees as an invitation.

Ibrahim passed his granddaughter over to me and she obeyed without any resistance.

"*Jambo!*" I said, using the most common word for "hello" in Swahili.

"Say 'Shikamoo' to uncle," Amani then said to his daughter.

She said it slowly and measuredly. I replied with the appropriate *marahaba*.

With that, she smiled. She then looked up at my hair. This was another part of the body that intrigued me the first time I saw a sub-Saharan African. Their hair is jet black and comes in tight curls. I particularly like the feeling when I rub my hands over the hair. So, it didn't surprise me that Amani's daughter took interest in mine. My hair was particularly long and so I pulled my ponytail around so she could hold it.

Amani's daughter hesitated at first and then slowly grabbed the end of it, pulling down but allowing the hair to slip through her fingers.

It was like a spell had been broken because once she had grown accustomed to this absolutely odd creature who had entered into her midst who in fact was as human as her father and mother, she reacted to me as if she had known me forever. The only problem was that when she spoke, I could barely understand her. This is a real problem when learning a new language. Young children speak in such a way that I find difficult to understand. I had to keep looking at Amani and Ibrahim for a translation although the translation was simply them resaying what she had just said in Swahili.

I then made a comment for Amani's wife to sit with us. Amani once again looked at his father who then welcomed the invitation. I could also tell that this was uncomfortable for Amani's wife. In the end, she came up with a compromise and brought one of the chairs from the diningroom set and placed it at a safe distance, holding her two-year-old daughter in her lap. It took a while to actually get the names of these three women. Amani's wife's name was Sarah, his elder daughter's name was Maryam and the younger was Upenza.

It was rather mean of me to show what clashes arise when trying to push multiculturalism on Ibrahim and this small part of his family but knowing Ibrahim I just knew that everyone would come out of the clash unscathed. But it was obvious that there was so much to consider in my forced experiment. According to Amani's culture, he now had three things at play: men and women socialised separately, the host had to please his guest and children had to respect their parents even when the children were grown up. So, how is a man in this culture to act when the man's guest invites the man's wife and daughters into the presence of the men while the man's father is also present, especially a father who probably brought the man up with the values of keeping women and men separate when socialising? Amani was fortunate that Ibrahim was aware that the interaction of men and women in the one place actually doesn't create a problem, probably as a result of his working at the International School, which is why Amani was not faced with the dilemma of trying to please a foreign guest who wanted the sexes to socialise together while a disapproving father did not.

But that was as far as the intermingled socialising went. When it came to having the evening meal, we men were seated at the diningroom table and served by Amani's wife who ate out of sight with her two children somewhere else in the house.

The food was brought out in different serving bowls and all of it smelt spicy and delicious. What intrigued me the most, however, was that almost all of the food was vegetarian. The only meat that was brought to the table was a plate with fish on it. Ibrahim naturally enough did not eat this. This was left for Amani and me. It appeared that despite Ibrahim's strong reasons to go vegetarian, this had not filtered down to his son. There were so many questions I wanted to ask about this. To what extent did Amani follow his father's very open and tolerant view of Islam?

Despite the discomfort of knowing that Sarah and the children were somewhere else in the house and unable to participate with their guest at least during the evening meal, the overall evening passed on pleasantly. Once we had finished, Sarah returned to pour water over our hands and then returned to clear all the eating utensils away from the table. I stood up at one moment to begin collecting plates together when Amani stood up and beckoned me to sit down and relax as I was his guest. Amani then began collecting plates and bowls with his wife and removing them from the table and the two of them disappearing into another section of the house. We were then invited back into the loungeroom where we were served more tea. Amani returned and once Sarah had once again served tea, she sat at a safe distance with her two daughters who looked on again at the strange new person in the room.

It was a pleasant evening. Amani definitely knew how to make me feel welcome which made me feel rather terrible for making him feel uncomfortable with my insistence of forcing him into a predicament.

At one stage, Ibrahim got up and went with Sarah and the children out of the room. I was left alone with Amani.

"More tea?" Amani asked. I replied in the affirmative.

There was a moment of silence as Amani poured the tea. He sat back, made himself comfortable and then took a sip of tea. He then put his glass back on the table, leant back and looked up at me.

"You love my father very much, don't you?" Amani asked without flinching. I thought I was going to spray my tea out I was so shocked by the comment. I then looked up at Amani as I didn't know exactly what to say. In a way, it was like payback for the uncomfortable situation I had put him in earlier in the evening although it probably wasn't his actual intention.

"What do you mean?" I then asked hesitatingly and measuredly.

Amani sat back in the lounge with absolutely no signs of discomfort as if this were a conversation occurring in a country full of freedom as in Australia, not in the closed society of Zanzibar.

"My father loves you very much," Amani continued.

It felt as if all the heat in my body was forced into my face.

"Don't worry," Amani reassured me. "I understand the situation."

He then laughed and he sounded so much like his father when he did so.

"I certainly don't understand it. But he is my father and he has always been a good man. In Tanzanian society, we have to honour our parents. I have friends who honour their parents because it is what society expects of them but their fathers have not been good people. But my father deserves the utmost respect. He was very good to his children."

Amani paused and then added, "He even looked after orphans."

I sat there for a moment and listened.

"He ensured," Amani continued, "that we all got a good education."

He then gave me a funny look.

"Not all of my father's children grew up with my father's good character, unfortunately."

Amani looked as if he had gone into reflection. But that was the only comment he made about a sibling who had strayed off the rails a bit and all I ever learnt about Ibrahim's other children from Amani. Amani then returned to the original conversation.

"When I discovered that my father loved you, I certainly was shocked. It's a pity, though, that he feels that he has to leave the country to live with you. I would rather he stayed here. You would be fine in Tanzania. Tanzania is a very peaceful country."

Everything, therefore, was out of the bag so there was no use hiding it. In a way, this relaxed me quite a bit and allowed me to then open up in conversation.

"Amani, it wouldn't matter to me where I lived with your father, here in Tanzania or back in Australia, because I simply want to be with him. The issue about living here, though, is that it is illegal. It's against the law and it's a crime which carries a criminal sentence."

"Bah!" Amani exclaimed with a dismissive brush of his hand in the air. "Yes, they say it's a crime. But these things go on here anyway and people ignore it. It might be in the law but no-one takes that seriously."

"That may be the case," I replied. "But it's there in the law. People may ignore this law. But if this law served their interests, they would use it."

Amani shook his head and screwed up his face to show his disagreeance with my statement. "I have never heard of cases in Tanzania of men being tried. True, in other African nations it happens but not here."

That you have never heard of such cases, I thought, doesn't mean that they don't go on. In the comfort of your heterosexuality, of course you would never hear of such cases, unless it occurred to someone you knew personally. I wanted to push this particular point but I didn't have any evidence so it wasn't a point of view I could substantiate.

I moved the conversation to other aspects of Amani's father, in particular his father's tolerance of other religions. Amani explained that he grew up with his father's views of respect for other religions. In his adolescent years, after his mother's death, his father took a further interest in the Torah and the Injil and explained to Amani the koranic basis for this respect. Apart from the idea that Christians view Jesus as more than simply a messenger, Amani agreed that by simply acknowledging that Jesus like Muhammad was only a messenger of Allah, the Gospels still could be appreciated by Muslims because the Koran itself still teaches that the Gospels like the Koran are a sign from Allah.

Amani hastened to add that as much as his father taught him this, this was still not well appreciated within the society on the island of Zanzibar or in greater Tanzania. It would take a complete societal overhaul within the Muslim majority to accept this view of Islam.

"But it's not your father's particular view of Islam," I objected. "Your father quoted this from the Koran."

"Yes, I know," Amani continued. "However, just because people say with their lips they believe in Allah and the Koran, this doesn't mean they actually show it by the way they live. Allah Himself says in Al-Ankabut 29:3 and 4, 'do men think that they will be left alone because they say, 'We believe', and that they will not be tested? And We did test those who were before them. So Allah will surely distinguish those who are truthful and will surely distinguish the liars'. Those of the Muslim community are being tested to see if they truly believe in Allah. Not many of them, however, are passing the test and the social unrest that results shows clearly what happens to those who fail. My father and I wish the rest of the Muslim community would recognise this."

I thought that this was an interesting analysis.

"Allah also says in the Injil," Amani continued, "through Issa, 'Not every one that says to me, Lord, Lord, shall enter into the kingdom of heaven; but he that does the will of Allah'. I feel sorry for many in the Muslim community who think they are going to heaven because they do things that they think are right in the name of Allah when in fact they are going against everything Allah taught them so much so that we can hear Allah still crying out today as He said through His messenger Isaiah in

Isaiah 29, 'people draw near to me with their mouth, and honour me with their lips but they have removed their heart far from me'."

As soon as Amani quoted from the Koran, the Gospels and the prophet Isaiah, I realised that the resemblance between him and his father was not only in appearance. Amani was in many respects a chip off the old block. I was intrigued, also, how Amani had altered the verse I was familiar with from the Gospel of Matthew from 'the will of the Father' to 'the will of Allah'. Was there anything particularly wrong with referring to God as one's father? I didn't think Christians understood this in a literal sense but more in a way to show the closeness between God and humans. Also, his quote from Isaiah was not exactly word perfect but it certainly was Isaiah's overall meaing.

"Unfortunately," Amani continued, "there are those who call themselves Muslims here but then they destroy churches and attack Christians. But they do this even though Allah says in Al-Hajj 22:41 that it is within 'churches, synagogues and mosques wherein the name of Allah is oft commemorated'."

Amani then sighed. "The father of our nation, Mwalimu Julius Nyerere, certainly brought us to independence in unity of tribe and religion. Those who create mischief here are going against both the father of our nation and the tenets of their own religion."

Listening to Amani speak, I could hear Ibrahim. Like father like son and amazingly so.

Amani then stopped and looked at me. He then smiled.

"At least my father has a nice *Mzungu* friend and one who speaks Swahili. That's really impressive."

"I'm amazed," I replied after a moment's pause to this statement, "that you both know the situation between your father and me, and that you accept it. How do the rest of the family feel about it?"

Amani shook his head and smiled.

"The rest of the family don't know about it. My wife doesn't know. No-one in the community knows. It is still considered here a disgusting and unacceptable thing. Tanzanian men are very macho."

"Yes," I replied. "I'm quite aware that in many countries relationships between men are not accepted because macho men feel this is some sort of threat to their masculinity."

Amani smiled, shrugged his shoulders and nodded.

"This is true," he replied. "After all, a man likes to be king in his family."

"And hold ultimate power," I replied. "And like a king, men like to boss everyone else around. In order to do that, there has to be an excuse for men in society to view themselves as better and higher than everyone else, and in particular, higher than women. Otherwise, if a man concedes equality with his wife, there are times when the man has to do things for his wife. But I can understand that. It's only human for us to want to be at the top and then boss everyone else around and have everyone fulfil our own personal desires without caring that those we boss around also have desires. I can see how religions, and in particular the Abrahamic religions, have exalted the man so high that their gods are purely masculine."

As soon as I said this, I thought of Ibrahim's explanation of God being both masculine and feminine. Even though Ibrahim's explanation was supported by the Torah, such an understanding in fiercely patriarchal, male-chauvenistic societies would never take root.

"But such societies," I continued, "are not just. They cause untold misery to everyone below them. And that's why men like your father and me are treated so despicably. That we form a bond in a similar way to a married couple in some way makes these men feel as if we have feminised these men's masculinity, as if feminising anything was something terrible, implying anything associated with the female is something inferior. Such a bond between two men forces them to see that they may actually need to share their power with women. And with everyone else for that matter."

"You sound just like my father," Amani stated and laughed. "I can understand why he loves you so much."

I smiled in acknowledgement to Amani's comment which was to a degree a compliment.

"The thing is," I continued, "that it doesn't make sense to me that men can consider themselves better and higher than women because we need both men and women in a community. Both play very much similar roles."

"But men are stronger than women," Amani replied. "You have to appreciate that."

"Yes, on the whole this is true," I replied. "But what tasks do men do today that require more strength than a woman? I mean, I'm a teacher. I would never make a better teacher than a woman simply because of my masculine strength."

"But in the family, you need one decision maker," Amani added. "If both are equal, then no decisions would ever be made in a family."

"Okay," I conceded, "perhaps in the end there needs to be one final decision maker. Probably better said, in the end there has to be one final decision. But why does it always have to be the man who decides? Or only the woman? Can't there be times when the man decides and another the woman? After all, if men are given the total power to be the decision makers, they will always make decisions that suit themselves without considering what women think of the decision. I don't see how that's fair. Nor do I see how that helps a family and a society to prosper."

There was silence after that comment. I reached over and took a sip of tea. I decided to use the silence to add a further comment.

"This, then, is why men like your father and me are not acceptable in many societies. Societies in which men are considered higher than women consider men like your father and me as an extremely dangerous threat. Macho men in these societies abuse, torture and kill men like your father and me not because our relationship is bad or affects anyone else but because relationships like ours threaten male dominance and force men to share their power with women."

"That is a point," Amani admitted. "I know that in western countries it is accepted that my father and you can have a relationship. Tanzania hasn't reached that point yet. Many Tanzanians still believe that it is a phenomenon introduced from western countries."

"How?" I asked almost as an outburst. "How can anyone introduce this to anyone? Who introduced this to your father? And those who say it was introduced from the west, it has to have been introduced after the 1970s because that's when it first began to become tolerated, at least in Australia. That means that there have never been men and women like this in Tanzania and indeed among the sub-Saharan Africans in the past before the coming of the Europeans. And that is totally untrue."

Amani shrugged his shoulders. "That's what people think here. They also say that it's not a part of Tanzanian culture and therefore that's why it is still looked on so negatively. African culture is for a man and woman to marry and have children."

I stared at the ceiling and then looked back at Amani. "But it's not a matter of culture, either. Your father and I have these feelings for each other irrespective of what the culture is. But if people in sub-Saharan Africa want to put culture before anything else, why did Africans struggle to stop the *Mzungus'* culture of the trading in African slaves? Slavery was once a part of their culture so why did the Africans insist on *Mzungus* changing their culture to be fairer and treat Africans as equals? And why did the sub-Saharan Africans insist that their countries become independent and not remain under *Mzungu* rule? I mean, just like men in this society want to be the boss, *Mzungus* in world society, at least back then, wanted to be the boss over everyone. It was not right for the *Mzungus* so it's not right for African men. Don't Tanzanian men see the comparison?"

Amani laughed. I was quite amazed at his ability to see into what I was saying.

"I don't know, Bwana Michael," he replied. "Maybe a new generation will rise up and see things differently."

"But you can already see this?" I asked.

"Bwana Michael," Amani replied. "To be very honest with you, if I had not known about my father, I would have maintained the same belief as all other macho Tanzanian men that this relationship between him and you was wrong. But my father was a good father to us children and worthy of respect, not only because it is in our culture to respect our parents but because my father was a great man. Because of this, I have had to change my thoughts about the whole matter. Also, now that I have met you, and from what my father has said about you and all the good things you do, that you came all this way to help someone out, and now listening to what you have to say, I am forced to think differently about it. And I can see that you will make my father very happy."

Amani stopped there which gave me a moment to reflect. Did you listen to yourself? I thought. Let's substitute a few other hypothetical aspects of a person and see if you could say the same thing. "If I had known that my father was a murderer/rapist/thief/child molester, I would have had to change my thoughts about murderers/rapists/thieves/child molesters." No, you would never say that. This just shows that your father's sexuality is not in the same league. It wouldn't matter how much you loved and respected your father in your childhood if one day you found out he made a practice of murdering people in cold blood, or raping people, or stealing things of great value, or molesting children. These would actually cause you to no longer respect your father, and in some ways fear him. The reason why you can continue to respect your father with this new knowledge of him is because deep down you know it is not inherently a bad thing. The only problem with it is that it makes people feel uncomfortable to know that people engage in such activities that others would never engage in themselves. Further, it upsets the view of male dominance because now there is a relationship in which both partners treat each other equally and forces heterosexual men to ask the question that maybe they should be emulating this equality with their wives and stop considering women as inferior.

What was particularly frustrating, I continued to say in my mind but not outrightly to Amani, was that your father had to exceed in goodness in order for you to accept his sexuality. But this contrasts starkly with these other aspects: it wouldn't matter how much your father exceeded in goodness, you could never accept his murders, rapes, thefts or child molestations had these been aspects of him.

Amani then broke through my thoughts. "It's sad, though, that you two cannot live here together. My father will be living very far away so I won't see him for a long time."

I was surprised once again by the assumption that Ibrahim was definitely coming with me to Sydney. It had not been established as far as I was aware that such a thing was possible. As for the point Amani made about me living with Ibrahim here in Tanzania, I also agreed with him that it was a shame that we couldn't live together in this way. I would definitely miss Polycarp and Jeremiah who I now considered very much my sons. However, I would have very much liked to have stayed in Tanzania and continued to help out at the Msingi wa Mungu Project or in a similar organisation and help children who had been orphaned or anyone else who was disadvantaged, especially the gay boys and girls whose voices I heard begging for my help during the debate at the Nyika. Both Ibrahim and I had the view that we wanted to give disadvantaged children a better education and disadvantaged people in general a better life. That we would be intimate with each other from time to time would satisfy a normal natural human urge as well as help to solidify our togetherness. But it would be such a small and private part of our lives. Ibrahim and I had no intention whatsoever of anyone actually seeing what we did together when we were intimate. It would only be a problem with the macho Tanzanians if they felt it necessary to actually try to imagine what Ibrahim and I were doing whenever we were together in private.

At this point of the conversation, Ibrahim came back into the room holding Maryam who once again had a finger in her mouth.

"I'm very sorry, Bwana Michael," Ibrahim said by way of apology as he entered the room. "One of the neighbours wanted to talk to me. But I'm sure my son entertained you well."

Ibrahim came and sat down with Maryam on his lap. Soon after, Sarah returned and took Maryam, saying that it was well past her bedtime. Ibrahim then made the comment that as it was Maryam's bedtime, in a way it was also bedtime for him and me as well.

Amani made a call on his mobile phone and soon he indicated for us to get up. We said goodbye to Sarah, Maryam and Upenza and left the house. Once outside the house, the taxi was already there waiting to take us back to our hotel. I felt so bad about Amani paying for such an expensive form of transport and so I nudged Ibrahim and secretly tried to pass money over to him so that he could pay the taxi driver on my behalf. Ibrahim in secret reply indicated to me to put my money back in my pocket in a way that he didn't want Amani to know what was going on.

Once we had arrived at the hotel, we said goodbye to Amani. I gave him a big hug and thanked him for his hospitality. Amani then spoke very quietly in my ear obviously to not allow his father to hear, "You look after my father." He then pulled away and while holding onto my shoulders added, "I'm sure you will."

Ibrahim and Amani then said their goodbyes in the same emotional way as they had greeted each other and soon Amani was back in the taxi and then disappeared into the night. Ibrahim then directed me to lead the way back up into the hotel room. It was later that evening that Ibrahim explained to me that as much as my gesture to pay for the taxi ride was nice on my part, this would have been considered a shame to Amani.

It was an interesting night and I was so glad to have been able to speak to Amani on his own. He caused so many thoughts to float through my mind.

The following morning we once again got up late. We were on holidays and I wanted to take things slowly. We didn't get downstairs to breakfast until rather late but it was still early enough to be considered breakfast and the cook was still willing to serve us. Breakfast consisted of an omelette on a couple of slices of extremely white and tasteless bread and a cup of coffee. Certainly not a filling nor appetising way to start the day.

Once breakfast was over, Ibrahim, the noble person that he was, asked me what I particularly wanted to do for the day. I simply wanted to roam around the township of Zanzibar, soaking up the atmosphere and letting it soak right through me.

Ibrahim took me out to an area of Zanzibar town called Stone City. Stone City is a labyrinth of small streets or alleyways so narrow that the only way to get through these alleyways is on foot. These small streets weave in and out between walls at times exposing a small shop here and a small market there. Even though the sun was blazing above us, once inside this maze of alleyways, we were hidden from the sunshine and walked in the semidarkness caused by the shadows cast by the tall walls on every side. But it provided great pleasure walking around.

There were times when we stopped to look at the wares on display in the small shops. The poor shopowners tended to think that they were in luck and about to get a sale each time we stopped to look at the goods for sale. I was simply curious to look at many of the odd objects on sale but had no intention of buying anything.

There was one shop that caught my attention. On one of the walls was an ornate calendar which displayed not only the months but also the signs of the Zodiac. Why it caught my attention was because of the artwork and the effort the artist went into to actually design the calendar in this way. The Zodiac sign that was the most prominent was Aquarius, draped in what looked like a colourful toga, bearing an amphora full of water ready to be poured. Some of the calendar was blocked by a cage with two yellow birds which I guessed were canaries. One of these birds was fluttering around agitatedly while the other just sat quite calmly. Soon the realisation as to why one of the birds was madly fluttering around was made apparent when I saw above on the rafters from which the cage was suspended a grey, mottled cat jabbing its paw at the top of the cage. I was captivated by the fact that only one bird actually was frantic while the other sat calmly, possibly because it had not at that point in time sensed the danger lurking above it.

We finished our wanderings through Stone City and began walking over to the shoreline. We walked along the road which ran parallel to the shoreline when I noticed that the building with the tower I had seen from the ferry was actually a museum. I told Ibrahim that I wanted to go inside.

The museum was absolutely fascinating. There were artefacts on display of typical objects of this part of the world both objects of every day life as well as traditional African art. Although the artefacts were of considerable interest, it was the information about the history of this part of the world that particularly caught my interest. From this I learnt a lot about the history of Tanzania and indeed much of Africa itself although with more focus on the eastern regions. What most fascinated me was that there was evidence of civilisations within the African continent which predated even ancient Egypt. There was a Kingdom of Nubia which was situated somewhere within the area of modern day Sudan. One of the great feats of this kingdom was the mastery of the smeltering of metals and the fashioning of tools from these metals, a skill that was later passed on to ancient Egypt. It was hinted that the Nubian kingdom actually originated further south in the area of present day Uganda. There was another kingdom which existed also around the time of the Kingdom of Nubia called the Kingdom of Kush. This also was a flourishing kingdom and a significant civilisation which also influenced the later developments in the well-known Egyptian Kingdom. Both the Kingdom of Nubia and the Kingdom of Kush were two great empires inhabited by black sub-Saharan Africans.

The information became more interesting when I read that the ancient Egyptians themselves were, in fact, a Negroid race. Evidence for this came from the writings of the Greek historian, Herodotus, who in the fifth century before Christ stated quite clearly that the Egyptians like the Ethiopians of antiquity were a race of people with dark skin and black woolly hair. When I read this section, I simply looked at Ibrahim and looked at these same features in this man here with me. Another piece of evidence was the comparison of the vocabulary of the ancient Egyptian language and various sub-Saharan tribes today where there were obvious similarities in the words and grammatical features amongst these languages. Further evidence which suggested that the ancient Egyptians were in fact inhabited by people with the same features of today's sub-Saharan Africans was the fact that many of the well-known gods of Egypt, such as Osiris and Isis, were often depicted with skin as dark as charcoal either painted onto a blank surface or fashioned from dark ebony.

Evidence also suggested that the people who inhabited other ancient civilisations which bordered Egypt such as the Canaanites to the north were also Negroid. I was especially struck by the Canaanites being black, and in particular having features like Ibrahim's. I was also struck by what was written here at the museum about the Canaanites, that they were in fact a civilised race of people. So the Canaanites were black and civilised? Does this therefore imply that the story of the Israelites coming into Palestine and invading the Canaanite civilisation was akin to the barbarians who came into Europe and brought the civilised Roman Empire to an end?

Centuries later, a flourishing trade developed between Arabia, India and East Africa. This began with the rise of the Arabian Empire in the 600s when the Arabs created an Empire which extended out from the Arabian peninsula as far east as India and as far west as Spain. Eventually the Arabs began trading with the inhabitants of the east coast of Africa. The people in East Africa were not simply primitive people living in mud huts. There had developed a great kingdom called Zimbabwe, which is now the name of the modern country which borders with Tanzania to the west. Zimbabwe was at that time a great kingdom inhabited by sub-Saharan Africans who transported goods to the east coast to trade with the Arabs who had sailed down this far south. Trade was so extensive in this area of the world and there was evidence that even ships all the way from China had sailed to the east coast of Africa.

It was in this museum that I discovered that the word *Swahili* came from the Arabic word, *sawahil*, which is the plural of *sahil* meaning "coast" so that *sawahil* means "coasts". When the Arabs came to this part of the world, they established the island of Zanzibar as a sort of headquarters from where they could conduct trade with other parts of the coastline. The exotic name *Zanzibar* came from the Arabic *zinj barr*, that is, "black land", that is, the Land of the Blacks.

Because of the trade and then the intermarriage between Arabs and sub-Saharan Africans, a new race of people and a new language developed, Swahili. The Swahili language structurally is an African language, belonging to what is known as the Bantu family of languages. However, about half of the words used in Swahili are of Arabic origin although the original pronunciation of these words has since been altered to fit the Bantu characteristic pronunciation. I noticed that this was similar to the way that a large amount of French vocabulary had infiltrated the English language but the pronunciation of these words has been altered to fit English pronunciation patterns.

The coming of the Portuguese to this part of the world was for us in Australia the first step in the final colonisation of Australia by the British. What this museum showed was just how European-biased our history classes had been. All we had known about this part of the world was Vasco da Gama's epic voyage around the Cape of Good Hope and his eventual arrival at Goa on the Indian coast and hence the beginning of European interests in this part of the world. What was not taught was how the Portuguese single-handedly destroyed the illustrious trade and hence the wealthy and advanced civilisations that had already been established along the eastern and northern rim of the Indian Ocean centuries prior to the coming of the Europeans.

The Portuguese certainly left their mark. Mozambique, the country directly south of Tanzania, was a country dominated by Portugal and today the inhabitants there still speak Portuguese as the official language. Portuguese had also left a few remnants of vocabulary in Swahili. This finally explained to me why the Tanzanians called the Bible *Biblia* which came not from Spanish but from Portuguese, and it was understandable why I originally thought it was a Spanish word because after all Spanish and Portuguese are very similar languages with a lot of overlap in vocabulary. A number of other words from the Portuguese language made their way into Swahili such as *bandera* for "flag", *pipa* for "barrel" and *padri* for "priest".

Eventually other European nations made their presence felt. In the late 1800s, the Germans came to this part of the world. They at first established a treaty with the locals of the area and developed trade. However, eventually the locals felt that the Germans were interfering too much in their locality and hence they led a revolt to get rid of the Germans. This had the reverse effect as the Germans were able to crush the revolt and soon Germany took control of this part of East Africa. Germany made Tanga, a city on the north coast of present day Tanzania, a military post and a type of a capital of the area. Germany began to call this area on the East African coast that it controlled Tanganyika, where Tanga was the name of the central town, and *nyika* was simply a word meaning "wilderness" or "grassland", something akin to the Australian outback, and a word I had become familiar with when the debate at the Msingi wa Mungu Project was carried out at the Nyika. Hence the name the Germans gave to their colony of East Africa meant something like "Tanga and the grassland", that is, Tanga and the stretches of land around it.

The Germans appeared to contribute little to the Swahili language, the only word I recognised as being German was *shule* meaning "school".

Germany lost Tanganyika to the British at the end of the First World War. The British had already taken control of Zanzibar Island and now after the Great War they had control of both Zanzibar and Tanganyika.

As a result, many words from English poured into the Swahili language. However, it was not all one-way traffic. A few common words from Swahili managed to make their way into English, such as *safari* which in Swahili means "a trip" or "a journey" and *mumbo-jumbo*, which literally translates as "things thing" or "problems problem". Also, the *lala* in the word *lalaland* in expressions such as "I think he's now in lalaland" meaning that he is now sleeping, comes from the Swahili word *lala* meaning "sleep".

Then Julius Nyerere arose to the scene. Nyerere led this East African nation to independence which it finally gained in 1961. Nyerere combined Tanganyika and Zanzibar to create one country. He took the first three letters of each country, namely Tan and Zan, put them together and added a final ia to the end of the word and finally came up with the present day name of Tanzania.

Although Tanganyika and Zanzibar are united today, Zanzibar is now fighting to become a separate state from Tanzania. A lot of this is because Zanzibar is inhabited predominantly by Muslims and hence the inhabitants want their island to be somewhat of a separate Muslim state.

The building itself in which the museum was held was actually a gift from the British to the Sultan of Zanzibar at the time the English had begun to establish colonial interests in this part of the world. However, later it became derelict. Fortunately, the building was once again revived and made into a museum.

The museum was a real eye-opener and it revealed to me how little I knew of Africa and of the history of the sub-Saharan Africans. Africa had always been considered the Dark Continent but this museum made me question who in fact was making it dark. But what I learnt from the museum made me want to investigate more about Africa and its rich past. However, unlike museums I had visited in the past, there were no books on sale in the gift shop which provided indepth information about any of this history on display.

But there was one book which caught my attention: *Nyerere, Freedom and Socialism, Uhuru na Ujamaa, A Selection From Writings and Speeches 1965 – 1967*. I knew that the word *uhuru* in Swahili meant "freedom" so I immediately made the connection that *Ujamaa* actually meant "socialism". I picked the book up once I had made this connection.

"Nyerere was a communist?" I asked Ibrahim in horror.

Ibrahim laughed. "No, he wasn't a communist, he was a socialist."

"So, all that you were saying about *Ujamaa* was actually about the political movement of socialism?"

Ibrahim laughed again. "Well, yes," Ibrahim confirmed. "Mwalimu Nyerere was all for socialism as a political movement."

"But we know that communism doesn't work, nor does socialism," I remarked.

Ibrahim breathed heavily through his nose. "Bwana Michael," he answered, "when I think of *Ujamaa*, I don't think of it in the political sense. Think of it more as a heart attitude, irrespective of the political party in power."

The puzzled look on my face caused Ibrahim to continue. "Bwana Michael, when you left your country and came to Tanzania to help Polycarp, you did this because of the principles of *Ujamaa*. Now that you look after Polycarp and Jeremiah as if they were your children, this is also because of the principles of *Ujamaa*. I'm sure that your country is not a socialist country. But you do this irrespective of the political ideology governing your country at the moment. I'm sure that it would not have mattered which ideology was governing your country, you would still be helping Polycarp and Jeremiah. So, in effect, you live your life according to the principles of *Ujamaa*."

It took a while for me to absorb Ibrahim's interpretation of socialism. However, the only way I could dissociate socialism as the political ideology and socialism as a heart attitude as Ibrahim indicated was to actually use the Swahili word *Ujamaa* to refer to Ibrahim's original explanation of the word he gave me when we travelled to Arusha. This certainly sounded like a better explanation of socialism and its political sibling communism. Ibrahim's explanation also made me even more interested to read what Nyerere had to say.

"Have you read this book?" I asked Ibrahim.

"No," Ibrahim confessed. "However, I am familiar with Nyerere's principles and I'm sure this will help you to understand more about what Nyerere was trying to achieve in the country."

I bought the book with the intention of reading it on my way home on the plane.

From there, Ibrahim and I wandered around aimlessly in Zanzibar until late afternoon. Ibrahim suggested we return to the hotel for a short break before going out again to get something to eat.

While we relaxed in the hotel room, I decided to have a sneak preview of Nyerere's speeches. I started with the introduction and hadn't gone far when I read something in Nyerere's speech which leapt from the page. Nyerere talked about how in a society built on *Ujamaa* people should not discriminate. There was mention that there should be no discrimination between people of different tribes or religions. But it was this stress on being non-descriminatory that caught my attention. This is the society we had established in Australia. Does this make Australia a society built on *Ujamaa*? This became especially apparent as later in this speech, Nyerere confessed that democracy was a part of *Ujamaa*. That comment certainly drew me in.

But there was a beautiful description that *Ujamaa* is built on the principles of upholding human dignity and respecting the differences found in different people. It didn't matter what the physical characteristics of a person were, whether the person was a man or a woman, and then this was followed by a long list of other attributes that make up the human species, such as skin colour, length of nose, height, physical strength and so on. Human differences were immaterial. In fact, what Nyerere actually said was despite the differences between the attributes of all humans, in the end, all humans are equal. I could easily read sexuality as another physical attribute within this long list. And in so doing, I felt that I was reading our anti-discrimination laws but in a very well and beautifully argued way. Yet, homosexuality was still considered a crime within

Tanzania. If the father of the Tanzanian nation was so revered for bringing the nation to independence based on the principles discussed in this book, I could well understand Ibrahim's comment on the bus ride from Moshi to Arusha that Nyerere had died and left the Tanzanians wandering in the wilderness. A society built on *Ujamaa,* so Nyerere argued in the very first speech recorded in this book, respected all people. How then could Tanzanians respect Nyerere but not respect this very principle? How could male Tanzanians continue to uphold a macho male attitude of treating women as lesser and inferior and at the same time revere the man who said that in a society built on *Ujamaa* everyone with their differences was valued and their differences harnassed to the benefit of this entire society irrespective of their gender and further of their sexuality? I could almost hear Amani's voice as I read this: "as Allah says through his messenger Isaiah in Isaiah 29, 'people draw near me with their mouth, and honour me with their lips but they have removed their heart far from me'."

I had to show Ibrahim this. Ibrahim acknowledged a familiarity with the principle even if he wasn't familiar with this particular speech. I was taken in by this. I wanted to read on but decided to leave it for later when I travelled home on the plane as I would have plenty of time to read the book then.

That evening, Ibrahim and I walked from our hotel to a place called the Wharf. It really was only a large open area where locals prepared local fair. This area was a mix of tourists and local Zanzibarians and there was a wonderful carnival feel to it. The flames from the barbecues lit up in the darkness and danced around like will-o'-the-wisps or magical night-time beings from a children's fairytale book. The smell of barbecued food wafted through the air and stimulated our appetites. There was one place where food on skewers, cooked over open fires, was sold. Ibrahim asked the chef if he could prepare a vegetarian skewer for him. He asked me what I would like. He hastened to add that if I wanted one of the skewers with meat on it that I was welcome to eat it. I looked at Ibrahim shyly and admitted that I did want the one with meat. Once we had eaten, we strolled around in the Wharf for a little while longer. I soon became tired and so we returned to our hotel to sleep off the excitement of the day.

It was amazing how so much had happened in so little time on the exotic island state of Zanzibar. Zanzibar has such an exotic name, almost like the name of a place in a dream. So much had happened here and so much I wanted to remember. I had also learnt so much about Africa and the people who inhabit this place. At the end of such an exhaustingly long

day, it was lovely to curl up with Ibrahim and enter the dream state within
this little dream state.

Chapter 18

The following morning we checked out of our hotel in Zanzibar and made our way back to the mainland of Tanzania. We travelled back on the ferry and all the while we sailed I watched the dhows sailing around, living remnants of a life from the past when travelling by sea like this in this part of the world was a common feature. And which still was. The sun shone down on us and with Ibrahim in close proximity to me, the feel of the sun, the smell of the salt spray and the spectacular view of the coast of Zanzibar Island on one side and the east coast of the African continent on the other, I couldn't think of a better time in my life.

Once we had embarked in Dar-Es-Salaam, instead of staying in the city, Ibrahim said that he wanted to take me to another place of historical significance to Tanzania and indeed to the east coast of Africa when the entire north western area of the Indian Ocean was once a thriving seafaring network of trade routes between the east African coast, India and the Arabian Empire. Ibrahim organised a taxi to take us up to a place about an hour by car north of Dar-Es-Salaam called Bwagamoyo. Back in the time when the east coast of Africa was part of the Arabian trading route, Bwagamoyo became a place where slaves captured in the interior of the continent were brought to a sort of holding station. From Bwagamoyo, the slaves were shipped to Zanzibar and from Zanzibar the slaves were sold to the rest of the known world at the time, the Arabian Empire under its various guises in the north, and then later to the Europeans who later found a way around the southern tip of the Dark Continent.

We came to the actual building and compound of the holding station which had been turned into a museum. However, it was obvious that it was not a museum well visited because the building showed signs of wear and tear with sections of the walls potted with holes where the concrete had fallen out.

We were provided a tour guide who took us around and explained the different sections of the area. It was more a depressing place than a place of enlightenment. What amazed me the most, however, was to discover how late in history slavery continued as an institution. On display in one section were various documents in German granting the bearer of the certificate his or her release from slavery. And they were dated in the early 1900s. I was just stunned. This meant that people living during my great Uncle William's childhood had been treated as no more than a mere commodity.

The historian who had set up the museum obviously was a native Tanzanian who took the opportunity to have a go at the Europeans and Arabs who in a former epoch had treated sub-Saharan Africans as less than human, probably to put those of us of European or Arabic heritage to shame for what our ancestors had done. However, this historian had either inadvertently or possibly intentionally used the opportunity to also poke a serious gibe at the religions the Europeans and Arabs had brought to this part of the world. There was an inscription on one of the walls of the museum. I read it with wonderment.

Europeans, so the text began, believed that trafficking in slaves was not only a lucrative practice but was also justified by their religion. The Europeans looked to the Bible and used the following to justify their trade in slaves:

Cursed be Canaan! The lowest of slaves will he be to his brothers.
Genesis 9:25

You shall not covet your neighbour's… manservant or maidservant.
Exodus 20:17

Your male and female slaves are to come from the nations
around you; from them you may buy slaves. You may also buy some
of the temporary residents living among you and members of their
clans born in your country, and they will become your property.
Leviticus 25:44, 45

Slaves, obey your earthly masters with respect and fear.
Ephesians 6:5

Slaves, obey your earthly masters in everything; and do it,
not only when their eye is on you and to win their favour,
but with sincerity of heart
and reverence for the Lord.
Colossians 3:22

Arab traders also justified their trade in slaves because in the Koran slaves were a possession, in particular, "what your right hands possess" and the Koran provides clear guidelines as to when slaves may be freed which meant Muslims must have had slaves in the first place.

Marry …what your right hands possess
Al-Nisa 4:4

Forbidden to you are married women, except
such as your right hands possess
Al-Nisa 4:25

Show kindness to… those whom your right hands possess
Al-Nisa 4:37

He who kills a believer by mistake shall free a believing slave
Al-Nisa 4:93

Allah… will call you to account for the
oaths which you take in earnest.
For expiation…give a slave his freedom.
Al-Ma'idah 5:90

Success comes to the believers… who
guard their chastity, except from…
what their right hands possess
Al-Mu'minun 23: 2, 6, 7

Disclose not their beauty save…
to what their right hands possess
Al-Nur 24:32

Marry…your male slaves and female slaves
Al-Nur 24:33

We have made lawful to you… whom your right hand possesses
from among those whom Allah has given you as gains of war
Al-Ahzab 33:51

Once I had read these verses, what formed in my mind's eye was the image of a European and an Arab trader, whips in hand while roughly pushing along a group of captured Negroid Africans. Another European and Arab with more sympathy towards humanity looked at them in anger and demanded how could they be so cruel and inhumane as to treat human beings as a simple commodity. I could then see the European and Arab slave trader stand tall with crossed arms still gripping their whips, tapping their foot like the Wicked Witch of the West and saying, "Well, the Bible/Koran says that we can have slaves so who are you to argue with Jehovah/Allah?"

As the guide continued our tour, I pointed at this on the wall and nudged Ibrahim to get his attention to look at it and read it. The guide, however, moved on without waiting for us. I decided to take a photo of the verses with my smartphone and show Ibrahim and discuss what I had read later with him.

If Bwagamoyo was designed to shame the *Mzungus* and the Arabs for the wrongs their forebears had committed in the traffic of slaves, the tour had its desired effect on me.

The tour ended with a walk to the driveway entrance to a hotel situated right on the coast. As we approached the main building, on the left was a large pyramid about two metres high. Attached to the pyramid was a small plaque which read

*Here is the place where the German Colonists used to hang to
death revolutionary Africans who were opposing their oppressive rule*

This was a double shame for me. Not only was the tour guide showing us where the Europeans hanged Africans who rebelled against the tyrannical European rule, the particular Europeans being aimed at were in particular the Germans, a people to whom I now realised I was kin. But in my now mixed heritage, there was a mixture of feelings. I felt ashamed of my German ancestors, those related to the Germans who had established a colony on the east coast of Africa and committed the atrocities against the local Africans, but also a sense of loss for my German-Jewish ancestors who suffered at the hands of these same Germans, and my German Australian ancestors who suffered under the Anglo-Australian authorities in Australia. Within my person I could feel all these feelings at once, the guilt of the oppressor and the remorse of the oppressed as if I were oppressor and oppressed all at the same time.

Being a part descendant of the former Teutonic Europeans who had come to this country which had already been inhabited by people who were then made their slaves, I asked the question, how could a descendant of someone who had been treated as subhuman and as a commodity seriously love me like Ibrahim did? But Ibrahim had also told me that he was part Arab part Bantu. I wondered if he was experiencing the same mixed feelings that I was experiencing.

The tour guide continued with his talk. He explained how the Europeans were at least in comparison to the Arabs much more humane. The Arabs, in contrast to the Europeans, once they had captured male

Africans, castrated them before taking them back to the Arabian continent and selling them on as slaves. The Arabs did not come to the east coast of Africa to proselytise the sub-Saharan Africans but to enslave them.

So how then did Islam become the established religion in this region of the world? When the Arabs first came to the east coast of Africa, so the tour guide explained, they took their slave bounty back to the Arabian Empire and sold this bounty off to prospective buyers. During their stay in Arabia, the slaves were forced to observe the rites and rituals of the Islamic faith and hence had learnt at least some of the common prayers such as the *Al-Fatihah* and the *Shahada*. Certain slaves, however, managed to escape and make the long trek down the east coast of Africa back to their homelands. Once they had arrived back in this area of East Africa, they explained to their fellow countrymen that if they wanted to avoid being captured by Muslim slave traders from Arabia, these East Africans simply needed to learn the Arabs' prayers. When the Arab slave traders again arrived on the east coast to take slaves, the East Africans simply recited the prayers to show the Arabians that they were brothers in the faith. If the East Africans were fellow Muslims, the Arabians could not take them as slaves as the Koran, so they had been told, only allowed for the taking of slaves who were of the infidel.

However, there was another story which explained the origin of Islam on the east coast of Africa. This story comes from the journal of an Arab explorer. In 920 AD, a group of traders from the Arabian Empire, so this journal reads, sailed along the coast of East Africa to a thriving city called Kanbaloo. However, there was a storm which drove them further south of this city. The inhabitants of this part of the coast of the Dark Continent were believed to be cannibals so when the inhabitants came out off the coast in their boats and approached the Arabs, the Arab traders feared for their lives that they would become the next meal of these sub-Saharan Africans. However, it turned out that the king of these people preferred to trade with them rather than eat them. Both these east coast Africans and Arab traders spent time with each other trying to establish business. Then the king of the people of the east coast was invited on board the Arab trading ship and offered a ride back to the Arabian Kingdom. However, the Arab traders, now far enough away from the coast, knowing that the king of these east African people would fetch a good price as a slave, betrayed the trust of the king and sold him into slavery. The king remained in the Arabian Empire for some time during which he learnt Arabic and became a convert to the Islamic faith. However, he managed to escape and make the long trek from Arabia down the east coast through Ethiopia, Somalia, present day Kenya and all the way back to his homeland south of the city of Kanbaloo. As he was king of these people, he was able to persuade the subjects of this area to convert to the Islamic faith and hence establish Islam as the religion in this part of the African continent. The same Arab traders once again years later sailed from Arabia to the city of Kanbaloo but once again were blown off course by a storm and once again were driven further south to arrive at the same place where they had been years earlier. They were brought ashore and to their amazement and terror discovered that the king whom they had years earlier sold into slavery in Arabia was once again on the throne back in his homeland. The Arab traders feared for their lives. However, the king spared their lives despite their betrayal. The king then told the Arab traders that they were now Muslims like the Arabs and so the Arabs had to trade with them and treat them like brothers.

Although this story was much more pleasant than the first one, there was something mythical about it, especially as the Arab traders miraculously were blown off course twice and forced once again into the presence of the king whom they had earlier sold as a slave. However, it still remained that the reason why Islam was introduced to the region was not because the East Africans were terribly convinced of the religion but because converting to Islam simply was an insurance policy against being made slaves by Arab traders. Hardly a positive endorsement for the Islamic faith.

The tour guide seemed to tell these stories with a subtle snub of the nose at the Arabs for their treachery in dealing with the Africans as slaves. I looked up at Ibrahim briefly to see his reaction but he did not seem to flinch or see any reason to see anything wrong with this.

What was further shocking about this monument was its location. A one hundred and eighty degree turn and you were facing a plush hotel on the shoreline of the East African coast. We took a stroll past this building and were soon on the beach. The beach was just spectacular. The view of pristine tropical beaches was an expectation on a deserted island in the remotest area of the Pacific Ocean. But to see the same on the coastline of Africa was just unbelievable.

But I could not enjoy the view or the luxurious hotel, however. I wondered who in their right mind chose to build a hotel on this very location. No doubt the descendants of those who were once the ruling class from Europe or Arabia came to this hotel to relax and get away from the rigours of their routine lives. But to come to this hotel required passing this monument. I wondered to whom this monument was making more of a mockery: the native Tanzanians from days of yore who would not bow the knee to the foreign oppressor and in their resistance faced this terrible fate only years later to find that the descendants of these oppressors succeeded anyway and though the Africans had gained independence these foreigners still find a place to rest and enjoy themselves in this country at the expense of the locals? Or was it towards the tourists whose ancestors were related to the ruling class which once ruled this country and put those whose country it was into slavery to make them feel guilty at the thought that relatives of their ancestors also once relaxed and enjoyed their leisure time in this place?

The trip to Bwagamoyo was mentally and emotionally draining for me. The shame of being the oppressed and the guilt of being the oppressor struggled together inside of me as if I were personally bearing all within my person. I could well relate to the oppression of the sub-Saharan Africans because my race was also an oppressed race. Homosexuals, bisexuals, transsexuals and all those who did not fit in neatly within the traditional mores of the general global society have for time immemorial been oppressed, crushed and killed for their resistance. Yet, unlike this monument in Bwagamoyo, I was totally ignorant of the existence of any monument made out to those of my race and species that had fought and lost against the oppressor.

When the tour guide had completed his job, he allowed us to wander around the Bwagamoyo compound and investigate it in more detail. I purposely pulled Ibrahim with me back to where I had seen the verses from both the Bible and the Koran which illustrated quite clearly that these holy books endorsed slavery.

When I pointed this out to Ibrahim, Ibrahim looked through the verses and then commented, "I'm sure these verses don't mean what they say they mean."

"It did when the Europeans and the Arabs came trading in this area of the world," I replied quite pointedly. "But not only that. Have a look at that first quote from Genesis chapter nine. Do you know the full story behind this curse against Canaan?"

Ibrahim admitted that he wasn't sure of the story.

"According to the Genesis story," I related, "Noah had three sons, Shem, Ham and Japheth. Shem was the father of the Hebrews, which is why we call these people 'Semites' today and use the expression 'anti-semitic'. Ham was the father of the black races, in this case, people like you. And Japheth was the father of all the Europeans, the *Mzungus*, people like me, although this makes it difficult for me because I now know that I am both a descendant of Shem and Japheth."

Ibrahim looked at me in deep thought as if he didn't believe what I was saying.

"It also makes it difficult for me because I am therefore a descendant of Shem and of Ham," Ibrahim replied.

"And you are not the only person I know who has a mixed heritage from Shem and Ham. Ishmael, Abraham's first son through Hagar, was like you, the child of a descendant of Shem through Abraham and a child of a descendant of Ham through Hagar, as the Torah says that Hagar was an Egyptian. It is said that the Arabs are actually the descendants of Ishmael and if the Torah is true, Ishmaelites have a problem because within their own person they have both the slavemaster and the slave within their physical makeup. I don't know how you feel about it but if it were me, I would find this unsettling."

Ibrahim then paused and said, "And the Bible says that about Noah's sons?"

"Not as clearly as that, but it doesn't take much to work it out. The name 'Japheth' comes from a Hebrew word which means 'fair' in both English senses, that is, 'good to look at' but also 'light-coloured'. Already the word carries prejudice because it assumes that *Mzungus* are better-looking than the other two races because of their fair skin, something which I certainly don't agree with. The name 'Ham' comes from a Hebrew word meaning 'hot' and by extension, 'burnt' that is, 'burnt like charcoal', that is, 'black'.

After Noah and his family came out of the Ark, Noah planted a vineyard and one day got roaring drunk. He was lying in his tent naked and his youngest son, Ham, came in and saw him naked. When Noah had sobered up and found out what Ham had done – and the Bible doesn't actually say how Noah found out so it's left up to us to guess – Noah then cursed Ham, but strangely, he did this by cursing one of Ham's sons, Canaan. The implication is that Ham's descendants would become the slaves of the descendants of Shem and Japheth, which was fulfilled during the trade in slaves in the 1700s, 1800s and early 1900s by the Europeans, and by what we have learnt today even earlier by the Arab slave traders. There is nothing in the Bible or in the Koran which indicates that slavery should be abolished and the verses displayed here show that."

Ibrahim gave a sheepish laugh. "But how can you be sure that Ham was the father of all the Africans?"

"Because," I continued, "in the next chapter, Genesis chapter 10, the four sons of Ham were Cush, Mizraim, Canaan and Phut. Cush is just another name for Ethiopia and Mizraim is just the Hebrew name for Egypt."

"Mizraim," Ibrahim repeated. "That's similar to the Arabic and Swahili word *misri* which also means Egypt."

"And," I continued, "it is evident that the Ethiopians are black. As for the Egyptians, the view that we have of them today as resembling Arabs may not actually be historically correct. Remember what we saw in the museum at Zanzibar where it said that even Herodotus said that the Egyptians had black skin and woolly hair, which describes sub-Saharan African features, not Semitic or Arabic features. This also implies that the Canaanites were black. This further shows the racism of the Torah against blacks because Abraham in Genesis 24 didn't want Isaac to marry a Canaanite and then in Genesis 28 Isaac tells Jacob the same thing, not to marry a Canaanite. Why? What was wrong with the Canaanites apart from the fact that they were black?

The Koran in a similar vein supports the idea that having black skin is something negative, in this case, that it is evidence that a person is a *kafir* and therefore evil. As it says in Al-Zumar 39:61 that 'you will see those who lied against Allah with their faces blackened' and in Al-Imran 3:107 it says that 'on the day when some faces shall be white, and some faces shall be black. As for those whose faces will be black, it will be said to them, 'Did you disbelieve after believing? Taste, then, the punishment because you disbelieved'.'

What amazes me about sub-Saharan Africans, both Christian and Muslim, is that many of them support the Bible and the Koran which are overtly racist against blacks and in particular sub-Saharan blacks. What you don't realise is that because you support these books, in time they will come back to bite you."

Ibrahim didn't say anything to that either way. In a way I felt bad about what I had said to him because I knew Ibrahim believed in these books as divine revelations from a compassionate God. But at the same time, I felt that Ibrahim really had to face the reality of these verses.

The trip from Bwagamoyo simply filled me with many thoughts but Ibrahim didn't seem to be fazed by any of it. He chatted to the taxi driver while I sat at the back of the car with my physical eyes looking outside at the passing view of the countryside but my internal eye flicking through the pages of history of humanity and the eternal struggle between the oppressed and the oppressor.

We eventually made it to Dar-Es-Salaam. The city was its usual tangled mess of cars and run down buildings. It was probably the worst time of the afternoon to arrive there because we got caught up in the late afternoon traffic. The roads were congested like nothing I had ever seen before with cars faced in every direction as if this were the vastest car park I had ever seen. The exhaustion of the day only was made all the more exhausting by being trapped inside a car in the middle of the traffic going nowhere or at least only in occasional bursts of movement only to be followed by lengths of time of immobility. How the traffic was untying the knots further down the line was totally unknown. It seemed ages before we managed to pass through what seemed to be the central part of the city and soon head away from the coast but in what direction I could not exactly tell, whether it was south west, north west or simply due west.

We eventually made it to what seemed like a small rundown suburban area of Dar-Es-Salaam. We left a tarred road only to bounce along a dirt track which was still wide enough to be considered a main thoroughfare and possibly from my understanding of Tanzania no doubt a relatively upmarket suburban area within the Tanzanian context. The houses looked considerably well-kept with only a few showing signs of neglect and the need of a fresh coat of paint on the otherwise bare concrete monolithic structure to bring it back to life.

We eventually arrived at a place with tall concrete walls which looked like the façade of a penitentiary. The taxi driver let us out and we soon found ourselves standing at the gateway of this large complex. The gates which led into the complex were open which to me was a good sign that it wasn't necessary to keep everything meticulously locked up and secure in an unsafe neighbourhood. In fact, a casual glance down the street revealed that there were signs of openness everywhere which helped me to feel relaxed and safe in this unknown area of the city.

We had hardly begun to enter the complex when what looked like a typical Muslim Tanzanian came out and greeted Ibrahim with the most expressive greeting which showed that Ibrahim and this man knew each other well. There were exchanges in rapid Swahili and then Ibrahim introduced me to this friend of his, whom I found out was called Hamadi, and we were welcomed into his home.

As we made our way in, it became obvious that within these walls were a number of small buildings which abutted against the periphery of the inside of the walled area. The central courtyard appeared to be a common area for all the residents in this enclosure. Certainly not very private.

Hamadi came across as being more Muslim than Ibrahim, at least in appearance, simply because of his facial appearance. He had a fully grown bushy Muslim beard. His clothes were somewhat Arabic, a long type of robe which reminded me of the toombarn that the Afghanis wore but which came down almost to the ground like a one-piece pyjama men of old or at least in cartoons and films from my youth wore which meant that they were ready for bed. His feet were sandaled as if he were about to walk the dry sands of the Meccan desert. My immediate aversion to his appearance being related to acts of terrorism against non-Muslims immediately filled me with fear but his friendliness towards me and his hospitality helped to assuage this fear somewhat.

Hamadi grabbed both my and Ibrahim's bags and led us inside his humble abode. And it was rather humble. We entered through the front door and stepped immediately into what could be considered the loungeroom. Inside this room were a few lounges and matching armchairs to form a lounge set with a coffee table centrepiece. The only thing was that the lounge set was rather large for this very small room that there was little space left to move around let alone place anything on the floor. It was as if Hamadi had seen the furniture on sale and simply bought it without taking into consideration the actual size of the furniture in relation to the smallness of the room it was soon to occupy.

We manoeuvred through this cramped room into another room beyond it. This was the bedroom. Inside was what I had become accustomed to, the large double bed so large that it looked as if it could have fit Hamadi, Ibrahim and me so comfortably that none of us would ever notice the other during the hours of sleep.

Hamadi was offering this bed for us to sleep in but there was no other bed in the room. Did this mean that we were definitely, all three of us, going to sleep together in the one bed?

Once I had a chance to take in the surroundings, I realised that there were a few rooms missing that we would have in a conventional residence at home. There was no kitchen and there was no bathroom. The thought was beginning to form in my mind when Ibrahim turned to me and asked if I wanted to have a shower – or as he liked to phrase it, a bath.

The shower was away from Hamadi's lodgings, a separate small building abutting the inside wall of this small castle-like enclosure. The shower recess was simply a small room with a wooden door, fortunately covering the entrance so well that no indecency could ever be exposed when the door was closed. The only trouble was that once inside, there was very little light except for that which crept in under or over what the door did not seal.

Once inside, I noticed that there was a tap and a shower rose with the now familiar one-tap-one-temperature I had grown familiar with. I had my shower and then Ibrahim decided to have his. This forced me to be alone with Hamadi for some minutes. I really didn't know quite what to say. Hamadi looked so much like the terrifying stereotypical Al-Qaeda bully except that he was extremely dark skinned in comparison. If by some misadventure I ended up in the same space-time dimension of an Al-Qaeda terrorist, what would be the topic of our conversation? This made me further pose the question: when two Al-Qaeda bullies were alone together, if they weren't talking about who or what they could blow up, did they engage in other topics of conversation? Did they reminisce about their childhood days, talk about the weather, their families, the latest football results, the latest TV sitcom, funny youtube sites or amusing anecdotes of events in their past? Was there ultimately something human below the hardened exterior they presented to the world?

The fluffy beard, also, was a typical characteristic of the devout male Muslim. Was it in the Islamic religion that the measure of one's righteousness was equivalent to the length of one's beard? What if you were someone like me who found it difficult to grow facial hair in a way that looked suitable if not at least presentable?

Hamadi broke through my thoughts by asking me some questions. At first I couldn't get past his fluffy Muslim beard. However, Hamadi obviously was used to foreign guests as he very quickly made me feel welcome and asked me questions about my trip in Tanzania, where I had been and what I had done. He listened intently and allowed me to elaborate. I found that quite fascinating. Like Ibrahim, he tended to listen intently and show interest in what I had to say.

Once the ice had melted and I felt more and more relaxed with Hamadi, the fluffy Muslim beard began to look less like the mask of a man with a sinister mission and more the face of a man who decided to grow a big, fluffy beard because he liked having a big, fluffy beard.

Through our conversation, I discovered that Hamadi had a wife and two small children who had gone to stay with Hamadi's wife's mother who was unfortunately rather sick at that time. Hamadi had remained at his home because of his work but also because Ibrahim had told him in advance that he was coming for a visit.

Eventually Ibrahim came back refreshed and as handsome as ever. Hamadi raced around Ibrahim as if Ibrahim were an imam from the local mosque. Hamadi at one point in humility told Ibrahim that he needed to step out for a little while and asked us to simply rest and relax until he came back.

This gave me the opportunity to ask more about Hamadi. I discovered that the little room at the back of this small house was where everyone slept as Hamadi's two children were still very small. Where they would sleep when the children grew older and if Hamadi and his wife had more children was a mystery. However, Ibrahim explained to me that for our one night's stay Hamadi would no doubt make other sleeping arrangements for himself and allow his two guests the comfort of his own bed.

Ibrahim then explained to me that Hamadi had been orphaned as a child and Ibrahim had welcomed him into his own family, even though Ibrahim already had four children of his own. The Koran, so Ibrahim explained, requires that people look after orphans and he answered this call. This really touched my heart and made me see further the depth in Ibrahim's beautiful character.

Soon, Hamadi returned. Ibrahim suggested that we go for a drink not far from Hamadi's home. In fact, it was barely a minute's walk from the entrance gate of Hamadi's compound to where we had a drink. We walked through the gate, turned a corner and before us was the stretch of dirt road we had ridden over in the taxi with a vacant lot on one side and high concrete fences, almost like a fortress, on the other. The fence led to what looked like a little shop where the shop front was simply an open window but heavily barred with thick metal meshing enough to be able to communicate through comfortably but not large enough to even insert one's index finger. Inside was a small young man sitting motionless, a series of candles providing the only light within and casting shadows on the walls as if the movement of dark images danced within and created the only motion. There was in one corner of this shop what looked like a very old refrigerator from antiquity.

On seeing the three of us arrive at his shopfront window, the little man at the counter immediately came to life. Ibrahim spoke to him and the little shopowner responded by leaving the shop at a side door which led onto what looked like a small passageway I guess to the shopowner's house. The shopowner soon returned carrying two plastic chairs and then walked across the dirt road to the vacant lot. Ibrahim by a hand movement made the indication for Hamadi and me to follow. Once the chairs were down, Hamadi motioned me to sit down in completely respectful gesticulations, and then did the same for Ibrahim. There was the respectful argument where both men told the other to sit down by which time the shopowner appeared back with a third chair and a plastic stool which he placed in the centre of the three of us. The shopowner then returned to his shop and in the shadows of the inside we could see him taking bottles out of the refrigerator and placing them on a tray before walking back over to us. He then placed the tray on the stool. I noticed that both Ibrahim and I had been served a beer but Hamadi was served a bottle of lemonade. This was the first time I had ever seen a Muslim not drink alcohol.

As was the custom, the shopowner then opened each bottle and poured some of the contents into glasses beside the bottles before retreating back into the shop and returning to his immobile state. The way he came to life and then returned to his motionless state gave me the impression that he was one of those mannequins at fairgrounds where you put a coin in the slot and the mannequin comes to life, sings a song or tells a story and continues until the value of the money has been consumed at which time the entire internals of the box return to its original lifelessness.

Once I had taken a few mouthfuls, the effect of the beer overcame me and the entire atmosphere became really wonderful. I sat on this chair out on a vacant lot down the middle of a street in a suburban area of Dar-Es-Salaam out under the starry night of the Tanzanian sky. I was with Ibrahim and in the company of a new Tanzanian friend. There was something so wonderful about that night. There was something very relaxing about this atmosphere.

This also helped me to relax and ask Hamadi about how he knew Ibrahim, even though Ibrahim had already told me. Hamadi confirmed what Ibrahim had already told me about him, how that Ibrahim had taken him in when his parents had died. Hamadi related all this with reverent awe for Ibrahim and threw in a few expressions of "praise Allah" in Arabic to substantiate his reverence. I thought to myself that Allah actually didn't do anything but rather it was Ibrahim who had done all the work, a thought, however, I kept safely to myself. As a result, Hamadi had made a vow that he would thank Allah for helping him by devoting himself to his religion.

It was a lovely and touching story. However, the thought went through my mind: wouldn't it have been better to learn from this experience that whenever he came across anyone in need that he helped that person in the same way as Ibrahim had helped him? Wouldn't that be much more beneficial to his community, his society and indeed to the rest of the world? Wasn't that Julius Nyerere's whole point when he tried to establish *Ujamaa* in Tanzania?

As the night wore on, more and more people came to this basic bar. Makeshift tables and chairs were scattered over the vacant lot as if the shopowner were the proprietor of this block of land. A few people recognised Hamadi and some even recognised Ibrahim as they came to this area of the street. At one time, Hamadi took out his mobile phone, made a call and I heard him telling the person at the other end of the phone that "Baba" was here. I guessed that this "Baba" was Ibrahim so I surmised that there was another sibling in the area. Eventually, two young men came and joined us. One was a dark-skinned African so I assumed he was a Tanzanian. His name was David and he gave Ibrahim a very warm greeting. It was obvious that David and Ibrahim were also very close, very much like Hamadi and Ibrahim. David then hugged Hamadi also quite overtly and emotionally.

It was obvious that David followed the Christian faith because he had a golden cross suspended from a gold chain around his neck. So this came across to me as extremely strange. Hamadi, obviously Muslim to an extreme, and David, a Christian from what his jewellery indicated, were both happy to sit and have a drink together. This Tanzania was showing me more and more that people of different religious persuasions could, after all, get along together if they really put their mind to it and these sub-Saharan Africans were truly leaders in this quest.

Then I found out that David also had been an orphan and Ibrahim had taken him in as well. Therefore, David and Hamadi had more or less lived together as brothers. I was overly intrigued because this meant that David grew up in a Muslim household and yet Ibrahim both took him under his care and allowed him to remain faithful to his religion. This really made me see more and more the deepness in Ibrahim's beautiful character.

The friend who came with David had a much lighter complexion and much more refined features than the average sub-Saharan African. Although he greeted all those around us in Swahili, when he continued talking, he spoke in English. This caused everyone at our makeshift table to shift to English as the main language of conversation. Ibrahim and Hamadi switched over quite naturally as if speaking Swahili and speaking English were speaking the same language. David's friend's name was Abdullahi and I found out that he was actually a Somalian refugee who had found refuge south of his country here in East Africa. A Somalian refugee in Tanzania. I had always assumed that only wealthy countries like Australia took in refugees.

I was aware that Somalia was traditionally a Muslim country and Abdullahi carried a typically traditional Arabo-Muslim name. But that was as far as the stereotype went. Nothing about Abdullahi revealed his Islamic background. For a start, he was clean-shaven. And then, he wore local African clothes. And when the shopowner like a small obedient servant came to serve him, Abdullahi asked for something which turned out to be quite alcoholic.

In fact, what he ordered to drink was in itself a fascination. The shopowner returned with a beer for David and then what looked like a plastic pouch made of clear plastic, inside of which was a clear, watery liquid. Abdullahi tore open the plastic pouch with his teeth and poured the liquid into his glass. On opening the pouch, the contents revealed themselves through the strong odour of some liquor, something which smelled of vodka or ouzo.

Abdullahi was particularly fascinated by me and it soon became evident as to why. I was a *Mzungu* from a wealthy *Mzungu* land and he was a refugee who wanted, like many of his compatriots, to find refuge in a country like mine and not stay in Tanzania. It was true that Tanzania had offered him refuge but as the conversation progressed, he was considered as an outsider and would, so it would seem, remain this way. This affected his status as a citizen in Tanzania and this hence was very limiting on the life he was allowed to lead. The only occupation he was offered was that of a labourer but it appeared from the way he described it that he was the next best thing to a slave.

During the conversation, I looked at Abdullahi, Ibrahim and Hamadi and the striking contrast between them. All three of them were Muslims but Muslims of such distinctive and obvious degrees. Back home we were constantly told that we had to respect Muslims for their beliefs. But it was obvious here that Muslims did not hold one purely, distinctive belief. There were variations on what was considered appropriate facial hair, attire and attitudes to drinking, very much as varied as it is amongst men in general in any society the world over. Take the word "Muslim" out of the equation and we simply had three men who held different beliefs about their personal aesthetics and the admission and prohibition of the drinking of alcohol. The religion starkly had nothing to do with it.

I had seen the same thing among Muslim women. You could place a number of Muslim women together and one would be dressed with her hair flowing unabashedly like any woman from any modern country, one would wear some sort of veil but loosely crowned to still reveal the hair above the temples, one who wrapped her hair in a cloth as if she had just stepped out of the shower and wanted to ensure all her hair was covered until it dried, one who covered much of her face so that all you could see were her eyes and then the woman who was completely covered in cloth to the point that she was indistinguishable as a human being. All these women could confidently claim that they were Muslim and yet the way they dressed their heads was so different. Could it be asked which was more Muslim than the other? Was it possible to have varying degrees of Muslimness? And what did this mean?

What intrigued me yet further was that in Islam the measure of how religious Muslims were was in the way they excelled in something as impractical as in the amount of cloth a woman wore over her head or how long a man grew his beard. In fact, this was where all religions had something in common. The more one exerted energy into some impractical exercise the more religious that person was. Christians are looked on as more saintly and more religious by the frequency they read the Bible or attended church or sat or lay on the floor and spoke to nothing but the air around them.

When I thought about it, why wasn't the measure of saintliness or the religiosity of a person the amount by which their actions actually made an impact on preserving the earth that religious people say their gods created than in engaging in such futile acts? Wouldn't it be more pertinent for religious people to say, "so and so is so religious. They don't waste food, they recycle all their paper and any extra food or money they make or every spare moment of their day they share it with those in their community who are in most need."

But the evening wasn't only spent in reflecting on religious oddities. It was a strange mix of five men with different stories to relate. I can barely remember the conversations now. What remains is that wonderful night under the stars, in some backstreet in Dar-Es-Salaam, in an atmosphere that was quite relaxed and personal. What further added to the wonder of the moment was knowing the deepness in Ibrahim's character of taking on these two young men who had been orphaned. This made me feel even more strongly than I had already towards this wonderful man.

That evening Ibrahim and I slept in the bed in the bedroom which served as the back room of the house. It was nice to curl up with Ibrahim but it was too daring to take liberties and do anything in what was actually Hamadi's bed.

When we had settled into bed, thoughts about Ibrahim and his growing up in Tanzania with feelings for men came to mind. I had never had the opportunity to ask him before and this particular night I wanted to know. How had Ibrahim dealt with this and reached a point where he felt comfortable within himself about such feelings even though the society around him had not woken up to the idea that it was simply a natural phenomenon? It took some time for me to get the courage to frame the question but at the same time I realised if I wanted to know I would have to ask him before he fell asleep.

Finally I mustered up the courage.

"Ibrahim," I started. The mention of his name in the otherwise complete silence of the night sounded as if I had yelled his name from the mountain tops. I felt Ibrahim move which meant I had his attention.

"Yes, Bwana Michael," Ibrahim replied. There was no tiredness in his voice so this meant that he was still quite awake.

"Ibrahim," I said repeating his name and then paused before bowling into the question on my mind, "how long have you known about yourself?"

"How long have I known what about myself?" I heard Ibrahim ask with a puzzled tone in his voice. This made me laugh inside. There was something comical about the way he responded to my vague question. I then turned back to a more serious tone.

"You know, interested in men."

I felt Ibrahim pull away from me and lie on his back, the movement of his arm indicating that he now rested his wrist on his forehead. For a moment, with the length of the silence after the question, I wondered if I had asked a question Ibrahim felt was too personal to answer.

"I...I'm sorry," I hastened to say. "I didn't mean to ask you this question if it was too personal or you didn't want to tell me."

Ibrahim rolled back on his side, placed his hand on my forehead and stroked back my hair.

"That's okay," Ibrahim said with a smile in his voice.

Every muscle inside me froze and tightened. Was this story that troubling? I had asked this question many times to many of my gay friends and there had never been any resistance or difficulty in relating their stories. This story, therefore, sounded quite frightening and I waited to hear it.

Ibrahim moved away from me again and rolled on his back. "It all started when I discovered that I was left-handed."

"Left-handed?" I echoed. I rolled onto my side and rested my head on my hand while my elbow dug into the mattress.

"Yes, left-handed. You see, according to the Islamic community, we must do everything using our right hand, especially eating and drinking."

Ibrahim paused and added, "Because Muhammad used his right hand, the general belief is that all Muslims must use their right hand. But if we are commanded by the Koran not to make a distinction between the prophets, then we must use the hand that all the prophets used. Was Issa right-handed, Moses, Ibrahim or any of the other prophets? I see some evidence that some of these prophets were, in fact, left-handed."

What evidence do you have? I thought to myself. I can only guess that Jesus was right-handed because he was biased towards the right hand, where God exalted him "with his right hand" as it says in Acts 5:31 and Jesus now sits "on the right hand of God" in Colossians 3:1.

"Evidence that some of the prophets were left-handed?" I echoed.

"Yes, you see," Ibrahim began, "when I was at school, when I started to learn to write, I automatically used my left hand. My teachers hit me across the knuckles with a ruler for doing so saying that writing should only be done with the right hand. My teachers made me even further embarrassed by telling me that my left hand was only useful for one purpose."

I knew what Ibrahim meant here. I had heard it said that before the advent of toilet paper or any material for a similar function, many cultures adopted the practice of keeping right and left hands separated in function. Because the right hand was the hand used most often in greetings particularly when shaking hands, it was important that everyone in that community knew they were being offered a clean hand. This then became extended to a strict rule that food could only ever be touched with the right hand and never with the left. Obviously this began in a time when no-one had heard of soap and hygiene.

"The teachers," Ibrahim continued, "insisted that I learn to use my right hand because it is the most natural when writing from left to right as it was the only way to see what we were writing. After all, they said, the right hand was the natural hand to use when writing.

I remember even as a child trying with all my might to learn to write with my right hand and each time I went to use my left hand, which to me was the side that felt the most comfortable and natural, I was filled with horrible guilt from what the teachers had told me.

Also, from the comments made by the teachers, I was mocked in the playground by the other children who then refused to get close to me and some would even hit me because they all thought that the hand that I offered in greeting was dirty."

What Ibrahim was relating to me made me feel so sorry for him. Ibrahim in every way was a really nice guy and I guessed he probably was a really nice kid. How could his teachers have treated him like that?

"Then, when I started attending the *madrassa*, I was further scolded for using my left hand."

"The *madrassa*?" I asked.

"Yes, Islamic school, where I learnt about my religion."

I guessed that the *madrassa* was similar to what we called Sunday School.

"You imagine," Ibrahim said, "the natural instinct for me is to use the left hand. I didn't choose this. One time when I automatically went to pick up a pencil with my left hand to write, my teacher got angry at me, telling me that it said in the Koran in Al-Ankaboot 29:49 that the right hand was the hand to be used to write with.

But then, when I started to learn to write Arabic, you know, Arabic is written from right to left. My teachers at school told me that it was natural to use the right hand to write from left to right when writing in Swahili and in English. To me, this meant that it should be natural to write using my left hand when writing from right to left when writing Arabic. This made me then think that written Arabic was invented by a left-handed person. Then when I discovered that Moses wrote the Torah in Hebrew and Hebrew is also written from right to left, this made me reason that Moses had to have been left-handed as well."

An interesting point, I thought to myself.

"At the *madrassa*," Ibrahim continued, "they also told me that according to the Hadiths the Prophet insisted on using the right hand and that this was *sunna* so I had to use my right hand."

"I'm sorry," I interrupted. "What's *sunna*?"

"Many Muslims say," Ibrahim replied, "that whatever Muhammad did, we should do as well. This is what is known as *sunna*. So, if Muhammad wrote with his right hand, we should write with our right hand. If Muhammad grew a beard, we should grow a beard."

The word *sunna* sounded so much like the word Sunni to describe one of the major sects of Islam.

"But does it say in the Koran that Muhammad wrote with his right hand and grew a beard?" I asked.

"No, this is all in the Hadiths."

This was becoming more confusing. Faraj had told me that the Sunnis didn't believe in the Hadiths, only in the Koran. But if they were called Sunni, I guessed this was because they believed in following the *sunna* of Muhammad. But Muslims only knew what Muhammad did from the Hadiths, not the Koran. I decided not to ask anything about this at this stage because it was obviously another long topic of conversation and it could wait for another day. I was more interested in hearing Ibrahim's story.

"Okay," I said. "So then what happened?"

"It was put to me that the use of the left hand was somehow evil, wrong and unnatural. Because I didn't want to be evil and wrong, I tried my best to use my right hand to write with, even though what I wrote always looked messy. However, when I was at home doing my homework, because I needed to get the homework done, I would revert to using my left hand, even though it made me feel guilty for doing so. But also, deep down inside of me, I kept thinking to myself that the only difference between me as a left-hander and other people as right-handers is that I function well using my left hand. I did learn to eat and drink with my right hand and make sure it remained clean when I offered this hand clean to everyone in my community. As I grew older, the teachers became less strict in insisting on using my right hand to write with although they would always make me embarrassed by telling me that if I write with my left hand, make sure I follow the usual conventions and only use my left hand for other base things. They even told me that they would never use any of my pencils because I used my left hand to write with. The other students as a result never shared my pencils."

This was just horrible, I thought.

"In a way, it was a good thing," Ibrahim then added. "No-one ever stole my pencils."

And he laughed at that. He then paused and became serious again as he continued.

"Then in my teenage years, I began to realise that I was interested in other men, well, boys of my age at the time. As I got to the age of about sixteen, the feelings were terribly strong and I was totally aware of them. But I knew what the Muslim community said of them. But it didn't make sense why I was attracted to men and not to women. I also knew there was no way I could talk about it. All my friends at school made fun of boys who were more timid and less masculine than other boys, saying that they must be gay because of their more feminine qualities. Because of this, I thought that to get rid of my feelings for men, I had to be more masculine. So, I got interested in sport. In particular, I played football."

When Ibrahim mentioned football, I assumed it meant what we in Australia call soccer. But his comment about the assumption that the smaller, thinner and weaker boys being treated as if they were gay because they came across as more feminine was very much the same as my experience growing up at school. And I approached it in much the same way as Ibrahim although I took up swimming whereas Ibrahim took up soccer.

"I exercised," Ibrahim continued, "and that's when I took up running. These days I just do it because it makes me feel good and it's a good way to keep my body healthy. But back then, it was my attempt to make myself masculine. And because at the *madrassa* and at the mosque we were always told to beware of the sins of the people of Luti, I devoted my every effort to Islam to cleanse myself of these desires."

I realised in context that 'Luti' had to be the Arabic version of the English 'Lot' from the story of Sodom and Gomorrah. This part of Ibrahim's story also sounded somewhat reminiscent of mine. When I was aware of my sexuality and then what the church thought of it, this made me more religious than ever and made me apply myself more to the religion so that I could find a way out of these so-called dirty desires.

"Then, one day," Ibrahim said, then took a breath, paused and then continued, "something terrible happened. I had a cousin. He was the only son of three children, the other two being girls. He was the eldest. He was only a year younger than me. We were very close, like brothers. He was such a bubbly sort of boy, cheeky and playful. But then one day he suddenly changed. He became more serious and more reserved. I noticed this change in him but could not work out why. He was like this for a long time. Then once he asked me if he could stay with my family. When he said he wanted to stay, I thought he meant for a couple of days. However, he meant he wanted to stay and live with my family. Of course, that was impossible because in Tanzania, children must stay with their parents until they are old enough to marry or if they have to move to a different location for school or work. However, he did come to stay for a couple of days during the school break.

Because we were cousins, we slept in the one bed in a separate room from the other members of the family. One night while in bed we got into a discussion about the Koran. My cousin asked me about what was written in surah Bani-Israil 17:24 where it says, 'show kindness to parents. If one of them or both of them attain old age with thee, never say unto them any word expressive of disgust nor reproach them, but address them with excellent speech'. He asked me if this verse was true. 'Of course, it's true,' I replied. 'And,' he continued, 'where it says in the Koran in surah Luqman 31:15, 16, 'And We have enjoined on man concerning his parents

…if they contend with you to make you associate others with Me of which you have no knowledge, obey them not, but be a kind companion to them in all worldly affairs,' do you believe that?' 'Yes, of course,' I replied.

My cousin then went very quiet. Then he started to cry. I was moved by his sudden change in emotions and tried to comfort him. I asked him what the matter was. He just sobbed for a while. Eventually he asked me, 'Was it Luti who destroyed the people of Sodom?' This was quite chilling because I knew what we were told as to why the people of Sodom were destroyed, for having the same desires for men that I knew I had. 'No,' I replied. 'Luti didn't destroy them. Luti told them in Al-Ankaboot 29:30 to stop their evil ways. The people of Luti replied, 'Bring upon us the punishment of Allah if you speak the truth' and because they said this, Allah destroyed them. So it was Allah who destroyed them, not Luti.

My cousin went really silent again. Then he finally spoke. 'When Luti told the people of Sodom to stop what they were doing, was it because the people of Sodom were doing it to Luti?' 'No,' I told him, 'not as far as I understand from the Koran.'

My cousin lay silent for a moment and then asked, 'If the people of Sodom had done this to Luti, would Allah have destroyed him along with them?' 'That would be totally unjust of Allah if He had,' I replied.

Eventually the truth came out. My uncle had been forcing sex on his own son, my cousin. This forced sex, so my cousin told me, my uncle said was okay because it was within the family. In the Koran, the people of Luti had sex with men who were not related to them, that is, with travellers and strangers. My cousin was also bound by the verses in the Koran which commanded children to be good to their parents and never say a word of reproach or disgust to them. This meant, then, that my cousin could not express his disgust to his father about the forced acts his father made him participate in. My cousin then found out that he had contracted AIDS from his father. AIDS, so we were told, was a punishment brought on by Allah towards those who practised abominations. But Allah, so we were also told, punished the perpetrators of the sin, not the victims. I then understood my cousin's question: would Allah have destroyed Luti along with the people of Sodom if the people of Luti had forced themselves on him? My uncle had forced himself on my cousin and both were punished. We found this out when both my cousin and my uncle were found dead. The evidence suggested that my cousin had killed my uncle and then himself."

I gasped at this story. This was awful, a very tragic story. Ibrahim took a deep breath.

"I was then afraid. I was afraid of catching AIDS and being punished because my feelings were towards men and not women. But I was also afraid of what would happen once I had sons. My uncle no doubt had strong sexual urges for men but in Tanzanian society this is completely unacceptable. That my uncle had contracted AIDS meant that he had picked it up somewhere in secret. But to find an outlet for his sexual desires and in a way that he thought would be secret he took them out on his only son. My uncle even had the Koran to back him up should his son not comply. Associating other gods with Allah is the worst sin. As it says in Al-Luqman 31:14 'associating partners with Allah… is the highest wrongdoing' and in Al-Nisa 4:117 'Allah will not forgive that anything be associated with Him as partner, but He will forgive what is short of that'. Thus if the parents, so the Koran says, commit this sinful deed, associating partners with Allah, the sons were to still respect their parents and not reproach them. This then meant because my cousin's father committed a lesser sin than associating other gods with Allah, my cousin was bound by the command in the Koran and could not reproach his father because it was a sin for the son to reproach his father.

I heard about other events of boys and girls committing suicide in their teenage years and other boys killing older men without giving a reason for the murder. I have wondered many times whether these murders were carried out for a similar reason as my cousin."

I was so struck by what Ibrahim was telling me. It was so disturbing that I wanted him to stop but at the same time I wanted him to go on.

"When I reached the age to marry," Ibrahim continued, "I married. I had to. I don't know what it's like in Australia but in Tanzania, as soon as you are old enough to marry, the whole family and even the whole community puts pressure on you to marry. It's not just the parents. Even the grandparents and other members of the family put pressure on you to marry. However, I also thought that perhaps once I was married and started making love to my wife, my sexual desires would naturally turn towards women and in particular towards my wife and I would no longer have these feelings towards men. So I married. But my feelings for men just didn't go away.

Then, when I had sons, I had to struggle with myself not to touch them. When they reached adolescence, it was difficult not to appreciate how handsome they were. I understood the conflict that my uncle had gone through."

I shuddered. Was Ibrahim now going to make a confession about his relationship with his sons? Ibrahim must have read my mind.

"I never touched my sons," Ibrahim continued. "Not even my adopted sons. Because of my cousin, I knew what could follow if I did such a thing. I mean, I also knew that it wasn't right."

Ibrahim paused again before continuing.

"At around this time, I got a job at the International School at Moshi. This got me in contact with people from other countries. This is when I learnt about western countries and how homosexuality had become legalised. This then made me question what would have happened to my cousin and my uncle had Tanzania made homosexuality legal. My uncle would not have forced his sexual energy onto my cousin but would have been free to express it with someone who was willing to reciprocate it.

Also, I discovered how AIDS actually spreads. Here in Tanzania there are many campaigns and advertisements warning about AIDS. However, it is only explained how to prevent catching AIDS when a man and a woman have sex. Because homosexuality is illegal in Tanzania, no-one mentions that AIDS can also spread when two men and two women have sex together. I can only guess that my uncle did not know that he could catch AIDS by having sex with a man who had AIDS. And this is a big problem here in Tanzania. Because homosexuality is illegal, the government cannot educate the people by showing how to prevent AIDS spreading when two men have sex."

This was a real tragedy, I thought. One of the benefits of the legalisation of homosexuality in Australia was that homosexuals could be educated in how AIDS spreads and learn how to prevent the spread of this disease. By making homosexuality illegal meant that no-one could talk about it openly. The problem was, and Ibrahim's uncle showed this, that by making homosexuality illegal did not stop the homosexual urge. The homosexual urge is just as strong as the heterosexual urge. But just because a country makes homosexuality illegal doesn't make the sexual urge go away. Rather, as it came out in Ibrahim's uncle's case, the homosexual urge finds an outlet whether that society likes it or not and the consequences can be quite disastrous.

"I also began to question," Ibrahim continued, "the view of homosexuality itself and compare it with my left-handedness. I had been told by so many in my community that being left-handed was somehow wrong and evil, even unnatural. And even dirty. But I kept thinking, it doesn't feel wrong, evil and unnatural for me to do everything with my left hand. In fact, it feels quite normal. I couldn't help but see that this was simply a prejudice of right-handed people against left-handed people. I appreciated that our community demanded the right hand to be clean so that when it was offered, all those in the community knew that everyone's right hand was clean. But when it came to writing or kicking a football or doing any other activity which required one of the two hands and one of the two feet to actually do something, to what extent did it affect everyone else in the community? In fact, my left-handedness became useful in football as I was given the position to play on the left hand side of the team.

Then I thought of sexuality. Was this the same with sexuality? In the same way that my left-handedness was viewed as wrong, evil and unnatural, so homosexuality is viewed as wrong, evil and unnatural. But that's easy to say when you are not left-handed and you are not homosexual."

When Ibrahim made this comment, an image formed in my mind of two men, one a protestant pastor, well-dressed in suit and tie, and an imam with a long, razzy beard in full Islamic attire, both of them arms crossed, with stern-looking faces and tapping one foot like the Wicked Witch of the West, saying, "Well, the Bible/Koran says that you should write with your right hand and you should only have sexual relations with someone of the opposite sex." Because the pastor and the imam were right-handed and heterosexual, it was so easy for them to be so condemning. There was absolutely no need for them to even consider the possibility that there were left-handed people in the world or that there were people who thought of the idea of having sex with someone of the opposite sex was actually detestably disgusting whereas with their own sex it was pleasurable. The pastor and the imam were right-handed and heterosexual and the Bible/Koran supported right-handed heterosexuality – although Christians had moved out of the phase that left-handedness is sinister, the word *sinister* itself showing the early Christian prejudice towards left-handedness as it is the Latin word for "left" – so why should the pastor or the imam even try to show any sympathy or understanding for left-handers and homosexuals? After all, it is more important for religious people to maintain the integrity of their holy books than it is to maintain the well-being and happiness of a human being.

"I began to go back over the verses in the Koran," Ibrahim broke through my divergent thought, "about the sins of the people of Luti. The verses to me were telling me that the people of Luti forced sex on men because of lust and greed. This meant that the victims of their lust did not agree to it, so in other words the people of Luti actually raped men. But there was one verse in the Koran which I still have trouble with today where it says in surah Al-Araf 7:82, 'You approach men with lust in preference to women'. There is a problem with this verse on two accounts. One is that this means men should approach women with lust, *shahwatan*, and yet we are supposed to approach women, in particular, our wives in love, not in lust. The other is that the expression 'in preference to', which in Arabic is *min dooni*, can also mean 'more than' so that this verse could actually read, 'You approach men with lust more than women'. This is not true for me. I don't prefer men more than women. In reality, I simply do not have any desire for women."

I was quite taken by Ibrahim's comment. This was the first time in the entire time that I had known him that he actually saw a crack in the belief that the Koran was perfect and true. Or at least, he was raising questions about the Koran.

"I don't want to break the flow of your story," I interjected. "But, you know, I was only recently reading the Torah in Hebrew and I realise now that the story of Lot and the cities of Sodom and Gomorrah has been totally misinterpreted and it's in fact not about homosexuality at all."

Ibrahim rolled over on his side and leant on his arm. "Really?" he asked.

"Yes," I replied. "When you read the story carefully, the men of Sodom did not want to have sex with the angels, who they thought were men, because they simply liked having sex with men. Rather, the men of Sodom wanted to rape the angels because they were xenophobic."

"They were what?"

I laughed. This word had become popular in Australia the day Pauline Hanson had been told that she was xenophobic and her ignorance of the word was used to show that she wasn't quite bright. The reality was that most Australians themselves didn't know what the word meant either but no-one ever admitted this and everyone tried to make sure they knew what the word meant from then on.

"They were suspicious of strangers," I continued. "Well, I'm actually reading into this but I have a reason for this interpretation. In chapter fourteen of Genesis, we read how a king called Chedorlaomer invaded and took the cities of Sodom and Gomorrah. Lot was living in Sodom at the time and when Abraham heard that Chedorlaomer had taken Lot, Abraham waged war with Chedorlaomer and freed the cities of Sodom and Gomorrah. So, you imagine at the time, any stranger who walked into your city after you had been invaded, you would be suspicious of them. What would these strangers be doing in your city?

Further, I think the whole reason why the men of the city wanted to 'know' the angels, as the Bible so delicately words it even in the Hebrew, was not because they thought the angels were good-looking but to let the strangers know that they were completely unwelcome and to let this be a warning to any stranger who wandered into their area uninvited. Now, I don't know about here in Tanzania and I have never heard about it in Australia, either. But a number of my Afghani and Iranian friends, particularly a good friend of mine, Faraj, told me that in their countries it is not unheard of that a group of men will rape a man as punishment. In fact, Faraj told me that even in one of the detention centres in Australia, there was one guard who the Iranians hated because this guard ill-treated them and so they decided to punish him by raping him. Faraj told them not to go that far so they simply had him on the ground and poked his butt area with their fingers. But the original plan, as it is in their home country, was to actually gang-rape the guard as punishment, not out of lust.

Now, when you read the Sodom and Gomorrah story carefully in Genesis 19, it makes more sense that the inhabitants of Sodom wanted to rape the angels as punishment, not for sexual pleasure. For a start, why was it that all the men of the city, the young and the old, all were determined to have sex with these two angels? Weren't they satisfied enough having sex with each other? Then there is no indication that the angels showed any signs that they were interested in complying in the act, so the Sodomites, each and every one of them, had planned to force themselves onto the angels. It finally becomes clear that their intent was not to fulfil sexual pleasure but to actually inflict harm on these supposed male-human strangers. When Lot told the Sodomites not to do so wickedly, the Sodomites got angry at Lot and told him 'now will we deal worse with you than with them'. That the men of Sodom were going to 'deal worse' with Lot than they had intended to do to the angels meant that their intentions were bad. I mean, any two people who want to be intimate, both people in the act want to ensure that it is a pleasurable experience for all involved. By contrast, the Sodomites wanted to 'deal worse' with Lot which means that they didn't want Lot or the angels to enjoy it but rather suffer from it. And the fact that they were going to 'deal' with the angels, who the Sodomites thought were only human strangers, implies punishment, not pleasure. In all probability, the men of Sodom were actually not gay at all. The whole motive behind the act was punishment."

Ibrahim's face brightened up and I could even see this in the semi-darkness. "This does explain what the Koran says about the people of Luti," Ibrahim replied.

"I mean," I continued. "When the men of the city came to Lot's place and demanded Lot to send out the angels, the angels didn't look at each other with sinister grins and say, 'Yeah! Alright! Let's go out and have a great time in this all-male orgy!' and then Lot turned to the angels and said, 'do not do so wickedly' to the angels who wanted to engage in homosexual lust as much as the inhabitants of Sodom. The angels were unwilling to participate and hence the motive of the inhabitants of Sodom was actually to force themselves onto the angels. There is nowhere in the story which indicates that the men of Sodom first asked the angels if they were willing to participate."

I sighed.

"What's worse is that those who look to the story of Sodom and Gomorrah as evidence that homosexuality is wrong, therefore implying that the inhabitants were all gay, don't realise that what they are implying is so insulting to gays. In all my encounters, I have never met one gay guy who would force himself on another guy, even a straight guy, no matter how enamoured he was by him. The story just shows that the inhabitants of Sodom were so bad that they would even gang rape a guy. I mean, I like guys as much as heterosexual women like guys but I would hate to be raped by another guy or even gang raped by a group of guys in the same way as a heterosexual woman wouldn't want to be either. So, that's a pretty ugly sin and I certainly wouldn't want it done to me."

There was some silence after I had made this comment. Then Ibrahim spoke.

"I wish I had known this story as well as you do," Ibrahim then added. "It would have helped me to see things in better perspective. Maybe it would have spared my wife's life."

Ibrahim then rolled on his back and then inhaled a noisy inhalation. "You know, I struggled with this all the time I was married. But then my wife died. There was a terrible bout of cholera in the Moshi area and my wife succumbed to it and died. I was heartbroken."

At this point, Ibrahim went silent. The story was already quite disturbing for me but I had to now hear to the end of it. But when Ibrahim went silent, I thought it was too painful for him to go on. I did not feel it was my place to urge Ibrahim on even though he was keeping me in suspense. I thought he might stop here and not continue because the story was just too disturbing for him. But he soon broke the silence.

"In some ways," Ibrahim continued, "I feel somewhat responsible for the death of my wife. At that time, I know my wife knew of my attraction for other men. I mean, I wasn't unfaithful to her, like other African men are although towards other women, not to men. I mean, I loved my wife, but I more and more realised that I did not love loving my wife. Even though I had managed to sire four children, once the children were in the family, it became harder and harder for me to want to be with my wife in this way. The idea that having sex with a woman would eventually help to erase the attraction for men and lead me to spontaneously be attracted to women, in particular, my wife, just wasn't true. Once the excitement of the first years of marriage were over, I could feel the feelings for men becoming once again stronger and stronger. My wife must have been aware of it because I just found it more and more difficult to bring myself to do it with her. I guess this disappointed her and hence when the cholera outbreak came, she just succumbed to it."

The religious homosexual nightmare. How many times had I heard this story? It was the first time to hear it from a Tanzanian, from an African man. But also the tragedy for the poor wife of the homosexual man forced to marry.

"Because of my continual attraction to other men," Ibrahim continued, "I applied myself more and more to my religion. I began to regularly read the Koran. My Arabic had become rusty because of my neglect during my study years but I applied myself once again and got back into the religion. I attended the mosque as often as I could, five times a day if I could make it. And I read the Koran and read it slowly and carefully, looking for answers to this dilemma.

I eventually decided to speak to an imam. But it's not an easy thing to go and talk to the imam about such an issue. I couldn't just go to the imam and tell him, 'I have desires for men and not for women. Can you explain why this is?' The imam would probably have tried to have me arrested if not at least thrown out of the mosque.

I couldn't ask the imam in any of the mosques in Moshi because it would have been easy for others in the community to find out. So, from time to time, I took bus trips to other cities in Tanzania. Once I came here to Dar-Es-Salaam, another time I went to Zanzibar.

The way I addressed the issue was to lead up to it. The question I wanted to ask had to be presented as a side issue, not as the main idea, so as not to make it obvious that I was talking about myself.

Each time I visited an imam, I spent hours with him. I asked a variety of questions and the imam answered them at length. I apologised for taking up his time each time I asked an involved question but the imam replied that it was good that I was a diligent Muslim searching the depths of the Koran and not brushing over it superficially like many Muslims do these days and don't really take the Koran seriously enough as I did.

Eventually I worked the conversation to the people of Luti. I asked about the verse in Al-Araf 7:82 where it says about the men of Sodom and Gomorrah that

You practise your lusts on men more than women

I asked the imam, why did this verse say this? It sounded as if men, all men, had sexual lust towards both men and women equally but good Muslim men practised this on women whereas bad people, and in this case the people of Luti who were exceptionally bad, practised their lust on men instead when they should have preferred and chosen to express their sexuality on women. Was this the right way to understand this verse?

The imam replied that it was not true that all men had the propensity to lust men. In fact, he bombastically stated that he had no sexual attraction for men at all and was sure that I didn't either, a good Muslim like me who diligently studied the Koran.

Just on this statement, I realised that this imam did not nor could not understand how a man could have sexual desires for another man. Further, it was evident that he thought the idea of two men having sex was disgusting and dirty. He also made the assumption that good Muslim men could not have sexual desires for men. It was a bold assumption on his part and it was clear that I could not confess to him the reality in me. This made me ask myself: am I then a bad Muslim, or worse, am I clearly a *kafiri* because of my sexual desires for men? This did not make sense. I practised as much as I could all the rites of a Muslim but my sexual desires for men were still there. I may not have been able to confess this to this imam but I certainly could not deny the reality to myself.

I then asked the imam, 'Where did these men get their lust for men? Where did this desire for men come from?' After all, the imam didn't have it and he assumed I didn't have it.

The imam replied that the natural order was that men are sexually attracted towards women. Homosexuality is a distortion of nature and hence the men of Luti were distorting nature and therefore distorting what Allah had intended from the beginning to be the union between a man and a woman. Who else would distort nature but the enemy of Allah?

If, then, I replied, Satan caused the distortion of these sexual desires in the men of Luti, to what extent were the men of Luti themselves responsible for committing these acts? If Satan distorted their sexual desires towards men, why didn't Allah simply step in and repair that which was distorted? If Allah Himself is so disgusted by this distortion, why does He allow Satan to distort Allah's creation while Allah stands by and does nothing? Further, why didn't Allah simply destroy the homosexual desire but instead destroyed the men themselves?

I continued with my questions. Does this mean that all distortions of nature are of Satan? When someone is born blind, or deaf, or without limbs, or with more limbs than they should, or mentally retarded, or albino, aren't all these distortions of nature? Are these all the work of Satan? Should these people give in to their deformities or should they go through life acting as if they were whole like normal people and if they acted out their deformity they should be put to death?

The imam was rather shocked and said I was being callous. But I wasn't being callous. I was raising an honest question. The imam replied that we should look on these people with compassion and help them despite, or because of, their deformities.

I left this imam with more questions than answers. But I was also frustrated by my sexual desires.

I decided to see another imam. This time, I addressed the issue by talking about a friend of mine who I thought was struggling with it and who wanted to see the imam but was too afraid and ashamed. I talked about this person so convincingly that for a while it felt as if the person I was talking about was not me.

This imam was a bit more sympathetic towards people like this friend of mine. He asked me questions about other features of this friend, what he was like as a Muslim. I told the imam that he was exemplary, an excellent example of what a Muslim should be.

The imam thought about it for a moment and then as if he had just had a revelation, he gave me an answer. Allah gives us all tests and therefore he must be testing this friend of mine in this way. Because this Muslim was such an exemplary Muslim, Allah wanted to test him.

I was quite disgusted with this imam's comment. Allah chose to distort His own nature? Allah distorted the natural sexual desire that my friend should have towards women which he now had towards men? How could Allah, the Compassionate, do such a thing? I thought about my own children. If I had the power, would I seriously change my children's sexual orientation from the opposite sex to their own? And then would I tell my children that if they enacted on this strong sexual urge that I had given them, I would ensure that they were punished by members of the community in the most demeaning and despicable of ways? And while my children kept begging me to change their orientation, I would continue to keep it towards their own gender? And what would be the test I was trying to give them? What lesson would I have taught my children from that?

The mere suggestion of the imam was disgusting to the point that I wanted to be sick. I made the excuse that I needed to go and simply left. But I continued to think on what each of these imams had said. One said that it was a distortion of nature created by Satan. But this had to mean that all distortions and therefore all imperfections in nature were of Satan. Mental retardation, deformities, black parents who have children with absolutely no pigmentation and therefore are completely white, all these are distortions of nature. Even my left-handedness according to Islam is a distortion because in Islam it is the right hand which should be the dominant hand. If Satan is the distorter of Allah's nature, then Allah allows these distortions because Allah is greater than Satan. But it made sense to me that Allah would only allow Satan to create distortions in those people who do not obey Allah. But these distortions were random. I was familiar with all of these so-called distortions in Muslims and non-Muslims alike.

The alternative was what the other imam said, that these distortions were a test from Allah. Already the thought was repugnant to me that Allah Himself would distort His own nature as a test. Not only was it a repugnant thought, it was also of necessity blasphemous. To associate the distortions of nature to Allah was to say that it was Allah who distorted His own nature and therefore Allah was somehow evil.

Further, once again, if this were a test, why did Allah only give this test to some Muslims, and only a minority? This imam had said that it was a test for those Muslims who were exceptional Muslims. So this meant only very good Muslims should be given this test. But then, why did Allah give this test to non-Muslims as well? What would this achieve? Allah already knew that non-Muslims were condemned anyway. So if Allah was causing these non-Muslims to have desires for their own gender, Allah also knew that without a belief in Him these non-Muslims would simply give in to their desires and commit the sin. And then what would Allah do then? Would He then say, 'See? I told you that you were wrong   to give in to your desires and so you are condemned'. This would make Allah into a sick and vindictive being indeed. Already non-Muslims are vulnerable to Satan and by Allah distorting their sexual desires, Allah was increasing their vulnerability in a way that Allah already knew where it would lead.

If Allah was doing this to some non-Muslims as a way to finally destroy them, why did He only do it to some non-Muslims and not all of them? Alternatively, if these distortions are from Satan, then these distortions should only occur in non-Muslims.

What was further evident was that I had spoken to two imams and received two very different answers. Both answers could not be right. One of the answers was right which meant the other was wrong. Or both were wrong.

But I was desperate for an answer. I went and saw yet another imam. This imam said that the answer was in the Koran. This sounded like relief because the other two imams I had approached had not used the Koran to help me with an answer. This imam justified his reasoning on the verse in Al-Hajj 22:53, 'Never sent We a Messenger or Prophet before you, but when he framed a desire, Satan put some more into his desire. But Allah cancels anything Satan puts in'. Even when Messengers or Prophets are sent by Allah, Allah puts desires in them and this becomes an obstacle that Satan uses. But when I read this verse, it was not saying what the imam told me it was saying. Rather, this verse implied that the desires were created by the Messenger, not Allah, and not by Satan either. Satan only added to the desire that was already framed by the Messenger. But then Allah cancelled the desire.

I asked the imam, then, that if this verse is true, this means that some of the messengers of the past also had these desires in them. The imam was quite disgusted with my comment saying that Allah would never allow good Muslims and in particular His messengers such disgusting desires. I asked the imam why then he had quoted this verse from the Koran when I had asked my original question. The imam thought for a little while then looked back through the Koran. He then referred to the verse in Al-Shu'ara 26:170 where it said that Luti called out to Allah to save him from what the people of Luti do. If Luti wanted to be saved from the actions that the people of Luti committed, it could actually mean that Luti had these desires, even though he hated the practice. Once he had called on Allah, Allah removed these desires from him and also removed Luti from these wicked people. If this friend of mine simply called out to Allah to remove these desires, Allah would remove them especially as the verse in Al-Hajj 22:53 said that Allah cancels the desires.

The imam further suggested that my friend fast and be in earnest prayer until he received an answer. He did not give any particular reason why I needed to do this. However, I was in desperation to be rid of these desires and so I chose to do this. I simply stopped eating and spent much of my time when I wasn't at work at the mosque praying.

One night after I had fasted for some days, I had a dream. In the dream I was incredibly thirsty. In the dream, I was somewhere in Zanzibar but it was not the Zanzibar of my reality. I was extremely thirsty and so I asked my wife to get me some water. My wife told me that she would have to get the water from somewhere else. For some reason, I understood that the water was not readily available and so I waited for her to come back. When she finally arrived, she told me that she had to get the water from her neighbour, and her neighbour got it from her husband, who had to get it from a merchant in the town, who got it from a market from the mainland, who got it from someone who had transported it from the centre of the country and who had sourced it from a river in the interior of the continent. But when I looked at the water, it was dirty to the point of appearing completely undrinkable. I looked back up at my wife but she was no longer there. Rather Michael the archangel was standing watching me. He then asked me, 'Why are you so disappointed? What did you expect? If you ask to get water and the water exchanges hands from one person to another until it reaches you, each person along the line will add something to the water they think will help to make it pure and so by the time it reaches you it will be undrinkable. If you are thirsty, why don't you go directly to the source? It is only there you will be fully quenched.'

'Because the source is so far away,' I replied.

'But the source is very close to you,' Michael replied. 'You have been told that the way to the source has been blocked off but it is open to all who will go there.'

I then began to make my journey and, sure enough, as the angel had told me, I arrived at the place. Even though I had only walked to the end of the road, the view below me was of a valley where there was a large river flowing into an immense sea. From my vantage point, I could see in the distance how that several waterfalls, absolutely beautiful, dropped down into this river. A strong wind blew across the river and over the vast ocean, a great ocean breeze, like a cleansing agent. And out of the sea arose a great light, brighter than the sun, that shone over the earth and brought back the world to paradise.

When I woke up, I realised it was only a dream, but then I really had to have a drink of water."

Ibrahim and his dreams! I thought. His dreams were bizarre but they certainly were entertaining. I nestled back into the mattress and listened further to Ibrahim's story.

"I decided to go back to the last imam I had spoken with," Ibrahim continued. "I asked him for further help. The imam then referred to the

Hadith for the answers. After he read to me the Hadith, something inside me, no doubt Allah, made me ask the imam who wrote that Hadith. The imam went back to the Hadith and read to me the *isnad*."

"The what?" I interrupted.

"The *isnad*."

"I'm sorry. What's that?"

"Well," Ibrahim replied, "the Hadiths are collections of sayings of Muhammad. But they were not written by Muhammad himself. Rather, they were written by those who said they had heard it from someone else, who had heard it from someone else, who had heard it from someone else and this continues until you reach the person who heard it directly from Muhammad."

"That's not really a reliable way to get information," I said.

"You know," Ibrahim replied, "I know what you are saying because it was then that the dream came to me. I asked the imam if each member in the *isnad* was a prophet. The imam laughed as if I were foolish and replied that they were not. However, he then went on to defend the position that as much as each person in the link along the *isnad* was not a prophet, they were all reliable. However, as the dream revealed to me, the Hadiths were like the chains of information that were brought from the source of the water and would not fulfil what I needed to know. I left this imam. I realised that the answer had to be in the Koran itself.

It was not long after that when I read in the Koran that the Koran itself is a fulfilment and a summary of the Torah and the Injil and the other prophets. In the dream, I saw several waterfalls. I realised that the water from these waterfalls falling into the river were the Torah and the Injil. But the Torah and the Injil were only two other sources."

Ibrahim stopped there and I thought he had reached the end of his story.

"And so?" I whispered into the night.

"My feelings for men continued," Ibrahim began again. "You know, Bwana Michael, I was faithful to my wife to the end. When she passed on, my family and friends encouraged me to take on a new wife and not be alone. I began to ask myself the question: why should I take on a wife? I already had four grown up children so I did not need a companion for the purpose of fathering more children. I knew when everyone encouraged me, my children, my mother, others of my relatives, my friends, that when they said I should find a wife as a companion, I knew that it was not merely to have someone to live with me as a friend. Part of that relationship would be intimate, sexual if you will. What difference, then, did it matter at my age to have a companion, an intimate friend, to share my life with and that friend be a man and not a woman? The intimacy was not supposed to bring forth more offspring therefore I saw no difference in having either a man or a woman as an intimate companion. I mean, this intimacy was private so what did it matter to everyone else who this person was I was intimate with?

I had gone about two weeks of fasting and praying -"

"You seriously mean you did not eat for two weeks?" I interrupted.

I could feel Ibrahim move to face me.

"Yes, I did not eat for two weeks. Bwana Michael, I was desperate for an answer."

I could well empathise with what Ibrahim had said. When you are told that your sexual desires for the same sex are disgusting and evil, it is amazing to what extent you will go to try and get rid of them.

"Sorry," I apologised. "Continue."

Ibrahim lay back in the bed.

"I begged Allah to show me an answer to my question. One morning while I was at home deep in prayer, a sudden gust of wind blew through the house. My Koran was on a table near the window and the wind blew it onto the floor. But the wind had blown so hard that the Koran fell onto the floor upside down and open. I went over and picked it up off the floor. But as I picked it up, I instinctively read the verse near where my thumb was holding the Koran. The verse was from Al-Rum 30:22 and it said

And one of His Signs is this, that He has created
spouses for you among yourselves, that you may find peace of
mind in them, and He has put love and tenderness between
you. In that surely are Signs for a people who reflect.

I realised then and there that Allah was answering my prayer."

Ibrahim stopped there for a moment as if he had decided to reflect as the verse bid him to do. He then added what came across as an afterthought. "What was interesting was that the word for 'spouses' in this verse is *azwajaan*. This is not gender specific. The word *azwajaan* simply means the pairing up of two things. This pairing is not necessarily male with female. After all, this same word *azwajaan* is also used in Ta Ha 20:54 where it says that Allah has created 'diverse pairs of plants'. We know that each individual plant produces both male and female flowers on the one plant so these 'pairs of plants' are not plants that depend on each other as male and female for reproduction. So, this word *azwajaan* simply means the pairing up of two irrespective of the gender of the two that make up that pair."

"Spouses, then," I replied, "or what we say in Australia, 'partners'. In Australia, we simply use the word 'partner' to mean the person you are paired up with, irrespective of whether you are a man or a woman and your partner is a man or a woman."

Ibrahim turned on his side. He touched my cheek with his hand.

"My partner, then," he half-whispered.

The touch was beautiful and reassuring. Ibrahim then removed his hand and then lay back on his pillow.

"But listen to the completion of the verse. In that surely are His Signs, *ayaatihi,* not *ayah,* a Sign, but *ayaat,* 'signs', for a people who reflect. Only those who reflect see this and understand this."

Ibrahim then mounted up on his side as if he were in urgency to tell me something.

"You don't have to reflect, to be clever, to see that all peoples and races of the world have couples who marry, between a man and a woman. So, there is no need for any of these people to reflect on anything. But only those who reflect will truly see the sign from Allah that the word chosen in this verse is not gender specific and should be applied to all of us who wish to find peace of mind, and that Allah has put love and tenderness between two people for this very reason. It also made sense because all the time I was trying to deal with my sexual desires for men, I was completely concentrated on myself and did not care about other people. I then realised that Allah was telling me, 'stop worrying about your sexual desires for men. I put them there for a reason. I will create of you and your partner who is to come *azwajaan.* This partner will respond to the desires I put in you for a purpose so that you will find peace of mind. And he will have the same heart attitude as you to want to help others. This will give you the comfort and strength you need to go out and help others in need'."

Once again, the beautiful tingling feelings that often went through my body whenever Ibrahim said anything that was so profound flowed through my body.

"Further, I read the verse in Al-Nur 24:33, 'Marry…your male slaves and female slaves'. In Arabic, the verb 'marry' here is masculine, that is, this verse really reads, 'You men marry…your male slaves and female slaves'. There are two forms of the imperative of 'marry' and indeed all verbs in Arabic. This verse could have been written in Arabic, 'you men marry your female slaves and you women marry your male slaves' but that's not how it is written. So, if men are allowed to marry their male slaves, this shows that men are allowed to marry other men."

This was quite striking on many levels. What Ibrahim said was quite a plausible way of viewing his understanding of the verse. But what intrigued me more was that the idea that Muslims were allowed to own slaves according to this verse didn't seem to bother Ibrahim. Or he didn't seem to notice or appreciate what it meant to make people a slave.

"Also," Ibrahim continued, "I appreciated that in the Torah, men making relationships with men, and women with women was originally *haram*, that is, forbidden, but then I remembered reading in Al-Imran 3:51 that the prophet Issa said 'I came fulfilling that which is before me, namely, the Torah; and to allow you some of that which was forbidden you'. There were certain things in the Torah that were originally forbidden but then Issa came and said these were now allowed. This therefore meant that this could include the relationship between two people of the same sex.

And I discovered that this was so. I decided to do as the Koran was telling me and go back and read the Christian Bible. I decided to start with the Gospels. There was a verse in Matthew 19:12 which talked about people being born eunuchs. It is usually understood that eunuchs are men who have been castrated. But this verse is not talking only about men but about all the followers of Allah, both men and women, and women cannot be castrated. I wondered then if the word 'eunuch' had other meanings. I knew from my studies of history when I studied the history of India that eunuchs are talked about in the *Kama Sutra* of Vatsyayana. I read an English translation of this text and whoever translated the word from the original language chose to use the English word 'eunuch'. But in the context, these eunuchs were actually men who liked having sex with men. Nothing in the text suggested that these men were castrated, simply that they were men who had sex with other men. I realised this was Allah's meaning. This then made more sense when I read the Acts of the Apostles in chapter eight when the Ethiopian eunuch became a believer. And this was significant to me. Why did this Gospel focus so much attention on an Ethiopian eunuch? Why was Philip told to specially speak with him? This made sense. I mean, there was no word at that time to describe what we call gay or *mshoga* and so the only word they used was eunuch. I realised then what Allah had been trying to tell me. This was one of those things that was originally *haram* but Issa had now made it *halal*, that is, permitted."

Once again, a tingle surged through my body when Ibrahim made this connection.

"And notice," Ibrahim continued, "that it was an Ethiopian. So it was a black man, a descendant of Ham, to whom Allah showed this sign. And it further made me realise how much Muslims should be looking back to the Torah and the Injil when they needed an answer because sometimes the answers are not complete within the Koran as the Koran itself is only a summary of the Torah and the Injil."

This was quite significant. If what Ibrahim was saying were true, then salvation to homosexuals came through a sub-Saharan African. One could also argue that the curse on Ham's descendants to be the slaves of Shem and Japheth had been removed as well through this Ethiopian eunuch. Strangely, or was this an insidious show of racism, the story of the Ethiopian eunuch is not terribly well-known. How many people even think about this story or have even understood or cared for its significance?

"You know?" Ibrahim continued. "This is the problem with Muslims in countries where there is constant war and unrest. These people have not found peace of mind. And why not? They do not reflect. They do not think. They act on their impulses like animals. Humans are not animals. We are made in the very image of Allah and we stand above the animals. What makes us above animals is our ability to think, reflect and reason.

This is what Allah is calling us to do. I mean, it finally made sense to me. Why is it that men like you and me who love each other, and women who love each other, are not given the space and ability to find love and tenderness like their heterosexual brothers and sisters? This is because people don't reflect. They don't ask themselves, 'what would it be like if I were a man who liked men or a woman who liked women? Is it possible? How would I feel in this world? If I were one of these people, would I make the rash judgements I make of these people?' To do this requires some imagination and intelligence, and requires people to rise up above their basic instincts and enter the world of their minds and reflections to find out what the situation would really be like.

Further, this is a lesson for all of us. Allah is telling us all that we should all reflect and think before we judge anyone. Think about it. Let me imagine I am this other person. How would I feel if I were that person?"

Of all the turbulence in the world of the Muslims, I was lying in bed with one, a male Muslim, who supported his religion from the very book I had been told was the cornerstone of the Islamic faith. And yet, the man lying next to me was totally opposite to anything like the reality of the violence and unrest in these countries whose basis was the Koran. How was it that these people, these Muslims, could say that they believed in Muhammad and this holy book and yet they became the violent and most unforgiving of people whereas Ibrahim, also a Muslim, was totally the opposite?

There was a moment of silence. I was in total awe of this man beside me, even though I was totally skeptical of the religions of the books. Would that Ibrahim were the first Abraham, the father of the three monotheistic religions and, as the Bible says, the Father of Many Nations. If this modern Abraham had been that ancient Abraham, how different the world would be today.

Ibrahim then turned back on his side, faced me again and then touched once again my cheek with his big hands, softly and tenderly.

"You know, Bwana Michael?" he whispered in the dark. "The archangel in my dream told me to wait and he would make of me and my partner *azwajaan* so that I could find peace. Now that we have found each other, eventually we will be able to fulfil Allah's plan and, now that we are married, we can work together to continue that plan."

This comment knocked the serenity of the moment out of me. Married? We were married? Then I thought back at the comments I had made in our little dormitory at the Msingi wa Mungu Project about how a man marries another man. I had simply said this as a joke but Ibrahim had taken it seriously. In his eyes, therefore, we were married. This meant that Ibrahim presumed that we would eventually live together. But how?

But this wasn't the only issue. My mind then fast tracked into the future. What would life be like with Ibrahim permanently in my home? I had lived on my own for years. My little flat, small enough to accommodate me and cheap enough for me to afford, while not the plushest and in the elitest of suburbs of Sydney, it still was my home, it was safe and I was free to come and go as I pleased. There was no timetable to observe, no houserules to follow, no strictures on the way I lived. If at 10.30 one night I suddenly wanted to go out, I just did it, I didn't have to ask anyone's permission. If I didn't feel like hanging my clothes up when I got home, I could simply toss them on the floor wherever I liked with the promise that I would put them tidily away when I felt like it. I didn't have to make my bed when I got up in the morning, I could go to the toilet with the door wide open, I could eat when I liked, sleep when I liked, be intimate with another guy when I liked.

But further, marrying Ibrahim meant that I was totally his. My body was not available to anyone else. This was the most difficult of applications. I liked the freedom to pick up a new partner, even for a quick one night stand, without the commitment of seeing this person again or holding any obligations to him. To be married to Ibrahim meant only being intimate with him and him only. But what would happen in the situation where Ibrahim was not in the mood for intimacy when I was? What would happen if Ibrahim just let his body go and grew extra luggage around his waist? What would happen if Ibrahim became disfigured through disease or injury which prevented him from being able to be intimate? What would happen if Ibrahim for years was unable to come to Australia?

All these thoughts began to impinge on me while Ibrahim held me tight and Morpheus reached down, took my hand and led me to the land of dreams.

Chapter 19

Not long after these cogitations, Ibrahim and I were walking along a semi-deserted place somewhere in Moshi in what was like a forest area or woodland. There was only the two of us. We were holding hands and walking along which within the Tanzanian context looked quite innocent. Oddly enough, I suddenly felt a sense of guilt as if what Ibrahim and I were doing was overtly a crime within the Tanzanian context and we were openly defying both the laws of the land and the sensibilities of the Tanzanian people through this outward expression of our love towards each other.

Things then happened very quickly. We suddenly realised we were trapped inside a large cage. Someone must have been able to strategically drop a cage right over the top of us and encapsulate us. We frantically grabbed at the ribbing and bars of the cage to try and get out when suddenly a figure appeared out of nowhere, clothed in what looked like an army uniform, a Tanzanian of richly dark skin. His eyes were bloodshot as if he had been drinking heavily or smoking marijuana but his glance, his staring was ominously fixed and determined, making him look like one of the evil creatures or devils in typical portraiture in Buddhist and Hindu artistry. His face was also quite familiar. Then I realised. It was Babeer.

Ibrahim suddenly became calm and collected but I was frantic, trying desperately to find a way out of this sudden prison.

Babeer looked at the two of us but seemed much more intent on Ibrahim as if he had a strong desire to be satiated by Ibrahim. Although not looking at me, I guessed he wanted the same from me.

"So," he seemed to say but I cannot remember seeing his lips move and it seemed as if his speech were taking place in my mind, not entering the natural way through my ears. "You two want to fulfil your wicked lusts. Well, I have a wicked lust and I plan to fulfil it. Your lust towards each other, although it harms no-one, is looked on with such disgust by society that it makes my lust look acceptable, even though it is more damaging."

There was a sinister coolness and calculation in his tone even though it did not seem that he was actually saying anything.

I became even more frantic and yet Ibrahim remained cool and confident as if he felt that he was protected. I frantically pulled and pulled at the bars of the cage when suddenly parts of the cage came away in my hand allowing me to escape.

I must have been extremely out of my wits because I felt as if I were higher than ground level looking back down at the cage. Babeer's burning red eyes looked up at me without any expressions or emotions at all and he seemed to just shrug me off with a wave of the hand as if to signal me to go. His entire insistence was on Ibrahim.

"Ibrahim, Ibrahim," I began yelling, "you have to get out. Get out! Get out!"

"But he can't get out," Babeer monotoned. "And he is the victim of my lust."

"No, no," I yelled in panic, "Ibrahim, get out! Get out!"

Ibrahim looked up at me. His face was shining as if it were polished ebony. There was a calmness to him as if his fate were sealed and he had accepted it, that he was about to become the victim of whatever Babeer's lust was.

I wanted to run away, to fly away, but I couldn't just leave Ibrahim here. But the look on Ibrahim's face was as if he were telling me that what was about to happen was ordained and he was ready to accept his fate.

I was in a panic. But then someone else appeared on the scene. This man was a *Mzungu* but oddly dressed and carrying a very large clay jug which looked very much like a Greek amphora. I was so intent on looking at the amphora which was clearly filled to the brim with water. This *Mzungu* looked so much like the caricaturisation of Aquarius, the Zodiac sign. I looked at the Aquarius with a sense of relief thinking that he was the deliverance we were looking for. However, I turned back to look at Babeer who had now advanced to the cage itself and was intent on sucking out all the water from Ibrahim's body. I don't know how I knew this. I looked back at Aquarius with earnestness as if to say, "Please give him your amphora of water so that you can satisfy the thirst of this strange creature." I looked back at Babeer now holding Ibrahim so firmly against the inside of the cage in a way that Ibrahim could not move. Ibrahim's body had become limp as if he had become complacent towards his fate. Suddenly, I was filled with unimaginable panic.

"Ibrahim! Ibrahim!" I screamed. "Ibrahim! No, please! Ibrahim! Ibrahim!"

Suddenly everything around me was dark. It took me a moment or two to realise that I was no longer in the woodland. The window to the left of the bed which allowed the extremely limited amount of night light into the room made me realise where I really was. I could feel the softness of the mattress under my body and I realised I was in a sitting position. I then felt Ibrahim's arms wrap around me.

"Bwana Michael, Bwana Michael," he whispered in earnest. "What is it? What is it? Are you alright?"

The reality of where I really was in the time-space dimension became lucid in my consciousness. When I realised in the quasidarkness that Ibrahim was safe and unharmed in the bed beside me, I just grabbed him tightly.

Ibrahim and I then lay back down in the bed and I clutched ever so tightly around his body and buried my head so much into his chest I could hear his heart beating. What I had just experienced in the world beyond our sleep had been completely traumatic.

"Hey, Bwana Michael," Ibrahim whispered in my ear. "It's okay. You're fine. You were having a bad dream."

It took some time to finally gain total composure and have complete control of my emotions. Ibrahim seemed to understand because for a while he just stroked my head but said nothing more until I could completely calm down.

The horror of the nightmare was replaced by total embarrassment for reacting in what I thought was a childish way. Since when did grown men of our age have nightmares which drove us to act so emotionally? Wasn't this really the realm of young, pre-pubescent children?

Once I had reached full composure, I pulled myself away from Ibrahim and lay looking up into the darkness then back at him. There was a moment of relief knowing that Ibrahim was here beside me, safe and sound.

The dream, which had seemed so real and disturbing while I was in it, now seemed rather stupid. But I recognised the elements of it. I had seen that birdcage when we wandered through Stone City and saw the poor birds captured inside and I had felt sorry for the birds. One fluttered around as if trying to escape while the other sat there morosely as if it were ready to die. The idea of me flying in the dream was my mind somehow transferring what I had seen to actually me being the bird flying around. I had taken on the feelings of the bird when I had walked past and this had left an imprint on my mind which manifested itself in the dream as me trying to escape the cage. That it was Babeer who tried to attack Ibrahim, the other bird in the cage, made sense because I remembered how the bare patches of hair, the wounded eye and the missing teeth all made him look like a stray tomcat, like the tomcat who had tried to grab the bird in the cage in Stone City. As for Aquarius, it was the image of that beautiful calender for sale with the twelve signs of the Zodiac illustrated quite clearly. That Ibrahim was the other bird which didn't move and simply accepted its fate simply was my transposition of Ibrahim and me being the two birds in the cage. If I was the bird fluttering around in fear and anxiety, Ibrahim had to be the other bird. Somehow this scenario had troubled me which is what led me to dream about it, even though the event had formed such a minor part of my day.

Ibrahim suddenly interrupted my thoughts.

"Are you okay now?" he asked so softly and sweetly.

"Yeah, yeah," I replied. "It was just a nightmare, that's all."

I proceeded to recount the entire dream to him. I thought the dream, now in my current lucidity, rather silly and that was the tone in which I delivered it. Once I had finished relating it, I felt Ibrahim's grip loosen from me.

"What's up?" I asked as I realised the way Ibrahim pulled away from me meant that something was wrong. Was there something about the dream which he didn't appreciate which meant that I had said something to offend him? I rolled on my stomach and placed my arm over his chest. Ibrahim responded by holding onto this arm and stroking it to signal that his reaction was misinterpreted.

"I see what that dream is about," Ibrahim replied.

"What?" I retorted, in a way to reveal that once again I really didn't believe neither Ibrahim's dreams nor his interpretation of my dream.

"We have to be careful, Bwana Michael," Ibrahim then whispered in my ear. "However, it doesn't matter how careful we are, just before you leave, there are those who know about us and are going to use this as an opportunity for them to extract something out of us, in particular, out of me, partly out of jealousy, partly out of greed. This is the lust that this person in your dream meant and he was right in saying that his lust is much more evil and more damaging than the love you and I share, which they interpret purely as animalistic and demonic lust. He will get away with it regardless, unfortunately, although not entirely. Allah will lead the way out and this person will be punished."

I pulled away from Ibrahim in incredulity.

"I think," Ibrahim continued, "this person will be after money because in dreams water is a symbol for money. In any case, I know who that person is. But he won't get away with it."

Oh, get off the grass! I thought but knew I couldn't say that out loud.

The only saving grace for Ibrahim was that I loved the guy very much.

Then I began to reflect on what my Chinese students often told me, especially about dreaming about water. They saw a connection between water and money as well. This was made more pronounced in Hong Kong with the building with the hole in the middle of it to allow the money dragon to leave the water and go up the mountain and then return to the sea to allow the flow of the water dragon because water symbolises money.

In a way, I could actually see a parallel in western culture as well between the flow of water and the flow of money through the economy, where a good economy meant there was a good flow of money in the same way as a flourishing landscape was one where water was flowing abundantly. Also, it was true that we talked of different types of money as being different currency, and this implied a flow of money. But it was simply a parallel and that was all. There was no definite link. It didn't follow, or so I thought, that there was a definite connection between money and water.

"Aquarius with the amphora, what did he look like?" Ibrahim asked.

I rolled over on my side.

"Ibrahim, you know what dreams are like. I at least knew it was a he. But like it is with dreams, his features were formless. He reminded me of the Aquarius I saw on the calendar in Stone City but even though I'm sure the Stone City Aquarius had definite facial features, the Aquarius in my dream did not. After all, the focal point of the Aquarius in my dream was the amphora which was full to the brim with water."

I paused and then as the feelings of the dream once again entered my consciousness, I added, "You know? The water in that amphora. There was something wonderful about it. I only looked in at the top and it was as if I were close up to the Aquarius and that I could see into the amphora. I remember the water looked so clear and so clean, and even though I didn't touch it, I could feel its purity and refreshing quality."

Ibrahim made a comment and there seemed to be the sound of frustration or annoyance in his voice. But then his gestures revealed a restrained despondency or acceptance of what the dream might mean. From the way he reacted to it, it sounded as if there were something ominous about to happen.

To me, however, it had simply been a dream. I could gather the fragments of the day in Zanzibar and understand how different elements ended up in my nightly cogitations. That to me was what constituted dreams, a mental replay of events in the past which had left a strong imprint on the mind which the mind felt it had to deal with and strangely did so by personalising the troubling event. But then, if Ibrahim felt he had to interpret something out of the dream, did it really matter to me if his interpretation was quite banal?

The next morning, Hamadi drove us to the central bus station in Dar-Es-Salaam so that we could make the voyage back to Moshi. This bus station was an amazing place. It seemed more noticeably amazing when we took the bus back to Moshi than when we had arrived here from Moshi some days earlier. It was packed with people at the entrance so it was just impossible for Hamadi to park anywhere conveniently. People were everywhere and it was as if some great personality was soon to arrive and be mobbed by the throng. I felt as if we were going to be torn apart by the people at the entrance yelling at us, and they were only yelling to find out if we needed a taxi. I stayed extremely close to Ibrahim the entire walk through the crowd.

We eventually made it to huge, barred gates which gave the bus station the ominous appearance that we were about to enter a maximum security prison. There was an office before entering and the person behind the counter checked our names and tickets to see if we were able to go inside. We finally made our way through oneway turnstiles and were soon within the large compound of the bus station. The contrast was stark between the choking crowds on one side of the fence and the sparsity of people on the other. Inside this large, open compound were many coaches parked waiting for passengers to board. There were not many people around.

We were soon on our coach and on our way back to Moshi. It was a long seven hour trip but I enjoyed every minute of it. The roads were well sealed and as we went further and further in a westerly direction, the crowds of people diminished. What intrigued me, however, were the colourful houses. People had painted their concrete houses in a blaze of colour which brought brightness to the place. Some were emblazoned with the ads for certain products, one for a laundry detergent, one for a popular soft drink, as if the houses themselves were bulletin boards. I wondered if the companies actually paid these people to decorate their houses in this peculiar way.

While we travelled, Ibrahim read a copy of the *Mwananchi* newspaper while I stared out and watched the country go by. We eventually came to a T-intersection and instead of continuing straight ahead, the coach turned right onto another main road. In so doing, we entered a town called Chalinze where we stopped to drop off and pick up passengers. While we stopped, people came running to each side of the coach, each with a pile of stuff to sell. They held each of their piles of merchandise on long sticks or with long outstretched arms for those of us high above in the coaches who wanted to purchase anything. I thought this was absolutely amazing. What was amusing were the types of items on sale. I remember someone having a box full of personal hygiene products such as bath soap and shampoo. Did these sellers seriously think that on our journey we would have oddly forgotten to bring such products along with us and hence would need to buy them here in the middle of our trip when we could no doubt buy them at a local shop at our final destination? Some of the products were useful, however, such as fruit and other foodstuffs. I was particularly intrigued by the long, thin packets of cashews, about the length of someone's forearm. I asked Ibrahim if he wanted to eat some cashews and to his affirmative reply I then negotiated the price to the seller below the bus in Swahili and with great dexterity carried out the exchange of money and goods in the most vertical exchange I had ever participated in.

We soon continued on. The journey was long but I was happy to just sit and watch the Tanzanian landscape drift by. The further we got into the trip, the more the landscape spread further and further out into the horizon.

There was a time when we came across plantations of a spiky plant that looked like cactuses. What on earth were the farmers there doing growing cactuses in Tanzania? I asked Ibrahim and with one glance out the window he commented that these were sisal plantations. Sisal, so he explained, was a plant with such fibrous leaves that the material was an excellent source for producing rope.

When we reached the middle of the day, the coach stopped at what was obviously a stopover for all coaches. The coach drove into a compound where there were other parked coaches scattered about. The coach driver announced what time we had to return to the coach so that we could continue our journey. Ibrahim and I followed the crowd to a sort of eatery. But it certainly was not the clean, modern, glitzy type of eatery that we would get at home. And there were no fast food outlets like MacDonalds or KFC. This made me realise something I had not been aware of until this time about Tanzania: at no time had I seen one fast food outlet in all of Tanzania. Wow! There was a world where fast food simply did not exist!

What was on offer resembled more of a family barbecue on a grand scale, with cuts of meat barbecued on large hot plates. There were even fried bananas. I decided to follow Ibrahim's lead and only eat vegetarian. The reason for my decision was simply that meat on the stomach while travelling tends to make me feel sluggish and uncomfortable. Ibrahim ordered us a helpful serving of fried bananas with bread.

Soon after, we were once again on our way. As we drifted into the afternoon, I noticed a set of mountains rise to our right. They were majestic to the eye and no doubt a precursor to the greatest mountain, Mount Kilimanjaro, which was further along the way. At other times, I noticed trees with long logs sealed at both ends hanging from the branches. It was quite disenchanting to see and my first reaction was to think that these were coffins. But eventually I plucked up the courage to ask Ibrahim about these macabre looking things only to discover that these suspended logs were not coffins but beehives. These logs were strategically hung from trees to attract bees which would then manufacture the sweet nectar for human consumption.

It was mid afternoon when Ibrahim got up and spoke to the coach driver. Not long after, the bus slowed down until it reached a wide enough area where it could come to a complete stop. Ibrahim and I then got off the bus. The bus then set off and we were left on the side of the main road. One quick look around to get my bearings and I realised we were back in the vicinity of Ibrahim's house. But we weren't staying for long. It was simply a stopover, a sleepover so that we could resume this long adventurous trip.

The next number of days were spent going north west of the country. We went to the Serengeti National Park and Ngorongoro Crater. I discovered that the word *Serengeti* was a Masai word for something like "outstretched plain", possibly the Swahili version of "nyika". The Serengeti was absolutely marvellous. Ibrahim and I spent a number of days there travelling around this vast grassland. We saw all the wild animals that I had seen in documentaries from my childhood, giraffes, zebras, hippopotamuses and elephants. And, of course, the prize of them all, the lions.

Although we had our own hired driver, this driver travelled together with a few other independent drivers to form a small convoy. I can only imagine that the reason behind this was because of safety in numbers. When we came across a pride of lions one afternoon, we were fortunate enough to actually see three prides together, mothers with their cubs and the males with manes fluttering proudly in the afternoon breeze. Though majestic to see, there was a moment in time when I got the whillies and had to draw my head down inside the four wheel drive from the sunroof. Ibrahim simply laughed. It was at this moment that I realised that there truly was safety in numbers. What would happen if our four wheel drive suddenly had a puncture, the radiator overheated or there was some other breakdown in the mechanics of the engine?

It is impossible to find the words to describe just how wonderful it is to actually see these animals in their natural habitat in real life. Seeing these animals in documentaries or even in zoos just doesn't capture the awe and the wonder of it all when you see them in the wild.

The Ngorongoro Crater, which we visited on our return journey, was just as amazing. The crater itself was supposedly formed by the collision of a meteor with our planet way back in the obscure past. I was fortunate to come at this particular time of year because it was at this time that the crater was populated by hundreds and hundreds of many species of wild animals, wilderbeest, zebras, ostriches, hyenas, all gathered together to eat from the lush vegetation and drink from the abundance of water. It was the pink carpet of flamingos that particularly filled me with complete wonderment.

Our driver finally returned us to Arusha where Ibrahim and I caught a bus back to Moshi and then a daladala from Moshi to Ibrahim's little house. It was a long but wonderful tour and I gained a real appreciation of this vast African country.

The following day was my last full day there. I simply wanted to purchase a few mementos of the place and also some gifts to bring back for family members and friends but also for Polycarp and Jeremiah who were themselves sub-Saharan Africans and there was so much merchandise that I knew they would appreciate.

I remember early in the afternoon as we made our way back in the daladala, where I was once again fortunate enough to have a front seat view, that I noticed the sky heavier than normal. Clouds had gathered around the mountain as was always the custom but this particular afternoon, the clouds looked darker and more forboding than I had ever seen them in this part of the world.

"It looks like we're going to have a storm," I commented to Ibrahim.

Ibrahim looked at the sky in the distance but instead of responding to my comment casually, he held a grave expression on his face and nodded, but the way he nodded and the way he looked at this climatic phenomenon was as if something had been planned that he had to fulfil.

When we reached Ibrahim's place, the sun was still shining in the west while the storm clouds gathered in the north around the mountain, dark heavy clouds which signalled a heavy storm. There was soon heard the faint but definite rumbling sounds of thunder. Ibrahim reacted to the sounds rather strangely, as if he were trying to listen to the message the thunder was conveying. We then felt a cool breeze come through the window and the coolness indicated that rain was soon to follow.

"Wow!" I commented. "It feels like we're really going to have a bad storm."

Ibrahim smiled at my comment but it was obvious that his mind had gone into contemplation mode. Was there something about the storm that meant something to Ibrahim? There certainly wasn't a storm in the dream I had related to him.

"I'm taking you back into town to the mosque," Ibrahim then said.

For what reason? I thought. I don't want to go to the mosque. And I certainly don't want to travel back into Moshi while we experience a downpour. I was about to raise my objections when Ibrahim continued.

"When we enter the mosque, all will be well. But when we leave the mosque, we will be confronted. When they see you, they will speak to you in Arabic. They will ask you who you are and where you are from."

Ibrahim then told me what the actual Arabic expressions the man will use.

"Remember what my mother said to you when you told her your name?" Ibrahim continued. He then repeated what his mother had said in Arabic and then translated it although I already knew both the Arabic original and what it meant, that I was Michael from heaven. Musa had drummed this Arabic expression into me long ago so there was no way I could forget it.

"That's what you say in reply. Then all will be well."

I looked on at Ibrahim in total disbelief. As wonderful a man as he was, he came out with such otherworldly nonsense. Could I really live with a guy who believed and lived by such things?

Ibrahim then told me to remain where I was while he went to his mother's house. Ibrahim left me for some time. The problem with Ibrahim's house was that there wasn't much to do. It wasn't like I could turn on the television or even a stereo to play music because Ibrahim's house had no electricity. So, I simply went out and stood in the courtyard and watched the storm clouds slowly gather. The clouds looked threatening but it appeared they had more bark than bite. They swished and swirled slowly around the mountain like a tumultuous ocean.

Eventually Ibrahim returned with a bundle of clothes draped over his right arm. The clothes were all white, so white that "no fuller on earth can white them" as the verse from Mark 9:3 came to me as I put the clothes on. The clothes came with the *kofia*, the traditional Muslim hat. I wasn't sure how to put the kofia on over my long hair but Ibrahim made the appropriate adjustments to keep the kofia in place. Ibrahim himself got changed into ceremonial Muslim clothes. Once in these clothes, I felt that there was something special about dressing up in these clothes. This is an aspect of religion which is quite captivating. There's something special about dressing up in different clothes, clothes that are not of the every day but are special to set aside for a ritual. Everything that made me scared of the Muslim faith disappeared as I accompanied Ibrahim, also similarly attired – and he looked even handsomer than ever – to the mosque dressed as we were and being accompanied by others attending the mosque for prayer.

When we left Ibrahim's house, Ibrahim locked the door and then called in at his mother's house. Ibrahim's mother looked at me in my outfit and made the comment that I looked just how she would envisage the angel Michael with his flowing hair would look dressed in the apparel I was wearing. I didn't know where they got the idea that Michael particularly had to have long hair.

"Michael from heaven," Ibrahim's mother once again said, and once again strangely not in Swahili but in Arabic.

Ibrahim entrusted his keys to his mother and then we walked down the dirt track to the main street.

"We need to get to the mosque quickly so we'll need to catch a bodaboda."

"We need to catch a what?" I asked perplexed.

"A bodaboda. It's like a taxi but it's a motorbike. The motorbike rider can take two passengers at a time. It's a little more expensive than a daladala but we need to be at the mosque on time."

"Why?" I asked. "In time for what?"

Ibrahim stood on the side of the ride and signalled the first bodaboda that came by. But he totally ignored my question. The determination in Ibrahim's countenance beamed off the message that he had a task to complete and nothing was going to sway him from what he had to do, even if I tried to find a reason.

A bodaboda soon stopped. Ibrahim and I climbed on the back and the bodaboda was soon roaring along the street. I had never ridden a motorbike without a helmet before and I was sure that my kofia would not offer me protection should we have an accident. I was also worried that my kofia would actually blow off along the trip and so I had taken it off and placed it under my clothes where it was safe.

It wasn't long before we had arrived in the township of Moshi. It was so different to the slow and staggered trip on the daladala. Once we had arrived at the mosque, it began to rain. Fortunately we had arrived at a place in the mosque where we were off the soil because with the rain coming down, our majestic white clothes would have become obviously dirt stained very quickly. Ibrahim helped me once again to put my kofia on properly so that it didn't fall off.

Ibrahim then took me through the ritual washing. Basically, he washed the appropriate parts of the body in the correct sequence and I followed as if I were his echo.

We then entered the mosque. I was captivated by the beauty inside. Again, I realised just how captivating the religious world was. Whenever I had entered a church, especially traditional Middle Age churches which are decked out and ornate, or synagogues of the same calibre, I noticed how for religious people there was that familiar underlying need to make the insides of the building different and other-worldly appealing. For a moment, while I entered the interior of the mosque, I didn't feel that I was entering something that was distinctly different to other religions which had holy buildings but rather this was a subdivision of the holy building genre.

While reflecting on this, my mind was cast way back into the past when I went to work with Markus. Markus had once said that although different religions have different buildings, when you consider them, they are after all similar in many respects, the way the building protects the devotees from the elements and what occurs inside is ritualistic. But further, I noticed here that the ornateness, the setting, the dress code, the arrangement, although it was distinctly Islamic, it was similarly religious. And somehow, although I did not ascribe to the religion, there was something underlyingly beautiful about it.

The ritual of prayer was rather involved. All those around me must have realised, apart from the fact that I was not dark skinned, that I was not a Muslim as I did not do the movements in complete unison with everyone else. Rather, I was like an echo but a clumsy one at that who followed everyone else. Yet, no-one seemed to make any indication that they cared.

Soon there were the rumbling sounds of thunder. They were distant but because of the contours of the countryside, the sound of the thunder rolled on and on as if great titanic beings in the heavens were having a serious debate. Meanwhile, the rain could be heard pouring down. Because the mosque was a concrete structure, this did not deter the proceedings in the building from continuing.

At one point we sat on the floor while the imam gave a sermon. However, he spoke in Arabic and as my Arabic was rudimentary, I did not understand much at all of what he said. Rather, I just looked around at all the other Muslims sitting on the floor. I could tell, however, that not all of them were listening, as some were chatting to each other. In any case, I listened to the rumbling sounds of the thunder and the heavy sound of water beating down on the soil surrounding the mosque area, noticeable but like background noise. Strangely, the combination of the subtle sound of thunder, the gentle beating down of rain and the sound of the imam giving a talk in Arabic was a harmonious mix of noise which made it feel as if we were floating in a dream.

At one time there was a loud clap of thunder and this caused the imam to stop for a moment. He made a comment and the other members of the mosque looked on in awe. The way they looked at the imam was as if the clap of thunder were God speaking and the imam had just translated the comment into Arabic.

The subsequent claps of thunder were heard in the distance again as if the storm no longer were posing a threat to our immediate vicinity. The sound of the rain had abated which indicated that the storm was moving.

Eventually the ceremony was over and we could leave. Ibrahim and I made our way back out to the entrance to put our shoes on. No sooner had I slipped my feet into my shoes when I heard someone yell out something in Swahili that did not sound very pleasant. When I looked up, I saw a middle-aged man looking across at Ibrahim. His face through his full beard said it all. He was not happy.

"Hey, you!" he called out in Swahili. "What are you doing in this holy house of God? You Muhammad-hater!"

This last comment made the atmosphere electric. Everyone within a ten metre radius stopped and altered their gaze at Ibrahim and me. Ibrahim then grabbed my hand and his grip was very tight. I wasn't sure if this meant that Ibrahim was afraid. However, I certainly was. I knew that Muslims were capable of killing anyone they considered a *kafir* and the statement that this stranger made to Ibrahim was enough to start a jihad. I stood in a way that I was hiding behind Ibrahim as much as I could out of this man's view but enough for me to be able to see him.

This man approached Ibrahim, his face displaying rage. But at one point he looked down and saw that Ibrahim's hand was holding mine. I could feel a flurry of nerves rush up through my face and could just imagine that this situation was going to get worse with two men holding hands inside a holy place. I wanted to let go of Ibrahim's hand but

Ibrahim's grip was so tight that I couldn't do it without it being obvious. The way Ibrahim gripped my hand, it was as if I would never be able to feel my fingers ever again.

The man then looked up at me and his terrifying rage turned to horror as if he had seen a ghost or at least he had seen a police officer just as he was in the act of committing a crime.

There was once again a clap of thunder, not frighteningly close but loud enough to create an impression. The man turned to look back as if the thunder had called his name. He then turned back to look at me but the look on his face was disturbing.

"*Anta*," he said. I knew this was the Arabic word for "you". "Who are you and where are you from?" he asked in Arabic.

Suddenly the whole situation went into slow motion. I was taken back to earlier in the evening when Ibrahim had told me that when we leave the mosque we would be confronted. This was happening right at this point in time and it was frightening. However, Ibrahim had also told me that the man who would confront me would ask me in Arabic who I was and where I was from and this was happening just as Ibrahim had told me. Ibrahim had also instructed me how I was to reply.

"I am Michael," I replied in Arabic. "Michael from heaven."

There was a communal hush through the crowd, not at least from this hostile man who suddenly went pale as if his entire colour were going to drain out from him. Ibrahim's grip tightened even more for a second and then loosened enough for me to feel the blood rushing back through my fingers.

There was a communal sound of surprise. This man who had earlier looked as if he were going to attack Ibrahim now looked on aghast. He then muttered something in Arabic. Ibrahim replied quite at length in beautiful sounding Arabic, melodious and mellifluous. It sounded as if he were delivering a sermon. I heard the word "Koran" mentioned a few times and the names of a number of surahs so I guess Ibrahim was quoting from the Koran in his speech. While Ibrahim spoke, he stood there tall and confident but squeezing my hand the whole time. Ibrahim finally came to an end of speaking and stood there silently. The crowd slowly dissipated. When almost everyone had left, I caught a glimpse of Babeer. He was also wearing traditional Muslim clothes which made it obvious that he had attended the mosque this afternoon as well. He had a rather arrogant look on his face. He raised his head with an overt sign as if to say "I've got you" and then, together with the first man who was enraged to see Ibrahim and then frightened on seeing me, he slipped out of the mosque.

When we were fully outside, the rain was pouring down once again. The others who had been to the mosque ran onto the main street to catch public transport and from there disappeared in the semidarkness in all directions.

"Do you want to wait till the storm has passed?" Ibrahim asked me.

"How long before the storm passes?" I asked.

Ibrahim understood my question. He then grabbed my hand, looked at me and the move of his body communicated what to do next. We dashed away from the mosque and onto the main street. Once we had arrived under a tall tree which offered some protection, we stopped for a moment for Ibrahim to weigh up the situation. The rain continued to fall relentlessly and so Ibrahim took the next step to dash towards a set of buildings in the main street which had shelter.

We kept on like this, at times running when there was nothing to shelter us from the pounding rain, stopping to stroll beneath shelter. My beautiful white clothes were getting wetter and wetter, clinging to my chest and revealing my poor passport hanging in a special pouch. I simply hoped that my passport wouldn't be soaking wet when I got home so that when I got to the airport the following day it would be a terrible mess to hand to the authorities at immigration. I also worried about the outfit I was wearing becoming dirty as it had looked so pristine and clean when I first put it on that it would have been a shame to get such a beautiful white outfit mud and dirt on it.

We finally made it to the bus stop to catch a daladala. There were a number of like-minded, or at least, similarly dressed people on the daladalas so I can only imagine that many of these people had also come back from the mosque. There were also other people making the trip home in the evening under the pouring rain, all looking washed out and all forlorn from the annoying cloudburst. The daladalas were all crowded as if the only reason why people had mounted them was to simply escape the downpour. It seemed so comical the contrast of the atmosphere of solemn serenity while we were wearing these clothes in the mosque to when we were wearing these same clothes now partly wet crammed unceremoniously inside an old, wornout minibus.

The trip back to Ibrahim's place was cramped and uncomfortable but for the love of Ibrahim I followed what he wanted me to do. When we arrived at the place to hop off the daladala, the rain had subsided to a gentle sprinkle of water. We still had to walk through the farmland track which had now become rather muddy and sticky.

We were almost at Ibrahim's mother's place when in the now silence of the night we heard footsteps behind us as if someone were hot on our heels. We turned around to see Babeer walking close behind us. Ibrahim greeted him warmly but I mouthed a greeting as if to make out that Ibrahim's greeting had drowned out mine.

Babeer accompanied us right up to Ibrahim's mother's home. We stopped and exchanged conversation with Babeer. While Ibrahim spoke with Babeer, I had a good look at him. The first thing that grabbed my attention was his scraggy beard. The poor man must have grown a beard simply because it was *sunna*. Because Muhammad had grown a beard, all Muslims who followed the *sunna* had to grow a beard. I sympathised with Babeer because like him, I could not grow a beard which would look presentable. I had tried to grow a beard on several occasions simply because I like facial hair on a man but my attempts were as scraggy as Babeer's which is why I remained clean shaven. Babeer would probably have looked a lot more presentable if he actually didn't have a beard at all. Even a simple moustache would have made his facial features a lot more appealing.

But this idea of *sunna* also troubled me. If everything Muhammad did was *sunna* and therefore all Muslims had to follow this, what happened if a physical attribute of a Muslim simply prevented one from achieving this? Babeer's patchy beard, Ibrahim's left-handedness and both Ibrahim's and my sexuality did not physically allow us to follow everything that Muhammad did. What about everything else about Muhammad? If Muhammad had blue eyes, did this mean everyone had to have blue eyes and therefore wear contact lenses if they had eyes of a different colour? If Muhammad's nose was long, did all Muslims have to stretch their noses out to the same length? If Muhammad had a chest like a shag pile carpet, did all Muslims have to have chests as hairy as his and artificially create this if nature simply failed them? What was also odd was that a requirement of all Muslims is the ability to read the Koran in Arabic yet traditionally Muhammad was illiterate. Shouldn't that therefore mean that to follow the *sunna* Muslims need to remain illiterate and only recite the Koran when the angel Gabriel visited them in a cave? To what extent were Muslims required to follow the *sunna*?

And, of course, if all Muslims need to follow the *sunna*, how do women achieve this?

The appreciation of *sunna* also made less sense in the light of Ibrahim's explanation that all humans are different reflections of the one God who is both a singularity and yet a plurality as Muhammad could only be one of these several reflections. Would God want everyone to imitate only a portion of His several aspects?

Ibrahim spoke cordially with Babeer and Babeer responded just as cordially but I was getting negative vibes from him. His patchy beard, missing teeth and the couple of scars on his face only accentuated what seemed to already be negative about him. He spoke pleasantly with Ibrahim but I kept having flashbacks of the way he interrogated me on my first night here, how he later strangely had injured himself while Ibrahim and I had the long discussion late in the night, and then of how he had followed out the man who verbally attacked Ibrahim at the mosque earlier this evening. He was bad news and I wished he would go away. Soon enough, my wish was granted and Babeer continued on to his house further along the track.

When we arrived at Ibrahim's mother's house, Ibrahim yelled out *hodi* and Ibrahim's mother soon came out and presented Ibrahim with his keys. Ibrahim then took us into his home and we got changed into some dry clothes. Once changed, Ibrahim's mother received our mosque clothes and then returned to bring us dinner.

Ibrahim served me. There was a rice dish that looked partly yellowish, partly brown and partly white. It smelt rather spicy. Ibrahim explained that this was biriani. It was a food preparation that actually came from India or so he believed. Ibrahim explained to me all the other dishes on the table. Not one of them contained meat. So it was obvious that Ibrahim's mother knew Ibrahim's unique Muslim dietary requirements.

But that wasn't what was on my mind at the time. What was sitting on my mind waiting for an answer was the event at the mosque. Once Ibrahim had served me and was putting food in his own plate, I spoke.

"That man was angry at you and called you a Muhammad-hater," I stated. "But you are a Muslim. How can you be a Muhammad-hater?"

Ibrahim smiled as he reached over to put one of the serving spoons back into the dish that held the food.

"Unfortunately, I am not really welcome at this mosque because many people know me there, particularly those my age. They don't like me and accuse me of being a Muhammad-hater because I have told them the truth about Muhammad and they don't like it."

"What truth?" I asked, the mystery becoming more intriguing.

"That we should not worship Muhammad. Muslims have gone too far in their veneration of Muhammad that they now worship him like Christians worship Issa. The way some Muslims venerate Muhammad, they are committing *sheerk*. Christians have done this for a long time, associating Issa with Allah saying that Issa is Allah or the Son of Allah when Issa was only a messenger. But so was Muhammad. What Muhammad said was not from his mind but straight from Allah."

"What do you mean?"

Ibrahim sat down and settled himself in his chair.

"Many Muslims say that we should grow a beard like Muhammad, we should do ablutions like Muhammad, we should pray like Muhammad, we should even include in our prayers an acknowledgement of Muhammad. Muslims criticise Christians when Christians say they should imitate Issa but then some Muslims do exactly the same with regards to Muhammad. At least Christians have a point because they believe that Issa *is* Allah even though Christians shouldn't commit *sheerk*. But Muslims don't believe Muhammad is Allah. They believe he, like all those before him, was purely a messenger. However, many Muslims then venerate Muhammad as if he were Allah when he was only a man."

I looked on aghast at Ibrahim. I was amazed he was still alive. But what he had to say was also true. This was another point about *sunna*. If Muslims were supposed to follow everything Muhammad did, this made it sound like Muhammad was God. And like Ibrahim said, I remembered as a Christian that I had to copy everything that Jesus did. At least there was a logic to it because as a Christian I had to believe that Jesus was God and therefore what Jesus did was what God did and what He wanted us to do.

"You think about it, Bwana Michael," Ibrahim continued. Ibrahim then picked up a glass of water. "Look at this glass of water. What refreshes you, the water or the glass that holds the water?"

"Naturally, the water," I replied.

"And what is the function of the glass?"

"To hold the water."

"That's right. So once you have drunk the water, will you praise the water that quenched your thirst or the glass which held the water?"

"Naturally, the water," I once again replied.

"And that's the same with Allah and His messengers. Allah's message is like water, sent to refresh our souls. The messengers are simply the glass that carries the water. There have been many messengers but the same water – the same message – has been delivered by these messengers. The water did not develop out of the glass itself but came from the well of everlasting water of Allah. And it is quite clear from the Koran. As it says in Al-Imran 3:81, 'It is not possible for Allah to bid you take the angels and

the Prophets for Lords'. There is only one Lord, the 'Lord of the worlds'
as it says in the Al-Fatihah. Allah is therefore my Lord, not Muhammad."

There was a bit of a shudder that passed through my body. If this
was something that Ibrahim said out loud within the Muslim community,
I was surprised he was still alive today and telling me of these events.
But then, what he had to say was quite logical so why would the Muslim
community get so upset for something that Ibrahim said especially as
he backed it up from the Koran? Weren't Muslims critical of people who
committed *sheerk* and isn't this what people were doing if they venerated
Muhammad as if he were God?

This also took me back to something else that Ibrahim had said long
ago about the relationship between what someone says and what they
do. In that earlier case, Ibrahim argued that just because people say with
their mouths that they believe in God and Muhammad, these were just
words that come out of these people's mouths. A true believer shows
belief through actions. In the same way, just because Muslims say with
their mouths that Muhammad is only a messenger and is not God, by their
very actions, there was nothing different between the way some Muslims
venerated Muhammad and the way the Christians venerated Christ.

"Many Muslims," Ibrahim continued, "rely too much on the Hadiths.
So much effort has been made to try and capture every word that came
from Muhammad's lips as if the words came from Muhammad and not
from Allah."

This was becoming more and more interesting.

"Allah doesn't need Muhammad," Ibrahim continued.

When Ibrahim said this, I thought I was going to choke on the food
that was in my mouth. Once again, I wondered how Ibrahim managed to
remain alive if he said this out loud.

"I don't mean that with any irreverence," Ibrahim continued.
"Muhammad was a great prophet and I respect him. But he was simply
only a messenger all the same, along with all the other messengers. As
Allah tells us in the Koran, in surah Al-Imran 3:85

> *We believe in Allah and in that which has been revealed to us, and
> that which was revealed to Abrahim and Ishmael and Isaac and Jacob
> and the Tribes, and that which was given to Moses and Jesus and other
> prophets from their Lord. We make no distinction between any of them.*

And again, in surah Al-Nisa 4:153

And as for those who believe in Allah and in all of His
Messengers and make no distinction between any of them,
these are they whom He will give their rewards.

Let me stress that: 'those who believe in Allah and in *all* of His messengers and make *no* distinction between any of them'. These are the words of Allah.

Allah reprimands the Christians in Al-Ma'idah 5:76 by saying

The Messiah, son of Mary, was only a Messenger;
surely, Messengers have indeed passed away before him

It is not simple coincidence that Allah says the same thing to Muslims when He says in surah Al-Imran 3:145

Muhammad is only a Messenger. Verily, all
Messengers have passed away before him.

This could not be any clearer."

Ibrahim took another mouthful of food as if what we were discussing was as mundane as the price of peanut butter. But I was absolutely flabbergasted.

"But what about Muhammad being the last and greatest prophet?" I asked. "I thought that was what made him special and above all the other prophets."

Ibrahim leaned back.

"If Muhammad is the greatest prophet and above all the other prophets, then we have a difficulty with the verses which say that we make no distinction between the prophets.

The verse in the Koran that is used to say that Muhammad is the greatest and the last prophet is in surah Al-Ahzab 33:41 where it is written

Muhammad is… the Messenger of Allah and the Seal of the Prophets.

Some Muslims take a momentous leap and then say, 'See? He is the Seal of the Prophets, therefore He is the last and greatest prophet'. But that's not what this verse is saying. The verse simply says that he is the *khaatama*, the *seal* of the prophets. And what is he sealing? He is sealing all the prophets together. Like a seal on an envelope which sticks all the papers inside together, so Muhammad sticks all the other prophets together because he acknowledges all the other prophets and brings them all together in unity. But that doesn't make him *better* than any of the other prophets. He simply fulfilled a function at a particular time in history when communication between the nations had been made easy.

Suddenly, people from different countries realised that other nations had prophets whom they respected. These nations didn't know how to react towards these other prophets. Muhammad simply sealed them all together, explaining that all need to be respected."

Ibrahim smiled and went to pick up his fork when he added, "Including your prophet, Socrates."

Once again I could feel a blush over my cheeks and a rush to my head. There was a silence while we both digested what Ibrahim had just said.

But then Ibrahim became passionate. Like a passionate pastor in a church and possibly like a passionate imam in the mosque, he extended his sermonising.

"The problem with some Muslims," Ibrahim explained, "is that they criticise Christians for believing in a Holy Trinity, venerating Father, Son and Holy Ghost. But some Muslims also worship a holy trinity, Muhammad, Mecca and the Koran. Muhammad is only a messenger, Mecca is only a place and the Koran is only a book."

This last outburst filled me with fear. What if Muslims in the vicinity heard what Ibrahim was saying? They would react violently, probably killing him, and possibly me as well simply because of my association with him. But it also filled me with curiosity.

"What do you mean?"

"As I said," Ibrahim continued, "Muhammad is only one of many prophets. He is important and he is significant. But we are commanded not to make distinctions between them."

"And Mecca?" I asked almost in a whisper. "Isn't this the holy place for Muslims?"

"Yes, it is a holy place. But it is still only a place. Allah is higher and more important than Mecca or any place on the earth. After all, Allah created the entire world so the whole world should be holy."

I sat there and listened, stunned at what he was saying. "So, what about Muslims praying to Mecca?"

"Muslims should be praying the *qiblah*. Some Muslims say that the *qiblah*, the direction of prayer, is towards Mecca. But which is greater? Mecca or Allah? *Qiblah* is simply an Arabic word and means 'direction'. Really, the true *qiblah* is the *qiblah al anzar*, the focus of attention, which is towards Allah. When we pray, we should focus on the *qiblah al anzar*, the prayer towards Allah whom we cannot see but when we close our eyes we can then focus on Allah who lives in the heavens, within a dimension beyond the one we live in now."

As soon as Ibrahim said this, I was taken back to the first time I had met him and the strange prayer that he prayed on the bed, almost like an Eastern form of meditation. Ibrahim's form of prayer was more like a yogic mantra than the active physical action of praying as the Muslims do in the mosque.

"How quickly Muslims have not listened to the prophets," Ibrahim continued. "Allah through Issa, in the Injil, prophesied that there will come a time when the *qiblah* will no longer be towards Jerusalem but will be towards Allah who is everywhere, all around us. This has been interpreted that the *qiblah* will be changed from Jerusalem to Mecca. And what is in Mecca that these Muslims pray to but a large rock? Allah is not a rock! Allah is constantly insulted by those who say they believe in Him but then pray towards a rock, something that is a mere creation, very much like an idol. And certainly no different to one."

Ibrahim appeared to be becoming rather agitated. I was becoming quite intrigued. What Ibrahim was saying was an interpretation of what Jesus said to the woman at the well in the fourth chapter of John. The contention between Jesus, who was a Jew, and the woman at the well, who was a Samaritan, was the location of central worship. The Jews claimed that it was at Jerusalem where the true worshippers were to worship God. The Samaritan woman claimed it was a place in the north of Judea where Jacob had bought a piece of land for his son Joseph.

But what Ibrahim was saying also made sense. Jesus came along and told the woman at the well that there would no longer be any dispute as to where worshippers were to worship God for "God is a Spirit: and they that worship him must worship him in spirit and in truth" (John 4:24). The logic was that if God is everywhere, as Jews, Christians and Muslims claim, there is no central place on the planet in which to worship God. Otherwise, that place is greater than God. But that it was Ibrahim who said it, someone who said he believed that Allah is God and Muhammad is His messenger, this was signficant.

"And Allah is not a book," Ibrahim continued. It was as if Ibrahim were preaching to me, as if I had to know. "The Torah, the Injil and the Koran are simply books. But these religious people treat these books in exactly the same way as idolators treat their idols. They venerate them, they clean them, they put them in honoured places and they kill those who damage them."

I was quite stunned by this statement. What was quite unnerving was that should unthinking, intolerant Muslims hear what Ibrahim had to say, they would kill him there and then. At least Jews and Christians would just become red-faced and call him horrible names or dream up terrible curses against him.

But then, this last statement sounded highly contradictory. Throughout all this time, Ibrahim had been quoting directly from these three particular sources of holy literature as if these books were the bedrock upon which he based everything he believed and now he was making this statement which did not make sense.

"But Ibrahim," I replied. I wasn't sure how to word this. To me, what he was saying was hypocrisy but Ibrahim always had a particular reason for what he said. I needed to find out what this reason was.

"Ibrahim, if you feel so strongly about this, why do you quote so much from these books?"

Ibrahim leaned back and laughed. "No, I don't think you get what I mean."

Ibrahim reached over and picked up a Koran that was lying somewhere within his reach.

"See this?" he asked me and held the Koran before my eyes. "It's just an object of paper."

Ibrahim then opened the book to the middle. He then held onto one of the pages and rubbed it with his thumb and forefinger.

"This is just paper and ink. It could just as well be the *Mwananchi* newpaper. Here, look," he said and then tossed the Koran on the floor.

I felt the entire Muslim community gasp in horror as he treated the Koran in what appeared to be complete disrespect.

"See? It's just an object. It is not this object of paper and ink that is important. It is the way you live your life in accordance with the words written inside. It is us, the way we live the Koran, or the Injil, or the Torah, and as it says in the Koran, how we live all three, and how we live *all* the holy books, this is where the holiness is, not in the actual book itself. It is in this way that many people err in their ways."

That word "err" intrigued me. I had never, ever heard anyone use this word before. It was such a religious word. But it sounded so beautiful coming from Ibrahim's lips.

But there was something eerily familiar about what Ibrahim was saying. I remembered long, long ago Markus, someone who I had loved deeply, who said something similar about my approach to the Bible, that I loved this book of paper and ink more than people. I was hearing this again, but this time through the voice of someone else whom I loved.

"But what about the reaction to me when that man asked me who I was?" I continued. "I mean, first of all, why did he ask me in Arabic? And why did he react the way he did?"

Ibrahim laughed.

"A long time ago, I was thrown out of the mosque here at Moshi because of my message. I tried to open the eyes of the people, to show them that the words I spoke to them were true. But no-one would listen, even though I showed them that what I said came straight from the Koran. Then one night I had a dream. I dreamt that Michael the archangel stood with me at the steps of the mosque, his clothes gleaming white, his long hair flowing down from his head and over his shoulders, like the rain of mercy from the clouds of Allah that tumbles down from the sky and washes away the filth of Satan. I understood the dream and so related it to the people of this mosque. I told them that they will see me again with Michael, and when they do, they will know that I have spoken the truth. They will know it is Michael because when they ask where he is from, he will say that he is Michael, from heaven. I told them that this would also begin the fulfilment of the prophecy in Al-Dukhan 44:11, 'But watch for the day when the sky will bring forth a visible cloud' and in Al-Furqan 25:26, 'And the day when the heaven shall rent asunder with the clouds, and the angels shall be sent down'. When that day comes, so I told them, they will be required to open their hearts and stop worshipping Muhammad, stop worshipping Mecca and stop worshipping paper objects. They were then to recognise that they are not to make a distinction between the prophets and how they were to do this was to enter a church or other holy place and ask Allah for forgiveness, that is, ask Allah, not Issa, not Mary, not anyone else but Allah. Then they are to start making peace with Christians and those of other religions by going out and meeting them, speaking with them, start building friendly relationships with them – "

Is that, then, how Ibrahim interpreted the view of the clouds that accumulated around Mount Kilimanjaro, dark and threatening, and then the resulting storm and downpour of rain?

Of all the wonderful things Ibrahim had to say to me, this was definitely not one of them. These words caused conflict inside of me. As much as I realised that my feelings for this man were deep, all this stuff about the holy books, angels, fulfilments of prophecy, and particularly my supposed role in the affair caused something inside me to snap. I had reached a point that I couldn't tolerate all this unfounded nonsense anymore.

"No, Ibrahim, no," I interrupted, half in a whisper, shaking my head vehemently. "No, I'm not an angel and you must know that. I am Michael Farril. I come from Sydney. I know who my parents were and now even my ancestors. I grew up in a small suburb way out in the west of Sydney, a very small and little-known one. I went to school just like your average person and later went to university. I go to work and come home, I get tired, I get hungry and I get thirsty like everyone else, sometimes I'm happy, sometimes sad and sometimes frustrated. This means that I am simply a human being. I am not a tool to be used in a religious play especially as there is no evidence to support any of this."

Ibrahim just looked at me calmly and did not say a word.

"You know, Ibrahim," I continued, "I know that you are religious and that you show respect to all the holy books, at least the Christian Bible and the Koran, and I think simply for my sakes you throw in Socrates because nobody else on this planet both past and present as far as I'm aware has ever considered Socrates anything more than just a philosopher."

Ibrahim looked on in silence but the expression on his face did not show exactly how he felt about what I was saying.

"But I want to tell you how I view things really and why I view them the way I do. This beautiful God you talk about, this wonderful deity who is full of compassion and wants us to protect the universe that He created, that He loves everyone and is struggling to protect us and all He has created from the Destroyer, as beautiful as this God that you love and worship is, this God you describe and follow isn't the God of the Bible nor of the Koran. The God of the Torah, the Injil and the Koran is just horrible!"

"No, it's not Allah who is horrible," Ibrahim contradicted. "It's the Destroyer which makes people believe He is."

"It's not the Destroyer which says it, but the very holy books themselves," I replied. "I mean, just the idea of a Satan, or what you say, the Destroyer, being something that God created already tells me that this God is not terribly nice. The fundamental problem with the biblio-koranic idea of Satan is that such a thing actually exists at all. The Bible hints at it and Koran states it quite clearly that God created Satan. But how can an Almighty God create a diabolical creature? Even if God did not create Satan to be an evil being, Satan turned out to be so. But if God knows the future before it happens and He knew that if He created this Satan, this Satan would turn out to be His enemy, why did God create Satan in the first place? Why did God create an enemy?

But further, not only did God create Satan, either intentionally or unintentionally to be the evil creature and the archenemy of God, God allowed Satan to exist and cause the confusion among us humans. As soon as Satan rebelled against God, why didn't God simply annihilate Satan there and then? According to the Bible, God will destroy Satan in the end because it says in Revelation 20:10, 'and the devil that deceived them was cast into the lake of fire and brimstone'. The Koran even confirms this by saying in Al-Shu'ara 26:92, 'And Hell shall be opened to those who have gone astray' including, as it says in verse 96 'the hosts of Iblis, all together'. So why didn't God destroy Satan in the beginning? The Bible does not provide an answer to this but the Koran does as it says in Al-Hijr 15:37 – 39 that Satan begged God to spare him and God granted his request. God granted Satan his request to spare him! Why? It wasn't because Satan was going to finally repent and worship God. Rather, God allows Satan to exist so that Satan can go out and get as many people into hell as he can. And God allows this which means that God Himself wants people to go to hell. When we read through the Bible and the Koran about Satan tricking people into believing that God does not exist, God punishes the people, not Satan, for being deceived by this powerful being, much more powerful than us human mortals. This is not an act of love! If God didn't want people to be deceived by Satan, if God really loved humans and His universe the way Christians and Muslims claim that He does, why doesn't God get rid of Satan now? It is already ordained that He will do it later, so why wait? Then there will no longer be this awful creature around to deceive people into believing God does not exist and then God's world would be perfect."

Ibrahim looked on but then smiled.

"Bwana Michael, it's not quite like that," he replied.

"But also," I continued, "we read that Jehovah is an awfully destructive deity. When we read the stories in the Torah, this ogre Jehovah is just awful. He is not the compassionate and kind being that the holy books claim Him to be. I mean, when I recently read the story of Noah and the Flood, my eyes were opened to just how horrible Jehovah is. We read in Genesis 6:5 that the reason why God decided to destroy the man He had created was because 'every imagination of the thoughts of his heart was only evil continually'. But then after the Flood when Noah and his family came out of the Ark to start the human species anew, Jehovah says in Genesis 8:21 that He acknowledged that humans were still the same and that 'the imagination of man's heart is evil from his youth' regardless. So, the Flood did not achieve anything but was simply a show of God's destructive rage. In other words, Jehovah destroyed all His creatures, except those who survived the Flood, in full knowledge that humans would continue to have evil imaginations after this utter destruction anyway. So, the Flood didn't do anything to improve on the humans God Himself had created but was more of a story to show how horrible Jehovah really was!"

"Bwana Michael," Ibrahim then said, "I don't think the story is quite like this."

"Well, the holy books testify otherwise," I replied. "The God of the Bible and the Koran is simply vindictive. He's just awful. In fact, the God of the Bible and the Koran makes Adolf Hitler look charitable."

Ibrahim's eyes widened in horror at this statement. "How can you compare Allah to Hitler?" Ibrahim gasped with a strong hint of anger in his voice.

"Because the similarity is there. What happened to all those caught in the Third Reich who did not believe that Hitler was a great guy, the great Fuhrer? Hitler put them in concentration camps. At least Hitler knew that these concentration camps were temporary for as long as the natural lives of those who were sent there. So, for Hitler, those he sent to concentration camps would eventually find respite from the horrors of the death camps by dying. But not with God. All three religions of the books, Judaism, Christianity and Islam, show a Hitlerish style of God who will put all opponents into eternal concentration camps much worse than Hitler's because in God's concentration camps, those punished will never find respite as God won't allow it. Hitler could not make those he sent to the concentration camps experience the horror of the concentration camps for eternity because Hitler did not have the power to keep those sent there alive for that long. But according to the Bible and the Koran, God does, and He means to use this power. As He says in Isaiah 66:24 those who He throws into hell will remain in a place where 'their worm shall not die, neither shall their fire be quenched'. That's horrible! Even gentle Jesus, meek and mild, who the Christians look on as this loving sort of character, says in the Gospels on several occasions that in hell there will be 'weeping and gnashing of teeth'. And he then says in Matthew 25 that the unbelievers will be sent to 'everlasting punishment' in the form of 'everlasting fire, prepared for the devil and his angels' to be as it says in Revelation 20:10 'tormented day and night for ever and ever'. And if that's not nasty enough, God says in the Koran in Ta Ha 20:75 that 'for him is Hell; he shall neither die therein nor live'. That is, those in hell will never lose consciousness but one could not call the conscious state in hell a life. So, the intent is to keep the person alive enough to feel the suffering forever. That would have been Hitler's dream if he had that power. But it's positively awful! But worse is how it is described in Al-Mu'minum 23:105 that 'the Fire will burn their faces and they will grin with fear therein' and in Al-Nisa 4:57 that 'those who disbelieve in Our Signs, We shall soon cause them to enter fire. As often as their skins are burnt up, We shall give them in exchange other skins that they may taste the punishment'. You have to have a brutal, vindinctive mind to even think like this. What is further vindictive is that God in all these holy books says that we will be thrown into hell simply for not believing in His existence. I mean, if God really wants us to know that He exists, all He needs to do is appear out of the sky and say, 'Look, guys! Here I am! I exist!' But He doesn't. Quite the contrary. According to the holy books, this terribly vindictive, awful God hides Himself and wants us to believe without any evidence of His existence. And then, on the Day of Judgement, when we will all supposedly appear before Him, we will finally see Him but, so the holy books say, it will be too late for us to say, 'Oh, finally we have evidence of your existence. Now I know you exist because I can see you.' He's going to say, 'Well, it's too late, now. When I provided you with no evidence of my existence, you didn't believe I existed. So it doesn't matter now that it is extremely obvious that I exist, you're going to burn in hell forever and ever, and I'm going to make sure that you continually have parts of your body to keep burning and feeling the pain forever and ever and ever'. And this will be our punishment."

I stopped simply to take a breath and then continued.

"And it's not even punishment. If we punish someone, we do something bad to them so that they learn not to do it again. But God's hell is not punishment. Once in hell, you never escape. So you don't learn anything. You don't learn to be a better person at all because you are there forever and never come out.

I mean, I don't know what they told you as a Muslim but as a Christian, I was told that the reason why we don't see God or have any perception of Him is because we are sinful creatures and God can't associate with sinful creatures. But then, on this supposed Judgement Day, those of us who have died in our sins will still be sinful creatures when we stand before the throne of God. So, we'll still be sinful creatures when we finally see God anyway. So, why doesn't God allow us to see Him now? How much easier would this make it to believe in His existence? And then there would no longer be any reason to simply believe He exists, we would actually know it and be certain of His existence because we will have hard evidence. Then Satan's deception would further have no power because when Satan whispers in our ear that God doesn't exist, we would have to say, 'Well, hello! I've actually seen Him with my own eyes and heard his voice'."

Ibrahim smiled. He actually smiled! And I had been so incredibly condemning of his beliefs.

"So, does that mean you believe that the Bible and the Koran are evil books?" Ibrahim asked.

In a way, I wanted to reply in the affirmative. Ibrahim taught history. Surely he had studied the history of Europe and probably the Middle East as well. As such, he would have read about the awful destruction caused because of disputes over religion and the resulting carnage that ensued. But I decided to answer it in a different way using the very books themselves.

"Ibrahim," I said, "why do we need the Bible and the Koran in the first place?"

"Because," Ibrahim replied, obviously quite unshaken by what I had just been saying, "these books help us to know what is right and wrong."

"But that's the problem," I replied. "These books themselves tell us that they are not needed. Right at the beginning of the Torah, we discover that books and messengers sent from God to tell us what is right and wrong are wholly unnecessary. We find this in the story of Adam and Eve. You know, when I was growing up, I was told that when Adam and Eve ate from the Forbidden Tree, they became sinful beings and this sinfulness was passed down to all humanity like a genetic disposition. But the Torah doesn't say that. Rather, before Adam and Eve ate from the Tree of the Knowledge of Good and Evil, they didn't know what right and wrong were. When they ate the fruit of this tree, they became like the gods, 'knowing good and evil'. So, the genetic disposition that was passed down from Adam and Eve to all their descendants was not sinfulness but the knowledge of good and evil. So, according to the story in the Torah, the knowledge of good and evil is already inherently intrinsic in us. No book or messenger can tell us more than what we already know, knowledge acquired through our first parents' act of eating of the fruit which contained this knowledge.

But also, you have mentioned several times that the Koran provides signs for those who reflect. If the Koran requires us to reflect, then we are not called to submit and therefore mindlessly obey. If we are called to submit and obey, then there is no room to reflect. You mentioned that you realised that all couples, man to woman, man to man or woman to woman, are all helpful to humankind. You did not get this as a directive from the Koran but on reflection. Societies which have allowed all unions irrespective of gender have also reflected before allowing such unions and none of this reflection came from the edicts from ancient manuscripts. So, if we are required to reflect, what need is there of the Holy Books?

I mean, you think about it. Soldiers in the army are required to obey without thinking. If they were required to reflect, they would question whether or not it was necessary to obey an order. Rather, they are taught to obey unquestioningly. Reflection requires questioning what one is told. Therefore, to reflect on what you read in the Koran means that you have to ask yourself whether or not certain commandments are actually beneficial or not. To submit to what it says in the Koran means you do it without thinking. To reflect on and to submit to what you read in the Koran are mutually exclusive. And yet the Koran demands that you do both. When the Koran commands you to do something that on reflection you see is a bad thing to do, do you continue to obey the edict as presented in the Koran or do you follow your reflection?"

Ibrahim just stared at me. There was some silence after my outburst.

I felt as if I had just vomited. There was some relief in getting out of the system something that was making the internals feel terrible. At the same time, the horrible mess that resulted was quite unpleasant.

There was a long moment of silence. What do we say now? I wished then that I was at the airport on my way home. Finally Ibrahim broke the silence.

"Bwana Michael," Ibrahim began unswavered, "I don't have answers to what you have said. But I still believe the Bible and the Koran are holy books from Allah. I admit that I cannot answer these questions for you at the moment but I am sure there are answers to these questions."

Ibrahim paused for a moment and then said, "I appreciate that you have difficulty believing the holy books."

He then paused for a little longer. Finally he added, "But does that mean you cannot love me?"

There was a plea in that question. I felt terrible and it took me a while before I could finally answer.

"Ibrahim," I replied. "How can you, a religious person, a very religious person, love me, someone you know questions everything about your holy books and questions the very existence of a god?"

There was a deathly silence in the room. It was positively awful. Why was it that the discussion of religious beliefs always seemed to muddy the atmosphere and spoil human relationships? But eventually Ibrahim broke the silence.

"If you don't believe in Allah," Ibrahim then said quietly, "nor in the Holy Books, I still love you, Bwana Michael. I love you because everything about you, your very soul is like one who is devoted to serving Allah."

I rolled my eyes and Ibrahim responded to this.

"Yes, I know," he hastened to add. "You don't believe in Allah. But your goal is the same as mine. You want to help people and so do I. You want people to increase their knowledge and so do I. You want to increase their happiness and well-being and so do I. You associate with people irrespective of their race or religion, and so do I. You believe in the preservation of the earth, and so do I. I acknowledge that we have different views of Allah and Holy Books, but beyond that, what we want to achieve in this world is the same. Is that at least enough for you to love me?"

This last question forced me to rise out of my chair, walk around to Ibrahim and hug him tightly. We held on to each other for some time and allowed the sound of the pouring rain and the distant thunder serenade us. Finally we moved apart. I suggested to Ibrahim that maybe we should clean up and make our way to bed.

Ibrahim and I returned to Ibrahim's bedroom. With the aid of a hurricane lamp, I did a last minute check of my luggage in preparation for the following day's flight out, that I had my passport and other flight documentation ready. Soon we had changed and were in bed.

I held Ibrahim tightly. I wasn't sorry for what I had said. I was sorry that it was something unpleasant for Ibrahim to hear and I told him so. I admitted that he as a religious man and I as a non-religious man can co-exist even intimately if our goals were ultimately the same. But also, we could co-exist if we loved each other.

And finally I told him that I loved him. I told him that despite his religiosity, I thought he was the most wonderful man I had ever met, that he had the most wonderful characteristics I had ever known in a person and that he had a beautiful heart. Ibrahim responded with similar comments. He told me that he could not and did not want to live without me. He told me that life would no longer be bearable if I wasn't a part of his.

We therefore shared a very pleasant night. This was our last night together. The following day I had to be at the airport and make the long flights back home.

You appreciate the person you love when you know your togetherness is temporary, and especially as our separation was quite vast. Eight thousand kilometres of ocean, four thousand kilometres of land and a lot of money kept us apart.

The next morning, Ibrahim told me that he wanted to stop at the Msingi wa Mungu Project before going to the airport. I really didn't want to. What I wanted was to spend the last number of hours just the two of us together while the sands of time went rushing through the hourglass. I don't know why I couldn't have just said this but for some reason I didn't. I nodded in acceptance, not in agreement.

Ibrahim had organised the same car and driver that picked me up from the airport to take me back. Once we had arrived at the project, Ibrahim asked at the entrance where to find Gordon. Gordon welcomed me back to Tanzania and then was engaged in what sounded like quite a serious conversation with Ibrahim. I did not quite follow the flow of the conversation and so I just looked around at the compound. Memories of my first time here came back, the time when I arrived, what I really felt of Ibrahim when I first met him and the amazing and beautiful turn of events that came out of it.

The conversation turned out quite serious between Gordon and Ibrahim as if something of extreme importance were about to happen. I simply guessed that there was an upcoming issue that Ibrahim and Gordon had to deal with and they were in preparation to deal with it once I had left.

Once this serious conversation was over, Gordon asked me about my stay in Tanzania and my trips around the country. I gave him a running summary of the events and the enjoyment it brought me.

"I wish you a safe trip back home," Gordon then said. And then as if it were an afterthought, he said to me something which seemed so strange and out of context, and without any particular meaning, "And everything will be fine. You will make it safely out of the country. And don't worry, everything will turn out well."

This made my heart freeze. Was that the serious conversation that Gordon and Ibrahim were having with each other? Was something terribly serious on a national scale about to erupt, some civil war, a rebellion, a coup that would make it difficult for tourists to get out of the airport and out of the country? And if it was going to be safe for me to get out, what would the situation be for those who were left? What further would occur from Ibrahim's prophecy?

A wisp of fear came over me. But before I had the opportunity to quiz Gordon, Gordon shook Ibrahim's and my hand, wished us well and signalled us to go.

I was beginning to feel ashamed and even frightened of my outburst from the previous evening after Ibrahim had explained the prophecy. Was my disbelief about to cause something to happen, or were terrible things about to occur in fulfilment of the prophecy despite my disbelief?

From the project we had to pass through the centre of town to get petrol. We passed a church and outside there were groups of people congregating and in deep discussion. It was obvious that there were two different groups of people, one lot wearing the type of clothes that Ibrahim and I had been wearing the night before and others wearing what looked like everyday attire according to Moshi standards. Hence one group of people were no doubt Muslims. Muslims attending church? I then thought of what Ibrahim had told me of the prophecy. But I just couldn't accept it. This couldn't be happening even though my eyes could see what was taking place.

This then made the trip to the airport much more of concern to me. Ibrahim's comment about the prophecy sounded quasi-apocalyptic. What made it even worse was Gordon's comment about me getting out of Tanzania safely. All these comments played again and again in my mind. At one time, I just reached over and grabbed Ibrahim's hand. Ibrahim looked at me and smiled, then placed our clasped hands on his lap, passing a loving and gentle rub over the back of my hand with his free hand, a non-verbal sign to acknowledge my presence but also to further acknowledge the bond that had developed between us.

But then, he simply looked towards the front of the car, past the driver, through the windscreen and into the distance ahead of us. His look was determined as if there was something serious that he expected to arise from the journey. The stare was soon followed by increasing pressure he exerted on my hand as he squeezed it within his lap.

We finally made it to the airport, the familiar little unassuming building I had become familiar with. Ibrahim got out one side and I the other while Ibrahim looked around pensively. This unusual behaviour was increasing the tension of the atmosphere. Already the separation was approaching and this was making the sorrow weigh heavily in my heart but this feeling of sorrow was becoming more and more replaced by a sense of anxiety by Ibrahim's irregular behaviour.

Ibrahim grabbed the larger of my two travel bags from the boot of the car. The driver then made a comment in Swahili but it sounded so mumbled I had no idea what he said. Ibrahim began to engage in a lively conversation with him but the driver kept his grim countenance and his insistence. Ibrahim then replied back in rapid Swahili and then held up his open hand with his five fingers open in the sign of the number five so I guessed that he was telling the driver he would be back in five minutes. Once we began walking to the airport building, Ibrahim confirmed my suspicions. This, then, explained Ibrahim's erratic behaviour, I thought. A sense of relief passed through my body coupled with an immense feeling of love. It was obvious all the time I had been with him that he loved me but this was yet another wave of confirmation of that love he had for me, so much so that this separation from me was affecting him as much as it was affecting me.

We arrived at the building. The entrance was unassuming and was supposed to be the echo of immigration in larger international airports like the one in my home city but this looked nothing more than an entrance to a small social hall in the suburbs. The official at the door who inspected my ticket apart from being dressed meticulously correct in uniform looked more like an usher in an old cinema than someone in an official capacity.

Before I entered, Ibrahim once again confessed that he had to go. What was it, I thought, about these people who brought us to the airport that made them suddenly want to keep tightly to time schedules whenever Ibrahim and I had to say farewell? Everything else about the country always occurred at a leisurely pace.

Ibrahim and I then embraced. I would have liked to have had one more passionate kiss but I knew this would have been totally dangerous in this place. It was a strong embrace, the tight embrace that communicated the impending separation, that this would be the last time we would be able to be in physical contact for a long time, a time period that had no definite end. I wanted to soak this moment in, to feel Ibrahim's body pressed close to mine, to smell his person, to soak in everything about him.

We heard the sound of an insistent car horn and it was obvious that this was the last trumpet sound which heralded the final separation from each other. Ibrahim pulled himself away from me and stroked my right cheek with his left hand without saying a word. His eyes were red and pools of water had formed inside them. He then turned and left, and I could tell by the movements of his left arm that he was wiping the tears from his eyes as he walked away. The water works were suddenly beginning to bubble up inside me as well.

I heard the voice of the official at the entrance to the airport in uniform say something which made me turn around. I had been blocking the entrance into the building. It was a very dispassionate address after a very passionate moment. I walked through the entrance and watched Ibrahim continue to walk away. But then he stopped. He turned and looked in the direction of the airport. At the same time, I heard an announcement of my flight and I knew I had to check in. The check-in counter for my flight was oddly empty. However, I went and did the check in as quickly as I could so that I could go back to the window that looked out onto the airport and watch Ibrahim continue to go. It was the speediest check-in by Tanzanian standards.

There was a row of windows inside this section of the airport which looked back out onto the carpark. Ibrahim had to have already gone by this stage but I decided to have one last look out onto the carpark. Contrary to what I expected, I could see Ibrahim but now he was not alone. There were various officials surrounding him. They were all dressed in uniform so I guessed they were police officers. Ibrahim was in the process of taking out stuff from his pocket and by the way the officials inspected what he had taken out, this had to be his identification. Suddenly, the anxiety I had felt on the way here returned. Had Ibrahim suspected something untoward was going to happen when we got to the airport? Then, even though they were quite far from me, I recognised, standing among the uniformed men surrounding Ibrahim, a person I now knew quite well - Babeer.

The next thing, the police officers began mishandling Ibrahim. They were doing this in full view of the public and the public looked on indifferently or at least in curiosity. But how could they be doing this to Ibrahim? What crime could he have committed? Holding my hand luggage, I made a dash for the entrance and would have instinctively run out when the official at the door yelled at me to stop. She told me that I had already entered and checked in, and therefore I could no longer go back out this way. If I wanted to leave the airport, I would have to go around the other way and she pointed in the direction I needed to go.

I made a dash in that direction. I found myself at immigration. Another official, a man this time, dressed once again meticulously but ominously and evidently wearing a gun yelled at me to stop.

"I want to go out," I gasped, trying to get a grip on myself and not reveal the urgency of the situation and not look like I was in the process of committing a crime.

"Then go to the counter here," he replied gruffly and pointed, "and then you can get through."

I got to the counter. The official behind the window was just as welcoming to see guests leave the country as the officials were whenever tourists entered. He took his time to go through my passport and stamp the appropriate places and for me to do the fingerprint checking before stamping my passport and letting me through.

I walked controllably a little way and then when I felt that I was out of view of officialdom, I began running inside this section of the airport, looking for the way out of the airport. In this section of the airport, the only view was out onto the tarmac, in the opposite direction to the carpark. There was no way, as far as I could see, where I could look back over the carpark and see what had happened to Ibrahim. I felt like a wild animal caught in a trap and trying to find a way out. Kilimanjaro Airport is quite small and it didn't take me long to realise that there was no other way out. I then realised what all these officials were saying to me when I said I wanted to get out. They obviously misinterpreted what I meant by "out" as they had led me through immigration and out of the country.

I began making my way back when suddenly two more officials came in my direction from the other side of immigration. One was a woman, the other a man, both stern-looking and with a look of evil intent. They came to the immigration desk and began asking questions. I couldn't see the man behind the immigration desk from the angle I was in because the light of the airport reflected on the surface of the glass screen behind which this man was now hidden. The officials then looked up at me and came determinedly in my direction and stopped. I was terrified.

"Michael Farril?" the male official grunted.

"Yes," I gasped.

"Your passport."

I dutifully obeyed and nervously took out my passport which was suspended under my undershirt. I fumbled through the pockets of my passport holder to finally pull out the desired article the official had asked for. The official flicked through the pages of the passport until he had reached a page of interest to him. He then closed it and roughly handed me back my identification.

"You've already crossed the border," he growled, almost in discontent. "So, I won't touch you. But we have arrested your friend out there."

"Arrested him?" I gasped almost in a whisper. My mouth went dry and my throat had constricted so much on my larynx I could hardly make a sound.

"Yes," the official replied gruffly. "Arrested him. Because he was suspected of committing lewd sexual acts. Had you not crossed the border, we would have arrested you, too."

What he had to say was so full of venom as if he had spat the words out like saliva right into my face.

"But," he continued, "you don't want to come back here. We don't want people like you in this country. If you try to step back into this country, you will be arrested as well. Your type really make us sick with your disgusting, shameful desires. We don't want this practice to catch on in this country. You're just dirt and not fit to be called human."

He had vomited out his disgust and the female official there with him showed by her facial expression that she was in total agreeance. The two turned and left, slowly and discreetly, as if they had accomplished after all what they had set out to achieve.

As they walked away, I looked on at the two of them. The hopelessness and the despair just hit me as they walked off. Though I was safe across the border, the one I loved, Ibrahim, was taken captive, prisoner in the clutches of a cruel, bitter society. The full realisation of what was happening finally came over me. I just stood there and soon that surge of bitter sorrow swelled up from within and flowed up and out through my throat and eyes. I began to weep uncontrollably. I couldn't even move. I just stood there. The last image I had of Ibrahim was when he was in the presence of the police officers and that they were mishandling him, out in public. The image of Babeer among the officers filled me further with anguish because I knew Babeer had to be bad news. What were they going to do to Ibrahim? Would they put him in prison? And if they did and the others in prison found out why he was there, how would they treat him? And there was nothing I could do. If I crossed the line back into the country, I was equally doomed. They would then put me in prison also. And then I'd lose my job, my rent wouldn't be paid, I would be evicted, the repercussions would be just devastating.

I just cried as I watched these two black sub-Saharan African officers walk off while the acid of their remarks slowly sank in.

"How can you say that?" a voice inside me yelled. "How can you say that? You, sir, you are a black sub-Saharan African. Cast your mind back into the past. Don't you remember when your ancestors had similar comments thrown in their faces? Don't you remember that for a long time similar comments were made about those of dark skin, how they were disgusting, that their dark skin was evidence of their disgustingness? Don't you remember how degraded and humiliated you felt when you knew that the colour of your skin was a natural phenomenon, a very part of your person? Wasn't it the right thing for the *Mzungus* to look into their hearts and realise that your skin colour does not make you disgusting but rather it was our *Mzungu* ancestors' attitude that had to change? Don't you see that you are now being called to look into your hearts and ask yourselves whether your disgust to us *mshogas* is truly the way to view us or that your attitude needs to change? And you, madam, don't you remember in the past when women were treated as less than men, simply as sexual objects whose role was to maintain the home, raise the children and be the recipient of heterosexual men's desires and that was all you were good for? Don't you remember the degrading comments heterosexual men made of you all because of a physical attribute that made you you, a physical attribute that you have no control over?

But my and Ibrahim's desires for each other, what are they to you? Don't you, sir, have a wife? Don't you, madam, have a husband? And if so, how would you feel if you had thrown at your feet that your desires for your spouses and your spouses' for you were disgusting? Those who threw this at you, what business is it of theirs anyway? If others around you thought it was disgusting to think of the two of you making love, does this constitute a right for those around you to stop you from engaging in this form of love? What right do others around you have over your body and over who can touch your body intimately and where you allow them to touch you? And what business is it of those around you to actually entertain the thought of you making love when you do it away from the public eye?

And further, don't you enjoy your spouses, to have and to hold, to be with, to talk with, to spend time together, to love each other? Don't Ibrahim and I, like everyone else on the planet, have a right to love? Why is it up to those around us to decide who we are allowed to love in all its forms, physically, mentally, emotionally, companionshiply?"

Each weeping heave was a further expression of my despondency and despair. People passed me as they shuffled in but they just stared and walked on. Suddenly I felt so cold and alone. I felt once again the loneliness of being gay and the way the world treats us with disgust. For a moment I thought of home, of Australia, and the geographical and chronological island I lived in where in this small moment in space and time I could live as close as an acceptable human being as ever one can where no-one minded and people actually treated me as a person. But here in Tanzania, I was forced back into the realisation of worlds where homosexuals were treated like nothing because of an attribute of their person they have no control over.

I stood there and cried. And the cries of the children in the Nyika sounded within me as if I could hear them in my ears once again, as if they all wept together within me. I stood there and cried. The helplessness and the despair of all the injustices of my world created an abyss of despair beyond anything I had ever experienced. I stood there and cried. Suddenly the despair that others felt because of similar injustices was felt within. I stood there and cried. I thought of Polycarp, first being forced to grow up in a world where he was considered as nothing more than a refugee and not quite a person, forced to continually move on from one country to another, his parents from Burundi, then Polycarp and his entire family from Rwanda, then from Tanzania as if he were simply surplus goods, a person nobody wanted. I stood there and cried. I thought of the discrimination against all those outside the accepted norm, blacks, Aboriginals, transsexuals, people with disabilities, people from all walks of life who for some reason were considered outside the ideal human form simply because of an aspect general society claimed was not human, and heard them cry together within me. I felt as if everybody's injustices had suddenly been channelled into the centre of my being and welled up like a fountain into my crying fit.

I stood there and cried. How would I ever see Ibrahim again? My way back into Tanzania had been closed tight. Ibrahim no doubt was about to suffer a long prison sentence. I didn't even have a decent enough job to earn the money to even buy him a ticket to come to Australia. And if he now had a criminal record from Tanzania, didn't this mean that Australia would never allow him to enter the country?

I stood there and cried. I had never felt so lonely in my entire life. Everyone, both white and black, just walked past me, looking on with bewildered looks and whispering as they went by but not one person stopped to ask what the matter was. I cried and cried until I no longer had any energy to cry any more, until the well had completely run dry.

I heard once more an announcement of my flight. I then turned around, went through the X-ray machine and sat and waited to board the plane.

Chapter 20

The plane arrived in Sydney, parked in its proscribed gate and the hundred-odd passengers began bustling with impatience to get out. I did not share this eagerness. On the contrary, I felt a numbing nothingness. There were moments when I reflected back on the various stages of my trip when I had tried to ring Ibrahim on my mobile phone, first at Kilimanjaro Airport once I had gotten over my crying fit, then on the various stopovers on the way back to Sydney. But each time I rang I received the message that the phone had been switched off and I should call back later. Not knowing what had happened to Ibrahim and the realisation that he was not contactable only increased the anxiety and the patheticalness of the moment and each time it had set off a new wave of weeping.

But one can only weep so much. My eyes were dry and sore from all the rubbing and I had a mild headache from the pressure of each sob. The crying seemed to have expended a lot of my energy as I didn't have much left to actually get up from my seat. It was an effort, once the other passengers began to leave, to actually get up, grab my bag and exit the plane.

In past trips from overseas, I walked almost at a sprinter's pace from the plane through the airport to immigration in the eagerness to get out of the airport. This time there was no eagerness. I had no particular destination I needed to get to. There was no expectation of a brighter tomorrow.

I reached the immigration desk and the officer who greeted me examined my Incoming Passenger card and then my passport before finally giving me the stamp of approval to continue onto the next step.

I wandered slowly down the steps to the baggage carousel where my luggage was soon to come. There were people everywhere, hovering around the baggage carousels right across the floor. Between two carousels, it was difficult to distinguish which passengers were waiting for baggage from which carousel. As a result, it was difficult to know where exactly to stand to be able to be in a position to grab my luggage once my luggage arrived.

At the opposite end of the carousels from where I was standing there seemed to be less people and a lot more standing room. The challenge was to actually get through the crowds of international travellers, especially the groups and families with trolleys aimed randomly at no specific angle like obstacles in an obstacle course.

I struggled my way through. There were a few polite responses and a few not so polite but the manoeuvre was worth it when I finally reached the other side where it was easier to breathe.

There at the end but obviously looking at a different carousel to the one from which I would retrieve my luggage was an Indian man. What caught my attention was how well dressed he was and how good-looking he appeared. There were grey specks of hair at the base of his sideburns on an otherwise jetblack head of hair cast on quite a dark set of skin. There was a roughness to the skin where his beardline would have been had he allowed his facial hair to grow and which betrayed that he was most probably middle-aged. I admired his fairly well-kept physique bound up tightly and neatly within a business shirt and tie. It wasn't so much the fact that he was quite a handsome man that struck my attention but the fact that he was no doubt of my generation and yet he had not let age swell his body as if this were an inevitability. His body was three-quarters turned towards me which gave me a good view of his body front on but his face was in profile and his left hand was held up at the cheek so that I could not quite see all of his face. My admiration of the man would have ended here had it not been for something familiar about him.

He reminded me of someone. Was it a former learner of mine? That was quite possible because I had had students from the Indian subcontinent from time to time, although I had always thought that such students would not have had the money to be travelling so freely nor had the type of job which required this exquisite apparel.

The Indian man moved and in so doing looked at me while I approached his vicinity. He looked straight at me and then turned away again which made it clear to me that he did not recognise me so it couldn't have been someone I knew. It was obviously an Indian man who simply looked similar to one of my past learners.

I continued on and let the thought of who this Indian man might be pass but the face once captured in my subconscious made the passage through the chambers of past images hidden from my consciousness and was compared with the faces of those who had passed through my life. Suddenly, a match between this fleeting image which had been photographed in my head and the image of an Indian-looking man from my past made a sudden match and made me realise who this man must be. A sudden jolt ran through my body like a mild electric shock.

At first I tried to convince myself that this man was merely a look-alike. But the more I watched his movements, the more I realised that this was actually someone from long ago, someone who had played a special role in my life, someone who meant something to me in times gone by. He had disappeared and I thought that I would never see him again. And suddenly, like an unexpected fulfilment of a dream, there he was.

Our separation had not been cordial and in fact I had been instrumental in making our separation an unpleasant one. This made the next step such an awkward one. Inside there was a burning desire, a deep longing to go up to him, be with him and to re-establish at least a shadow, a remnant of the beautiful relationship we once had. But then, how would he feel about it? Would he greet me like Esau greeted his brother, Jacob, after their many years of separation, where Esau promptly forgave Jacob's connivances and trickery against his elder twin brother, and let all that had caused their separation to remain in the past? Or had the wound of my separation from him remained a bitter memory, a scar that wouldn't heal?

I stood in momentary suspense. But I knew I had to act. At any moment, this man's luggage would arrive and once done, he would disappear and I would be left wondering forever.

I turned and walked over to him. I tapped him lightly on the shoulder and he turned around. I looked into that face, into those brown eyes, somewhat less glittering from age but still the eyes of the one whom I had loved so long ago. But his eyes gave no sign of recognition and he waited in expectation to find out why a stranger had tapped him on the shoulder.

"M...Markus?" I stammered. "Markus? Is that you?"

Markus smiled embarrassedly.

"Yes, it's me," he replied.

There was a momentary pause and I could tell he was trying in vain to work out who this person was who out of the blue knew his name.

"It's me," I said almost whispering. "Michael."

"Michael?" Markus asked. It was obvious that even my name no longer held any meaning.

"Michael Farril. Remember? We once..." I began. The magic memories of the distant past came to me but I couldn't mention that here. "We once worked together."

This was in a way a euphemism, although there was truth in the statement. We had worked together long ago in the days when I worked as a research chemist.

I could see as if it were lights going on inside his eyes once he had made the connection between the person in his distant past and the person standing before him.

"Oh, Michael," he said quite flatly. "You have changed so much! So, how are you?"

His statement, although said with a smile on his face, was devoid of any expected emotions that I thought that he might have. Our times together were swimming around in my consciousness to the point that here in the airport I just wanted to embrace him and relive those blessed memories from the past. But Markus' reaction was dry and emotionless, polite but distant, not unfriendly but not passionate either.

"I...I'm well," I replied. I didn't know what else to say. There was a short lull and then Markus broke the silence.

"So, you've been away on a trip, have you? Where did you go?"

"To Tanzania," I replied. I could feel once again the passions within me welling up inside. But Markus was not responding with any emotions and this was very disheartening.

"And you?" I then said back to him.

"I'm back from Sri Lanka. I run a business now between Australia and Sri Lanka so I have to travel back and forth between the two countries from time to time."

"Oh, I see," I replied because I really didn't know what else to say.

Markus cast a glance at the carousel and because the desired luggage was not there, he turned back to me. He placed his left hand on his face as if he were meditating on something and with that I noticed a ring on his finger. Markus noticed where my attention had been diverted.

"Yes, I'm finally married," Markus said with a laugh as if this had been the natural course of his life, as if what had occurred between us years ago had never happened, that our desires, or at least his desires, had never been towards men but had always been naturally and expectedly directed towards women and therefore allowed the predictable course of life to occur.

His comment under normal circumstances would have been met with some sort of compliment and a word of congratulations but it took the wind out of me and caused a lump to form in my stomach.

"You're married?" I asked to make sure that I had heard right. This preliminary conversation we were having was only further adding to my distress. Didn't Markus have equal pleasant memories of us together in a time far in the past? Didn't he have joyous memories of a time when the two of us were in a way a pair? But the way he responded to me was as if the only connection that had ever been between us was simply the work relationship. Had he completely blocked out all his feelings for me?

It was distressing. But at the same time, my guilty conscience was telling me that this was after all my fault. I had created the split between us and no doubt this had broken Markus' heart. Decades had passed, circumstances had changed, life had moved on.

"Yes, married, children, a house in the suburbs, a mortgage," Markus said with a cheery voice devoid of any regret as if he had achieved what he had wanted to achieve.

My own shortcomings, the fact that I lived alone, I had a part time job and made only little more than enough to survive, that I rented a cheap flat in a cheap area of Sydney, that I really hadn't advanced that much in life suddenly made the chasm between us feel twice as wide as it originally had felt.

Markus cast another glance at the carousel and then turned back to face me.

"Would you like to see my wife and children?" he asked and before allowing me the opportunity to reply, as the reality was that I really didn't want to, Markus had his smartphone out and began tapping on the screen until he had found what he was looking for. His wife was Indian, or I guess she was Sri Lankan like he was, about the same colour of skin and wearing traditional Indian clothes.

A flurry of jealousy came over me as I looked at the photo of this woman, elegant of dress and prettiest of smiles, the smile of a happy wife content with her situation in life, that situation including this beautiful man, a man I had once loved. I could have been in her place.

This feeling of jealousy was replaced by a feeling of despondency. I had created the unattached man that Markus had become which therefore made him available for someone else to have and to hold. If I had broken up with Markus, I could not continue to hold him at a distance on a leash and not allow him to become emotionally involved with someone else.

There was once again a momentary pause when Markus then threw the questions at me.

"So, what are you doing with yourself?" Markus asked.

"I'm a trainer," I replied.

"A trainer?" Markus commented with a smile. "Wow, that's a career change!"

"Yeah, I know," I replied. "I was unhappy being a research chemist and anyway jobs as research chemists were becoming scarce so I retrained and got my teaching qualifications, which are now only recognised as training."

"So, you train…what?"

"I train adults. Refugees mainly. People who have fled their countries to come to Australia and so need to learn English to become a part of the country." I had a quick glance at Markus' elegant and meticulous attire. "It's certainly not a lucrative job!" I then added.

"Money isn't everything!" Markus threw in.

Yeah, that's true, I thought. But it certainly helps. A greater amount of money would help me immensely. But I was not the type of person who could perform in a job that gives a great income. The idea of sales, marketing or IT are just not me and they are not jobs that would suit me.

"And," Markus added and then left a pause before continuing. "Are you married also?"

His words were measured as he said it, with purposed spacing as if he were expecting a certain answer.

"No," I replied quickly. I wanted to leave it there but Markus obviously had to know more.

"And is there…or has there…been anyone special in your life?"

Feelings welled up inside me. But Markus' neutral responses created the feeling in me not to care anymore what his reaction might be. There appeared to be no recollection of the beautiful times we had spent together. This then meant that when we separated ways from this airport, this would be the last time I would ever see him again unless we once again inadvertently crossed each other's paths.

"After you," I said slowly and measuredly, "there has never been anyone special. Until now."

Markus' reaction this time showed some emotion. It wasn't evident at first if it were a positive or a negative one.

"So, tell me?" he asked which was a strange thing to say in question form.

"His name," I said slowly so that the masculine form of this pronoun was quite clear, "is a man called Ibrahim."

"A man called Ibrahim," Markus echoed as hollow as any echo. There was a momentary pause.

"Michael, what happened to your belief in God?"

That question caused tears to well up in my eyes. So much was in that question, the memories of the past in the days when I was an avid Christian but at the same time had a temporary fling with Markus, a fling that was developing into a serious relationship. But then I had broken up with Markus because of this God I once believed existed because I thought this God said that this relationship building between Markus and me was sinful. Then not too long after that, I realised that Markus had been right that the Bible which I had believed in had let me down, which then caused me to lose both the Bible which I loved and Markus who I loved even more. There were also the feelings of seeing him here now in front of me and yet there was no possibility of re-establishing the beautiful relationship we once had. There was also the feelings for Ibrahim and a partial feeling of betrayal, that my love for a former lover still formed a part of my being and had the potential to hurt the new person I loved. And there was the feeling of jealousy that someone else now enjoyed the intimacy with this man whom I had once loved and could have continued to love and be happy with had other things not gotten in the way. And the knowledge of what had occurred to Ibrahim just as I was about to leave him all jerked the tears back out. Feelings like the chaos of Tiamat whirled inside of me.

And then Markus showed the first sign of recollection of the beautiful things between us. He reached out and hugged me. People around us just stared at us because it was the most unusual sight to behold. But the emotions inside me were much stronger than how much I cared what those around us thought.

Once I could get a grip on myself and actually articulate the words, I just said to Markus, "I am so sorry, Markus. I am so sorry."

With these words, I felt Markus grip me even tighter. When it seemed that I was able to compose myself, Markus pushed me away to allow him to see my face. He had a gentle smile on his face and this smile seemed to betray that he now acknowledged that there had been beautiful times together.

"It's alright," Markus said softly. "It's all in the past. All is forgiven."

I pulled a handkerchief from my pocket to wipe my eyes and blow my nose.

People were shuffling their way past us so we moved slightly to let them pass.

I felt as if I could speak again without my emotions taking over.

"I am so sorry, Markus. And, God, I missed you. I even went looking for you but you had completely disappeared."

Markus laughed somewhat sheepishly. "Well, you could say that I had."

Markus held my face in his hands and looked me straight in the eyes.

"When you left me, I couldn't stay here any longer. I could no longer bare living in Sydney because everything about the city reminded me of you. So I got a job in Melbourne and moved down there."

That just affected me even more and I started to sob. I had been the cause of this.

"Michael, don't worry. It's all in the past. As they say, 'Time heals all wounds'."

"And so are you living in Melbourne?" I asked.

"No," Markus said as he removed his hands away from my face. "Obviously God wanted me back in Sydney. I suppose it was a bit like Jonah and Nineveh. The company I was working for decided to move to Sydney and so I moved with it, which caused me to return back."

"And you got married?"

"Yes," Markus sighed. "I got married. Unfortunately, that's the advantage you have of being an Anglo-Australian. You and your family have moved with the times. Those in my family and my community still support the old traditions even though they moved to this country to embrace the new life that this country offers. Some of the new things in this life they haven't been able to accept. You don't know the pressure parents of my background put on us to get married."

"You mean to say that you would have married even though we were…um…sort of…together?"

"Michael," Markus replied. "When I met you and I saw how things were developing, I was ready to defy my entire family to be with you. I had already made the move to go against my parents' wishes when I first left home and lived on my own. My parents weren't happy about that but they at least consented to it, especially as I had put up a strong enough argument that it was easier for me to live in a unit close to where I work than commute back and forth between my parents' home and my workplace. I still had to call in from time to time at my parents' home as is my duty as one of their sons."

Markus stopped there and took a deep breath.

"When I met you, Michael, I knew I had reached a crossroads. There were my parents and family on the one hand urging me to get married. And being one of their sons, there was a lot of weight resting on my shoulders to fulfil the family obligation of carrying on the family name. And then there was you, my feelings for you and what I believed was what God was showing me to do. Things were developing between me and you, and they made me believe that God had made things to be this way and that God was teaching me to have the courage to follow His plan which would then help my parents to understand His plan. However, near to the time I had decided to lay everything on the line with my parents, you left. I couldn't cope so I went away. But God was obviously showing me that this was cowardice and that it was important for me to face up to His plan whether I wanted to follow it or not. I came back to Sydney, got a job here and my parents finally arranged a wife for me."

"But are you happy?" I gasped.

"I'm content," Markus replied but that choice of adjective and his body language spoke more than what the words that came from his mouth conveyed. "I mean, everything in my life is stable. I have a good job. In fact, I have my own company now. I have three good children, a nice family environment and I am accepted and remain a part of my extended family."

But is that enough to make you happy? was what I wanted to ask but Markus' answer pretty much said it all. It was a heavy choice. On the one hand there was accepting his homosexuality and living openly as a gay man who made relationships with men and not women at the expense of losing his entire family network and in some ways his social acceptability. On the other was the road he chose, to follow the traditional family line, get married and sire children despite his inner sexual feelings which whether we like it or not are somehow mixed up with our feelings of love which meant that Markus did not love his wife as fully and intimately as he could another man.

To look at Markus from the outside, he was the ideal successful man of the twenty-first century, successful in his own business, a wonderful nuclear family, an upright, respectable work and family man. But inside, I knew what it must really be like. He was playing a charade. He was acting out a part. But if anyone could break through the shell and see what was inside, no doubt they would see that inside it was totally empty because the inside lacked a way out to express the essence of what made Markus the person he really was and so a part of that inner self simply could not continue to live.

"So," Markus broke me from my thoughts. "Where is this new man in your life? Is he travelling with you?"

This question, as innocent and sweet of Markus to mention simply allowed the water works to open once again. Markus looked at me perplexed but then reached forward and held me close to him. Markus' reaction made it feel that he already understood what had happened.

Eventually I was able to pull myself together enough to be able to at least in summary form relate what had happened at Kilimanjaro Airport before I had left and what had been going on to make me react in this way.

"Oh, Michael, that's terrible," Markus said by way of consolation. "Is there anyone in that country you can contact to find out what has happened?"

"I think the people at the Msingi wa Mungu Project may be able to help. They know Ibrahim, and I can only guess that Ibrahim at least tried to contact them when the authorities took him."

"At the airport?" Markus then asked with a puzzled look on his face.

"Yes. And I would have been arrested also had I not gone through immigration and hence was considered to have crossed the border out of Tanzania."

Markus looked at me with question marks in his eyes.

"Michael, that doesn't sound right. There has to be something more to the story than what you're telling me."

The look in my eyes must have indicated to Markus that I didn't quite understand what Markus meant.

"Like, did they catch you in the act?"

"No, no," I replied. "And I don't even know how they would have known because we were so careful not to make it obvious." But once I had said this, the image of Babeer came to view in my mind's eye.

Markus looked at me thoughtfully.

"Michael, had the authorities any proof of the accusation, they would have arrested you despite the fact that you had crossed the border because you would have committed a crime inside the country and you would still be guilty irrespective of whether or not you had already crossed outside of Tanzania's jurisdiction. I know how countries like this operate. Your friend, Ibrahim, has been arrested simply out of corruption. He has something someone in the area wants and this is simply an excuse. Maybe they have suspected something between you and Ibrahim but it can't be proven but that is being used as the surface accusation to hide what they really want."

This did not make me feel any more comforted but it did provide an additional and in some ways a hopeful dimension to the events.

"Don't let it worry you too much. He will come out of this in a short time."

Markus paused and then smiled an authoritative smile.

"Michael, don't you see how this occurred to Ibrahim just before we met here at Mascot International Airport after many years of not seeing each other?"

I looked on at Markus perplexed. I didn't understand what he was saying. His words were too cryptic and my mind was too tired to try and decipher the cryptogram.

"Michael, when you get home, you're going to fall asleep and despite what has happened, you will have a pleasant sleep. When you wake up, you will know what to do."

I looked in Markus' face but wasn't sure what he meant.

"Michael, reflect back on the events of your life. They have all happened for a reason. They have made you the person you are today. Love, in all its forms, has led the way and you have followed it. I mean, not the treacly, mushy love, I mean the pure love, the love of all humanity, that deep, mystical love which contains a yearning to search the truth and not just sit around lazily accepting what everyone tells you, the pure love which contains the strong desire to do whatever it takes to increase the happiness of others. You have used this love as your guiding principle and this love will reward you. Keep following it."

To this day, I have no idea what made Markus say this. It made no sense at the time but what he said later turned out to be creepily insightful.

Markus paused and then continued.

"This friend of yours, Ibrahim, he will come to you. But this time you won't make the same mistake. You know that it doesn't matter what happens, you know to hold onto him and not let him go."

On that thought, I took a glance at the carousel and saw my bag in the distance slowly coming in our direction. The number of people who had been waiting at the carousel had now diminished by half and I could have walked over to get my bag but I decided to let it come to me.

"Well, my bag's coming," I said to try and hide the real feelings I had inside because I felt as if I wanted to just burst into tears again.

"Yeah, my luggage has arrived, too," Markus replied. He paused and then added, "Actually, I have seen it go around the carousel about three times now but I just wanted to spend this moment with you."

After that statement, I had to hug him. Feelings from the past came rushing through as I held him. I then let him go, turned to the carousel and then took my bag. When I turned around again, Markus was at the other carousel doing the same.

We both made our way towards the bag inspection area.

"Would you like my number? Maybe we could get together for a coffee sometime," Markus said to me when we had stopped momentarily on the queue.

Markus took out his phone. I told him my number and he punched it in. He then rang my phone so that I could save his number in my address list.

"How are you getting home?" I asked Markus.

"Oh, my wife should be outside. She's picking me up."

"Oh, okay," I replied. This was like a secret message passed on to me that when we exited this part of the airport, we had to act as if we had never known each other nor even had this casual conversation. Markus had items to declare and was stopped for a bag inspection whereas I had nothing and hence we parted ways. Once I was through the last automatic glass doors, as I walked down the ramp towards the awaiting crowd, I could see a woman who looked similar to the woman in the photos from Markus' smartphone. I just walked past her.

I watched other heterosexual couples where one of the spouses greeted the other after their long trip. I wondered how lucky it was to be a heterosexual. You don't have to make choices in life. You don't have to make the choice between forming a relationship with someone with whom you can enjoy the act of lovemaking according to your body's dictates, and getting married and being accepted by the family. When you are heterosexual, both of these go automatically together.

I followed the signs that led to the train station. Once on the train, I thought back to the events in Tanzania before I had left and once again tried to ring Ibrahim. Once again I got the same message that the phone had been turned off or was out of phone range and that I should try again later. This was further painful and very anxiety-filling.

Who should I speak with next? Who should I contact? Who should I turn to for a shoulder to cry on? It was far too early in the morning anyway to ring or visit anyone in Sydney. I was also exhausted from the long trip and could feel the tiredness of the trip and the anxiety like heavy weights around my body. The train trip from the airport all the way to the station closest to the suburb I lived in and then the long walk from the station to my home was enough to drain any strength I had left in me.

Once I had opened the door of my flat, the stale smell of a closed-in unit welcomed me. I went around opening blinds and windows to let both the light and air of the outer world into my unit to drive away the staleness of the past couple of weeks. I left my luggage unopened then went straight to my bed and lay down.

I closed my eyes. I was still awake and could hear the outside noise, neighbourly noises and the noise of nature. The noises were familiar and homely. They were comforting and provided me with some relief from the tension and the trauma of the troubles that were happening in my waking world. I could hear in the distance the neighbours' children playing. I could hear the sound of a child's laughter.

Then I could see the source of the laughter. It brushed past me, what looked like two streamers, one thin and white, and one thick and pink. Once my view was clear, I could see that the streamers were long strips of either paper or plastic at the end of a stick that a little girl was holding as she ran around, as if she were a band leader. She was a very young girl. She looked about three or four years of age. A little sub-Saharan black girl. Her hair was done up in the traditional African way with white, purple and red beads scattered throughout her hair as much as decoration as to hold her hair in place. She was wearing a lovely pink and white dress, with white socks and pink shoes.

And she laughed as she played. Her laughter was contagious. It was the laughter that was carried by eternal joy emanating from deep within one's being. Her being. She was so full of energy, running about on the lush green grass. There was an elderly gentleman there with her, a white man, a *Mzungu*. Although evidently elderly, there was evidence that he still maintained the vigour of life as he watched on. This little girl ran about and the elderly man chased her. At one time, the man just stopped and allowed the little girl to run until she had reached an invisible barrier and then by an invisible thread was drawn back to him.

I smiled at the gentleman and he smiled back at me. The little girl laughed and her joy was contagious. I just wanted to catch her, hold her, hug her and squeeze her, and allow all that joy that seemed to ever bubble out of her to become as much a part of me as it was of her.

The little girl turned and saw me. She smiled. She laughed. Her laughter was a welcoming laughter. It was as if she had always known me, that I was no stranger to her. She had a cheeky look on her face and then she started to run. I realised she wanted me to run after her. I looked up at the elderly gentleman but he was no longer there. The yard was no longer there. The fence that bordered her in was no longer there. The land had opened up. And the little girl ran. And I ran after her.

We were in a park. There were two park benches up in the distance, at an angle from each other as if the two park benches were two sides of a triangle. The benches were shaded by a large eucalyptus tree. On the left I saw a man, well-dressed, in a smart shirt open with a V and smart trousers and shoes. He was standing behind the bench on the left. He was smoking a pipe. I realised as I chased the girl that she was leading me to the tree and this gave me a better view of the man. Soon I recognised who it was. It was Troy Krisston.

Troy Krisston. Oh, Troy! I thought. He was my first true love. He was a fellow student when I was at secondary school. I was amazed at how much he hadn't aged in all these years. He still looked like the handsome late adolescent that he was when I last saw him, although his stance betrayed that he was now a man. When he saw me, he nodded his head, winked and smiled in consent with a tug on his pipe.

The little girl laughed and her streamers fluttered in the air. Then I saw who was on the right bench. There was a young woman sitting on the bench with three children around her and a gentleman standing behind her. I then recognised that it was Ruth Carpenter, another school friend who had been significant to me during my high school days. She reached down to one of the children at her feet and, as she moved to sit back up, she turned to see me and smiled. She then hugged the child she had picked up, pushing her cheek against the cheek of the child.

The little girl with the streamers laughed. She ran in a direction away from the tree. Her streamers fluttered in the wind as she ran and she skipped at the same time, the wind blowing carelessly and carefree through her lovely dress.

She ran up a hill and from the top was a view that sloped down to a fence which then led to a cliff which dropped down into the open sea. The girl laughed and a man at the railing looked up. He was wearing a black kippah. He wore round glasses. He had a long razzy briar salt and pepper beard that went down to his chest. He was dressed in black garb. He was holding a book in his hand. When he looked up, he smiled and winked at me. It was Joseph, my old Jewish friend from university. He tapped twice on the book he was holding and then nodded in consent. The little girl with the streamers laughed. She kept running along. I was compelled to follow her. Joseph waved and nodded in acknowledgement and understanding.

She ran past a beautiful big bush. The bush was like a dense leafy wall but covered in pink flowers. In front of this sat two women on what looked like park benches, a round glass top table in front of them. They were drinking from white mugs. They were wearing white. They had white ribbons in their hair, their dresses were white, they were wearing white slacks that went down to their ankles. They were wearing pure white shoes. They were drinking from their mugs, looking at each other and laughing. A few pink flowers dropped and fell around them. It was Rosemary. She had been my friend at church long, long ago. We had been friends for a while before she decided to become a Mormon. At that time it was devastating. But now it didn't matter. She and the other woman were laughing as if they were telling each other funny stories while sipping from their mugs. The little girl with the streamers laughed and the girls turned to look at me. Rosemary looked at me and grinned. She took a sip from her mug and then waved to me. I waved back.

The little girl stopped, turned to look at me and smiled an open mouthed teethy smile. She then laughed and began skipping, the streamers trailing behind her in the wind. Then she ran on. She ran past a tall eucalyptus tree, its rich green leaves blowing in the breeze, the trunk in artistic colours of grey and brown stood firm against the blue backdrop of a summer day's sky. Beside it an Aboriginal man was performing a ceremonial dance, stamping the ground furiously with his feet which caused clouds of dust to blow up into the air. His dark chest juxtaposed with the white painted markings in florid design painted on his chest, with the hair on his chest like a lush garden. Dark of skin and his face betraying typical Aboriginal features, as soon as he saw me, without interrupting the dance he smiled. The smile led to the recognition of this man. "Oh, Elliot," I thought aloud, "It's you. How I missed you." Elliot kept dancing but he opened his mouth in a broad smile and lifted the spear in his right hand high above his head. He then winked at me and blew a kiss before continuing with his dance.

The streamers of the little girl fluttered in front of my face and the little girl laughed. I really wanted to interrupt Elliot and simply hold him tightly one more time. But the girl ran on and I was compelled to follow her.

The little girl ran past a bush. Beyond the bush was a river. There was a man on the bank of the river sitting on a picnic blanket. No, it was a Persian rug. The man was wearing a karakool, peerhan and toombarn, traditional Afghani clothes. He had a dark beard. He was sitting on his haunches as if he had just done obeisance. It was Faisal. The little girl laughed. Faisal looked up. I stopped for a moment. "Faisal, I have missed you so much," I said. Faisal simply replied with a smile. He reached for a book on his rug, a green book with ornate decoration on the cover. Faisal kissed the book and then winked at me.

I felt the pink and white streamers brush across my face and then move forward. I was compelled to move on. But the streamers were not streamers. They were the wings of a beautiful pink and white butterfly with white, purple and red spots throughout the design of the wings. The butterfly continued to fly in its usual sporadic way. I was compelled to follow it.

It flew out onto the street. There was a small red car parked along the kerb with a jack holding the car up while a man dressed in overalls was at work fixing the wheel. I could see from the black curly wool-like hair that he was sub-Saharan African. Although sitting he was incredibly tall. I heard the clinking sound of a spanner hitting the ground and then watched the mechanic pick the spanner up. The sound as I put my foot on the gravel caused him to turn. It was Daniel, once a learner at Tevah Am, who I had looked after and helped to get a job as a motor mechanic. With the spanner in hand, he saluted me and smiled. He then saw the butterfly. He pointed at it as an indication to follow it.

The butterfly flew on. It flew past a window. Inside a well-built man was wearing only T-shirt and sport shorts. He was lifting weights. I could hear the clunking of the weights on the frame that held them. The leaf litter outside the window rustled with the sound of someone running through it. I was running through it. The man turned to look out the window. It was Faraj. Beautiful and well-built. Tough and yet gentle. As soon as he recognised me, he threw me a cheeky smile. The butterfly kept on. I was compelled to keep moving.

I heard a noise of cheering to my left. There in the distance was a large imposing building with beautiful colonnades at the entrance which led down a series of stairs to an open area. There were people coming out of the building cheering. They were wearing graduation clothes and holding diplomas in their hands wrapped up in cardboard and tied up in a ribbon. Among them was Polycarp. He had graduated. He had finally graduated. He was hugging his classmates and cheering. I felt so proud. My son had finished studying. My son had finally completed his studies. Polycarp looked over in my direction. He held up his diploma, the blue ribbon tied up in a bow waving in the wind. He smiled. It was the smile of satisfaction. He called out to me but I couldn't hear him at first. "What?" I kept saying, thinking I was yelling it but it sounded as if I had only mumbled it to myself. "What did you say? I don't understand."

"*Kipepeo!*" he yelled pointing with his diploma at the butterfly, "*Kipepeo!*" It made no sense and yet it made every sense.

I turned away from Polycarp to look at the butterfly and realised I was now standing on a high place looking out over a great plain which ended with a shoreline and then the open sea. Way over on the horizon the sun was shining. It was setting. I couldn't look directly at the sun because it was so bright. But I could feel the warmth on my face.

The butterfly continued to fly towards the sun but I could not follow it. I was at the edge of a high cliff. In the distance I saw a high mountain and from it arose two lines that merged into one and then disappeared into full puffy clouds surrounded by stars, some of which fell gently like snow onto the shoreline. I watched the butterfly fly into the wind and could see its silhouette as it faded out of view and leave an imprint on the surface of the sky, and finally transform into the constellation of Orion.

And then I heard someone singing. It was a song which had such feeling, such longing. It was Markus' voice, soft and melodious. The song was full of past sorrow but at the same time of future hope, a yearning for what had not been but yet what should and could be, a regret of the past and yet a desire and a promise for tomorrow. I could feel the sorrow, the regret, the yearning deep within me, the longing for what might be, what could be, what ought to be.

I looked out onto the scene of the dusky night sky, the stars glowing brightly, the Orion constellation now shining brightly but not alone but as one constellation among many. The stars shone so brightly, the contrast between the brilliance of the stars and the dark backdrop of the sky was immensely beautiful. The soft, yearnful singing continued. I stared out onto the majestic scene below of a shoreline, the sound of the waves far below breaking onto a clean, white beach and the feeling of a gentle breeze blowing gently across the surface of the waters as if calming the rage. The singing continued, full of yearning, full of hope. The beautiful feelings deep within me made me feel as if I were floating and all was at peace.

And then I heard the strange but joyful sound of jungle music, an upbeat rhythm that sounded as if what was being played was a xylophone made of glass. The sound was so intense that the view suddenly dissipated and all went dark. The upbeat music played on.

I began to realise that the sound was my mobile phone. I had set the ring tone to something called *Glass* and this was creating the sudden noise. The ringing of the phone brought me out of my sleep although I was deep in it that it was difficult for me to climb out. Also, there was a reluctance to climb out of sleep after such a beautiful dream.

The phone kept ringing but I was battling to open my eyes. I picked up the phone and struggled to read the name of the person ringing. With a few blinks, I was able to make out the name of the caller. It was Polycarp.

I still wasn't fully awake. Even if it were an emergency, my mind was still partly back in the world of dreams for me to be able to engage in a lucid conversation. I had to let the phone ring through. Before I could hold an intelligible conversation, I had to force myself out of bed, drown my body under a warm shower and make myself a cup of strong coffee to finally get my mind back into physical reality. Once done, I called Polycarp back.

"*Naam*," I heard Polycarp say as he answered the phone, using a Swahili word meaning "yes". We exchanged the typical Swahili greetings before getting to the point of the call.

"*Baba*, are you back from overseas?"

I wanted to give a smart answer and say that I wasn't but I was in fact still in the aircraft on my way home but then realised that it was the twenty-first century and we could after all phone people in any part of the world.

"Yes, yes," I replied. "I was just asleep. I'm a bit jetlagged. Are you alright?"

"*Pole sana!*" Polycarp replied, using a Swahili expression to show that he empathised with my tiredness. "Are you awake now?"

No, I'm still asleep, I wanted to reply. But Polycarp was such a nice kid so I just couldn't say anything sarcastic to him.

"Yes, I'm awake now. Is anything the matter?"

"Can you come over and help me? I need to write a letter."

I rubbed my eyes.

"Yeah, okay. A letter to whom?"

Polycarp mentioned an Aged Care centre and that he needed to write an application letter for a prospective job. This was wonderful news. Polycarp was applying for a job. If he were to finally get a job, that would be fantastic. He would be on the way to being settled in the country.

When I arrived at Polycarp's place, Polycarp was alone. Jeremiah had gone out with his church on an outing. Polycarp told me all about the prospective job and how he simply needed to write an application letter and submit a recent resume. All this he needed to do on-line. Polycarp had already made an attempt and simply needed me to fine-tune the English. He then had to write a resume. Polycarp had never written a resume before and asked me for help.

We finished putting the resume together and all that was left was a section to include referees. I asked Polycarp who he wanted as a referee. Polycarp's answer was immediate and to him quite self-evident.

"That's fine," I replied. "I'm happy to be your referee. But you need a second person. Don't you have someone from your church?"

"I don't. I don't trust them. I only trust you," Polycarp said adamantly.

"But surely people in the church are there to help you," I said by way of defence.

"*Baba*, there are not many people in the world whom I can trust. When I was in Tanzania, I couldn't trust the Tanzanian authorities. I couldn't even trust my fellow Rwandans. You know, even now I don't trust those from my own community."

I was quite taken aback by this statement.

"And me?" I said almost in a whisper.

"*Baba*, you have always been there. You have always helped me. You have always been honest with me. You give of yourself and you don't ask for anything in return. You have helped me and Jeremiah for all this time. You have done for us what a real father does. In fact, you act like our Heavenly Father acts towards us."

I could feel a flush in my face as he said this. It was a lovely compliment.

"And because you have been open and honest with me," he added, "I have learnt to trust you, so I am open and honest with you."

You have been open and honest with me. Those words were like the opening of a door. Was this the moment? Was this the time to tell Polycarp once and for all? I was in a commanding position. Polycarp needed me. And did it matter to him now what I did in my private life? What I did in the privacy of my life would not affect Polycarp in the slightest. But it was now time for Polycarp to know this aspect of me.

The timing was also perfect because Jeremiah wasn't around. There was only Polycarp and me.

I sat back from the computer and crossed my arms. I then grabbed my chin with my left hand as I gathered my thoughts together. I then cupped my hands together on the table and looked Polycarp in the eye.

"*Mwanangu*," I said using, as was now the custom, the Swahili expression for 'my son'. "Yes, I have always been open and honest with you. But there is one thing I haven't told you before and it's time that you know."

Polycarp didn't flinch. He just looked on.

I then readjusted my seating position and sat up.

"You may have realised that I am not married, that I have never been married and that I don't have any children. It is because of this that I have been able to spend the time looking after you and Jeremiah."

Polycarp's face showed no recognition of the implication of what I was saying or where it was leading.

"The thing is, *mwanangu*," I continued, "is that I love guys. That is, *mimi ni mshoga*, I am gay."

Polycarp's facial expression changed to one of deep thought and deep concern. He then slowly folded his arms across his chest in protection.

"Is that why," Polycarp started slowly and measuredly to say, "you have looked after me for all this time?"

I knew what Polycarp meant. Had it been someone else, the comment would have made me angry. But Polycarp was such a nice kid that I just couldn't feel angry or hurt or offended by his comment. But it demanded an explanation.

"No, *mwanangu*," I replied. "I have helped you and Jeremiah for all this time because you and Jeremiah have needed help and I have had the means and the ability to help you."

I paused for a moment.

"*Mwanangu*, one day you and all Christians and Muslims and all religious people in general are going to have to realise that gays are not the evil people that the Bible and the Koran and any of the other religions portray them as being. Everything about us is the same as you. We are human beings just like you. We hunger, we thirst, we need to go to the toilet, we get hot, we get cold and we get tired. We also have sexual desires and the majority of us, just like you, don't force our sexual desires on other people. All people who hate homosexuality have to finally realise that when we *mshogas* demand to be treated equally as all humans who have sexual desires, we are not saying that it should be compulsory that all men have sex with men or all women should have sex with women. What people also have to understand is that we *mshogas* are a part of the human race and sometimes parents will have *mshogas* for children whether they like it or not because sexuality, both heterosexuality and homosexuality, is very much a part of nature. And we *mshogas* are stuck with our sexual attraction towards our own sex whether other people like it or not, and whether we ourselves like it or not, and we cannot change our orientation. There are many straight people who tell us that if we try hard enough, we can become straight but they have no idea of the extent to which many of us have gone to try to change our sexual desires but with no success."

When I made this statement, I thought of Ibrahim not eating for two weeks. I also reflected on how both of us did sport and other what we considered masculine things to become more masculine thinking this would remove our homosexual desires. I thought of how we both had had sex with a woman as our first sexual encounter thinking that by having sex with a woman our sexual orientation would naturally turn. I thought of how we both immersed ourselves completely in our religions with a dedication unsurpassed by the average religious person to try to rid ourselves of our sexual orientation. I also thought of Nikita and what she had told me about the extent she had gone to try and change her sexual desires so that they would be towards men but to no avail. And I thought of all the other men and women in my past who had told me of what they had done to themselves to try to get their sexuality to change, some even going so far as to inflict terrible pain on themselves in order to get their bodies to obey what their mind wanted, all to please those around them, but their homosexual orientation remained fixed.

If only people in the community at large could finally realise this and adjust to it.

"We are stuck with these desires," I continued. "And in the end, these desires are no different to the desires that straight people have. It's just directed at our own sex. Apart from making straight people feel uncomfortable when they imagine what two men or two women do together in sex, the sexual behaviour of *mshogas* doesn't affect people in society in any way."

Polycarp looked on at me in wonderment. I kept going.

"But apart from my sexual desires, which in reality are only a small part of me, like all people who have sexual desires, whether for the same sex or the opposite sex, I also want to feel that I belong to a family, to a tribe, to a group, not to a group of only gay men, but to a group of all humans, a group with men, women and children in it, with brothers, sisters, cousins, uncles and aunts, even with people to whom I'm not directly related. I also want to love and show that love in the way I care for people, in the way I have cared for you and Jeremiah. There is and will be one love that I will show to a special person and that love will include the sexual expression. But there are other loves, and I express those loves to others in different ways. And you are the same. One day you will meet a woman and fall in love with her and the way you express your love will be intimate, sexual, between you and her. But this will not be the limits of your love. You will continue the love you have for Jeremiah, to me – hopefully – and to anyone else in the general community."

Polycarp looked on at me with a serious expression which slowly relaxed.

"Well, this is a shock," he replied. "However, I can't get inside your body or get your blood and put it in my body and fully understand how you feel about having sex with men."

I was quite surprised at how quickly Polycarp understood my situation. But he continued.

"I don't think the Bible, however, says bad things about *mshogas*, though. And you have a good heart so you must be a Christian of some kind, at least by your heart attitude."

No, the Bible does say bad things about homosexuals, I wanted to argue. But to what gain? Polycarp knew everything about me now and in contrast to the way my parents had reacted when they found out I was gay, Polycarp was quite accepting that he had a father who was gay.

"And do you have anyone special in your life?" Polycarp added.

My thoughts were taken back to Ibrahim about whom I had heard nothing. This formed a lump in my throat.

"Yes, there is," I half-whispered.

"I guess I will have two papas, then."

This comment brought tears to my eyes. I reached over and gave Polycarp a hug which he responded to. I then began to cry again. Polycarp, the angel that he was, patted me on the back. He made the comment that I would always be his papa because I had always been there for him. But this wasn't why I was crying. I had to allow the convulsions to stop before I could sit back and pull myself together. I then related the story of Ibrahim up to what had happened as I was leaving to return to Australia. This was the special person in my life and so easily he had slipped through my fingers.

When I had finished explaining this, Polycarp looked at me thoughtfully.

"Your friend, Ibrahim," he said. "He wasn't arrested because he was a *mshoga*. I know how it works over there. They wanted money. They probably wanted to get money from you because you are a *Mzungu* and they assumed that you, being a *Mzungu*, have lots of money. So they probably made up the charge that it was because you and Ibrahim are *mshogas* simply to bribe you. You give them money, they will drop the charges. It was simply a way to extract a lot of money out of you out of greed. But they couldn't arrest you or capture you after you had gone across immigration not because they no longer had any power to do so but because they had no proof for why they were arresting you which means they weren't even arresting you for that anyway even though they said they were. Maybe someone told them about you two but that was not enough. The police could have captured you while you were in the country and made up any excuse but once you had gone through immigration, they would have had to have some proof if they wanted to really arrest you. Ibrahim is probably in custody and he will stay in custody until someone pays the police corruption money to get him out. They are probably expecting you to pay."

"But how can I? I don't even know what happened after I left."

"The police don't care. They will assume that Ibrahim has lots of money through you somehow. The only thing to help Ibrahim is to get someone to pay for him to get him out but also he might have to leave the country to prevent himself getting into more trouble."

This news sounded a little better than what I had thought before. It also made a little more sense. But it also was still just as complicated a situation.

"Papa, don't worry. I will pray for you. As it says in James 5:16, 'The effectual fervent prayer of a righteous man availeth much'. I will pray that Ibrahim will be alright. And if you love him like you say you do, I will pray that you will be together."

I just had to hug Polycarp. It was a false hope, a deluded hope but it was a nice gesture.

"*Mwanangu,*" I replied, "You are my beloved son in whom I am well pleased!"

Polycarp and I hugged once more. After a long moment of silence, I sat up.

"I suppose we had better finish this letter," I concluded.

The days rolled into weeks and I heard nothing from Tanzania about Ibrahim. I had contacted the Msingi wa Mungu Project in North Parramatta but the people I spoke with there could not provide me with any information. I eventually sent a letter through the post addressed to Gordon with the hope that he would be able to provide me with some information. Weeks rolled by but I heard nothing. I was reaching a point of despair when one day I received an email message. It was evening and I had just got home from work. I was putting my phone on my charger when I noticed that there was an email message. The phone was on the charger and I thought I would quickly find out who the sender was before going to the kitchen and cooking tea. As soon as I pressed on the email icon I noticed that the message was from Ibrahim. I could feel my heartbeat immediately speed up to double its pace. I tapped on the screen to reveal the message. The message began with a greeting that could have made me sing: "My dearest, loveliest Michael".

Those four words were enough to know that Ibrahim was alive and well. He must have also been somewhere where he was free to express his feelings towards me, the feelings of one man to another which was forbidden in Tanzania and for which, I had presumed, had caused his arrest, feelings that had been forbidden in many countries in time and space around the globe, a secret love, a different love and yet a well-known and common love.

Ibrahim's email began simply with the expressions of his love that truly came from the heart. However, when it came to what had happened to him, Ibrahim simply glossed over this, putting it aside with a comment that hinted that he would discuss it later. And then the great surprise. Ibrahim was coming to Australia. He was coming to Sydney. His working visa had finally been approved.

His working visa. He had mentioned this right at the very beginning of our meeting and it had completely dropped out of my memory. Ibrahim was coming to Australia! The excitement that went rushing through my body. Ibrahim is coming! Ibrahim is coming to Australia! I read the email again and again to make sure that what I was reading was not a dream. Ibrahim is coming to Australia!

I went out onto my balcony and looked out into the night sky. I wanted to yell out my delight to the entire universe.

I then made a mental calculation of the time difference between Sydney and Tanzania. Surely at this time of the evening it would be the middle of the day over there. I allowed the impulse to overwhelm me and so called Ibrahim on the phone. As soon as I heard Ibrahim's voice and his terse "hello?" I just blurted out, "Is this true? Are you coming to Australia?"

"Hey, Bwana Michael!" Ibrahim replied a few seconds after my outburst.

It was great to hear Ibrahim's voice. But it wasn't his voice that I wanted. I wanted to feel his presence, to feel him beside me, to feel him close to me.

Our conversation was stilted and I could only guess that Ibrahim's feelings were making it difficult for him to speak as my feelings were for me. Ibrahim gave me the details of his coming to Australia. It seemed an eternity away. I felt as if I had received a second wind.

Once off the phone, I couldn't contain myself. I told everyone. I told Khatyn. I told my sister, Karen, and her husband, Peter. I told Faraj who shared my happiness. And I told Polycarp.

The next time I saw Nikita, I told her as well. It was hard not to show my excitement but at the same I had my reservations.

"And he's definitely coming?" Nikita asked.

"Yes," and then I told her the date.

"That's not long away! You must be excited!"

However, my face obviously portrayed what I was thinking and it wasn't what Nikita expected.

"You're...not...excited?" Nikita asked slowly and measuredly with a deep furrow and a serious frown.

"Yeah, I am," I replied hesitantly.

"But?" Nikita filled in my thoughts for me.

"You know, Nikita, I realise I hardly know the guy. Yeah, each time we've been together it has been wonderful. But they have been very short moments. His religiosity annoys me somewhat but apart from that, he seems like a great guy."

"But?" Nikita once again teased out my thoughts. In a way, I hated her reading what was on my mind.

"But what happens when we finally live together and he turns out to be, well, not someone I would like to spend the rest of my life with?"

"Michael," Nikita said. "How long is he coming out here for?"

"I think he said he had a year's contract."

"And at the end of that year's contract, then what?"

"I don't know. Maybe he will return to Tanzania," I replied. "But then, what happens if we do get on well together but he has to return?"

"Michael, Michael, Michael," Nikita sighed. "Has anyone told you that you are never satisfied?"

This comment was like a smack on the face. It took me a moment to respond.

"Well, it's not like he's a local and we can have a trial relationship and if things don't work out he can go back to his place. We're dealing with crossing international borders here."

Nikita laughed. "And you have the best situation in the world before you. This Ibrahim is coming and you can have that trial relationship. If you don't like him, he has to return to Tanzania. If you do like him, then you can sponsor him to stay. If only we all had that opportunity."

What Nikita was saying was correct. However, it was also an oversimplification because I was sure that if things did turn out, the sponsoring process would not be easy. But then, for anything we particularly want, it is never easy.

But still I had my reservations. Nikita once again could see that I was hesitating.

"Okay," she then added. "Now what's the problem?"

I smiled. I smiled because I liked it that Nikita knew me well enough to know what must be going on in my mind.

"You and Pace, like," I stumbled, "like, do you always get on?"

Nikita laughed. "Michael, we've been through this conversation before. Which relationship is perfect and idyllic? It doesn't matter if you're straight or gay, as soon as two people live together, you have your great moments and you have your down moments. There are times when I hold onto Pace and think that I'm the luckiest woman alive and there are other times we have some real humdinger arguments." She stopped there. "But even then, I still think I'm the luckiest woman alive. We have our clashes but we have our wonderful moments as well. Sometimes I feel I want to have a fling with someone else but I have to honour the commitment I made with Pace. Whether you finally decide to live with Ibrahim for the rest of your natural life or to remain single, ultimately you have to make that decision and either decision will have its positives and negatives. Personally, I prefer my partnership with Pace than not being in a relationship at all. But I can't make that decision for you. Only you can make that choice."

The morning of Ibrahim's arrival finally arrived. I had tried to sleep but to no avail as I was completely excited. Ibrahim was due on a morning flight and so I had to take a morning off from work. I paced around my flat for some time because I was unable to settle down and also was unable to actually concentrate on doing anything. If I picked up a book, I lost interest in it, if I turned on the TV, the program didn't hold any interest. I felt the same as when I was a child on the night before Christmas. But also I was supersensitive about the condition of my flat. Was it clean enough? Was it tidy enough? I spent much of the night dusting and cleaning, making sure everything was away in its proper place.

At one point in the morning, I still had a few hours before I needed to go but then decided to simply go to the airport and wait. I could deal with the waiting better at the airport walking back and forth, and watching Ibrahim's flight on the big screen.

I hastily left my flat and headed for my car. I hopped in and turned on the ignition. The car tried to kick over but it simply spluttered and then stopped. I tried again. And then I tried again. And then I tried again. My car just spluttered and then stopped.

"What?" I shrieked in horror. "No! I don't believe this! It can't be happening!"

I kept turning the key. There was noise and there was splutter but there was no engine kicking over.

I was now in a panic. And yet, it was like there were two of me. Another side said to me, "Did you hear what you said? You said you don't believe this is happening. If you believe with all your heart, will this make the car start?"

I started banging on the steering wheel as if it were the car talking back to me saying this stupid statement.

"Come on, you stupid car," I yelled. "Start, for goodness sake! You can't do this to me!"

"Are you talking to your car?" this inside voice then said. "Can your car hear you? Will your car respond? Is your car a person? Personification? Personification?"

"Alright, alright!" I yelled at the top of my voice. "I get the picture."

But who was I yelling at? Strangely this calmed me down somewhat and allowed me to evaluate the situation. My car hadn't decided to fail me today simply to be vindictive because cars can't be vindictive. The reality was that for some reason my car failed to start this particular morning.

Just call the NRMA, I thought to myself. You're a member of their roadside service so you may as well use it. Maybe they can get your car going.

The number for the NRMA Roadside Service was on a service card inside my wallet. I reached around, grabbed my wallet and then removed the card. I then placed my wallet on the seat beside me and took out my smartphone. I was about to punch in the NRMA Roadside Service number when my smartphone started ringing. The phone nearly jumped out of my hand. I looked at the screen and saw that it was Polycarp.

"No, not now," I said to myself. "Polycarp, I love you, you are my son, but I really can't help you at this moment."

I balked at replying. The phone kept ringing. My conscience then got the better of me and forced me to answer.

"*Mwanangu*," I spat out.

"*Baba*," Polycarp replied. Polycarp then went through an elaborate respectful greeting. I nodded my head and hmmmed in the hope that he would eventually get to the point.

"Are you busy?" he asked so sweetly and innocently.

"Yes, yes," I snapped exasperatedly through the phone.

There was a moment of silence. I already regretted the outburst. It wasn't Polycarp's fault. But Polycarp beat me to the next step, not allowing me a chance to apologise for my outburst.

"Are you okay?"

"No," I spoke loudly, "I'm not okay. My car won't start and I'm supposed to pick up Ibrahim from the airport."

"Now?" Polycarp peeped.

"Yes, now!" I snapped as if it were Polycarp's fault.

"Well, I can come around now and drive you to the airport."

It took a moment to register what Polycarp had just said. My frustration was suddenly exchanged with hope.

"You drive me to the airport?" I asked now lowering my voice to humility level. "But you don't have a car."

"Yes, I do. I bought one last week," Polycarp replied so innocently. "I need one for work."

He bought a car last week? He told me nothing of any plans to buy a car. Didn't he want to consult with me, as his father, as to the right car to buy, how to buy one, and all that is needed to actually get a car? However, I was just as proud that he was able to purchase a car all on his own.

And a job? So, did that mean he actually got the job with the Aged Care centre? Then why hadn't the company rung me as a referee?

I agreed for Polycarp to come around and decided to leave ringing the NRMA for later. Getting to the airport was the most important thing to do at this time.

It didn't seem to take very long for Polycarp to come. I imagined that he must have been sitting in the car ready to set out when he had rung me. When he arrived, I jumped in the passenger seat but tried not to make it look like I was feeling desperate to get to the airport.

"Polycarp, thank you so much! You are an angel," I praised him.

Polycarp just looked at me and smiled.

"*Baba*, it's no problem. Anyway, you have done so much to help me in my life in Australia, how can I not help you when you need me?"

I then looked at Polycarp's shirt. The design on the top left corner of the shirt caught my attention. I pulled at that part of the shirt to make him turn around a bit.

"What is it, *baba*?" he asked.

He was wearing what looked like a polo-shirt. On the top left hand corner was a logo to show that the shirt was part of a uniform for an organisation of some kind. When I looked closer at it, I saw that the logo was a red fish and instead of an eye there was a Christian cross. Below it was written The Way.

Polycarp looked down at what I was reading and then looked at me. He realised what I was looking at.

"This?" he asked. "This is just my The Way shirt."

"What's that?" I asked.

"The Way is just an organisation at my church. It's where we organise activities, do volunteer work and so on."

"And their emblem is a red fish?" I bemused.

Polycarp didn't get why I had asked the question and I just told him it was nothing. Polycarp then set off for the airport while what passed through my mind was that this was just too bizarre for words. It was mere coincidence, I knew it, but what frighteningly bizarre coincidence.

"By the way," Polycarp continued, "I rang you this morning because I submitted my resume and the Aged Care centre rang me for an interview."

"That's great!" I exclaimed. "So, when's your interview?"

"I had it yesterday," Polycarp replied. "I just wanted to tell you that the company said that they will call my referees and that I need to let my referees know that they will be ringing. They might ring you today."

"Polycarp," I stated again, "you are an angel!"

Polycarp looked ahead as he drove but when he thanked me, his voice indicated that he felt that he didn't quite deserve the compliment.

"But I'm a human being just like you, *baba*," he replied with all seriousness.

This then made me reflect back on Ibrahim. I had had a go at Ibrahim for telling me that I was Michael the archangel and I was quite adamant that I was only a human being and no angel. Was Ibrahim telling me that I was an angel in the same way as I had told Polycarp? And yet my reaction to Ibrahim was a lot harsher than Polycarp's reaction towards me.

We finally made it to the airport. Polycarp found a suitable parking spot. We got out of the car and I pulled out my smartphone to check the time. Once I had dragged down on the screen to activate the phone, the phone indicated to me that it was now raining where Polycarp and I were standing, yet although a few scattered clouds were apparent in the sky, it was a beautiful sunny day.

"Look at that," I told Polycarp and showed him my phone. "My smartphone says it's raining but look around us. It's sunny!"

"My phone does the same," Polycarp replied. "There have been a few times I have adjusted my plans because of the weather on my phone only to discover that my smartphone was wrong. I mean, which are we supposed to believe, what is on our smartphone or what we actually see around us?"

I then tapped the screen to reveal the clock and noticed that there was still quite a bit of time ahead of us before Ibrahim's arrival. Polycarp and I then walked to the airport building. I checked Ibrahim's flight and then walked over to the entrance where Ibrahim was due to arrive. While we waited, this gave me an opportunity to talk to Polycarp about Ibrahim.

"Polycarp," I started, "this Ibrahim who is coming to Australia, this is the special guy in my life. He's a Tanzanian guy. He's also Muslim."

As soon as I said this, the look on Polycarp's face said it all.

"Yeah, I know," I continued, interpreting Polycarp's facial expression. "But he's not quite like the average Muslim that I know."

"Papa," Polycarp then said. "Are you sure Ibrahim is not using you simply to come to Australia?"

"I don't know, *mwanangu*," I replied. "To be really honest with you, I know this is a possibility. However, there are a lot of things about him that show me that he is a serious and trustworthy guy. But I also acknowledge that I don't know him enough. And I really need your help. He's an African just like you and I know you will pick up things about him that I won't which will show just how serious he really is."

"So, where is he going to live?" Polycarp asked with an interrogative expression on his face.

"I have invited him to stay with me. He originally had accommodation planned for him but I asked that he stay with me."

"So, you're not sponsoring him?" Polycarp asked.

"No, no," I replied. "He's on a work exchange program with an International School here. So an Australian teacher has gone over there for a year while he teaches over here."

Polycarp looked at me in thought.

"Yeah, I know, *mwanangu*," I continued. "Look, another thing was that the director of the project told me that he was a trustworthy man. He did confess that *Mzungus* have to be careful with Tanzanians because Tanzanians will take advantage of *Mzungus* thinking that *Mzungus* have lots of money which Tanzanians can deftly take from them. I stayed with Ibrahim on two trips to Tanzania and on both trips Ibrahim never asked me for a cent. In fact, he paid for lots of things for the both of us and he even invited me to stay at his place and he provided everything."

Polycarp looked on in reflection before speaking. "Well, that is a good sign," he replied. Polycarp then grabbed my left hand.

"Don't worry, papa," he then said. "I'll keep an eye on him. You have protected me. I will now protect you."

I just turned and gave Polycarp a big squeezy hug. While holding him, I was taken back to when I had first met him and the realisation that it was because I had decided to take on the responsibility of looking after him, this inevitably led to my meeting Ibrahim.

Polycarp and I waited a while. People came out in dribs and drabs, sometimes in crowds and sometimes there was no-one for some time.

Then finally, the automatic doors opened and out came the face I longed to see. My heart began to beat at twenty beats a second. Ibrahim walked down the ramp carefully, looking in different directions, trying to work out where I was. I had to grope through the throng. Finally Ibrahim realised where I was and came in my direction.

We grabbed each other and embraced. And kissed. On the mouth. I didn't care. I had seen men and women hugging and kissing in welcome embrace before Ibrahim had arrived. I thought it was disgusting to see a man and a woman kiss but they made a public display of it. So why couldn't Ibrahim and I do the same? Especially here in Australia? Once we had separated for a breath of air, I could see that Ibrahim's eyes had watered and I could feel mine had as well.

"*Karibu kwetu*! Welcome to our country!" I stated. I didn't know what else to say after that. Then I remembered poor Polycarp who was with me and this was most probably the first time he had ever seen two people of the same sex actually engage in an intimate kiss.

"I'm sorry, *mwanangu*," I said as I turned around. "Polycarp, this is Ibrahim. Ibrahim, this is Polycarp."

"I believe you are my other papa," Polycarp said.

"Then I believe you are now one of my sons," Ibrahim replied. Both Polycarp and Ibrahim hugged. Just to watch the two of them especially after what they had said to each other, I just wanted to weep with happiness.

Both Polycarp and I took one each of Ibrahim's bags and led Ibrahim out to the car. I invited Ibrahim to sit in the front passenger seat next to Polycarp. Although Ibrahim and I were now in a country which allowed the expression of love free course in all its forms, I thought it rather crude if Ibrahim and I sat in the back seat and let our feelings express themselves freely in the presence of Polycarp even though I knew Polycarp would have tolerated it. Once home, Ibrahim and I had all day for that anyway.

It also was a strategy to allow a conversation between Ibrahim and Polycarp to develop so that they could start to get to know each other. After all, it was a case of father, son and friend, and I wanted this friend to fit in with my father-son relationship. Not that I had any doubts because I knew the temperaments of both Polycarp and Ibrahim, and they were likely to get along anyway, at least superficially on their first meeting. I also needed Polycarp to act as a spy to suss Ibrahim out to make sure that it was a serious relationship and check that Ibrahim was not using me to achieve another end.

There was a lull in the conversation between Polycarp and Ibrahim at one stage as Polycarp was concentrated fully on driving. I used this opportunity to fill in a gap in recent history.

"Ibrahim," I said getting Ibrahim's attention, "what happened?"

Ibrahim turned around to face me.

"What happened when?" he asked.

"What happened when I left you in Tanzania?"

Ibrahim smiled. I wondered why he smiled. Was it really an amusing story to relate? Ibrahim then explained. Ibrahim at first mentioned that "someone" wanted money from him. It was honourable of Ibrahim that he didn't want to name this person. But I knew exactly who it was.

"Babeer!" I exclaimed.

Ibrahim hesitated and then finally admitted. "Yes, it was Babeer. Babeer has always been jealous of me."

"Why?" I asked.

Ibrahim shrugged his shoulders.

"What makes a person jealous? Jealousy is like a disease in my community. Babeer was most affected by this disease."

The story Ibrahim related to me was of very sketchy detail. Ibrahim knew Babeer from the mosque although later he discovered that he was the son of one of his parents' neighbours, and subsequently became Ibrahim's neighbour when Ibrahim moved back to live on the same plot as his mother. Simply, Babeer was jealous of Ibrahim and for years had been looking for an opportunity to get at him, in particular, to get money out of him. Ibrahim did not furnish any of the details as to why Babeer particularly had it out for Ibrahim. However, because Ibrahim worked for the Msingi wa Mungu Project, an organisation sponsored from outside by *Mzungus*, Babeer knew he could extricate money out of Ibrahim in this way. When Ibrahim told me that part about Babeer, I was wild. That money that Babeer wanted to get out of the Msingi wa Mungu Project was for the poor and needy, and Babeer did not look like he was in desperate need of anything. Didn't Babeer know or did he even care that the money he wanted to get out of the Msingi wa Mungu Project he was actually taking from the mouths of the poor and the orphans the Msingi wa Mungu Project was trying to support?

Babeer had suspected the relationship between the two of us when I arrived on the scene. This explained Babeer's interrogation the first night I had met him. It also made sense that Babeer was further convinced of our relationship because he had overheard Ibrahim's and my conversation later that evening, the time when he had fallen in the dark. When Ibrahim and I appeared in the mosque the night Ibrahim declared that I was Michael from heaven in order to fulfil a prophecy, Babeer had incited the hostile man to attack but unfortunately this backfired when the hostile man spoke to me. Babeer then went and made the report himself to the police of Ibrahim's suspected lewd sexual practices with me. Although there wasn't any particular evidence to support it, Babeer assured the police that there would be a reward if Ibrahim and I were arrested. The police, led by the promise of money, subsequently made the arrest.

"That means," I interrupted, "that they were actually able to use that law against homosexual practices."

Ibrahim looked at me but didn't understand my comment.

"When I spoke with your son, Amani," I explained, "Amani said that although there was a law which said that homosexuality was illegal, Amani said that this law is largely ignored. But it's still there and it can be used when it suits the Tanzanians. And this is an example."

The look on Ibrahim's face showed that he did not quite understand what I meant so I just told Ibrahim to continue with the story.

Ibrahim was duly arrested at the airport as I was witness to. However, because of the dream I had at Hamadi's place, Ibrahim knew in advance that he would be caught and I would be set free and that the only way Ibrahim could get out of the situation was for someone to pay the corruption money. He had told Gordon on the way to the airport so Gordon knew that he needed to bail Ibrahim out as soon as money could be arranged. This explained the Aquarius carrying the amphora of water. This pure water in the amphora was money paid from the Msingi wa Mungu Project, money that was pure and used for the helping of disadvantaged children at the project. Gordon was the one, the Aquarius, who came and paid it.

This was once again creepily coincidental, my dream and what occurred as a result. But it didn't make full sense. My dream was based on what I had observed at Stone City. But I couldn't deny that Ibrahim's interpretation of the dream fit the details of the events that occurred not long after this. It sent a shudder up my spine but I said nothing more about it. I then said that I would work hard to raise the money that was used by the Msingi wa Mungu Project to release Ibrahim and pay back the Msingi wa Mungu Project.

We finally made it back to my place. Polycarp helped me to bring in Ibrahim's luggage and then stayed around a bit to speak with Ibrahim. Part of me wanted Polycarp to go because there was so much lost time to make up for but another part of me was happy that Polycarp felt relaxed enough to actually engage in conversation with Ibrahim for this long.

Eventually Polycarp had to leave and this left Ibrahim and I alone. And so we engaged in our first romantic encounter in my little unassuming flat in a suburb of Sydney. Unlike in Tanzania, it wasn't imperative to ensure doors were locked and windows were sealed closed to avoid being caught out in a crime, although it was still prudent to do so simply because it was not a spectacle for the public eye.

Once over, we engaged in ablutions together but this time during the wonderful yet wasteful moment under the spray. Then it was my turn to keep a watchful eye on the time and not allow Ibrahim to sleep too long so that he would at least be able to sleep properly later that night.

While Ibrahim slept, curled up and holding me close, gently breathing in complete serenity, there was a wonderful moment of happiness to finally have this beautiful man I loved, yes, that I loved, here with me, at least for the year that lay ahead. Ibrahim claimed we were married. He said this because I had told him how men marry each other in Australia even though what I had told him was in actual fact tongue-in-cheek. But now, for the first time in my life, I realised that I was ready to enter the marital state with a man after all and that being married wasn't as ludicrous and pathetic as I had long ago surmised. It may not be an institution for everyone but I now realised that with the right person, this could certainly be the case for me.

However, because of a physical attribute of people like Ibrahim and me, a significant proportion of the world's population is denied the right to marry. But our case is not unique. In the early 1900s, Aboriginal Australians were denied the right to marry and could only do so with the tacit approval of the government. There was also a time up until the late twentieth century when marriage was denied between a descendant of Ham and a descendant of Japheth, or simply put, between people of different racial backgrounds, especially if they had different coloured skin. That Ibrahim and I would be denied a right to marry was therefore not unique in history. What was surprising, however, was that Article 16 of the United Nations Declaration of Human Rights clearly states that "men and women of full age, without any limitation due to race, nationality or religion, have the right to marry", the only limitation being that they need to be of "full age" and one would think that nations which bought into the Declaration of Human Rights would actually abide by it. Unfortunately, as Amani had once said, many pay only lipservice to ideals no matter how lofty these ideals were, ideals of their religion and even the ideals of remarkable historical figures, such as Tanzania's Julius Nyerere. There was, therefore, still a huge struggle ahead of us.

If Ibrahim's dreams were anything to go by, there was an exceedingly tall mountain that we needed to climb over even before Ibrahim could finally settle with me here in Sydney simply as my partner, let alone being granted the right for the two of us to legally become *azwajaan*. But if Ibrahim's dream was prophetic, eventually we would get over this mountain.

Ibrahim truly believed in his dreams, and on the whole the fulfilment of his dreams was remarkably coincidental. But even so, I could never be completely sure and could only simply wait and see.

Epilogue

"And you think they are not talking about the universe in which we live?" Ibrahim asked as he grabbed my hair with his right hand and started to brush it with his left.

"No, not at all," I replied in all seriousness, my head being pulled back each time Ibrahim took a stroke. "I mean, if you go right back to the beginning to the Creation Story as it is recorded in the Torah, the picture we have of the universe is of a bottomless pit and stuck inside is a round disk, the round disk being earth. Above the earth is an empty space which according to the Genesis story God called 'heaven' – and just as an aside, there is nowhere in the Bible that I'm aware of that says that when people die they go to heaven, simply because heaven throughout the Bible is the sky above us. As another aside, it is in this air bubble that God sits on His throne, not in some spiritual, ethereal dimension beyond our five senses. And above this empty space called heaven we have more water like an overriding arch. This picture of the universe remains consistent throughout the entire Bible and even in the Koran."

Ibrahim kept brushing energetically. His voice revealed that he wasn't convinced of my comment. "Surely it's not that specific."

"Well, it's quite clear that this is the picture the writers of the Bible and the Koran had of the universe when these holy books were written. The Bible writers continue to maintain that the earth is flat such as when Isaiah wrote in chapter 26 verse 15 that God has glorified Himself to 'all the ends of the earth'. A sphere has no ends but a flat object like a circle does. The Koran also says that the earth is flat by saying in Al-Baqarah 2:23 that God 'made the earth a bed' where the Arabic word for 'bed' is *firaashan*, and this word comes from the Arabic *farasha*, meaning to 'spread out'. The Koran says again that the earth is spread out in Qaf 50:8 where it says that, 'the earth – We have spread it out' and in this case the word 'spread out' comes from the Arabic *madda*, meaning 'to extend' or 'stretch out'. Also, in Taha 20:54 it is written that God 'has made the earth for you a cradle' and the word 'cradle' here is in Arabic *mahdan* and comes from the Arabic *mahada* meaning 'to flatten'. This last verse could probably just as well be translated that God has made the earth for us as a flat place. So, the Koran talks about the earth as a place that is stretched, extended and flat. However, the actual planet we live on is a sphere and spheres are not spread out and definitely are not flat."

Ibrahim kept brushing.

"Bwana Michael," Ibrahim commented, "perhaps when it says that Allah spread the earth out that He spread it out in the formation of a ball."

"That's a way to understand it, I guess," I replied, "but I see this as more of a way to change the understanding of the word to fit the modern idea of the world, an idea that those in the seventh century were unfamiliar with. That it says the earth was flattened out, however, makes it very clear that it's not talking about a spherical earth."

Ibrahim stopped brushing for a moment. "I can't answer you on that now without going back and looking at the verse in the original," he replied. "But I'm sure the description of the universe we know today can still be appreciated by what we read in the Koran."

Ibrahim then resumed his brushwork.

"I think that's a stretch of the imagination," I replied. "However, let's leave the description of the earth and look at the sky. Not only do the Bible and the Koran talk about a world where the earth is flat, they talk about the sky being a ceiling of some kind. In the Genesis story, the roof of the sky is more water. This is quite clear and it is not ambiguous at all. But then there is a little confusion about what actually constitutes the heaven itself. In Genesis 1:8, God called the air bubble between the earth and the lower surface of the upper waters 'heaven' so it is assumed that heaven is in fact empty space. But then both in Ezekiel 1:1 and in Revelation 19:11, the two visionaries who wrote these books write that they saw 'heaven open'. This either means that the Bible writers actually didn't know that God had called the empty space 'heaven' because empty space cannot be opened as there is nothing there to open, or this makes the heaven sound like the actual roof of this arch above the earth which can be opened up. Isaiah further writes in Isaiah 34:4 that 'the heavens shall be rolled together as a scroll'. Empty space cannot be rolled like a scroll so the heaven that Isaiah is talking about is made up of a solid substance. The Koran also holds this image of heaven where it is written in Al-Anbiya 21:105 that God will one day 'roll up the heavens like the rolling up of written scrolls by a scribe'. Also it says in Al-Rahman 55:38 'when the heaven is rent asunder', that is, broken apart. Empty space cannot be 'rent asunder' or broken in any way.

The Koran then makes it clear that the heaven is a roof because in three separate surahs, in Al-Baqarah 2:23, Al-Anbiya 21:33 and Al-Mu'min 40:65 it says that God made 'the heaven a roof'. In fact, the Koran shows that heaven is really a solid object when we read in Al-Anbiya 21:31 that 'the heavens and the earth were a closed-up mass, and We opened them out'. The word used in the Arabic to describe 'a closed-up mass' is *rataqan* coming from the Arabic *rataqa* meaning 'to sew together' and the expression 'opened them out' is in Arabic *fataqnahum* coming from the Arabic *fataqa* meaning 'to undo the sewing'. So the image is of two pieces of cloth sewn together and then God came along and cut through the thread so that the earth as one cloth and the heaven as another were no longer joined together. Certainly a lovely, poetic image of the universe but definitely not describing the one we actually live in."

Ibrahim got the brush caught in a knot in my hair and tugged energetically until the brush finally was once again free to move. This caused me to stop for a moment. But once the knot was untangled, although there was some pain while Ibrahim tried to force the brush through the knot, it was a pleasurable relieving feeling once the brush moved freely through my hair.

"However," I continued, "the reality is that the earth is a relatively small spherical rock moving around a very large star we call the sun and that we can move out in all directions from the earth but we will never come to any roof at all."

"Isn't the way the heaven is described in the holy books simply a metaphor?" Ibrahim asked.

"If it is," I replied, "then explain the metaphor."

"What do you mean?" Ibrahim asked.

"In every case that a metaphor is used, we know that the metaphor is not explaining a real situation in the world we touch and see. However, the metaphor will also have a concrete understanding that we can explain in literal terms. So, if the Bible and Koran writers metaphorically meant that heaven will be rolled together as a scroll, for example, although this is the metaphorical expression of the event, what is the literal explanation of the event?"

Ibrahim stopped for a moment. "I'll have to think about that one, Bwana Michael," Ibrahim replied and then he resumed brushing.

I looked up at Ibrahim. "Ibrahim, you know you can simply call me Michael. I'm your equal. And we're in Australia and in Australia we don't need to use these words of respect."

I paused and then added, "And I'm definitely not an angel."

Ibrahim laughed, grabbed my head and kissed me on the forehead.

He then resumed the brushing. "I never said you were."

"Well, you certainly implied it on many occasions," I refuted. "When you had dreams of Michael the archangel you implied that this Michael was also me."

"Michael, Michael, Michael," Ibrahim stopped brushing and leant forward. "When are you ever going to learn that Allah operates on different levels? When Michael the archangel appeared to me in my dreams, it wasn't you but Michael the archangel acting a part to show what my future was going to be. There's Michael the archangel in my dream and he is one entity and there is Michael, my partner, who is the other. I never said that you were actually Michael the archangel."

When Ibrahim had said this, my next thoughts were that I wondered really how long this relationship would last. Ibrahim made the situation rather difficult for me because he had to believe in angels because the Koran insisted that he did so and it would appear, at least from his perspective, that he had evidence that such beings existed because he had visitations from one. And this belief was supported from the Bible, especially from the prophet Joel who said that old men would dream dreams.

However, despite this bizarre otherworldly appreciation of the universe, Ibrahim was a really lovely man with a beautiful heart and had an outlook on life of wanting to help people in need as much as I did. Also, Ibrahim didn't mind me voicing my contrary opinions to his beliefs and this was another wonderful characteristic I found in him.

"Okay," I replied. "I take your point."

Ibrahim resumed brushing.

"Back to what I was saying," I continued, "the Bible and Koran writers also all live in a world where the sun moves and the earth remains stationary. We have the story in the Book of Joshua where Joshua commanded the sun to stand still and then later in II Kings 20, Isaiah made the shadow go back ten degrees which means he made the sun move back in the sky. In Al-Fatir 35:14 we read that God 'has pressed into service the sun and the moon, each one runs its course'. That the writers of the Koran talk of both the sun and the moon following a course comes from the ancient belief in a stationary earth where the sun and moon equally move across the sky. Later, in Ya Sin 36:39 it is written that 'the sun is moving on the course prescribed for it. That is the decree of the...All-knowing God' and then two verses later in verse 41 the Koran says 'it is not for the sun to overtake the moon...both of them float in an orbit'. This is clearer in Al-Anbiya 21:34 where it says that 'the sun and the moon, each gliding along in orbit'. Clearly, the writers of the Koran believed that both the sun and moon move in an orbit because the Koran lumps these two heavenly bodies together which shows that the writers of the Koran believed that the sun and the moon were similar in the way they moved in relation to the earth."

Ibrahim laughed. "Okay, Bwana Michael, that is, Michael," Ibrahim corrected himself. "but maybe there is a different way to understand these verses."

"But I cannot see how these verses can be understood in any other way," I replied. "Further, if these holy books are supposed to be forever accurate, what do the teachers in Jewish schools, Christian schools and Muslim schools teach their children in the science classroom about the workings of the universe? Are they even allowed to describe the universe according to what is observed and therefore contravene the writings in the holy books or are they supposed to teach the structure of the universe according to the holy books and then reinterpret the observations to fit?"

Once I had said this, I thought back at the times when I had looked at my smartphone. On many occasions the weather conditions indicated on my smartphone said one thing but what I observed around me was totally different. I couldn't help seeing the same with the religions of the books. The religious books said one thing but what we observed was totally different but oddly enough believers in the books preferred to continue to believe the books than what was actually observed.

Ibrahim laughed. "But the Bible and the Koran are not science textbooks."

"No," I replied, "nor are they scientifically accurate. But I hear the people of the books sometimes refer to certain scientific discoveries to prove that the holy books made claims a long time ago that science only much later proved to be right and therefore they use this as justification that the holy books were inspired by an intelligence much greater than our own. Although I am not convinced that these claims ring true, it is at least clear when it comes to cosmology and astronomy that the writers of the books were actually unfamiliar with the universe we now know it to be today based on observation."

"I'm sure Allah knew what He was doing when these books were written," Ibrahim then commented. Ibrahim paused for a moment.

"And what about Socrates?" Ibrahim then asked. "Does Socrates describe the universe more accurately than the holy books?"

I laughed. "You mentioned him because you know how much I admire Socrates."

"Well, of course," Ibrahim replied. "Because I want to show you a comparison."

"Okay," I answered back taking up the challenge. "Socrates' description of the universe was also inaccurate. Plato has Socrates saying that where we live here on earth, it's like we're living in little ponds. If we could go higher up into the sky, we would see that we are inside little ponds around the world. But this is not the reality."

Ibrahim then placed his hands on my shoulders and I felt the brush on my left shoulder. "Then, if Socrates was not correct about the universe, why do you admire him?"

"Because of the things he did say which speak to me," I replied. "There's one big difference between me and the people of the books. I admire Socrates, I enjoy reading Plato's dialogues where he has Socrates speaking. I enjoy Socrates' argumentation. Socrates speaks to a part of me which I find uplifting and indeed Socrates has uplifted many people which is why he was so influential and still is today. However, I also appreciate that there are many out there who find the dialogues of Plato, in which Socrates presents his argumentation, confusing and incomprehensible, and this therefore means Socrates does nothing for them. And I acknowledge that. This is why I don't bring Socrates' beliefs into the public sphere and say that we should make certain things law because Socrates said so because he received messages from God. Rather, Socrates speaks to me in a way which makes me feel I have a place on earth within the scheme of things. I also like Socrates because he says that he is neither an Athenian nor a Spartan but a citizen of the world which shows that even back then he had a universal view of humanity. Socrates was also very supportive of women and regarded them equally as men stating that they had an equal place in society."

"The holy books," Ibrahim then threw in, "also teach equality and tolerance."

I looked up at Ibrahim. "Well, not really," I replied. "Rather, the Judaeo-Christo-Muslim texts teach *intolerance*. And they are fiercely religio-racist."

Ibrahim shook his head and smiled. "They are what?"

"Religio-racist. Religio-racism falls within the category of the words 'racism' and 'sexism' and all other such 'isms'. Religio-racism is simply a form of racism where there are only two races of people, the believers and the unbelievers. In the same way that a racist is someone who thinks someone else is a lesser human being simply because of their race or a sexist is someone who thinks someone else is a lesser human simply because of their gender, a religio-racist is someone who thinks someone else is a lesser human being simply because of their religious belief. Most religions I'm aware of, and not just the three Abrahamic faiths, teach overt religio-racism. And by logic they have to. If the God of one's religion is good, those who believe in that God are good and hence those who don't believe in that God can only be bad. It is not logical in any religion to think that someone is still a good person if that person doesn't believe in the God of that particular religion.

We see this in the Bible. In the Old Testament, there is a close connection between race and belief where only the descendants of Abraham, and by extension, only the descendants of Judah are of God. Jesus says this quite clearly to the woman at the well in John's fourth Gospel when Jesus says that 'salvation is of the Jews' and not of the Samaritans. Throughout the Old Testament, we have the recurring story of keeping the Jewish bloodline clean of strangers. Isaac and Jacob were told not to marry a Canaanite but only marry someone from Abraham's family. Then when the Israelites entered the Promised Land, the Israelites were to destroy all the inhabitants. Very few of the Canaanites survived the onslaught and those who did survive were reduced to slavery. And there was to be no intermarriage between Jew and Canaanite. And to really make it clear that Jews were to keep the bloodline pure, we read in the Book of Ezra how Ezra separated those of mixed heritage from those of pure Jewish descendancy. Just looking at it in this light, you can already see that as much as I may have Jewish ancestry on my mother's side, because of my Gentile ancestry on my father's side, the Old Testament clearly puts me outside of those considered as the pure race.

As an aside, this no doubt would have caused a great identity crisis for me had I been living in 1940s Germany because the Jewish community would have rejected me because I wasn't purely Jewish, and the Aryan Germans would have rejected me because I wasn't purely Aryan - well, the Germans would have put me in a concentration camp along with the full-blooded Jews who didn't accept me as a Jew because of my Jewish heritage.

Then, the New Testament is also full of religio-racism. Christians are told in II Corinthians 6:14, 'Be ye not unequally yoked with unbelievers'. This means that a Christian cannot marry a non-Christian but also means that close friendships should never develop between Christians and non-Christians either. Even Jesus taught in Matthew 18:17 that Christians are to treat 'ethnics', that is, those outside the Christian community, differently and with some sort of contempt. This comes from Jesus' teaching that if a brother offends you and you tell him privately, then with a couple of witnesses and then finally to the whole church, if the brother refuses to listen, you are to treat this person as 'an heathen man' - and the Greek uses the word *ethnicos* from whence we get the English word 'ethnic' - so there are people outside the church that Christians are to treat as 'ethnics', that is, like a race or nationality outside the Christian 'race' and in this context lesser than the average person. Also, Paul tells Timothy in I Timothy 6:4 to keep away from non-Christians because they are 'proud, knowing nothing but doting about questions and strifes of words'. And St John writes in his general epistle that what is in the world is 'the lust of the flesh, and the lust of the eyes, and the pride of life' and that the non-Christians are 'of the world' whereas the Christians are 'of God'. I remember in my church that we were taught exactly that, that non-Christians were simply awful and untrustworthy people because they didn't believe in the Christian God who was love and goodness.

The Koran is no different. The Koran teaches in Al-Ma'idah 5:52, 'don't take the Jews and the Christians for friends'. Further, the Koran teaches in Al-Taubah 9:29 'fight those from among the People of the Book who believe not in Allah'. Although the word translated in the Koran you gave me is 'fight', the original Arabic uses the verb *qatala* and I believe this verb can also have the meaning 'to kill'."

"Dearest Michael," Ibrahim interrupted me, "no, you're not correct here. The word is translated correctly as 'fight' and not 'kill'. I understand your confusion because, yes, the words 'fight' and 'kill' are similar in Arabic. For example, in Al-Taubah 9:111, these two words appear where it is written, 'they fight in the cause of Allah, so they kill and are killed'. The phrase 'they fight' is in Arabic *yuqatiloona* which is the third person plural of the imperative *qatiloo*, that is, 'fight' in the verse you quoted in Al-Taubah 9:29, but the phrase 'they kill' in Arabic in this verse is *yaqtuloona*."

"I take your point, Ibrahim," I replied. "I stand corrected."

I appreciated Ibrahim's point here and I acknowledged that Ibrahim knew the Arabic better than I did. However, I was at least familiar with the fact that the words 'fight' and 'kill' are related through the Arabic *qatala*, and that the consonants are important in Arabic and not the vowels, which made *yuqatiloona* and *yaqtuloona* creepily similar. Not to mention, how were believers in the Koran required to fight? With words? With weapons? And to what point? At the end of the verse, Muslims are required to fight until non-Muslims pay something called *jizya*, an unspecified sum of money non-Muslims are required to hand over to Muslims for simply admitting that they don't believe in the Koran. How far in their fighting are believers in the Koran required to go if non-believers in the Koran adamantly refuse to give Muslims *jizya*?

"But also," Ibrahim continued, "this is possibly not the original way of understanding this word. I've read this word and pondered on it. In Arabic, the vowels are not written, only the consonants. Also, there are some letters which differ only by a dot. For example, the letter t and the letter b look the same except that the letter t has two dots above it and the letter b has one dot below it. In the original Koran, these two dots above the letter t and the one dot below the letter b were not written. These dots were added later. This means that this word could be read as either *qatala*, which as you say means 'to fight' or 'to kill', but also as *qabila*, which means something like 'to treat kindly' or 'to get along with'. It is the Destroyer who wants us to read the Koran in a way that makes humans believe they should go out and kill and destroy."

"But I thought," I protested, "that you said some time ago that the Koran says that God's word never changes."

I felt Ibrahim press on my shoulders.

"And indeed it does," Ibrahim replied. "The original manuscripts of the Koran did not have the vowel points or the extra dots to tell the difference between letters. These were added later. The original Koran has not changed but the addition of the dots has changed much of the original meaning. Allah wants to create peace and unity among humanity, not call people to kill."

"Then what about what it says later in the surah, in Al-Taubah 9:123, to 'fight such of the disbelievers as are near to you and let them find harshness in you'?"

"Again," Ibrahim said as he sat back and resumed brushing my hair, "that word *qatala* probably in the original was derived from the verb *qabila*, and the word translated as 'hardness' is believed to come from the Arabic word *galaza* meaning 'harshness' but the difference between *galaza* translated as 'harshness' and *galita* meaning 'error' or 'mistake' is only in a dot and this verse probably meant in its original something like, 'get along with the disbelievers as are near to you and let them not find fault in you', that is, let them see in your conduct that you are upright and blameless, that is, blameless of killing and hurting people and blameless of killing and hurting anything within Allah's creation. In other words, Muslims are supposed to get along with those who don't believe and convince the unbelievers through their upright conduct the goodness of Allah. What better way to create a world of peace?"

I didn't know enough Arabic to say anything either way to that.

"Then," I then said, "what about what it says in Muhammad 47:5 that 'when you meet those who disbelieve, smite their necks'? This is hardly teachings of tolerance and equity among all people."

Ibrahim continued to brush my hair with determination.

"I'd have to look this up in the original. I'm sure there is an explanation when we examine the original Arabic without the vowel points and the dots around the letters which were added later."

In a way, I thought it was commendable of Ibrahim to view the Koran with verses which read differently produced a doctrine more peaceful than what is generally interpreted.

"Well," I continued, "this would make the verse in Al-Hijr 15:4 make more sense where it says that believers in the Koran are required to leave non-Muslims 'alone that they may eat and enjoy themselves' because otherwise there would be a contradiction where on the one hand the Koran teaches to fight non-Muslims but on the other hand leave them alone to enjoy themselves.

However, even though the Koran might say believers have to be nice to unbelievers, and the New Testament says the same thing to some degree, the religious books still teach intolerance when it comes to belief. I mean, I have heard many religious people say that religions all teach tolerance. I remember when I first heard about the Msingi wa Mungu Project that this project was supposed to be built on the premise that religions teach tolerance which is why the different religions can work together. But in fact what the Bible and the Koran teach is entirely the opposite. These books teach total intolerance. There is nothing in the Old Testament, the New Testament or in the Koran that says we should respect the religious beliefs of other people. What you say is that those who believe in the Koran might have to be nice to unbelievers but still the Koran like the Bible teaches that those who don't believe in these holy books are condemned at some time in eternity. Because of this intolerance of alternative beliefs, this has made believers in the books intolerant towards those who hold different beliefs. A quick glance at history shows quite clearly just how intolerant religious people have been to those that these books call unbelievers.

Further, what is not clearly understood by those outside the faith is what, to religious people, an unbeliever is. When I was a Christian, anyone who was an unbeliever was someone who wasn't a Christian. Sounds logical and straightforward at first. But there is more to the meaning than meets the eye. Because I was a Protestant Bible Christian, unbelievers to me also included Catholics, Mormons, Seventh Day Adventists, Jehovah's Witnesses, Anglicans and any other Christian who did not believe the Bible exactly the way our family viewed it. My parents even used to say that our pastor was an unbeliever because he didn't follow the Bible in exactly the same way that my parents thought he should. By the time I was in my early twenties, from this view of Christianity, the only Christian believers were my parents, my sister and her husband, and me.

And I now know it's the same with Muslims. To a Muslim, let's say you are a Sunni Muslim, then unbelievers, *kafirs*, include Shi'ite Muslims, Wahabi Muslims, Ibadi Islam Muslims, Koranist Muslims, Yazdanism Muslims, the Nation of Islam Muslims, Sufi Muslims, Salafi Muslims, Al-Ahmadiyyah Muslims and all Muslims who don't follow exactly what the Sunni Muslims say about Islam. Even you yourself have experienced this. For all the time I have known you, I have never once heard you deny your belief in the Koran nor in Muhammad. However, even you yourself admitted that you were thrown out of the mosque at Moshi, not because you said you no longer believed that Allah is God and Muhammad is His messenger, but because of the way you understood the Koran.

I mean, it would be a terrifying thought if the Koran required believers to kill the *kafirs*. This would mean that no-one, even those who believe the Koran is the Word of God, could find any comfort in this book because although those who believe the Koran is God's Word may believe they are true believers, Muslims of rival sects would simply view them as *kafirs*. I mean, just say I were a Sunni Muslim. I would be led to believe that I can take comfort in the Koran because only *kafirs* are to be killed. But while I believe I am a believer, to a Shi'ite Muslim, I am a *kafir* which would give the right to a Shi'ite Muslim to kill me, marry my wife, make my children slaves and take everything I own. The commandments in the Koran, if they are to be understood at least as it is written in the translation you gave me and what I understand of the word *qatala*, these commandments put believers in the Koran in a position where they would have to say to others, including Muslims of different sects, 'you are a *kafir* when you don't understand and follow the Koran in exactly the same way as I do so I am commanded by the Koran to kill you'. If we took this to its logical conclusion, a true nation of Islam could only be made up of one person who had managed to murder every other single human being on the planet from existence and he or she could stand there alone congratulating him or herself for triumphantly succeeding in finally freeing the world of the infidel because this person would simply assume that because no-one else understood the holy books in exactly the same way as this triumphant person did, every other person on the globe would by this line of thought be considered by him or her as an infidel or *kafir*."

"Well, Michael," Ibrahim replied, emphasising his comment with a gentle whack on my left shoulder with the brush, "the Koran does not call us to kill willy-nilly. And our fighting isn't necessarily with weapons. We fight with our words and we fight using our upright conduct, our example of good citizenry and our respect towards all humanity because this is the surest way to make people believers."

I rubbed my shoulder and then looked up at Ibrahim. Ibrahim then rubbed the shoulder he had hit and then kissed me on the forehead. He then resumed brushing my hair.

"The problem with that, however," I replied, "is that I don't know how well that would work because the Koran says that God makes unbelievers 'unbelieve'. For example, in Al-Anam 6:126 the Koran says that 'whomsoever Allah wishes to guide, He expands his bosom for the acceptance of Islam; and as to him whom He wishes to let go astray, He makes his bosom narrow and close'. In Al-Araf 7:102 it is written that 'Allah seals up the hearts of disbelievers'. In Al-Kahf 18:58 we read that God has 'placed veils over their hearts' – that is, the unbelievers' hearts – 'that they understand not, and in their ears a deafness.' In Bani-Israil 17:46, 47 God says 'And when you recite the Koran, We put between you and those who believe not in the Hereafter a hidden veil. And We put coverings over their hearts lest they should understand it, and in their ears a deafness'. In Al-Araf 7:156 it says that Moses said to God that 'You cause to perish whom You please and guide whom You please'. And according to Al-Nahl 16:10 it says that if God 'had His will, He would have guided you all', the implication being that it is God's will that He does *not* guide us all, which means that God makes sure some people don't believe. Further, God says in Al-Sajdah 32:14 that 'if We had enforced our will, We could have given every soul its guidance, but the word from Me has come true: 'I will fill Hell with Jinn and men together'.' This further shows that not only does the Koran teach religio-racism, God Himself causes people to not believe to ensure that the believers have unbelievers in the world to be religio-racist against, and in this last verse, that God will have enough people to fill hell to fulfil His own prophecy."

Ibrahim kept brushing my hair quietly but when I had finished speaking, he made a movement with his head that showed that he really didn't accept everything I had said.

"So, what do you think we should do with the Bible and the Koran?" he then asked and wrapped his arms around my shoulders and brought me up to his chest.

"Put them in their proper place," I replied. "Like the *Iliad* to the Greeks or Shakespeare's works to the British, the Bible and the Koran have a place in history because of how they affected the course of history. But they are still only books written by humans. They have inspired people and definitely made people feel good about themselves but just as equally been the hurt and destruction of others. Like all written documents, they are open to being questioned."

"Or possibly updated?" Ibrahim asked. This comment made me look at him with surprise.

"Updated?" I asked inquisitively.

"Michael," Ibrahim then said and sat back. "It is written in the Koran, in Al-Furqan 25:33, 'Those who disbelieve say, 'Why was not the Koran revealed all at once?'' And as it says in Al-Baqarah 2:107, 'Whatever verse We abrogate or cause to be forgotten We bring one better'. What we hold in our hands of the Koran, it has not all been revealed at once as there is more to be revealed as the Koran prophesies. And in the new revelations, Allah will abrogate, that is, replace verses that were once in the Koran and cause others to be forgotten in order for Allah to bring us a better Koran. This doesn't mean that Allah will change His word, He will simply make adjustments to it."

I frowned at this statement because this did not make sense. But then I thought that it wasn't worth a comment.

Ibrahim continued. "As it says in Al-Luqman 31:28 that 'if all the trees that are in the earth were pens, and the oceans were ink, with seven oceans swelling it thereafter, the words of Allah would not be exhausted'. This means that there are more of Allah's words to be revealed apart from what we have now and of the four missing books of the stars of Orion. I can see what Michael the archangel was trying to show me, that the waters that flowed from the different waterfalls and into the one river continued to flow into a vast ocean. In the new Koran which is to come we will read of how Allah will blow away all the works of the Destroyer, that once the Destroyer has been conquered, the great light will shine over the paradise Allah had intended for us in the first place, a paradise where all people are equally respected, men, women, black, white, *mshogas* and non-*mshogas*, people of all races and all tribes. And all of Allah's creatures will live once again in peace as it was in the beginning. The spirit of Allah will spread to the seven seas and enlighten us all."

And the gods in unison blew over the waters to assuage the confusion and brought forth light, I thought, which was a loose translation and a fresher interpretation of the verse in Genesis 1:2. This image fit in with what Ibrahim was describing of paradise.

What Ibrahim was saying certainly sounded beautiful. It was a prophecy of a brighter tomorrow. I wasn't sure if Ibrahim believed that the prophecy would fulfil itself independently of any human intervention or, as he had implied for other prophecies, that we as humans had to do something to make the prophecy come to pass.

However, whether the Koran, the Bible or any religious texts need changing or updating is immaterial to me. Rather, to me it is quite clear that religious people need to change their focus, taking on the view that it is important to preserve the happiness and well-being of each human being before focusing on the preservation of religious practices or one's culture in order to enter into paradise, which in effect means creating a paradise on earth.

And is it really important what people believe about God and the godhead? In what way does believing Jesus is God or believing that Issa is only a messenger make any difference to our happiness and well-being? If the Koran teaches that children should still speak well and not reproach their parents if their parents believe that Issa is God, isn't there a lesson in this that those who believe in the Koran should still be nice to all people who believe Issa is God? And if one person believes there are many gods, another believes there is only one god and a third that there are none at all, is it necessary to fight to the death over these beliefs? If God or the gods haven't made it unequivocally clear to us of their existence and how many of them there are, and who is and who isn't God, isn't that a sign that it doesn't matter what each person believes about the deity?

In any case, those who believe that Issa was a messenger of God, whether as the Son of God or simply as a prophet like all the other prophets, are actually not supposed to worry about the nature of the deity anyway but rather change their focus from the deity they can't see onto the earthly representatives of the deity they can see. In the teaching of the Sheep and the Goats in Matthew 25, Jesus teaches that if religious people want to do anything to please God, what is of primary importance, what matters first and foremost before anything else to God is that believers look after and treat well all those around them, the hungry, the thirsty, the sick, people in prison, people in hospital, and by extension all people in general, especially those who are destitute or who are treated unfairly, because whatever good thing one does to a human being, as God says, "you have done it unto me".

This then means for those who believe the Torah is a revelation from God, where it says in Exodus 20 in the very first commandment of the Ten Commandments that "you will have no other gods before me", religious people are to have their focus first on God before any other "gods", and in light of the Sheep and the Goats, this means that their focus should first be on human beings. If by looking after and treating well each human being is in effect looking after and treating God well, this means that the happiness and well-being of God in the form of each and every human being on earth come first before anything else that people treat as "gods", such as cultural expectations, religious practices, sacred sites and holy books.

The forked road in the stars that Ibrahim saw in one of his dreams presents itself to all of us, the downhill road to destruction and the uphill road to paradise.

But one thing is certain: we can either work together and create the world we live in a paradise of joy and happiness for all humanity or we can continue to slowly destroy ourselves till there is no life left on the planet.

What the future holds is entirely up to us.